BY MOON AND STAR

Also by Goldeen Ogawa

THE ADVENTURES OF BOURAGNER FELPZ
Volume I: A Study of Magic
Volume II: Anatomy of a Magician

PROFESSOR ODD
The Complete Season One (Episodes 1-6)
Episode 7: The Dogs of Canary Island
Episode 8: Chronostrophe
Episode 9: Star Walkers
Episode 10: The Thousand Songs
Episode 11: Davebot

For a complete catalog of titles, please visit us online at
HELIOPAUSEWEB.COM/FICTION

GOLDEEN OGAWA

BY MOON AND STAR

WHEEL 1

a HELIOPAUSE PRODUCTION

For Hailey and Taylor, sisters in arms.

CONTENTS

For the fool who takes a rod to wield
Before the shadows that surround them yield
Follow the path by moon and star,
Ride a red ram, with a sword and shield.

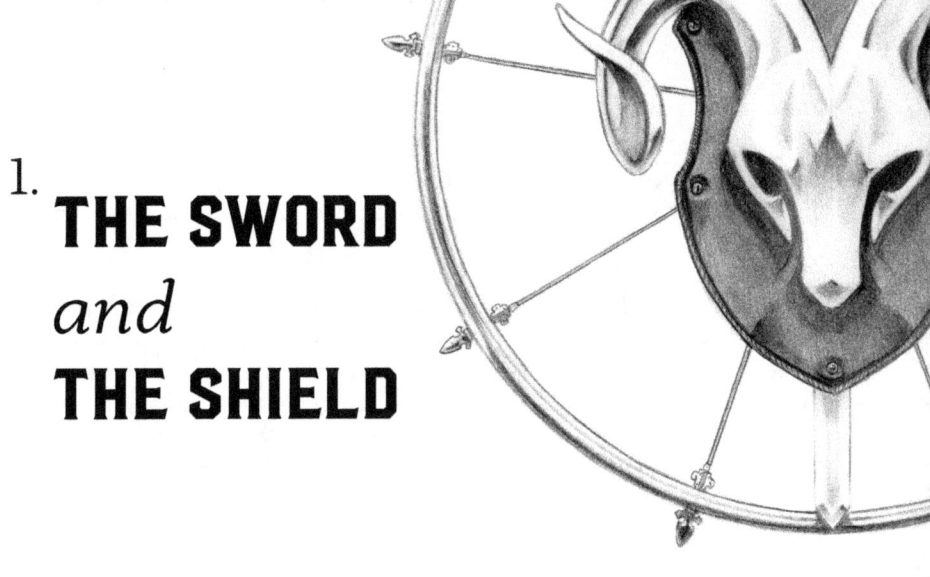

1.
THE SWORD
and
THE SHIELD

ALONG A DESERTED STRETCH OF HIGHWAY, under a pristine night sky, a black motorbike roared. Its headlight glared ahead at the cracked pavement as its tires ate up the miles. On and on stretched the road, and the night stretched on with it, the desert swallowing the sound of the motorbike's engine as it grumbled into the distance. The person riding it wore black leather from head to toe; a black helmet with its visor down hid the face. The night was young, and when you wear black leather from head to toe, night is when you move in the desert.

Night is when you hunt.

The truck stop off Interstate 40 was disappointingly empty. That was, it was disappointingly empty of obliging truckers heading west. The door to the little diner slapped shut behind the figure marching out into the night, and if you had been in that parking lot, this is what you would have seen: a young woman of medium build, her skin the color of milk chocolate, a black curling tangle of hair falling off her head and over her shoulders. Her eyes were big and dark, and her lips—though they were set in a frustrated line— were very full and red. Not the red of lipstick, but a lighter, more natural, pinkish red. She wore sensible boots, faded bluejeans and a khaki work shirt, rolled up over her elbows. On the right shoulder of this shirt was an embroidered rainbow appliqué; red, orange, yellow, green, blue and purple, with three black X's underneath. Over her shoulder was slung a duffle bag, and as she marched across the parking lot it clanked against her back.

There was a noise like: *Drrrriiiiip.*

The woman stopped. The sound could have been made by a great many things: a leaking faucet, for one, or a car dribbling fluid onto the asphalt.

Or a dead body. Dead bodies dripped. If they were dead because they had been ripped open. Or poked full of holes.

In an instant the duffle bag was on the ground, unzipped, and the woman rose, holding a long shotgun.

Again the noise came: *Drrrriip.*

Like the needle of a compass swinging north, the woman turned slowly on her heel. The sound had come from a dark semi truck parked on the edge of the lot. Slowly, silently, she began to pace toward it. The yellow lights around the diner fell across the vehicle in bars, making the pool of liquid slowly oozing out beneath its tires look black. The woman sniffed, but with all the smells of diesel and dirt clogging her nose she couldn't tell if it was blood or oil. That question wasn't answered until she came around to the far side of the cab and found the door open, the owner of the truck sprawled halfway out, his head hanging at an alarming angle. Blood was oozing slowly from three large holes in his neck, and crouched above him was . . .

Well, it was something the size of a small bear with long sticky claws and a wide hungry mouth. It had dead black eyes and a ridge of spines down its back. Its breath smelled of putrified meat.

The woman barely brought her gun to bear before she pulled the trigger. The creature staggered back under the impact of the shot, then turned and dove through the windshield, scattering chips of glass and leaving gashes down the hood as it slid off, hitting the ground with a wet *smacking* noise and taking off toward the highway.

The woman was already running after it. Rabid chupacabra don't feel a thing and keep going until they are dead. Even injured, this one was leaving her behind, and she took another shot—but it was hard to aim in the dark while running flat out, and she missed.

Behind the pounding of her heart, behind the furious roar of her breathing, the woman thought she heard another roar: the deep thundering roar of a motorcycle engine.

Then the chupacabra reached the highway, almost at the same time the roaring rose to a deafening howl. Something went *swish*, the roar decreased, and the chupacabra fell to the asphalt—neatly cut into two pieces.

Light erupted from the black motorcycle's headlamp as it slowed, turned, and then came rumbling back. The rider helped it along with one foot on the ground. He had only one hand on the handle bars, for in the other he held a long sword, which had something black dripping down its blade.

The bike stopped, its headlight illuminating the dark and sticky remains of what had been a rabid chupacabra. These were already melting away into the pavement, becoming another stain of a past roadkill.

The woman pulled up next to the bike across the black puddle of ooze, resisting the urge to clutch her knees as she caught her breath.

"You . . . bastard . . . " she gasped eventually. "You . . . you stole my kill!"

The biker looked from the stain on the ground, then to the sword he still held in his right hand. He reached into his pocket, pulled out a black cloth, and began to clean the blade.

From the truck stop there were sounds of commotion, of people shouting and the slam of doors. And she had left a duffle bag full of guns, knives, and ammunition lying out in the middle of the parking lot. Curses.

"Fine, I'll give you that one," she said, edging toward the side of the road. Once they found the dead trucker she could probably sneak around and pick up her bag.

There was a shout, a cry, some horrified yelling.

"That's my cue," she said to the stoic rider, who still sat astride his bike wiping his sword.

That's an innuendo I could have done without, thought the woman disgustedly. But she tossed the rider an easy salute, "Next one's mine, remember that!" and took off for the parking lot.

The rider watched her go, expression impenetrable under the helmet's dark visor.

"You're welcome," said the rider, and if the woman had been within hearing distance, she would have been surprised at how light and musical that voice was. Downright *feminine.*

The rider finished cleaning her sword, slid it carefully back into the sheath strapped to her back, and carefully trundled the bike around. A moment later the night air was again filled with the roar of its engine, and a bright single light appeared on that deserted highway. It moved, faster and faster, into the west.

University of California, Santa Cruz, two weeks later

J ILL HAMILTON (second year graduate student, evolutionary biology) checked her phone for the third time in as many minutes. No messages. This was unlike him. Ever since Christian had got his internship with Portola Equine he had been methodical with his updates, despite emergency farm calls and surprise cases of colic and all the other distractions one could expect as a first year large animal vet intern. Jill knew it was noon when her phone made the happy *ding, ding!* of a new text message coming in.

Now it was 12:34, and Jill chewed her grilled chicken sandwich without really tasting it, staring at the screen of her phone which displayed a string of messages—all outgoing, unanswered messages from *her.*

The latest he had ever been before was ten after noon, when he had texted her a simple ":'-(" unhappy face. She later found out this was because an old blind mare had wandered out onto the road in Los Altos Hills and gotten hit by a car. She hadn't made it. (Neither, Christian noted, had the car, but that didn't exactly make things better.)

12:40. Jill sent one last text:

heading back. lecture until 2. hope you okay. <3

She wrapped the remains of her sandwich in its papers and pushed away from the café table. She checked her phone one last time before slipping it into her pocket, and tried to ignore the unreasonable tightness in her chest as she made her way back to the physical sciences building.

Her phone buzzed half an hour into the lecture. Behind her open laptop she discreetly checked her messages: a missed call . . . from Christian's mother.

Jill Hamilton knew something was wrong then. Christian's mother never called if she could help it. She sat through another five minutes, feeling numb, before she closed her laptop, stuffed it blindly into her bag, and ran. She called the vet office as soon as she was out in the hall.

"Oh good, it's you," said Lisa, the desk worker. "Have you seen Christian? He never signed in for his shift this morning, and he's not answering his cell *or* his pager. I've tried—"

Jill didn't wait to hear what Lisa had tried. "I'll call you back!" she gasped, and hung up. She ran flat out down to the parking lot, flinging her bags into the back seat of her battered old Honda, and pulled out.

The last text she had from him, he'd said he was leaving home.

Jill's fingers were white as she gripped the wheel, turning out onto the highway.

Christian shared a house over the hills from the city with four other vet techs; an arrangement that was supposed to be temporary until Jill completed grad school and got a job of her own. Now she pulled up outside the house with a nervous jerk. Her body went cold when she saw his truck still sitting in the driveway, its driver's door wide open.

That truck, a molten red Dodge Ram dually, was his pride and joy; a graduation present from his uncle, Christian seldom went anywhere without it. Even on the rare occasion that their schedules allowed them to go out together he insisted on driving his truck, even though Jill's Civic got better mileage *and* was easier to park.

Jill nearly tripped over her own feet getting out of her car. She dashed up the drive, then skidded to a halt five feet from the truck. As if afraid of spooking it, Jill slowly approached the vehicle, running her hand up over the hood. It was cold. Peering inside the open door she saw the key still resting in the ignition.

That did it. Something terrible *had* happened; she just didn't know what. Up until that moment Jill had been worried, but she hadn't panicked.

The sight of the key in the ignition was the last straw. She lost it. She was no more Jill Hamilton, just the panic banging around in her chest. The panic ran inside the house, screaming for Christian. It ran up the stairs, turning the bedrooms and the closets inside out. It ran down into the basement, knocking over old boxes and nearly crashing into the water heater.

When Jill came back to herself, she was sitting on the front porch staring at her phone. She should call someone about this. Question was: who?

There was a *snap* of a branch, and Jill looked up. The drive was lined with rose bushes, and now she noticed what her panic had missed: one of them was torn out, almost to the root, and lying on its side. Like something had been dragged over it. Something large. Like a body.

On trembling legs Jill got up and walked over to the bush. Beyond it there was a trail of bent and broken grass, disappearing into the undergrowth of the small wood that surrounded the house.

Jill followed the trail to the edge of the wood. From there she saw it continued, down into a dry gully. Walking doubled over and pushing the branches out of her way as she went, Jill scrambled down the bank.

Christian was lying at the bottom, one arm folded under him, his face to the sky. Whatever had torn his shirt off had torn away a good deal of his chest as well.

Later—*much* later—after the paramedics and then the fire department and then finally the police had gathered in front of the house, nearly hiding it from view, two figures came and stood at the end of the street, watching the commotion.

One of them, a black woman in jeans and an olive green work shirt, turned to her companion and said: "I thought you *tracked* him."

Her companion, an imposing figure dressed all in black biking leathers and a full-face helmet, slumped its shoulders. The voice that emanated from behind the visor was muffled, but distinctly feminine: "I was too late."

The shorter woman snorted. "So, what do you think this is?"

The tall figure shrugged

After a while, they left. No one saw them go.

Grief takes different people different ways. For Jill Hamilton, a sort of numbness settled on her in the days after Christian's death. It was like the part of her mind that had feelings and emotions just shut down; as if it had blacked out from the pain. In its absence the cold, analytical side of her brain took over, and did the only thing it knew how: it analyzed stuff.

There had been something wrong the moment she set eyes on Christian's body—and not just the fact that he was ripped open and dead. If it had been a mountain lion attack—which was what the police thought it was—Jill couldn't imagine a mountain lion going to that amount of trouble to make a kill and then *not* eat it. Why had it ripped open his chest and left the easily accessible arms and legs alone? And he had been lying in such an odd way: one arm folded at the elbow beneath him, and the other folded over his belly. His neck was perfectly straight, his head level. His legs were straight and his feet together.

It was all wrong. You didn't fall into a position like that. You were *placed in it.* Mountain lions didn't arrange their food. And anyway, who heard of a mountain lion hunting in *midday?*

Later still, after the coroner had also ruled the death a lion attack and after the yellow police tape had been cleared away, Jill went back to the gully. Nature had taken its course in the intervening weeks: more leaves had fallen, obscuring the place where the body had rested. It didn't matter to Jill, who would have been able to pinpoint the spot no matter what.

She started by clearing the leaves from where Christian had been. Sure enough, there was still a little blood visible in the earth beneath.

And *that* was wrong too. Something tears into your chest, cutting through the bone and ripping straight to the heart, you lose your blood in a big way. This was not enough blood. Logic told her he must have been killed elsewhere, and then dragged back and placed here.

Jill crouched by the little patch of blood, scanning the branches and the undergrowth of the forest around her. *Fool* not to have done this before. Now, of course, any sign would have been covered by the free fall of leaves.

Or would it?

A body being dragged wouldn't just crush leaves. It would snap branches. Its clothes would catch on things. Jill began looking for broken branches, or pieces of cloth caught on twigs. She began moving outwards from the site of the body in a slowly widening circle.

She did not find any pieces of clothing. Instead she found a patch of shrub whose leaves were caked in the cracked, brownish substance of old dried blood. From there it was suddenly easy to see how *that* branch had been stepped on, and over *there* was another spot of old blood.

Like someone following a trail of macabre breadcrumbs, Jill began working her way down the gully.

The patches of blood and broken branches led her more or less straight down, and after a while she stopped looking for signs of a trail, and started peering about for signs of a struggle. She was so concentrated that she didn't notice how her own clothes were getting ripped and torn from scrambling through the undergrowth, how her shoes were filling with sand, or how her hair was collecting twigs.

At last she came upon a wide wash, where some flood from years past had piled a sandbar in the middle of the ravine. The sand was trenched and scattered, as if a fight had taken place in it, and in one spot there was still a small puddle of blood—the earth dyed brownish red for three feet around it. A few flies buzzed about its edge.

Jill found she had to go sit down on a rock and put her head between her knees until her brain stopped spinning and her vision cleared. Then she got out her phone. She wasn't sure who she should call—only that she should call *someone*—and that no mountain lion she'd ever heard of dragged its prey back *toward* civilization.

There was the crunch and rustle of something moving about the undergrowth above her, out of the gully. Jill looked up, expecting to see a flock of quail or maybe a deer.

What she saw instead was a four-legged black creature the size of a small horse, its fur sticky and stiff with dried blood, and its mouth pulled back into a terrible snarl. It had a lot of sharp teeth, and they were stained black and brown.

Jill found, to her intense disappointment, that she could not move.

There was a shout from behind her—high and wordless—and the beast leapt. It arced through the air above Jill's head and came crashing down on the tall figure in black leather who had appeared behind her.

Jill stared in astonishment. The person wore a full-face motorcycle helmet with the visor down, and was over six feet tall. It dwarfed the creature, batting it aside with one hand. Then it drew a huge sword—no joke!—out of a sheath strapped to its back, and as the beast turned, lunged again, the figure dodged sideways and caught it a deep slash across its throat.

The beast took a surprisingly long time to die. It thrashed around in the sand, black blood pouring from the gash in its neck, its jaw snapping at nothing.

The figure in black leather just stood, its sword still at the ready, and watched while the beast slowly lost energy, fell to its side, twitched horribly, and finally lay still.

The figure in black relaxed visibly. It reached into the pocket of its leather jacket and removed a long piece of black cloth, which it used to wipe down its sword. This done, it re-sheathed the sword and turned to Jill, holding out the cloth.

Jill realized she must have been sprayed with blood when the creature had been killed, and looking down she saw her shirt was speckled with red—there also was something wet dripping down the side of her face. But she didn't take the cloth. Instead she huddled backward on her rock, wishing her legs felt steady enough to make a run for it.

"I will not harm you," said the figure, the voice muffled from within the helmet. It sounded wrong: too high and soft. Then, as if seeing Jill was not going to calm down any time soon, the figure reached under its chin, undoing the snap of the helmet, and in one fluid motion pulled it off.

Jill found herself staring at the angular, pale face of a woman with bright blue eyes. Her cheeks were flushed pink from the fight, but her mouth was a calm, narrow line and she wasn't even breathing hard. And she was as bald as a monk.

The woman tucked her helmet under one arm and bent forward—she really was impossibly tall—and offered the cloth again.

"My name is Clara," she said, looking earnestly at Jill. "I am here to help."

Dumbly Jill took the cloth and wiped the blood from her face. When she was done Clara took it from her limp fingers, folded it carefully, and replaced it in her pocket. Gently she took Jill by the arm and helped her to her feet.

"Is that . . ." Jill said, staring at the corpse of the dog-like thing. "What *is* that?"

The tall woman barely glanced at it. "Bulldog."

"Bull*crap!*" said Jill, whose analytical brain was reasserting itself. She pulled her arm free from Clara's grasp and walked unsteadily over to the body.

In the stillness of death it was more grotesque than ever: she could see its scaled underbelly and the strange spines protruding from its back. It had fallen face first into the sand when it died, and as Jill came around she reached out her hand.

"Give me that cloth again," she said.

Wordlessly Clara handed over the cloth. Carefully covering her hand with it, Jill pulled at the creature's head so she could get a good look at its face. A little more blood oozed out from its cut throat at the movement.

On closer inspection it was not so much like a dog's face, Jill thought. It was flatter, and the eyes were too far apart. The mouth, as she remembered, was filled with sharp teeth in the manner of a shark: row upon row of little triangular blades arranged on a roll of bone, so that new teeth would move forward as old teeth grew dull and dropped off.

"This . . ." Jill said, staring at Clara over the body. "This is *no* dog."

Clara shrugged unhappily. She seemed a little annoyed, as if Jill had discovered something she'd rather have kept secret.

"Right. Help me carry it," said Jill.

"What?"

"You heard me," Jill said, standing up. "This is like no animal I've ever seen before—it's like no animal I've ever seen *documented* before. We have to save the body for study!"

Clara's face was quickly becoming bewildered. "Study," she repeated in a dull voice.

"Yes," said Jill, surprised at the woman's inordinate calmness. She had only just killed a probably new to science creature *with a sword* and she seemed surprised that Jill wanted to study it. "Now *please* help—there's *no way* I'm budging this thing on my own."

A battered old jeep lurched down the road to the house that had lately been occupied by Christian Wosely. It pulled up behind a similarly battered blue Honda Civic, and a young dark-skinned woman with frizzy black hair climbed out. She had to climb because the driver's door was jammed shut—had been ever since an unlucky collision with a possessed cow. She walked around the black motorbike that had been parked haphazardly in the driveway, and tried the front door. Locked. Casually, as if she did this sort of thing all the time (which she did) she pulled out a set of lock picks and was making good progress on the deadbolt when there was a crashing in the undergrowth behind the house, and the tall, bald biker woman appeared, carrying what looked like a chimera slung over her shoulders. Right behind her was the small white-faced woman she recognized as Christian's girlfriend. She was carrying the chimera's head cradled in a piece of cloth.

"What . . . did you . . . ?" the woman with frizzy hair stood up from the door, the lock picks forgotten.

"Friend of yours?" asked Christian's girlfriend, seemingly not seeing that the woman had been well on her way to breaking and entering. Well, *picking* and entering.

The dark woman and the bald woman glanced at each other.

"Sort of . . ." the bald woman began.

"Co-worker," said the dark woman, firmly. She put on a tight, fake smile and stretched out her hand. "Selene Shields. I see you've already met my colleague . . ."

"Clara Nordstern," said the bald woman with equal firmness. She jerked her head at the smaller woman. "This is Jill Hamilton. She knows it's not a bulldog."

The fake smile on Selene's face became, if anything, even wider, and her left eye twitched.

"*Does* she now?" she said forcefully. "*Well,* that's great—because it's . . . not a bulldog! Of course it isn't! It's a . . . it's—"

"It's like no animal I've ever seen," Jill said, giving Selene a critical look-over. The rainbow appliqué on the shoulder of her work shirt clashed with its drab olive green color, and there were some rather suspicious splatters of something dark across the knees of her worn jeans.

"Oh, you'd be amazed at some of the crazy critters that are out there," Selene said through her teeth. "Fact is stranger than fiction and all that jazz."

Jill straightened up to all of her five feet, three inches, holding the decapitated head like a ceremonial helmet in the crook of her elbow. She narrowed her eyes.

"I am studying to be an evolutionary biologist," she said. "I know from strange and impossible, and *this*"—she gestured with the head toward the body Clara carried—"is impossible."

"Yes!" Selene exclaimed, eagerly. "Impossible—it must be. Probably had a few too many beers last night, or the stress of studying—"

"Either it's the best damn hoax *I've* ever seen," Jill interrupted shrilly, "or it's an animal new to science that defies all previous documentation, and I could be the first scientist to get my hands on a specimen. *In either case* you can be sure I'm going to study it down to the *molecular* level. Now do us a favor: go open up the back of that Civic—it's not locked—there's a tarp in there."

Through all this Clara had stood stoically, holding the dripping body and staring resolutely over the heads of the shorter women. Now she glanced down at Jill. She seemed resigned.

"I think it's a chimera," she said blankly, and went over to the little blue car and opened the hatchback one-handed. There was a small tarp folded in a corner, and she shook it out with her free hand, trying to keep the headless body from dripping on the car.

"Clara," said Selene in a warning tone.

"Chimera?" said Jill, coming over and setting the head reverently on the curb before going to help Clara spread out the tarp and lay the body on top of it. She frowned. "What *kind* of chimera?"

The other two women stared down at her.

"What . . . kind . . . " something inside Selene seemed to pop. "It's a *chimera!* Are you *happy* now? It's a magical, supernatural creature that shouldn't exist! It's a monster! A *real* monster! I mean, *look at it!*"

"I have been," Jill said calmly. She went and got the head and laid it gently down next to the body. "But 'chimera' can mean many different things. I take it this is not *the* Chimera from ancient Greek mythology—I distinctly remember it had three heads, and I seriously doubt it would still be alive after thousands of years—"

"You'd be surprised," murmured Selene, rolling her eyes.

"—and it is probably not a blood chimera, though I'd have to make a much more thorough study to determine that. So. What *kind* of chimera *is it?*" She glared back and forth between Clara and Selene.

Selene just stared blankly back. Clara looked at the corpse thoughtfully.

"The dog kind," she said decisively.

Jill whirled around on her. "The *dog* kind? As opposed to *what?*"

"I killed one that looked like a bear, once."

"How do you know it wasn't a bear?"

Clara blinked down at Jill, who couldn't help but notice how shockingly blue her eyes were. Icy and pale, like shadows in snow.

"Bears don't have antlers. Or snake tails," she said blankly.

"Did you save any part of it?" Jill asked sharply.

"I cut off its head and burned the corpse."

"You *what?*"

"It's standard procedure if we're not sure what will kill something," Selene said with a sigh.

Jill's eyes narrowed sharply. She went to sit on the tailgate of her car, then remembered it had a dead monster in it, and settled for folding her arms across her chest. A whirlwind of emotions raged inside her head; all mixed up with the terror and confusion of being attacked was an intense excitement at a possibly game-changing discovery—tempered with her natural skepticism, and under it all the big, harrowing hole where Christian should have been; the horror at what had happened to him. Out of this whirlwind one thing Selene had said crystallized in her mind.

"Who . . . are . . . 'we'?" she asked, speaking slowly and carefully. "Who . . . are . . . *you?*"

Clara straightened up. She seemed about to speak, but then appeared to change her mind. She abruptly turned on her heel and marched off toward the motorcycle parked in the driveway. Throwing a leg over the seat she strapped on her helmet and walked it backward out the drive.

"Where are *you* going?" Selene asked, sounding annoyed.

"I don't have time for this," Clara said from under her visor. "They are out in daylight. Someone is controlling them. I am going hunting." And with a grumble and a growl the motorbike came to life, and she roared off down the road.

"Hunting . . . " Jill echoed numbly as the sounds of the bike faded into the distance. "Is that what you do? You're . . . " she was having a hard time saying it, even though it was the most obvious thing to say. "You're *monster* hunters?"

Selene Shields shrugged. Then she threw her hands up.

"Yes, all right? Yes!" she said. "Happy now? Monsters exists, ghosts too. Every urban legend you've ever heard has roots in something that really happened—most of the old legends do too. They're rare—people don't see them unless they want to—and they don't work by our rules. If the government knows about it they're not *doing* anything about it, which leaves people like me—and the biking giant over there—to clean up when it starts making messes."

"It?" repeated Jill. It was a trick she'd learned from her father: repeat one word as a question to keep them talking. Keep them explaining.

"*It!*" Selene waved her arms. At the dead monster in the car. At the world in general. "The *super*natural, the *para*normal. The *other side.* All that messed up stuff that doesn't obey the laws of nature. Normally it hides in the shadows, in the dark, where people can't see it. Sometimes it bites. We're just the people who go into the dark and bite back."

Jill looked at the corpse. It was definitely very much like nothing she'd ever seen before, but equally as real. It was starting to attract flies.

"Okay," she said. She closed the hatch and went around to the driver's side door.

"Where are you going?" Selene asked sharply.

"Campus," Jill said, pulling open the door. "They have an exam room in med lab, and I want to show this to Professor Okedo. What are *you* doing?" For Selene had run over to the jeep, pulled a worn duffle bag out of the back seat, and was now walking purposefully toward Jill's little Civic.

"Coming with," she said frankly, shoving the bag in next to the corpse. "You're boyfriend is the latest in a string of vet victims. I have no idea how much danger you're in, but you've just kidnapped the body of a supernatural creature. That—" she climbed into the passenger seat "—*never* ends well. You think I'm gonna let you drive off on your own? That'd be as bad as putting a bullet right in your face. Now drive."

Jill drove.

The med lab was, by some small miracle, deserted. Jill backed her car up to the cargo dock and Selene rolled the body into the tarp so that they could carry it, one on each end, without anyone seeing what it was.

"You got a basement or anything?" Selene asked as Jill pushed open the door. "Somewhere we won't be . . . disturbed?"

Jill shook her head. "We'll use the main lab. Better lights there. They use it for student necropsies sometimes, so it has a recorder and all the tools I'll need."

"Tools—just what are you planning on *doing?*" Selene asked.

"I'm going to examine it," she said simply. "Lift your end, you're dripping."

The exam room gave Selene the willies, which was an odd thing because Selene could be quite at home crawling through sewers where rats were the friendliest things you could hope to find. But the bare sterile walls and the fluorescent lighting and the racks upon racks of instruments for cutting and dissecting, not to mention the calmness with which Jill was laying out one such rack beside the corpse, was seriously putting her off. It reminded her too much of other rooms, in other places, where she had been the one on the table, and not nearly so comfortably dead. She shivered.

"Something wrong?" Jill asked, looking up.

"Flashbacks," Selene said, tightly. "What are you doing?"

Jill had put on a rubber apron, a mask, and a pair of elbow-high rubber gloves and was unwrapping the tarp, pulling it back and then working it out from under the corpse. She placed a large pan on the floor at the foot of the table, under the drain from the groove that ran along its length. Almost at once it began filling with the thick, black blood of the chimera.

"I'm examining it," she said flatly, her voice a little fuzzy from under the mask. Slipping off one of the gloves she got out her phone and brought up its recording function. She started it going, then reached up and pulled down the overhead mic that fed into the official lab tape. She started that going too.

"Wait, what?" Selene backed away from the mic as if it would bite her.

"Standard procedure," Jill said, putting her glove back on and getting out a measuring tape.

"Oh no, no it's not," Selene said, looking around the room as if she hoped to find a club to start bashing it to pieces. "Standard procedure is burying your head in the sand while people like *me* clean up the mess—"

"Be quiet," Jill snapped, pointing at the mic. She stood over the corpse, gloved hands resting on the edge of the table, and began to speak in clipped, even tones, her voice an emotionless drone.

"Unknown creature, deceased due to exsanguination. Decapitated post-mortem. Roughly canine in shape. Measurements..." she got out the tape and began measuring the thing. The length of the head (14 inches), the width of the head between the ears (10 inches), the length of the neck (approximately 9 inches when intact). She measured its spine, the circumference of its chest, every one of its legs, and its stubby tail. She examined its paws and discovered that it had three toes on all its feet but the left front, which had four.

She was well on her way to counting its teeth, having convinced Selene to don an apron and gloves and hold its jaws open, when the door to the lab slammed open and a young Indian woman came into the room and screamed.

Jill's shoulders slumped. She straightened up and turned around, eyeing the newcomer with disappointment.

"Hello Sabi," she said, under the woman's continued shrieking.

Selene, who was used to this sort of reaction from people, stripped off her gloves as she came around the table and put the poor woman into a firm hold, clamping her hand over her mouth.

"Thanks," said Jill. "Now, Sabi, would you go fetch Professor Okedo? He's not answering his texts, and he needs to see this."

Selene felt the woman nod shakily under her hands, and she stepped back.

"But—" Sabi glanced nervously at Selene.

Jill tapped the exam table sharply. "It's *important*, Sabi."

With a dirty look thrown at Selene, the young woman backed through the door, her feet echoing down the hall outside.

Jill turned back to the corpse. She cursed under her breath.

"Selene, do you remember where we were?"

"Is this what killed Christian?" Jill asked an hour later. Professor Okedo had still not shown up (Jill had received a text from Sabi saying he was stuck in some sort of meeting), and having finished with her preliminary examination Jill had taken tissue and blood samples and now they were waiting while the various tests she had set up ran their course.

"Generally speaking, yes." Selene said, her big brown eyes crinkling unhappily. "I don't know if it was *that* chimera specifically or if it was a chimera at all, but his death matches a pattern of unexplained disappearances I've been tracking the last few weeks."

"What kind of disappearances?"

Selene shrugged. "Vet technicians, usually. Sometimes interns. They go missing, turn up days later with their chests ripped up. Cops put it down to wild animal attacks every time, which is what I'm sure whatever is behind this *wants*."

"You don't think it's just . . . rabid chimeras?"

"Chimeras aren't like normal animals, Jill. They are *made*. Made for a purpose. And each chimera is a little different. But there's always been something bigger and badder behind them, in my experience."

"What do you think it is this time?"

Selene looked unhappily at the corpse, now covered with a sheet. "I've got no idea." She turned back to Jill, her brow furrowing. "But I *will* find it."

Jill leaned back on the counter, careful not to disturb any jars of chimera. She was skating around the question of just who Selene was and what she did. It felt like skating around the edge of a giant whirlpool into someplace dark and deadly, so she remained silent.

Then to her surprise, Selene began to talk on her own.

"*We* will find it," she said. "Clara and I've been on its trail for a month now. Started in New Mexico, ended up bumping into each other in the dark—literally. She's impossible, Clara is, one-track mind—but that one track is hunting monsters, which makes her the best I've ever worked with."

Selene looked cautiously at Jill, as if summing up her state of mind.

"It seemed to be heading north up the coast, so we began trying to get ahead of it. Clara was checking up on all the vets in this area, but when she got to . . . er . . . Christian . . . she was too late."

Jill worried at her lip, staring at the worn linoleum of the floor. There was a big, icy pit inside her where Christian was concerned, and if she didn't think too hard about it she could manage not to fall in.

Selene was also staring at the floor. She seemed to be coming to a decision because then she looked up, took a deep breath, and said: "Clara found him before they were . . . finished. The chimeras tried to run off with him, but she . . . stopped them. She was going to bring him—his body—back to the house, but then *you* were there so she . . . left it."

A cold silence stretched out after Selene stopped talking. Jill was still staring hard at the floor when there was a horrible buzzing noise, and Selene slapped a hand to her pocket and pulled out a battered old phone. She frowned at the number, but answered anyway.

"Who is—" she began. Then: "*Clara?* Where did you get a phone—oh. *Oh.*" As Jill watched, her eyes went wide. "I'll be right there," she said shortly, and started for the door. Then she stopped. She swore. Turning back to Jill she said, "Can I borrow your car?"

Jill seemed to come back to herself. She frowned. "Where are you going?"

"Clara found another vet tech—only this one's *alive.* Borrowed her cell to make the call. She's up in Boulder Creek—I need to talk to her, Clara's no good with people."

"I'll take you," Jill said without hesitating.

Selene stared at her, flabbergasted, as she marched to the door.

"Are you coming?" Jill asked. "I have to lock up."

"What is *wrong* with you?" Selene exclaimed, waving her hands expressively. "You—people like you don't *do* this! You go home, lock your doors, and let me and Clara kill the monsters. Then you go back to your life and live happily ever after. You *ignore* the things in the shadows. Trust me, Jill," she said earnestly, "there are things out there it is better *not to know.*"

Jill looked at her evenly. Her eyes were cold and hard, and her mouth was a humorless line. "It is *always* better to know, Selene." She jerked her head toward the door.

The first thing they saw was Clara's bike, propped by the side of the road. The next thing Jill saw, as she climbed out of her car, was a young woman in jeans and a polo shirt, half covered with Clara's black leather jacket and sitting on the ground. Clara was sitting on a rock behind her, somehow managing to blend in with the dappled afternoon sunlight falling through the trees. In just a tight black turtleneck she looked much smaller, though Jill noticed in a detached sort of way the definition of the muscles in her arms where they rested on her knees. She looked strong enough to pick up an ox.

The young woman looked up as they approached, and she tried to stand, but Clara placed a heavy hand on her shoulder and pushed her back down.

"These are my friends," she said simply. "Tell them what you told me."

It was not as simple as that, of course. The poor woman was in shock, and kept asking what time it was—as if she had somewhere she needed to be.

"Hey, hey," Selene said, her voice soft and soothing. She went down on one knee and touched the young woman gently on the arm. "Everything's going to be all right, hey? You're all right, okay? What's your name, sweetheart?"

"Je-Jenny," the woman said, looking wildly around at them. "Wh-who are you?"

"We're here to help," Selene said smoothly. "Now, Jenny, can you tell me what happened here?"

"I don't— I can't." The young woman looked about helplessly. She glanced back at Clara, who nodded jerkily.

It eventually came out that she was an intern at the Boulder Creek Animal Hospital. She had been answering a house call about a sick dog when *something* had jumped in front of her car.

"It *wasn't* a dog," she said, as if trying to convince herself of the fact.

"Where is her car now?" Selene asked Clara. Clara pointed mutely behind her, where the hood of a small white truck was just visible poking out from under some branches. It had been driven clean off the road.

"What did it do?" Selene turned back to the young woman, gently touching her shoulder.

She looked up at them with wide, frightened eyes.

"I *don't remember!*"

A wind rustled in the branches of the surrounding trees, and a lone bird chirped.

"I heard the crash," Clara explained later. *Much* later, after Selene had made an anonymous call, and after they had waited at a prudent distance until the first responders had arrived. Now Jill's car was parked in a dusty turnout and Clara was leaning against her bike, watching the sun settle into the Pacific Ocean. "They were dragging her out of the truck when I got there. They ran away."

Selene rubbed her face in her hands. "I need a beer. Or several."

Jill's phone sang. It was the special ringtone she had assigned to Professor Okedo, and she scrambled to answer it. Selene and Clara watched in silence as she took the call.

"Professor, I—" "What?" "No, it *isn't* a joke." Then a long silence. Jill's brows came down over her eyes, which stared at the world like it was a rug that had just been pulled out from under her. "What do you mean it's *gone?*" she said in a quiet, frigid voice.

Selene and Clara both went deathly still, tense and glaring at each other.

"Has Sabi, or anyone else been into the lab?" Jill asked.

"What did you do with the head?" Clara asked Selene darkly.

Selene's complexion did not allow her to get very pale, but now it was making a valiant go of turning white. "We left it on the table . . . *next to the body.*" She was so frustrated she actually punched Jill's car with her fist. Jill put a finger in her free ear as Selene subsequently hopped up and down swearing.

"Were there any windows broken?" Clara asked, looming above her. Jill repeated the question into the phone. The faint response was drowned out by Selene's colorful language as she kicked a rock off the road, but Jill managed to hear.

"No," she said.

Clara's eyes narrowed to little glittering blue slits, and she looked around at the road, at the trees and at the sky as if she expected something to jump out from behind any one of them.

"He says the door was left open," she added.

Clara looked over at Selene, a question unspoken in her eyes. Selene heard it anyway.

"That sucker was locked down when we left," she snapped. "I'm not *stupid.* Where are you going?"

For Clara had marched back over to her bike and was in the process of putting her helmet on. She pulled it back off to say: "I'm going to *find* that chimera, and kill it. *Properly* this time," she added, glancing meaningfully at Jill, before she shoved it down over her face, revved the engine, and sped off in a shower of pebbles and leaves.

"Yes, Professor," Jill said into the dusty sounds of the motorcycle accelerating away. "Yes, I'm sorry. I'm going to figure this out. No, *look* at the tests I've set. Seriously. Okay . . . yes . . . bye."

She looked over at Selene, her eyes like saucers.

The dark woman laughed a little weakly. "Hey, we don't call it the *super*-natural for nothing!"

Jill did not laugh back.

It was completely dark when two cars (a little blue Civic and a battered brown Jeep), turned down a quiet, dead-end street lined with trees and houses. They pulled into the yellow swell of a streetlight and stopped.

"Nice digs," Selene remarked, looking up at the house in front of them. It was a crumbling two-story building with an oak tree growing precariously close to it; an untended garden sprawled between it and the street.

"My father left it to me," Jill said in a hollow voice. She was tired and wrung out; the adrenaline from the day had long since leached out of her system and left her with a cold, sick, shaking feeling. She wanted nothing more than to curl up in her own bed with something alcoholic and drink herself to sleep, but Selene had insisted on following her home, and was now taking her duffle bag out of the back of her jeep and pulling something long and cylindrical out of it.

"Is that a *shotgun?*" Jill asked incredulously.

In the split between the night and the yellow street lamp Selene's grin looked rather ghoulish, her white teeth standing out prominently against the dark of her face.

"*This,*" she said, hefting the weapon, "is a 1963 Winchester Model 12 pump-action trench gun, one of the last ones they made."

"Oh," said Jill in a small voice.

"His name's Freddie," Selene added affectionately.

"That's . . . nice," Jill said.

Selene checked the magazine of the gun, carefully slung it from its strap—which, Jill couldn't help noticing, had a little rainbow tassel on the end—over her shoulder, then reached again into her bag and pulled out a much smaller gun, which was still twice as long as Jill's forearm.

"And this," Selene announced, as proud as if she were showing off her own children, "is his little brother, Elvis." She cracked the gun open, loaded it, and snapped it shut again. "Unlock the door," she said, gesturing with the handle to Jill's house. "Then let me go first."

Jill had watched movies where trained assassins or cops would creep into a building looking for an enemy. Selene did not move like them. She did not creep. She did not duck and roll or stare for long periods of time into dark corners.

She marched inside and turned on all the lights. She checked behind the door, under tables, chairs, couches, in cupboards and on top of bookcases. She made a note of all the air vents. And she never, as far as Jill could see, actually put her finger on the gun's trigger.

"Basement?" Selene asked when she had been all over both floors of the house.

Jill pointed wordlessly to the door next to the broom cupboard. Selene disappeared through it.

She reappeared five minutes later, the sawn-off shotgun tucked comfortably at her side, looking far more relaxed. "Your house is clean," she said, going to sit at the kitchen table.

Jill looked around at the clutter and mess of her living area, then gave Selene an odd look. "I'm assuming you mean there are no monsters," she said.

"None yet," Selene said cheerfully, pulling up another chair and putting her feet on it. She wore scuffed cowboy boots, Jill noticed. "But you never know. In my experience, it's always when you're ready to put your gun away and call it a night that they decide to show up. Almost predictable, really, so you go on—" she flapped a brown hand at the stairs "—go hit the sack. I'll get intimately acquainted with your collection of instant coffee and keep watch."

Just like that, Jill felt all the fight go out of her. It had been a long day; there was nothing more she could study clinically in order to keep the roaring storm of grief at bay. She went to the cabinet and pulled out a bottle of red wine—a gift from Christian, of course. She felt the lump rising ominously in her throat, and she knew it would be mere moments before she started crying.

"What about you?" she managed to get out, not turning to look back as she left the kitchen. Turning back would mean Selene could see her face, and she did not want that.

"Ah, I'll sleep when I'm dead," Selene said cheerfully. "You go crash, girlfriend."

Jill went. She stumbled up the stairs and nearly tripped over the threshold of her room. She flung herself face first into the pillows, biting down on the cloth to muffle the sobs which, after a day of being kept forcefully down, were now storming up and demanding to be let out.

Sleep was a blissful, dreamless refuge. Jill's mind surfed on the dark waters of unconsciousness, untroubled, unburdened, the salve of forgetfulness soothing her worn and ragged mind. Then slowly she was buoyed up, rising to the surface to find herself warm and comfortable with the gnawing feeling of something awful, just on the edge of remembering, that yawned beside her like a black abyss.

Christian. Christian was gone. She would never see him smile, hear him laugh, or get angry at him for leaving the toilet seat up ever again. She would never be able to jump on his back and hug him from behind, or hear the annoyed huffing sounds he made when he studied. She would never be able to play with his hair, or touch his funny pointed nose, or wake up to the crushing weight of his arms around her, holding her like she was something precious. She would never . . .

She was crying again, the tears flowing across her face and soaking the fabric of her pillow. She felt her sinuses clogging and she sat up to grope around for a tissue—

There was something in the room. Something crouched in the shadows by the open window—which she could have sworn she'd locked and closed—that was large and smelled vile.

Jill had never been able to understand why characters in horror movies seemed to be struck dumb at the sight of some monster. Now she found that her throat stuck to itself, making it alarmingly hard to make a noise.

So she took a deep careful breath and then forced it all out in one long, inarticulate wail.

Several things happened at once.

The beast by the window sprang. The door slammed open. The lights went on. And a sound like a small thunderclap tore the air in the little room.

The chimera—for chimera it was—jerked sideways under the force of the shot, which caught it square in the shoulder. It fell on the bed next to Jill, and Selene nearly stepped on her as she jumped up and got out her sawn-off shotgun and methodically put rounds in the creature's head and its heart. It rolled off the bed with a groan, then scrambled across the floor, trailing black blood, until it was out the door.

Selene, reloading as she walked, followed it down the stairs and to the front door, where she found its corpse, headless once more, lying across the doormat with Clara standing over it, looking grim.

Selene sagged against the bannister, tired and annoyed. "You really gotta stop stealing a girl's kills," she said.

"Honestly, you're taking this so calmly I think *I* might just freak out," Selene said about thirty minutes later. They had spread an old sheet over the solid oak kitchen table and laid what was left of the chimera on that, and Jill was currently arranging bowls and dishes to catch the blood that was still leaking freely from its neck and all the gunshot wounds.

This Jill could deal with. It was actually a welcome relief, having something real and tangible to work with. Anything that could push back the big storm of grief. She put on her rattiest apron and second pair of rubber gloves, set up her desk lamp to shine full upon the creature's severed neck, and then pulled her entire knife drawer out of the counter and laid it on a chair next to the table.

"What are you doing?" Clara asked. She was standing uncertainly in the doorway, still holding the chimera's head.

"I'm going to find out what makes this thing tick," Jill said. "This is the same chimera you killed earlier today—"

"Yesterday, if we want to get technical about it," Selene interrupted. She pointed at the digital readout above the microwave, which was glowing a bright green 2:32 AM.

"I want to know how it got its head reattached after suffering full cardio-pulmonary arrest, not to mention a severed spinal column. Give!" She thrust a hand imperiously at Clara, who backed away uncertainly.

"Oh, let her have it," Selene said, twirling a chair around so she could straddle it and rest her arms on the back. "I mean, what can it do with both of us watching it like hawks?"

Clara glared back and forth between the two of them, then with a roll of her crystal blue eyes she held out the head.

Jill took it and laid it beside the body. She put on a headlamp and took out a magnifying glass, then began going over the severed ends of the neck with a toothpick. Clara came and loomed over, her bald head nearly knocking against the hanging overhead lamp.

"What are you looking for?"

"Some sign of scarring—yes! Here it is!" she pointed triumphantly at a ridge of rough, whitened skin that crossed over between the severed ends of the neck. "Here is where it healed the first time, and if we were to leave the two halves in close proximity for the next few hours I expect it would reattach again."

"Yeah, let's *not* do that," Selene suggested from the chair. "Ammo ain't cheap."

"My sword does not run out of ammunition," Clara stated. "But I agree: I do not see the point."

"It would be fascinating to observe," Jill said. "But under the circumstances I think it would be better to find a way to prevent it reattaching. How sharp is your sword?"

Clara blinked at her. "Very sharp."

"Good," said Jill. She stood back from the cadaver. "Cut it open."

Clara gave Jill a puzzled look, but under her instructions she rolled the chimera onto its back and cut it open from sternum to pelvis. Then she patiently held empty tupperware containers for Jill to scoop organs into, labeling them with a sharpie marker on post-it notes.

On the chair, Selene quietly went to sleep, the gun Elvis still in her hand. It was only a light sleep, however, her consciousness ghosting under the surface of slumber, and she heard in a fuzzy, indistinct way, the conversation that was taking place across the dead monster.

"Heart, liver, lungs . . . all fairly normal."

"What is that?"

"That's a bullet, Selene put it in him."

"No, *that.*"

"That's . . . another bullet. It appears the heart has healed around it. Well, that would explain why it barely slowed him down."

"You are certain it is male?"

"Yes, here are his testes."

Spluurrt.

"I see."

"Hand me that BBQ fork, would you?"

Slowly, despite Selene's best intentions, she felt herself slipping further down, down into true sleep. It felt like it was only for a moment, but then Jill was shaking her excitedly, and she was fumbling for Elvis out of pure habit.

"Success!" Jill cried happily, and held up two ziplock bags, each with something gooey and yellow the size of a walnut in them.

"What are those?" Selene asked fuzzily. "Lemon-flavored mouse brains?"

The bags were whipped away, replaced by Jill's frowning face. "Of *course* not. Mouse brains are smaller. No, I think *these* are the key to its regeneration!"

Coming fully awake, Selene saw the chimera, still lying on the table, but now stitched back together, even its head reattached with what she could only guess was dental floss. That made her jerk upright.

"Don't worry," Clara intoned from where she was standing over the creature's head. "There have been no signs of life."

"Because I removed *these!*" Jill said excitedly, waving the bags. "One from under the liver, one from behind his amygdala—well, what could be *called* his amygdala, between us our friend over there was not very emotionally developed."

"But—how do you know?" Selene began, trying to rub life back into her brain through her eyes.

"Watch!" Jill practically crowed. With what appeared to be some effort she separated the two bags, holding one in each hand, then brought them slowly together again.

When they were about three inches apart, they swung together like magnets and stuck with a smack. They began to pulse before Selene's eyes, leaking a clear, yellowish fluid that now filled half the bags.

"This stuff," Jill said, tapping the bulging side of the bag with one finger, "is like stem cell juice on steroids. It promotes cell regeneration to an unbelievable degree; I used it to heal some of the superficial injuries on our friend here. *This* must be what allows them to come back to life—and to even reattach their own *heads.*"

"Fascinating," Selene said, wrinkling her nose at the bags, which were almost full now. "Perhaps you want to, er, separate them?"

"Oh, yes!" Jill trotted around the table and pulled two glass jars out of a cupboard. They had "Mary's Best Preserves" written on their lids, and Jill carefully transferred the bags's contents into them. "You realize what this means, of course?" she said as she poured.

"The . . . damn thing won't come back to life?" Selene offered.

"This . . . will *revolutionize* medicine!" Jill cried, turning around with a jar in each hand, a strange, wild light in her eyes. "Forget liquid bandages and disinfectant, just a little bit of this and we could have people recovering from lacerations in seconds—broken bones in minutes! It could be used to help patients recover from invasive surgeries—the list goes on and on . . . I *have* to show this to Professor Okedo!"

She turned to head for the door, as if she were going to tell him right that moment, despite it being four in the morning, but Clara loomed pointedly in the way.

"Don't act too rashly," she said gravely. "Some things beyond our understanding are not meant for us to meddle with."

"Yes, of course. There's no knowing what the possible side effects could be. For all I know it causes cancer," Jill said brightly. "All the more reason to *study* it! This may be too big for UCSC—but Okedo has friends at *Cornell . . .*" she clutched the jars to her chest, seeming to quiver with excitement.

Clara just stared at her, and after a few minutes the energy appeared to leave Jill and she went to sit on the kitchen stool, staring at the rectangular pattern of the linoleum.

Selene followed her with her eyes, then she got up off her chair and came over, gingerly taking the jars and setting them on the counter. "You need to get some sleep. Come on." Taking the smaller woman by the elbow she hauled Jill to her feet and turned her toward the stairs.

"But the . . ." Jill made a feeble gesture toward toward the body on the table.

"I will watch him," Clara declared firmly.

This seemed to satisfy Jill, and she allowed herself to be put to bed.

Sunlight rose on the house in Santa Cruz. It was going to be one of those brilliant California autumn days that seemed more like summer, though the shower of leaves shaken loose from the giant camphor tree by the morning breeze were suitably red and gold.

Inside the house, on the sofa in the living room, Selene rolled over under her borrowed blanket and buried her face further into the armrest. Years of hunting things that went bump in the dark had had an odd effect on her circadian rhythm, and now her body associated the night with work, activity and sudden danger, and sunlight with safety and rest. Selene found she couldn't really sleep properly unless the sun was out, though she still had trouble when the bugger was shining directly into her face.

At last she found an angle that cast her eyes in shadow, and was just sinking back into a pleasant golden slumber when there was a god awful pounding on the stairs, and Jill Hamilton charged across the room and into the kitchen, as if she had not spent half the night dissecting a chimera. Selene swore under her breath and turned to face the back of the couch, pulling the blanket right up over her head.

On arriving in the kitchen the first thing Jill saw was the dead chimera lying on the table, exactly as she had left it. The sight sent a thrill of something through her veins, and, in keeping with her capricious mood swings, she gave a little hop of excitement.

Clara, who had moved only to sit in a chair at the head of the table, raised her pale, almost nonexistent eyebrows.

Jill waved a hand at the body. "I told you, it *worked!*"

"Yes, it appears so," Clara agreed gravely.

Jill drank in the sight of the dead, *dead,* monster; the deep whirling storm of grief under her ribcage getting pushed back by the excitement of discovery. She turned to the giant woman, who had crossed her arms and was still staring intently at the body.

"Do you like eggs?" she asked brightly.

* * *

The sound and smell of frying food at last dragged Selene off the sofa. She staggered into the kitchen, Jill thought, like a zombie.

Then she paused, and wondered if zombies existed.

"Sweet Jesus, Mary and Joseph in a hand basket, do you have any bacon to go in that?" Selene asked, pointing at the huge pan full of egg and cheese Jill had frying on the stove.

Jill froze. She never ate bacon, but Christian loved—had loved it. He'd kept a secret stash of it behind the mustard in the refrigerator door; he thought Jill didn't know about it, but it was forever falling out whenever she used the mustard, and she hadn't the heart to tell him. Now she couldn't. She couldn't—

Jill realized she had frozen, wooden spoon in one hand and Selene staring at her expectantly over the door of the fridge.

"D-door," she gasped, pointing with the spoon, and quickly turned back to the stove so they would not see her blinking furiously.

"What concerns me," Clara said over the sizzling and spitting as the bacon was added. "Is why the creature returned to Jill. Why did it attack her in the ravine in the first place? She does not fit the profile of the previous victims."

Selene turned from her contemplation of breakfast, annoyed. "Maybe it was in the ravine for a different reason, and she surprised it?" she suggested. "As for last night . . . I dunno . . . maybe it held a grudge?"

"Why are they attacking people in the *first place?*" Jill exclaimed suddenly. "It doesn't make any sense!"

The two hunters looked at her sympathetically. Selene opened her mouth to say something about sense and how it was a precious and rare commodity in their line of work, but the young women plowed on, waving her spoon for emphasis: "A predator wouldn't go to the trouble of stalking and killing its prey just to leave it for someone *else* to find. Unless they had an alternative source of food . . . *or* they were working on behalf of something else . . . like hunting dogs." She glanced over at the table, where, in a half-hearted attempt at sanitization, the dead chimera had been covered with a cloth. "*Who* sent them?" she whispered.

Selene heaved a great sigh and pulled up a chair. "That's what Clara and I have been trying to figure out for the better part of a month," she groaned. "I still think it's a shaman or a witch, though what they need with a bunch of dead vet techs I don't know."

"You don't have any clues?" Jill asked. "Or . . . I don't know, a chimera expert you can ask?"

"This stuff ain't exactly taught in elementary school," Selene said. "Mostly we have to go on what some crazy scholar or monk wrote down in the dark ages—there was a lot more of this stuff around back then. It doesn't always translate to the present day though."

Clara, who had been staring thoughtfully at the corpse for the past few minutes, looked up and said: "We could always ask an oracle."

Jill stared at them.

"There are *oracles?* Real oracles?"

"Not here there aren't," Selene said. "That's sort of the problem. Oracles only exist in the spirit world, so to talk to them you need a door to the spirit world—and not just any door, the *right kind* of door that won't let through a flood of bad mojo we don't ever want to deal with."

"You need to do it from a node, a place of power," Clara said.

"They're like little windows into the spirit world, but they've got all these protections around them so the two worlds don't bleed into each other. They're *everywhere* in Europe, I hear. Out here though . . . " she flapped her arms. "Not so much. They usually look like crazy roadside attractions—like the House on the Rock out in Wisconsin."

"That one is very crowded now," Clara remarked. "Everyone knows about it since a writer put it in his book."

"I hate that guy," Selene said casually. "I mean, how can you know *so much* and not *do* anything?"

"I think writing books *is* his way of doing something," Clara said thoughtfully. "We can't all be warriors."

"If he would just stick to the *facts* I wouldn't have a problem," Selene snapped. "But he mixes it up with enough made-up stuff that those books are pretty dangerous—I mean, a vampire would *never* help raise a child, he'd *eat* it!"

"Maybe you haven't met the right vampire," Clara suggested innocently.

"I dunno, I've met a *lot* of vampires. And by 'met' I mean *killed*," she added reassuringly to Jill.

Jill wasn't listening. She switched off the gas on the stove and turned around, a piece of bacon dangling from her spoon.

"You said . . . tourist attractions? They can be like . . . these windows?" she said.

"Uh . . . yeah," Selene eyed the bacon, which was tipping precariously. "Weird places, historical curiosities, the stuff people go to see."

Then Jill's eyes fell upon Selene's trench gun, which was hanging next to the door, and something in them seemed to focus and harden.

"Then what about the *Winchester Mystery House?*" she asked. "It's just over the hills, in San Jose."

"Is it *actually* haunted, then?" Jill asked as they chugged up 17 in her little blue Civic. Selene was lounging in the passenger seat, one booted foot resting on the dashboard. She had a set of lock picks and was polishing them as they drove.

"The Winchester Mystery House?" she said, looking up. "Nah. Well, not any more haunted than your regular house. Which is not very. What makes it special is what happened *after*. Sarah Winchester spent almost forty years building that sucker—rooms within rooms and windows in the floor and stairways that go to the ceiling and that stupid fixation on the number 13—and now people come from all over to look at it. They pay tribute in the form of their time and their little plastic cards," she grinned. "It's a funny kind of worship, but it's what makes places of power like that tick."

"Do you think . . . " Jill still had trouble getting the words out. "Were there ever any actual spirits?"

Selene shrugged. "Spirits exist. We're going to talk to one now. Whether any of them talked to Sarah Winchester . . . I dunno. She'd lost her daughter and her husband . . . is it so hard to imagine that she was just a woman with a fortune and out of her mind with grief? After all," she glanced sideways at Jill, "people do crazy things when they're upset."

Jill nodded, not seeming to make the connection, and drove on. Ahead of them, Clara gunned the engine on her bike and disappeared around a turn in the road.

Imagine a house with too many spires, gables, and oddly jutting façades. Imagine it with a round tower half covered in trumpet vines and a wide green garden in front filled with graceful curving hedges and dotted with statues and fountains. Imagine it a rambling thing, full of awkward protrusions, yet contained within the chaos is an impeccable sense of style and taste: the fish-scale siding, the elegant windows and eaves, everything is constructed with the ideals of beauty and craftsmanship at heart. So even though there is a door set suddenly eight feet up the side of a sheer wall, it is a very *nice looking* door. Imagine a house that has been designed with an eye for the details, rather than the big picture, and you will have a pretty good mental image of Llanada Villa, better known today as the house of Sarah Winchester, widow of William Wirt Winchester, and heiress to the fortune of the Winchester Repeating Arms Company.

"They *say* she built the place to appease the spirits of the Native Americans her husband's guns killed," Selene remarked, leaning back against the hood of the Civic.

They were parked in the deserted lot outside the gift shop, which had a big, helpful "CLOSED" notice in the window, and the mansion loomed as a spiky silhouette against the evening sun.

"That is only partly true," Clara said, walking over from where she had been rummaging in the panniers of her motorcycle. She carried a small box in both hands, as if it were something precious.

"Oh yeah, and what's your theory then?" Selene asked.

"I don't have one," Clara intoned heavily. Her shoulders drooped, then rose again, like an inverted shrug. "Sarah Winchester . . . was protecting herself from the God of Ruin."

"The god of what?" Jill asked, raising an eyebrow.

"God of Ruin," said Clara. "An old god. Mostly forgotten now. All ruined and abandoned things belong to him, and those who dwell in them may be taken as his slaves. He took Sarah's daughter and husband. Sarah was very wise: she thought if she never stopped building her house, it could never be ruined and so he could never come for her."

Jill frowned. "How old did she live to be?"

"Eighty-three," said Clara.

They fell silent, looking up at the house with a cautious kind of respect.

"What about the number thirteen?" Selene asked suddenly. "It turns up all over the place."

Clara turned her head and blinked down at the dark woman. "For Jesus Christ and the twelve Apostles," she said, as if this were obvious.

"Even Judas?"

"*Especially* Judas."

"This is fascinating," Jill said, cutting off Selene's next remark. "But we have to think practically: how do we *get in?* We can't just buy a tour and then stop halfway to summon a spirit—besides," she squinted through the fence at the sign on the shop door, "it says the last tour left two hours ago. I don't suppose you two have, I don't know, supernatural investigator cards that give you special access to places like this?"

Selene laughed, throwing back her head and flashing her white teeth. Even Clara smiled a little.

"I wish," Selene chuckled. "Yeah, but no. I mean, I've met a few guys who use fake IDs, and some chicks who've, you know," she wiggled her fingers expressively, "*slipped around* security, but I prefer the old fashioned cat-burglar approach." She pulled out her chain of lock picks and jangled them cheerfully.

"What about security?" Jill asked, hanging back nervously as Selene approached the locked gate.

"Sweetie, I've broken into places what had twice the security this does," Selene said. "Nothing's secure from me unless it's buried two miles under the ocean and encased in concrete."

She was just bending over the lock when Clara coughed meaningfully behind them. Jill whirled around, her deeply law-abiding heart expecting to find a troop of angry security guards storming across the parking lot, but it was just Clara, still holding her little box. Carefully, as if she were afraid of spilling the contents, she pried it open.

"Or we could use these," she said, holding it out to them.

Selene sucked in her breath so sharply she whistled. Jill leaned forward, curious.

Inside the box, lying on a bed of oil-stained cloth, were two lumpish metal rings. They seemed to have been made of three threads of wire—one silver, one copper, one gold—twisted around each other and then melted together, blobs of metal distorting the outside of the ring, while inside it was smooth and circular. One of the rings had a piece of diamond embedded in it and looked rather battered, and the inside of it was shiny from wear. The other had a deep red ruby, was rather smaller, and looked tarnished all over.

Jill felt then as though she had stumbled into a conversation in a foreign language.

"How long can you last?" Selene asked.

"Two hours," Clara said modestly.

"I hate you," Selene said, in that casual way which seemed to mean she really didn't. "I can do forty-five minutes on a *good* day."

"I will take Jill then," Clara declared. "We will be even."

"You're pretty practiced at this?"

Clara did her little inverted shrug again. "My sister was better. She taught me. You?"

"Sorta had to learn on the job. Ex-girlfriend let me borrow hers a few times—oh *what?*" she broke off, seeing the look on Clara's face.

"Nothing," Clara said, looking down awkwardly at the box. After a time she said: "You . . . were involved with another warrior? That never seems to end well."

The chill which had crept into the conversation suddenly lifted. Selene tossed her head. "I'll have you know *all* my exes are alive with their souls and memories intact—I abide strictly by the campsite rule—*anyway!*" Her hands fluttered over the box, but never actually touched the rings. "Shall we?"

"I don't understand," Jill cut in, hoping to steer the conversation back into a language she knew, or at least get the equivalent of a rough translation. "What. Exactly. Are we doing?"

Selene turned to her, grinning again. "These little babies," she said, waving at the rings. "Think of them as . . . backstage passes. Yeah. Only backstage is kinda like going up to twenty-six thousand feet above sea level; we can't stay there for very long or our bodies shut down and then we die. Ooh . . . " she said, her eyes lighting up. "But this is going to make summoning an oracle *so* much easier!"

"I still don't understand," Jill said. "What is 'backstage'? And why would it make a summoning easier?"

Clara sighed. "There is our world," she said. "Then there is the spirit world. They lie together, one on top of the other. These rings let us walk between the walls of the worlds—'backstage' as Selene likes to call it. We will still be in our world, we will still be able to interact with it, but no one will be able to see us or hear us. And because we are closer to the spirit world, it will be easier to make contact with it."

"Wow," said Selene, after a moment of silence. "I think that was the most words I've heard you say at one time—ever." She patted Clara on the elbow. "I feel like I should give you a cookie or something."

Clara just glared at her.

"Okay," said Jill, taking a deep breath. "Let's do this."

* * *

Selene went first. After she had gotten both her guns and checked their ammunition ("Do bullets even work on ghosts?" Jill had asked. "I don't use bullets," Selene had replied. "I use iron pellets and slugs. Iron works against a lot of things, and a 12 gauge iron slug will slow down just about anything."), she slung the trench gun over her shoulder and the sawn-off shotgun under her arm, took a deep breath and spread her hand over the little box that held the rings.

"See you on the other side," she said, and grabbed up the tarnished ring with the ruby.

To Jill, it looked as though Selene blinked out of existence, leaving a Selene-shaped afterimage, like you get when you go from staring at a bright object to a dark thing very quickly.

Clara turned to her, taking one hand from the box to work the leather glove off with her teeth. Her hand, when it was revealed, was big and pale, with wide stubby fingers and the curving stroke of what must have been a tattoo peaking out from under the cuff of her jacket. Carefully she took the remaining ring (the other having disappeared with Selene), in her still-gloved hand, then shut the box and put it in the pocket of her coat. She held the ring out between two fingers, and looked at Jill very seriously over the top of it.

"We must touch it together, at the same time," she said gravely. "Otherwise I will not be able to take you with me. If you ever feel like you're dying, *let go*. Understand?"

Jill nodded. She held out her hand, which seemed tiny and childlike in comparison. Clara took it in her ungloved one and guided it forward.

Their fingers met the cool metal of the ring at the exact same moment.

It was like being plunged deep into ice-cold water. Jill felt the shock of it on her skin, and instinctively she shut her eyes and held her breath, but she heard Clara's voice almost in her ear saying "Breathe!" so she took a gulp of air. That made it worse, the chill shooting inside her and making her seize up. She nearly lost hold of the ring, but this was because Clara was maneuvering it onto her finger, so she could hold Jill's hand against it more easily.

Eventually the the shock subsided, the cold settling into a dull ache under her ribs. Jill opened her eyes and looked around and found the world not much changed. The colors were a little muted, and the sunlight was a little dimmer, but the gift shop and the parking lot and her car and Clara's bike and the house itself all appeared unchanged. Beside her, Clara was the only thing in full color she could see. Indeed, she seemed more full of color than she had before, her eyes unearthly blue and her skin radiant, like a rose petal with light shining behind it. Looking down at her own hands Jill saw the same thing had happened to her.

"Will you two stop cloud-gazing? We don't have forever, you know!"

Turning around she saw Selene, who seemed to have gone darker and more vivid. Her skin was glossy and almost bluish, and her wild hair had come partly loose from the knot it was usually kept in, floating around her head as though she were under water. The only bright thing about her was the ring she wore, the ruby burning like a hot ember.

She had been busy while Jill was adjusting to the sudden change. When they approached the gate her picks were already sticking out of the already-sprung lock. Selene pushed the gate open and they passed into the grounds of Llanada Villa.

They did not go in through the front doors. They did walk past them, but Clara explained that they had been shut for a reason and that to open them would be " . . . rude." Instead she led the way beyond, past the statues of Greek goddesses that guarded the entrance (Jill got the uncomfortable feeling that the statues turned to look at them as they walked by), and around a corner to what appeared to be a blank wall. Then she looked up meaningfully.

"There is always one door they leave open," she said, and pointed.

Sure enough, eight feet up the side of the house, there was a door. It was cracked partially open, and through it Jill could glimpse the shadowy interior of the house. Above it was a modern-looking sign that read: "The Door to Nowhere"

"Nice," said Selene sarcastically. "Did you bring a ladder?"

"Don't need one," Clara said, offering her free arm to Selene.

With a grin Selene scrambled up onto Clara's sturdy shoulders, and from there stepped easily into the house, kicking the door the rest of the way open as she went. Then she turned around and lay on her belly to help Clara lift Jill up. This was a harrowing experience for Jill, who clutched awkwardly at Clara's ring hand, fearful of losing contact and finding herself jolted back to the real world six feet up in the air. There were a tense couple of seconds when she was suspended between the two of them, before Selene's ring hand closed on hers.

Switching between the two rings was like having the worst ear popping ever, and Jill's head was spinning as Selene hauled her inside.

"What about—how will Clara—?" she gasped, tripping over ceiling beams and dust.

For answer Clara's hands appeared on the threshold of the Door to Nowhere, then like a rock climber she pulled first her head, then her shoulders up and over, bracing her feet against the side of the house. She jerked stiffly, so the sword slung over her back wouldn't catch on the doorframe, and then she slithered, like a giant leather-clad snake, into the house. She got up, brushing the dust off her front, and offered her ring hand back to Jill.

The popping was significantly less this time, and Jill saw Selene heave a sigh of relief before she turned and walked carefully over to where a red rope marked the area where people usually went.

"What are you thinking, the Ballroom?" she asked, once they were on firmer ground. This area of the house seemed to have been damaged at one point, with plaster flaking off the walls and the floor only covering half the room. "Maybe the Seance Room?" she suggested.

Clara shook her head. "We'll need the Tiffany window. It has the most power."

"What's the Tiffany window?" Jill hissed. Something about the house made her feel like it would be wrong to speak loudly, though she had no idea why.

"Maybe you've heard of Tiffany's of New York?" Selene said, peering around. "Well, this one was designed by *the* Tiffany. Cost a fortune, beautiful cut glass and crystal, designed so that when light shone through it you'd get millions of rainbows all over. And what did Winchester do? She installed it against a *wall!* So it'll never shine, not properly. It's got *the most* potential power in this entire house. We've got about thirty minutes before I expire, so let's split up and start looking." And with that she took off into the twining corridors of the house.

Clara sighed. She tightened her grip on Jill's hand and led the way in the other direction.

It was frustrating going. Clara seemed to be following a plan of the house that was entirely different than the one used by the traditional tour, if the number of times they had to climb over red rope was anything to go by. The fourth time this happened Clara lost patience, got out her sword, and cut the rope neatly in half. After that she kept her sword out and simply sliced through any ropes that crossed their path.

Clara was silent, intent, and moved swiftly from room to room. Jill caught brief glimpses of tasteful sitting rooms with delicate sets of china laid out on neat little tables, of antique kitchens and numerous closets with windowed doors showing toilets on the other side. Along almost every wall ran water pipes connected to a complex system of sprinklers mounted to the ceiling.

"It will be a long time before the God of Ruin claims this house," Clara remarked once as they descended a set of narrow stairs that switchbacked within themselves, making Jill a little dizzy.

Eventually they passed a glass-walled room, inside of which was another glass-walled room, inside of which a giant statue of an eagle spread its wings. Then they were outside again in the dim, colorless evening light, in a courtyard filled with tables, benches, and neatly trimmed trees with strings of lights draped between.

Clara cursed, turned around, and dragged Jill back inside. They passed by a wood-paneled room with a huge organ and stained glass windows ("Wrong ones," Clara said in response to Jill's inquiry), and took a turn up a staircase that dead-ended in the ceiling. Then they bumped into Selene coming through a secret passage hidden in a closet, looking frazzled.

"This is worse than the McCready House," she said, running a hand through her wild hair.

"What's the—" Jill began, but Clara cut her off.

"A house in the spirit world manifested in ours right on top of the McCready's family homestead. So there were two houses in the same space. It got complicated."

"But at least there was a *plan!*" Selene wailed. Jill noticed that she had begun to go a bit fuzzy around the edges.

"Keep moving," Clara said. "Or we will never find it."

They did find the Tiffany window, eventually. It was actually quite near the Door to Nowhere, and Jill wondered if perhaps they had walked right past it when they first came in. It didn't look like much: a modestly sized arched window with tasteful flourishes and raindrops set in tones of pink, yellow and green, with white crystal diamonds marching up the center. It appeared dead and lifeless, looking onto a plain dark wall, and easy to miss. It was set above a stairwell so the three of them could stand behind the railing above and see it almost at eye level.

By this time Selene looked like she was behind a plate of foggy glass, an indistinct shape in the shadows of the house. Her voice when she spoke, however, came through loud and clear.

"We'll need to do this fast. We're using the *English* Gunn Summoning, right?" she said, standing on the other side of Jill.

Clara nodded. With her free hand she reached into the pocket of her leather jacket and pulled out the stump of a candle, which she set on the bannister. The indistinct shape of Selene produced a box of matches, slid out a single, and held it at the ready. Then, a little awkwardly and out of sync, they began to speak.

> *Scatter, scatter, three-headed queen*
> *Light along the trivial path.*
> *Shatter, shatter, spiderglass mirror,*
> *Let your prisoners go.*
> *For the life of a candle, cross over the veil, lift the curtain that*
> *lies between us and eternity.*

Selene struck a match, which flared like a small star in the dark room, and brought it to the candlewick. As the flame began to take, the light that was reflected in the Tiffany window grew and grew until Jill thought that she had been wrong, that the window *did* look upon the outside, and that the sun was rising behind it. Little perfect rainbows were thrown in profusion on the floor and the walls around them, and as the light intensified the room was cast in a brilliant multitude of colors. She felt something hard and cold grip her other hand, and she realized it was Selene, who appeared to have firmed up under the lights.

"Here it comes," she whispered, giving Jill's hand a reassuring squeeze.

Something rose up behind the window, a shadow in the light. It rose up until it filled the window, cutting out all but the streaks of light that escaped around the edges. Then it appeared to step through into the room, the light pouring in around it like a rush of water, and came to stand on the other side of the candle.

It was tall, man-shaped, but so black it was impossible to tell whether there was anything within the shadow. It put a shadow hand on either side of the candle, and leaned forward as if to get a better look at them. Like that, its face was finally illuminated, and Jill felt her heart seize up and her stomach go plummeting.

It was *Christian*.

On either side of her Jill felt the hunters tense, but she found it distant and unimportant. She would have leapt over the railing and thrown her arms around him, but both her hands were held in vise-like grips. And . . . there was something a little wrong about this Christian. It was him, down to his stupid pointed nose and the mole on his chin and the floppy bangs she had always bugged him to get trimmed, but the expression on his face was not his. It was too blank, too vacant. It looked down at her distantly, as if she were a stranger to him.

And then . . .

Then he *smiled*, and all the old warmth and life flooded back into his face, his eyes lit up and he bent down over the candle.

"Hey Jill." His voice was all over the place, like the little rainbows cast by the light behind the window, and there seemed to be another voice under his, a dark, cold voice that put Jill in mind of a cave.

"Is that you, Chris?"

"Mostly, yeah."

"I miss you."

"Miss you too."

"What—why are you here?"

The candlelight flickered across his face, making it look for an instant like a stranger's once more. Then Christian was back. He seemed a little sad now.

"Someone has to speak for her," he whispered, and Jill could almost see the dark cave yawning behind his face. He straightened up, and for the first time glanced at Selene and Clara. "She has something for you, each of you."

"We have a question," Clara said gravely.

The shadow of Christian nodded. "And she has an answer. But first . . . " he fell silent, a look of incense concentration on his face. Then abruptly he looked up, and it was as though there was something else entirely peering out of that cold, dark cave and through his eyes. Something inhuman and impossibly ancient.

It spoke to each of them in turn, and when it did there was almost nothing of Christian's voice left; it was all harsh, cold, and dark. To Selene it said:

> *When wandering the moon it seeks*
> *To kiss the flame from the devil's cheeks*
> *And on the bough, before the storm,*
> *With a shattering, the earth it weeps.*

From the mystified look on Selene's face this clearly meant as little to her as it did to Jill. Then the thing in Christian turned to Clara and said:

'Cross a thousand shining frozen seas
A sword sailing high on a bloody breeze
To plow the field, to ride the storm,
And scatter wide, stars across the trees.

Clara just nodded impassively, as if she received surreal poetry every day. Then finally it turned to Jill, and she found it hard to look at the thing now it was not really Christian. But she heard him choke and in his own voice he gasped, "Listen to this bit, Jill, it's *important*—" and she looked up in time to watch him as the other thing said:

For the fool who takes a rod to wield
Before the shadows that surround them yield
Follow the path by moon and star,
Ride a red ram, with a sword and shield.

"I don't understand what that means at *all*," Jill said, a little desperately, since it appeared Christian wanted her to know it.

The shadow of Christian gripped the rail, as if doing so would bring him closer to her. He leaned right down so his face was nearly in the candle.

"She's doing her best, but it's *hard* for her, you know? She doesn't think in your dimensions. She sees the path you're on, Jill, she knows it's going to kill you if you don't have protection. But you've already *got* your sword and shield, Jill. Your moon and star." He glanced quickly at Selene and Clara, who were both frowning at him. "All you need is the *red ram*, and I gave you that. I know I did. Tell them—" his shadow flickered. The candle had become nothing but a puddle of wax, and the flame was dying. "—tell them to look in the will."

Having gotten this out, the shadow of Christian seemed to relax. He looked up at Clara and Selene and smiled just a little.

"The answer, by the way, is the mother," he said. Looking back down at Jill he reached out a hand, as if he were going to brush her hair out of her face, like he had done countless times when he was alive. But he stopped himself, and took his hand away again.

"I'm glad she let me come," he said softly, and it was all his own voice now. Big and warm, just like he had been. "Because there was something I wanted to say, that I couldn't. Most people can't." He leaned right down over the dying candle, so close Jill kept expecting to feel his breath on her face.

"I wanted to say *good-bye*, Jill." His voice was hardly more than a whisper. "Good-bye, and I love you."

He leaned in, and it was such a casual, familiar thing that Jill didn't think not to respond. Never mind that the shadow was cold and black and made her skin tingle uncomfortably, it was *Christian,* and this really *was* good-bye. She ripped her hands free and surged forward to kiss him, to feel him, to run her fingers through his hair one last time.

Instead she was plunged into darkness, coming up against a wooden beam that dug sharply into her belly. There was no Christian, no candle, no Selene and no Clara. The window was dark and the only light was a filtered gray glow coming in from another room. Warm air that smelled pleasantly of wood and a little of dust came rushing into her lungs, purging the clinging ache that had spread through her bones.

It did not purge the other ache, the one that had lodged in her throat, and Jill bent over the bannister, shaking, the tears running down her face and disappearing into the dark.

After a little while first Selene and then Clara winked into existence behind her. They looked at each other, Selene a little guiltily; Clara impassive as always. Jill's sobs had by then devolved into little dry chokes, and she allowed herself to be led away, lowered out the Door to Nowhere onto Clara's shoulders, and then furtively across the grounds, over the fence, and toward the car.

Selene drove. Jill didn't argue. She curled against the door, pressing her face to the window and watching as the night went flashing past.

The sun lit a band of fire along the ridge of mountains as it rose, burning away the fog and chasing back the clouds that had gathered low in the night. Halfway up the side of a mountain, where a dirt road ended in a wide turnout, the sound of a motorbike engine cut through the quiet morning air as Clara rolled slowly up the road, a trail of dust rising behind her. She parked the bike at the edge of the circle farthest from the little blue Civic, got off, and unloaded a stack of newspapers from one pannier, a bulging plastic bag from the other. With both hands filled she walked over to the rumpled figure sitting in a pile of blankets on the scrabbly edge of the road, facing away from the sunrise—out to sea.

"Praise the never-present lord," Selene said, raising her hands to take the plastic bag, out of which the smell of french fries and pancakes wafted enticingly.

"Better this morning?" Clara asked, opening the top newspaper and skipping to page three.

"Me, hell yeah," said Selene, unwrapping a plastic fork and popping open one of the styrofoam containers. "Aw, sweet! It's got blueberries!" she exclaimed, emptying the entire maple syrup packet over the stack of pancakes within. "As for Girl Genius, she's finally asleep. I think she'll be all right. You know, as much as anyone who's lost the love of their life *can* be all right. Didja get what he said about the chimera?" She stuffed a forkful of pancake into her mouth and chewed vigorously.

"Yes. It is the mother. I'm looking for signs," Clara said from behind the newspaper.

"Jeez, do you *ever* take time off?" Selene asked, her mouth full of pancake.

"All Hallow's Eve," Clara said, putting aside the paper and picking up another. "It's traditional to call a truce that night."

Selene rolled her eyes, and seemed about to make a sarcastic reply, when she evidently thought of something and changed her mind.

"So . . . what'ya think of that freebie prophesy she gave us? I can only remember the first part: *when wandering the moon it seeks* yada yada. My name means 'moon,' I think she was talking about me."

"*'Cross a thousand shining frozen seas, a sword sailing high on a bloody breeze. To plow the field, to ride the storm, and scatter wide, stars across the trees,*" Clara said. "That is the second verse, which applies to me."

"Oh, how do you figure that?"

Clara seemed to retract in on herself, as if trying to hide behind her paper. "I just know."

Selene swallowed. "That just leaves Jill's verse, which I hope she can remember. The vessel went all distant and fuzzy when it talked to her, as if it didn't want us listening in."

"The vessel was her dead lover," Clara remarked. "What was said between them is not for us to know."

Selene chewed thoughtfully. "Maybe. I don't suppose you've got coffee?"

Clara reached into her jacket and pulled out a thermos which she passed to Selene, who chugged several gulps before she sat back, wiping her mouth with the back of her hand.

"Mystical prophesies aside, what's our plan for taking out big momma chimera?"

"Our plan?" Clara raised an eyebrow, which, because her eyebrows were the color of finest platinum, meant that it looked like one side of her forehead got wrinkled.

"Hell yeah *our* plan," said Selene, carefully closing the styrofoam box and putting it back in the bag. "Because teaming up has been working *so* well for us."

"I cannot tell if you are being sarcastic," Clara said, moving on to her third newspaper.

"I hope you weren't," said a small, gray voice from behind them. Both the warriors turned with carefully measured speed, and saw Jill standing there. She was wrapped in a tattered blanket, her hair twisted into a bird's nest on the side of her head.

"Hey hey, look who's back in the world of the living," Selene said. "Sit yourself down, sister, and have some of the best fast food Santa Cruz has to offer." She rattled the remaining styrofoam container enticingly.

Jill only shuddered and shook her head.

"*C'mon,*" wheedled Selene. "You'll need to keep your strength up. Life goes on and all that jazz."

Jill looked at Selene, and her eyes had that strange intensity that Selene was starting to associate with the young woman announcing her intention to do something crazy.

"But don't you think of—" she began, but too late.

"I want to come with you," Jill said. "When you find this . . . mother chimera thing."

"Look, Jill, I like a spot of vengeance as much as the next person, but practically speaking it's never actually been that helpful—"

"This isn't about revenge," Jill said, and her voice was so level and emotionless that Selene almost believed her. The woman glanced briefly at the ground, then looked up again. "This is about understanding what's going on."

Selene stared at her blankly, and Clara went back to her papers. After a while Selene sighed, and thrust the box of fries at her.

"Here's the deal: you eat, you haul your own weight, you don't get in our way, you can tag along and take notes—that's *all*."

Jill pursed her lips, but she nodded tightly and took the box. As she settled down to gingerly pick over the limp french fries, Selene helped herself to one of Clara's papers.

"Right," she said, pulling it open. "What are we looking for?"

"Signs," Clara said. "Reports of animal attacks. Things that are not right."

"Huh," said Selene, scanning a page at random. Then she froze, folded the paper back, and held it up. Speaking slowly and clearly she read: "Local no-kill pet shelter to close after outbreak of rabid dogs kills three, area in lock-down quarantine, eight disappearances in the neighborhood in the past week." She turned the paper around and showed it to Clara. "That seem *not right* enough to you?"

Clara read the headline, took note of the address, then got up in a shower of papers and strode off to her bike.

"Where are you going now?" Selene called after her.

"Scouting," said Clara, buckling on her helmet. "Get your arsenal and meet me there. Bring—" she waved a gauntleted hand at Jill "—if you must."

"Get your arsenal?" Jill said, licking the grease off her fingers as Clara roared away again. "What does that mean?"

Selene sighed. "It means, sister, we're gonna be taking *my* car."

The building was a plain, square one with small windows set high up near the eaves. In the afternoon light it was stained a warm peach color, and it would have looked entirely innocuous save for the hastily erected chain-link fence decorated with bright orange tape with QUARANTINE printed along it. Two vans with "Animal Control" blazoned across their backs were parked outside the main entrance, which Selene and Jill observed from the safety of some nearby bushes.

"It looks deserted," Jill whispered.

"I expect they're lying low, using the rear entrance," Selene said, and turned back to her jeep. Across the seat was laid an array of daggers, knives, ammunition, a sniper rifle, and a giant hand cannon. This last

Selene had picked up and was adjusting the sights on, carefully twisting knobs and screws and sighting through a crosshair mounted on the barrel.

There was a quiet crunch of gravel under boots, and Clara appeared around the corner of the car, bent double with a streak of grease down one cheek. Jill jumped in surprise, but Selene only looked up from adjusting her gun.

"Well?" she asked.

"It's the place," Clara said, gracefully dropping to one knee so she could hide behind the car.

"Were you spotted?"

"I don't think so."

"Good." Selene slipped the massive hand cannon into a leather holster, then strapped it to her back. She slid a vicious-looking machete into the sheath strapped to her thigh, then removed the smallest knife—still in its own scabbard—and presented it to Jill. "Just try not to cut your own hand off, will ya?"

Jill took the knife with a frown. "I am not a fighter."

"And I don't expect you to be," Selene said briskly. "But you'd be a fool to go in there unarmed."

"Oh." Jill looked down at the knife. Its handle appeared to be made of polished horn, and the blade, when she partially removed it, was serrated and slightly curved. "If it's all the same, I think I'd prefer one of those nice guns."

"Ah ha ha ha—*no*," said Selene.

"Why not? It'd make it easier to kill those things."

"It would also make it easier for you to kill *us*, by accident," Clara said quietly. "That knife is a good weapon. It will serve you well." She stood up, looking over the roof of the car. "Now follow. Stay between me and Selene."

With that she crunched around the car and began walking purposefully toward the chain-link fence. Jill followed a little reluctantly, suddenly conscious of what they were about to do—walk into a nest of vicious beasts—and also because Clara's comment about guns had her weary of walking in front of the person who *was* carrying one. Several, in fact. But when she glanced back over her shoulder Selene had her trench gun pointed at the ground and was walking sideways, crablike, so she could keep an eye out behind them.

There was a metallic clatter as a section of the fence came down—Clara having used the hilt of her sword to break the joints between them.

"They'll have heard that," Selene remarked, still looking behind them.

"I want them to," Clara said.

No sooner were the words out of her mouth than something large and black launched itself from the roof of a nearby building.

Selene coolly raised her gun and shot it in midair, shot it again when it hit the ground, reloaded, and finally a third time as it leapt awkwardly toward her. The third bullet caught it in the left eye, and Jill flinched at the eruption of dark blood that came pouring out. The chimera was still running, but clearly suffering from its wounds; it careened into the fence and flailed there for a moment.

A moment was all Selene needed. She leapt to its side, pulling the machete from its holster, and proceeded to hack its head off.

Jill was still staring, mostly from shock, then Selene looked up, looked past her, and shouted "Clara! *Drop!*" at the top of her lungs, even as she raised her trench gun—the machete hanging off one finger by a loop of string attached to the handle.

Jill whirled and dropped, saw Clara flatten herself against the ground, and then a shot rang out over their heads, catching the chimera that had appeared on the roof of the stricken shelter. It yelped, a horribly canine sound, and disappeared over the edge.

"In, now!" Clara grunted, moving smoothly from a crawl to a run as she made for the entrance. Selene caught Jill by the elbow as she climbed clumsily to her feet and half dragged her after, spinning them in a slow circle as they went so she could still cover their backs.

Clara did not kick the door open. Rather she turned sideways and threw herself, shoulder first, at the locked door. It dented on the first hit, groaned on the second, and came off its hinges on the third. Clara ripped it roughly from its lock and moved inside, using the door as a makeshift shield. From the way it jerked under her hand, Jill guessed there were a number of angry chimeras inside. Clara spared one hand from the door to draw her sword, and shot jabbing thrusts around the edge as she crept further into the building. Every time her sword came back out it was darker and darker from all the blood on it.

"You wanna do this the hard way or the easy way?" Selene called over the din of growls and barks and angry claws against metal. She had put away her machete and slung her trench gun over her shoulder, and was now holding the hand cannon purposefully.

Clara didn't answer, but she thrust the door forward with an almighty shove from her arm and leg, then leapt backward, rolling sideways outside the doorway.

Jill caught a glimpse of a crowded darkness full of teeth and angry, glinting eyes, and then Selene fired her hand cannon.

The *bang* was so loud it felt like her ears had been blown off, and at the same moment there was a sickening explosion from within; the doorway was filled with acrid yellow smoke that came billowing out in waves.

After a moment a chimera, streaming black blood from a wound in its shoulder, came leaping out of the smoke. Clara was ready, and she cut its legs out from under it as it landed, then on the upswing all but cleaved its head off at the shoulder. This staggered the creature, its head hanging at an odd angle, and with the next swing she struck it down.

"How are you doing?" Selene asked in an undertone, and Jill realized she was leaning heavily against the other woman.

38

"Fine," she said in a weak, shaky voice. She jerked herself upright and did her best to look alert and not at all like she wanted to vomit.

The smoke had cleared from the doorway and Clara was creeping cautiously inside. But there were no sudden grunts or growls or sounds of her sword being put to use, and after a moment her arm appeared, gesturing them to follow.

There was still the hot smell of gunpowder and something worse, like capsaicin, in the air when Jill and Selene followed Clara inside. What had been the lobby was a mess of blood—some old and brown, some new and shiny-black—and the lumpish shapes of chimera bodies. Apparently having large chunks blown out of them also induced a temporary death. Clara unceremoniously pushed one off what had been the front desk and leaned over, peering at something.

"What'chu looking for?" Selene asked, after she had ascertained that there were no monsters hiding behind the overturned chairs or clinging to the ceiling.

"Fire-escape map," Clara said briskly, swinging herself over the desk and going to examine the wall behind. "If I have an idea of the layout I could guess where the mother is nesting."

But there was no fire map, and so they moved in formation—Clara, then Jill, then Selene—from the wrecked lobby through the only door, which stood under a sign marked "private." This led to a brief hallway, smeared with blood and other, less savory smelling liquids, which then opened out into the body of the building.

Here was what once had been the primary living area for the building's original tenants: enclosed dog runs and cat runs, stacks of cages and a few carriers piled in one corner. All empty, all with their doors torn off—some of them had little piles of brown, goop-covered bones, in others there were more substantial leftovers.

"This . . . was a *no-kill* shelter," Jill said weakly, then had to cover her mouth to keep from vomiting. There was a smell here, like warm wine and fermented meat and frying fish and old fruit all mashed together into something truly gut-churning. As they moved through the carnage small clouds of flies rose from the puddling remains.

"Yeah, well, we don't call 'em *monsters* for nothing," Selene said.

Jill swallowed dryly. "There is nothing unnatural about carnivores feeding upon smaller, defenseless creatures," she said, her tongue sticking to the roof of her mouth. "But that does not make this any less horrible."

"Most carnivores," said Clara quietly, "do not keep their future meals in cages." She had stopped before a large run, in the back corner of which huddled a truly miserable mutt. Silently Clara opened the door, pushing aside the remains of what had been its cage-mates. She looked up and fixed Jill with a sad look. "And us humans, of course." She moved on.

Through the festering slaughterhouse they went, finding a few more survivors as they progressed. Clara opened their cages, but made no other effort. She was constantly pausing, looking around, as if getting her bearings. Finally they came to an avenue created by many cages having been pushed to the side, and a streak of drying, brown blood painted down it. This led to a door that had been not so much smashed as clawed open. It led to a steep flight of metal stairs and Clara whispered "Basement, as usual," as she began descending them.

Jill heard Selene patting her hand along the wall as they followed Clara, and a moment later a string of fluorescent lights blinked into life, illuminating the stairs—and the chimera that was waiting at the bottom of them. It stared up at them out of wide, red-tinged eyes. Then it ran, scrambling away behind a water heater and into the depths of the basement. Clara cursed in a Nordic-sounding language.

"It runs," she explained. "Now I worry."

"Going for friends?" Selene suggested.

"Going to warn its mother," Clara growled.

But the basement appeared deserted as they explored further, dim and quiet. Quiet, that is, until they rounded a corner and came face to face with a corpse hung from its heels. Then Jill gave a little, choked gasp.

It was a young woman, no older than Jill, a little gold hoop in her left ear (her right ear appeared to have been bitten off), and one eye staring at them blankly.

There was a snaking sound in the darkness behind the corpse, like a worm sliding through dry leaves, and with a jerk the corpse was pulled down, dragged away into the dark. But it only disappeared for a moment—Selene, resourceful as always, found the relevant switch and then the whole terrible scene was cast in a harsh light.

A dozen chimeras hunched in the depths of the basement, crowded around a figure that was both animal and human. It was animal in that it had what appeared to be antlers and a long snouted face, and human in that it stood on two legs. Before it was the corpse, right-side up now and suspended by the creature's two long, tentacle-like arms. One disappeared into the dead woman's back, while the other snaked around and plunged into her chest.

Right where Christian's fatal wound had been.

Jill felt her heart turn cold.

The corpse shuddered from head to toe, convulsed as though electricity had been run through it, and then took a rough, rasping breath. Without really looking at them, it spoke in a voice that was still recognizably human, but with a strange slur to the end of its words that made them hard to understand.

"Why-errr do you come-err herrrree?" it drawled, its mouth hanging open after, the tongue thick and purple, bleeding from where it had been bitten.

"We'll go away again if you promise to stop killing people?" Selene suggested hopefully.

Not the corpse, but the thing behind the corpse—the mother chimera, Jill guessed—turned to look at Selene. It seemed to gather in on itself, then came forward further into the light.

It really was horrible to look at, and yet Jill felt none of the emotions she expected. No great drive for revenge or fury consumed her, and neither did feelings of disgust or revulsion. Rather she was fascinated by this creature, as she had been by that first chimera.

Its head looked rather elk-like, save the long sharp teeth, and the eyes, which were too close together and deep pure black. Its torso was covered in dark fur, and its legs were digitigrade, like a dog's. Its arms were long and boneless, made of pure corded muscle, and covered at the tips with scale-like protrusions that glistened sharply.

"I am-err rrraising my brood-err," said the chimera mother through the dead woman's mouth. "Go away orrr stay and die-err."

"Yeah, not gonna happen," said Selene, carefully arming her hand cannon.

"What—" asked Jill, and her voice was so high and shaky she had to stop and take a proper breath before she could continue. "What do you need that poor woman for? Why have you been kidnapping and killing people?"

The mother chimera looked at her. It seemed puzzled, as if her questions made no sense. Through the corpse it said: "Someone-rrr must speak-err forrr me-err. I need theirrre minds to-err think."

"Why vets then?" Jill pushed. She cut herself off before she added *Why Christian?*

"They know-err what I need-err . . . " the mother chimera moved slowly forward, holding the corpse before her like a puppet. Almost at once Selene and Clara took half a step forward, raising their weapons, and oddly enough the only thing Jill could think of was Christian's ghost saying *"You've already got your sword and shield."*

The mother chimera—the real creature, not the corpse puppet—made a sound like a food grinder. Jill thought it must be laughing. "This one-err is almost-er gone-err," it said through the corpse. "I will take-err you-errrr allrrrrrr—"

To Jill's horror the corpse's mouth kept opening wider and wider until its jaw split right off as the tip of a lithe arm erupted from within it. Then the body was torn to pieces as the mother chimera freed her arms, spatters of blood and organs went everywhere as those arms snaked through the air toward them. At the same moment, the pile of chimeras that had been waiting at their mother's feet surged to life and lunged at them.

Clara and Selene closed together in front of Jill, and she heard rather than saw the hand cannon go off. Clara grunted as a chimera launched itself out of the smoke and managed to latch onto her arm. Jill saw her calmly drive her sword into its neck, before her own feet were jerked out from under her by what felt like a snake wrapped around her ankles.

She fell into Selene as she went down, which was a lucky thing since otherwise the hunter might not have noticed in all the chaos. As it was she looked down over her shoulder at Jill, shouted *"Mind the tail, Clara!"* and swung her sawn-off shotgun under her elbow and fired one-handed at the long coiling appendage that had captured Jill.

The shot hit it about a foot from where it had attached itself to Jill, and at once she felt the muscles constricting her go limp and she kicked herself free.

She saw, over the smoke, Clara leap across the backs of the chimeras, dead and alive, and throw herself at the mother. Then the two were hidden in smoke, and Selene was busy firing point-blank at any creature that got close enough.

Somewhere in all the panic and adrenaline flooding her brain, Jill found the presence of mind to unsheathe the knife she had been given, and not a moment too soon; a chimera pounced on her from behind and she went down again, rolling as she fell and lashing out blindly with her knife. She felt it connect with something, realized she had shut her eyes, and opened them to see the knife buried up to the hilt in the neck of a chimera whose jaws had snapped closed inches from her face. The stared at each other for a bleak moment, and then the muzzle of Selene's hand cannon appeared pressed against the side of its head. Jill just had time to squeeze her eyes shut again and turn her head away before the shot went off.

She felt rather than heard the bang. In the ringing silence that followed she felt her face splattered with something wet that was probably blood, and something sharp that was probably fragments of the thing's skull.

And then there was silence. Real silence—not just the ringing daze left from having a gun fire inches from her ear—and then the dead weight of the chimera was pulled off her and Selene was gently rolling her onto her side, pulling her knee forward so she wouldn't fall onto her face.

A hand gripped her shoulder. "You okay?"

Jill opened her eyes and found herself sighting along her arm to where her hand still gripped the knife. She found this somehow comforting. The wind was still knocked out of her and her left ear was still ringing something terrible, but she found herself nodding and even smiling a little. "Yeah," she said quietly. "I'm good."

"You just stay down," Selene said, giving her shoulder a pat. She stood up and picked her way through the field of corpses until she came to where Clara stood over the headless body of the chimera mother, calmly wiping her sword down. The taller woman looked up as she approached.

"It is finished," she said.

"Awesome," said Selene, picking a strip of chimera gut off of Freddie. "Beer's on me tonight."

*   *   *

As it turned out, of all the problems connected with their hunt for the chimera mother, Jill Hamilton was the biggest.

For a start, she would not let them burn the bodies.

"This is prime research material!" she insisted, even while still covered in chimera viscera. "At this rate, Professor Okedo *must* pay attention. And the mother's corpse is especially valuable."

She even wanted to save their clothes, so she could pick through the remains that had stuck to them. In this she was unsuccessful; Clara snuck off and cleaned her biking leathers before Jill could stop her, and Selene flat out refused to part with her boots, jeans, or jacket. She did give Jill her undershirt, though, as a peace offering. And she convinced Jill to let them burn the majority of the chimeras: they numbered almost thirty and it would have been difficult to transport them all. But Jill insisted on keeping three, and all the pieces of the chimera mother they could find. She also insisted on staying until Professor Okedo arrived.

The professor turned out to be a middle-aged man of mixed African and Asian descent, a naturally big person, comfortably padded. He took one look at the row of bodies they had lined up outside the shelter and insisted on calling animal control. Jill thought they should call some university on the east coast. Clara and Selene snuck away while they were still arguing.

For Jill Hamilton, the next two days passed in a blur of hectic activity. She attended the reading of Christian's will, where she discovered he had left her his truck, along with its remaining payments. The red Dodge Ram truck she had always thought of as a waste of space and fuel. Now, in light of recent events and the cryptic prophesy, it gave her ideas that two weeks ago she would have thought were crazy. She still thought they were crazy, but now they also sounded exciting. So after a night of agonizing and weighing the possibilities up and down and sideways she went to a realtor and made a very important arrangement. Finally she went to Professor Okedo—who was up to his neck giving interviews and talking to everyone from a biologist from Germany to the *National World Weekly.* The news of the chimera bodies had stirred all sorts of pots—in some cases tipped them right over—and the small lab at UC Santa Cruz was quickly filling with grad students and doctors from all over the country. When Jill arrived the professor was trapped in his office by a crowd of very small and very serious Japanese women, who were speaking in a hurried mix of English and their native language.

Professor Okedo appeared to be in the process of placating them, but when he saw Jill peeking around the door he sent them all packing.

"This is a nice kettle of fish we seem to have opened," he said, scratching at his thick black curls. "Now the wackos have got wind of this I'm getting all kinds of unverifiable reports about *other* supernatural phenomena. You know, I can actually see why your friends wanted to keep it quiet."

Jill nodded sympathetically. "It's actually about that that I wanted to talk to you. See, I have an idea . . . "

She laid it out for him.

Professor Okedo frowned and rubbed his forehead.

"I don't know, Hamilton," he said heavily. "That's a pretty radical decision. In fact, it's crazy. I could probably get you a little funding, but it won't be enough to live on . . . "

"Oh, that's all right," Jill said, with the brightness of one who has committed to her crazy plan. "I've already decided to sell my house—I've put it on the market at a moving rate, which should get me a comfortable amount of cash fairly soon. If I can't convince someone to fund me properly by the time that runs out I'll quit—but I sincerely doubt it. Not with the stuff I think is out there."

"But what about your education, your career? Your whole life here?" Okedo waved an arm expressively. "Are you sure you want to throw all this away?"

Jill leaned back in her chair and looked up at him, her eyes big and earnest. She thought about trying to explain how 'her whole life here' had died with Christian; how now that he was gone it was only a hollow shell of what she had dreamed, painful reminders of what she'd lost studded everywhere like nails.

Instead she just said, simply, "Yes."

Okedo sighed. A really big, deep sigh that came from every part of his large body.

"I'll make the necessary arrangements with the college," he said reluctantly. "I'll also see about getting you a decent mobile lab—though you'll need a bigger car than that little Civic."

"I have a truck now," Jill said. "A Dodge Ram. It's got an eight foot bed and a crew cab. Would that be big enough?"

Okedo whistled under his breath. "Yeah, that just might be. But Jill, have you thought about this seriously? From what you've told me things got damn hairy with those monsters—chimeras—whatever. I don't want you doing something that could get you killed. And this could *kill* you."

Jill nodded serenely, and smiled. "Oh yes, I thought of that." And to Professor Okedo's immense confusion she said: "I'm going to get a sword and shield."

The afternoon sun glinted off a spotless black motorcycle parked at the end of a dirt road halfway up a forested mountain. It would have glinted off the little battered Jeep parked nearby, but the thing was so covered in dust it had been made entirely matte. Two women stood a little awkwardly between the vehicles. One was impossibly tall, pale and bald, the other was shorter, slimmer, dark-skinned with a mane of frizzy black hair. Eventually the dark one gave a little shrug and said:

"Well, I guess I'll see you around."

"Maybe," said Clara.

"I gotta say . . . it's been . . . nice, you know, having a partner."

"And you," Clara said stiffly.

"Well," said Selene, rocking back and forth on the balls of her feet. "You've got my number, if you ever need some help."

Clara pulled out a slip of paper from her pocket, checked it, then put it back. "I do."

"And the minute you get a cell phone of your own you *call me*, okay? So I can get yours."

Clara stared at her blankly. Selene sighed. "Girl, this *isn't* me hitting on you. If I get in over my head I just want to be able to call a six-foot-five amazon warrior with a big honkin' sword to come save my ass."

Clara actually smiled a little. "I am only six-four," she said modestly.

Selene threw her arms up in the air. "Well, *never mind* then," she said with a laugh.

It died away between them, and the two hunters stood, not turning, not leaving, not ready. Yet.

In the silence they heard, distant but growing steadily louder, the deep grumble of a diesel engine approaching up the road. When they looked all they could see was the dust cloud the vehicle was raising as it climbed until it rounded the final bend, and a huge dually pick-up truck, blood-red and gleaming, emerged from the cloud and crunched to a halt. The engine died with a sputter and the driver's door opened to let a figure, tiny in comparison, climb out.

It was Jill Hamilton. She had to take a bit of a leap even from the running board, and as she walked away from the truck she fondly ran a hand along the side of its nose.

Selene let out a low whistle. "Sister," she said. "Where did you get that ride?"

Jill just smiled, a little sadly. "You like it?" she asked.

"*Like* it?" Selene sputtered. She pushed past Jill to give the truck a look-over. It was so big her head couldn't clear the hood, and she had to stand on the running board to peek into the bed. "Dodge Ram, Cummins engine, 3500," she said approvingly. "Longhorn? Wait, no, Laramie. What year is he?"

"2010," Jill said, a little bemused.

"*Sweet,*" Selene practically squealed, handing herself along the crew cab so she could pull open the driver's door and stick her head inside. "Is he a stick? Oh-ho *yes he is!*"

"You like him?" Jill said. "If you come work for me, I'll let you drive."

Selene pulled her head out of the cab so fast she nearly over-balanced backwards. "Work for you—*what?*"

Clara frowned at them, but not in a way that suggested she was angry; instead she seemed to be concentrating. She looked at the truck, at Selene, and at Jill, and she ran what she remembered of the oracle's prophesy through her head. A picture had been slowly forming in her mind, and now it clarified enough for her to walk over and lay a hand on the nose of the truck, just above the grill, where there was set a silver ram's head with curling horns. She wiped away the dust that had gathered there, and looked over at Jill.

"*Ride a red ram,*'" she said. "Jill, what are you planning?"

Jill went over and hung her hand from the supports of the rearview mirror, and sighed.

"It's like this," she said. "The whole *problem* with going public on the existence of impossible animals is that now anyone who's thought they've seen a ghost or a werewolf or bigfoot is knocking down my door—well, Professor Okedo's door—trying to get their stories heard, when all we've actually *got* is a half-dozen corpses we've barely had time to study yet. *So* there was this particular kind of chimera, and it had a *particular* kind of queen-bee sort of mother; that *doesn't* prove the existence of chupacabras or mermaids or unicorns—though a lot of people seem to think it *does*. So what can we do? We can't believe any old wives' tale about the supernatural—we've got to know which ones are real and which ones aren't, and of the real ones, *we need to know how they work.*"

She looked from one hunter to the other, a steely glint in her eye. "That's where I come in. Okedo has agreed to set up a lab at UCSC, and I'm going to send him specimens and reports from the field." At their blank looks, she went on. "I'm going to do some *research*. On the *supernatural*. Because we desperately need it. We barely understand how this—" she waved a hand "—*normal* world works. To find out there's a whole *other* world, with a *completely different set of rules?* It needs to be studied. And I'm going to do just that."

Clara blinked. Selene coughed, then she said: "Girlfriend, have you got a *death wish?* You don't just waltz up to a werewolf and give it a survey to fill out! You'll only get yourself killed, you mark my words."

"Oh yes," Jill said, with unnerving cheer. "That's where you and Clara come in. I want you to come work for me."

"What, as bodyguards?" Selene sniffed.

Jill shrugged. "Partly. Hunters too. I want you to keep doing what you've always done—going into the dark and biting back or whatever—only let me *study* whatever you have left over. Let me observe. Let me *learn*. And yes, protect me. I think you're meant to, anyway."

Selene looked at her incredulously, but realization was dawning on Clara's bluff face.

"*For the fool who takes a rod to wield,*" Jill quoted. "*Before the shadows that surround them yield, follow the path by moon and star, ride a* red ram—" she patted the truck "—*with a* sword—" she looked at Clara "—*and* shield." She finished, returning her gaze to Selene.

"Oh *hell* no," said the black woman. "*That's* what your verse meant?"

"You said your last name was *Shields*," Jill persisted. "And Clara, you even *use* an actual sword—what?" For Clara was shaking her head.

"That is not the reason why," Clara said, her shoulders drooping. "It is all in the names. And my name, my *real* name, is not Clara." She looked down at them through narrowed eyes, as if she hated to admit this. "It is *Claymore,* after the Scottish broadsword. I am Claymore Nordstern, your sword."

"Oh damn," said Selene. "I just thought of something. My name—my *other* name—is the moon. Wasn't there a bit about—"

"By moon and star," Jill finished. "Clara—er, Claymore, what does *Nordstern* mean?"

"North star," the woman replied, looking resigned. Then she brightened. She looked over at Selene and she even smiled a little. "It looks as though you will have a partner after all."

Selene, however, remained unconvinced. She eyed Jill skeptically. "You said *work*. Does that mean just work, or work as in 'we protect your ass and you pay us?'"

Jill looked surprised. "I'll be paying you of course, and I'll make sure you get the proper medical treatment should you be injured."

"Would this be on a weekly or per-case basis?"

"Weekly," said Jill. "Your job is to protect me, then kill monsters."

"But I would still get to hunt them?"

"I want you to. I have no idea how to find the supernatural."

Selene shifted from foot to foot, looking restlessly from Jill, to the ground, to the truck... lingering on the truck.

"You said... I could drive?"

"As much as you want," Jill said.

"What about Clara?"

"It's got a full crew cab," Jill pointed out. "It'll seat six."

"No," said Clara, shaking her head. "I'll work for you, I'll hunt for you, but I ride Unicorn." She pointed at the black motorbike.

Jill nodded. "Fair enough, but we're getting you a phone."

Clara nodded assent.

"Hey," Selene said as she climbed into the cab, running her hand over the interior upholstery. "Has he got a name yet?"

"How do you know he's even a *he?*" Jill asked.

"Well, men are always naming their ships and planes and cars and things after *women*." She looked at her two companions. "Do you *see* any sausages present, ladies? I don't *think* so. Seems only fair, and ..." she glanced nervously at Jill. "Correct me if I'm wrong, but, this was your boyfriend's truck, wasn't it?"

"We're not naming him Christian," Jill said icily.

"Of course not!" agreed Selene. "Terrible name for a truck!"

Clara left them to argue ("What about Chuck?" "Chuck the Truck? Really?" "Sounds catchy!") and ran her hand over the wide, sloping hood, down to the ram's head ornament. It twinkled at her in the afternoon sun.

"The ram is an arcane symbol, like the goat," she said, derailing the naming discussion.

"Yeah, so?" said Selene.

"The arcane is all the things you think of as supernatural. The arcana is what you are getting yourself into." She smiled a little, as if at some internal joke. "Why not call *him* the Arcana?"

"Arcana," repeated Jill, as if trying the word out. "Ar-cay-nuh . . . huh."

"No, not just Arcana," Selene corrected. "Arcana is the plural. So he's *the* Arcana. Don't you know your latin?"

"Arcana," repeated Jill, not seeming to hear. She smiled, and patted the wheel well. "Right then, he's Arcana." She looked up at Selene. "Get your things. And remember, you're driving."

It was early evening when a red Dodge Ram truck pulled onto Highway 1 South, followed closely by a black motorcycle. As it left the lights and the traffic of Santa Cruz behind, accelerating into the night, in the passenger seat Jill leaned back and closed her eyes. She listened to the deep rumble of the engine, a pervasive purring hum that filled the cab under the soft tunes Selene had coming out of the radio. The song changed, and to Jill's surprise she recognized it.

"Hey," she said, still not opening her eyes.

Selene, who had been singing along under her breath, froze. "S'matter, Jill? Don't like Technorhyme?"

"No, it's not that," said Jill, blinking at her. "Turn it up."

Selene raised her eyebrows, then she chuckled. "At least you respect the classics," she said, cranking the volume up. "Maybe I will like working for you after all."

Accompanied by the pulsing beat of a song that until then Jill had never quite understood, Arcana roared on into the dark.

Turning 'round
the world spinning
Turning down
this dark beginning
Like nothing that's come before.

We're spinning 'round
but we don't see it
We're falling down
but we don't feel it
And we won't take it anymore.

Paint my life across the sky
Is that too much for me to ask?

I've gotta ride, though it might leave me numb
I've gotta ride, ride on over, ride forever
I've gotta ride, blow along my smoking gun
Now I've got my guiding light, though it's distant, it's so distant.

The Sword and the Shield

The world is a cold place, and I never asked to be here
All I can see is the crimes that I can't fix, hell no
My sword and shield, they can't protect
I've got this twisting dark in my heart, my heart

Like a star on the run
A valkyrie riding a smoking gun

I've gotta ride, though it might leave me numb
I've gotta ride, ride on over, ride forever
I've gotta ride, blow along my smoking gun
Now I've got my guiding light, though it's distant, so distant.

Ride on baby, oh
Gotta ride on now, baby
Gotta ride hard now, baby
Oh, gotta ride on . . .

—I've Gotta Ride, *Technorhyme*

HIGHWAY ^{2.}
UNICORNS

Somewhere in California
November, Present Day

ON A DARK HIGHWAY, in a remote house at the end of a dirt drive, lights were on inside. They turned the windows into squares of yellow. A door slammed, and voices escaped into the chill winter night.

"*Dammit Lola, why do you get like this?*"

It was a man's voice, slurred around the edges and angry.

"*Josh, I don't want to talk about it right now.*"

A woman's voice, clipped and short. She was frightened.

"*Why do you do that?*"

"*Josh . . .*"

"*Why do you put me off like I don't matter?*"

"*Don't be ridiculous, Josh.*"

"*Don't take that tone with me! Jesus, Lola, you don't* care, *do you?*"

"*Josh, please, you're scaring me—*"

"*Where are you going? Don't you turn your back on me, woman!*"

"*Josh, I think you need to leave now.*"

"*You do* not *tell me to leave my own house, god-dammit—Christ, you care more about that filthy animal than your own* husband—"

"*Josh,* please—"

"*Don't give me please, you've had your chance! Listen, you call the vet* first thing *tomorrow morning and get that animal* disposed of or I'll *take care of it in the back yard!*"

"*Josh, you wouldn't—*"

"*It's a waste of money and space, Lola, it's a lost cause.*"

"*Josh . . . please . . .*"

Another door slammed. Inside the house the lights went off one by one, the yellow squares eaten by the dark.

* * *

The next morning Lola went out back and checked on Barney. The skinny horse nickered at her as she filled his feeder with soft hay and then went around to check the wrap on his hind foot. It was holding together well, but the poor horse still couldn't rest his weight on it. Lola added an extra scoop of painkiller to his grain and placed the bucket in his feeder. Then she dusted off her hands and went to work.

When she returned that afternoon, the truck, trailer, Josh—and Barney—were gone. Lola flew around the house, hoping she was mistaken. When it was clear the place was deserted she picked up the phone, feeling sick to her stomach as she hit the speed dial for Josh's cell.

"Hey hon," came his voice, cracking over the line.

"Josh, you *didn't*," Lola began, her own voice breaking.

"Already done, hon."

"No . . ."

"Sweetie, the thing was dead on his feet—what was left of his feet. It was *cruel* to keep him alive."

"Josh, *no*," Lola began to shout, drowning out the man's response. "No, no, *no!* You had no *right!* He was getting *better!* He was *happy!*"

"The vet said—"

"I don't *care* what the stupid *vet* said!" Lola screamed into the phone, cut the call, and threw the receiver as hard as she could toward the wall. Its cord pulled it up short, and it swung back and hit her in the chest. Lola sank into a corner, still screaming faintly, and buried her face in her arms. After a while she crawled outside and into the empty barn, curled up on the bales of wood shavings that would now never be used to bed Barney's stall, and cried. And waited. And cried.

And waited.

But she never heard the rumble of Josh's truck, never heard its tires crunch on the dirt drive, never heard the squeak of the door as he got out.

Because Josh, and the truck, never came back.

It was a narrow highway; two lanes separated by a thick double yellow line with gravelly shoulders on either side. It stretched and wound through rolling hills dotted with farms and vineyards, accompanied only by the procession of power poles a few yards to one side. These stuck up, dark against the pale late-autumn sky, and provided perches for flocks of blackbirds, retreating from foraging parties in the fields below. It was almost deserted.

Almost.

A rumble in the distance signaled a traveler on the road, and as it grew nearer and louder it clarified into the hard bark of a motorcycle engine. Three motorcycle engines, in fact.

Vrrrrrrooowm!

Vrrrrrooowm!
Vrrrrrooowm!

They went zipping past. Three dirty white bikes, they powered around a corner where the road curved to accommodate a hillock and disappeared. Not just from the sight of the blackbirds perched on the power lines, but out of the world altogether. The *other* motorcyclist, riding at a more sedate pace down the road from the opposite direction, never saw them.

Again the rumble of an engine, deeper this time, and another motorcycle—a black one—came around the corner of the hill. It was not exactly a cruiser (the rider sat too far forward) and not exactly a sport bike (it had hard-case panniers on either side of the passenger seat). Someone who knew motorcycles might have thought it looked very like a Yamaha V-max, but a little rounder and a little heavier—and it had a single spike of black anodized aluminum welded above the main headlamp. In old and patched silver paint across the gas tank was written *Unicorn* in a careful hand.

In defiance of law and common sense the rider had her black full-face helmet off and clipped under one arm, with only a pair of sunglasses to protect her face from the wind and insects. She rode, relaxed, leaning as far back as possible while still keeping hold of the handlebars.

She was remarkably tall for a woman, and her long, leather-clad frame almost overpowered her already-powerful bike. Her head, bald as a newborn babe's, shone in the weak sun as she coasted down the hill and then powered onto the flat. Along her back was slung a wide sword in a worn leather sheath.

Clara Nordstern liked riding. It was why she kept Unicorn going year after year when a car would have been more practical. That and other, more personal reasons she didn't like to think about too much. Clara liked to consider herself the perfect hunter: concentrated, pure, undistracted. She allowed for emotional upheaval and irrationality in *other* people—but not herself.

But she liked to ride, and the narrow highway leading out of Hollister had looked attractive, so she decided to take a quick out-and-back joyride while she waited for Selene and Jill—currently stuck in traffic on 101—to catch up.

Cruising around another corner she had to fight the urge to brake hard out of pure surprise: a truck and trailer had jack-knifed across the road, tipping over onto their sides. The truck's windshield was broken, and there were dents all along its visible side, as though something had trampled it. The driver's door—which faced the sky—had caved in completely. Not far from the truck was a lump that had once been a man, lying in a puddle of dark liquid.

Clara came to a gentle halt beside the crash and extended one long leg to rest on the ground. She pushed her sunglasses up, revealing cold blue eyes, and surveyed the damage thoughtfully. Then she killed the engine of her own vehicle, pushed down the kickstand and dismounted.

First she went over to the man—what had until quite recently been a man, anyway. She discovered she could do nothing for him. With gentle hands she carefully rolled him onto his back.

He had been a big man: barrel-chested with thick gray stubble over his chin. Half his face had been crushed in, and that eye bulged from its destroyed socket, leering at Clara. Further examination revealed that his chest and abdomen had been crushed in a similar fashion. Indeed, the man looked as though he had been trampled just like his truck.

As there was no hurry to save anyone's life, Clara left the man in the road and went over to the truck, a blue Ford that had been used hard even before this calamity.

Reaching in through the driver's window Clara switched off the engine—which was still bravely turning over—and peered around the cabin. Thrown against the passenger window was a thick braid of dark hair—horse hair, she thought—tied at the top with a blue satin ribbon. Next to it was a frayed brown halter with a striped red and white lead rope. Clara frowned, and went around to investigate the trailer.

As she expected from the mementos in the truck, it was empty. But there was green hay in the feeder and fresh horse manure thrown against one wall along with the shavings that had originally been on the floor.

Clara stepped away from the trailer and looked over at the corpse in the road.

"A grim end to a grim journey, my friend," she said quietly, returning to stand beside the body.

She had gotten her phone out and was on the verge of calling the authorities—cleaning up car accidents was not *her* job—when something about the dead man caught her eye.

When she had moved him his button-down shirt had pulled open at the collar, revealing the corner of a black stain that disappeared under the blood-soaked cotton.

Still with her phone in one hand Clara bent over and pulled back the fabric, which revealed a mark the size of a liberty dollar. It was simple enough: a rough circle with a single dot in the center and a slanting gash that cut through the rim and pierced the dot. Anyone else would had written it off as some odd tattoo, but the sight of it made Clara's already pale face turn white. Standing up suddenly she looked sharply around, as if expecting some hidden enemy to spring from the vineyards on either side of the road. But all was empty and quiet. Above her on the power lines, a blackbird defecated serenely.

Clara looked back down at her phone and dialed a different number.

Miles away from where Clara stood by the wreck and the corpse, a different truck—a dark red Dodge Ram—rolled into the parking lot of a motel, and a woman—as petit as her truck was huge—jumped out. She had light brown hair and a pair of no-nonsense glasses balanced on her nose, and her feet tapped briskly over the pavement as she walked into the office. Behind her, from out of the truck, a dark sleepy face with a head of frizzy black hair emerged and blinked into the late afternoon sunlight.

Selene Shields rubbed the sand out of her eyes and yawned. Gingerly she climbed out of the truck and stretched her shoulders—after a night of driving and a day of sleeping in the back seat she felt like an old dog, and according to her reflection in the rearview mirror, she looked like one too. Her phone buzzed in her back pocket, and she groaned as she pulled it out and flipped it open.

Jill Hamilton's head was full of thoughts of a shower and bed when she exited the motel office, a room key clutched in one hand. But Selene was waving at her from the truck, very much awake, and very much excited.

"Pull up your pigtails, honey," she said. "Clara's found you a *case*."

Clara Nordstern heard the distinctive growl of Arcana's engine long before the huge red truck rolled into view. She had moved Unicorn off the side of the road to make room, and had been furtively going through the contents of the wreck's glove box. Furtively, because a lone motorist had been by and reacted as any ordinary person would react, and Clara had been forced to play the good samaritan and call the authorities after all. She gave them a half hour, and so was relieved when she emerged from the truck to find Arcana pulling to a stop and Jill and Selene tumbling out.

Jill—who had been driving—leaned back against Arcana's side as she took in the scene. This was not her first dead body, nor even her first dead human, but the shock of it there, on an otherwise idyllic country road, left her reeling.

Selene, who had become so inured to death and gore that it was no more remarkable to her than the hedges or the power lines, came around to where Clara stood by the truck and gazed down at the dead man impassively.

"Tell me there's more to this than a single-vehicle accident," she said.

"It wasn't," said Clara. "There was another. Perhaps several." She walked the length of the stricken truck, one gloved hand running along its battered side. "These dents," she explained as she walked, "did not come from the rollover. They were inflicted before the truck rolled, while it was still upright."

"Someone rammed this guy?"

Clara nodded with a grunt, coming around to the front. She pointed at the battered driver's door; the broken windshield. "This was done after. The victim crawled out here—see his blood on the hood? He had cut his hands on the glass, as you can see. He made it . . . " Clara pivoted slowly around and took two long paces to where the corpse lay, broken and twisted. "Here," she finished.

"Nice work Sherlock," Selene said, raising an appreciative eyebrow. "So why'd you call sounding like a ghost had punched you?"

Clara showed her.

Selene let out a low whistle.

"Hey sister," she called to Jill, straightening up. "You'll want to come see this."

Reluctantly Jill approached the dead man, bending low to see what Selene was pointing at. She stomped down hard on the initial rush of nausea, and tried to concentrate on the body analytically. It had, quite clearly, been trampled; there was a compound fracture in one arm and both legs, and the skull had been crushed. Trying to avoid the eye leering from the ruined socket she peered past Selene's dark finger to the strange little tattoo on the man's chest.

"Funny tattoo," she said, bringing out her phone and snapping a picture without really thinking.

"Not a tattoo," said Clara.

"That's a death mark," said Selene softly. "I've never seen one so black."

"Death mark . . . a what?" said Jill, straightening up.

"Death marks are . . . uh . . . " Selene pulled at her already wild hair. "Well, you ever read *Treasure Island?* Remember the Black Spot? It's kinda like that, only magic. A death mark means you're literally marked for death, and it calls to the person or thing that's going to kill you, so they can find you. Witches use them in their feuds—but they're usually a lot lighter than this."

"This was not done by a witch," Clara announced, producing a worn halter and a braid of dark hair. "At least, I do not think so."

"Where did you get those?" Jill asked sharply.

"The truck," Clara replied.

Eyeing the trailer Selene said, "Is the horse . . . ?"

Clara shook her head. "There is no horse."

"No," said Jill softly, "there wouldn't be."

Clara's cold blue eyes met Jill's warm brown ones, and the two women came to a silent understanding.

"Am I missin' something?" Selene cut in.

"That's a horse's tail hair," Jill said heavily. "They cut it off sometimes . . . as keepsakes. An empty trailer, an empty halter, and a horse tail . . . " she looked sadly down at the corpse.

"He was returning from taking a horse to be euthanized," Clara announced. "And on his way, he was trampled to death."

"Trampled?" Jill wondered aloud.

For answer Clara knelt by the body and pulled up the shirt over the man's abdomen. There was a horrible wound there, like a crescent had been gouged out of his side. Blood and gore was pooling in it, but the shape was distinctive.

"A hoof print?" Jill said, incredulous.

"I think," said Selene after a while. "That I'd like to see the horse he took to be put down."

Clara produced a receipt stub and handed it to her. "Hollister Valley Animal Control," she said. "Ask for the horse that Joshua Gobel brought in."

"Where are you going?" Jill asked.

Clara produced the truck's registration papers. "I am going to talk to Lola Gobel, his wife." She pressed the halter and the tail into Selene's arms. "Take these, they belong with the horse, and you might need them."

Jill and Selene watched as Clara pulled her motorcycle out of the bushes and pushed it up onto the road, watched as she mounted the bike, started the engine, and roared away.

"Does she know something we don't?" Jill asked, when the engine was fading thunder on the wind.

Selene, her arms full of halter and horsehair, shrugged. "She's a giant bald lady with a sword who rides a motorcycle named Unicorn—'course she knows things we don't!"

The sun was close to disappearing behind the western hills and it was growing cold in the barn. Lola sat on a bale of shavings despondently petting Cowbell, her shaggy gray cat, who in the nature of cats was more concerned with getting his dinner than the emotional well-being of his mistress. She was just beginning to think she might be able to manage a can opener without hurting herself when she heard the unmistakable sounds of an engine and the crunch of gravel under wheels.

Anger surged up in her, past the sadness and despair. She shot to her feet, displacing Cowbell, and stormed out of the barn and around the house, ready to do battle with her wayward husband. But even as she walked a part of her mind said, *that didn't sound like our truck . . .* and sure enough, there was no truck: instead a muscly black motorcycle was cooling in the drive, and the rider was just in the process of removing his—no, *her*—helmet, and coming toward the house. She was a giant, easily over six feet tall and broad-shouldered, bald, and there was something that looked like a sword strapped to her back. Lola gazed at the apparition, bewildered.

"Lola Gobel?" the woman asked. If she had said "*Sarah Connor?*" with a deep Austrian accent Lola would have been less surprised, but the bald woman had a pleasant, light voice, though her words were clipped and short.

"Yeah, th-that's me," said Lola, trying to keep the shake out of her voice.

The woman nodded to herself, as if this was what she expected to hear. Then she said: "You had a horse—a black one, or dark bay, I wanted to talk . . ." She trailed off into silence, for Lola, at the mention of poor Barney, had broken down into tears once more.

The woman seemed taken aback, and understandably, but only for a moment. Then she came forward and, ever so gently, took Lola by the elbow and led her toward the front door.

"You did not want him to be killed," she heard the woman say under her breath. "I had not realized."

Fiercely wiping away her tears, Lola got herself under enough control to say; "Who are you? Don't tell me you're his *family?*"

The woman shook her head. "Not I," she said. "But I am looking for them." She had a funny way of talking, Lola thought. Stiff and formal, like she ought to have an English accent, but she didn't.

"I rescued Barney from Animal Control," Lola explained—later, after Cowbell had been fed and coffee had been started. "They were going to put him down—he had terrible abscessing in his hind foot and damage to the leg—we think it had been caught in a fence—but I saw him, and he was so sweet and alive and the way he looked at me, like he knew I was going to help him, that I was a good person—I *couldn't* leave him there to be . . . k-killed." Her voice choked up again. Clara waited patiently.

"Anyway," Lola continued, heaving a deep breath. "I had my vet look at him, and she said the foot would be salvageable if the abscess hadn't gotten into the bone—which it might not have. So she cleaned it out as best she could and we packed it and bandaged it—but he still had trouble walking on that foot. Then yesterday we had him down for x-rays and . . . and . . . " she had to swallow hard, took a break to poor coffee.

"It wasn't just the abscess," she said when she came back. "One of the tendons on that hind leg—you know how horse legs are all bone and tendon down there—well, one of those tendons, a big one, had been ripped clean through. Probably from a wire fence, the vet said. And, well, that was that. He'd never be sound again, even if he did recover from the abscess. We could keep him comfortable, but he'd always be dragging that hind leg around—he could never work or be ridden. Josh and I had a fight about that. Josh said we'd never be able to adopt him out—we can't afford to keep a horse, you see—and I said we could do our best and maybe there was some charity or outreach program that would take him. He had such a beautiful soul, you would agree if you ever met him, I thought maybe he could be one of those therapy animals or something. But he . . . Josh said . . . if I didn't then he would . . . and . . . "

She trailed off, staring into her untouched coffee.

The house phone rang, loudly, and Lola jumped. Excusing herself she went and inspected the caller ID, and with a bewildered expression she picked up the line.

Behind her, unseen, Clara watched intently.

"Hello?" she said. Then . . . "He never keeps his phone on, I'm not surprised. They want what? No . . . I mean, yes, yes I suppose that's good. His body won't go to waste, then? No, no I don't want anything. Yes, thank you."

Click.

"That was funny," she said, sitting back down at the table. "Two women from some college just turned up at Animal Control asking for Barney's body. The college wants to buy it and study it—isn't that weird?"

Clara looked at her impassively. "Yes," she said, in her strange, stiff way.

Lola eyed her then, a little apprehensive. "This whole day has been weird," she said, suddenly wanting this big, strange woman out of her house. It had been good to vent, but now she wanted to be alone with her thoughts. As if sensing the change in her demeanor the woman carefully pushed her chair back and rose, her head nearly brushing the low-hanging lamp.

"I am sorry," she said, but for what she didn't elaborate. Lola supposed, for the whole business in general. She sighed in relief and showed her to the door.

"Good luck . . . finding Barney's family," she said, seeing Clara off into the evening. "Though the kind of people who let this happen to him . . . I'm not sure they deserve to be found."

"I do not think," said Clara quietly, "that it was his family that did this to him." She paused, there on the doorstep, and Lola suddenly worried that she might ask more questions. But she only reached into her pocket and pulled out a pad of paper and the stub of a pencil. Jotting down a number she tore the paper free and handed it to Lola.

"If anything else . . . *weird* . . . happens," she said. "If you are frightened, or think you're in danger, call me."

Lola laughed, but she took the paper. "Why would I be in danger?" she asked.

Clara just looked at her with those pale blue eyes. She looked, Lola thought, immensely sad, and a little worried. She seemed on the verge of speech, but then came the sound of a car approaching, and looking toward the road they saw a highway patrol crunching down the drive.

"I'm sorry," said Clara, and she seemed to mean it. She pulled on her helmet and mounted her bike, pushing herself slowly down the drive and past the approaching car.

Lola waited in the door for the state car to park and the officer—a rotund middle-aged woman—to climb out. One look at her face and Lola knew something was terribly wrong.

"I can't believe that worked," said Selene, once they were alone.

"It was the truth," said Jill briskly, pulling on her gloves.

It had been surprisingly easy and relatively cheap to purchase the body of the abandoned horse. Getting it to a place where Jill could perform a necropsy—that had been the hard part. It had taken almost three hundred dollars and the commandeering of the clinic's backhoe to maneuver the corpse onto the flatbed trailer Jill had purchased, which was then hooked up to Arcana and positioned under the floodlights behind the clinic—since by this time they had lost the sun and it was growing dark.

Now the bored tech who had sold them the body had gone back inside, and Selene was holding a flashlight for Jill as she worked her way around the stiff corpse, checking its eyes, nose, feet, and other dark areas. There had been a bandage of duct tape over its right hind hoof, and this Jill had removed one strip at a time. She gave a little *"Oh,"* at the sight of the gaping hole in the hoof beneath, packed with gauze and smelling strongly of iodine.

"Is that why they put him down?" Selene asked. She didn't know much about horses, but she had heard that problems with their feet tended to escalate to life-threatening situations for mysterious reasons.

"Possibly," said Jill, moving back up along the horse's body.

He had been a tall, thin horse—Selene lost count of his ribs, and his hipbones looked like coat hangers. Lying on his side with his legs stuck out straight from the rigor mortis, Selene thought he looked like a model of a starving horse that had been tipped over.

Jill moved on up to his long head, taking the flashlight and peering into the one available eye.

"Huh," she said, and looked closer.

"Huh, what?" said Selene, who pulled her coat tighter around herself. It was getting colder, and she was growing bored of watching.

"He has white sclera," said Jill, pointing at the eye. "Most horses, they have black sclera—that's the part of the eye around the iris—"

"I know what the sclera is," snapped Selene. She could see from where she stood that the horse's eye, instead of being a pool of dark, seemed to leer at her because of all the white around the edges.

"I thought he looked like a thoroughbred," Jill mused. "But you don't get white sclera next to dark skin except on appaloosas."

"So . . . he's an apple-what's it?" Selene said.

"I don't know, I can't find any mottled skin and he hasn't got striped feet and . . . " Jill gestured at the length of the dark body under the harsh floodlight. Selene thought he looked black, but Jill had insisted he was a dark bay. "No spots," she said.

"How d'you know so much about horses?"

"I don't," Jill said tightly, running a gentle hand over the horse's unresponsive ear and through his thick forelock. "But Christian was a large animal tech . . . I picked things up."

Her voice had gone distant and hollow, the way it always did when she talked about her dead boyfriend. Selene mentally kicked herself for stepping into that hole, even if it had been by accident.

Fortunately, Jill's probing fingers felt something then that distracted her, and she began to comb both her hands through the horse's forelock, which was so thick and bushy this was almost impossible. But she did manage to pull it aside and up, exposing his forehead.

"That's weird," said Jill clinically. Selene came up and leaned in over her shoulder.

In the exact center of the horse's forehead, where all the short, soft hairs twined together into a little swirl, there was a bald oval patch rather larger than a half dollar coin. But instead of exposed skin there was a raised lump of something smooth and bone-like, and in the center of it, emerging like new growth from the center of a tree stump, was about a quarter of an inch of tiny, spiraled horn.

Gently, Jill ran a finger over the destroyed horn.

"Is this what I think it is?" she asked softly.

Selene didn't answer. When Jill turned to look, she found the other woman had backed off and was pressing her fist against her mouth as if to plug a scream. Her eyes were wide as saucers and they darted all around, as if expecting an ambush. She looked, Jill thought, almost as though she were going to be sick. Finally she took her fist out of her mouth and said:

"They killed a unicorn. A real, live *unicorn.* Bloody mother, Jesus, Mary, and Joseph in a laundry basket—they killed a *unicorn!*" She gave out a short, harsh laugh. "Oh, we are *so screwed.*"

"Okay," said Jill, rubbing a tired hand over her face as Arcana rumbled back toward town and their hotel room, the trailer loaded with dead unicorn rattling behind them. "Explain to me why it's bad that we've got a dead unicorn—like, why is it worse than a dead anything-else?"

"You don't kill unicorns," Selene said tightly. "You just—don't. Heck, I've never even *seen* one before this—almost didn't think they were real— but it's just something, you know? Like, don't kick puppies, don't rape children—and *don't kill unicorns.*"

"So, like common decency? But what if this was a mercy-killing? It's called euthanasia for a reason."

Selene shook her head as she drove. "It's not worth it—look what happened to his owner. *Christ,"*— she slapped the steering wheel—"what was he *doing* with an injured unicorn in the first place?"

"Perhaps Clara will know," Jill suggested.

"Let's hope so." Selene ground her teeth. "One thing's for sure; this explains the death mark on that poor bastard's chest."

Jill blinked. It had been a long day, and aborted necropsy notwithstanding, she had a hard empty feeling inside rather like hunger. It made it difficult to think.

"How so?" she asked.

"Unicorns use death marks," Selene said absently, as if thinking of something else. "According to the stories, anyway. Kill a unicorn, and that unicorn's family will hunt you down and kill *you*—there's a big reason not to kill them—death marks are their way of . . . well, of tracing you."

"Can they really do that?"

"What do you think killed Joshua Gobel?"

Jill thought about it. Then said:

"He was in a truck."

"Yep."

"On a highway . . ."

"*Yep.*"

"They got him anyway."

"That right."

Silence. Arcana grumbled over the asphalt.

"Drive faster?"

For answer, Selene gunned the accelerator. "Have you heard from Clara yet?" she asked.

"Still not picking up. I think she's out of service range."

Selene cursed under her breath, but the words were eaten up by the roar of Arcana's engine.

As it turned out, Clara was just very bad at answering her cell phone; when they pulled into the motel's parking lot (the corpse carefully hidden under a tarpaulin), she was leaning against her bike waiting for them.

Selene jumped out, pulling her duffle bag filled with guns after her. The two hunters exchanged a silent look filled with meaning.

"It's a unicorn," Selene said shortly. "But you knew that already."

Clara nodded; one sharp jerk of her chin. "I didn't know which room," she offered.

"Then follow me," said Jill, slinging on her backpack and leading the way.

Ten minutes later they were assembled around a table; Selene was unpacking the leftovers of a cold lunch for dinner, and Jill had her laptop open. Clara sat like a large, leather-clad boulder, her arms crossed, having just recounted her interview with Lola Gobel.

"Okay," Jill said, businesslike. "I've entered the info from the notes I took this afternoon—and Mrs. Gobel's testimony. Now, you two, tell me everything you know about unicorns."

Selene paused with a handful of limp fries halfway to her mouth. Then she pushed them the rest of the way in, chewed, and swallowed.

"Don't know much for certain," she said. "They're not like werewolves or vampires; they don't exist in this world naturally."

"Vampires and werewolves exist naturally . . . " Jill repeated, pulling up a new file on her computer and adding a note. "Go on."

"Well . . . by all accounts they are very magical . . . " Selene continued. "But they need at least a little magic to manifest in our world at all. They can . . . um . . . cure injuries and illness . . . or cause injuries and illness. They can appear and disappear at will . . . "

Jill frowned. "If they're so magical," she said, her nose wrinkling. "How did this one end up dying like a common horse?"

Selene, her mouth full of fries, looked pleadingly at Clara.

With a sigh, the large woman unfolded her arms and leaned them on the table, her leather jacket creaking as she did so.

"What Selene says is true," she began. "Unicorns *are* magic. You hear of witches, how they *do* magic? Yes, they do. But where does that magic come from? From things like unicorns. Creatures that *are* magic. A unicorn's magic is strongest in its horn, mane and tail. The horn mostly—but the hair of a unicorn is still powerful good luck. Unicorn horns and hairs are ingredients in a lot of spells and form the core of many artifacts of power.

"But to kill a unicorn is a grave crime, and carries a heavy penalty: all blood relations of that unicorn will feel the death, and they will seek out those they judge responsible for the crime and kill them. As we have seen. So what is done by some people is to trap a unicorn—which is possible, with the right spells—and cut off its horn, mane, tail. This will leave the unicorn powerless and vulnerable, but alive."

Clara paused, and for a few moments all was silent except for Jill's clickety-clack on her keyboard. Selene chewed her fries unhappily.

"Manes and tails grow back fast," Clara went on. "But horns take years. They are the core of a unicorn's power, after all. During that time the unicorn will appear as an ordinary horse; it will be unable to take itself home, and will be forced to live in our world until it recovers. Some . . . " she looked past Jill, past the drawn blinds, to where they all knew Arcana and the trailer were parked. "Some don't survive."

"Hmm . . . " said Jill, her fingers flying.

There was subdued silence for some moments, until Selene decided to break it.

"*Wow,*" she said, swallowing the last of the fries. "Is it just unicorns, or are you secretly a walking encyclopedia of fantastical creatures? Ask her another, Jill!"

Clara gave Selene an unreadable look. "I was thirteen years old," she said. "I wanted a unicorn to ride instead of a pony. My sister built me a motorcycle instead, and named it Unicorn. I learned all I could about them so I could pretend she was one. I *remember.*"

"Well, I'm taking this all under consideration as unproven hypothesis," Jill said, pushing her laptop away. "What you know may or may not be true. I'll have to examine the body more closely, and for that I'll need sunlight." She stretched, yawned, and rose from her chair to crawl over to the nearest bed, pausing only to kick off her shoes. "Please don't wake me unless someone is dying," she said, stuffing her head under a pillow.

"Aye, no fear there," Selene said with a chuckle. She nodded at Clara, who was still sitting with her arms defensively crossed. "You go ahead, I'll take the first watch."

Clara shook her head, rising from her chair like a mountain unfolding. Wordless she went to the door.

"Where are you going?" Selene called after her.

Clara stood in the open door, her broad back hunched in the frame. She tilted her head just slightly, so one eye was visible, and said: "To hold his vigil."

The door clicked shut behind her.

Out in the parking lot Arcana and his grim cargo were just visible on the edge of the streetlight's glow. Clara went first to her bike, where she took the helmet from the handlebars, then went over to the truck. She undid just enough of the ties on the tarp so she could pull back a corner to reveal the unicorn's head. Reverently she stroked a gloved hand down his long nose, then pushed aside the bushy forelock to reveal the stubby, partly-healed horn.

She stood like that in silence for some time, half bent over the body. Then, as if finished with some silent prayer, she mounted by the trailer's hitch and came to sit on the tailgate, her feet resting on the rear fender. She pushed her helmet on (for the night air had grown cold), and unsheathed her sword from its scabbard on her back. Resting the naked blade across her lap she placed one hand on the hilt, and the other (carefully) across the flat of the tip.

There she sat: a black figure in the black night, so still one might have mistaken her for a statue. She sat and she waited, the naked sword across her lap. She held vigil.

Highway 25 was a notoriously fun drive . . . in a sporty car . . . in the daytime. Late at night, after a hard day being the on-call vet for county animal control, in an old Chevy with a temperamental steering wheel, it was not.

Still, the section between Hollister and Paicines was a drive that Harvey Cline, DVM, had made so many times that his hands and arms practically remembered the turns for him. He drove on autopilot, leaning into the curves and casually speeding, not bothering to check his brights—as there was practically no traffic on Highway 25. Except . . .

Vrrrooooowm!

Guy could get hurt if he crashed at that speed, Harvey thought to himself as he watched the taillights of the motorcycle retreat into the distance. He idly shuffled the tuner on the radio, looking for that one station that wasn't static or Mexican or Christian rock. He was peering at the dusty display, trying to make out whether that was a 101.7 or a 101.1 (did he need a new prescription already?) when there was another *Vrrroooowwm!* and a motorcycle passed him so close he was surprised neither of them lost paint. He was still cursing under his breath when . . .

Vrrrrooooowm!

There went another one.

What had today been? Wednesday? Why should there be so many bikers out on a weeknight?

Harvey was shaking his head to himself when he came around a corner, and there was the single headlamp of a motorcycle—*heading straight for him!* Instinctively he wrenched the wheel—overcompensated—and he felt the right wheels riding up onto the bank beyond the shoulder. The motorcycle whizzed by on his left.

"Mother of *Christ!*" he gasped as the truck returned to the road with a jerk. He had to swing again—he nearly went off the road on the other side—and by the time he had the truck back in its proper lane the taillights had vanished once more.

Now there were two headlights ahead of him, barreling down the road. Too far apart to belong to a car, they could only be the other two motorcycles.

Swearing fit to burn, Harvey slammed on his brakes, the tires squealing as they skidded along the asphalt. The two bikes parted, one swerving to either side, and Harvey was sufficiently distracted that he did not notice the third bike, which had come around and was running toward the back of his truck.

He did notice when that bike mounted the bed, engine growing, tires crunching, as it rolled on, on, and *up*.

With a crash of glass and buckling metal the bike rode clear up and over the cab, broke the windshield into smithereens, and ruptured the hood before returning to the ground.

The engine died violently, with a hiss and a gurgle, and Harvey came up against the seatbelt with a jerk. There was broken glass everywhere, and something liquid was running in his eyes—though he couldn't feel the pain through all the adrenaline.

Those bastards!

In shock, Harvey grabbed the crowbar he kept on the floor by the passenger seat and fumbled his way out of the seatbelt and the door.

From what he could see his truck was totaled and there was no sign of the motorbikes. He pulled his phone from his pocket, scraping his hand on some glass shards that had settled in the folds of his clothes, and woke it up.

No service. Of course. It was patchy and unreliable at best on this road.

Vrrrrrrrrrrooooooooooooo OOOOOOO W — WOOOO W WOOWWWMMM!

The noise of the motorcycle engine grew suddenly close. No— *engines*—here came the two again, back up the road, their headlights blazing like angry eyes.

Harvey was no fool. He knew it was idiocy to run along the road. So he ran across it—toward the shoulder and the ditch beyond, where motorbikes couldn't follow.

He only had a dozen or so feet to cross, but the motorcycles came on incredibly fast—they almost seemed to leap through the air toward him.

Lit red on one side from his truck's taillights, Harvey at last saw them clearly.

That's impossible! he thought. *They don't have riders!*

After that, Harvey Cline thought nothing at all.

Selene woke early, an uncomfortable thought gnawing on her mind. She got up, showered, dressed, and went out to Arcana where Clara, that crazy girl, was still sitting, holding her vigil. Now it was light Selene noted with relief she had covered the unicorn's head, and the body was an unrecognizable mass under the tarp. People would think they were just transporting a sofa, or something. Yeah.

Clara didn't move even as Selene opened the back door and rummaged in her other duffle. Finding what she wanted she took it and walked briskly across the street to the diner that advertised a $4.99 breakfast special. She had a feeling it was going to be a long day, and a girl needed fuel.

Jill found her some hours later, after inquiring of Clara (eating breakfast out of a paper bag) and following the silent, pointing arm, in a little booth near the back, the table littered with the remains of a greasy breakfast. Black earbuds protruded from her ears, the curling wires trailing down to where they disappeared under her jacket.

"What are you—?" she began, but Selene held up a hand to silence her. Shrugging to herself, Jill ordered a pot of coffee and a plate of what she hoped would do the least damage to her heart.

After a few minutes Selene pulled the earbuds out and looked over the table at her, grimly.

"So, the unicorn mafia will go after anyone they think is guilty for their relative's death, right?"

"That's what Clara said," Jill replied carefully, pouring herself a cup of coffee.

"So they go after the guy who takes the unicorn to be euthanized—makes sense but isn't there at least one other big player?"

Jill sipped her coffee and thought about it for a few moments; but she didn't need to wait for the caffeine to kick in to realize who the obvious target would be.

"The vet who performed the euthanasia!" she cried, half standing.

Selene motioned her to sit and pulled out the receipt Clara had given her the day before and slapped it on the table.

"His name was Harvey Cline," she said. "I put a call through to his receptionist, but he hasn't gotten back to me yet." Replacing the earbud she added, "Now I'm scanning the police and highway patrol radio, but nothing..." she trailed off, her eyes going so wide the whites could be seen all around her dark irises. "They found him," she said softly.

"The police," said Jill, "or the unicorns?"

"Both," whispered Selene.

Clara was just rising stiffly from her post when she saw the other two women walking hurriedly across the street toward her. She read the morning's events in their faces.

"The vet?" she asked.

Selene gaped at her as though she had sprouted horns, but Jill just narrowed her eyes.

"You knew?"

"I feared."

"Why didn't you say anything last night?"

Clara pulled her shoulders down, then raised them; her trademark reverse-shrug. "He *did* kill a unicorn."

"And you think that *justifies* getting turned into road pizza?" Jill said, a little shrilly.

"That justice is beyond me," Clara returned after a long pause. She locked Jill with her steely blue gaze. "But I cannot bring my heart to grieve for him."

"*Okaaaay,*" Selene said, sliding between the two of them. "Let's just . . . oh . . . set the existential eye-for-an-eye argument *aside* for a bit. Think *practically* here. We've got two dead men, one dead 'corn and an unknown number of live and angry ones running around. What do you want us to do?" She wheeled on Jill, who pushed her glasses up her nose in surprise.

"Me?"

"This is your case, sister. We don't *hunt* unicorns."

"Oh," Jill looked down at her feet for a moment. She was unused to giving orders so directly, but her natural assertiveness soon trampled over any concerns about social expectations.

"Clara," she said. "I want you to go investigate the crash site: it's out Highway 25, near Paicines. Selene, if there's any way you can get a *look* at Harvey Cline's body . . . it would be good to know whether he carried this death mark also."

"And you?" Clara asked.

Jill seemed surprised at the question. "I'm going to stay here," she said, as if this were obvious. "Selene, help me move the trailer to some place private with good light: I want to take a closer look at our specimen."

"You will defile the body?" Clara said, her normally light voice dropping to a growl.

"I'm going to *study* it," Jill said, rounding on the taller woman, like a magpie going after an eagle. "It's what I *do.*"

"What if she puts everything back where she finds it?" Selene said quickly, laying a soothing hand on Clara's elbow. "Doesn't take anything *away.* So, no samples, Jill. Just notes."

Clara shrugged off the motion, jamming her helmet back on and flipping the visor down. "If she violates the corpse," came the muffled voice, "it is not I to whom she will answer."

Selene and Jill watched the tall dark figure walk across the lot, pulling her bike upright and kicking a long leg over the seat.

"What do you *mean* I can't take *samples?*" Jill said. "You were happy enough when I cut up those chimeras!"

Selene gave her a tired look. "Joshua Gobel? Harvey Cline? Do you *really* want to risk it?"

"That's what I've got you and Clara for," said Jill.

Selene let out a sad laugh. "We can't protect you from everything, hon."

The weather had turned cold overnight, and there were clouds banking to the north as Clara sped down Highway 25, leaning into the curves with practiced ease. Out of the city, winding through hills, up and down, past the fatal stretch where Joshua Gobel had met his end. Clara didn't even slow down; there was nothing left for her to find there.

Further on she rode, long past the point where the weak cell signal gave out altogether. The terrain had subtly changed: the hills moving to either side and growing taller and steeper, mountains creating a shallow valley in which the road ran. Still it wavered and wobbled to navigate the stray hill that sometimes crept onto the floor of the valley. It was past one such hill that Clara found the spot where Harvey Cline had met his demise.

There was nothing obvious to say that a human being had died here: the highway crew had already come and gone, and what was left of Harvey Cline was likely in the morgue. But there were still signs of a crash: alarming skid marks that curved wildly across the road, chips in the asphalt, and here and there a deep stain of something that had resisted all attempts at washing.

Clara slowed Unicorn to a gentle halt and walked her carefully off the road and onto the meager shoulder. Leaving her at rest a safe distance from the scene, she dismounted and approached the site, trying to reconstruct from scattered bits of glass and plastic what had unfolded the night before.

One element was easily established: Harvey Cline's place of death. Though the road crew had neatly washed all traces of blood from the asphalt, they had not been so careful with the gravel on the far side of the road. Here Clara found flecks of newly dried blood—some of it still luminous red—concentrated in the dirt near the road.

He must have bled quite a lot—been smashed to death as much as trampled—to have flung his blood so far.

But there was not what she had wished to find: clear prints in blood of the unicorns' tracks. Either they too had been cleaned away by the ignorant road crew, or they had faded with the coming dawn. Or they had not been left at all.

Still, there were distinct motorcycle skid marks, and so many, and so far around the place where the truck had clearly crashed, that she doubted it was a single machine. Two at least, perhaps more.

No hoof prints, however. Which meant nothing to Clara: she was convinced that it was the unicorn's family that was enacting this bloody revenge, and if they had to transform into motorcycles to do it then it would not have been the strangest thing she had seen in her life.

She looked back down the road to where her own bike waited patiently, its black metal horn catching the winter sunlight.

"It's not such a far leap," she said to herself.

While Clara was out tracing skid marks and turning over blood-stained pebbles, Jill was engaged in the altogether less pleasurable task of dissecting a dead animal.

Selene had found her a suitable deserted dirt road not far out of Hollister, and there unhitched the trailer to leave it, and its increasingly ripe cargo, with Jill before taking Arcana back into the city on a quest to locate Harvey Cline's body.

Now that the truck's rumble was but a memory and Jill was alone with the corpse to do as she liked—no brooding Clara to make vague, threatening comments—she had expected to feel released from the promise that had been made for her.

This was a find of incalculable worth. She had called Professor Okedo, and they had agreed that rather than trying to ship the thing back to Santa Cruz she should do her own field dressing, and send the artifacts of interest back in smaller, easier-to-mail packages.

Clearly, the item of greatest interest was the horn, and there Jill ran into her first problem: did she saw it off, or send the entire head? Was it a horn, proper, being part of the bone as were ram and goat horns? Or was it actually an antler, like that of a moose? Or was it a concentration of keratin, like a rhino's horn? How it connected to the body of the unicorn would tell them much, and Jill was loathe to destroy evidence.

As she pondered this, she found herself gazing down at the unicorn's dead face, and she got the strangest feeling that it was looking back at her. Its dead eyes were dark and sad, and seemed to be imploring her. Though to what end Jill could not possibly guess.

She stood there, knife in hand, while a few curious and hopeful ravens congregated on a nearby power pole. It was their cawing at each other that finally jerked her out of the daze.

Jill was not a superstitious person, but she remembered ravens were quite common in fairytales and mythology. Pointing her knife at the crowd of black bodies atop the pole, she said aloud:

"You'll be my witnesses, I'm not taking *anything.*" And she climbed up onto the trailer next to the dead body and began going over it with a magnifying glass.

She eventually took many things from the corpse, but they were intangible things such as measurements and observations—knowledge gleaned from deduction and inference.

The horn, she decided, was closer to bone than antler or keratin. Its growth pattern was such that, though it appeared to be a straight rod, it was actually formed of a tight coil of thinner horn, which had grown in a spiral on itself. Smooth and cold, its coils had faint growth rings laid upon them, like that of a tree. Jill spent an hour counting them, using the tip of her exacto-knife as a marker. The rings on the stump were packed so close together they were almost impossible to count—she hazarded somewhere on the order of a hundred or so—but on the tiny, new growth they were much farther apart. This new horn was pale with a pearly sheen and held a grand total of seven rings, about two per complete coil. If each ring did indeed represent a year, then this unicorn had been running loose for quite some time.

Jill moved down to the mouth, popping it open with improvised forceps—though what she wanted was one of those contraptions used to hold a horse's mouth open while having their teeth floated. She had seen Christian use one once, and she suddenly found herself wishing for his vet supplies.

Then, having thought of Christian, she had to sit down on the edge of the trailer and have a good cry.

It had been a month, and Jill was only just beginning to be able to keep his memory safely tucked away. While she could do that, she could function, but even the slightest reminder brought on a debilitating bout of grief. So she sat and wept for the memory of Christian, and for the unicorn too, she supposed, until her body had wrung itself out like a sponge, and she was able to think clearly again.

When at last she returned to the unicorn's mouth she found a surprise: not only were the teeth remarkably white and clean, but there were huge canines in the place of the usual gap where, in an ordinary horse, a bit would rest. Anyone trying to put a bridle on this beast would have been in for a nasty shock. Jill took measurements, pictures, and notes, and wondered how his human caretaker—let alone a vet—could have missed this. Perhaps they were too distracted by his rear end, where the obvious damage was.

Everything else about the unicorn was practically indistinguishable from an ordinary horse: his hooves were wide and dark, with paler hoof showing near the bottom where a farrier had clearly been at work. His mane was as long and bushy as his forelock, as was what was left of his tail: all the hair below the bone having been neatly cut off and currently lying in the braid beside his head. He was also, Jill noted with interest, intact; though he did not display the prominent neck ridge she usually associated with stallions. Still, he would have been a powerfully built equine, if it weren't for his emaciated state.

The only point of interest on the rest of his body was his injured hind leg. Though he was laid on his side, with rigor mortis in full effect his upper legs were stiff as pegs, jutting away from his body. The injured hind leg was one of these, and unlike the front leg, whose hoof was held in a more-or-less ordinary position with regards to the rest of the leg, the hind hoof hung down from the joint. It wobbled a little when Jill tested it.

This had been the bandaged hoof, and now in the daylight she could see more clearly the huge gaping hole that had been carved in the sole to allow what must have been a terrible abscess to drain. He might have recovered from that, she thought, but the limp way the hoof hung suggested further injury. Jill guessed that one of his flexor tendons, perhaps also the suspensory ligament, had been severed. Further examination of the leg revealed an ugly scar that stretched all the way around the hock in narrow bands.

"Wire fence," Jill muttered to herself. She shook her head. With such damage to the leg, he would barely have been able to walk, even without the abscess. Unthinking, she reached up and stroked the animal's flank.

Some miles away Lola Gobel sleepwalked through her day. The officer had said she shouldn't be alone, but her nearest relative was a sister who lived in Flagstaff, and she wouldn't arrive until tomorrow.

So Lola ghosted through that strange limbo of time where her head felt neither here nor there. She fed Cowbell, she petted Cowbell, and she washed dishes. Then she went and took a very long, hot shower.

It wasn't until after, as she dried herself, that she noticed a strange dark mark on her shoulder. Wiping the condensation from the bathroom mirror she peered at it through the steam.

It was a circle the size of a liberty dollar, with a dot in the center and a gash through it.

Lola rubbed at it with the towel. It remained.

She stepped back into the shower and tried to scrub it off with soap.

No difference. If anything, the mark was blacker than before.

The sight filled her with a strange, primal fear. She had never seen that mark before, and yet she knew on some gut level that it was *bad*. A worse-than-cancer kind of *bad*.

She thought about calling her sister, but Maria would be on the road by now. But who else *could* she call about grief-induced hallucinations? Or was this even a hallucination? It was so *weird* . . .

That word triggered a memory. A recent one. Someone saying, "If anything else . . . *weird* happens . . . " and a piece of paper with a number on it in rough pencil.

Lola had already run into the kitchen, snatched the paper from the pile on the counter, and had halfway dialed Clara's number before she realized how silly she was being. Then she glanced down at the strange mark.

"Hell," she said to herself. "This *counts*." She finished dialing, and held the receiver to her wet ear.

It rang for so long she wondered if she had been given a prank number. Then at last she heard the line get picked up—and a computerized voice was telling her that "Clara Nordstern" was not available.

Lola stared blankly out the window, a sinking feeling in her stomach.

It was late in the afternoon when the crunch of gravel and the grumble of a diesel engine announced Arcana's return. Jill sat on a cooler some ways from the corpse—now decently covered with a tarp again—picking at a sandwich.

"He still in one piece?" Selene asked, coming around Arcana's big, blunt nose.

Jill set the sandwich aside. "We can give him an open-casket funeral," she said dryly. "How did your day go?"

"*Well*," said Selene, flinging herself onto the ground beside Jill. "Let's just say I am *not* the Hollister deputy's best friend, and if anyone comes asking for one Annie Slick she skipped town yesterday, the heart-breaker. *But . . .* " she reached into a pocket of her coat and pulled out Jill's digital camera. "See for yourself."

Jill raised an eyebrow at Selene's implied escapade, but she took the camera and began looking through the photos. The very first one contained an expanse of white, hairy skin, in the middle of which was a dark mark identical to the one on Joshua Gobel.

"Harvey Cline?"

"A part of his back, anyway," said Selene, helping herself to Jill's abandoned sandwich.

"Then, is that the end of it? I mean, what will the other unicorns do now?"

Selene shrugged. "Have a beer. Read sad poetry to each other. *Heck* if I know—they're unicorns! Go back to wherever unicorns go when they disappear, I suppose."

Jill glanced toward the trailer, where the lump of tarp represented the reason for all this hassle. "What will we do with the body, if I'm not allowed to take samples?"

"Clara will probably insist on giving it a Viking funeral or something," Selene said, rolling the paper the sandwich had come in into a ball and tossing it over her shoulder. "C'mon, let's grab some proper eats and then head back to the motel—I'm interested to know what the giant's found."

Clara, however, was not yet back by the time they pulled into the parking lot, and they shared take-out Chinese alone in the room until after dark, when Clara loomed in through the door looking haggard and tired.

"We saved you a spring roll," Selene offered by way of greeting.

Clara barely glanced at the food, making her way across to the little bathroom where not long after the sound of running water could be heard. The towering woman emerged a few minutes later, a towel covering her head and water still dripping into her eyes.

"So . . . tough day?" Selene asked as Clara laid herself out on the nearest bed.

"Frustrating," came the quiet response. Then, guessing she would not be left in peace without a full explanation, Clara sat up again. "I have spent the past day riding up and down Highway 25 looking for unicorns."

Jill snorted some of her noodles. "Come again?" she said. "Why?"

"If I knew how to find them, we could return the body to its kin. It is the right thing to do," she said, over Jill's half-hearted protest.

"But why Highway 25?" asked Selene, leaning back in her chair and crossing her legs.

Clara gave her an annoyed look, as if she did not wish to talk so much. But she continued mildly: "Unicorns need a bit of magic on this side in order to cross the border between worlds. Roads have a certain kind of magic; I supposed they were using that."

"Yeah, but why Highway 25?" Selene persisted. "Why not Jack Random Lane? Officer Douche-face Memorial Freeway? Main Street! There are a lot of roads in this world, sister."

Clara stared down at her hands, thoughtful. "Highway 25 is . . . special."

"Special?"

" . . . Yes."

"*How?* It's just a road!"

"Perhaps it's the remoteness: there's no cell service along most of it," Clara suggested, snappishly. "Perhaps it runs on a ley-line; perhaps it's *just special.*"

"What's a *ley-line?*" Jill asked with almost predictable promptness.

Clara groaned and flopped back on her bed. She felt something twitch against her side, and she rolled over so she could fumble in her pocket. In the background she heard Selene doing her best to explain transdimensional rifts to their employer.

"So you know how there's tectonic plates," Selene was saying. "And where they meet up there's . . . well, a fault line?"

"The San Andreas Fault," Jill suggested.

"Yeah! Like that! Well, ley-lines are like fault-lines, only they're faults in the fabric of *reality*—where two *worlds* meet."

"But it's the same world on both sides of Highway 25," Jill said, confused.

"I didn't say Highway 25 *was* a ley-line, only that it might be built along one. You don't see them normally—but weird things happen along them; bits of one of world start bleeding through into the other. Like . . . well, *unicorns.* Oi, help me out here, Clara!"

Clara didn't answer, however. She was sitting up on the bed. Her phone—which had been flashing "No Service" for the better part of the day—had finally seen fit to check her voicemail, and was now replaying Lola Gobel's increasingly desperate and frightened messages. As she listened, her face went perfectly white, and she gazed in horror at her two companions.

"*I keep hearing motorcycles,*" the little recorded voice said in her ear. "*At first I thought it was coming from the road, but now they sound like they're circling the house. What's going ON Clara?*"

Slowly, Clara lowered her phone.

"What's going on, Clara?" repeated a voice, in the room with her this time. She looked up, and found Jill gazing at her expectantly.

"They've marked *Lola*," she said in a hoarse whisper.

"Lola . . . " Selene frowned. "Lola . . . Gobel's *wife* Lola? But I thought you said she *rescued* the poor guy!"

"This is not right," Clara declared, rolling to her feet and making for the door.

"Hell no it's not," Selene agreed, half rising from her own seat. "They got the dude who took him to be killed and the dude who actually killed him—what have they got against *her?*"

72

"Unicorns are medieval creatures," Clara said, pausing with her hand on the door. "Perhaps they considered her culpable because she failed to protect her charge." She swallowed hard at the thought, steeling herself. "But that is not justice. She does *not* deserve to die. I will not allow it."

"What are you going to do about that?" Jill asked.

For answer, Clara wrenched open the door and stormed out into the night.

"Where are *you* going?" Selene shouted, running to the door after her. "Just tell her to stay inside—keep off your stupid Highway 25!"

"She *lives* on Highway 25!" Clara shouted back from halfway across the parking lot. She had her phone to her ear, and was listening to it ring . . . ring . . . *ring* . . .

"H-hello?" gasped a frightened voice.

"It's Clara, are you hurt?"

"N-no, not yet," Lola's weak voice had a hysterical tinge to it. Clara wished she could have spoken calmly; told the poor woman that everything would be all right, but she was too naturally honest.

"Listen, I am coming. Stay *inside*. Do you have iron in the house?" She had reached her bike, had her phone in one hand and her helmet in the other. She would need it tonight.

"An iron?" now she sounded confused. "Y-yes, I've got an iron. What good will that do?"

"No, *iron*, the metal," Clara said. "Pots and pans. Put iron at the four points of your house: north, south, east and west. That will confuse them. I need you to hold out for fifteen minutes—can you do that, Lola? I'm on my way."

She hung up over Lola's stuttering questions. There was nothing more a phone call could do. She roughly unstrapped her panniers, pushing them at Selene, who had followed her into the parking lot. Ignoring Selene's protests she pulled her helmet on, flung a leg over Unicorn's back, and accelerated out of the parking lot so fast she left a track.

Selene rocked backwards from the sudden blast of sound, nearly dropping the heavy bags.

"What do we do?" Jill asked, gingerly removing her hands from her ears.

"Get'cher car keys," Selene said, diving back toward the room and her duffle bag with all the guns in it. "She's gonna need backup."

In her cold little kitchen, Lola Gobel stood and stared at the dead receiver in her hand, the orange rectangle blinking "Call Ended" seeming to mock her.

Sometime in that interminable afternoon she had gotten dressed, picking the same clothes she had worn the day before up off the floor. Now she pulled her sweater closer about her shoulders and looked around for iron.

She had two cast-iron frying pans, wedding gifts from her mother-in-law. She pulled them out of the cupboard and then stood, wondering how to tell where the points north and south lay in her house. She knew the general direction from observing the sun, but the seasons skewed everything, and the irregular shape of the house made it harder. In the end she placed the larger of the two pans on the floor of the bathroom that attached to the north side of the house, and the smaller on a table by the big south-facing window.

As she paced about the house looking for something that could cover the east and west sides, Lola wondered why she was so willing to obey Clara's instructions.

As if in answer, from outside there came an angry roar of motorcycle engines, and the sick crack and splinter of broken wood. Lola didn't bother going to the window: that had sounded like the front garden fence going down. She also didn't like the look of those motorcycles: they were big, scary things, and despite how hard she looked, she could never make out their riders; they hunched too low, and they drove too fast.

Lola pulled an iron poker from beside the disused fireplace, and put that by the back door, which she thought ought to be close enough to west; she would sit on that porch to watch the sunset. She was at a loss for where to find the fourth piece of iron until she remembered the monstrosity of a dutch oven that was currently hiding in the back of a cabinet in the kitchen. She had to get out the stepladder to bring it down, and by the time she had, the sound of engines had drawn closer still; it sounded as though they were running across her front lawn.

She placed the cast-iron cooking vessel in a corner of her own bedroom, beside the window that was the first to let in the morning sunlight.

As soon as it was in place, the noises outside stopped.

Slowly, irrationally fearing that the slightest sound would alert them to her presence, Lola rose and looked out the window.

Parked in a line across her gravel drive, just visible in the light from her window, were three dirty, white motorcycles. They had heavy plating over their engines, making them more aerodynamic, more like futuristic space bikes than motorcycles.

Then where had the riders gone? Lola found herself panicking, running around the house and locking doors. By the time she was finished and back at her window, the line of bikes had gone: she could still hear them, though, gunning it up and down the road before her house.

Lola sank down beside the wall of her room, crouching miserably on the floor. She wished for Cowbell's comforting presence, but the cat had long since hidden himself. Lola wondered if she too could hide until this strange trial was over; the thought of locking herself in the closet was not unappealing, but the uncomfortable prickling of the mark on her shoulder told her otherwise. The motorcyclists would find her wherever she hid, she just knew it.

The engines were getting closer again, slowly this time, so she didn't notice until one of them must have blazed by right outside her window. It gave her such a start that she gave a small, involuntary cry.

A rumble of engine, revving angrily. Light flooded in through the window, bleaching the drawn curtains. With a shaking hand Lola pulled herself up and peered under the hem. What she saw nearly gave her a heart attack.

A motorcycle was sitting *right outside* her bedroom window, engine grumbling, headlight blazing, and no sign of a rider.

Lola dropped to the floor again. It had been a long time since she had done anything remotely religious, but a Catholic childhood was a hard thing to shake off. Without thinking she crossed herself, murmuring a prayer in Spanish.

As if in answer the sound of the motorcycle drew away, the light fading. Lola felt her chest loosen from its panic seizure, and was just about to utter her heartfelt thanks when there was a horrible crashing sound from the living room.

It sounded like a bang, mixed with the snap and crunch of splintering wood—followed by a heavy *thud.*

Lola was so shocked she scrambled to the door of the bedroom and down the hall to see, stopping dead in the doorway to the living room.

The front door was a wreck of splinters and broken wood, the hole had cracked across, tearing gouges out of the drywall.

Sitting in the living room, the debris of wall and door cluttered about its wheels, its engine still running and its headlight casting the room into harsh light and shadow, was a riderless motorcycle.

Like a cat zeroing in on its prey, the front wheel—and the headlight—turned to Lola. All on its own the engine revved, and across the ruined carpet the riderless motorcycle leapt toward her.

Lola pushed herself off the doorframe, scrambling down the hall. She heard the motorcycle follow her, and she darted sideways into the washroom.

A small part of her head was still protesting that this could not be real, that a riderless motorcycle chasing her in her own house was beyond belief. But that was effectively drowned out by her raging self-preservation instinct, that said she could wonder about it later, when she was not in danger of being run over.

Lola scampered through the laundry room and out the back door, forgetting for a moment that there were two other motorcycles outside.

She remembered when she came around the barn and found them waiting for her in the drive. They were motionless and riderless, but Lola did not let that fool her. She froze in their headlights, a small, squishy, frightened animal, as from behind her she heard the third motorcycle come crashing out the back door.

So far she was too scared and deafened by the noise to notice the addition of a *fourth* motorcycle, running at top speed down the drive, until it shot into view, turning hard into an arc that sent a spray of sharp gravel at the riderless bikes.

It was bigger, blacker, with a prong of metal mounted above the headlamp. As it came to a halt beside Lola, she saw it *had* a rider: dressed all in black with a visored helmet, and holding at the ready a long broadsword, leveled over Lola's shoulder at the motorbike behind her.

Lola barely had time to register this before Clara grabbed her by the wrist and pulled her onto the little seat behind her, guiding her hands around her waist so she could clutch at her own wrists.

"Whatever happens, do *not* let go," came the voice, muffled but distinct through the helmet. In one fluid motion the rider brought her sword up and around, sliding it home into the scabbard across her back, the hilt coming to rest inches from Lola's face. She clutched at the rider's leather jacket, at her own hands, finding them cold and wet. Her feet flailed, then found the little footrests.

The riderless bikes were bearing down upon them, but Clara opened up Unicorn's engine, and left them in another explosive spray of gravel.

For one glorious moment Lola thought they had left the nightmarish visions behind, but Clara had to slow down to make the turn onto the highway and she heard them again, hard on their tail. Abruptly Clara turned, putting a foot down for balance, and accelerated over the road the opposite way—away from town.

Once more they left the other motorcycles behind, but they were caught at the first turn of the road; Lola saw one of them draw even, and it was just leaning in to ram them when Clara braked—*hard.*

Lola felt the rear wheel fishtail under them as Clara brought the bike to a standstill, and the two bikes that had been flanking them nearly collided with each other, shooting around the bend in the road, unable to stop in time. Clara began walking her bike around in a tight circle, using her inside foot as a pivot.

Then they were off again, accelerating so fast Lola thought she would leave her stomach behind. She clung with cold, numbing hands, her cheek pressed against the rough leather and metal buckles of Clara's scabbard. Her hair was whipping furiously, lashing her cheeks, and all she could see was the rushing blackness of the night, partly illuminated by the motorcycle's headlamp.

Clara tore along the road, crouched forward and taking the turns on the edge of crashing, swerving freely back and forth across the double yellow line. They shot past Lola's driveway and on the straightaway following picked up even more speed. The night closed in black around them, and the yellow beam of Unicorn's headlight showed only empty road. Clara dared take the next turn at something more closely resembling a reasonable speed, only to accelerate again as soon as they were clear.

It was not enough: two headlights, gaining steadily, appeared around the corner behind them. A moment later the sound of angry engines reached their ears through the whistling wind. Clara's response was to lean into the next turn as far as she dared, Lola balanced precariously behind her, and for a moment the headlights were cut off—but not for long. Soon they appeared again—and closer.

"What *are* they?" Lola cried. Though she was shouting practically into Clara's ear the other woman didn't answer—whether because Lola's words were lost in the wind and the roar of engines, or because she was concentrating on outrunning a pair of sentient motorbikes, was uncertain.

The riderless bikes gained, pulled even . . . and Clara let Unicorn go.

Unicorn had been a powerful bike even before she had been modified by Clara's older sister, and Clara had faithfully maintained her ever since with the love and devotion she would have shown a family member. As such she possessed not merely the raw power of her engine, but that particular magic that is unique to machines that are accorded the same kind of love as a living being.

Now she practically *flew.* The front wheel lifted gently from the road as the motorcycle named Unicorn reared up and shot forward, first opening a gap, then leaving the unicorns in the shapes of motorcycles behind entirely.

They raced forward, the still night air whipped into a storm around them. In the jumble of dark night cut by yellow beams one light held steady, a single point that grew larger as they approached the lone motorcycle which waited in the middle of the road.

With a roar that screamed it took off, blaring down on them.

Clara didn't waver, didn't even check her speed. The two machines shot toward each other; the one carrying two hunched figures; the other nothing at all.

The distance between them vanished as if devoured by a hungry beast, and at the last the riderless motorcycle seemed to leap through space, jerking suddenly forward as though teleporting from one spot to next.

But Clara had already leaned, drifting her bike ever so slightly, and the two machines passed within an inch of each other. Lola felt the shock of the motorcycle's wind like a physical blow on her side, its engine an angry scream in her ear.

Then it was past and gone, skidding to a stop, turning around and giving chase with its fellows, but Unicorn was well away and flying, the night dark and the road clear before them.

Around one last turn, and there suddenly was a car. A huge red pickup truck parked across both lanes of traffic, its emergency lights ablaze and its engine running. Seeing them it rolled forward, opening a small gap to the right. Clara aimed for it like an arrow, and Lola just glimpsed a dark woman with wild, frizzy hair, standing in the bed of the truck, leveling a shotgun at the road behind them.

Clara shouted something, but muffled in the wind and the roar her words were lost.

They shot through the gap, and Lola thought she heard a *bang*, but it was muffled by the deep rumble as the truck turned to follow them.

Clara didn't look back, didn't wait to see if the truck followed, but headed into town, turning off at the first substantial street that presented itself. Only then did she slow, waiting until the reassuring bulk of Arcana loomed into view, then took off again, heading for the motel.

The adrenaline had subsided, and Lola was shaking furiously when Clara helped her off the bike. Arcana pulled up beside them, and Selene hopped down from the back, taking one look at Lola before hitching her bag over one shoulder so she could help lead the poor woman inside.

"I d-don't understand," Lola was chattering through her teeth as she tripped between them. "Wha-what *were* those things?"

"I take it you found the unicorns?" Jill said briskly, appearing by their side.

Clara glanced at her, sharply. "You didn't see them?"

"I fired a warning shot, then we were off after you," Selene said. She turned back to Lola. "Easy now, babe, we've got you. You're gonna be just fine."

"Wha-what *unicorns?*" Lola said, beginning to sound hysterical.

"Your rescue horse, Barney," Jill said matter-of-factly. "He was actually a unicorn. Clara here thinks his relatives are hunting down everyone they feel is responsible for his death. For some reason they've latched onto *you.*"

"But . . . they were motorcycles . . . " Lola's eyes were wide and frightened.

Jill and Selene glanced at each other in surprise as Jill unlocked the door.

"Unicorns *can* appear as different things, if they want," Selene said.

"They are motorcycles," Clara said grimly, heaving Lola into the room and setting her in a chair. "Three of them. They are confined to Highway 25, for now. It's only a matter of time until they find the means to manifest elsewhere." Clara knelt before the shaken woman, who had begun to cry with relief and confusion.

"Lola," she said softly. "Lola, you said you found a mark on your arm, may I see it?"

With shaking hands Lola rolled up her sleeve. There, plain as day, was another death mark, dark and vivid against the woman's skin. Selene sucked in a sharp breath when she saw it, and Jill got out her phone to take a picture.

"It t-tingles a little," Lola offered.

Clara looked up at her earnestly. "Lola," she said quietly. "This is a dangerous thing. It will lead the unicorns to you. It binds them to kill you. But I will not allow that. I'm going to do something about it, but you must trust me; it won't hurt."

Lola met her eyes, held them, and steeled herself as she nodded. Clara rose and walked briskly over to her panniers, which Selene had dumped on the second bed. Opening one she removed a small bottle of rubbing alcohol, a packet of sterile gauze pads, and a roll of medical tape. Then she leaned over and pulled a small knife out of her boot.

"Clara, what are you doing?" Selene asked, a warning in her voice.

Clara didn't answer. She had laid the sterile pads out in a line across the bed. Now she opened the bottle of alcohol and poured it liberally over the blade of the knife, which she then laid carefully across a pad. She put the cap on the bottle and paused.

"*Clara?*" Selene was beginning to sound alarmed.

"This is not for her," was all Clara said.

In one smooth motion she shrugged off her sword harness, then removed her leather jacket. She pulled off the glove on her left hand—only the second time, Selene realized, she had seen her without her gloves—and began rolling up the cuff to reveal her bare arm.

There was a long, curving black mark, like a wide brushstroke, running down the outside of her forearm, and similar marks on the back of her hand. Selene caught a brief glimpse of them before Clara turned her palm skywards, pushing her sleeve up past her elbow.

With a businesslike briskness that was frightening to behold she uncapped the bottle of alcohol and poured some into the crook of her elbow, letting it run down her arm. Then she wiped it away with another pad. She tore a length of tape from the roll and affixed the last pad to it, leaving it adhesive side up on the bed.

With an expert hand she smacked at the flesh of her forearm, clenching her first to bring the vein to the surface. At last she paused and looked around uncertainly.

"I need a small bowl, or a cup," she said. "Glass would be better."

There was no such object, but Jill helpfully produced her own ceramic coffee mug.

"It's clean," she said as she offered it.

Clara nodded her thanks. She sat on the floor beside the bed and rested the mug in her lap. Then before Selene could so much as shout in protest she took the knife and carefully cut into her own arm where the vein ran, greenish under her skin. She carefully angled the knife so the blood that erupted flowed down the blade and dripped into the mug.

Selene did protest then, and Lola gasped in shock, but Clara ignored them both. Her back was a tense line as she waited until at least two tablespoons of blood had accumulated in the cup before she removed the knife (resting it blade down in the mug), and, taking the piece of gauze and tape, pressed it against the small cut on her arm, smoothing down the adhesive and holding it there firmly for some moments before pulling her sleeve down again.

Then she reached over, took the alcohol-soaked pad the knife had rested upon, and used it to clean the blade before sticking it back in her boot. Rising to her knees she took the cup of blood and crawled over to Lola, who recoiled in her seat.

"I promise it won't hurt," she said. "Please, let me help you."

"Clara. *What. Are. You. Doing?*" Selene sounded downright upset now, but had not the nerve to interrupt the proceedings.

Holding the mug in her gloved hand, Clara dipped her bare fingers in the blood and gently painted it over the mark on Lola's arm. Lola shivered at the sensation, but didn't speak.

When the whole area was covered in a thick coat of the viscous liquid, Clara took a cloth from her pocket and gently wiped it away.

It came off easily enough, except for the blood that had covered the death mark; that remained as though glued to the skin, turning the mark a bright, luminous red.

Clara nodded to herself, as if pleased with the result. She pulled off her other glove, and pressed her newly-bared palm against the bloodstained mark.

"Oh!" cried Lola, so suddenly that Clara brought her other hand up to steady her arm. "That tickles," she added.

Clara did not smile. Slowly, gently, she peeled her hand away, and Selene gasped at what it revealed.

The death mark had gone, leaving Lola's arm bare and clean once more.

"You can't do that," Selene whispered, torn between amazement and horror. "You can't remove a death mark, not without killing the thing that put it there. You *can't* . . ."

Clara sat back on her heels and sighed. "I *didn't* remove it," she said. "I just transferred it." She raised her right hand and held it, palm out, to Selene and Jill.

There in the center, black against her pale skin, was the death mark.

"I took it upon myself," she said grimly.

Jill looked confused. Selene was speechless with shock and horror. Lola was beginning to shiver. Clara got up and went to the TV cabinet to retrieve the room's extra blanket.

This seemed to jerk Selene out of her shock. She reached across the bed to the nearest pillow and hurled it, hard, at Clara. It struck her on the side of the head and bounced off, harmlessly, and Clara turned to look sadly at Selene.

"C-could someone p-please explain?" Lola said in a small, shaking voice. "I don't understand."

Jill, who could empathize, took off her own coat and draped it over Lola's shoulders. Sitting down beside her she began to recount everything from their investigation, from Clara's discovery of the first crash, to Barney's true identity, to the second death, and finally Lola's own rescue.

Lola took it with a sort of detached calm that worried Jill. She wondered whether laying everything out was the right thing after all. But when Lola looked up alertly, her eyes darting to each of them in turn, they seemed more focused now.

"So . . . that mark. They were coming to kill me?"

"Not anymore," Selene said heavily. "Now they'll be coming for *Clara.*"

Lola's eyes went to the woman in question, who stood towering over them all. She had rolled her sleeves back down and put on her jacket, but had left her right hand bare.

"But Clara . . . you'll be able to fight them, right?"

Clara's whole frame seemed to droop.

"No," she said grimly. "I will not fight. That will only cause more bloodshed."

"But . . . they'll kill you."

Clara shrugged. "I am a warrior. It is better me . . . than you." The words came out with some difficulty.

Jill looked up sharply. "That was a little irresponsible," she said.

"Understatement of the week," Selene snorted.

"Did you forget you're not on your own anymore?" Jill snapped. "What about your obligation to *me?*"

Clara regarded her evenly. "I did not," she said simply. "A life seemed more important."

Jill glanced down to where Lola sat, looking very small and sad, and found she could not argue.

"So what do we do now? Wait for them to find us?"

"That would be pointless," Clara said. She went over to the bed and began re-packing her panniers, buckling on her sword. "I will go," she said. "And return the body."

"You're going to *what?*" Jill exclaimed, seeing her prize specimen disappearing before her eyes.

"It is what we should have done all along," Clara said.

"Like hell you're going alone," Selene said, surging into motion. "Those 'corns ain't getting near you before I give 'em a piece of my mind. C'mon Jill, let's go hook up the trailer; Arcana can tow him out there."

Clara looked around, a little flabbergasted.

There was a soft rustling sound, and they all turned to find Lola on her feet again. One hand gripped the chair for support, but her gaze was steady.

"I will come, too," she said through clenched teeth.

It was ten o' clock on an autumn night, on a deserted stretch of country highway. There was a rumble of engines, and a beam of light washed over the green, shield-shaped sign with a big, white 25 in the center. Its reflective surface shone blindingly bright for a moment, before fading as the source of the light passed.

Arcana drove slowly, not out of any practical necessity—he was more than capable of pulling a light trailer with one dead horse (or horse-shaped animal)—but because he followed closely on Clara's taillights, and Clara was creeping along at a snail's pace.

Selene drove. For once the radio had been turned off, and only the muted growl of Arcana's engine filled the cabin. Jill sat shotgun, while

Lola crouched in the back, leaning forward between the two front seats. None of them spoke.

They rounded the shoulder of a hill, and at the bottom, where there were wide gravel shoulders to either side, Clara stopped. She walked Unicorn off the road and set the kickstand. Then she dismounted and walked back to where Arcana sat, idling in the road.

Silently she took off her helmet and sword and laid them in the bed of the truck. The little knife from her boot followed, and then a fair-sized dagger from who-knew-where. They joined the sword with a clatter.

Selene cut the engine, but left the key in the ignition and the lights on. She pushed open the door and got out.

"Now what?" she asked.

"We must walk him from here," was all Clara said. She would not meet her gaze. "I need a guide for the nose, but if you unhook the trailer I can push it."

"Yeah, but why here?" Selene insisted.

Clara looked up, as if she were surprised at the question.

"This is where they killed Joshua Gobel. This is where it began. It seemed a right place for it to end."

Without further protest Selene followed the taller woman around to the back of Arcana, where she helped her unhitch the trailer. It was the triangular kind with two large wheels on either side, bracketing the dead unicorn, and a third at the nose which could be let down when not hooked up to a truck. Using the handle attached, Selene quickly turned it sideways so the whole trailer did not begin rolling down the gentle grade.

"Seriously, Clara," she said, leveling a hard look across the tarp-covered body. "What happens if they try to kill you?"

Clara was busy undoing the straps that secured the tarp, pulling it back to reveal the unicorn. She paused at Selene's question and gave her an open look of infuriating calm.

"Then I die," she said simply.

Selene looked like she was going to protest further, but at that moment Jill and Lola came around the truck to help and she bit off whatever she had been about to say.

Lola had to go over and pet Barney's head one last time. Strangely, she no longer felt like crying. The grief and turmoil of the last two days had settled into a sort of dull ache. There would be more tears later, but for now she had a task to complete.

"Here," she said, and took a spot beside Selene, on the other side of the trailer's nose.

With Lola and Selene at the head, and Clara and Jill pushing from the rear, they maneuvered the trailer out into the road, around Arcana's bulk, and down onto the straightaway. When they had reached the edge of Arcana's headlights Clara called a stop and came up to stand at the nose.

"It is my life that is forfeit," she said. "The rest of you should leave."

Jill and Selene made faces and retreated—but only to the back of the trailer. Selene had left her shotguns in the truck, but she still placed herself protectively in front of Jill.

Lola remained; she stood across the nose from Clara, one hand resting on the trailer.

"I don't want to leave him," she said quietly.

Clara gazed at her, a troubled ridge rising between her invisible eyebrows. But at length she nodded and said; "Yes, that is your right." Then she turned and looked resolutely down the highway, never sparing another glance for her companions.

They did not have long to wait.

Out of the darkness three lights appeared. They moved swiftly closer, and the distant sound of engines reached the ears of the waiting women. But it was a broken, uncertain sound, and as they watched, the lights began to dance, to leap and weave about. As they did so the sound slowly changed from that of motorcycle engines to the no less thunderous noise of hoofbeats on pavement. They clanged, as though they wore shoes of metal, and the road shook as three huge pale horses, each with a horn of shining light growing from its forehead, emerged from the night and bore down upon them.

They never checked their pace, nor did they swerve. The lead unicorn, who glowed silver and moon-white, ran with its head raised high, its long horn a beacon.

Clara stood like a stone, and the other women followed her lead, though a little uncertainly. Lola was gripping the trailer with both hands, as if to keep her legs from carrying her away.

In a swift, steady motion Clara brought her right hand forward, palm out, presenting the death mark to the unicorns. As if in answer they slowed, almost imperceptibly, and then came to an abrupt halt mere feet from the trailer.

Two pale gold horses with horns of shining light stood on either side of the road, while the third—the silver one—dissolved into a billow of white mist, out of which walked a tall man.

At least, he *looked* like a man. But there was something wrong about his feet, the way he walked, and there was still a luminous horn growing from his forehead. His skin was white as paper, his hair a waterfall of silver down his shoulders, and he wore an old-fashioned tunic and hose with knee-high boots—but again there was something wrong with his feet: it looked as though he walked frozen on the tips of his toes, like a ballerina. Even without this he was incredibly long-limbed, and he towered over Clara as he approached.

His face was angular and bony, not naturally cruel, but it wore such an unpleasant expression that it appeared sinister. His eyes were set wide on his head and slanted downward toward the middle, and his ears were long and curved, though at the moment they were laid back along his head and barely visible.

He walked right up to Clara so that he nearly touched her raised hand. Then abruptly he bent his head to her, leaned forward, searching her face with his eyes.

Clara bore this examination stoically, returning the unicorn's gaze with one of perfect blankness. Then, as if in answer to some unspoken question, she said:

"I have come to return the body of your kin, and to atone for what was done to him."

The unicorn pulled back sharply, his nostrils flaring. He looked across at Lola, then at Selene, then at Jill. His eyes narrowed as they turned back to Clara.

In a voice like a waterfall, the unicorn spoke at last.

"There is one here who owes us a life," he said. "But it is not yours, knight-errant."

Clara's gaze remained steady. "Nevertheless," she said. "It is mine that has been claimed."

Behind their leader the other two unicorns snorted and tossed their heads. When they moved, Jill noticed, they left a faint afterimage of sparkling dust.

The leader, the unicorn in human form, paced back and forth in front of Clara, his boots making soft *clopping* sounds on the pavement. His horn kept coming back to point at her raised hand, like the needle of a compass.

"You have put me in a difficult position, knight," the unicorn hissed. "You have denied our justice."

"I deny you nothing," said Clara, and there was a strange edge to her voice. An undertone, a slight hint of . . . could it be triumph? It was still there as she continued: "Two already you have taken in payment for the one. Three strikes me as unnecessary, but if you truly require it then take mine as it is freely given. *Not* hers," she said, following the unicorn's eyes as he glanced at Lola. "I will not see her punished for an act of kindness."

"She was his *guardian*," said the unicorn, sounding anguished. "She failed him in her duty. Our brother she allowed to be taken from her care and killed. She bears as much responsibility as the other two!"

"I do not see it that way," Clara said, quiet but firm. "And I back my opinion with my life." She stretched out her hand again, palm up, inviting.

Behind the trailer, Selene's arms were locked on the rail like steel clamps, her eyes riveted. Jill wore an expression of shock and horror; Lola had covered her eyes.

The unicorn paced again, but this time it was Clara's eyes that followed him, cold and steady.

"Take what you are due, unicorn," she said at last. "Take it, and nothing more."

The silver man froze, gazing at Clara was such a look of hatred that Jill's stomach churned. But then he stalked past her, along the trailer, and pulled the tarp completely off the body. Jill did not need Selene's warning touch on her shoulder to fall back. From a distance of a few feet she watched as one of the horse-shaped unicorns came forward and gently touched the tip of its shining horn to Clara's palm. There was a flash and a glow, like a fire flared up, then died, and the unicorn walked on to join its brother, leaving Clara to turn and stare after it, her face a blank mask.

The humans drew back further from the trailer as the three unicorns encircled it, nosing at their dead brother, stroking his mane with their horns, while the leader climbed up beside him, finding the braided tail and stroking it reverently. Then all three of them leaned forward so their horns intersected over his head, and a deep calm settled over the area.

In it, as if in a dream, Lola saw Barney begin to glow from within, like his body was filled with burning embers. As she watched, the embers grew brighter, and the dark body melted away. The red and gold sparks hung in the night air in the shape of a fallen horse, and then they too faded away— leaving nothing but a flat trailer with a crumpled and bloody tarp.

Flowing into equine form again, the silver unicorn led his siblings away. The glow from their horns became bobbling lights in the darkness, and then they disappeared entirely; their hoofbeats slowly fading into nothing.

The four women stared after them in silence.

"Where did they go?" Lola asked in a quiet voice.

Clara just shrugged. "Where do all magic things go, when they are not here?"

"So, it's over then?" Jill hissed.

"Looks like," said Selene.

"But Clara's *alive*."

Clara turned to look at them. She seemed tired, but she was smiling faintly. She held up her right hand, and they saw that its palm was clean and bare; the damning mark had vanished as if it never was.

"For now," she said.

"All that time . . . I had a *unicorn* and never knew it?" Lola said.

She sat slumped at her kitchen table, cradling a cup of hot coffee between her hands—they had all long since given up getting any sleep that night. Selene and Clara were busy about the house, sweeping up broken glass and plaster and propping the ruined front door back on its hinges. There were tire tracks on the carpet in the living room and on the linoleum by the back door, but besides that and the mess there was no sign of the unicorns' presence.

"We think he was caught in a witch's trap," Jill explained seriously. "They do that, you know, to harvest their horns—kind of like rhino or elephant poachers. Only they know not to kill the unicorn, because that would alert their family. So the unicorn is let go, but without their horn they can't access much of their magic, it seems. So your Barney was stuck as an ordinary horse—and fared about as well as one."

Lola shook her head slowly, gazing into her coffee. Cowbell came and curled up on her lap, purring like a small motor.

"Then you came along," Jill continued. "It looks like he was getting better, until your husband—well, you know the rest."

She was not sure Lola heard. The woman was stroking her cat and staring off into space.

"A unicorn . . ." she murmured. "I always wanted a real unicorn, when I was a little girl, I mean. Be careful what you wish for, huh?"

Jill contemplated this, and found she had to agree.

"Do you think she'll be all right?" Selene asked, eyeing the house in Arcana's rearview mirror as they pulled away. They had waited out the night there—though Clara made a trip in the early morning to retrieve the rest of their belongings from the motel and check them out—until Lola's sister had arrived. She seemed like a brisk and competent woman, and so the three took their leave as quietly as they could.

"Not for a while," said Jill, with some certainty.

They reached the highway, and Jill signaled to turn toward the city.

"Hold on a sec," Selene said, surging forward again. "We checked out, remember? Why not take 25 all the way south? It ends at 198 and we can take that over to meet up with I-5."

"It'll be slower," Jill said, uncertain.

"Who cares!" said Selene. "There's been such a hubbub over this damn road, I want to see what's so special about it."

Jill looked unconvinced, but she obligingly flipped the signal stick over, and instead of turning left toward Hollister, she turned right onto Highway 25 and pulled onto the empty road. Behind Arcana the flatbed trailer still rattled—though it now carried a different unicorn: Clara's bike was strapped firmly to the middle, and Clara herself was laid out on the back seat of Arcana. After two nights without sleep, a motorcycle chase, facing down her impending death, and some moderate home repair, even Clara was too tired to ride.

But she would not be allowed to sleep yet. Something had been nagging at Selene ever since the unicorns disappeared, and only now that they were alone did she feel comfortable asking about it. She twisted around in her seat to get a good look at Clara.

The woman, all six feet and four inches of her, was crammed on her back with her feet propped against the window. She had her arms—covered and gloved once more—folded behind her head, and her eyes determinedly closed.

"Yo, Claymore," Selene said, using her real name for a change.

For answer, Clara grimaced.

"Why didn't the unicorns kill you? Did you *know* they would spare you? *Why?*"

Clara opened one blue eye and glared at Selene.

"I knew nothing for certain," she said grumpily. "I am a warrior. I must be prepared to die at any time. I was ready for it last night."

"Huh," was all Selene said, and she did not turn around. Her patience was eventually rewarded; Clara opened her other eye and seemed to come more awake.

"I did . . . hope," she admitted. "Unicorns *are* medieval in nature. Though I believe the lore of a unicorn laying its head in the lap of a virgin is likely a fabrication of male scholars to perpetuate the hypocritical glorification of feminine virginity . . . I couldn't know it had no basis in truth. It did occur to me that, perhaps, they would find me an unsuitable sacrifice due to my . . . condition. But it was no guarantee." She lay back and closed her eyes in relief.

At the wheel, Jill snorted. Selene stared.

"What—you? You've never . . . ?"

"I have killed men," Clara stated, not bothering to open her eyes this time. "But I have never lain with one."

Selene opened her mouth, ready to protest that, if they were measuring virginity by the amount of intimate experience a woman had with a *man* than she was every bit as much a virgin as Clara—maybe more so!— but Clara raised a tired hand to silence her.

Jill's chuckle broke the tense moment.

"Somehow I'm not at all shocked," she said through her grin, and drove on.

Lola was alone in the house when there was a cautious knock at the front door. Cautious, probably because the door looked like it was held on with duct tape. Which it was.

As Maria was out buying groceries it fell to Lola to drag herself over to the door and answer it. She had to physically lift it by the handle and drag it away, and once she had she stared at what was on the other side.

A man she had never seen before in her life stood on the porch, smiling uncertainly at her. He was a tall man, worn and thin with a dark, lined face. Nevertheless his eyes were alive with a light that danced when he saw her, and he smiled. He wore a rumpled black suit, and there was a cane hanging off one arm. In his hands he held a small bundle wrapped in tissue paper.

"Mrs. Lola Gobel?" he asked in a soft voice.

"Y-yes, that's me," Lola said, unconsciously trying to hide behind the door. She had had altogether enough of strangers who knew her name.

But all the man did was present the bundle to her. "I want you to have this," he explained. He seemed earnest, and a little sad. "Especially after all they put you through. I never wanted you to come to any harm."

Lola took the bundle. The paper crinkled under her fingers. There seemed to be something soft inside.

"Thank you?" she said uncertainly.

The stranger had long, shaggy black hair that fell over and around his face, making his expression hard to read. It might have been kind, or sad, or satisfied, or all three at once.

"My name is Beauceros," he said, with the same sad earnestness. "I thought you should know. Good-bye, Lola Gobel." He turned and began to walk away. He had to lean heavily upon his cane as he did so, for it seemed his right leg pained him.

Lola heaved the door shut and stood in her ruined living room as she opened the bundle.

The thin paper fell away easily, and from it emerged a thick braid of long, coarse black hair. It shimmered red and copper where the sunlight hit it, and the ends glowed like fiber-optic filaments. Now it was tied at either end with pieces of black string, but she still recognized it.

The last time she had seen it, this braid of hair had been tied with blue ribbon, and laid across Barney's dead body.

This was Barney's tail.

Unicorns can appear as different things, if they want.

Lola shot back to the door, the braid of unicorn hair in one hand, the paper in the other. Again she heaved it open—but when she stuck her head out the man who called himself Beauceros was nowhere to be seen. Her driveway stretched on to the highway, empty.

In the distance she could hear a motorcycle, the sounds of its engine slowly fading into wind.

Blinking back tears, Lola Gobel waved good-bye.

Arcana was just passing a sign informing them that they were approaching The Pinnacles, National Monument, when they themselves were passed at a searing pace by a group of motorcycles.

Vrrrroooooooooowwwm!

Vrrrroooooooooowwwm!

Vrrrroooooooooowwwm!

And, a little ways behind the others . . .

Vrrrrooooooooooooooowwwm!

Jill swore, riding Arcana far to the right after the fact.

"You could get killed, riding like that," she said.

Selene, who had been dozing in the passenger seat, sat up alertly.

"Did you see their riders?" she asked suddenly.

"Not really," Jill said. "They were those big, racing bikes. The riders were all sort of hunched down."

"No," said Selene seriously. "Did you see their riders. I mean, *did they have riders?*"

Jill rolled a wide eye at Selene.

"Actually . . . no," she admitted. "I mean, I don't know. But . . . they couldn't have been the unicorns! There were *four.*"

At that, Selene could say nothing.

Unicorns are more than the flesh and blood they appear in, Clara could have told them. She could have told them also that there was a practical reason for returning the body intact and unviolated, and that the taking of the lives responsible for the death was more than an act of vengeance. She could have told them, but she was too busy pretending to be asleep so they wouldn't bother her.

Still, she couldn't help smiling to herself.

Arcana rumbled on, swinging his trailer wide around the curves of the road. Far ahead, along a deserted stretch of remote highway, four motorcycles rode in a close line. Three of them had dirty white coats, but the fourth one, which had a mangled rear fender, was glossy and black.

The still air of the highway was split by the scream of their engines as they flew down the road.

We can ride on
(We can be wrong)
Out on this lonely road
on a run for blood.
We're going long
(We can be wrong)
Flying high—flying blind
on the road of blood.

Run, run,
with a twister.
Run, run,
withered sister.
Run, run, 'cause if you stop, baby, she dies.
Run, run, there's a whirlwind of hate in your eyes.
Run, run, hide your children, baby, he's keen.
He's a long man, rides the toughest bike you've ever seen.

There he goes again
Here he comes again
Run, run, girl, be strong
There you go again
Here you come again
Run, run, girl, ride on.

We can ride on
(We can be wrong)
Out on this lonely road
on a run for blood.
We're going long
(We can be wrong)
Flying high, flying blind
on the road of blood.

We're on a road
We're on a road of blood.

She's a free girl with a black bike under her knees
She's got a red rage in her black heart that she feeds
She's got twin guns, eyes like ice in the thaw
She's burning rags and she won't stop til she's raw.

There he goes again
Here he comes again
Run, run, girl, be strong
There you go again
Here you come again
Run, run, girl, ride on.

We can ride on
(We can be wrong)
Out on this lonely road
on a run for blood.
We're going long
(We can be wrong)
Flying high, flying blind
on the road of blood.

We're on a road
We're on a road of blood.

Raise your sword up woman of thunder
Cause they'll try to take you down tonight
Get your arms up girls of wonder
You gotta chase 'em down before they fly.

You know death is all that awaits you
If you choose to ride the road of blood
Better still to just take the highway
The road of miracles and unicorns.

Or die.

Death is all that awaits on the road of blood
Ride the highway of miracles and unicorns.

—Miracles and Unicorns, *Princess Die*

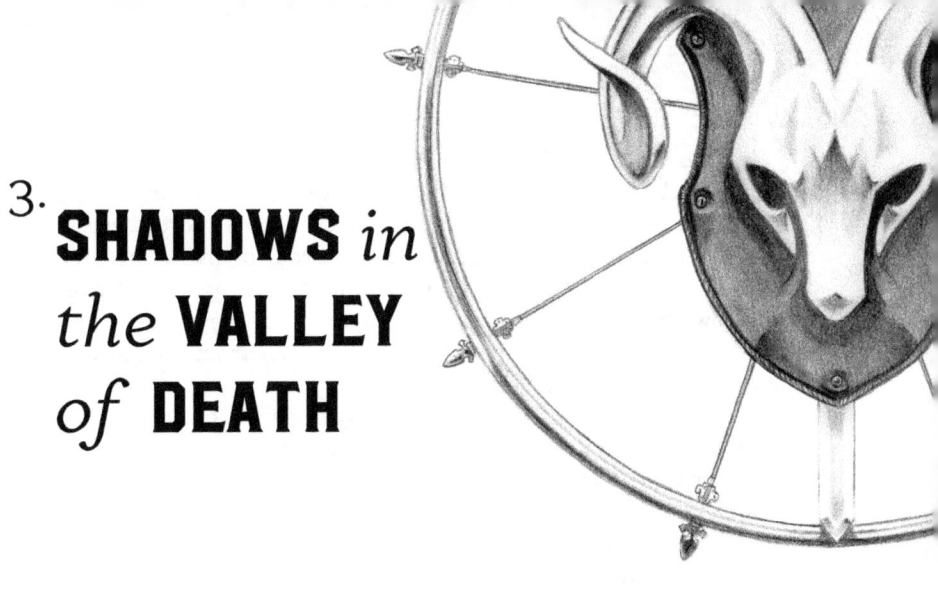

3.
SHADOWS *in* the VALLEY *of* DEATH

Death Valley National Park, California

THERE ARE MANY WAYS to go missing in the wilderness. Step on the wrong rock, put your hand down the wrong hole, or set up your tent in the wrong clearing, and all manner of nasty things can happen to you. Even without the help of bears, cougars, rattlesnakes, scorpions, or particularly vicious spiders, the desert of Death Valley has a number of ways to make people disappear. In the summer, there is the heat. In the winter there are flash floods. All year round there are abandoned mine shafts, and of course the isolation. Get stranded on the wrong back road and it could be days—weeks—before someone finds your lifeless body.

Then there is the classic example—dating back to William Lewis Manly's crossing in December 1848—of someone simply wandering off into the desert *and never being seen again.*

Never before, however, had anyone gone missing from the Furnace Creek Visitor Center.

"Explain this to me again," said Deputy Sheriff Belinda Sparks. "Your fiancé disappeared . . . from the *flash flood* exhibit?"

Hilary Castillo stared at her out of wide, panic-stricken eyes, her mascara only slightly smudged. She hugged her thin arms around herself, and shivered.

"We were looking at the table, the one with the rolling wooden bits," she said, pointing. "Andy pushed the button to start the demo, and we were watching the little video screen."

"Yes, and?" prompted the deputy.

"Well, it does this thunder and lightning sound effect," said Hilary. "And Andy was being all dramatic, making funny noises with his mouth and waving his hands, and then . . . then . . ." The young woman swallowed. "The lights, they sort of *flickered*—"

"On the video screen or—?" began Deputy Sparks.

"No, all over," said Hilary. "The whole room went dark and light, dark and light, and . . . in one of the dark patches . . ." Hilary trailed off. She found she still couldn't articulate the sensation she'd had, of a great yawning mouth opening behind her, and a distant roaring like an ocean of people screaming. It had only been for a moment, and she'd felt it like a cold feeling down her back more than anything, and now Deputy Sparks—solid, rotund and reasonable—was shifting impatiently from foot to foot. "He disappeared," she finished lamely.

Deputy Sparks shot a look over Hilary's head at the ranger who had called her in. The look said: "I could be putting my feet up in my office with a beer right now, but *you* had to jump for a cute girl in high-quality makeup."

Rodriguez raised his hands in defense of the look. "It's true, he's *gone*," he said. "He hasn't been back to his car; their tent is unoccupied; his cell won't pick up—"

Sparks waved an impatient hand. "His cell wouldn't pick up in ninety-nine percent of this *park*," she snapped.

"We put his description out to Stovepipe, Panamint, Scotty's Castle—no one's seen him since Hilary here."

With a sinking feeling Deputy Sparks rubbed her tired eyes. "I'll add him to the list, then," she sighed.

"List?" said Hilary, looking up suddenly. "What list?"

"Your boy ain't the first kid we've had up and disappear into nowhere," said Deputy Sparks, resentfully. "I expect they are conspiring to work me into an early grave. Your man—"

"Andy Woods," Hilary said.

"Woods," repeated Sparks. "He's not a member of a secret society of pranksters, is he?"

Hilary Castillo screamed. It was not a scream of terror or shock; it was simply the scream of a woman whose nerves had been fried to a cinder and could not take any more.

"Is there *anyone*," she cried, "*anyone* who will take me *seriously?!*"

Somewhere off Interstate 5, California

QUESTION," said Jill Hamilton, sipping her coffee.

"Why do you say that?" Selene retorted from under the *LA Times*. She was lying across the second hotel bed, scanning the paper for possible cases. Jill sat at the little table nursing her coffee, having surrendered her laptop and its Google access to Clara—who had proven quite adept at scanning the internet for possible incidents of interest—or lack thereof.

"Say what?" said Jill.

"When you have a question," said Selene. "You start by saying: 'question.' Just *ask* the question already."

Jill pushed her glasses up her nose, and thought.

"Explain this to me," she said instead.

Selene threw her paper aside and folded her hands behind her head. "Explain what?"

"If these . . . *supernatural* things . . . chimeras, werewolves, unicorns . . . if they're all real—why haven't people *noticed*?"

Selene shrugged.

The leather-clad bulk that was Clara shifted behind the laptop.

"Mother always said humans were very good at coming up with reasonable explanations for unreasonable things," she said.

Jill was already shaking her head vehemently. "No, no, *no*," she said. "Humans are *great* at coming up with—and sticking *to*—unreasonable explanations. We're so good at it, we've spun whole webs of lies to make us feel better about the natural order of things. Humans will build up just about anything as proof of whatever delusion they subscribe to. Look at ghost hunters, or people seeing Jesus in their toasted bagel."

Selene tapped her chin thoughtfully.

"You know," she said. "It's a funny thing, but most of those things—famous hauntings, alien conspiracies—*are* fake. It's like, you think there *must* be something behind it if everyone believes in it, but usually that's not the case. There really *are* rational explanations for all those phenomena you mentioned. Crystal Ball fantasies, I call 'em. But when it comes to the *real* supernatural, the *real* paranormal . . . people can be . . . weird. It's like, it's fun to take ordinary stuff, like wind and electrical shorts and say it's ghosts . . . but when it's *actually a ghost,* well . . . let's say most people prefer to say 'funny weather, eh?' and leave it at that."

"They refuse to accept the world as it is, for the true supernatural is just as unyielding as the rest of the world, and therefore far more terrifying than any fantasy," announced Clara. In the thoughtful silence this generated she slid the laptop around. "I found us a case," she said.

"Andy Woods, twenty-five, of Orange County, California," Jill read from the online article. "Disappeared from Death Valley National Park, Furnace Creek Visitor Center, at approximately 3:30 PM on January 13th. Missing Person report filed by his fiancé, Hilary Castillo, on January 15th. Mr. Woods is the seventh sudden disappearance reported from the greater Death Valley area in the past month. He joins Martha Bickman, Jeremy Jones, Robin O'Hare, blah blah blah . . ." Jill skipped forward over the rest of the names. "Sheriff's Deputy Belinda Sparks was not available for comment, and there has been no evidence of foul play."

She blinked over the laptop at Clara. "What makes you think this is something for . . ." she waved a hand, ". . . us."

With a sigh Clara reached around and switched to a different tab.

"Look at how they disappeared," she said.

"Martha Bickman disappeared at sunset at Ubehebe Crater." Selene spoke up from under her paper. The other two turned to her in surprise. She folded aside a corner and wagged her eyebrows at them. "Would you believe, a *newspaper* has information! Listen . . . Jeremy Jones was hiking in one of those canyons, and he climbed down under a ledge to pose for a picture and—poof. Gone. Robin O'Hare, he vanished—wait, says *she,* whoops—she vanished in front of her friends' eyes: they say some clouds rolled over and when the sun dipped behind them Robin disappeared. Then there's Harry Goodman and his son Rodney; they left Scotty's Castle at sunset and were never seen again. And Danny Ferrero, he was exploring one of those ghost towns . . . says here he was last seen going into an abandoned bank vault."

Jill blinked at her. She was aware that a pattern existed, but she could not put her finger on it.

Selene spread her hands out over the paper. "It's the *shadows,*" she said. "They all disappeared *in shadow.*"

Jill frowned.

"Martha Bickman," said Selene. "Sunset. Night. Same with the Goodmans. Jeremy Jones, he was in the shadow of a canyon. Robin, clouds. Danny, an abandoned building."

"And Andy Woods?"

"His fiancé said that they were watching an exhibit, and the lights flashed on and off," said Clara. "In between on and off, and on again, he left."

Jill raised her eyebrows.

"What could cause that?" she wondered aloud.

"That's what we gotta work on," said Selene. "Nice catch, Clara." She threw aside the paper and bounced off the bed. "Up, up, girlfriends," she said. "We're not gonna stop evil by sitting on our butts. Let's boogie!"

The Ram dually truck, deep red with a light coat of dust, was almost too big for the station—its huge double rear wheels nearly filled the aisle, and Selene had to squeeze between the cab and the kiosk to get at the pump. "We really better go to truck stops," she said as she started the first tank filling. "They've got these pumps, y'know, with like, huge nozzles. For the big semis. Wouldn't take an hour and a half to fill Arcana up."

"Is that diesel?" Jill asked from around the truck's nose. She had climbed up onto the front tire in order to reach across and clean the windshield.

Selene rolled her eyes expressively. "Do I *look* like the kind of person who would put gasoline in a diesel truck?" the eye roll said.

"Then I don't care," said Jill cheerfully, correctly interpreting the expression.

"Think he'll make it across Death Valley on this?" Selene asked, climbing up on the other side with another windshield squeegee.

"Don't they sell fuel in Death Valley?"

"Gas, sure. Dunno about diesel," Selene shrugged. "And it'll cost you an arm and the better part of your leg. And—" she would have gone on to espouse the shortcomings of vehicular service in the desert, when there was a deep guttural roar, and Clara, an imposing figure with her visor down, rolled past on her black motorcycle. The afternoon sun glinted off the metal spike mounted above the headlamp.

"I'm going on ahead," she announced, her voice surprisingly light and musical from inside the helmet.

"Oi!" called Selene, leaning off Arcana's hood. "You can't keep ditching us like this! What if Jill needs you?"

Clara's black shoulders shrugged. "You're the shield," she said, and drowned any retort with the bark of her engines as she rode away.

"Bah." Selene spat onto the pavement.

Jill, who was still too full of broken glass emotionally to be physically able to laugh, nevertheless smiled to herself as she ran a rag over Arcana's bumper. The deep red paint gleamed.

It is a long way to Death Valley, whichever way you approach it. This is because Death Valley is only one of several long, deep desert valleys separating what are currently the states of California and Nevada. To get there you have to drive across miles and miles of desert and up and down a couple mountain ranges, just to get to something that is, when you get right down to it, more of the same.

Still, it had a certain something to it, Jill thought as she looked out across the valley unfolding before her.

They had stopped at a rest area perched on the slopes of the western border mountains for Selene to use the bathroom. While she waited Jill climbed out of the truck and ambled to the end of the cement walkway, where a small plaque proclaimed the parking lot to be *Father Crowley Vista Point*. Jill went and stood, leaning her back against the stone.

The valley, brownish gold and streaked with blue-gray shadows, faded to a gentle purple in the distance where the mountains on the opposite side rose like a spiky wall. If Jill had been a fanciful person—which she wasn't—she might have compared them to the spiny ridges of a dragon's back. Because she wasn't, instead she thought of wind and water erosion, and how defenseless the naked earth was without its armor of trees, shrubs and grass, with their absorbency and stabilizing root systems.

"You noticed it too, huh?" Selene remarked, jolting Jill out of peaceful contemplation of geology.

"Noticed what?" she said.

Selene waved a hand at the valley.

"The shadows. They're not right."

"There *can* be cloud shadows in the desert," Jill said. "It's not uncommon for Death Valley to even have some precipitation in the winter months."

"That's as may be," Selene said, and there was a tight edge to her voice that made the hairs on the back of Jill's neck prick. "It'd be fine for clouds to cast shadows on Death Valley. Not saying they couldn't. Would be upset if they *didn't*. But in that vein, Jill, *look at the sky.*"

Jill squinted up into the bright, pale blue sky. Pale, *clear* blue sky.

She looked back at the valley and the long streaks of dusky grayness that slanted across it. They were just the kind of vague, gentle shadows to be cast by high, thin clouds.

Of which there were currently none.

"Wait . . ." said Jill. "Wait—*what?*"

"Something weird's definitely going on with the shadows here," Selene said smugly, then: "What are you doing?"

"Documenting an unexplained atmospheric phenomenon," Jill said. She had taken out her phone and was snapping pictures like mad. "Of course, skeptics will say these were photoshopped—which they *should*, that's what we have skeptics *for*—but there may be something going on that we're not seeing yet. Something *else* affecting the behavior of light. How long would you say those shadows are? One, two miles on average?" Now she had switched to a notepad app and was tapping in notes with little *pic, pic, pic-pic* noises.

"I'm not getting paid enough for this," Selene murmured.

"I'll give you a raise as soon as the sale closes on my house," Jill assured her. "Now look at that shadow nearest. Would you say it resembles that cast by an altostratus or a cirrostratus?"

It was a long time before they reached Death Valley proper, and the little ranger's station at Stovepipe Wells Rest Area was deserted. There was no cell phone reception, and no sign of Clara, either. There were a lot of flyers with headings like "HOW TO SURVIVE IN THE DESERT" and "SURVIVAL TIPS FOR DEATH VALLEY" taped on all the buildings. They looked new. Selene read them while Jill worked the automatic ticket dispenser outside the locked door.

They all said more or less the same thing: tell people where you are going. Bring extra water. Don't go alone. Take extra water. The desert can get surprisingly cold at night; bring warm clothes. And extra water. It was enough to make you thirsty standing in the cool twilight.

Speaking of twilight, the strange shadows had disappeared with the setting of the sun, replaced by the all-encompassing shadow of night. Selene tried not to get twitchy, but as someone to whom being twitchy in shady places had been the reason for her continued existence she found it difficult.

"No way we're getting through to Clara tonight," Jill grumbled as she came away from the machine with a little white printout and a pink square of paper.

"We can try Furnace Creek," Selene offered, crunching over the gravel to Arcana.

"That won't help if *she's* not in range," Jill pointed out.

"Yeah, but maybe she's had the same idea," Selene said, climbing into the driver's seat.

Arcana's lights came on, big and bright and yellow, chasing the shadows of evening back as it rolled out onto the road. Selene tried to concentrate on what was within those beams of light, rather than the thickening darkness that lay beyond.

Clara was not at Furnace Creek. Jill did get reception and used it to call Clara, but the woman didn't answer. Instead she sent a report to Professor Okedo while Selene organized them a campsite.

"Don't you need a ... I dunno ... tent or something?" Jill asked as they rolled into the campground.

"Probably," said Selene, carefully squeezing Arcana into a parking space meant for a sedan.

They laid down the back seat, and Selene produced a threadbare sleeping bag and ratty pillow. Then they took turns sleeping in it for two hours at a time while the other sat on the cargo trunk in the bed of the truck, keeping watch. Jill spent the time entering notes on her phone, and dozing. She couldn't fathom the logic of watches. It just meant both people would be cranky and sleep-deprived the next day. Besides, people camped out all the time in the wilderness and slept unmolested.

Mostly.

Selene spent her watches stargazing, and listening.

You learned to listen, in the dark. It was probably a load of bull that blind people developed heightened sensitivity in their remaining senses, but Selene thought they definitely paid more attention to them. The same thing happened in the dark: you noticed the sound of wind in leaves; learned to distinguish a palm tree from a creosote bush; you started making guesses at how large an animal just stepped on that twig.

Selene had the last watch: those two hours before dawn when all was silent and still. It is not true that the hour before dawn is the darkest, but it is the quietest.

Selene sat, her trench gun, Freddie, resting between her knees, and waited for the stir: the subtle shifting of air and the creeping grayness in the east that would signal the coming of the sun and the new day.

She waited a long time.

It never came.

Selene checked her watch. It said 7:34. If it was correct—which she was beginning to doubt—it should have gotten light half an hour ago. She frowned.

They had been timing the watches using Jill's phone, which had the advantage of not running slow or stopping. Perhaps she hadn't been waiting as long as she'd thought.

Or ...

Selene shook that idea out of her head. She had a somewhat broader scope of credence to give the universe when it came to improbable phenomena than Jill, but she was not a fanciful person. She began counting minutes.

One thousand, eight hundred and some seconds later Selene had to admit something had gone wrong, and it wasn't her watch—which was reading a cheerful 8:00.

She looked at the impenetrable blackness of the night around her, glanced at the all-too-distant stars, and then carefully climbed down from the bed and pulled open the rear door.

"Sorry hun," she began. "You better rise and shine, 'cause the sun's taken a day off—and I do mean *off*—" she stopped.

There was no one in the back seat.

Not only that, it wasn't even laid down any more; the seats were up in their normal position, and her sleeping bag and pillow were gone.

The first thing Selene did was look behind her. She swung Freddie in a large arc where she stood, but her gun met no resistance.

Having ascertained that there was nothing waiting to eat her in the immediate vicinity, she took a few steps back from Arcana and squinted at its dark shape.

It seemed . . . smaller? No . . . *bent.* Or maybe crippled. Its outline looked pockmarked, as if damaged by acid.

Selene reached out and shut the door.

The black outline of Arcana crumbled like dust and scattered into the night.

Suddenly a whole lot of subtle *wrongness* that had been gathering in the back of Selene's mind pushed to the front: *no other* lights were visible—none in the campground, and none from the direction of the visitors' center—where there was, she remembered, a yellow streetlight—and everything eerily silent.

In the silence and the dark, Selene Shields stamped her foot and swore.

She took stock of what she did have: a fully loaded shotgun with two rounds in reserve, a knife sheathed in her right boot, and a watch, compass, Leatherman multitool, and a spare bandana.

Her phone, water bottle, and the rest of her arsenal had been inside Arcana.

"Well . . . *damn it.*" She swung Freddie over her shoulder and began walking toward where the visitors' center should have been.

Jill had trouble getting to sleep after her second shift. The problem of the shadows played over in her mind like a tape stuck on loop. In the way of indecisive insomnia, she finally drifted off just as a pale pink glow began spreading behind the eastern mountains. She dragged a fold of pillow over her head, and slept.

She woke with a horrible crick in her back—from sleeping diagonally across Arcana's back seat—to find the sun shining full into the cab. Checking her phone, she discovered it was almost ten—that meant she'd slept a solid five hours at least! Good. One of them would be functional today.

With a groan she pushed open Arcana's door and poked her head out.

Selene was nowhere to be seen.

I hope she's gone for breakfast, Jill thought as she pulled out her phone and hit Selene's speed dial.

There was a harsh tinny sound from Arcana's front seat that soon grew into an obnoxious default ringtone. Letting her own phone drop from her ear Jill leaned forward between the seats, an icy feeling of dread crawling up out of her gut.

Selene's phone lay on the passenger seat, its digital display reading "Boss Jill calling . . . "

Jill killed the call. She didn't panic. She pulled the door shut, then leaned across the driver's seat and hit the power lock. Then she called Clara.

Ring.

Selene didn't attach the same kind of importance to her phone that Jill did, but she wasn't a scatterbrain.

Ring.

She understood the importance of communication, and being accessible, unlike Clara.

Ring.

Selene was not—*was not*—the kind of person to wander off without her phone. Not unless she'd been compromised in some way.

Ring.

Jill could feel her heart pounding in her chest, and willed it to slow down.

Ring—BEEP. *Hummm . . .*

"What is it?" Clara's voice said.

"It got Selene!" Jill practically shouted.

There was an ominous silence on the other end of the line.

"What?"

"Whatever's been nabbing people here? It got Selene last night."

"Where are you?" There was a sharpness to Clara's tone now.

"At Furnace Creek," Jill said. "Okay, so *maybe* this is a false alarm and she just left her phone by accident, *but—*"

"You stayed *the night* in the valley?" Clara exclaimed.

"Um . . . yes? We couldn't contact you!"

On the other end of the phone, Clara swore in Danish.

"But you saw the shadows?" she asked.

"Of course!" said Jill.

"Do you still have Arcana?"

"I'm *in* Arcana," Jill said. "The doors are locked."

"That won't do much good," Clara said. "You need to get out. Get out of the valley. Do not leave the truck. Just . . . *go.* Take the highway north until you come to the Beatty cutoff, then keep heading east. I'll come meet you."

"Where *are* you anyway?" Jill asked.

"Beatty, Nevada," Clara said, as if this should be obvious. "Are you driving yet? I'll stay on until you've got Arcana running."

"What about Selene?"

"We'll take care of that later," Clara said. "First, we need to get you out of there. Drive, and *do not stop* driving until you're out of the valley. Understand?"

"But what if I'm wrong and she's—" Jill began, having a sudden attack of doubt.

"I'll find her," Clara said. "First. You. Out. *Drive.*"

Jill scrambled into the front seat, pulling her key out of the cup holder. She put Clara on speaker phone while she buckled herself in and turned on the ignition.

For one wretched second Jill thought she had somehow stumbled into one of those stupid horror movies where otherwise reliable engines suddenly don't work as the monster is sneaking up behind the vehicle.

Then Arcana came to life with a roar.

"Remember," Clara's voice hissed from her phone, "highway north, take the Beatty cutoff, keep heading east. I'll meet you." Then she hung up.

At about the time Jill was peeling out of Furnace Creek, Selene was casing the visitors' center. She'd already been to the gas station next door and found it deserted. The door to the food mart had been unlocked, however, and Selene had helped herself to candy bars and bottled water from the shelves. She'd even left a crumpled twenty by the register—what else would she use it for?—and now, hydrated and fueled by sugar, she cautiously approached the low, angular building that was the visitors' center.

A wind, sudden and surprising in the stillness, rushed through the trees and blew her hair sideways. Strange, but it had almost sounded like Arcana's engine. Selene shook herself, and concentrated on the building.

It was as still and dark as everything else, but as she'd passed it on her way to the gas station Selene had heard something that wasn't wind in leaves, or the footfalls of unknown animals, but the low murmur of human voices. Selene had learned long ago that just because something sounded human didn't mean it was, and even if it was, that did not mean it would help. Humans—*civilian* humans—could be singularly *un*helpful when it came to supernatural phenomena.

Now Selene crouched by the large wooden slab of a sign by the entrance walk, Freddie held lightly in both hands. The building had great big wall-wide windows, but they were tinted dark—no doubt against the sun that was currently AWOL—and she could see nothing through them.

Leaving the front door—*never enter by the front door*—Selene began making a circuit of the building, looking for alternate entrances.

She found three. The first two doors were locked, but the third was a swinging glass door that gave under her push.

Selene took her hand away immediately, checked behind her one last time, and then slowly—*slowly*—pushed the door open.

Bless the National Park Service and their attention to public image; the thing made not a sound, and Selene slipped inside, dark and silent as the shadows that surrounded her.

Out of habit more than anything else, she tried the first light switch she found. It didn't work, of course, but Selene took it in stride. She felt her way along the dim wall, careful not to breathe too hard, using the muzzle of Freddie as a probe.

Around a corner Selene got the sense of a large space opening in front of her, and at last she heard the sounds of other human beings.

They sounded like two men, and unsurprisingly, they were arguing. Selene turned her back to the direction of the voices, leaned against the nearest wall, and listened.

"Listen, man, you just got here so I'll cut you some slack," said one voice. It was high for a man, and sounded frazzled. There was a waver in it that spoke of madness and panic, barely contained. It still held an undercurrent of natural confidence, however. Its owner was used to getting his own way, to being given things as a matter of course.

White male, between twenty-two and thirty-five, Selene guessed, wrinkling her nose.

"You don't *go* outside. There's *things* out there, in the dark. I *heard* them."

"Did you see them?" A deeper voice, raised in alarm, with a slight musical quality that suggested it was perhaps more comfortable in Spanish.

"What? *No* I didn't *see* them! Can you *see* anything, Jorge?"

"My name is Brian," said the Hispanic voice, all trace of an accent deserting it on the name.

"Whatever man. I'm just saying, I've *been here* for a while. *Don't* go outside."

"But there's no one here. There *should* be people here. There *were.* We've got to go find them. I know they're looking for you, and they'll start looking for me soon as my shift starts and I don't show."

The white guy laughed. That laugh rang all sorts of alarm bells in Selene's mind. She began to worry for Brian. At the same time she wished the other guy would stop laughing. There had been a sound, muffled by his voice, that had not come from any human throat.

Fortunately, Brian was on that.

"Hey, hey *cut it out,*" he said, and with a muffled thumping the laughter cut off abruptly. *"Did you hear that?"* he hissed.

Selene had: the *clatter clatter* of sharp little feet on metal, coming from somewhere above them.

Giant killer centipede in the air ducts, in my professional opinion, Selene thought. Which I *am* a professional now, she thought with an inner grin. At the same time a little voice that sounded like Jill said "Be sure to save some samples for analysis!"

Selene told it to shut up.

The men were talking again, arguing about what they had heard, and they were making it difficult for her to track whatever was in the ceiling.

"Man, man we *got* to get out of here," Brian was saying.

"You don't *understand*," shrieked the white dude. "There was another *girl!* This *chick!* She went out there—I couldn't stop her—and a minute later I heard this—"

There was a clang and a skittering sound.

"*Madre de dios!*"

"Holy shit! Your *leg!*"

"FREEZE!" shouted Selene, coming around the corner at a run. It was a dark confusion in front of her, and she clipped the side of a low table, painfully, as she went. Fortunately the surprise of her entrance caused one of the dark shapes near the glass door—which let in the faintest of filtered starlight—to still. That allowed her to concentrate on the writhing mass on the floor.

Poor Brian was gibbering in Spanish—not all of it words—and when Selene grabbed him by the shirt she felt resistance; something was trying to drag him the other way.

To Selene's poor human eyes it appeared only a darker shape in the rest of the blackness, but she put her knees on Brian's shoulders to hold him still, and aimed Freddie down his body.

The gun flashed briefly as it fired, and for an instant Selene saw the glinting of a segmented carapace over countless little claws: a creature the size of a bulldog, its mouthparts firmly clamped over Brian's left leg.

There was a hiss of escaping air. Brian shrieked and kicked. Selene pulled out her knife and stabbed down at where she'd seen the creature. Her knife met resistance, then stuck in the floor. She felt something wet and sticky seep into her hand.

Brian was wriggling backward out from under her, so that was okay. Above her, she was aware of the other guy hyperventilating. Right. Time to do damage control.

"What the *hell?* I'm serious, like, *what the HELL?*" he shrieked.

For any given value of "control."

"Cut that out," Selene snapped. "Do you have a light?"

"None of the lights *work*," groaned Brian. He sounded like he was in shock.

"I know," said Selene. "I meant a *lighter*, light. As in *fire*."

"We sell novelty lighters behind the front desk . . . " Brian mumbled.

The hyperventilating stopped, followed by the thump of feet.

"Be *careful*—" Selene began, but was cut off by a string of curses as the other guy ran into the table.

"Hey, hey . . . " Brian's voice was slurring now. Did that thing have a poisonous bite? Damnit, she needed to *see*—" . . . are you that chick?"

"I'm not a chick," Selene said firmly, putting Freddie under one knee and feeling gently down Brian's injured leg. Luckily, the creature had let go when it had been shot. She felt blood and torn clothing, but didn't palpate the wound with her hands covered in goo.

Unsteady footsteps approached, and a bright light flared over her shoulder.

She almost wished she hadn't sent the dude for a light. Freddie's shot had torn away half the thing's head, but what was left gaped at them eerily in the flickering light. It looked indeed like a millipede crossed with a bull-dog. (*Get samples!* shrieked Jill's voice in her head. Selene ignored it.)

"First-aid kit?" she asked Brian.

"B-by the restrooms," he stammered. Not sounding good. Damn.

"Go get it, uh—" she realized she still didn't have a name for the other man, who was standing uncertainly by with a lighter in one hand.

"Andy," he said, almost as if he were challenging her to deny it.

"Great. Wonderful. *Andy*, do me a solid and go get the first-aid kit. Oh, and water."

Andy looked like he was about to refuse, but then he took another look at Brian's leg. "Yeah," he said. "D-duh."

The little light moved away, past some racks of books, and Selene felt behind her for the table she and Andy had both run into. It was better to have your back to something solid.

"Brian," she said, as gently as she could manage. "That is your name, right? Brian?"

"Uh . . . yeah, that's me."

"I'm going to move you, Brian. But only a little ways. It might hurt some." Gripping him under the armpits she carefully began dragging him backward. He was a generously built man, but the floor was smooth.

"Wh—what was that *thing?*"

"Whatever it *was* it's dead now," Selene assured him. "Don't worry."

"Is there more of it?"

"Maybe. Don't worry, you're safe with me."

"'Cause you've got a *shotgun,*" Brian slurred.

"That, and . . . " there was just enough light for Selene to see his face. It was a wide, pleasant face. It seemed wrong for it to be so contorted in pain. She flashed him an encouraging smile. "*And* I'm a *professional.*"

Andy returned with the kit, and thrust the lighter at Selene.

"Sorry?" she said.

"Hold my light," he said. Andy was an improbably blond-haired, blue-eyed man in his early twenties. A pinched quality to his mouth and around his eyes suggested he was used to being in control of things, and was des-perately trying to regain that.

"Uh-huh," said Selene, sneaking a hand past the proffered lighter and to the gray box clutched in his other hand. "Andy, have you *ever* dressed a serious wound?"

Andy snorted. "*Sure.*" Like it was something everyone did on a weekly basis.

"Are you an EMT?"

"A what?"

"Thought not," Selene grabbed the first-aid kit and tucked Freddie under one arm while she popped it open. "Hold the light higher, it scatters better," she ordered.

After a dumbstruck moment, Andy obeyed. "You sure are a *bossy* one," he muttered, getting to his feet.

Selene paused in sorting through the bandages, packets of disinfectant, topical anesthetics, scissors, tape, and temporary casts, to give Andy a penetrating stare.

"I *am* the boss," she said. "Hold the light. And don't look at *me*, look out—" she waved her spare hand "—for more of *those*." She pointed at the bulldog millipede. Turning back to the kit, she found it contained rubber gloves—nitriles, in fact. Bless the National Park Service.

Jill passed a park ranger's truck as she headed north from Furnace creek. She didn't think much of it until, having turned right at the road marked "Beatty Cutoff," she was passed by a string of law enforcement vehicles, including an ambulance, driving the opposite way.

And then . . .

Vrrrrooooooooowm!

Something black and motorcycle-shaped whipped around a corner. Jill twitched so hard in surprise that she caused Arcana to skitter sideways across the road. She felt a wave of indecision overtake her; should she turn around? Stop? Wait? *What?*

Her questions were answered a few seconds later when Clara appeared in her rearview mirror, riding sedately at a safe distance behind Arcana. One black arm rose, waving her forward. Jill drove.

Up out of the valley, while the sun arced high above them, following the narrow road as it twined through red-brown hills, then out and up over the fan of sand and dried mud spewed long ago from the mouth of a canyon. They saw no one else.

At the top of the fan, where the road disappeared into the peaks of the bordering mountains, Clara signaled a halt.

With a sense of relief Jill pulled Arcana off the road, sending up a storm of dust and rocks from the soft shoulder. Clara gave her a wide berth as she passed, and stopped on the edge of the road.

"Talk to me, Clara," Jill said, even as she was climbing out of Arcana's cab. "What's going on?"

Clara, masked under her helmet, was unreadable. Silently she pointed behind Jill, to Death Valley laid out below them.

Jill turned to look; her jaw dropped.

She could see the road they had climbed up, see it descend into the valley, joining the highway that ran north to south. She could see the glitter of the salt flats, see the pale haze over the sand dunes, even a faint cluster of white squares that she supposed was the Stovepipe Wells way station.

All of it lay under a deep, dark shadow, which stretched up to the fan they had just ascended. Above them the sky was a clear, hazy, blue. It was as though a patch of the previous night had simply decided to *stay*.

It was amazing. Impossible. Fascinating. And, Jill thought with a lurch, vaguely terrifying. It was so . . . so *wrong*.

"Explain this, Clara," she said, even as she got out her phone and started taking pictures.

Clara's huge shoulders dipped and rose, her head tilting to one side.

"I *can't*," she said unhappily. "But the valley isn't safe anymore, and we're not out of it yet."

Something in her tone made Jill look at the shadow again. Was she imagining things, or were the shadows deeper at the center of the valley? And was its edge creeping closer up the road?

"Then why did you stop?" she snapped, setting up her phone to take a panorama.

Clara sighed. "Because you needed to see," she said in a long-suffering tone.

When the shadow had crept up over the nearest mountains, and lay on the road only a quarter mile away, Jill's nerve broke, and she scrambled back into Arcana.

Clara followed, acting as rearguard, until they had climbed out of the valley entirely and were crossing the high desert plains west of Beatty. They passed a large sign informing them that they were now leaving Death Valley National Park, and Clara gunned her bike past Jill. She made a beckoning motion with her arm as she did so—*follow me*.

Jill followed without question, and did not look back.

"All right gang, refuel," Selene announced, dumping out a pile of granola and chocolate bars from the backpack she had borrowed from the visitors' center gift shop.

Andy, still clutching the lighter (his fourth) eyed the food like a madman presented with a barrel of gold. She took the lighter from him, and he dived for the pile.

"Don't hurt yourself," she muttered, and turned to Brian.

The bite had not been nearly as bad as she'd feared—only a couple stitches necessary—and after she'd washed the goo off and bandaged it up tight he could even limp on it. But there hadn't been any ibuprofen or aspirin in the kit, and now she rattled a bottle at him.

"Eat first," she said, handing him a box of cereal bars. "Then take three."

Brian nodded silently and took the box. Selene wondered if he was this agreeable when not injured, and vaguely wished it had been Andy who'd taken the bite.

Andy, who was currently trying to eat two chocolate bars at once. By Selene's estimate, he must have been in this shadow-world for *at least* two-and-a-half days.

"Andy," she said gently, sliding the box of granola bars further away. "When was the last time you had something to eat?"

Andy stopped mid-chew and screwed up his face. "There was this couple a while back—man and a woman—they came over from the resort a little while ago, and they had food. They shared."

"What happened to them?" Selene asked.

Andy glared at her, as though this were all her fault.

There was a horrible screeching from outside, and something smacked sickly against the glass front doors.

Andy shouted in alarm, threw down his chocolate, and backed away until he ran up against the puppet display. "Th-*that* did!" he cried.

"Hold this," Selene said to Brian, handing him the lighter, and then vaulted the table and crept toward the door.

Whatever had struck the door was not dead—not yet. It was moaning faintly, and its arms flailed. Selene thought it was a woman. She pulled the door open, grabbed the person by the shoulder seam of her jacket, and dragged her inside. It was a woman, and she thrashed and screamed at Selene's touch.

She'll live, thought Selene, dodging a leg.

"Addison! *No! Addison!*"

"Who is Addison?"

The woman gulped, blinked up at Selene.

"My *daughter!*"

Daughter, right. Of course. White women could be so weird about names.

"Andy, I need you!" Selene shouted.

"I'm *not* going out there!" Andy called.

It was Brian who came limping over, carrying the flickering lighter.

"I'll watch her," he said tightly. "You go, get the girl."

Yeah I wish, Selene thought as she slipped out the door and checked Freddie.

Seven shots. That was all she had. And by the sound of it, there was a whole pack of large, angry somethings out there in the dark.

She stood with her back against the door, every muscle in her body singing with tension, until she heard what she was waiting for.

There. In among the beastly growls and padding of paws, there were the high, panicked gasps of a human—punctuated by little squeals.

Just save some breath for running, Selene thought as she took off across the parking lot.

It was relatively light out here: the stars were extraordinarily bright, pricking the velvet blackness of the sky. They cast the parking lot and the trees beyond in a dim gray light, and Selene could make out dark shapes moving toward the campground.

Taking a deep gulp of cold dark air, Selene bellowed at the top of her lungs: "*ADDISON!*"

A startled gasp from the direction of the trees. Selene altered course just in time to dodge the slinky, vaguely feline shape that darted from the shadows. She turned, whip-fast and adrenaline-fueled, and caught whatever it was across the head with Freddie's butt. The animal staggered, and Selene used the moments of its disorientation to slip her knife into its jugular vein.

Dark blood spread out in a growing puddle below the body, but Selene was already on and running, diving into the trees.

"Addison!"

"Mom?"

The voice came from surprisingly high up.

"Your mom's okay!" Selene shouted. "Where are you?"

"Up here!"

"Where?" Selene growled. There was another animal in the shade, and Selene wanted it to think better of attacking her all on its own.

"Tree!" cried Addison. "I climbed."

She sounded maybe sixteen.

"Keep talking, I'll find you!" Selene called, and started slashing her way through the shrubby bushes toward the voice.

Movement at her ankle. Selene didn't even hesitate. She dropped Freddie's nose and let off a shot directly into the head of what looked, in the brief flash of light, like a mountain lion with scales.

Huh—was all that went through Selene's mind as she followed Addison's wavering call. Some heavy rustling in the branches of a nearby tree guided Selene to the base. She could just make out the silhouette of a young body, clinging belly down to the lowest branch.

"Careful!" Addison cried. "There's one—"

Whack. Slash. Stab.

"Not anymore," Selene said. "Get down, fast. Jump. We gotta move."

"I *can't!*" cried Addison.

"You *can*," Selene said, grinding her teeth. "Throw your legs down and relax."

"N-no *way!*" Addison said, her young husky voice taking on a determined undertone. "It's too far!"

This is the problem with teenage girls, Selene thought bitterly. They had it pounded into them as children that they were delicate princesses, and they hadn't yet figured out what a load of crap that was.

"Addison," she said, backing herself up against the tree and scanning the undergrowth. "I'm trying to help. Really, I am. But I'm not *made* of bullets, and there's more of those things. Now, you can jump, and risk bruising your pretty little feet, or you can stay up there and get eaten while I go back to your *mother* and tell her 'Sorry ma'am, tried to save your kid, but she couldn't *jump out of a tree* and—'"

Thump.

"Oww . . ."

"Good girl," said Selene. She grabbed a bony elbow and began dragging the girl back toward the visitors' center.

The door was locked when they got there. Not for the first time Selene wished she could shoot laser beams out of her eyes. Laser beams would shatter glass, right?

She had only banged twice, however, when Brian opened it for her.

"You *made* it," he said, blank with shock.

"Told ya I was a professional," Selene said as she pulled Addison inside after her.

"We thought—well . . . " Brian limped aside as Addison's mother came charging forward.

Under the tearful reunion of mother and daughter, Selene looked around to find Andy approaching with the lighter. Strangely, the sight of two distressed females was motivation enough for him to get his own hysteria under control. He practically swaggered over and offered soothing words to Addison's mother, who had burst into tears.

"How's the leg?" Selene asked Brian.

"Hurts," he said. "But I can walk on it. Don't think anything important got broke."

"Good," said Selene. "You'll need it for the push outta here."

"Out?" Brian said sharply.

"Yeah," said Selene, pulling out her knife and wiping it down with her bandana. "We can't stay here. I'll explain the plan when they've calmed down a bit." She reloaded Freddie. *Six shots left.*

Addison, with the natural resilience of those under twenty-five, quickly shrugged off her brush with violent, fanged death, and transitioned to mortal embarrassment at her mother's emotional response. She looked like a willowy teen, wearing skinny jeans, sensible shoes—thank goodness!—and her long straight hair up in a lopsided ponytail. Her mother was a wide-set middle-aged woman in hiking pants and sandals, who looked like she'd spent the previous weekend shopping for outdoorsy clothes because she'd never had any need of them before.

"Okay, introduction time," Selene said, when she felt the woman would listen. "I'm Selene, this here is Brian. Mind his left leg, he got bit by a giant killer millipede. That there's Andy. Everyone this is Addison, and . . . " she trailed off.

"Miranda," Addison supplied.

"Miranda," said Selene. "Ordinarily I'd love to hear y'all's stories about how you got yanked into the wrong side of Oz, but we don't have time. We gotta get out of here. And by *here* I mean this godforsaken valley. Since I haven't seen any cars, this means walking. Lots of walking. So . . . to begin at the beginning . . . Brian's gimp leg notwithstanding, does anyone here have any medical complications I should know about before we get started?"

They stared at her in varying states of blank befuddlement.

"Oi, hey," said Andy. "Who died and made *you* the boss?"

"Nobody," Selene said simply. "I'm only the boss if you want me to be. And you *want* me to be the boss if you want to get out of this alive."

She glared around at the assembled circle, as if daring them to challenge this.

Andy drew in a breath.

"She *does* have a shotgun," Addison pointed out. She turned to Selene. "I'm allergic to bee stings. But not badly. Mom's diabetic. Type 2."

"Anyone else?" Selene asked.

For once, Andy remained silent.

"Okay," she swept on. "Here's the plan."

She told them.

"*Walk* out?" Brian exclaimed when she had finished. "But it's *miles* to the nearest town!"

"Around forty," Selene agreed, nodding. "And we'll get there a lot faster if we're not sitting on our butts in here."

"Yeah? Well *I'm* not going," declared Andy.

Selene gave him a blank stare.

"Shouldn't we wait?" quavered Addison's mother. "Wait for help to find us?"

"Don't you get it?" Selene growled. "*I'm* the help. But I can only help you if you *work* with me. Now, we don't know what's out there, but we don't know what's *in here* either. In here all we can hope for is for things to *miraculously* go back to normal—which in my experience they *do not*—or we can do the responsible thing and try to get ourselves out. We might still get killed,"—she shrugged, just to show them how little the idea meant to her—"but that way we actually have a *chance* of escaping."

"You said 'walk out,'" Addison repeated thoughtfully. "You think it's night just here in the valley? If we get out of the valley, we might . . . uh . . . get out of this night?"

"That's what I think," Selene said. *What I hope. Hope against hope against—*

"What *is* going on?" Miranda asked.

"If I could explain that," Selene said, patting her gun. "I wouldn't need ol' Freddie here. Now," her gaze shot across the four of them. "We have supplies to pack."

The highway out of Death Valley came through a saddle in the mountains and suddenly changed its name to Main Street and got wider. A sign, rather the worse from years of ultraviolet radiation, welcomed them to Beatty, NV: *Gateway to Death Valley.* Bleached, rundown houses lined the street, interspersed here and there with abandoned lots.

Clara cruised into the roadside parking lot of a hotel that, had it not been painted a bright mint green, might have slipped past Jill's notice. She pulled Arcana in behind and parked it next to the motorcycle.

"Okay, *what*—" Jill began, before she'd quite gotten out of the truck.

"Inside," murmured Clara, locking her bike and tucking her helmet under one arm. In the daylight Jill saw deep shadows under her eyes, and a wary press of her lips that suggested she too was running on a less-than-optimal amount of sleep.

Then again, Jill had seen Clara perform beautifully even after staying up for two days straight. She pressed on mercilessly.

"You can't tell me no one else will have noticed," she said as Clara unlocked the door of a room.

"Bring your computer," was all Clara said, and disappeared inside.

Jill nearly stumbled over her own feet scrambling back to Arcana, whose door still stood open. She grabbed her backpack, locked the truck, and followed Clara.

Inside it looked like a criminal investigation was underway. Clara had clearly forbidden the housekeeping staff from setting foot inside; Jill was certain they would have objected to the wall covered in photocopies, printouts, and newspaper clippings. Clara had stripped one of the double beds, and tacked the sheet across the wall. This supported all the papers. She had also drawn lines connecting certain articles with certain photos, with notes printed in neat capitals in the margins.

Jill dumped her backpack on the stripped bed and gazed at the wall in awe. Now she took the time to read some of the headlines and Clara's larger notes, she began to have a new respect for the woman.

It was a both a flowchart for all the disappearances in Death Valley over the last week and a record of unusual weather. There were also notes on the correct time the sun should rise and set, and the phases of the moon.

In the very center of all this, printed on the back of a meal receipt, were Clara's guesses as to the cause. Jill read:

MALICIOUS SPIRIT(S)/GHOULS
BENIGN GHOST(S)   *(unlikely)*
DISTRESSED GHOST(S)
REALM INCURSION, DIRECTED/UNDIRECTED
DEMON
ANY COMBINATION OF ABOVE

Jill put a finger on the last line. "That's helpful," she said.

"Different causes require different treatments," Clara said, unzipping Jill's backpack and pulling her laptop out.

"Such as?" Jill prodded.

Clara gave her a stricken look over the computer, as if her train of thought had acquired a team of hijackers.

"Malicious spirits and ghouls are easiest," she said in a monotone. "They can usually be neutralized by the Gunn Classic. All ghosts, in fact. But it's better to find out what's gone wrong with the benign or distressed ghosts, and solve that. Realm incursion is bad. So are demons. And they usually go together."

Jill looked again at the list.

"I bet it's a realm incursion directed by a demon," she said.

Clara's head shot up. "What makes you say that?"

Jill shrugged. "Because in my experience, the correct answer is *usually* the worst possible option."

Clara flashed her a brief, humorless smile and went back to the laptop. "What *is* 'realm incursion' anyway?"

"Exactly what it sounds like," Clara answered without looking up, and Jill had to content herself with that.

The group of five walked two abreast down the empty highway, with the teenage girl in the lead. Selene brought up the rear with Brian, who sometimes had trouble with his leg. She'd put Andy next to Miranda, with the thinking that Miranda was the sort of person Andy liked to help, in his condescending way, and so was less likely to cause trouble.

Addison had been a bit of a gamble, but she was proving a competent lead. She probably had the best vision of the group, and since Selene had made them travel without light they were navigating by the faint glow of the stars.

Selene kept glancing up at the stars. There was something not quite right about them. Not quite *wrong* either. She couldn't quite put her finger on it, until the moon rose.

To some people the phases of the moon are random and mysterious. Those who are interested enough generally know about angles and why the moon changes phase, maybe they understand how and why eclipses happen. They might even be able to tell whether any given phase is waxing or waning.

Selene, who had taken a particular interest in the moon ever since she'd learned what her first name meant, had learned all this. She had also learned where to spot the moon, day or night, at any given time during its cycle.

Now, as a waxing crescent climbed up over the eastern mountains, she felt a deep lurch in her stomach. It was a strange mash of panic and relief. Panic, because a waxing crescent—and this one was close to first quarter—should never be seen *rising* in a dark sky. When things were working properly, it appeared in the sky in the late afternoon. Relief because, well, it meant that time at least was still moving. They hadn't been frozen in time; they were just stuck in eternal night.

This *was* day. Just a day without a sun.

Without sun*light.* Clearly, the moon was still enjoying its regular day and night cycles. Selene wondered briefly what this patch of darkness would look like to an outside observer.

The new influx of light from Selene's namesake better illuminated the desolate landscape through which they walked, and allowed Selene to spot the dark lump of a jeep parked on the shoulder of the road.

Andy gave a glad shout and broke into a run. Selene had to grab him by the back of his shirt to stop him.

"Don't be an idiot," she hissed in his ear over his loud protests. "Have you *seen* any vehicles around lately? No. So what's up with *this* one? Why is it still here? More importantly, is there anything large and unpleasant with sharp teeth waiting for us inside? *Think!*" She shook him by the collar.

Andy said a rude word and brushed her off angrily, but he didn't try to approach the jeep. Miranda clutched Addison by the shoulders, and Brian wobbled uncertainly.

"Let me clear it," Selene said. "You four wait here, and make a ring facing outwards, then you won't get snuck up on."

"Yeah, and what do we do if something *finds* us, huh?" Andy sniped.

"Scream like a girl," Selene told him shortly. At his offended grimace and Addison's sniggers, she added: "The high pitch carries better."

With that, she turned and crossed the last few yards to the jeep. It had been northbound as well, pulled over on the right shoulder with no real amount of care. The driver's door stood open, and it was dark inside.

Selene crept up to the open door as softly and gently as if she were stalking a den of tigers. Which, for all she knew, was what waited inside the jeep. Dropping to her knees she crab-walked under the windows, and peered in over the driver's seat.

The first thing she saw was the silver glint of metal dangling from the ignition. The second was the dark shape slumped in the passenger seat, its head hanging forward over the seat belt.

With a sinking sensation Selene climbed over the driver's seat and felt over the body riding shotgun. It was a woman, middle-aged, and there was a neat bullet hole directly between her eyes, which had frozen open.

Selene climbed out and went around to the far side of the car, where her party on the road could not see, and checked the back seat.

At first she thought there were two bodies, but then she found the third: half the size of an adult, and nestled in the arms of the one by the driver's-side door.

They had all been shot, with more or less precision, in the head.

Selene felt like her stomach filled with ice even as the bile rose in her throat. She forced herself to remain still, to breathe normally, and to pull slowly out of the jeep.

The others could not—*must* not—see this. She stared at the moon for a few moments, while all the little things that she had been noticing but hadn't been paying attention to presented themselves for inspection.

Four bodies. Four bullet holes. Presumably four bullets, then. Where was the gun?

It had not been dropped outside the jeep. It was not on the floor, as far as she could tell. It was not on any of the bodies. Selene checked carefully as she pulled them out of the jeep one by one and dragged them behind the nearest boulder.

Last of all she carried the smallest in her arms. It had until recently belonged to a boy of about eight, and still wore his *Jurassic Park* T-shirt under a grubby jacket. Selene laid him reverently with the other three, beside the one in whose arms she had found him.

She felt split in two. One half of her was filled with cold, hard fury at the universe, at the people in it, at the dark, and *everything*. The other half was systematically going over the evidence and coming to some unsettling conclusions.

What she had were four dead people with no obvious traces of a struggle, each killed with a single bullet.

They might have been asleep when they were killed — or drugged, though Selene doubted this—but unless there were four assassins ready to execute them simultaneously then the first shot would have woken the rest. They would have resisted. Fruitlessly, probably, but they would have resisted.

Judging by the size of the car and the empty driver's seat, Selene guessed they had originally been a party of five. Now the driver was missing, along with the gun.

Three at least had been awake. And he or she must have shot them one by one.

Madness.

Or mercy.

Where was the driver? Chances were, if they had the ammo, they would have finished with their own damn self. And if they hadn't?

Selene walked back to her own party with dark troubles swirling in her mind.

"Had some junk in it," she said in answer to Andy's inevitable question. "Jeep's clear now. Come on over, and I'll see if she starts."

She did start, after a few coughs. She was almost empty, and Selene weighed the chances of coaxing gasoline out of the Chevron at Furnace Creek. She decided not to try; so far nothing electrical had worked, and she doubted the gas pumps would. It would only slow them down and give Andy something to complain about.

She piled them into the jeep; Brian went shotgun, and she put Andy between Addison and Miranda in the back. They weren't happy about this, but Selene had long since taken Andy's measure; he was that most frustrating kind of sexist: the one who doesn't recognize that he is one. He would respect and defer to women, but only as long as they looked and acted a certain way. Selene wasn't that kind of woman, but she guessed that Miranda, and possibly Addison, were. With any luck they would keep him under control.

The jeep's headlights didn't work, but that didn't faze her. The road stretched out, empty and inviting. The fuel they had wouldn't get them out of the valley, Selene guessed, but it would get them somewhere.

When your only thought is survival, every little bit helps.

"Just a fair warning," she called back over her shoulder as she pulled onto the highway. "If we run into anyone on the road, they're probably not in their right minds. Oh, but if they've got a gun, don't worry, it's empty."

In the stricken silence this caused, Selene acceelerated along the desert road.

Clara and Jill sat, slowly eating increasingly cold bowls of chili, as Clara scrolled through the list of all the new disappearances.

"There were *five* last night, not including Selene," Jill gasped.

"Those are only the ones that have been reported," Clara pointed out. "Probably there have been more."

"Why would someone not report?" Jill wondered.

"We didn't report Selene," Clara said. "Some maybe haven't been missed yet."

Jill scrolled down the list. "Aw geez," she said. "One of them's a *kid*."

"Kids usually do better," Clara said. "They recognize the dangers that adults try to rationalize away."

"Oh really?"

"I did."

"You did this . . . " Jill waved her hand at the room cluttered with case notes, " . . . *when you were a kid?*"

Clara's mouth shut like a trap, her thin lips sealing together. She stared vaguely across the room as if wrestling an internal adversary, and then her whole posture changed: the stricken look evaporated from her face, and the line of her body straightened. She pushed the computer onto Jill's lap and stood up. She crossed the little room in two strides and stopped at the bedside table. There had been piled the heap of newspapers she'd had to make do with before Jill arrived with her computer and therefore access to the internet.

They had been arranged with no great care, and folded on top was the local rag, the kind of thin, twelve-page weekly that did interviews with the local schoolchildren and pleased itself to call that news. This particular copy was from nearly a week ago, and on its front was a picture of modern art currently on display at the local historical museum. Clara picked it up and shook it out. She nodded once sharply to herself, then threw it down and went over to the makeshift whiteboard.

Jill carefully set aside her computer and picked up the discarded paper. The black-and-white picture showed a couple of women standing beside some rather ugly surrealistic paintings and smiling. The caption said they were Jenny Hurlin and Isobel Meeks, curator and assistant curator of the Beatty Historical Museum, seen posing with three paintings by Ben Wool, some high-class painter who had passed through Beatty and done a series of paintings inspired by the surrounding desert. Jill took another look at the artwork, and wondered what they were putting in the paints these days. Then she looked over at Clara.

Clara had drawn a line from *Realm Incursion* downward, connected with a + and then another line down to where she had just finished writing *Night God.*

Jill came over and stood next to her.

"Night god?" she said.

"It fits," said Clara, her voice like sharp steel. "We need to get the fetish."

"Fetish?" Jill said, feeling like the quicksand she had been treading was suddenly turning to pea soup. "People have erotic fantasies about incomprehensible art?"

Clara snatched the paper from her. "A *fetish* can also be a small object used in the worship of a deity, religious figure, or folk hero," and she pointed at a corner of the picture.

Jill squinted at the dark, blurry image there. In order to get the women in frame, the photographer had been obliged to back up sufficiently that a part of the neighboring exhibit was also visible. There, tucked in an unassuming corner, was the creepiest mask Jill had ever seen. She hoped it was just a bad photo, but she doubted it.

"Tell me you're not thinking of *stealing* it," she groaned.

Clara gave her a tight, blank look. Jill carefully refolded the newspaper and then slapped it against her face.

"So, when you say this thing is a god . . . "

"A night god."

"Yeah, night god. Whatever. But is it like, a *god* god? Like, would I have heard of him?"

"It." Clara corrected her.

"*Well?*"

"Probably not. It is not a god in the spiritual sense, only the general sense."

"Explain."

Clara paused on the edge of the road, waiting for a line of cars to pass, her eyes screwed up against the afternoon sun.

"It's just semantics," she said after the roar of the cars had died down. They hurried across the highway. "*God* can refer to any anthropomorphic personification of sufficient extraordinary power. They can also be called demons, angels, or just *spirits.*"

"The difference being?"

Clara shrugged. "Not much. Gods have a greater opinion of their own importance? We use the labels almost interchangeably. No one's ever gone through and catalogued the supernatural beings the way you scientists have with mundane animals."

Jill frowned to herself. "Someone *should,*" she stated.

Clara raised an eyebrow, but because her hair was such a pale yellow, it just looked like half her forehead had got a surprised wrinkle.

They stopped. In the curious way of small towns that lived off one arterial highway, the historical museum was just across and a little ways up the road from the motel where they were staying. A number of signs executed in varying levels of professionalism informed them that the faded blue building with the steepled roof was the Beatty Historical Museum, and that it was OPEN and to please COME ON IN! This last sentiment was repeated on signs tacked over and on the door, and on an old plow parked nearby.

Jill regarded them skeptically.

"Do you think it's open?" she asked Clara with a grin. Clara just grunted and pushed the door open.

Somewhere overhead a bell tinkled. The first thing Jill noticed was a bearded doll of the sort that came to life and tried to kill people in horror films. Despite her excellent grounding in reality, even the kind that contained inexplicable shadows, Jill had to suppress a shiver.

A woman in jeans with a mouth like a prune was talking to an elderly white-haired couple at the front counter. Jill caught her eye and smiled shortly. Clara, moving like a shark through a reef, melted behind an antique piano and moved off toward the back room.

Jill, beginning to feel like the chili had turned into a horde of bees in her stomach, made a show of admiring a display of truly horrible-looking women's shoes from the 1880's, before looking around for her companion in an exaggerated way and then darting down a short hallway lined with faded photographs.

Clara was standing in front of a scene containing more creepy mannequins dressed in female pioneer costume. One of them, clearly the grandmother, had a mass of white wool for hair. It looked like she was wearing a dead sheep.

"Talk about uncanny valley," Jill said. At Clara's blank look she added: "It's a thing . . . where the closer something looks to human, if it's close enough, suddenly it stops looking human and looks really, *really* wrong. It's called uncanny valley."

"Hmm," said Clara.

"Well?" hissed Jill.

"Well what?"

"What about . . . the fetish?"

Clara gave a half-shrug. "There is no fetish," she said, her voice even more of a monotone than usual.

Jill looked around. Sure enough, there was the display of surreal paintings—they were not improved by in-person viewing—but the collection of Native American artifacts next to it contained only old spearheads, a few moth-eaten beaded dresses, and one rusty machete.

When she looked back Clara was already moving toward the exit. She could walk very quietly for someone so big, and in motorcycle boots too. Jill scurried after her.

They were almost at the front door when a voice, rough from twenty years of cigarettes, called after them.

"Ladies ... er ... sir?"

Jill froze. Clara paused, her hand on the door.

The woman behind the counter had a puzzled look on her face, as if she were trying to decide which pronoun to apply to Clara.

"Yes?" said Clara.

A red flush rose in the woman's lined cheeks.

"Sorry ... uh ... ma'am ... would you ... er ... *ladies* like to sign the guest book?" She offered them a battered book and a pen on a string.

Clara didn't budge, but Jill, her cheeks aflame, ran over and took the pen.

"Lovely place," she mumbled as she scribbled incomprehensibly—she hoped—*It's all for the best, really. —J*

"Thanks so much," wheezed the curator. "Have a great trip!"

With a heroic effort, Jill managed to walk—not run—to the door and slip out behind Clara.

The jeep rattled on through a dead, dark landscape. The only sound was the shrill whine of its engine. In the comparative blackness of its interior, Selene could see in her rearview mirror the vast expanse of night desert stretched behind her. The mountains were black sentinels on the horizon, tinged gray in places by the light of the moon. She had the window open, but all she heard was the sound of the engine and the buffeting wind.

The jeep had gotten them to the Beatty Cutoff, and now they had passed through a range of low hills that looked like they'd been carved out of mud. They were on a long, straight run up a fan of broken rock and sand to where the real mountains started in earnest, when Selene spotted in the middle of the road, ambling right along the double yellow line, what she'd been half-expecting to see for the past ten miles: a man-shaped patch of deeper darkness against the dark road.

He was walking slowly now, favoring his left side a bit, and wobbling slightly along his path.

He was nearly invisible. Selene might have hit him—would have hit him—if she hadn't spent the past half an hour with her eyes peeled for him—or someone like him. She drew gently off to the right, as far as she dared without putting the jeep's wheels on the soft shoulder, and moved past at a sedate speed. Inspecting her rearview mirror, she determined that, yes, he *did* carry something in his right hand. She sighed.

"Hey, wasn't that—" Andy began.

"Yes," said Selene.

"Was what?" said Brian, who had, against all odds, been dozing.

"It looked like a *man!*" cried Addison.

"Aren't we going to, y'know, *help* him?" Andy asked, almost accusingly.

"I'm going to try," Selene said through gritted teeth, and stopped the car.

There was no sense in pulling over; there was no other traffic. They were about fifty yards from the dark man-shaped thing on the road, and Selene estimated that was far enough. Not far enough to mute the sound of a gunshot, if it came to that, but then, in this strange, dead silence, she was not sure anything could.

She cut the engine and put on the hand brake, then got out—taking the keys with her. She put her head back in through the window.

"This might take a while. You see or hear anything bad, give me a scream."

From the back seat, Addison's voice, carrying the self-assurance of one who knew exactly what she was capable of: "Leave it to me."

"Good girl," said Selene, and began walking back down the road.

She walked slowly, first checking to make sure Freddie was fully loaded and ready, and then slung him casually over her back by his strap. She didn't want to appear any more threatening than usual.

The man shape grew closer, but no more distinct. With a slight jolt, Selene realized that the man didn't have a face. Or any other recognizable characteristics. He was just . . . a black, man-shaped patch of darker darkness.

Selene hesitated, eyeing the revolver-shaped silhouette that still hung limply from his right hand.

"Hello?" she tried when she was still ten feet away.

The man kept walking slowly toward her down the double yellow line.

"Can you hear me?" she called, a little louder now.

The man shape paused. His head swiveled around, as if trying to place a sound.

"I'm right here!" Selene shouted. "Can't you see me?"

He definitely heard that. His head swung round to face Selene, and he put out his free hand, groping forward blindly.

"If you want my help—" Selene bellowed, as if she were talking to someone on the other side of a busy street "—take one step *back!*"

The man shape wobbled. He seemed confused. Then he staggered backward.

Close enough, Selene thought. She ran forward and grabbed the shape by his still-outstretched hand. Her fingers sank into the darkness by half an inch before they met resistance in the form of a fleshy arm under what felt like a cotton shirt.

"Got you!" she hissed, and pulled.

The darkness came away from him like the rubber packaging on a toy. Easier, actually. Selene peeled it off him in ribbons. His arm, then his face and torso and finally his legs became visible in the faint moonlight. Selene helped him step forward out of the puddle of darkness, whereupon it melted into the road.

Selene frowned at that. It should have told her something about the nature of her predicament, but she had other things to worry about.

Namely, a distraught man with a gun. Quite probably an unloaded gun, but *still*—bludgeoning instrument, and all that.

He was, in a word, a mess. His shirt and jeans were rumpled and torn, and there was a dark stain on the knees of his pants, as though he had knelt in something. His hair was standing up from all the times he had run his hands through it, and there was dirt on his face. He had a graze on his left cheek, and when he raised the hand with the revolver, Selene saw his knuckles were red and raw.

"Easy there son," she said, raising her own hands, palms out. "I'm here to help you."

"*You!*" The man's voice was a choked, hoarse whisper. Selene waited patiently for him to continue. "Your voice—I thought you were one of *them!*"

She didn't have to ask who *they* were. Four bodies in a jeep, one bullet each. She swallowed.

"Just take it slow, son. I'm here now. Things are gonna be A-okay . . ." she slid her feet forward down the road, inching her way closer to the man. He really did look terrible. Like he'd been through hell and wasn't out the other side yet. Which was accurate enough, Selene thought.

"Things are *not* okay!" the man screamed. Then he dropped his voice—thankfully—and continued in a whisper: "Don't you *understand?* I *killed* them! *Me!* I did that! But we decided . . ." he doubled over, gasping, shaking. Selene took the opportunity to close the distance further. She was almost within reach.

In a voice that was barely there; more like a weak exhalation, she thought she heard the man say, " . . . we thought it was for the best. I could hear the howling . . . the howling . . . "

"Hey, what's going on here?" Andy said, coming up suddenly and striding past Selene.

"No, *don't*—" she began, but the man had already hit Andy across the face with his gun, and as he staggered back, the man raised the weapon and pulled the trigger. Selene saw his finger move.

All that happened was a sad *click*.

She took that opportunity to grab the gun—and by association the hand holding it—and pull it roughly away. She turned, reeling the man in, bringing his arm up over her shoulder and then . . .

 . . . then it was all a matter of *leverage*.

The man grunted as he was jabbed in the gut by Freddie's stock, wailed as he felt himself lose his battle with gravity and go sailing in a gentle arc over Selene's shoulder, and finally grunted again as he hit the ground.

He lay still. Selene twisted the revolver out of his limp hand, checked to see that it was indeed empty, and stuck it in her belt.

"What the *hell?*" said Andy.

Selene ignored him, and knelt beside the strange man. She'd been careful to throw him so that his back and shoulders took the brunt of the impact, but he appeared stunned nonetheless. His eyes stared glassily up at her and refused to focus. She held a hand up to his mouth and nose and felt a breath that was barely there.

"Seriously, what the hell?" Andy said. "You just ... you just ... *threw—*"

"Help me move him," Selene said. "You take his shoulders—his *shoulders* Andy. Grab under the armpits, are you *trying* to dislocate his arms?"

Andy made a face, but reached under and took hold of the man as instructed. At this the man blinked once, then Selene saw his eyes roll back in his head, and he went entirely limp.

Well, that was a small mercy, Selene thought as she grabbed his knees and they began crab-walking back up to the jeep. She hadn't been sure how she was going to coax him back into the selfsame car where he'd done something unspeakable, not to mention explain his half-coherent ramblings to the others.

As it was Selene just hauled the jeep's hatchback open and laid him, as gently as she could, across the jumper cables. On second thought, there was something.

"What are you *doing?*" Andy protested as she took the cables and roughly secured the man's hands and feet.

"I don't know what he's gonna do when he wakes up," Selene said. "And I'd rather it not be *strangle the first person he sees.*"

"What's this about *strangling?*" Miranda said sharply, twisting around in her seat. Selene looked up into two pale round faces (Addison had also turned to watch).

"Picked up a stray," Selene said, gesturing at the man on the floor. "Dunno what he's seen out here. He was kinda ... loopy when I brought him in."

"*Did* he have a gun?" Addison asked.

"Yep," said Selene.

"*Was* it loaded?"

"Nope," said Selene. "Luckily for Andy."

Even in the dark she could imagine his cheeks going red from the inarticulate sounds of protest he was making.

A kind of screeching scream came rolling down across the pitch-black mountains.

It was high, short, and cut off sharply. Selene heard Miranda give a little yelp in sympathy, and Andy dove for the door of the car.

Silence descended again. Utter silence: no one spoke.

Then, from another direction entirely, a long painful wail. It warbled and weaved, rising and falling. It sounded like a creature in pain.

It *meant*, Selene knew, "Gather round all ye eaters of human flesh, for I have found dinner."

"Addison," she said. "Can you drive?"

"She has her learner's permit," Miranda said conscientiously. "But I can—"

"I'll drive!" Andy said decisively.

"*No!*" shouted Selene, so forcefully that Andy actually looked hurt. She took a deep breath. "Sorry. I'm asking *Addison.*"

She peered at what she could see of Addison's face in the darkness over the back seat. The dark line of her mouth trembled, then was pressed out of sight.

"I can drive," she said quietly. Firmly.

"Then get up there," Selene said, pressing the keys into her hand. She took them and began wriggling forward. "Andy, *in.* How are you up there, Brian?"

"Holding up," came Brian's strained voice. "I think my leg is swelling."

"Try elevating it," Miranda offered helpfully. Selene shut the hatchback on her words, and shooed Andy in beside her.

"What are *you* going to do?" he asked. It was mostly a challenge, but there was an honest query in there somewhere.

"Don't think there aren't things out here that can hunt down a moving car," Selene said. "I'm going to take care of them."

She climbed up, using the open driver's window as a foothold ("Mind yer fingers, Addison"), and pulled herself up onto the roof. The jeep had a luggage rack, and here Selene braced herself—one foot forward, one foot back; secure, but not entangled. She leaned down toward the driver's window, then paused as another scream ripped through the air.

It's meant to frighten us, Selene thought. *They're trying to panic us, scare us out of our wits.* Oddly, Selene felt a sense of relief. In truth the great black emptiness had been spooking her. Like waiting for a sword to drop. Well, here it was.

"Any time you're ready," she said to Addison's shadow.

Addison poked her head out the window. She had a stubby, freckled sort of face. And young, so young. *Was I ever that young?* Selene wondered. But there was also a hunted look behind her eyes that gave weight to her stare. Selene knew that look well.

"Why me?" the girl asked, quietly, so the others couldn't hear.

Selene gave her a brief smile. "Because I trust you, kid."

It was not exactly the truth, but it was what she needed to hear.

The truth was Selene didn't trust Miranda or Andy not to get ideas in their heads of what *should* be done, and she didn't want to put Brian, with his injured leg, in control of a large moving metal object. Addison would do what she was told, and that was enough for Selene.

Addison's face actually seemed to glow in the dark. Her head whipped back inside, and a moment later the jeep chugged to life.

The sound of the engine, and of the wind whipping past once they got up to speed, helped to fill the great black silence. It was not loud enough to cover the screeches that pierced the sky, and Selene was glad: she could track whatever was making the noise by its call, and with everyone safely inside the car, she had taken Freddie out and trained his barrel upward.

"C'mon you bastards," she murmured. "Come to mama."

It felt like forever. The wind rushed, the jeep chugged, the dark shapes of mountains ate into the starry sky. The moon was high above them—it must almost be evening again—and Selene wedged herself more tightly against the luggage rack. Addison could drive all right, and apparently she was using this opportunity to break all the rules she'd been taught in drivers ed.

Then, out of the darkness, and closer this time, another scream. But before that, under it, the sound of leathery wings cutting through the air—from an entirely different direction.

Selene turned just in time to see something that looked vaguely like a pterodactyl come swooping down at her. Its wings flared wide at the last minute, its clawed feet extended, grabbing.

She barely had to aim.

The force of the shot hitting and entering the creature's chest from such close proximity sent the huge body jerking back. Selene saw it hit the road and flop to a pathetic halt, before being consumed by the creeping shadow.

"Got one!" she called in triumph toward the driver's window. One down, and five shots left, she couldn't help thinking.

The cool wind whipped past her face, numbing her cheeks and nose. Her hair had pulled loose from its ponytail and was stinging her eyes, but she didn't dare relax long enough to fix it.

The screams continued, but they were less frequent, and when they did come, they sounded farther and farther away. Perhaps the other creature had been warned off by the fate of its companion. Perhaps it was waiting for a better opportunity. Selene wedged herself more firmly against the bars of the luggage rack, and waited.

The road was twisting seriously now, climbing steeply through a range of sharp, rocky mountains. Selene wasn't sure how much farther they had to go, but she was fairly certain the jeep would run out of gas before then.

They made it to a summit of sorts, a saddle between two shoulders of hill, and then the road began a serious descent.

As if on cue the jeep's engine coughed, chugged, made a few half-hearted attempts at turning over, and then died completely. In the relative silence Addison stuck her head out of the window.

"Now what?" she called up to Selene, over the babble of concerned voices inside.

"Put her in neutral and coast for as long as you can," Selene replied. "Don't worry about carrying too much speed, just get us to the bottom safely."

Selene could hear Andy giving advice. Addison snapped something at him that made her mother scold her. Brian groaned.

The night closed in around them, dark as ever. This worried Selene. By her internal map she guessed this was the eastern border of the valley. Now they had crossed the pass, they would be heading down to the high plain east of Death Valley. If the night was a local phenomenon, they should be coming out of it by now. She glanced at the moon. It was high in the sky, not having begun its descent into the west. Selene held up her watch, trying to catch enough light with it to read the position of the hands. This was made more difficult by the constant weaving back and forth Addison was doing, trying, despite Selene's instructions, to carry as much momentum as possible down the road.

Somewhere around four, Selene guessed, squinting at the tiny face. Not late enough for it to be naturally dark. In any case, the night had a wrongness about it that was beginning to grate on Selene's nerves; there was no way she'd mistake it now for ordinary night.

They came around a corner (Selene had to spare one hand from Freddie to hang on) and Nevada opened up before them: a flat, almost featureless plain of shrubs and rock, with another range of mountains decorating the far side. The road cut across it in a dark line so straight it looked like it had been drawn with a ruler.

They coasted down the last, gentle grade, and finally rolled to a halt—fittingly enough—within spitting distance of the "Now Leaving Death Valley, Come Again!" sign.

There was a creak as Addison put on the parking brake, and then her head emerged once more. Selene thought her hair must be blond, or at least very light brown, but it was hard to tell in the dark.

"Now what?" she asked in a small voice.

Selene was about to tell them all 'Get up, get out, start walking . . .' when there was a shift in the wind. That was to say, there hadn't been any since they'd stopped. It had made the air feel comparatively warm. Now a faint breeze picked up from the south, lifting the sticky hair that clung to Selene's neck. It brought with it the thick smell of dirty hair, filth, and a tang of what was probably blood.

"Stay put," she said sharply. "Roll up the windows."

"But there's no—"

"You got ignition?"

"Er, yes."

"Use it. Oh, one other thing . . ."

Addison paused her fumbling in the dark.

"Get your mom to pass me up one of those bottles of water we packed. I'm parched."

The water bottle was produced. Selene twisted the cap off and chugged the whole thing in one go. Then she crushed the plastic bottle between her hands and threw it back down the road out of sight.

There was a snapping sound, a crunch, and then a disappointed spitting noise.

Ah well, thought Selene. *Here comes nothing nice.*

* * *

The fetish turned out to be a fairly ordinary wooden mask. Clara produced it from under her jacket as soon as they were back in the room. It was old, clearly, the primitive paint faded and chipped. Jill took a scraping of the wood from its back, put the shavings in a tiny glass vial. This vial went into a case filled with other vials, so far empty. Jill couldn't help feeling pleased that she'd finally managed to collect something.

The mask still looked creepy though. If you turned your head slightly the expression appeared to change, but only from one kind of pained grimace to another. It had been carved of a light red wood, which had been stained dark. Then the outer dark layer had been gouged away to produce intricate curving lines of reddish brown. Further details and decorations had been added with paint, but a lot of these had chipped off over time. It was an eerie half-face that looked up at them, made even more grotesque by the fact that it was lying on a tacky motel bed.

"Explain," said Jill, gesturing at the mask. "How is this a god?"

Clara sighed. She had been doing a lot of that lately. Jill wondered if for Clara the worst part about losing Selene was not anxiety over the fate of their companion, but that now it was her job to answer all Jill's questions.

"This is not a god," Clara said laboriously. "This is a fetish. Something someone made while *thinking* about the god. Something used in connection with their worship."

"I never heard of a night god."

Clara's ice blue eyes—they really were extraordinarily light, like crystals—fixed on her. "There are many gods," she said gravely, "that you have not heard of. Some of them have always been; they are archetypes, changing and adapting to a growing world. Some of them are created, by humans and their extraordinary ability to imbue the things they believe in with reality—whether by design or accident. The night gods are very old; they came from our primordial fear of dark places and the things with sharp teeth that live there. They are worshipped every time you walk a little faster home after dark, every time a mugger jumps out of the shadows and attacks someone, every time you curl up under your blankets after a specially bad dream. You feel their presence in the night, the thing that tells you 'it's not safe here.'"

Jill sniffed. "That's a biologically evolved response to nocturnal predators," she said dryly.

To her surprise, Clara nodded. "Like I said, they're very old. They evolved with us."

The way Clara spoke of gods, as if they were real people, was beginning to get on Jill's nerves. As a scientist, she'd always held that belief was not part of her mental equation. An experiment worked, or it didn't. You didn't believe in something science told you couldn't work, because that was stupid. And if science told you it worked, then you didn't *have* to believe in it. People could say she believed in *science*, but Jill didn't think that was true either; it was just that science had worked for her so far, and if it ever stopped working she'd find another method.

Science was having some difficulty reconciling Clara's words, but Jill reminded herself that they were just that: words. A secondhand hypothesis. She needed evidence—testable material.

"What are you going to do with that mask?" she asked.

"This mask was carved by someone afraid of the night. They wanted to put a name—a face—to their fear. It is a direct link to a night god. I will use it to establish a link to their realm, force them to manifest as a physical avatar on this plane, and then I will kill them."

Jill actually felt her mouth drop.

"You'll *kill* . . . a *god?*"

"An *avatar*," Clara snapped. "Though you can kill gods. Just not with swords." Seeing Jill's expression, she went on: "There is night in Death Valley. Unnatural night. If I'm right, it's because a night god has forced some of their realm into ours—a *realm incursion*. Within this realm they are all-powerful, but if pulled completely into ours they would become mortal, vulnerable. If I can kill their physical avatar, that should disrupt their powers sufficiently to force them to release their grasp on our dimension. In other words: to go away and leave us alone."

Jill nodded, a fixed grin on her face. "Back up a mo," she said. "I get the killing part; big sword and all. How do we use that mask to get it to come all the way into *this* world?"

"We'll need a few more supplies," Clara admitted. "And a good place to perform the ritual."

Jill threw up her hands. "Give me a shopping list," she said.

It was late afternoon by the time they left the motel. Jill drove, while Clara rode shotgun and studied an old piece of paper she had removed from her saddlebags. It looked like a hand-drawn map, from what Jill glimpsed of it.

The contents of the shopping list lay on the back seat. They were actually a fairly mundane set of items: five bags of flour, a small bowl, a bag of bamboo skewers, two balls of string, a funnel, and one roll of bright orange masking tape. Jill felt like she was seven again, heading out into the hills behind her house with her friends to perform Scientific Experiments of the sort that usually didn't work and made a giant mess.

"Now we just need . . . what? A good place?" she asked as they picked up speed.

"A place of power," Clara corrected her.

Jill's heart sank. "You mean like the Winchester house? Clara, I don't know if there's anything like that around here."

"No, not like that. That was human-made. We need a place of natural power."

"What? You mean places of power come in regular and organic?" Jill asked.

Clara looked up from her map, frowning. "Those words are not accurate descriptors," she stated. "Places of power can be created over time by human activity, but they can also be created by intense natural forces. Everyone can sense these. Have you ever come to a place and thought 'this is magical, this is special?' Natural places of power feel like that. Humans have even come up with a system for protecting the most powerful of them: you call it the National Park Service."

Jill nearly pulled Arcana off the road. "We are not, *not*, going back into Death Valley!" she declared.

"Of course not," Clara said calmly. "That would be suicidal. The night god is already utilizing the innate power of the valley to push his realm into ours. We need to find a place on the edge, where I can tap into its power yet not be within reach of the night god's realm."

"Great, great," said Jill, taking a firmer grip on the steering wheel. "You got any ideas?"

Clara was silent. She went back to studying her map. Jill drove.

They wound their way out of Beatty, through a cleft in a small ridge of rocky mountains, and out past the base of one scarred from a century of mining. Facing almost due west now, with the low sun shooting beams of fire over the next range of mountains, Jill was in the action of pulling down the visor on her half of Arcana's windshield, when Clara said abruptly: "Turn here."

She almost missed the little road, saved only by the fact that it had a wide mouth. Arcana threw up a cloud of pale dust as his tires crunched on the shoulder, and Jill saw a sign there as they rolled past: *Rhyolite Ghost Town.*

"A *ghost* town?" she asked incredulously.

"No, not the town," said Clara. She was leaning forward in her seat, like a dog trying to catch a scent. "Slow down," she said. Jill did. Clara directed her to take the first left, away from the little cleft in the mountains where Jill had glimpsed the pale skeletons of a few houses, and out toward a nondescript plain with nothing but a red barn-shaped building, and a piece of stone wall half fallen down.

Arcana rolled ponderously down the narrow road. The low sun cast the red barn—which looked more and more derelict the closer they got—bright and vibrant against the tannish ground.

"Here, stop," Clara said.

Jill pulled over onto the shoulder, a respectful distance from the barn. Even from the truck she could spot no less than four "No Trespassing" signs.

"Are you sure we're allowed to be here?" she asked as she climbed out.

Clara was already outside, filling a backpack with the items from the back seat. She heaved it over one shoulder, and shrugged with her other one.

"Probably not," she said, pushing the remaining two bags of flour into Jill's arms. "But we need to be here."

Here looked to Jill very much like somewhere in the middle of nowhere. The paved road had ended, but the road itself widened and spread into a dirt rectangle that sloped gently upward toward the dilapidated barn. This had a pair of wide doors, chained shut, a small junkyard off to one side, and a wire fence stretching a few hundred feet on the other. A bare rocky peak, stained pink by the setting sun, rose in cliffs and tumbles of stone behind it.

Clara's heavy-soled boots crunched on the stray rocks as she marched across the lot, and the stiff breeze blowing out of the west caught the small puffs of dust and whipped them away across the ground. Jill pattered after her, marveling at the contrast between the plain gray backpack slung casually off one shoulder, and the broadsword in its sheath, belted across her back with leather straps.

Like someone out of a comic book, Jill thought, rolling her eyes.

As she walked up the gentle rise, Jill gradually became aware, under the constant buffeting of the wind, of a distant hooting noise. Dispersed among the hoots were faint chinks and chimes. Like a tree full of metallic owls, she thought at first.

Clara had stopped at what was more or less the center of the dirt lot, but Jill kept walking. The sound seemed to be coming from the fence, and as she drew closer she saw why.

Glass bottles—hundreds of them, probably— had been hung from their necks on the wires of the fence. The chiming was made by the bottles, jostled by the breeze, gently chinking against the fence. And the hooting, now Jill was close enough, resolved itself into the voice of the empty bottles being played like so many reed pipes by the persistent wind. Jill had done it herself long ago with half-full root beer bottles. Now an adult, she stood and watched, listening to the sound of the wind playing on hundreds of bottles at once, as enchanted as a child.

"It's a wind speaker," Clara said.

Jill, who hadn't heard her approach, jumped.

"I thought you said we needed a *natural* place of power," she said.

"We do," said Clara, blinking in surprise. "We have found one."

"But," Jill waved a hand at the fence, "*Humans* made this."

"Sometimes humans, by their actions, will imbue a place with power. Sometimes, the power inherent in a place causes humans to take action." Clara spoke with assurance, but with a difference cadence than she usually did. Jill thought she must be quoting someone.

"How do you tell the difference?" she asked.

Clara's eyes shifted. A sideways blink that only lasted a moment. "You get a feeling for them, after a while. Now come over here, I'm going to need your help."

Jill followed Clara to where the backpack lay, and thankfully put down her bags of flour.

"Okay," she said. "What are we doing?"

Clara inhaled, her natural reluctance when it came to explaining things clashing with the necessity to share this information.

"We're going to make a summoning and containment array. This will create a safe corridor for the night god to transfer to our dimension without undue malevolent reactions."

"Did you just say it's going to make it so we can pull this god thing out of its world and into ours in such a way that it can't wreak havoc here?" Jill asked, just to be certain.

"That's the idea," Clara said. "The best array is still the Gunn Standard, but it's become more and more ineffective, so I'll add a Nordstern orbiter as backup."

"Sorry," said Jill. "A gun what? And when you say orbiter, I don't think you mean a satellite that goes round and round a planet, but other than that I have no idea."

Clara had turned away and was unpacking the backpack.

"Not gun, like the weapon. Gunn, two *N*'s. The Brothers Gunn. They were . . . hunters. Warriors."

"They fought monsters?"

"They fought the dark," Clara said cryptically. "Until they became the dark. This was . . . oh . . . almost fifty years ago now. We still use most of the techniques they developed. That's been the problem; so many people using the Gunn Standard or the Gunn Trap, demons get wise to it, so we have to keep changing the pattern."

"Like bacteria resistant to penicillin," Jill said, on firmer ground here. "So a Nordstern orbiter is . . . ?"

Clara popped the plastic wrapper off one of the balls of string. Finding the loose end she tied it in a loop and handed the end to Jill.

"Hold this," she said. "An *orbiter* is an outer ring of runes that you put around your main array to strengthen it, or give it extra attributes. The Nordstern orbiter works like a magnifying glass; intensifying the power of whatever it contains."

"Nordstern . . . did *you* invent it?" Jill asked, not even trying to mask the admiration in her voice. She respected innovative people.

"No," said Clara, so shortly Jill thought that would be the end of the conversation. But she went on, as if the words were crowding their way out of her mouth. "My mother invented it."

"Your mother's a . . . hunter?" Jill said.

"She was the best," Clara said quietly, taking up the ball of string and a bag of flour. Jill caught the past tense, and didn't ask any more. She watched in silence as Clara walked away, unreeling the string until she had almost fifty feet laid out. Then she took the bag of flour, and slipping her knife out of her pocket, cut a small hole in the side. She shook the bag, to get the powder flowing. Then, carefully holding the string taut in the same hand as the bag, she began to walk.

"Keep facing me," she called over the windy lot. "We need to make the circle as clean as possible."

Obediently Jill held her loop of string and pivoted on her heel as Clara began to walk in a wide, slow circle, holding the bag close to the ground so the wind couldn't whisk the flour away.

When Jill had first seen pictures of crop circles, her thoughts had not been wonder at what phenomena had caused them, but rather dubious respect for the people who made them. It must have been tough, she thought, to get the circles so round, and the plant stalks all lying in a particular way.

Watching Clara draw an array on the ground in flour, she quickly developed a whole new level of respect.

It took a great deal of time. First Clara traced a large circle. Then she traced a smaller one within it. Then a still-smaller one. By this time the sun had set, and a blue twilight settled over the plain. The wind shifted, changing the tone of the singing bottles.

After the third circle, Clara got out a compass and began dividing the smallest circle into sections. One line ran north to south (Jill noted with approval that Clara corrected magnetic north to geographical north) and one line east to west. Then she took the funnel and attached it to the last bag of flour, and began filling in the quarters with . . . Jill didn't know what. To her eyes they looked like a bunch of squiggly lines, but considering how carefully Clara went, and how many times she cursed and rubbed a mark out with her foot Jill guessed she was making something very precise.

They lost light entirely before Clara had finished the fourth quarter. Jill went over to Arcana (careful not to smudge any of the flour lines), and got a flashlight. (And a jacket, because it was getting cold.) Then she stood above Clara and held the light while Clara finished the last quarter.

The lines reminded Jill of some kind of writing, now she could see them as they were formed.

"What does it say?" she couldn't help asking.

Clara stood up and stretched her back. "In a very specific and special way," she said. "It says: 'Come here.'"

They were still not finished. Jill had to hold the flashlight for at least another hour while Clara filled the space between the two outer circles with . . .

"Are those *runes?*" Jill asked.

Clara nodded. "Nordic ones . . . my mother's family comes from there."

Jill didn't ask any more.

They finished the circle around nine o'clock by Jill's phone, at which point she was cold, hungry, and stiff from holding the flashlight.

And *still* Clara wasn't done. She made Jill help her line the outside of the whole array with a fence of bamboo skewers, and then run strips of masking tape between them, like a tiny version of police crime-scene tape.

"Tomorrow you're going to make me a chart of all this," Jill said when they were finished, her fingers sticky with tape glue. "And explain exactly how it all works."

Clara just grunted. She took out the horrible little mask and put it in the bowl. Then, stepping very carefully so as not to smudge any of the lines, she walked over to the center of the array. There she set the bowl aside, and drew her sword. She squinted over to Jill, shading her eyes against the glare of the flashlight.

"Turn it off," she said. She could speak normally now: the wind had died completely; the bottles were silent.

Jill switched the flashlight off. She could not see what Clara did, but she heard a metallic *chunking* noise, like the woman had just rammed her sword into the ground. There was the whisper and creak of leather as she moved, and then a snap, and a tiny flame flared at the end of a match. Jill saw it illuminate Clara's face for a moment, and then it fell, its light reflecting off the metal of the sword.

It should have gone out. It was only a tiny wooden match.

Clara shouted a word that was eaten up by the darkness.

Fire flared up around the sword, raced down its blade—which was indeed stuck in the earth—and then out, tracing along the lines laid down in flour. The wave of flames hit the fence of bamboo skewers and shot up easily five feet into the air. Jill, who had been slowly backing away, fairly jumped backward.

For one blinding instant the whole array was picked out in lines of fire. In that moment, Jill felt something . . . *shift*. Nothing visible, nothing she could feel on her skin or with her hands, but deep in her bones she felt something go *clunk*. Like a great gear slotting into place and beginning to turn.

The fire went out. There was the slither of metal over dirt as Clara extracted her sword.

"You can turn your flashlight on," she said. "It worked."

Jill, whose hands were inexplicably shaking, had to try a few times before she got the light on again. When she had, its beam showed that Clara had set the bowl with the mask at the center of the array, and was now picking her way carefully out of it.

"And now?" Jill asked in the eerie silence. The air was warmer, from the fire and from the stillness. It felt unnatural, but there was no sign of any monster.

"We must wait for the array to draw them out," Clara said when she reached the perimeter. "This array works as a drain upon his domain. It may take some time." She crunched around uphill of the circle, to a piece of ruined wall that jutted out beside the bottle fence. She sat down, her sword flat and naked across her knees. After a few moments Jill went and joined her.

"Turn off your light," Clara told her as she sat down. "You will see better."

Jill did so.

In the silence and the night, the two women waited.

* * *

Not so many miles away and only a little earlier Selene also sat in the darkness and waited, but it was anything but silent. Her finger ghosting over Freddie's trigger, her breathing so faint and slow she might have been a statue, she sat and listened to the quiet sounds of clawed feet moving through brush and over concrete.

Four of them, at least, she counted. Four of *what* was a question she couldn't answer, and inside her head she kept repeating the mantra: *five shots left; five shots left.*

She was so concentrated on what was circling the jeep on the ground that she didn't pick up the faint whisper of wings until it was almost too late.

Almost.

She jerked sideways as soon as she heard it, and the claws that had been meant for her neck slid down across her left shoulder in three streaks of sharp coolness, too quick for pain. The pain would come later, Selene knew, but she also knew that she should still have full use of that arm, and at least thirty seconds before the searing agony pierced the haze of adrenaline that filled her head.

In those thirty seconds she spun, got the creature a mighty whack across the head with Freddie's butt, and followed up with a mad slash from her knife. It hit resistance, and she stabbed.

The great leathery form whose wings had been beating around her suddenly went rigid. It thrashed and she pushed it away, felt something graze her face, and then it was falling in a limp tumble down the jeep's side.

One of the things on the ground took that as a cue to leap.

Selene saw it as a black shadow moving across the star-pricked sky. She aimed Freddie at the center of it, and fired.

It twisted in midair, hit the side of the jeep—someone inside screamed—and slumped to the ground.

Four shots left.

Claws scraped on metal. Selene pivoted, grimacing as the motion dragged cloth over her gashed shoulder, and saw what looked like a mountain lion crouched on the hood of the jeep.

She shot it in the head, then turned and beat at the thing currently trying to sink its claws into her leg.

Three shots left.

She pumped the gun one handed while she stabbed at the thing with her knife and kicked. It reeled backward. Before it could fall out of sight she took off most of its face with a point-blank shot.

Two shots left.

She felt light-headed, almost immaterial. There was a haze before her eyes that clouded out all sensation except the weight of the gun in her hands and the flicker of movement beyond the jeep that was all she could see of the animals closing in. Yet they appeared all the more clear to her in this strange tunnel vision.

Two came up over opposite sides, and then it was all fight. Thrust. Slash. Shoot as soon as a target presented itself. Pump the gun.

One shot left.

Selene wasn't thinking about strategy anymore. She wasn't thinking about how the creatures seemed not to care about their fallen companions, nor seemed all that interested in taking the jeep apart beneath her. She was not thinking about what she was going to do after her last shot, because she was already doing it.

Fight. Head down. Punch, slash, hit as hard as you can. Ignore the blinding pain in your knees from where they struck the metal rack, ignore the slippery wetness of blood running down your arm—when had she been bitten?

A wide head appeared next to hers. Putrid breath washed over her. She stabbed it in the eye.

Something got its claws in the fabric of her jeans and started dragging her toward the edge of the roof.

If they get you on the ground, you won't get up again. She knew this with a deep, dreadful certainty.

Gritting her teeth against the searing pain from her shoulder as it dragged against the luggage rack, Selene managed to get Freddie pointed down between her legs. Throwing her free foot clear she fired one last defiant shot just as she went over the edge.

There was a moment of supreme confusion—something jabbed into her injured shoulder and she might have screamed—and then her feet hit asphalt. She buckled her knees, then threw herself upward again, her back against the rear door window.

"Oh my *god* are you okay?" Miranda's muffled voice sounded behind her.

No, I'm not okay, Selene thought. *In a few minutes, you will not be okay. None of you will be okay.*

Unless she kept fighting. That was the thing: you could never stop fighting. Fight on, past the point of no more bullets, past the point of blinding pain. Past the point of despair. Fight with everything you had—and anything you had to hand.

They came at her thick and fast now. There was no counting them, no tracking individuals; there were only wild strikes and fierce cries, trying to carve a little no-go space in the area around her very soft and squishy—and increasingly blood-soaked—body.

The hatchback of the jeep flew open. Grunts and yelps suggested it had hit a few targets. The wild man with the tattered clothes jumped out, swinging the jumper cables like whips. He shouted something. Something that sounded like a war cry.

Or a death wish.

Maybe both.

As one the pack turned, saw a new target, and lunged. The man went to pieces under their teeth. For once, Selene was glad she couldn't see very well.

She used the diversion to scramble around to the back. She saw a dark shape lunging toward the open door, heard the shocked screams from inside.

She slammed the door on its neck. When she pulled it back, the beast dropped to the ground. Selene shut the door, put her back to it, and leveled her toothless gun at the semi-circle of dark shapes pacing around her.

And somewhere, deep in the marrow of her bones, something went *clunk.*

She thought she heard a satisfied voice say "*Ah!*"

As one the dark beasts shrank back, turned tail, and ran.

Selene stood and watched, listened as their footfalls faded into nothing, and the silence of the night returned.

Leaning on her good shoulder, she slid slowly to the ground.

In the car, Andy was shouting. Had been shouting on and off ever since the first shot. Mostly it was just inarticulate swearing, which Miranda had long since ceased to protest, but now it had developed into a sort of rambling monologue.

Addison leaned forward on the steering wheel and tried to ignore him. It was impossible to see what was going on, but she heard the bangs, the grunts, and one gut-wrenching scream.

"That's it, she's finished," Andy said, but he was drowned out by Miranda shouting "Oh my *god* are you okay?"

Something struck the passenger window hard enough to crack it. Brian whimpered. Addison reached out and found his shoulder with her hand. She squeezed.

It felt like her heart was pounding in her throat, the blood in her ears so loud she didn't hear the shifting in the back until Andy started screaming in earnest.

"What the—" he spewed out several curse words that would have gotten Addison a spanking if she'd ever said them aloud—though in truth she'd been thinking them rather a lot lately.

The man Selene had put in the back was awake. He was struggling. He said something.

"What? *Hell* no! They'll *kill* you!" Andy shouted.

More muffled speech.

"Mom, what's he saying?"

"Not *now*, sugar," her mom said.

There was a *thump*. Her mom gasped.

"Don't open that—" Andy began, and then the rear door was pushed open, and all of a sudden the snarls and roars got a lot louder. The man shouted something, and then there was a wet crunching sound.

Addison felt like her stomach filled with toxic waste. She had just the time to turn her head away from Brian before she was sick all over the steering wheel.

Her mother screamed. Andy screamed. Real, guttural screams of pure terror.

There was a *slam!* A *crunch.* The noises got a lot quieter. Something went *clunk.* Addison thought maybe something important had been ripped off the car.

Andy was still shouting.

"This is *so* wrong! We haven't got a *chance!* Why the *hell* did she waste that ammo on those *things*—we should have just taken turns with that gun until there was no one left—"

"Andy!" Miranda gasped, appalled.

"—then at least we wouldn't have been *eaten alive*—"

"Andy," Brian hissed.

"We're all *dead!*" Andy wailed. "Don't you understand we're all gonna *die?* Just like them out there! And she *knew it!* What do you think was *in* this jeep to start with? I'll tell you, because I've figured out what I've been sitting in this whole time! Blood, I tell you. It's *blood!* There were *bodies* in here. *That* was the 'junk' she had to pull out before she let us get in. We didn't have a chance *and that dumb, dyke ni—*"

"Andy, *shut up!*" Addison screamed. Her voice was so high, so piercing, that it actually shocked Andy into a few seconds of silence.

Silence. All around them.

"You're not *listening*—" he began.

Addison twisted around, leaned back between the two seats, and slapped Andy across the face so hard her hand stung.

"No," she hissed, wringing her hand. "*You're* not."

"What the *hell* is wrong with you?" Andy gasped, making a snatch at Addison. She leaned back just in time.

"Addison, *what* was that?" Miranda said in a tone that promised a lot of trouble later on.

"Be quiet, all of you!" Brian shouted.

They reluctantly fell silent. And finally noticed what Addison had been aware of for the past few minutes.

It was awfully quiet out there. No sound of footfalls, no shots, no shouts.

"If y'all are quite finished in there," came the muffled sound of Selene's voice from somewhere near the back. "Could someone bring me one of them first-aid kits?"

Addison snatched a kit from Brian's lap and jumped out before her mom could protest.

It was comparatively light outside, and Addison could see the dark shapes of several bodies lying on the ground. One of them was vaguely human, and looked like its guts had been ripped out.

Addison steadied herself on the side of the jeep and made her way around to the back. There she found Selene, resting against one of the rear wheels. She was clutching her left arm.

"What *happened?*" Addison blurted out.

"Not sure," said the woman. "But they're gone now. Here, get me out the disinfectant, and then there's a bandana in my pocket we can use as a tourniquet."

With shaking hands Addison opened the box and began taking out all the bottles and holding them up to the faint starlight, looking for the beta-dine. Selene waited patiently, but Addison could tell by her hissing breathing that she was in a lot of pain.

She'd fought off a hoard of monsters to protect five people she barely knew, two of whom, Addison was certain, would soon as spit on her as look at her, in ordinary circumstances. And now she was lying up against a jeep that was out of gas, with a gun that was out of bullets, slowly running out of blood.

The night stretched out all around them, and Addison suddenly felt very, very alone.

"We're not gonna make it, are we?" she said in a small voice.

Selene's head lifted. Her face was a black shadow, but Addison could tell by the set of her shoulders that she was being glared at.

"You can't think like that," Selene said, and made a grab for the bottle in Addison's hand.

"I can't read the labels," Addison said.

"Then open it, let me smell it."

She did so.

"Rubbing alcohol," Selene said after a moment. "That'll do. Pour it here, don't be stingy—*ouch!*"

"Sorry," Addison mumbled.

"I'm serious, you *cannot* think like that," Selene said after a moment. "*He* thought like that."

Addison very carefully didn't look at what remained of their mysterious passenger. "But—"

"Here's my bandana, I need you to tie it on for me."

Selene held her arm up; she'd wrapped the bandana around the puncture wound, leaving the two ends loose.

"Andy says there's blood in the car," Addison said quietly as she knotted the ends tightly.

Selene grunted. "I expect there is."

"Is it true . . . there were . . . *in there*, when you found it? *That* was the junk you had to clear out? *That* was how you knew his gun would be empty?"

"Because if he'd had a bullet for himself, he would have used it," Selene sighed. She leaned forward. "Now my back, the side that's all tore up. Pour it on, you can't miss it. *Gnnh.*"

"So . . . there were bodies?"

Selene was very quiet for a moment.

"If I'd told you before, would you have gotten inside?"

Addison put the cap back on the bottle. "If you'd told me to," she said. "Probably not my mom, or Andy."

"And then we'd still be stuck in the valley."

"Are you sure here is any better?" Addison asked. It was what had been really worrying her; how the strange night went on and on, seemingly forever.

"It's somewhere else," Selene said. "That's something you gotta understand, kid, we *have* to keep moving. Even if it feels like there's no point. Even if it looks hopeless. We stop moving, we die. You gotta survive *to* survive, if that makes any sense."

"And that's something you're good at?" Addison asked. "Surviving?"

With a grunt Selene hauled herself to her feet, using her gun as a cane. The black outline of her face stared into Addison's, and there was the faintest flash of white teeth as she smiled.

"I'm a black, gay, woman," she hissed. "I am *nothing* if I'm not a survivor."

It made absolutely no sense, but to Addison, those words were the first glimmer of hope in a darkness that stretched back much farther than this strange night. She got to her feet, still clutching the first-aid kit.

Selene walked over to what was left of the man, took up his arms, and began dragging him to the side of the road.

"What're you doing that for?" Addison asked.

"We can't take him with us," Selene grunted. "This is the last thing I can do for him."

She laid the body by the side of the road. She didn't touch the trailing organs, but she folded the man's hands over his chest, turned his head to the sky. Then she straightened up, and stood for a while looking down at him. After a while Addison came and stood next to her.

"I don't know why he did it," she said. "He woke up and went crazy, got the door open and jumped out. What did he think he could do?"

"I don't think he was doing much thinking, there at the end," Selene said. "I think he'd been wanting to die for some time. Just a matter of finding a way to go. He quit." She didn't sound judgmental; if anything, Addison thought, she sounded sympathetic.

Addison was on the verge of asking more questions. Questions along the lines of "Have you ever done anything like this before?" and "Are you speaking from personal experience?" But Selene turned away to go bang on the door of the jeep before she quite got them out.

"All right, gang," she shouted. "Coast is clear, let's get up and at 'em!"

Reluctantly, three doors opened, and three heads poked out.

"What do we do now?" Brian asked shakily.

"What everyone does when they don't have cars," Selene said. "We're gonna walk."

*　　*　　*

It started slowly, and so gradually that Jill could not later say exactly when it began. It might have begun as soon as the flash fire had died away, but she rather thought they had a good ten minutes of ordinary night before the wrongness started bleeding through.

She first noticed it as a patch of night sky that seemed somehow darker than the rest. Over the next hour, the whole sky followed suit. While she was still puzzling over this she felt Clara tense at her side; heard her exhale sharply. Dropping her eyes to the array, Jill squinted into the darkness, but saw nothing.

Saw nothing, but smelled something sharp and unpleasant, like iodine. It seemed to be coming from the mask, but it was hard to tell.

"You should leave," Clara murmured. "I cannot guarantee the ring will contain him."

"What, watch from the car?" Jill said scornfully, but she knew Clara had a point. Still, she was loath to sacrifice a first-hand encounter with the supernatural. She felt torn between self-preservation, and an over-whelming curiosity to *see what was going to happen.*

"Get in Arcana," Clara said. "Drive away."

"Will you give me a full and detailed report later?" Jill asked testily.

Silence.

"I can't *see* you shrug in the dark, you know."

"I can't guarantee that I will be able to protect you if you stay," Clara said frankly. "I cannot even guarantee that I will succeed in slaying the night god."

Those words sent an icy spike through Jill's gut. The feeling made her snappish. "Well, that's great. What happens if you don't succeed?"

Clara did not answer, and Jill did not leave.

They waited an hour like that. Then another. And then . . .

Jill did not need to hear Clara's sharp hiss of indrawn air to alert her to the change. She shot to her feet and stared.

The mask was glowing.

Or: some unidentified source of light had appeared behind the mask. It shot three wobbly beams up through the eye and mouth holes. It was a pale, whitish light, utterly devoid of color. It did not behave quite like light ought, and this kept Jill staring longer than she should have.

Abruptly the light exploded skyward, carrying the mask with it. Behind it a column of light rose, burning Jill's eyes. Strangely, it did nothing to illuminate the ground around it. It was as though its light shot clean through earth and rocks, leaving them dark.

The light ceased to come out of the ground and was replaced with a thick whorl of black smoke. It rolled out of the center of the array, but when it hit the orbiter it stopped as though there was a wall of plexiglass between them. Things flashed and snarled in the smoke; teeth snapped. Jill thought she heard a howl.

Above them the column of light had condensed into a single speck. Then, almost imperceptibly, it reached its zenith, before falling to earth again, growing larger as it came.

It hit the center of the array and caused a shockwave that shook the ground beneath Jill's feet. It also shattered the invisible barrier that held in the smoke.

This came rushing out at them so fast there was nothing Jill could do. It swept past her legs, smelling strongly of iodine. It was painfully cold.

Something in the smoke began to laugh. Jill thought she saw, in the strange way one sees things in the dark, a tall, thin figure standing up in the smoke. It had long, spidery hands and a wide smile full of teeth.

Clara pushed her shoulder.

"Run," she hissed. "Run, *now!*"

Jill ran. The thing in the smoke leapt.

She should not, by rights, have gotten away. The thing was strong and fast, and Jill's boots slipped on the loose gravel hidden beneath the freezing smoke. She'd left Arcana parked down by the pavement—over forty feet away. She wouldn't reach the truck in time.

But she must have misremembered, because Arcana was *here,* appearing out of the smoke before her like another apparition. But the metal was solid and cool under her fingers and she pulled the door open and threw herself inside. Adrenaline truly was an amazing thing.

Pulling her legs in after herself she slammed the door and hit the automatic locks just as something else slammed into the side so hard the huge truck rocked on its wheels.

There was a face pressed up against the window. Jill carefully didn't look at it as she pulled out her keys and started the ignition. It was the face of her nightmares, she knew this by instinct.

Arcana roared to life like a beast unchained. Jill flicked on the lights, and by them saw Clara fight her way out of the smoke, sword flashing. She reversed, hard, and the thing clinging to the window was swept off. She backed in a wide, blind half-circle, and then accelerated down the road.

Standing knee-deep in a frothing river of black smoke, Clara leveled her sword and the night god slowly rose to their feet.

They still looked vaguely human, but Clara supposed they would, to her. She was human, ergo this personification of the primordial fear of the dark would also appear human. Sort of.

They were easily seven feet tall, wire thin with long, bladelike hands. Their face kept changing; lost in shadow it morphed from one set of three dark spots to another. It was an idea of a face, not a real one at all.

"Sorry," grunted Clara, kicking her way out of the smoke—which had become quite solid. "I haven't got any nightmares left for you to feed on."

The night god inclined their head, as if conceding the point. Then they began to drift away after Arcana's retreating lights.

"No," said Clara, and she stepped up behind the god and hit them across the back with the flat of her sword. "I did not bring you here to continue with your invasion."

The night god turned, their face a gray blur above dark, bony shoulders. The bottom spot, the one that resembled a mouth, moved, and words blossomed in Clara's mind. A question.

"I brought you here to kill you," Clara answered bluntly. "But you can make it a lot easier on both of us if you leave now. Remove your influence, and return to your own realm."

The night god sighed like wind whistling over a desolate plain. Another question formed in Clara's head. There was undercurrent of challenge this time.

"Or I will send you back there by force," she said.

The night god laughed at this. It was not a pleasant noise: it crept into Clara's bones and made them feel like they were filled with water.

For answer, she struck the god's left leg out from under them. Clara's streak of honor and fairness was strong, but it only ran so far.

The god gasped, stumbled, caught themself on one long arm, and gazed at her in mixed horror and fury. Dark smoke billowed about them, buoyed them up. Their arms lengthened, grew blades of pale bone. They snicked together like a pair of scissors.

Clara raised her sword.

The night god struck.

The party of five crept at a snail's pace along the desolate highway. Brian had begun limping almost at once, and Selene had ordered Andy to support him before it could get any worse. Andy had made a snide remark about "Bossy chicks ... " but he helped Brian. Selene got the feeling that saying things like that was what allowed him to follow her orders.

Selene herself walked in back, careful not to move her left side too much. Only Addison knew the extent of her injuries, and she intended to keep it that way. She watched the girl's straight back marching down the center of the road and felt her mind wander off, out of her current predicament, and down dark alleys and into unpleasant memories she'd not touched in many years. She wondered about secrets, about why people acted the way they did, feared what they did, and what they did about it.

They walked in the center of the road, clustered around the double yellow line. It was easier to see in the dark, and it had the advantage of giving them the most warning if something moved out of the shrubs on either side of the road. Not that the warning would do much good, Selene thought bitterly. But the countryside remained quietly deserted; even the wind had ceased. In the moonlight Selene could make out another range of mountains rising up out of the eastern horizon. There was a cleft between the lowest two peaks, and the road ran toward it in an unerringly straight line. Selene locked her eyes on this point and concentrated on walking.

They had been limping along in this way for what felt like hours, passing through a desert plain filled with coarse shrubs and crisscrossed by dirt tracks, when there was a blinding flash of white light from the hill rising to their left.

As one they stopped, and Selene stared, her heart beginning to pound, at the column of white light that had risen out of the earth less than a mile away.

"What the *hell* is that?" she heard Andy say.

No one answered him. They were all staring at the light, which had risen some ways into the sky before condensing into a single bright point. Then it plummeted earthward.

Selene stared, trying to fix that location in her brain.

There was a distant rumble, and she felt the earth shift uneasily under her feet.

"Was that an earthquake?" Miranda asked.

"Felt like one," said Brian.

"That was no earthquake," Selene found herself saying. Paying no heed to her burning back she slung Freddie over her shoulder and began walking faster down the road.

"Selene, what was that?" Addison called, trotting to keep up.

Selene paused, looked around at her sad little party.

"Now see here," she said. "I've gotten you as far as I can. You keep following this road until you get to Beatty. If things go normal there, then great. Don't you worry about me. If things ain't normal, hole up there, and I'll meet you. Either way, I gotta go check that out, and I don't have the time to take ya'll with me." She turned to go.

A hand caught her sleeve.

"You're *leaving?*" Addison gasped, appalled.

"I'll come back for you," Selene said, gently removing the girl's hand. "You keep this lot on the road, you hear? Stay on the road, stay together, and I'll be able to find you."

Addison's hand clenched on nothing, but she nodded.

"Good, I'll see you in a bit." She turned, and broke into a jog.

Behind her, Andy was shouting something. She ignored him. Her movement disturbed the still air, and a gentle breath of wind caressed her face.

A part of her feared for her party. A part of her rejoiced at the freedom of being on her own. A part of her desperately hoped that that light had been Clara's work.

A road opened up to her left, branching off the main highway. It ran uphill, toward the base of the towering mountain, toward where the light had been.

She was tired, injured, and dehydrated, but she couldn't help herself. Selene fairly sprinted up the road.

* * *

Clara sidestepped and slipped in blood. It was not hers, but it could be in a matter of time if things kept on the way they had. The night god she had been prepared to take. The night god plus a few shadowy doglike creatures was a challenge, but doable—especially considering they stayed dead once she'd killed them. No, the problem had been the giant raptors, which swooped in and out of vision, making dives for her head.

She slashed, by instinct more than anything, and felt her blade connect. A moment later something ran into her leg, and teeth bit down on her thick leather greaves. Taking her knife up in her left hand she cut down and up on the creature's neck, shook her leg loose.

No skin broken, but bruised—badly bruised.

She cut in an arc around her feet—struck something that moved like a snake but wasn't.

The god, on her, bone-white arms flashing in the dark. Block, jump, try to make contact—blocked by their right arm.

Clara jammed her knife into the face of the next creature that lunged at her—left it there so she could have a hand free to grab the night god by the elbow and pull herself inside their reach. Just in time, by the sound of frustrated screeching in her ear. She got two good punches in their midsection with her fist before their other arm came up. She blocked it with her own—felt a bolt of pain down to her fingertips—and rolled free.

She'd lost track of the knife—she couldn't be sure which dark corpse was currently doubling as its sheath—so she switched both hands to her sword and concentrated on fighting the god back into the array. They would be weaker within the orbiter, even if it did not have complete power over them.

They must have realized. Suddenly the barrage of strikes from their arms redoubled, and Clara was forced to give a little ground. She stepped on something that moved, and then next thing she knew the something was trying to eat her right leg.

She spared her sword for a second to dispatch it, then lunged away as the god's blades came in after her. She heard them slice into the earth behind her, and she rolled all the way upright again, using the momentum to propel herself to her feet.

The night god towered above her, their lower half disappearing into black smoke. Their face was as vague as ever, yet still managed to give off the impression of a smile.

Words began to form in Clara's head. She tried to shut them out, but it was too late.

The god was *enjoying* this.

"Oh, I just *bet* you are," Clara ground out through gritted teeth. She stamped her right foot, assessing the damage. Not critical. She took up a neutral stance and waited for the god to come to her.

They did not make her wait long.

* * *

The problem with adrenaline is that it is not, as far as human hormones can be concerned, a sustainable resource. It can get you very far in a short amount of time, but in the long run you can seriously hurt yourself with it.

Currently Selene's back, arm, legs and lungs were all calling up to complain, in the most vehement terms, about their treatment.

Her foot hit a stray rock, and she stumbled so badly she nearly fell. She slowed to a jog, wincing, panting, her blood pounding in her ears.

From the dark before her there rose a deep rumbling growl, and the next instant the darkness was washed aside by the twin lights of a huge truck barreling down the road toward her.

Selene was so shocked she stood still, literally an animal caught in the headlights.

Jill slammed on the brakes and wrenched the steering wheel. She felt the tires lock up, and Arcana skidded the last few feet before coming to a halt.

Jill rolled down her window and stuck her head out.

"Selene?" she cried. "Oh my god—*Selene!* Are you all right, don't move, I'll—"

But Selene was already climbing up onto the running board, leaping into the back where she opened the locker and began digging out her ammo cases. She could have wept with relief and joy.

"Turn around," she shouted down at a confused Jill. "Take me back to where the light came from!"

"You saw the light?"

"Damn straight I saw the light."

"It's Clara, she's called up this night god which—"

"He won't be alone," Selene said darkly. She'd finished loading Freddie and had now pulled out her sawn-off shotgun, Elvis. "Drive," she said, a gun in each hand.

The difficulty, Clara decided, was that the night god didn't fight with any kind of pattern or style. They just cut, as hard and fast as they could, with random retreats and relapses that made leading them impossible. There was no tell, no opening for Clara to exploit.

Or perhaps there was, but she couldn't find it because of the continuing distractions caused by the shadowy creatures that kept jumping up and trying to bite her.

Nevertheless, she managed to work her way around until she held the high ground, and there she stalled, trying to draw the god into making a mistake. It took all her concentration, and so she didn't notice the distant rumble of Arcana's engine coming nearer. Not until it came around a corner, and the full force of its headlights blazed across the scene.

The night god looked into the blinding twin lights—a faint, wraithlike shadow under their glare.

"Heeeeey *asshole!*" shouted a voice that sounded remarkably like Selene's.

The next second the god's head exploded in a puff of smoke.

Their body wavered for just a moment, then fell, almost elegantly, to the ground. It lay full in the beam of Arcana's lights, and did not move. The shadowy creatures wavered, then vanished.

A crunch of footsteps, and the lights danced with shadow as Selene marched out of them. She carried her trench gun slung under one arm, and seemed to be favoring her left side.

Without a word to Clara she came up beside the taller woman and calmly emptied the remainder of her shots into the night god's body.

Bang. One arm gone, scattered into the dust. *Bang.* And the other. *Bang.* Torso gone. *Bang.* Pelvis gone. *Bang.* The last of the god's shadowy body disintegrated and bled away into the earth.

Something that had been hanging unseen over the sky faded, retreated, and disappeared.

Jill switched off Arcana and got out into a night that was suddenly quiet.

Only not silent. The wind had picked up again, blowing briskly up the hill. There, under the gusting and the buffeting, was the faint hooting and chiming of the bottle fence.

"Tell me it's finished now," Selene said in a tone that brokered no contradiction.

Clara cocked an ear to the gently singing fence, and she smiled a little ruefully. "As far as the night god is concerned, yes, it's certainly finished for now."

"Great," said Selene. "I take it you'll clean up here then? Good? Good. Jill, gimme a ride down the road: I need your help for one last thing."

"Did you feel that, mom?" Addison asked.

"Feel what?" said Miranda distractedly. Brian and Andy were arguing. Andy thought he should go on ahead and try to get help. Brian thought they should stick together.

"About five minutes ago . . . did you notice something . . . change?"

"Like what?" Miranda said.

"Like . . . I dunno . . . " Addison cast about for words her mother would accept. It was something she was used to. "Like it was foggy, or smoggy, and we just got some fresh air?"

"I don't know what you're talking about," Miranda said.

Andy chose that moment to storm off in a rage.

"Serve you all right if you turn into monster chow!" he shouted over his shoulder.

Almost as if in response there was a distant roar.

Andy made a strangled yelping noise, and his step faltered. Then the exact nature of the roar was revealed when the headlights of a giant truck came into view not far down the road.

As one the group huddled together, uncertain, while the vehicle approached.

It rolled to a stop a few feet away, and the passenger door opened.

"Glad to see you took my advice," Selene said, hopping to the ground. "Now everyone climb on in. Congratulations, you made it."

"Made it? Made *what?*" said Andy.

The driver's window rolled down and a small feminine head appeared. Light glinted off her glasses as she straightened them.

"We have successfully curtailed a realm incursion from a night god," she said in a crisp, businesslike voice. "Now which one of you is Brian? Selene tells me you've hurt your leg."

Things happened in a bit of a daze for Addison after that. She remembered Selene coming around to help Brian into the front seat. She remembered asking the strange woman, as she climbed in the back, "I don't understand. We haven't made it out, it's still dark!"

"Of course it's dark," the woman replied. "It's just past midnight. I should *hope* it would be dark. Now buckle up."

Addison thought about asking to ride with Selene, who was crouched in the bed of the truck. She desperately needed to talk to Selene, she realized, but one look at her mother's face told her there would be hell enough to pay after all this. She clicked her buckle shut, and leaned back against the truck's soft, clean seats with a cautious sigh of relief.

In the end, none of them ever got to bed that night, and many more were gotten up out of theirs to attend to the sudden influx of distress calls coming from the area. When Jill dropped Selene's party off at the local medical center it turned out they were not the only group of injured people. The harried night receptionist was bouncing from phone to phone, and barely glanced at their bedraggled party.

"Yep, I think I've got the first batch here," she was saying as Jill headed back out to the truck.

Selene had climbed around into the cab and set up her radio scanner. They listened to the ranger and police frequency as they drove back out to pick up Clara and while they helped her brush away the remains of the array and pick out the bamboo skewers.

There was no sign of the night god, or any of the shadowy monsters, about which Jill was extremely bitter.

"They did not belong here," Clara explained soothingly. "Once the anchor holding them here was destroyed, they returned to their native realm."

"And the night god?" Jill pressed. "Is it dead?"

"Gods do not die the way animals do," Clara said diffidently. "But for all practical extents, and as far as they applied to this world . . . for now, yes. They are dead."

Jill was going to ask what "for now" meant, but Selene hushed them. On the scanner, there was a somewhat hysterical sounding deputy talking about dead bodies along the side of the road; four of them.

Selene refused to go to the emergency room, even after Jill had taken a look at her injuries and told her all about the risks of open wounds acquired from unknown animals.

"Yeah, yeah," said Selene. "Stitch me up, would ya Clara?"

Jill was forced to sit and fume while Clara carefully washed and sewed up the gashes on Selene's back, then the puncture wound on her arm. Then Selene got up and went outside, climbed into Arcana's bed, and sat down with her back against the cab.

She stayed there until the sky turned from deep blue to blue-gray, growing lighter and pinker around the eastern horizon, until finally the mountains in the west caught fire, and the first rays of the sun struck out across the sky.

Then, at long last, Selene leaned back and relaxed.

Jill stared at the television in horror. The newscaster was talking about all the bodies that were turning up in Death Valley this morning. So far, they all matched descriptions of people who had gone missing under mysterious circumstances. The ones that were still recognizable as people, anyway. Some of them had been mangled rather horribly.

"Come," said Clara. She had spent the wee hours of the morning packing their bags and taking down the sheet covered in pictures and clippings. Now Arcana was loaded, Selene was sitting in the bed—she seemed not to trust the sun to stick around if she didn't keep an eye on it—a certain package had been placed on the steps of the historical museum, and they only needed to drag Jill away from the TV in order to leave. Except.

"We have to stay," Jill said, waving her hand at the television, which was now showing one of the people they'd helped last night—a man—with his arm around a teary-eyed woman, talking about the strange hallucination he'd experienced. "We have to explain what really happened. They need to know."

"They won't believe it," Clara said. "And you can't prove it."

"I know," said Jill, clenching her teeth. "But they shouldn't *have* to believe it. I *should* be able to prove it." She reached forward and switched the set off. She pushed her glasses up her nose and glared out at the morning. "One day, I *will*," she whispered.

* * *

Addison sat in the sheriff's office's waiting room, chewing her nails while her mother gave her statement. Miranda, unlike Andy, was less apt to believe in the fallibility of her own mind, and after talking it over with Brian they decided to report as much as they could. Addison was glad, because they'd made her wait out with the receptionist—the first time she'd been out of her mom's presence since those few grim minutes outside the jeep.

She'd been thinking, picking away at a feeling that had been growing stronger all morning. The way Selene had taken off at the sight of the light, just dropped them like they were so many stones weighing her down, had truly hammered home to Addison how much it had taken to baby them along all that way. Selene might have made it clean out of the valley without even a scratch if she hadn't had to look out for Andy, or slow down for Brian. She could have ditched them at any point.

But she hadn't. Not until there was something even more urgent. And somehow, Addison was sure, the sudden change from bad night to normal night had been in some way Selene's doing.

Addison got up. She pointedly went and asked the receptionist where the bathroom was, and then walked down the hall toward it. But instead of going into the ladies' she went through the back door and stepped out into the early morning sunshine. She began to walk purposefully toward the center of town.

She had no idea where Selene was, but if she'd been staying in Beatty that giant red truck would be parked outside one of the many hotels that lined the main street. That, at least, would be hard to miss.

Clara tapped Selene respectfully on the knee. Selene glanced down, blinking.

"We're ready to leave," she said. "Jill says she's up for driving south as far as Indian Springs."

"That should be far enough," Selene mumbled. She was just leaning forward to climb down when she glanced up and saw a familiar figure walking along the side of the road.

Clara followed her gaze, took in the bedraggled teenager, then glanced back at Selene.

"One of yours?" she asked.

Selene nodded.

"Five minutes?"

"Five should do it," Selene said, heaving herself out of the truck.

Addison stood at the edge of the parking lot. She had her hands clasped behind her back, and she was standing awkwardly on one foot. The other was kicking a small hole in the dirt shoulder. Her face lit up at the sight of Selene, then shuttered.

"Hey," said Selene.

"Been listening in at the sheriff's office," the girl mumbled. "They're talking about how, like, they're finding all the people who went missing before us."

"Uh-huh."

Addison stared up at her. "They're saying, that . . . apart from us . . . they're all *dead*."

Selene nodded, but didn't say anything.

"A few people went missing *after* we did. They huddled up in the visitors' center. Some of them are still alive."

"That's good," Selene offered.

"*Some* of them," Addison repeated, giving Selene a hard look. "And it got me thinking . . . if you hadn't come along, if you hadn't been there . . . we'd have all died. And the people in the visitors' center, they were only saved because the . . . it . . . the weird night thing, ended. It ended because *you* figured out a way to stop it, didn't you?"

Selene ducked her head modestly. "I had some help from my friends," she admitted.

"Yeah, well," said Addison. "Then you came back for us and everything. So . . . why? Why did you help us, when you probably could have done a lot better on your own?"

Selene shrugged. "It's what I do," she said.

Addison bit her lip. She peered around Selene's shoulder to where Jill and Clara were puttering around Arcana, trying to look busy. "Those your friends?" she asked.

Selene nodded.

"Who's the big guy?"

"That's Clara."

"*That's* a woman?"

"Women come in all shapes and sizes," Selene pointed out. She looked long and hard at Addison. It was the first time she'd seen her in good light: a tall, wiry girl in jeans and a boy's T-shirt, her sandy hair up in a sensible pigtail. Her trainers were dusty and scuffed now, but they had once been red. She was shifting from foot to foot. She seemed uneasy, as if waiting for another shoe to drop. Selene might have puzzled over that one for a while, but in her sleep-deprived, aching mind, some things became immediately clear.

"Addison, you wanna walk with me?"

They crossed the highway and ambled down to a small coffee shop. At first Addison was silent, but when Selene made no attempt to spark conversation she gave in.

"I don't **understand** what happened last night, but I get it, I think," she said. "Andy's convincing himself it was all a hallucination, but it was real. It *happened*."

Selene nodded. "And now you're wondering, who are these people, who roll into town in their big shiny truck and beat up the monsters?"

"*No,*" said Addison, with every ounce of teenage scorn. "I know who *you* are."

"Oh really?"

"Yeah," said Addison, somehow managing to make it sound like she was saying *duh.* "You're the ghost hunters, the paranormal experts. You probably drive around *looking* for these sorts of things. You've got files and files and files on all sorts of weird things . . . which of course you can't tell me."

Selene's face curled into a wry smile. "You know," she said. "You're not *entirely* wrong."

Addison nodded, as if this was just what she expected. "No, it's not that." She went quiet again for a few more paces. Then she said all at once: "HowdoItellmyparentsImgay?"

Selene blinked, mentally parsing that last sentence. Then she shrugged, and pushed open the door to the café.

"Depends," she said. "How do you think they'd react?"

"My dad would probably kill me," Addison said matter-of-factly. "My mom . . . well. There was a boy a few grades ahead of me. He came out. My mom convinced his parents to send him to one of those . . . *you know* . . . ex-gay camp things."

Selene shuddered. She bought Addison a blueberry muffin and got a cup of decaf coffee for herself—she didn't plan on being awake much longer.

"Don't tell them," she said as they left the shop.

"What?" said Addison around a mouthful of blueberry muffin.

Selene nodded. "If you think they'll hurt you, don't tell them. Not until you're well clear. Honesty's a great thing and all, but sometimes you gotta just keep your head down and . . . "

" . . . and survive to survive?" Addison said in a small voice.

"Yeah." Selene took the lid off her coffee so it would cool faster. She blew on it. "Wait until you're eighteen, move out—go to some big city with a lot of friendly drag queens—" Addison choked on a piece of muffin "—and get some crappy job to pay rent, and then . . . *then you can tell your parents.*"

She saw Addison's face fall, and cast around for something more encouraging.

"Look," she said, "I know it might seem like some endless nightmare now, but you keep yourself safe, keep yourself sane, and keep pushing forward—even if it seems you're not getting anywhere. Even if it looks like the night is never-ending and you'll never get out of it. Because if you survive long enough, well . . . " she looked around at the bright morning light, breathed in the crisp, cool air, and whispered, " . . . *eventually* the sun will come up."

Addison ate her muffin in silence for a while. Selene sipped her coffee. Up the road at the hotel, she could see Clara and Jill sitting in Arcana's bed. Clara seemed to be drawing something on a sheet of paper, while Jill leaned over her elbow.

"Is that what you were telling yourself last night?" Addison asked.

Selene laughed. "Kid, it's what I tell myself every god-damned day. But you'll see. The world ain't all bad. You'll meet other people, *good* people. People who'll accept you for who you are, who'll have your back."

They stopped across the road from the motel. Addison looked over thoughtfully, finishing her muffin. "Like you've got Clara?" she asked.

"Yea—no," Selene corrected herself, seeing the way Addison was eyeing them. "Ah, no, not like *that*. Clara's just a . . . um . . . co-worker."

Addison raised an eyebrow.

"And straight," Selene said firmly.

Addison peered over at the tall, leather-clad figure.

"You sure?" she said, sounding disappointed

"*And* at *least* ten years older than you," Selene said sternly. She patted Addison on the back and made to start crossing the street.

Then she stopped, turned around, walked back.

"Give me your phone," she said.

"What for?" asked Addison, but she handed it over.

Selene took it, opened up the address book, and made a new entry.

"Now, I can't promise I'll be able to answer, or even if I'll be around," she said as she punched in her number. "But if you ever get into trouble, *serious* trouble . . ." she handed the phone back. "Give me a call,"

Addison took the phone as if she were receiving a holy relic.

"You don't mean 'monsters under my bed' sort of trouble," she said. It was not a question.

"Could be that sort of trouble, could be the 'my parents are monsters and sending me into ex-gay therapy' trouble." Selene said with a shrug. "It's your call. Good luck."

She crossed the street. When she looked back, Addison was walking away down the road again, shoulders squared as if going into battle, the phone still clutched tightly to her chest.

Clara looked up at the sound of Selene's step. She passed the clipboard back to Jill and swung her legs down over Arcana's side.

"Finished?" she asked.

"Not really," Selene said, pulling open Arcana's back door and climbing inside. "I did what I could, though."

"I'd say you've done more than enough," Jill said, climbing into the driver's seat. "Now, I'm taking us outta here because you and Clara seem hell-bent on avoiding the authorities, but I tell you, the minute we get to Indian Springs you are *going* to see a doctor."

"Yeah, yeah," Selene murmured, pulling her duffle bag up under her head as a pillow. She hadn't told Addison that the sun coming up brought with it a whole new set of problems. But Selene had decided a long time ago that they were, on the whole, a better set of problems than the kind one found in the night.

Arcana rumbled, comforting and strong, and the tires crunched on the gravel drive. Selene was asleep before they reached the highway.

On a road in the desert, under a bright and shining sun, a black motorcycle ran. It was followed not far behind by a giant red pickup truck. They raised a pale cloud of yellow dust in their wake.

Oh, no . . .

Oh-ho, no . . .

See that dark one walking there
See the moon caught in her hair
No . . .
She's not your daughter.

See that lead pipe in her hands
She walks firm on foreign lands
No . . .
She's not your mother.

You can call her beast, call her a villain
She'll find a way to settle the score.
She sits in the dark her finger on the trigger
Don't doubt her blood's redder than yours.

See her walk out in that night
See her walk without a light.
No, no . . .
She is not your sister.
She's not your wife either.

Standing under the moon's wing
She's a different song to sing.
If you dare to turn your back
You know your world will go black.

She's a ghost among your men,
She's a dark one understand!

No daughter, no sister, no mother, no wife
No daughter, no sister, no mother, no wife
Her water is fire, your death is her life.

Oh-no . . .

You can call her beast, call her a villain
She'll find a way to settle the score.

Shadows in the Valley of Death

She sits in the dark
her finger on the trigger
Don't doubt her blood's
redder
than
yours.

—Dark One, *Rook Parliament*

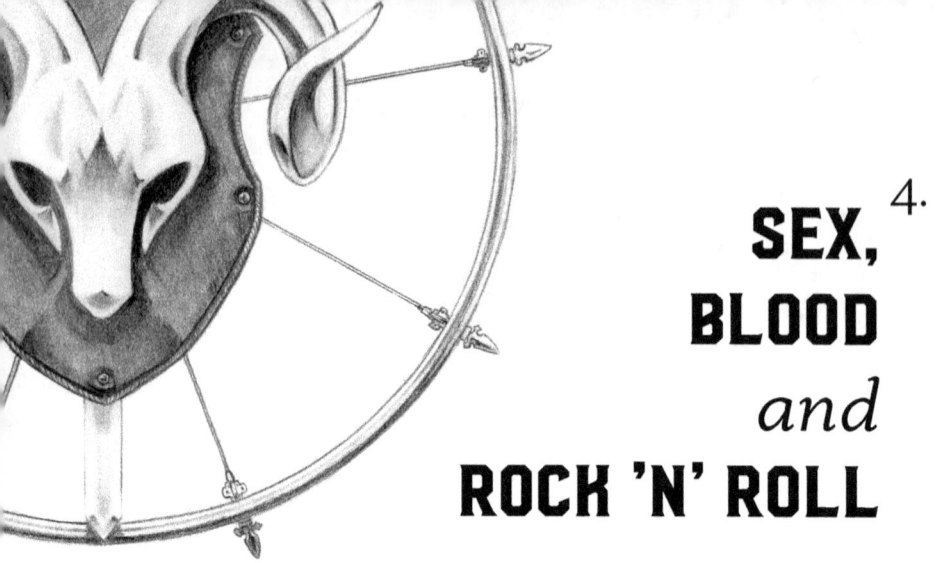

SEX, ⁴·
BLOOD
and
ROCK 'N' ROLL

Well I'm a jack ripper
And I'm a greedy god
I'm an idol for the opiate masses
Maybe I'm not your savior
But I'll still have your
Love and lust and guts and blood.

Sex, blood
Rock and roll
Sex, blood
Rock and roll

You wanna give me life
Well I will give you death
I will give you all the things that you want to fear
In return I ask for your worshipful heart
And the hearts of the gods you created!

THE MUSIC FADED OUT, and the camera, clearly handheld, panned across a line of people dressed in everything from fishnets and leather to fishnets and nothing else. Hair styles were spiked as high as white glue and hairspray would allow, and on the ground, groups had formed around those members with the foresight to bring their makeup supplies. Others, not so fortunate, stood resolutely in the Nevada sun while heavy eyeliner smudged and white foundation became streaked with sweat. Despite this there was a general air of excitement and happiness—almost rapture— among the crowd. The announcer's voice, clipped and professional, spoke over the ambient murmur.

"Outside the Hotel Castle in Las Vegas, Nevada, fans of Johnny Bathory have been standing in line since early this morning, hoping to win one of the five coveted backstage tickets. Originally these were sold to the highest bidder, now Bathory chooses the recipients himself, and they must present themselves for inspection before the show. With attendance in the thousands, only a few dozen will actually be seen by the rocker; the rest will be turned away as soon as the five have been chosen. Asked about the fairness of the situation, Bathory is unapologetic . . . "

There was a fade, and a man's face filled the screen. It was difficult to tell what sort of face it was since half of it was painted dark red, the other half white. Three jagged lines, like claw marks, ripped over from the red side to the white side, crossing his nose and mouth. He wore obviously fake contact lenses, which made his eyes look bright yellow with pinprick pupils, and his hair seemed to be a bird's nest of improbably black locks. The voice that came out of the face was similarly disconcerting: soft and weak, hoarse from too many cigarettes and too much shouting.

"It used to be, you know, I'd be getting people paying ridiculous amounts of money for these tickets. In the beginning it was great—I needed the money—but after a while it just felt greedy. So I started donating the money to charity. Oddly, people were willing to pay more because of that. I had this heiress once—they won't let me say who—who wanted to basically have her bachelorette party in my hotel room after the show, with four of her best friends. And she—well, her father—named this ridiculously high number, and I had to tell him no. Because what had happened was these people who had and were willing to pay out their asses were not actually people I wanted to hang out with. I didn't like them. And that's what the backstage tickets are all about; getting to hang out with some of my fans. What's the point of doing that if they're not people I like? So now we have this much better system; all you need to get a backstage ticket is to be there when I come out to choose people. You don't even have to have bought a regular ticket."

"But what about the sheer number of people who turn up?" the interviewer asked. "You can't possibly see everyone. Realistically, only the first fifty or so actually have a shot—because you usually pick the five from them and that's it."

The man stared past the camera, his face expressionless. He didn't blink.

"You know, before the show is a real hectic time," he said. "There's sound checks, light checks. We have a pretty big production and I need to be there for most of it. So I only have maybe fifteen minutes to see people beforehand, and I'm just looking for people I think would be fun to hang out with. Usually, I find those five people in the first batch. But sometimes it takes longer than that. You never know."

There was a cut again, this time to a crowd of people packed into what looked like a holding pen, with the man with yellow contacts standing on a platform above them. A line of large, humorless men stood on the ground, keeping people back. Even so, the crowd's arms were outstretched, reaching for the man on the platform as if he were some kind of idol. The announcer's voice spoke over it:

"As to the allegations that only the young and the beautiful have a chance of being chosen, and that he unfairly favors female fans, Bathory merely says . . . "

Fade back to the yellow-eyed man with half a red face.

"I mean the biggest demographic of my audience is people aged fifteen to twenty-four. They're *all* young and beautiful. And you know, most of the people who go for the backstage tickets *are* women. So yes, I'm going to favor them. But I had a guy up the other night, you know, and he was wonderful."

"What about the allegations that you use these fans, many of whom border on obsessing about you, for easy sex?"

For the first time, the faintest expression flitted across the man's face, under the makeup. It happened so fast it was impossible to tell just what it was. The next moment the man rolled his yellow eyes extravagantly and laughed.

"Yes," he said. "Because after two hours of dancing around on stage in high heels and leather underwear"—the camera cut to the same man doing just that—"singing my lungs out, getting all sweaty"—cut to a shot of the man, in profile, backlit, shouting into a microphone so forcefully that flecks of spit could be seen arching through the air—"what I really want to do is the horizontal tango with a person I've seen for maybe thirty seconds in a crowd three hours before."

"It's totally an orgy, isn't it?" asked the interviewer, but there was a teasing tone in her voice.

At last the man cracked a grin. He had very white teeth, and the canines were noticeably longer. "Yes, Margie," he said, with complete sarcasm. "Yes, that's exactly what we do."

"Many Christian associations have decried Bathory, some going so far as to call him a devil-worshipper, and several right-wing groups have staged protests at his shows. Nevertheless, attendance remains high and—"

Selene paused the video and hit "escape" so that the window shrank and the rest of Jill's screen came into view.

Jill, who was sitting next to Selene on the hotel bed, looked at her skeptically.

"Really?" she said.

"You asked if there were vampires," Selene said. "That there is the most famous vampire today."

"But . . . Johnny *Bathory,*" Jill said. "Even *I've* heard of him. It's an act. A show. Like Alice Cooper and that band Snog—"

"Kiss," Clara interjected from behind a mountain of newspapers.

"Whatever." Jill forged on. "I've read his *Wikipedia* entry, Selene. His real name is Doug Reed, he was born in *Minneapolis* or something. And you're telling me . . . he's a *vampire*?"

Selene raised an eyebrow. "Is it *really* so hard to believe?"

"Belief doesn't enter into it," Jill said. "There is evidence that shows him to be an ordinary human being—albeit one underneath a lot of makeup—and none that I've seen which would point to him being a vampire. What exactly *is* a vampire, anyway?"

At this, both Clara and Selene stared at Jill as if she had sprouted a second head.

"Puh-*lease* tell me you've seen *Buffy the Vampire Slayer*," Selene moaned.

Jill blinked at her, hard-faced. "I don't watch television," she said. "And I'm serious: what's a vampire? Because in every book or movie they're always portrayed differently. They are weak to crosses . . . or they're not. They burst into flames in the sunlight . . . or they don't. They can dissolve into mist, turn into bats . . . or they can't. About the only thing that's consistent is that they drink blood. But sometimes it's the blood of a human, or animal . . . or it can only be from a living human . . . or . . . "

Selene put her hands up, as if to shield herself. "All right, all right. I get it."

"What is a vampire, exactly, and *how does it work?*" Jill pressed on.

There was a rustling as Clara put down her paper. Her huge form—all six feet, four inches of her—spilled out of the flimsy motel chair in the form of long, leather-clad legs like tree branches. She had her leather jacket unzipped, cracked open to reveal the tight black undershirt. Above this her pale face hovered, angular and high-browed, her light yellow hair shaved right down to the quick. She rubbed a hand over the back of her head as her brow furrowed in thought.

"A vampire is a form of the undead," she said. "Similar to wights and zombies, but far more sophisticated. A vampire will present as dead, with no heartbeat and no pulse. They are defined by their need to feed on living blood in order to survive. Other than that . . . " she shrugged. "It depends."

Jill frowned, nonplussed. "Depends?" she said. "Depends on *what?*"

"It depends on the vampire," Clara said simply. "Their capacity to withstand sunlight, their susceptibility to Christian or other religious iconography, their taste in blood, and their . . . other abilities."

"Other abilities?" Jill said, pulling her computer onto her lap and beginning to take notes.

"You mentioned a few yourself," Clara said. "Powers of transformation, illusion, transmutation, mind control, flight . . . "

"Whoa, whoa," said Jill, hitting backspace several times. "Did you say *mind* control? And . . . and *flight?*"

"I tracked a vampire in Texas once that could fly," Selene mused. "That was . . . annoying."

"Did you catch him?" Clara asked, with professional interest.

"*Her,*" corrected Selene. "And yes, boy did I ever."

"Okay, so vampires can do pretty much everything," Jill said, skepticism positively dripping from her words.

"Not any *given* vampire," Selene said. "You don't get *flying* vampires much at all, and sun-resistant vampires rarer still. I think it's just skill. Different vampires develop different skills. Like some humans can do backflips, or figure skate, or play the trumpet. Vampires learn to manipulate people's minds, move super-fast, transform into animals, or mist, or fly. *Most* vampires can't do a fraction of that; they can only manage a little misdirection or mental pushing here and there. But they're pretty strong overall."

"What about sunlight?" Jill asked.

"Now, you'd think *that* would be universal," Selene said with a grin. "And actually, most vampires, they don't like the sunlight too much. Think really bad, really fast-acting sunburn. They don't *actually* burst into flames—not unless you douse them in kerosene first—but it ain't pretty, and it slows them down but good. But some vampires . . . I dunno . . . they just have a natural immunity, I guess. They are super-rare, though. I've never seen one."

Jill looked at her notes in some perplexity.

"Aren't you going to ask how to kill them?" Clara prompted.

"How they die does not interest me so much," Jill said, rubbing her chin. "I'm more interested in learning how they *work*. Still, it could tell me something about how they function. Yes. How do you kill a vampire?"

"I am *so* glad you asked!" Selene said, heaving herself off the bed. "Okay, so first, beheading. In fact, *always* try beheading first. It pretty much works on anything. Unless it's a hydra and then you're totally screwed. But we don't get hydra in the Americas, so don't worry too much. Anyway, yeah. Okay, a stake through the heart *does* work. Sort of. But not as well as in the movies. See, they don't explode in dust or goo . . . the stake just sort of . . . I dunno . . . *stuns* them, I guess. Makes them *act* dead. But if you take it out, then up they get again. Also, you actually have to get it *through. The. Heart.*" She emphasized this with prods of her finger against her own chest. "That means carefully angling it through the ribs or smashing them open. Not easy to do in a hurry. Oh, but you don't have to use a *wooden* stake. Iron nails work just as well, and fit better too. Let's see . . . "

"Silver," Clara said.

"Right, silver!" Selene grinned. "Silver is a good vampire deterrent. Works against a lot of magical stuff, actually. Kind of like beheading. What else . . . oh yeah. Fire."

"Fire?" said Jill.

"Fire," said Clara.

"When in doubt," Selene said, miming a flicking motion with her hand. "*Burn 'em.*"

"Well," said Jill after a thoughtful silence. "That is very interesting. But how do they *work* exactly?"

Selene and Clara exchanged a look. It was a look Jill was becoming used to. It seemed to mean: "How are we putting up with this woman? Oh right, she's *paying us* . . . "

Clara said:

"We don't know for certain."

Jill nodded to herself, went back to her computer. "But you are certain Johnny Bathory is a real vampire?"

"Yes," said both the other women in unison.

"Okay," said Jill. "I'm gonna need to talk to him."

They stared at her. She looked up, her expression open and innocent. She adjusted her glasses. "According to his website, his band is playing in Las Vegas for the next week. We could be there by tonight. Or tomorrow morning, if we don't want to leave right away."

Las Vegas sits like a glittering jewel in the middle of a vast, dusty desert. It is only a glass gem—not real diamond—but it is set about with such lights and sounds that it appears more brilliant than any precious stone. Dive beneath the city, beneath the neon-lit strip with its hustlers and tipsy tourists, and you enter an altogether different world, one built out of concrete and flooded with cast-off water, decorated with graffiti and the furnishings scrounged from the dumpsters and back alleys of the city.

Getting water in the desert is a trick, but what do you do with the water when you're done with it? Hence the extensive system of flood drains and sewers that stretch out beneath the famous city. Unseen, unthought-of, but certainly not uninhabited.

People live there, just as they do in the city above. People die there, just as in the city above. And there are other people—people you won't find in the city above—and what they do down there is debatable. You could call it living, but—as Jill would be quick to point out—to live first you must *be alive.*

Currently, two such people stood in the bright strip where the sewer opened to the sky and cattails grew thick in the mucky water, which reflected the vivid yellow light from the streetlamps. They were arguing.

It was nearly midnight, but you wouldn't have guessed it from the noise filtering down from above. Not unless you were experienced in the nightlife of Las Vegas.

This noise was what allowed the two people to argue freely.

One of them, who was smaller and vaguely female shaped, stood with her knees locked and one hand on her hip, while she used the other to jab an accusing finger into the chest of her opponent. He was bigger, leaner, but he cowered away from her nonetheless.

"What were you *thinking,* Darryl?" the smaller one was saying in a harsh rasp of a voice. "What is the first rule of the clan? If *they* find out about us where does your protection go then, Darryl?"

"That's why I *called* you," Darryl wailed, cringing. "We can hide the body. No one has to know!"

"Do. Not. Feed. On. Surface people!" the woman yelled. "You were told when you joined us!"

"But her kind disappear all the time!" snapped Darryl. "They overdose, or they get lost. Sometimes . . . *they just die*, okay?"

"This isn't any *ordinary* surface girl, she was one of *his*," hissed the woman. "But you knew that, Darryl. And you drained her anyway. You're gonna get *his* attention this time, and I won't take the fall for you. This is *your mess*, and you can clean it up or take your chances upstairs."

"That will *kill* me, Martha!" Darryl pleaded, then burst out, as the woman—Martha—turned to walk away, "You leave me here, you've as good as killed me!"

Martha paused, the line of her back tense in the artificial light. Then she was a blur, a darting shape lost in the confusion of water reflections.

"You had to ask," said a hoarse voice by Darryl's ear.

There was a small *snick*, and Darryl opened his mouth to scream. Nothing came out.

He heard, somewhere below him, the sound of his body falling into the water. Then Martha's face came into view, hard and jagged. His mouth moved open and shut; he tried to yell.

"G'bye, Darryl," she said, and dropped the head.

Darryl saw the water rushing toward his head—and then nothing. Whatever had kept him going, it was gone by the time he hit the surface.

Martha walked back into the sewer, disappearing into the shadow.

"It's an *amazing* experience!" said the girl, her eyes like stars inside the black splotches of makeup decorating her face. "They make you promise not to say, of course—I mean *really* promise—but it is *so* worth it, you know. He is *such* a generous artist!"

The video showed a crowd of people, all dressed in varying amounts of black leather and fishnets, lined up in the sun outside the back door of a theater. The narrator's voice, calm and cultured, spoke over them: "It is the hope of sharing the experience of fans like Belinda that keeps these devotees of Johnny Bathory standing in line outside the stage door for upward of twelve hours. Some fans arrive days in advance, bringing supplies of food and toiletries. Local authorities have since required Bathory to restrict the amount of time they may spend waiting in line for safety reasons. Now any backstage ticket hopeful may arrive twelve hours before curtains up at the earliest . . . "

"Are you watching *videos*?" Selene said incredulously. "How can you *do* that?"

Jill paused and looked up from her computer. Arcana swooped and dipped as they ran over a rough patch on 95 South. "I have a strong stomach," she said. "I loaded these up before we left. I'm trying to figure out the best way to actually *talk* to him."

Selene laughed. "It won't be easy. Bathory's the most famous vampire for a *reason*."

"He's the only one on MTV?" Jill guessed.

"*That,*" Selene admitted. "And he's the best protected. Not a hunter in the Americas doesn't know Bathory's a vampire, but I don't think a single one has gotten within shooting distance. *Think* about it: he's got bouncers, he's got agents, and he's got an army of fans who would die for him if those fail. Perfect cover, when you think about it. Honestly, I don't know why Clara said yes. My guess is she thinks she can sneak you backstage or whatever using her spirit ring. *Literally* going backstage," Selene chuckled.

Jill remembered Clara's rings: small, lumpy things made out of braided metal. Wearing them phased you out of the real world and into a sort of ghost land. Jill accepted the hypothesis of how they worked, but she still didn't understand the physics of it. Last time there had been other things on her mind. Now she began picking at the question in her usual way.

"So these two worlds," she said. "The ones we go between when Clara—or you—puts on one of those rings. There's our world—"

"And there's the spirit world," Selene said, nodding. "Which is where this world gets all its magic from. There's a certain amount of bleed-through between the two, from what I understand."

"Is it anything like the infinite multiverse?" Jill asked. "Like, where history could go two ways, so that means there's two universes, each with a different version of history? And it keeps splitting and splitting, because of all the little differences and variations. Instead of one universe, there's an infinite multiverse because of the infinite possibilities?"

Selene raised an eyebrow at her. "You know, for all you say *my* work is unbelievable, sometimes your science can sound just as crazy."

"My science is supported by demonstrable evidence and peer review," Jill said. "Your claims are just that—*claims*—until I can see some evidence."

"You mean there's *evidence* of multiple universes?" Selene nearly spat over the wheel.

"Not yet," Jill said calmly. "For now it's just a hypothesis."

"Ha. Okay," Selene gave herself a little shake. "All right, here's my . . . um . . . *hypothesis* about this world and the spirit world."

"I'm listening," Jill said.

"Well, *our* world is our world, right? It's made up of physics and stuff. Okay, well, the *spirit world* is the world for, well, the spirits. It's where your nightmares go to be real. That sort of thing. When you make up an imaginary friend, say, that friend only exists inside your head . . . but in the spirit world *they really do exist*. And I think the spirit world is a lot bigger than this one, with lots of little sub-worlds inside it."

Jill nodded. "Like dark matter and energy."

"Sorry?"

"Dark matter and dark energy," Jill said, "are just names for all the matter and energy in the universe that we can't directly observe. They aren't necessarily *one* thing—more likely they are many things, it's just we haven't been able to figure out what they are. But we know *something's* there, and so we call it dark matter, or dark energy."

Selene shrugged. "Maybe they're the same things?" she suggested.

Jill leaned back in her seat and stared out at the road, which was currently stretching on and on through nothing much of anything. "That would be . . . convenient," she admitted. "But not likely."

Selene hummed, and drummed her fingers on the steering wheel. A little frown that had come to rest on her forehead put down roots and grew until she was scowling at the road.

"Something wrong?" Jill asked.

Selene grimaced. "Ah, it's just—I dunno. Makes me uncomfortable the way you're so cool about all this."

Jill raised an eyebrow at that.

"*You* know," Selene said, sparing a hand from the steering wheel to flap it expressively. "The way you don't *reject* these things, but you don't accept them either. I show you a dead unicorn, you don't say: 'this is fake; this is impossible' you say: 'I've never seen anything like this before . . . *I'm gonna poke it until I find out how it works.*'"

Jill frowned and blinked. "Why should that make you uncomfortable?" she asked.

Selene groaned.

"I'm gonna regret saying this, but . . . well. This stuff. It's been around a while. No one's ever *really* studied it before. Not the way you're going at it."

"Your point?"

"Maybe there's a *reason* no one's studied it? What if there are things out there that aren't *supposed* to be studied? From my experience, there are things that really don't want you to know about them. What if you run into something that *you're just not meant to understand*?"

Jill was already shaking her head. "That has never been *my* experience. Humanity has never improved itself or the world through ignorance and apathy. We *must* question, we must continue to study, to explore, to further our understanding of the world—or *worlds*. It is only through knowledge and discovery and understanding that we can hope to survive."

Selene glanced at her out of the corner of her eye, then rolled it skywards. Jill didn't see; she had gone back to her computer. She took out a pair of headphones on thin white cords from her pocket and stuck the buds into her ears as she plugged them in and went to the next video.

Selene drove, and after a while the nothingness around them was gradually replaced by the suburbs, the sprawl, and finally the towers of Las Vegas.

"Johnny Bathory, now, that can't be your real name, can it, sir?" The talk show host with the plasticky hair had an air of cordial superiority as he leaned back behind his desk and folded his hands.

Sitting on the couch next to his desk, lounging on the conservative navy fabric like some exotic and deadly animal, was a man wearing tight leather jeans, boots with four-inch soles, and a studded leather jacket. His bare chest underneath was lean and pale and crisscrossed with delicate silver chains. He wore a leather collar as high as his neck, which forced him to keep his chin up. His hair was a wild, black bush and the face underneath it was powder white. He wore heavy black lipstick and heavier black eyeliner, and contacts that made his eyes appear yellow.

"Of course it's my real name, Gerry," this person said. He had a hoarse, quiet voice, at odds with his striking appearance.

"But according to your biography your legal name is Douglas Reed," said the host coaxingly.

"Yes, yes," said the man. "That's the name my parents gave me. But it's not my real name."

"But you picked your stage name?"

"That's correct."

"What was the reasoning behind your choice?"

"Well, when I was growing up there was this kid, see, and his name was Johnny. And when I was nine years old he cut his own throat—"

"Oh my goodness!"

"—and in the note they found with his body it just said 'don't forget me.' And I felt real bad, because he was my age, see? And so I thought: *I'll* be Johnny, that way Johnny won't ever be forgotten. And I've been Johnny ever since. And Bathory, that's easy. That's my family name. I'm descended from Elizabeth Báthory."

"The Hungarian countess?"

"The Hungarian vampire. When I say she is my ancestor I mean my maker line descends from her."

"Ah. Of course. Yes. Now, let's talk about this vampire persona of yours . . . "

"It's not too hard to believe, is it?" Johnny Bathory said with a grin, showing off his fangs. "I mean, I'm a rock star. We're practically nocturnal. We take way too many drugs, have way too much sex, and play way too much loud music. Any rock star that makes it past twenty-seven, I assure you, is actually a vampire. I'm just the only one who's open about it."

Clara was waiting for them outside a modest motel just off Highway 95. It had slot machines in the lobby, only one of which was unoccupied, and it smelled of cigarettes.

"Why not stay on the Strip?" Jill asked, poking her head out. "I'm sure we can get a room for the week."

"This is cheaper," Clara said.

"You let me worry about that," said Jill, with the confidence of one whose escrow payment just came through.

Selene gazed at Clara imploringly. "Come *on*," she said. "How often do you get to stay at a four-star Las Vegas hotel?"

"The last time I was here I stayed at the Venetian," Clara said. "I was not impressed."

"Technically, Strip hotels aren't *in* Las Vegas," Jill pointed out. "Most of the Strip is actually in the unincorporated community of—"

"But that's the one with the *canal*," Selene sputtered. "And . . . how did *you*?"

"I did them a favor," Clara said shortly.

Jill sighed. "Staying at the Castle gives us much better access to Johnny Bathory. It makes *sense*."

Although Clara looked unconvinced, and Selene seemed less than enthusiastic to be staying in close proximity to a vampire ("Why not the Bellagio? It has this *great* fountain!") eventually Jill and her all-powerful credit card won out, and they continued south, out of Las Vegas proper, until the looming replica of the Eiffel Tower announced they had arrived at the resort capital of the new world.

Arcana, woefully out of place among the sleek limousines, cabs, and billboard trucks, lumbered down the Strip like a dusty cowboy through a fancy club. After a certain amount of confusion Jill got them pulled into the entrance to the Castle, which sat at the south end of the Strip, its fake stone ramparts in sharp contrast to the otherwise modern-style buildings. The jarring transition was exacerbated by the enormous LCD screen over the portcullis entrance showing a looping video of Johnny Bathory—wearing a pair of devil horns and a leather speedo, prancing about with a microphone practically in his mouth—with flashing words running across the bottom proclaiming, "JOHNNY BATHORY, LIVE IN CONCERT—THIS WEEK ONLY."

Arcana pulled up behind a Las Vegas Metro squad car, which Jill barely glanced at as she jumped down and hurried inside, Selene on her heels. Clara parked her bike behind Arcana and waited there, her arms folded in silent disapproval.

The lobby of the Castle, in keeping with the overall theme, was built after the design of a medieval keep, with shields bearing coats of arms lining the high walls. There was also a huge fireplace set behind the check-in desk, with roaring fake flames projected in it. As a result, the clerks looked as though they were standing in an inferno. A large sign at the end announced "ALL BATHORY SHOWS SOLD OUT. STAND-BY TICKETS ONLY."

The place was filled with a milling crowd: middle-aged white men in T-shirts and shorts, middle-aged women in obnoxious print dresses, and between the adults, dozens of children from toddlers to teens, some of them wearing princess tiaras, others carrying fake swords. Many of them (young and old) carried huge paper bags stamped with the Castle's emblem (a large stylized C with little turrets woven into the design). Luggage trollies wheeled this way and that, maneuvered by porters dressed as pages.

Jill stared at the scene, and glanced at Selene a little skeptically.

"And he's a *real* vampire?" she asked, just to be sure.

Selene actually buried her face in her hands. "*Yes*. Okay? *Yes*. Check us in for three nights, would you?"

While Jill did this Selene surreptitiously checked the exits. It was a habit.

When they emerged it was to find Clara bracketed by two police officers. Selene froze in the doorway, hands automatically going for her guns—which were at Jill's insistence safely locked in Arcana—while Jill frowned and strode toward the group purposefully.

Yet as she approached, it appeared Clara was not in any sort of trouble. She looked resigned and long-suffering, but the officers were smiling and laughing. Almost *relieved*, Jill thought. She cleared her throat.

One of the officers, a jovial, overweight man with a red face and yellow hair, turned to her and schooled his expression.

"Clara?" Jill asked, trying to convey in a single word the questions, "What is going on? Are you in trouble? Are *we* in trouble? How much do they know?"

Clara just looked at her impassively and said: "We have a case."

They turned out to be Officers Nescal and Dunes. Nescal was olive skinned with lank dark hair, while Dunes was the blond one. He gave Jill a hard look, and Selene a harder one when she shifted uneasily.

"Officer Dunes," Clara finished, "this Jill Hamilton and Selene Shields. They are friends of mine."

"Friends?" said Officer Dunes, and threw a look at Clara which implied more than his spoken question. In answer, Clara nodded sharply.

Officer Dunes heaved a sigh like a horse, his great frame swelling and relaxing with a shudder. "Well I suppose you'd better come along. I expect you'll find out on your own anyway."

"I'm sorry . . . *what?*" Jill said, making a slicing motion with her arms as the officers moved toward their squad car. "What *case* Clara? What's going on?"

Clara's shoulders sagged. "There have been . . . complications," she said. "Officer Dunes is requesting our . . . expert opinion on a. . . . " She looking questioningly at the officer.

For answer, Dunes held the door to the nearest squad car open. "I'll explain when we get to the morgue," he said.

"Riiiight," said Selene, drawing the syllable out in her sarcasm. "We'll be taking our *own* car, thanks very much."

Officer Dunes shrugged. "Suit yourself." He climbed into the car, and Nescal slid into the driver's seat, and they pulled out into the road. Clara followed at a sedate pace on Unicorn, while Selene and Jill sat in Arcana and waited. When the squad car noticed Arcana was still sitting in the parking lot, it calmly pulled over to the curb and waited. Selene cursed and started the engine.

"What's going on?" Jill asked.

"Ask the giant," Selene scowled, pulling out of the hotel's driveway.

Following on the heels of the cruiser and the motorbike, Arcana made its way back out onto the Strip, turning north toward downtown.

"You don't work with local law enforcement?" Jill asked as they stopped at a light.

"Nngh," said Selene. "Try not to. Ask too many questions. Usually try to arrest me."

"For carrying unlicensed firearms?" Jill suggested innocently.

"*Those* are easy enough to hide," Selene said. "If you know how. If you see 'em coming. Which I do. No . . . I think it has more to do with *this*," she waved a hand in front of her face.

"What . . . because you're African-American?" Jill asked, surprised.

"Because I'm *Black*," Selene corrected testily.

Jill blinked at her. "Really?" she said incredulously.

Selene nodded.

The light turned green.

"*Really?*"

"You know," Selene said, easing Arcana forward. "I read in one o' them crap mags this column where it said *everyone* should try having gay sex at least once in their life, just to see what it's like, y'know? Well, *I* think it'd be better if we could change skins. And everyone had to spend at least *one day* with a different skin color. Just to *see what it's like*."

Jill fell silent at that, shrinking back into her seat.

Arcana chugged through the city, following the police cruiser and the black figure on the motorcycle.

"I just hope Clara knows what she's doing," Selene grumbled, shifting into fourth.

Jill didn't answer.

The city morgue turned out to be a gray, humorless building with half-washed-out graffiti on one side. They parked Arcana out front, a tactful distance from Officer Dune's cruiser, and piled out. Selene grabbed Clara by the elbow as soon as she had dismounted and dragged her around to the back of the truck.

"*Tell me,*" she hissed, viciously prodding the larger woman's chest, "what [prod] is [prod] going *on?*"

Clara looked over to where Officer Dunes had gotten out of his car and was waiting, leaning his forearms on the hood. She looked back down at Selene.

"I saved his life the last time I was here," she said. "Helped him with a possession case. He knows enough to be afraid."

"And now . . . what?"

"He has something he wants me to see. I thought Jill would appreciate being able to contribute. Why did you come?"

Selene punched her lightly in the arm. "You know why," she growled. "Come on, let's get this over with."

* * *

The body of a woman lay on the cold, stainless-steel table. She was remarkably pale, even for a corpse, almost gray as a stone. She looked like she had been fairly young in life, with dyed black hair and a lot of piercings—now empty. Officer Dunes took a tray from a nearby table and handed it to Clara.

"We had to remove her jewelry, but you can take a look if it helps."

Clara brushed the tray aside; Selene took it instead. The taller woman stalked around the body, her head cocked to one side, frowning. She came to a stop beside the corpse's head and held out two fingers over her neck. Coming around the bulk of the officer, Jill saw that there was an ugly wound there, as though something had bitten into her neck above the right carotid artery. Jill looked up at Clara, her eyes very wide.

"Don't tell me . . . " she whispered.

"Was this woman exsanguinated when you found her?" Clara asked.

"It was actually Nescal who found her," Dunes said, jerking his head toward the dour-faced officer. "But yeah, the coroner determined that she died from loss of blood. And that's the thing: there is *no* blood in her, and I mean *nothing*. She's not drained, she's *dry*."

Selene, who'd been idly going through the contents of the tray, froze. Clara nodded, as if this was what she expected to hear. Jill looked between them, her eyes narrowed.

"Most of the department thinks it's some sick joke," Nescal said, his voice a little hoarse. "What with that vampire rocker in town, they think maybe some psycho got it into his head to dress up a kill—make it *look* like a vampire. But Dunes told me about the case you helped him with in Henderson, and we got to thinking . . . "

Clara straightened up. "You thought right," she said.

"This . . . " Jill said, coming forward to get a better look at the body. "This is a victim of a *vampire* attack?" She froze, her hands outstretched. "Gloves," she said sharply. "I need gloves. And a rubber apron." She looked around hurriedly.

Dunes provided both gloves and apron with amusement in his face, while Clara looked across the body at Nescal and asked:

"Where did you find her?"

"Outside a storm drain in Winchester," the officer replied, shying away slightly as Jill dove at the corpse with surprising enthusiasm. "Your friend, is she a doctor?"

"Not yet," Jill answered. She was palpating the wound, peeling away layers of skin and muscle. "This is *fascinating*," she murmured. "Selene, can you take notes?"

But Selene had begun laying out all the ornaments collected from the corpse on a nearby table. Dunes obligingly brought down the morgue's microphone and hit record.

"This too," Jill said, handing him her phone. "I can't work it through my gloves—thanks."

She leaned forward again and pointed excitedly at the wound.

"It's not a sucking wound," she said. "Well, that's inaccurate. What I mean is, whatever drained her, it didn't *suck* the blood out. It opened her carotid artery and let her heart pump the blood out. Probably had an anticoagulant agent to help the flow. Do you have any swabs? I need swabs. And tweezers."

When these were provided she used the tweezers to prop the wound open—Nescal suddenly became very interested in what Selene was doing—and swabbed the inside.

"Not that I'll get anything," Jill muttered. "She's dry as a mummy. But look! You can see where the first incisions were made. I make that two teeth, very long and sharp—possibly with a slight curve. They were inserted once, here, where they missed the artery, and then again, here, where they punctured it. Then the owner of the teeth pulled back, rupturing the artery and doing significant damage to the soft tissue of the neck. There's some additional damage that suggests the victim struggled. I don't suppose you found any bruising? No, of course you didn't."

Clara left Jill to her study of the corpse and went over to Selene. After seeing a few dozen vampire victims, they all started to look the same, and while Jill was obsessed with the minutiae, to Clara it had long since congealed into a single picture that screamed "vampire attack!"

"What have you found?" she asked, leaning down to get a better look at Selene's array of rings and studs.

Shooting Nescal an unloving glance, Selene pointed to the little piles of black and silver jewelry.

"I got them sorted," she said. "Earrings, nose stud, lip ring, tongue stud, finger rings, something that *could* be an ear stud but might be a belly button stud. Nipple rings . . ."

Nescal coughed and turned away.

"Lot of metal," Clara remarked. "Any silver?"

"Not that I can see," Selene said. "Stainless steel all the way. But look at this." She had arranged the finger rings in a line along the bottom of the pan. These ranged from thin silver bands to thick ones with huge stones set in them. One which held a large black stone had a frame in the shape of an open mouth with elongated canines. Another was a signet-style ring bearing an upside-down cross with a crescent moon at its head.

With hardly a pause Clara singled this one out. She picked it up carefully and held it up to the light.

"'I am no Christ but which Christ do you know?'" she whispered under her breath.

"Say what?" said Selene.

"Johnny Bathory. That song's been going through my head. And this is his emblem."

"You got that right," said Selene. "And here, look: a bat pendant, fang pendant; the skull has little fangs too."

"So?" said Nescal. "She was some goth-punk JB fan. They're pretty thick on the ground these days."

"Yeah, *exactly*," Selene said, giving the officer a hard gaze. "She was a Johnny Bathory fan."

Nescal's lined face twisted in thought. "So?" he said.

"She was killed by a vampire," Clara announced. "Johnny Bathory is a vampire."

The tightness in Nescal's face dissipated like a cloud in the desert. "Oh," he smiled. "*Everybody* knows that. It's part of his act."

Clara and Selene just stared at him.

"I mean . . . uh . . . it *is* part of his act. Isn't it?"

"What have you got, Jill?" Selene asked, turning away from the tray of jewelry.

"We-ell," said Jill, still bent over the body. "Her neck was brutalized. And the loss of blood is the most complete I've ever seen. There is a partial dislocation of her right shoulder, which suggests she was forcibly restrained. There is damage to her fingers and nails which seems to indicate she clawed at her attacker, but I can't find any trace of skin or tissue under her nails. I don't suppose your forensics cleaned them out?" she asked Officer Dunes.

The man coughed uncomfortably.

"To tell the truth, forensics haven't *seen* this body," he said. "Junkie groupies go missing all the time. Sometimes they turn up alive . . . sometimes not. We're working on getting a positive ID on her—she didn't have a wallet—but the Sergeant didn't think we needed forensics. I wasn't going to pursue the matter, but then we were called in to break up an altercation at the Castle and up came Clara on that bike of hers and I thought—*well damn,* she'll know what to do with this." He shrugged expressively. "And now you're telling me it's *vampires*?"

"*A* vampire," said Clara. "I cannot be sure if there are more."

"With the flood drainage system Las Vegas has got?" Selene said. "You'll be lucky if you haven't got a *colony* living down there."

"But," said Nescal, who was still grappling with events. "The drains are full of people."

Jill stared at him.

"*Normal* people," he said. "Homeless people, that is. We would have heard—"

"They wouldda *told* you if they thought there was a colony of vampires living in the dark and selectively feeding on them?" Selene said, every word dripping sarcasm.

Nescal folded his arms defensively. "We would have heard something, I'm sure."

"Vampires do not need to breathe," Clara said quietly. "They do not eat or drink—they feed on blood, that is their only sustenance. They can live in places humans cannot. They can feed on people and *not* kill them. They are very good at hiding themselves. They have to be; for although they are powerful at night, day is anathema to them, and all an enemy need do is discover their location during daylight hours and they are as good as destroyed."

A respectful silence followed this speech, until Dunes broke it by coughing. "So . . . what do we do with this?" He waved a hand at the body on the table.

Clara dipped and raised her shoulders. "Identify her. Notify her family. Leave the vampires to us."

"We'll need to search the area where she was found," Selene muttered into Clara's arm. "Someone messed up here. There's bound to be . . . other evidence."

"Yes," agreed Clara. "We will need access to the storm drain in which you found her. Preferably soon, while it's still light."

The mouth of the drain yawned before them in the form of three gaping black holes, each separated by a concrete pillar. A smell of pungent pond weed wafted out at them.

"We found the body just here," Dunes explained, politely lifting the police tape and unlocking the metal gate. "Scrub crews have already been through, I'm afraid."

Clara nodded, as if this did not surprise her. "You will leave us here," she told the officer.

"Like hell we will," Nescal protested, almost laughing. He stopped immediately when his partner put a hand on his arm.

"You weren't around for the Henderson case," Dunes said. "When Nordstern says leave her to it, you're better off as far away as possible." He gave Clara an apologetic look. "It's safer for everyone that way."

"What about *her*," Nescal said, pointing at Jill.

Jill, who was trying on a pair of Selene's combat boots, looked up and raised an eyebrow.

"What?" she said. "I could be a tracker."

"Hunter," Selene corrected out of the corner of her mouth. "And no, sweetie, you couldn't."

"We have a . . . an *arrangement* with Jill," Clara said stiffly.

"I will attempt to document what we find in full detail, and report back," Jill offered.

The other two women glared at her, but this seemed to mollify Nescal.

They entered the drain with the afternoon sun at their backs, their long shadows stretching out to meet the imposing blackness of the cavern. Selene, who had strapped a flashlight to her gun Freddie, took the lead, while Clara walked behind Jill, casting her beam side to side and behind them.

The drain went down a ways, and the water rose to mid-calf. The temperature dropped dramatically, and the darkness pressed in on all sides.

Then they rounded a corner, and daylight streamed in; about twenty yards along, the drain ran out under the sky. There, in response to the sun, reeds and rushes and other plants grew in thick bunches from the ripe water. Insects hummed and a startled bird rose up in surprise, its wingbeats cutting through the air until it disappeared beyond the concrete lip above.

Selene paused in the shadow just before the open space. The rushes had clearly been trampled recently, with two discernible tracks of bent and broken stalks. In one patch, it looked like something had been burned right off the water's surface.

Jill tried to make a beeline for it, but found the back of her jacket held in Clara's iron grip.

"Let me sweep it first," said the tall woman, and stepped out into the sun.

Jill waited in the shadows with Selene as Clara crossed the strip of sunlight, carefully hugging one side of the channel, and disappeared into the darkness beyond. They could still see her as a black shape silhouetted against the erratic beam of her flashlight.

She reappeared a moment later, having crossed over and now walking back along the other wall. She put her flashlight away and beckoned to them.

"Stay away from the middle," she said.

"Why?" asked Jill, but she obediently veered away from the strange, burned patch and came to stand next to Clara. Carefully she pulled out her phone and began taking pictures.

"Because that is where he died," the woman answered.

"He died?" Jill echoed. "*He* died? *Who* died?"

"The vampire," said Selene, and pointed at the burned patch. The rushes there were crumpled and singed, and there was a thick bed of ash floating on the surface of the water.

"Wait," said Jill. "A vampire died? I thought the vampire killed that girl!"

"Yes, one did," said Clara, moving out toward the patch of ashes like it was a skittish cat she was trying to capture. "*And* one died here."

Jill frowned, then predictably latched on to the one thing that did not make sense in her mind.

"Why do you think it was male?"

Selene rolled her eyes.

"It is a statistical probability," Clara said, but she sounded distracted. She bent over the bed of ash and carefully lowered her arms into it. Her face crunched into an expression of the utmost concentration as she felt about under the surface.

"A lotta vampires tend to prey on people who resemble the class of person they felt the most resentful of in life," Selene explained dryly while they waited. "So you get a lot of male vampires hunting human women. And vice versa. White supremacist vampires are the *worst*. Also the most satisfying to kill."

"Ah," Jill said, and found nothing else to say.

Out in the center of the channel, Clara made a small noise of satisfaction.

"You found something, girlfriend?" Selene called out.

Clara grunted in response, both hands sunk elbow-deep in ashy water, but she did not straighten up. "I think," she said, still feeling around under the surface. "I think I've got his head."

Selene straightened up and Jill surged forward, saying, "Really? Bring it up, let's see!"

The two hunters gave her exasperated looks.

"It's a *vampire* head," Selene said tiredly.

Jill thought about this.

"But you said they don't burst into flames when exposed to sunlight," she said.

"Yeah, doesn't mean that sunlight don't do bad things to their bodies. As is exemplified by Clara currently standing in the middle of one. You better roll it, honey, I'll cover you."

So as Clara began the odd-looking task of rolling the unseen object along the bottom of the channel, dragging it through rushes and weeds, Selene took out her gun again and stood above her, sweeping the area.

"Why so cautious?" Jill asked, ducking to keep out of the gun's line of sight.

"To say vampires are helpless during the day is an over simplification," Selene said. "Technically, they're powerless against *sunlight*. These drains are *perfect* for them for more than one reason. You get complete darkness even during daytime." This last was spoken as Clara reached the edge of the shadow of the nearby drain and stepped inside.

Jill hesitated for a moment, but only a moment. She came up next to Clara's side and got out her flashlight and her phone.

"Well, come on," she said. "Let's see it."

Water streaming from her leather sleeves and gauntlets, Clara slowly raised her find up out of the muck. It was grayish in color, with pale splotches and bits of green algae sticking to it. The top was a mess of limp, gray-brown hair, and the rest . . .

"Well, what do you know," said Jill. "It *is* male."

"Was," Clara corrected mildly.

It was not a pleasant face. The features were twisted, and the open eyes, though covered in a thin whitish film, were stained red underneath. But by the width of the jaw and the stubble on the chin, it was recognizably male.

Handing Selene her phone, Jill stuck the flashlight between her teeth and pulled on a pair of latex gloves. Gingerly she took the grisly specimen from Clara and turned it over, examining the mouth, nose, ears and eyes. She lifted a lip and looked in perplexity at the more or less ordinary (if badly maintained) set of teeth.

"Here," said Clara, and deftly pushed up against one of the canines. It slid back easily, and from the opening a long, curving fang descended into view. Delicate and graceful as a cat's claw, it was half covered with membrane with only the pearly tip visible at the end.

"Well I'll be . . . " Jill murmured around the flashlight. She mimicked Clara's motion with the other canine, producing the same result. "Fascinating," she said. "Selene, take pictures of these."

With a sigh Selene obediently began taking pictures.

"There's no sign of putrefaction," Jill went on.

"What?" said Clara.

Balancing the head on one hand, Jill took the flashlight out of her mouth. "No putrefaction," she said. "Which is strange. Even if he was killed recently, there should be some signs of animal activity—considering he was lying in a veritable haven for microbes, worms, and other scavengers."

"Vampire flesh is toxic to most creatures," Clara announced. "Werewolves are the only ones who can eat them, but I hear they don't taste very good."

"Werewolves, huh?" Jill said, and Selene shut her eyes as if bracing for a physical blow. Glancing up, Jill saw her expression and relented. "We'll save them for another day. Hold him, Clara, I want to try something."

With Clara holding the remains firmly in both hands, Jill borrowed one of Selene's knives and cut a small piece of tissue from the vampire's neck—near where it had evidently been severed with a meat cleaver.

"Uh, Jill?" Selene said uncertainly as Jill, holding the piece of flesh at the end of her finger, inched toward the strip of blinding sunlight.

"I just need to see—oh, whoa."

As soon as Jill's finger, with the piece of dead vampire at the tip of it, emerged into direct sunlight, the piece of flesh began to smoke and sizzle. It bubbled, boiled, and finally ignited in a brief flash. Then there was nothing but a thin layer of pale gray ash.

Jill raised an eyebrow.

"They don't burst into flames?" she asked sarcastically.

"Living ones, no," Selene said. "Dead ones? It's pretty much like, y'know, what's that stuff that blows up when you put it in water?"

"Alkali metals," Jill murmured, pulling back into the shadow. Taking a vial from a pocket she carefully shook the ash into it. She took further samples from the head's hair and neck tissue, storing them similarly. Finally she took another strip of flesh and, holding it between two fingers, plunged her hand into the water.

A foot below the water's surface, invisible in the murk, there was no reaction when exposed to sunlight. Slowly raising her hand, however, caused the strip to warm gradually, and by the time Jill could see her own hand (barely an inch from the surface) the piece of flesh ignited, very much like a chunk of sodium in water, and flared brightly for a moment. Jill felt it, like the scorching of a candle flame, and then the coolness of the water rushed in; the fire had punctured her glove.

"Well, *that's* interesting," she said, straightening up and stripping off the glove.

"Yes," said Clara impassively. "May I burn this now?" she asked, indicating the head.

Jill's eyes veritably bugged out in horror. "Absolutely *not*," she said, snatching the head out of Clara's grip, heedless of her bare hand. "This is the most valuable specimen we've found yet. You *will not* destroy it. Now lend me your coat."

"What?" Clara's tone was chill.

"Lend me your *coat*," Jill insisted. "We need something to keep the sun off him until we get him a light-tight box"

"That won't matter in a few days," Selene said, even as Clara recoiled backwards. "Vampire decomposition—"

"He's *not* decomposing," Jill snapped, tugging at Clara's sleeve.

"—doesn't work like human decomposition," Selene finished. "He'll be dust in forty or so hours, no matter what you do."

"Well, then I *want to see that*," Jill insisted.

In the end it was Selene who sacrificed her work shirt to form a makeshift shroud, wrapping the head up in an awkward bundle, which Jill carried protectively clutched to her chest the rest of the way back.

Dunes was waiting for them at the exit of the drain.

"You found something?" he asked with barely concealed surprise as he let them out.

"It's not conclusive," Jill said. "Open up your car. I'll show you."

Dunes, to his credit, only whistled at the sight of the vampire head, unwrapped on the back seat.

"And you found this?" he said, turning to Clara.

"I expected to," she said.

"I can't be positive," Jill said. "But if you compare his bite to the wound on your victim's neck, that should be enough to identify him as her killer."

Officer Dunes rubbed the back of his neck unhappily. "Yes," he admitted. "It could. But you see our problem now, don't you?"

Clara and Selene exchanged bewildered glances, but Jill frowned thoughtfully.

"We don't have just *one* victim anymore," Dunes said, and the two hunters groaned. "We have a dead girl, and maybe this is the head of her killer. *But he's dead too.* Which sorta demands the question: *who killed him?* I don't think it was the lady we got back in the morgue."

"He was decapitated cleanly," Jill offered. "Some irregularity in the soft tissue suggests his assailant used a knife—a small but sharp one—as you can see that, although the spine has been severed, there is some tearing around his trachea and skin."

"Must have been a strong someone," Nescal, who'd been lingering by Dunes's elbow, pointed out. "Exceptionally strong." He shot a glance at Clara.

"Given the weapon used," Jill said. "I doubt it was someone with less than supernatural strength. I'm sure Clara could do this, but she uses a *sword.*"

"There would be no tearing," Clara announced. "And I would not have left the head for someone to find." She sniffed disdainfully.

"*And* we only got here this morning," Selene pointed out, a little defensively.

"You said vampires were strong," Jill said. "Strong enough to do this?"

"Oh, *easily,*" Selene assured her.

"But why—*sorry* if this is a stupid question," Dunes said. "*Why* would a vampire kill *another* vampire? *If* this thing *is* a vampire head . . . "

"Why would a human kill another human?" Clara countered. "Vampires are by nature a proud and violent race—much like humans. Just because they prey on us does not mean they do not attack each other."

Officer Dunes rubbed his eyes.

"Yes, of course. *Thank you,* Clara. And thank you, Miss, er . . . "

"Hamilton," Jill provided.

"Miss Hamilton. And I'm sorry about this, but I really do need to take your . . . um . . . *find.* For evidence."

Selene and Clara sighed, but they seemed resigned.

"*What?*" said Jill. "Oh no, *I* found him. I haven't properly studied him yet. You'll give me copies of the necropsy report *at least* . . . "

"Now, you know I can't answer that," Officer Dunes said, reaching to re-wrap the head. Selene snatched her shirt back before he could grab it.

"At *least* check his bite," Jill insisted, even as the head was carefully boxed up. "And keep him out of the sun, and record his rate of decomposition, and . . . "

"*Thank you,* Clara," Dunes said, lowering himself into his cruiser. "I'll call if something comes up."

Clara just gave one of her inverted shrugs.

The three women watched as the police cruiser pulled out into the evening traffic and disappeared into the hoard of cars, glimmering in the last rays of the sinking sun.

"Well *crud,*" said Jill, putting her hands on her hips.

"Ah, don't you worry," Selene said, patting her on the shoulder. "We'll get you another vampire, I promise."

"Honestly, I'd prefer to *talk* to one," Jill admitted as they walked back to Arcana. "The wealth of information we could gain . . . if like you said, there are vampires around who are hundreds of years old. It could revolutionize our history. Not to mention our understanding of biology."

"Yeah, yeah," said Selene, getting into the driver's seat. "The *trick* would be finding a vampire who's *actually willing* to talk to you."

"There's still that Bathory guy," Jill pointed out. "I'll ask Clara about getting me an interview with him."

"An interview with a vampire," Selene said, grinning humorlessly as she followed Clara back toward the Strip. "We all know how well *that* goes."

"Ha ha," said Jill.

Getting at Johnny Bathory, however, proved to be more or less impossible. Aside from the practical roadblocks put in place to keep the ordinary masses out of his hair before, during, and after the show ("It really is an ingenious defense system," Selene admitted with grudging admiration. "What will protect you from a deranged fan also goes a long way to protecting you from a determined hunter.") Clara's attempt to scope out the landscape using her spirit ring proved equally fruitless.

"He has *wards*," she said disgustedly, after disappearing for a mere fifteen minutes. "It would take a magician to get through them."

"A magician," said Jill. "There are *magicians*?"

"It's a general term for someone who studies or practices magic," Clara sighed.

"Oh. Can we hire one? I mean, this *is* Las Vegas..."

Selene laughed at that. "Sorry, they don't have *our kind* of magician here."

And there it rested. Jill dejectedly ordered room service and sat up late entering her notes from the day into her laptop while Clara and Selene slept in shifts.

"The vampire this... it's sort of a metaphor for life, you know," said the man with spiky, bleached-blond hair and heavy eye shadow. The tag at the bottom of the screen identified him as Clark Wuornos, the keyboardist for *Johnny Bathory*. "Because... like... vampires are *dead*. But they're also alive. That's sort of the act we have going on with Johnny B. Life and death go together. So we're celebrating death, this thing that's going to happen to all of us eventually. But we're also celebrating the fact that we're alive to have all this. Sex, blood, rock n' roll and all that."

"Don't you mean drugs?"

"Sorry?"

"Isn't it sex, *drugs* and rock n' roll."

"Oh, yeah. Ha ha. But blood works too... because—you know—*vampire!*"

"The vampire thing is pretty exciting."

"Well, yeah. I mean a vampire is basically the ultimate combination of life and death. They're scary and attractive at the same time. It's really the sexiest thing in the world to be a vampire..."

"I have an idea," Jill said as they gathered for breakfast in the Castle's main cafeteria—a restaurant made to look like the banquet hall of a medieval keep. "You think it was another vampire who killed the vampire whose head we found yesterday, right?"

Selene, stooped over a monstrous cup of coffee, silently covered her eyes with her hand. Clara, who had a bit more self control, nodded.

"Well," said Jill, neatly folding her napkin. "Then why don't we go find *that* vampire? Should be easier to get into those drains than past Bathory's bodyguards."

Selene actually put her head on the table at that.

"Not a good idea," Clara said.

"Why not?"

"Vampires are fast. Dangerous. Unpredictable. We would not be able to adequately protect you."

"Not even if we went down there during the day? I mean, I know it's dark so they can get about. But wouldn't just the fact that it *was* daytime sort of . . . um . . . slow them down?"

Clara frowned, considering this.

Selene's head rose up off the table.

"You got a death wish, girl?"

"I want to *learn*," Jill insisted. "I mean, it's not like I want to *kill* them. I just want to talk."

Selene laughed humorlessly, stuttering to a stop when she caught sight of Clara's expression.

"No," she said. "You can't be seriously . . . "

Clara gave one of her inverted shrugs. "If we put her in enough armor . . . I think my gauntlets might fit if we cinch them down all the way."

"But . . . "

"What—armor?"

"They *are* slower during the day. And I have flares."

"*What armor?*" Jill insisted.

The armor turned out to be leather. Mostly. When it was laid out on the hotel bed it looked rather like a particularly hard-core outfit worn by a fantasy role-playing actor. It was odd, however, in that it seemed designed to protect the joints and the interior of the arms and legs more than the knees, elbows, chest, and other places usually covered by such things. It wasn't until Jill realized that it had been designed to protect the wearer's *arteries* that it began to make sense.

The leather was hard and shiny, scuffed in places and clearly well used.

"You'll want to wear comfortable clothes underneath," Clara said. "Otherwise it chafes."

"I'll bet," said Jill, gingerly picking up a thigh guard. It looked almost like a piece of a robot's exoskeleton, save for the enormous buckles on the outside. "Where do you *keep* all this?" she asked.

"Usually I'm wearing it," Clara said mildly. At their surprised looks she just shrugged. "I've been ambushed enough times."

The armor turned out to be mostly too big all over. The legs were too long to be any use, but Jill found the upper-arm guards fit around her thighs almost perfectly.

"Go figure," Selene said with a wry smile.

They used the forearm guards for Jill's upper arms, and wrapped her legs from the knees down with strips of what Clara called "kevleather." They did the same with her arms. Finally, after some fiddling, Clara got the neck guard carefully buckled on. This piece stretched down over Jill's collar bones and up to her chin. With it on it was impossible to look down, and nearly as difficult to turn her head.

"Will this actually work?" she asked, pulling at the neck piece. "Isn't there more to protecting yourself against vampires?"

"Not really," Selene said. "I told you, religious paraphernalia isn't always effective, garlic just makes them sneeze, and silver is only a minor deterrent. If you want to use magic against a vampire, you need a real magician who really knows her stuff. Pretty much, your best bet is a good physical barrier between their teeth and your soft bits."

Jill tapped at the leather gauntlet on her arm. "And this will stop them?"

"Stop a determined vampire?" Selene said. "Nyah, but it *will* slow them down. That's all we need."

"What about you?"

Clara sighed. "With vampires the best strategy is to kill them before they attack you. That's what we'll do."

"Don't you *dare*," said Jill. "I want to *talk* to them, remember?"

"I will keep that in mind," Clara said gravely, even as Selene rolled her eyes.

The armor was stiff and uncomfortable and made Jill feel like she was in a robot costume. It was also hot, and she was sweating before they got to the sewer.

"How do you *stand* this?" she asked Clara while they waited for Selene to pick the lock on the gate.

Clara, who was wearing her thick leather biking pants and padded leather jacket, lowered and raised her shoulders. "I got used to it," she said.

"What about in the summer?" Jill persisted. "Don't you get heat-stroke?"

Clara's face took on a vacant, closed-off expression.

"No," she said.

There was a clink of chains, and to her evident relief Selene announced the gate was open.

This time, without the overbearing presence of the police officers, Selene had opted to bring out what she termed "the big guns." These included her trench gun, Freddie, her sawn-off shotgun, Elvis, and a strange tubular contraption she called "The Sparkler."

Clara drew her sword as they descended into the drain, out of the light, and Selene switched on the flashlight she had attached beneath Freddie's barrel. The beam, bright in comparison to the inky dark, illuminated a wide swath of graffiti on the wall, and reflected from the ripples on the surface of the water in dancing patterns above them.

Selene led the way, keeping her gun poised but her hands relaxed, her footsteps measured, with every so often a hitch in her stride as sore joints and bruised muscles—left over from their previous misadventure— protested the use. She was also, Jill noticed now, protecting her right side, where there was a cracked rib barely two weeks healed.

"Will you be all right?" Jill asked her.

Selene paused so she could peer around in the darkness at the smaller woman.

"You're asking me this . . . *now*?" she growled.

"Um . . . yes?" Jill mumbled, embarrassed.

Selene shook her head and kept walking. "Don't you worry about *me*, once the adrenaline kicks in I won't feel a thing."

They progressed slowly further into the drain, through the patch of sunlight, back into the shadow, and on and on. The ground rose and fell in smooth inclines which were strangely awkward to navigate on foot. They passed out into open air channels more than once, where Jill could hear the noise of traffic just beyond the concrete lip above them, and then back down beneath the streets and buildings.

Deep into one of these tunnels Selene paused. Three giant, circular apertures opened up high along the side of the channel they were currently in, out of which drifted thick, tepid air.

Selene and Jill waited, ankle deep in water, while Clara climbed up and investigated. After due inspection she sheathed her sword and crawled bodily into the middle one. Turning around and poking her head out, she said: "This one," and extended an arm.

Selene helped Jill up, then climbed Clara's arm as if it were a tree branch, slithering past Jill to take the lead once more.

Now they crawled, or walked bent over when the tunnel expanded, and soon Jill's back and knees began to complain. But neither Selene, with her injuries, nor Clara, who was almost a foot taller than either of them, complained, and so Jill remained silent, grimly pushing herself along.

Eventually the tunnel opened onto a wide cistern with several more tunnels (blessedly large) leading off from the other side.

There was a scuffle in the dark, and Selene swung her light—and her gun—around to a low ledge that jutted out into the shallow water. There a jumble of cardboard boxes had been arranged, and as they watched, a disheveled head appeared, its eyes bloodshot and the pupils tiny pricks in the middle of washed-out, hazel irises. A tangle of white hair drifted like spiderwebs against the dark backdrop.

"Hello," said Jill. "Sorry to bother you."

The man stared at them sullenly. He didn't seem to notice that Selene had a gun, or that Clara had a large sword.

"They don't like light," the man mumbled, retreating back into the shell of cardboard that served as his home. "They'll get you if you don't turn off your light."

"Who will get us?" Selene asked sharply.

"Nngh," was all the man said, and they saw no more of him. After a while they moved on.

They did, however, see more evidence of human habitation: they crossed the cistern on a path of wooden pallets which led out to the center where a wall of plastic crates gave some privacy to what looked like an improvised bedroom: a rocking chair, mattress, and bedside table were set out (also on pallets, to keep them out of the water). A few stray splashes and a knocked over crate suggested it had been vacated in a hurry.

"Sewer people," Jill remarked. "I remember reading about this once. They have them in New York City and Paris, too."

"Homeless buggers, drunks and junkies," Selene said. "Perfect for vampire fodder."

"But wouldn't they . . . um . . . *notice?*" Jill asked, carefully stepping around the bed.

"Surprisingly, a lot of people don't." Selene checked behind a wall made of flattened cardboard boxes. "This way."

"Sorry, *what?*"

"Vampires have ways of . . . altering a person's conscious state," Clara said. "We don't fully understand it."

"For obvious reasons," Selene added dryly.

A part of her, Jill realized, was becoming more and more alarmed at their situation. It was pointing out how they were walking into the territory of an unknown entity, whose powers she did not fully comprehend. But it was drowned out by the rest of her, which was so skeptical that she dearly wanted to prove Selene and Clara's outrageous claims false—or, excitingly, *true.* This part was having such a difficult time grasping the idea of vampires—as Selene and Clara described them—as real things, that the idea of being attacked by one registered as a probability of something like getting hit by lightning or eaten by a shark. It could happen, sure, but it was so unlikely she was having a hard time taking her fears seriously.

Mostly, she was so very curious.

There was a wide streak of wetness coming out of a tunnel that opened some three feet above the cistern's floor. This was not running water, but merely wet concrete where water had been left by the passage of someone with wet feet. After examination, Selene announced they had been coming *out* of the tunnel—the opposite direction from which Jill's group was headed.

"We go in," Clara said, sounding resigned.

They did, and encountered more water on the floor. It smelled old and stale, but not particularly vile. Some of it had been splashed along the tunnel walls, as if someone had run down the tunnel in a hurry.

They found the remains of another homestead about thirty yards in. This one had been merely a collection of blankets and old cushions on cinderblocks, but now they were scattered and soaked in the water.

"Where did everyone go?" Jill wondered aloud.

"Better question," said Selene. "*Why* did everyone leave?"

They continued up the tunnel in close formation, Clara walking sideways so she could keep an eye out behind them. She was so near that her left elbow kept bumping into Jill's back. For her part, Jill kept stepping on Selene's heels. She stopped apologizing after it appeared the hunter was more annoyed by her whispered *Sorry*'s than she was by the physical distraction.

Then, quite abruptly, Selene stopped. A moment later she shut off her light.

They stood perfectly still, and in the dark they heard it.

Voices, raised in argument.

Too faint for the words to be made out, the tones spoke clearly enough on their own. They echoed so it was almost impossible to tell where one voice ended and another began, and as the group inched closer it became apparent that there were, in fact, *many* voices, all raised in protest.

Words solidified out of the chaos of sound. Someone said:

"We outnumber *and* outgun him—we could just—"

Someone else said:

"Have you *seen* his guards?"

"*Yeah,* but he's not gonna be stupid enough to come down here on his own. Besides, they're *human!*"

"The brothers *Gunn* were human," said a sharp and scratchy voice, cutting through the others with an ease born of absolute authority.

"Only *one* of them," mumbled a voice, quickly hushed.

"What I am trying to make you dead-brainers understand is that the fight for our rightful place—not least our *continued existence*—has been brought to a head by the unacceptably rash actions of a *certain individual,* and unless you get your acts in line we are all . . . "

The speaker trailed off. There was a sound of many voices speaking in undertones together.

Jill felt Selene, who was in front of her, reach past her in the dark. She must have given some physical signal to Clara, because all of a sudden Jill felt large, strong hands on her shoulders, and she was being gently dragged backwards.

And because Jill had never received any sort of combat training, and because she was mostly thinking about setting eyes on the owners of the voices, she said out loud:

"What are you *doing?*"

Only the first three words got out properly because Clara clapped a hand over her mouth and it came out more like:

"What are you *doimph—*"

Something big dropped from the ceiling of the tunnel between Jill and Selene. It made a splash as its feet hit the water, and she felt something cold, very much like a hand, land on her face.

The fingers tightened.

Selene's flashlight, when it went on, nearly blinded her. It *did* blind the person who had a grip on her face that was quickly becoming painful.

With a slither of metal against leather and then a dull *thunk*, the hand came away at once.

By the slanting light of the torch Jill saw a man in a black, button-down shirt and tight leather-looking pants. He had skin so pale it was almost greenish in places, and currently he had Clara's sword sticking out of his chest.

It looked *wrong* somehow. Jill's mind told her it must be a trick—like those fake swords that are broken off halfway down the blade so actors can hold them against their bodies and make it *look* like they'd been stabbed. But she knew Clara had a real, long, and very sharp sword—not to mention she was certainly strong enough to drive it into someone's chest.

Then it clicked: the man was not bleeding. There was a sword driven clean through his sternum and his shirt was torn, but he was not bleeding.

In fact, he was hardly moving either. He stared at them blankly. Then Selene stepped up and, taking out a huge knife—almost like a meat cleaver—swung it at his neck.

The knife met the spine and stopped. Selene yanked it out and struck again. And again. On the fourth stroke the man's head sort of lolled off to the side, and Selene grabbed it by the hair and tore it away.

Clara removed her sword, and the body crumpled into the water.

Jill found her heart was pounding, her head felt like she'd done a dozen somersaults in a row, and she'd forgotten to inhale.

She took a deep breath. The first words out of her mouth were:

"But I wanted to *talk* to a vampire!"

Clara gave her a look like she wasn't certain she didn't want to stab Jill next, and Selene rolled her eyes.

"He tried to bite your head off," she said. "I don't think he'd have talked to you even if we asked nicely."

"Retreating," said Clara.

"What?" said Jill.

"That's what we're doing," Clara said. "We're *retreating*. Now come, the others will have heard us."

They ran. They only got about twenty feet before another dark shape lunged at them from out of what Jill had thought was a sheer wall.

"Ass *hat!*" Selene screamed, firing her gun in the direction of the body even as Jill and Clara dove for the ground. "Clara, we got a shifter!"

"Not for long," Clara growled through gritted teeth.

Jill knew better than to ask what a shifter was. She huddled on the ground, the water seeping up the back of her jeans, with her knees in her chest, while the fight went on above and around her. The tunnel suddenly filled with smoke, cold and smelling of stone tombs. It was such a different smell than the dull musk of the drains that for a moment it was almost refreshing. Then it abruptly solidified into a human shape, and the next moment the sharp end of Clara's sword exploded from its chest.

This time the vampire was not paralyzed. It struggled, kicked, and nearly writhed itself off the sword. Before it could break free, however, Clara's other hand, which now held a wicked-looking knife, appeared by its face and stabbed repeatedly into its throat.

Clara did not so much cut the creature's head off as shred its neck, and it wobbled sickly for a while, until with a rip and a crunch, Clara managed to tear the head off.

Jill found herself bracketed closely by the two women, each with their back to her and retreating slowly down the tunnel. Jill tripped and crawled as best she could, trying to ignore the echoing gunfire that Selene was using to cover their retreat, but every shot sent a shudder through her body and made her ears ring.

Clara said something, but it was lost in a bang from Freddie.

"Say what?" said Selene as she reloaded.

"Hold your fire," Clara said. "They aren't following us."

"H-how do you know that?" Jill gasped.

"Because they are in front of us," Clara said.

They had reached the end of the tunnel and emerged into the wide cistern where they had met the sewer dweller before. Now, as Selene shined her beam around the vast cavern, it illuminated a crowd of pale-faced people. They ranged in age from late teens to early forties, but few of them had graying hair or showed signs of extreme age. They were dressed in a variety of clothes, some of them rather old fashioned, but mostly in dark combinations of black and blue. They were predominantly white, Jill noted with interest, though there were a few people whose whiteness was tinged with a warmer green, whom she guessed might have been Latino or Asian, judging by their features.

They were, as one, staring at them with eyes that glinted red in the beam of the flashlight. In their center was a small woman with a mess of auburn hair. Unlike the majority, she showed noticeable signs of age in her withered face, and though she was barely taller than Jill, she stood in such a powerful way (legs apart with her hands on her hips) that it was clear she was the most important individual present.

"*Now* can I t-talk to them?" Jill stuttered.

"I think the time for your kind of talking is past, hon," Selene said, putting a firm hand on Jill's shoulder. Leaning in she whispered: "Keep your back to the wall and your head down. There is a chance we might not all die here."

"But—" Jill began.

"Either you two are the *dumbest* hunters I've ever met," said the withered woman with auburn hair. "Or that mundane is paying you *way* too much."

"I am Claymore Nordstern," Clara said, and Jill, despite her growing horror, started at the use of her real name. The large woman gestured casually with her knife hand at Selene, who was holding Freddie under the crook of her arm and the cleaver knife in the other. "This is Selene Shields."

The lead vampire twitched her head to the side and back again, her wire-thin mouth cracked into a sort of grimace. "Oh, so you want to do this the *old-fashioned* way," she said with a sneer. "Well, you can call me Martha, and these here . . ." she nodded at the assembled crowd around her. "*These* are my babies."

"Very well," Clara said. It sounded like she was passing sentence. "Martha. We did not come here hunting. We will leave in peace if you allow us."

Martha shook her head, sending her hair tossing. "Too late for that. You've already killed two of my brood."

"Because they *attacked* me!" Jill gasped. "We're *very* sorry!"

Selene groaned.

Martha laughed.

"Funny kid you've got there," she said. "Thanks for giving me the only good laugh I've had all week." She made a clicking noise in the back of her throat, and jerked a thumb in Clara's direction. "Get 'em," she said, her grating voice a low rasp.

The vampires moved so fast they blurred around the edges. Jill saw one come practically flying at Clara, and the big woman went over sideways under the force of the impact. She was up again in an instant and beating the thing back with her sword, but by that time they were already encircled in a ring of sneering white faces. Selene and Clara closed, back to back around Jill, their weapons at the ready.

There was a flurry of action: Freddie went off practically in Jill's ear, and Clara grunted under the force of a vampire slamming into her. Jill had the sense to duck down, covering her ears with her hands, even as a vampire went sailing above her head. This one landed on Clara's shoulders, and she saw the vampire, his mouth opened wide, and there was a strange, gleaming fluid dripping from his snakelike fangs.

Something thick and dark ripped through the air. It cleaved the head off the vampire that was menacing Selene, and neatly bisected the one riding on Clara's shoulders. As always there was no blood, but Jill still felt her stomach give a little turn at the sight of the upper half of the vampire, his eyes still blinking in confusion, as the pale gray innards slowly distended from his severed waist.

Clara didn't hesitate. She brought her sword around in a clean arc and mercilessly hacked his head off.

And then there was a strange silence. Selene swept her light over the room, only to discover a wide swath of headless vampire corpses where before a small army had stood.

The only one still standing was the auburn-haired vampire, Martha, and she was held in the firm grip of a tall, pale man with lank, black hair. He wore sagging, worn-out jeans and a threadbare t-shirt.

The two exchanged words, too quiet for Jill to make out, and then with a neat flick of his wrist the man decapitated the auburn-haired woman with his fingernails. Her body fell to the ground, but her head remained, hanging by its hair from the man's other hand. He appeared to study it thoughtfully, and then tossed it aside with an uncaring shrug. He glanced at them, and gave them a rueful sort of smile.

"Sorry," he said. "I had to wait for them to be distracted. Thank you for that."

And, though his eyes were red now instead of yellow, and his fangs were much smaller and infinitely more wicked, Jill recognized him.

As one, Clara and Selene moved to close in on him, weapons at the ready.

"Stop that *at once!*" Jill screamed, and they froze out of pure surprise.

The man, who Jill was increasingly certain was actually Johnny Bathory, dusted vampire corpse off his hands and turned to leave.

"Wait!" Jill cried, running after him. She avoided Selene's grasping hands and made it a few more feet before Clara caught her in an iron grip.

Johnny Bathory—it really *was* him—paused and turned back to look at her quizzically.

"*What?*" he asked.

"You—" Jill found she had to gasp rather hard to force the words out. "Why did *you* kill them?"

Johnny Bathory looked around at the mayhem of corpses as if surprised to see them there. "Do I need to give you a reason?" he asked. His voice was deeper than Jill remembered from the interviews. Richer and fuller, with a slight twist to the ends of his words that suggested a foreign accent heavily diluted by use of American English.

"Why did you kill *them* and not *us?*" Jill forged on.

"What, do you *want* me to?" Johnny Bathory pivoted on one heel and began to saunter toward them.

Clara's hold on Jill's arm tightened, and she raised her sword.

Johnny Bathory gave the weapon a disdainful look, and sneered so that one fang was clearly visible against his red tongue.

"No, *no*," Jill said. "I just—I want to *understand* . . . uh . . . you. Vampires. I . . . I just have some questions."

Johnny Bathory came up to the very edge of Clara's sword range, and then leaned in.

"Are you asking me for an *interview?*" he asked, a sly smile creeping up his face. Up close Jill could see his skin was pockmarked with old acne scars, and there was a thin line of perfectly white tissue running up from the neckline of his shirt and over his chin.

"I ... guess?" Jill said uncertainly.

Johnny Bathory straightened up, turned, and began walking away again.

"Three p.m.," he said. "Today. The backstage-pass signup area. Come *alone*," he added, flashing a grin over his shoulder at Selene and Clara. "Wear something *nice*."

He disappeared into the shadows, melting away like ink into dark water, and then they were alone in the field of dead vampires.

Jill was shaken. She insisted she was shaken, and Selene believed her. She had a little difficulty believing Jill was not in shock as well as she coolly went over all the vampire bodies, measuring and tagging them and taking clippings of their hair and fingernails—even scrapings of their skin.

But for once she was not interested in taking any actual dead bodies with them.

"We will notify Officer Dunes," she said with grim satisfaction. "He should know about this." And she would not stop badgering Clara until she gave her the policeman's direct number. Jill called him as soon as they got out of the drain and left a terse message. Then she had Selene drive her back to the hotel where she took a very long shower.

When she finally emerged, dripping but clean and wrapped in one of the Castle's princess-style bathrobes, there was a hard glint in her eye that set off warning bells inside Selene's head.

"You can't be seriously considering that psycho's offer?" she blurted out.

Jill looked up and frowned at her.

"I asked him for an interview," she said with a shrug. "He said *yes*. I *finally* have a shot at interviewing a vampire. I *have* to go ..." She gave a little start, as if coming out of a daze. "I have to go *alone*," she finished.

Selene slowly raised her eyebrows, in the manner of one watching someone realize the obvious.

"*Ye*-ah," she said. "That's *kind* of a deal breaker."

"No," said Jill, going over to her suitcase and fishing through its contents. "No, no. I have to go anyway. I may never get a better chance."

"Your life will be *filled* with better chances!" Selene assured her. "Clara," she tried, turning to the large woman who had been sitting, silent, in a corner. "*Talk* to her. You tell her!"

Clara chewed thoughtfully on her lower lip.

"Clara ... " Selene said in a warning tone.

Clara shifted uncomfortably. "Johnny Bathory is unusual in many respects," she said.

Jill paused. "You don't think he's a good example?" she said with a frown.

Clara seemed confused by this. "Not at all. What I mean is . . . there *is* a chance he will not kill you on principle, as any other vampire would."

"Oh, so there's a *small* chance?" Selene said, covering her face in her hands. "Well, *that* makes it all right. Look, Jill, I won't stop you doing what you feel you need to do. I'm your bodyguard, not your babysitter, but I'm telling you girl, it's gonna be a lot harder to keep you alive if you don't even let us *do our jobs*."

"I understand," Jill said, pulling out a black sweater, holding it up, frowning, and then tossing it aside. "And I am open to any pieces of *practical* advice you may have to offer."

Selene threw her hands in the air, in the imitation of an explosion, and stomped off into the bathroom. Clara did one of her inverted shrugs.

"Wear white," she said.

"What?" said Jill.

"Wear white," said Clara.

"I don't think I even *own* any white clothes that aren't *underwear* . . ." Jill began.

"It doesn't have to be clothes," Clara allowed. "But Johnny Bathory is granting you a truce. You should show that you are conscious of the honor."

"You've been accused by members of the Christian church of being . . . well, basically of being the spawn of the devil. That you're intentionally corrupting today's young people into being . . . what did that one fellow say?"

"Minions of Satan," Johnny Bathory said with a wry smile.

"That's right," said the interviewer. "What do you have to say in response to that?"

"I really don't know, actually. I mean, what *can* you say to that? Do they want me to say sorry or something? I mean, I guess I could say that, but I wouldn't mean it. I'd keep on doing what I'm doing. And being a minion of Satan, I think, really isn't so bad. I mean, you read the Bible, look at all the horrible things God has done, all the horrible things *His* minions have done, and you compare that to Satan . . . I dunno, I almost feel like the Devil is the better one. At least he's *honest* about being evil."

The interviewer laughed nervously. "But what do you say to people who accuse you of corrupting today's youth? Of introducing them to the sex, drugs and rock 'n' roll lifestyle?"

"Look," said Johnny Bathory, adjusting himself in his chair. "I'm not corrupting or introducing anyone to anything. What I try to do with my music—what I've always tried to do—is to give a voice to the people who have no voices, or who haven't been heard. When I'm up there performing, I'm not just performing for . . . *at* the audience. I really am performing *for* them. I think every one of my fans would do what I do if they could, but they can't, so *I* do it *for* them. I do it for all of us. And if that looks ugly or scary, well, maybe you should worry more about what's being done to these kids in school or at church or at their jobs than the stupid stuff that's coming out of my mouth."

Jill stood in the baking hot afternoon Nevada sun and felt horribly out of place. She'd ended up digging out her last remaining pair of jeans that didn't have rips, tears or stains on them, and pulled on the most edgy top she owned. This was a black, strappy, spandex exercise top with a shelf bra that never failed to make Jill feel like a flat-chested boy. Tied around her waist with the ends hanging to her knees was a strip of white cloth—actually torn from one of the Castle's bedsheets. She wore a pair of running shoes (Selene had insisted) and no makeup.

She stood in line with hundreds of other young women in sheer black outfits and elaborate face paint, and felt more and more uncomfortable. Like the rest of them she'd been given a yellow wristband with a number on it as soon as she arrived and said she wanted to enter for a backstage pass, but aside from that she could not have looked more different.

They all wore heels, for a start, and most of them were in strategically ripped pantyhose. Many were in corsets—black shiny ones or velvet red—and they all had heavily decorated faces. Some of these designs were clearly modeled after Johnny Bathory, others were more standard Goth, while others seemed to have tried to come up with designs of their own, with more or less success.

They were all very excited and intent, and talked among one another in cliques of threes and fours. Jill caught snatches of conversation like . . .

"This is my fifth concert . . . "

"You lucky cow!"

"Is it true he picks the winners *personally*?"

"You mean we actually get to *see* him? *Eee!*"

Jill stood alone, letting the motion of the crowd push and pull at her, felt hotter and hotter, and wondered if this had been one great setup. The vampires in the sewers seemed a long way away now she was in the hot sun surrounded by ordinary (if extraordinarily dressed) humans. She was glad Selene and Clara had been made to wait out front, where they couldn't see her.

Slowly the sun went down and the pavement cooled. It cooled so much Jill was glad Selene had made her bring a coat. She put it on.

A little before seven, after she had been standing on increasingly sore feet for almost four hours, there was a hum of excited conversation near the front of the crowd, and slowly the line of people began to move. They shuffled forward and down a side street and finally filed into the back lot of the hotel. Just after Jill passed under the archway sign—"Castle Back Lot, registered vehicles only"—there was a commotion behind her, and she looked back to find a couple of burly men in black t-shirts rolling the gate closed, much to the consternation of those shut out. Then she slammed into the person in front of her and stopped. The lot was packed beyond capacity, with people pressed in and up against one another. Jill, wedged against a woman in a corset and a feathered headdress on one side and the cool metal of the gate on the other, was comparatively lucky.

In the harsh yellow floodlights, she saw a little stage at the other end of the lot, up against the side of the hotel. High enough to be visible above the heads of the crowd, it stood below a rusty and battered iron door onto which had peen painted "PRIVATE" in big letters. Two more burly and humorless men in black t-shirts stood flanking it, and more were arranged in a human barricade around the base of the stage.

There was an excited hum as a small man in ripped jeans and a dirty t-shirt stepped out of the door. He wore a backwards baseball cap with his plain sandy hair sticking out beneath it. He held a clipboard, and as Jill watched, he took a cordless microphone out of his back pocket and tapped it.

There was a dull *pthud pthud* sound from all the speakers arrayed around the parking lot.

"Good evening ladies," he said in a pleasant and surprisingly British voice. He squinted into the crowd. "And . . . gentlemen. Yes, there are some gentlemen here, lovely, how nice to see you all. So, as you can probably tell I . . . am not Johnny Bathory. In fact, it's not at all important who I am, just what I'm about to tell you. Now, as some of you have doubtless done this before . . . "

There was scattered laughter from the crowd.

" . . . you are probably already aware of the rules. But I must ask you to please be quiet and listen, as we may have some backstage virgins and we want them to understand this, don't we?"

The crowd mumbled assent. Jill rose on tiptoe for a better look.

The man with the microphone held up the clipboard with a flourish and began to read dramatically.

"In order to qualify for a backstage pass, you *must* be wearing that little yellow wristband we gave you when you arrived. You must also step up onto the stage if you are chosen. We have some kind men to help you do this if you require assistance.

"You must *not* scream too loudly, since I need to hear what Johnny tells me and 'sides it hurts me ears. You must also not rush this little stage area, or throw anything—including yourself—at Mr. Bathory. As soon as you rush the stage or toss *anything* toward it he goes back inside and *no one* gets to come backstage.

"There will be five *and only five* backstagers chosen. You cannot bring a plus one, you cannot bring cameras or phones or any recording devices. We will hold these items in a secure place if you are chosen, don't worry, but you *cannot* bring them with you backstage.

"You *may* give gifts . . . to one of the nice gentlemen down here. Because Johnny goes straight from here to his warm up he cannot accept gifts. If you are chosen, and you have a gift that is small, you may present it to him after the show. If he does not pick his five from you lot here, you will be dismissed and a new batch shown in.

"Now, are there any questions?" the man asked.

Jill put her hand up immediately, to ask if having a notebook and pen was also not allowed. She'd thought ahead and brought one, in case they did take her phone.

It seemed, however, that questions were answered based on how loudly they were shouted. Near the front someone screamed: "When do we get to see Johnny?!"

"That's a very good question," said the man, grinning. "I'm so glad you asked that. Because the answer is . . . you get to see him . . . *now!*"

The roar was so loud Jill had to clap her hands over her ears, and she winced, looking down. Because of this she missed the moment when Johnny Bathory actually appeared, but she assumed he'd come through the same battered old door as the man, because when she looked up there he was.

He was wearing a pair of tight-fitting black underwear, black leather chaps, boots with one-inch soles and four-inch heels, a lot of makeup and a long leather coat with a collar that stuck up behind his head. His hair stood wildly on end, and the deep black rings around his eyes made the yellow irises stand out in a ghoulish way. Or made him look a little like a raccoon, Jill thought.

He looked exactly like he did in interviews and performances, and nothing like the man Jill had seen earlier in the drains. It was only his body language—the set of his shoulders and the careful way he walked in those ridiculous shoes—and the particular shape of his chin and nose under all that paint that convinced her this was the same person.

Johnny Bathory did not speak; he walked from one end of the stage to the other, one hand resting contemplatively on his chin.

The attention of the crowd went with him; Jill felt the other people sway around her as they leaned toward the man on the stage with every fiber of their being. She wondered how he would do the picking. Would she have to wait until the last name was called? Was this whole thing a setup?

Johnny Bathory looked out over the crowd, but Jill could not tell whether he was looking at them or merely gazing off over their heads.

Then he raised a hand and pointed one black-painted nail into the crowd.

The girl next to Jill screamed. It was a scream of excitement and exultation, and Jill felt as though her eardrums might have ruptured.

As suddenly as the scream came, it cut off abruptly; Johnny Bathory was shaking his head, *and still pointing.*

In a daze Jill realized he was pointing at her.

Cautiously she raised her hand and waved.

Johnny Bathory nodded.

The crowd around her erupted in cheers, and the girl who had screamed before turned to Jill and gave her a wet-faced hug. In the way of crowds they opened before her and pushed from behind, forcing her to the front where one of the humorless men gave her a leg up on stage.

Jill scrambled to her feet, glad of her sensible shoes, and stood in a daze. She was aware of Johnny Bathory standing mere feet from her, and of the thick crowd of faces below, but only in the most general sense. She realized now the reason they could see Bathory so easily in the dim twilight was because there was a spotlight pointed at the stage, and now it was shining right in her face. How Bathory could see to pick his backstagers was beyond her.

One of the men by the door led her helpfully to a white line painted on the stage, and put her at one end of it. There she stood while Johnny Bathory picked his remaining four. These were in turn cheered, pushed up to the stage, and came to stand next to Jill.

They were an odd assortment. One was a lovely, teenaged girl dressed in a lacy black short skirt and corset, striped stockings and a tiny hat, affixed to her head with numerous pins. She was also, Jill noted with distant surprise, an amputee; her left arm ended in a stump just below her elbow. She'd decorated it with red paint so for a moment it looked as though her arm had just been bitten off. She was quivering with excitement when she came to stand on the line, and kept whispering, "*Oh my god. Oh my god. Ohmygod . . .*" under her breath.

The third to be chosen Jill thought was an especially tall woman, until she got up to the stage and turned out to be a tall, fine-boned man in remarkably good drag. He wore an overbust corset and fishnet tights and improbably red pumps. He was laughing deliriously and hugged the one-armed girl when he came to join them.

The fourth was a punkish young woman covered in tattoos with a fluffy bleached mohawk. The fifth was a comparatively ordinary woman in ripped jeans and a Johnny Bathory t-shirt. She had a nose piercing and wore horn-rimmed glasses.

When they were all assembled, Johnny Bathory walked up and down in front of them, as if surveying stock he was about to take home from market.

Jill kept thinking about how he'd decapitated the vampire in the sewer. *With a flick of his wrist.*

Then he smiled at them, a leering grin so over the top Jill went back to feeling this was just a show, something exciting and fun for the fans of a rock star.

"See you later," he whispered in his weak, hoarse voice, and exited the stage.

They did not follow him. They waited on the stage while the lot slowly emptied, and then they were led around to the side and taken in through a door marked Staff Entrance Only.

Somehow Jill had forgotten about the concert. Between what had happened in the drain and the shock of being physically pulled up on stage, she had wanted the whole ordeal to be over with so much that she'd assumed they'd be taken straight to the dressing room or something.

But no. They were led through a narrow corridor with naked pipes running overhead, up some stairs and then through another door marked Stage Mait. Here a friendly tech came up and collected their phones and cameras into a little black lockbox, and they were shown to a set of five folding chairs that looked out on a strange landscape of boxes, cables and platforms constructed of pipe and black-painted wood.

It took Jill a moment to realize they were looking at the stage—from the *side*.

"Wouldn't want you to miss the show," their guide said with a chuckle as they took their seats.

Jill sank gratefully into the nearest chair available, while her fellow backstagers squealed with excitement and fairly shivered into their seats.

The pre-show started not long after that. It was all very loud, even though they sat behind the biggest speakers and so were not subjected to the full blast of sound the regular audience received. If she craned her neck Jill could just see them: a crowd of people pressed against the human wall of security down at the foot of the stage, and more in the boxes above her head.

Then the band came onstage and the noise fairly doubled. It was hard to see the band from this angle—Johnny Bathory was mostly eclipsed by his guitarist, and the keyboardist was half hidden behind the drummer's stand. The other backstagers didn't seem to mind this: they whooped and hollered with the rest of the audience, and Jill joined in. At first she did it so that she would not raise suspicion, but after a while she began to actually *listen* to the music, and found herself genuinely applauding after every song.

It was not pleasant music. It was dramatic music. It was not relaxing or soothing: it was hard-edged and heart pounding. But the songs, as they were arranged, seemed to have some internal narrative and kept Jill's attention, ever after she had to cover her ears from the sheer volume.

Johnny Bathory did not just sing: he danced, he kicked and strutted. After a while his jacket came off, and then his chaps. He danced around in just the underwear for a while (extra loud screaming from the contingent backstage) before he disappeared down a trapdoor in the stage floor.

The next time he appeared he was wearing what looked like a ragged evening dress with shreds of cloth hanging down below his feet, and he was being lowered by wires out of the rafters from the ceiling. He held his arms out stiffly to either side, looking like a well-used children's doll.

As soon as he hit the stage a grip in black ran up and unhooked something from his back, and he began to dance and sing once more.

The dress came off him in pieces over the course of the next few songs. Jill wondered if they had to get a new dress every night, or if it was a special one that you could take apart and put back together again. Underneath it he wore a corset that seemed to be mostly made of belts, tight black underwear, and thigh-high leather boots with stiletto heels.

He finished the performance in those heels, something Jill watched with numb fascination, her feet hurting just to look at the way he jumped and slid around.

After a particularly long and rambling song, the show ended. The audience roared. The curtain came down, and in the dark there was a muddled thumping and the sound of a person in high heels staggering past them.

"For the love of all hell," someone said. "Turn on the stupid light, Jerry."

The light came on, and there was the band. Jill got one glimpse of the five men in various stages of makeup and undress before the other back-stagers mobbed them.

She stood awkwardly on the edge of the crowd, uncertain what to do. Fortunately a couple of burly stage hands intervened and herded them all down some stairs and along a corridor.

Someone was fairly shrieking "Johnny, Johnny, *Johnny!*" and there was the sound of laughing and giggling. Then they were bundled into a huge lift.

"Is this the *service* elevator?" someone asked.

One of the band members—the keyboardist, Jill thought—huffed a laugh and said: "Believe it or not, it's the best ride in the place. No one else gets to use this lift!"

It was a large elevator, but Jill was crammed into a corner by the crowd. It also moved incredibly slowly: there was no feeling of being pulled upward, and the only assurance she had that they were moving at all was the lighted display that told them they were on Floor 5 . . . Floor 6 . . . Floor 7 . . .

Jill sank to a crouch in her corner, concentrating on watching the progression of floors, and trying to ignore the increasing ruckus of the band and their fans.

It was at Floor 38—the very top of the building—that the elevator finally stopped and the doors opened. The whole crowd tumbled out, leaving Jill to drift in their wake.

This floor was even more opulent than the others, with tapestries on the wall and a thick, soft carpet. The window at the far end of the corridor showed a glimpse of the lights of the Strip.

"You Miss Hamilton?" a deep voice asked from several feet above her. She turned to find a dour black man in modest jeans and a black t-shirt with "MINION" in big white letters waiting patiently beside the elevator.

"Um . . . yes?" she said.

"You go this way," he said, and led her down the corridor, turning at the window, to where it dead ended in a door. Using a card key on a chain he unlocked it and held it open while she drifted inside. The door shut with a soft *click* behind her.

Jill found herself alone then, in what must have been the Castle's Presidential Suite.

It was enormous, with steps leading down from the door and out into a spacious lounge area. There was a wet bar beside a floor-to-ceiling window, and plump, fluffy couches and chairs set out around a heavy wooden table. There was a display of waxily perfect dahlias there, the color of dark red wine.

As Jill wandered further out into the room she noted several other doors leading off it. One was left ajar, and through it she glimpsed a room with an enormous four-poster bed in the center of it. Around a corner where the wall protruded into the room, she saw there was a kitchenette, with a bowl of fruit set out on the counter. The bowl had little lion feet on it, like the ones sometimes found on old-fashioned bathtubs.

"It is a bit contrived, isn't it?" said a hoarse voice from behind her.

She turned, and found Johnny Bathory just shutting the door to the bedroom. He was still mostly in costume: leather underwear and thigh-high, stiletto-heeled boots. The corset he'd been wearing at the end of the show was unlaced but still clung resolutely around his waist. His makeup—white with heavy, dark eyeliner and a black stripe that covered his chin and lower lip—looked a bit smudged. Unless that was intentional. Jill couldn't tell.

"I'm sorry?" she said, finding her voice at last.

Johnny Bathory gestured at the room.

"It's typical Las Vegas, isn't it? Trying to be like something else, only entertaining. So it winds up being *nothing like* what it's trying to imitate."

His voice had dropped. Now it sounded more like it had earlier, in the sewer: deeper, rougher, and with a slight twinge to the ends of his words that suggested some well-smothered accent, too faint for Jill to recognize. She thought it suited him much better.

"I guess," she said, backing and turning as the man advanced into the room. He fumbled with something behind his back and then pulled the corset off, tossing it onto a nearby chair. Then he went and sat in it and began un-strapping his boots.

"It's sort of tragic, I think. I mean, spending all this time trying to re-mind people of something real, when the real thing is so much better you couldn't possibly hope to top it. Best they do is *remind* people of the real thing, and all those people think is how crappy their model is."

He kicked his boots off and stood up, rolling down the fishnet stockings that were revealed beneath them. Jill wondered if she should look away.

Johnny Bathory didn't seem to care. He stripped off the stockings, draping them over the back of the chair, and walked past her in nothing but his underwear to another door, which turned out to lead to a bath-room. He left it open behind him, and a few seconds later the leather un-derwear sailed out of it and landed next to the boots. Then there was the sound of running water and some splashing.

"Have you eaten yet?" he asked from the bathroom.

Jill was at this point so nervous the very thought of food made her feel like vomiting. But she hadn't eaten all afternoon, and was feeling a little shaky. Unless that was the nerves, too.

"No ... er ... but I'm not hungry," she said.

The water shut off. Johnny Bathory came out wearing a towel and nothing else. He had a damp cloth in one hand, and was scraping makeup out from behind his ears. His wet hair hung limply at his shoulders. He had an odd sort of tattoo above his left bicep. It looked like it had once been a circle with something inside, but it was ripped and scarred, black around the edges. It reminded Jill a little of the death marks the unicorns had used, only rougher and older.

"I only asked," he said, "because the Castle caters dinner for us every night. I usually give my share to the bouncers, but I figured ... " He made a shrugging motion at Jill. "It's not like *I* can eat it."

Casually he reached into his mouth and, with a small popping noise, took out a set of dentures. Underneath them his teeth appeared a little crooked and yellow, but not otherwise extraordinary. He put the discarded dentures on the coffee table—Jill saw they were indeed the oversized vampire fangs he displayed in interviews—and wandered off into the master bedroom.

"What ... cr ... *do you eat?*" Jill asked quaveringly.

The rummaging sounds from the bedroom stopped, and Johnny Bathory stuck his head back out. Without the makeup his face looked astonishingly plain, apart from the prominent acne pockmarks and pale scar. He was not a particularly handsome man—his face was a little too long, his eyes a little too deep set—but without the radical face paint he didn't look like someone Jill would have paid any notice to on the street.

Now one eyebrow was raised in surprise.

"You really need to ask *me*?" he said. "Surely your sword and shield could have told you *that* at least."

"They are secondary sources," Jill said. "And I meant ... specifics. Like ... how do you ... *feed?*"

Johnny Bathory's whole face seemed to droop in disappointment. "You don't have to talk about it like it's something *dirty*," he said, a little reproachfully. "We all do it."

His head disappeared into the bedroom and Jill was left standing awkwardly in the main room. Belatedly she remembered her pen and notepad, and got them out and wrote down a heading.

Interview w/ J Bathory, vampire
Notes ...

She was chewing on the end of her pen when Johnny Bathory came out of the bedroom. He was wearing a pair of frayed, brown corduroy pants and a t-shirt with a faded print of a dragon's head on it. His hair, neatly combed, was pulled back into a ponytail, and he was barefoot. He looked ... well, he looked a little nerdy, Jill thought.

Except for the eyes. He had taken out the yellow contacts, and now his irises were vibrantly red, and even more unnerving.

In long, loose strides he crossed the room to the kitchenette. He took two glasses from a cupboard above the sink, then paused.

"Just water for me," Jill said hastily.

Bathory shrugged, filled one glass with water from the tap, then opened the freezer and took out some ice.

"Usually, I don't," he said.

At Jill's befuddled expression he smiled a little and added: "Feed, I mean. On blood, anyway. I don't need much anymore. But as tonight is a special occasion ..." He opened the refrigerator, and there was a clink of glass as he pulled out a bottle of dark, viscous liquid. Twisting the lid off he poured himself half a glass and stuck it in the microwave.

"I love these things," he said, tapping the humming machine. "Time was I had to re-heat the stuff over a fire. It's not bad chilled," he allowed. "But room temperature?" he made a face Jill recognized from the show, twisting his mouth and sticking his tongue out so that the tip nearly touched his chin.

"You don't ... um ... prefer it ... fresh?" Jill asked in a small voice.

"Of course," Bathory said with a shrug. "But fresh as in spurting from someone's neck?" He shuddered. "That's just ... rude. And a bit sloppy, between you and me."

"Ah," said Jill, making a note in her book. Now that they were talking and she had so far not been attacked, she was beginning to get her confidence back. "There are some sources that imply there is a ... um ... *sexual* connotation to your method of feeding, is that true at all?"

Johnny Bathory made a stifled choking noise, and his shoulders shook. He shot Jill a deprecating grin.

"That, I can only imagine, is entirely a *human* invention," he said. "From my experience, vampires don't fetishize their feeding habits any more than humans do. I'm not saying there aren't vampires who *do* but ... if there *is* a sexual connotation, it's mostly in *your* heads, not ours."

"Interesting," muttered Jill, writing this down. "And can you subsist on the blood of other organisms?"

"Okay, first, it's not the blood." The microwave beeped and Johnny Bathory took his glass out. He stirred the contents with a spoon and blew on it. "Not ... in the nutritional sense. We *are* technically dead. We don't have a pulse. We don't have an active digestive system. We don't even need to *breathe*. I only got into a habit of it because it's hard to sing otherwise. And it helps to suspend people's disbelief."

"That ... you're a vampire?" Jill asked.

"That I'm a human *pretending* to be a vampire," Johnny Bathory said. He held out the glass of water and ice.

Forcing her legs to work, Jill walked stiffly over. She took the glass, trying to avoid touching him without looking like it. Bathory just grinned at her with his yellow, crooked teeth, his red eyes gleaming, and raised his own glass.

"Cheers," he said, and knocked back the contents in a single gulp.

Jill sipped her water thoughtfully. The coolness in her mouth was a pleasant physical anchor.

"How *does* it work, then?" she asked.

Johnny Bathory laughed, but he looked a little sad. "That's the . . . what do you call it? Sixty-four thousand dollar question." He moved past Jill and back out into the living room, where he sat down in the biggest chair, folding one leg comfortably beneath him. He gestured to the couch oppo-site. "Please sit down," he said. "You look like a stiff breeze could knock you over."

Reluctantly Jill came and sat down on the edge of the couch, putting her glass on the table next to Bathory's discarded dentures. She held her pad and pen protectively in front of her chest.

"As best I can tell," Bathory said after thinking a minute, "it's about the energy. Blood carries life: living cells and with them the means to keep the body to which it belongs alive. *That's* what we feed on; that pure life force. Does that answer your question?"

"It is useful information," Jill said, scribbling on her pad. She glanced up to find Johnny Bathory looking at her with an odd, intent expression. She couldn't tell if it was more like the way a cat watches a bird in the grass, or the way a horse freezes at the sight of a potential predator.

"What else," Bathory said—and this time Jill noticed how he had to inhale before he spoke—"what else did you want to know?"

Jill tapped the end of her pen against her pad of paper. "As much as you can tell me," she said frankly. "I'd also like to take some . . . um . . . physical measurements."

Johnny Bathory seemed amused at that. "If I'd known, I wouldn't have bothered to get dressed—" he began.

"Nothing like *that*," Jill cut in, flapping her free hand. "I just . . . well, I'd like to get a good look at your fangs."

"Most people do," Johnny Bathory said with a grin.

"Your *real* ones," Jill insisted. "It's for science," she added.

Bathory made a facial motion that suggested an eye roll without any actual eye movement. But he leaned forward obligingly and opened his mouth. With a flick his yellow human canines popped back up against the roof of his mouth and in one slow, smooth movement the long, sharp fangs descended from the gaping holes in his gums. They were a little longer than the ones Jill had observed on the dead vampire, but otherwise iden-tical: narrow and slightly curved. The thin membrane that covered them was pinkish and transparent.

"May I?" she asked, holding up a fresh piece of paper.

Johnny Bathory shrugged. Taking this as a yes, Jill placed the paper carefully behind the left fang and made a quick trace. By the time she had finished it was already leaking a pale, transparent liquid, which dripped on the paper, threatening the ink.

"Sorry," Bathory said as soon as Jill snatched the paper away. "It's a reflex, like drool."

"Is it toxic?" Jill asked, holding the paper awkwardly away from her.

"Not particularly. It's an anticoagulant and a sedative."

"That makes sense," Jill said, feeling about on her person for a spare cloth. She ended up using the white sash Clara had made for her to wipe the paper down. "Could I take a sample?" she asked.

"No," Johnny Bathory said, quite pleasantly. "You can ask more questions, though."

"Oh," said Jill, momentarily deflating as she realized she had left the list of questions on her phone . . . which was down in a locker somewhere. After some thought she decided to go with:

"How . . . er . . . how did you become a vampire? The mechanics of it, I mean."

Johnny Bathory leaned back in his seat and folded his arms. "I don't feel like talking about that," he said quietly.

Jill sighed and made a mark on her paper. "How dangerous is sunlight to you, really?"

"Pass," said Johnny Bathory, a small smile tugging at the side of his mouth.

"You know," Jill said, a little frustrated. "There's a lot of information *about* vampires out there in the world already. *Fictional* vampires. Some of it is *misinformation,* as I have learned—but I have no way of knowing which is true or false unless *you* tell me."

"Most of it is inaccurate," Johnny Bathory allowed. "Though you have to understand, all vampires are individuals. We're all a little different from one another in our abilities and . . . tastes."

"Like you're different from that vampire in the drain?"

"Yes."

"Why did you kill her, anyway?"

Johnny Bathory put his head on one side to look at Jill piercingly. "Why should it matter to you if one vampire kills another? I would think, from your point of view, the less of us the better."

"I don't know," Jill said. "I'm not a hunter. I just want to *understand.* For all I know, vampires fulfill some obscure but important biological niche."

Bathory gave her a critical stare. Then he leaned forward (Jill instinctively leaned away) and inspected her closely. His eyes were more than just red, she noticed; they were so vivid they almost appeared to glow.

"Great Hecate," he murmured. "You really mean it."

He got up and paced around the chair, leaning his arms on the back. Nervously he flicked at a piece of invisible dust on his shoulder.

"Vampires are made . . . " he began, "by the exsanguination of a living human by another vampire, and then the addition of that vampire's blood.

It's all very . . . messy. But that is how I—and every other vampire you meet—were made. More or less." He swallowed. Inhaled.

"Sunlight. That's different. It depends on the vampire; how strong the blood is and of what lineage they are."

"Does moonlight affect you adversely?" Jill asked.

"What?"

"Moonlight is just sunlight," Jill explained. "Reflecting off the moon and back to earth. Same thing. Does it bother you?"

Johnny Bathory gave her a funny look, as if he didn't know whether to be amused or annoyed. "No," he said at length. "Neither does starlight, before you ask."

"Interesting," said Jill, making a note. "And, getting back to an earlier question, can you survive on the blood of other organisms?"

"If it's red," Bathory said. "It works for us."

"What do *you* usually feed on?"

Johnny Bathory grinned. He had pulled his fangs in and snapped his canines back, but the smile was still off-putting. "Donations," he said.

"So . . . you prefer to feed on human blood?" Jill prodded.

"Most of us do."

"And these feedings . . . how often do they result in the death of the human involved?"

"Sometimes," Johnny Bathory said calmly. "Depends on the vampire."

Jill looked up at him and frowned. "That doesn't bother you?" she asked.

Johnny Bathory shrugged. "If I make an effort, it does."

"What does *that* mean?"

Bathory straightened up and looked at her with a sort of intense interest. Definitely catlike now. A cat who sees a mouse wander out of its hole, oblivious to all danger.

"Something you must understand about us," he said quietly. "As a human, you are *alive*. As such, you can *die*. You do not know what death *is*. And so you fear it, like you fear everything that is unknown and unknowable. You build imaginative castles all around it, to protect your delicate psyche. As a vampire . . . I know death. I *have* died. It holds no mystery for me or for any vampire. As a result we have, as a group, lost some respect for it. We think that because we have died once we cannot die again. We have no sympathy for things, such as you, who have yet to experience it and so hold death in a higher regard. In short, we do not feel it is such a big *deal* to die, or to cause the death of another . . . whether they are vampire or human."

Silence stretched on after this as Jill digested what had just been said. During this time Bathory seemed to consider his words, and added:

"Of course it is a false security; we *can* die . . . again and again and again. But it is still an effort for me to remember that; to remember what death looks like from your side of the wall. It is an effort that most of us do not bother to make. Does that answer your question?"

Jill nodded stiffly.

"How old are you?" she asked.

"Older than you."

Jill snorted in annoyance.

Johnny Bathory folded his arms over the back of the chair and gave her half a grin. "In all honesty, I'm not exactly sure anymore. They changed the calendars a couple times, and I lost track. I did tally it up once, but that was a while ago."

"Can you give me an estimate at least?" Jill asked. "It would be helpful."

Johnny Bathory got a distant look on his face, staring off into space over Jill's shoulder. He frowned. "I remember when there were still packs of werewolves in the forests of Deutschland," he said softly. "I remember when a Sami witch was something to be feared. I remember when the world was quiet and the skies were dark." He sounded a little wistful. Jill listened with what she felt was commendable patience, and then scribbled *pre-industrial revolution?* in the margin of her paper.

"Do you sleep?" she asked.

"Sleep?" Bathory seemed surprised by the question, or perhaps the change of subject. "No, not exactly. I can hibernate. I used to suffer from loss of consciousness during the day, but I grew out of that."

"Do most vampires . . . uh . . . lose consciousness during the day?"

"Only the young ones. It depends on how strong their blood is."

"You've mentioned this 'blood' before," Jill pointed out, flipping to a new page. "What exactly is that?"

She looked up to find Bathory examining her with marked interest. She raised her eyebrows at him.

"It's *our* blood. The essence of a vampire," he said simply. "My blood is my maker's blood, which in turn was *her* maker's blood. All the way back to the first vampire. Or one of the first vampires, depending on who you ask."

"Explain," Jill said.

Bathory inhaled. "There are some," he said, "who believe that all vampires can trace their blood back to a single, original vampire. Like the way your navel orange trees are all just shoots of that one navel orange tree some medieval monks managed to splice together. The same way all navel oranges are, in essence, the original navel orange tree, so all vampires are just branches off the original vampire."

"And what do *you* believe?" Jill prodded.

"I make a practice of not *believing* things," Johnny Bathory said. "What I *think* is that there was not one, but several proto-vampires, if you will. You will find many variations in ability and power among us, and because we cannot breed, cannot *evolve*, it means there are different *lineages* of vampire. It looks to me as though there are several strains, each with its own unique subset of strengths and weaknesses. For example, many of the vampires you will find in the Americas have the same blood as those from central and eastern Europe. However, a small number of them have blood—and therefore powers—which are completely different. *Ethiopian* vampires are so different they're hardly recognizable. There's a lineage of vampires from Russia who are almost entirely immune to the adverse effects of sunlight, though they are so mentally unstable they don't last very long."

"Fascinating," said Jill, writing industriously. "How many different strains are you aware of?"

"About seven," Bathory said. "It averages out to one per continent. Though most of the vampires you'll meet will be of the European lineage, like myself."

"And . . . what do you think these proto-vampires *were*?" she asked.

"I'm sorry?"

"Where did *they* come from?" Jill pressed on. "Were they just bigger, badder versions of vampire, or were they something else entirely?"

Johnny Bathory grinned at her. "That's where *you* come in," he said.

"What?"

"You're the one who's studying us." He raised his hands and slowly extended and contracted his index and middle fingers. "For *science*. Did it ever occur to you that the only reason you're *here*, talking to *me*, is that I'm *also* curious? That I'm tired of just accepting the world for what it is and I'd also like to understand *why* it is? And for once, I'm taking a stake in this game. Because I want to know just as much as you do."

"What do you mean by that . . . taking a stake in this game?"

Bathory cast a look of cheerful pity at her. "Come now, you don't think you're the first person to wonder: 'hey, what's up with all these hauntings and curses and angelic interference?' The reason your world doesn't know about us is not because no one's ever thought to *study* us . . . but because no one's lived long enough to tell their tale."

Jill felt a deep stillness settle in her stomach. It was not exactly like ice; more like a glacier covered in snow that spread out to the tips of her fingers. She clutched her notepad tightly.

"So why . . . " she began, but her voice caught in her throat and she had to cough a little before she could continue. "Why did you pick me? Why help *me*?"

Johnny Bathory stood up and moved out from behind the chair. He did not approach, but Jill was suddenly conscious of the fact that there was nothing between them now. He put his hands in his pockets and smiled blandly.

"Because, despite all appearance of a complete lack of self-preservation," he said, "you're not entirely stupid. Because you actually *do* have a chance. You have the tools and the talent to uncover things I couldn't, not in five hundred years. You, unlike your predecessors, have arms and armor. You have a sword and shield."

"Not right now," Jill pointed out, drawing her knees up into her chest and resting the pad on top of them.

"True," Bathory allowed. "And that's why I knew it had to be *me*. Before you tried to pull a stunt like this with someone like *Martha* again."

"Because you also want to understand the supernatural?"

"Because I want to understand why I'm here. Why do I burn in sunlight? Why don't I dream? Where do I come from? Where did *everyone else* come from?" Johnny Bathory said. "For a time there it seemed like all the old powers had gone to sleep. Every year there were fewer and fewer of us. But now things are changing. Old shadows are creeping back in around the edges of the world. Unicorns have been seen in the wild again. I know I'm part of a bigger, more mysterious world, but I really have hardly more knowledge of how it actually works than you do. And I hate that."

"So why don't you come out?" Jill asked. "Tell the truth about being a vampire—not just this mocked up version you do for show?"

Johnny Bathory folded his arms defensively. "Because I don't want things to go back to the way they were. Back to the days when people were more superstitious; when ordinary people would hunt and kill my kind if they knew what we were—would even hunt their own kind, if they thought they were vampires. Now that it's just die-hard fanatics like your sword and shield, things are much easier. A part of me doesn't want that to change. A bigger part of me wants to understand."

"Even though the prospect scares you?" Jill pointed out.

Johnny Bathory shrugged and smiled, putting his hands back in his pockets. "It's been a long time since anything scared me," he said. "Honestly, I kind of enjoy it."

He glanced sideways, at the clock in the kitchenette. It was now almost midnight. "One more question," he said, and there was a tightness in his shoulders and in his voice that put Jill on edge.

"Oh," she said, dismayed. Her mind was suddenly flooded with questions. *Why exactly is sunlight so destructive? Discuss effects of religious paraphernalia? Racial demographics among vampires? Extent and limits of various abilities? Are the other members of your band vampires as well?* With an effort she shut her eyes and closed her notebook. When she opened them again it was to the sight of Johnny Bathory gazing at her from out of his blood-red ones.

"Any advice for me?" she asked.

Bathory looked pleasantly surprised at this. "Oh yes," he said, his voice dropping to a growl. "Don't do anything this stupid ever again."

There was a flickering around his feet, and he glanced down. Jill saw his shadow, which by rights should have been pooled beneath him from the overhead light, was instead stretched out—*toward her*—and it was the silhouette of a thin, ragged man, the arms thrashing and grasping silently against the carpet.

Slowly, Johnny Bathory took his hands out of his pockets to let them hang at his sides. They were clenched in tight fists, which made the contrast with the wild, thrashing, clawing hands and arms of his shadow even more disturbing.

"It's time for you to go," he said.

"Why is that?" Jill couldn't help asking, even as she slowly unfolded her legs.

Johnny Bathory looked resigned. "It's been a long day and I'm *tired*," he said. "The longer you sit there, unthreatening and unguarded, the harder it is for me to remember that you are a *person*, and not some animal to string up and drain in the bathroom."

"Is that what you do to the others?" Jill asked in a small voice.

Bathory snorted in disdain. His shadow *writhed*. "Nothing so radical," he said. "There's a reason I pick *five*. Split between them and under the influence of my venom they don't even notice the loss. I told you, I don't need much these days."

He took a step forward. (His shadow leapt across the floor, nearly reaching Jill's feet.)

"What I *need* and what I *want*, however, are two very different things."

Jill stood up.

"Don't run," Bathory said. He words were a little slurred now, and Jill saw it was because his fangs—his real ones—were extended again. "Don't turn around. I told you, it's an effort—and I'm *tired*."

Pushing her notebook into her pocket Jill felt around for the back of the couch, stepped up onto it, and then lifted one leg over the back and gently lowered herself to the floor, pulling her other leg after her. Trying not to scramble, she walked backward in the direction of the door, all the while keeping her eyes locked on the vampire.

"Thank you," she said, proud of how she kept the wobble out of her voice. "You've been *very* helpful, and I appreciate it."

"Thank me when it's over," Bathory said, his voice a low growl.

Jill's searching fingers met the cool metal of the door handle. She glanced around the suite, and confirmed that this must be the door she came in by. A deep sense of calm settled on her, and with it a realization dawned.

"It'll never be over," she said.

Johnny Bathory nodded.

"Good-bye," said Jill, and let herself out. She held his gaze until the door shut between them.

The large black man was waiting for her out in the hall. From two doors down came the raucous sound of partying.

"Ready to leave, miss?" he asked.

"Yes, please," said Jill.

The man nodded. "Good," he said, and presented her with a tray holding her phone. "There are two women waiting for you outside the stage. They've been getting impatient."

Clara and Selene seemed both pleased and surprised to find Jill alive and in one piece. Jill didn't know whether to be amused or offended. She was beginning to shake, a deep trembling that started in her hands and knees and traveled upward and inward. Clara ended up more or less carrying her back to their room.

They wanted to know what had happened, but after everything, Jill found it difficult to speak. Thinking was becoming more difficult too, as fatigue and hunger began to catch up with her. What she did know was that she could not spend another night in the Castle. Not with Johnny Bathory and his wild shadow there. She made them pack up and check out, though Selene insisted she eat while they did so.

Then, having eaten, and safely tucked in the passenger seat of Arcana, she promptly passed out.

She was woken almost immediately when Selene pulled into the parking lot of a motel at the edge of the city, and Clara carried her to bed, but her eyelids felt like they were made of lead and her body like a limp noodle, and she was barely coherent enough to hear Selene say, "I'll take the first watch . . ." and thus assured, she went straight back to sleep.

She did not sleep well. It was a restless, fitful slumber, and lurking in the back of her mind was the feeling that *something* was watching her. Waiting. And if she drifted too deep it would open wide jaws and snap her up. More than once she woke with a start to find her heart pounding, and each time it was harder and harder to go back to sleep. Then at last she opened her eyes to find it was light outside, and got up with relief to go get breakfast.

When she returned, Clara was on the phone looking annoyed.

"Officer *Dunes*," Selene mouthed, taking a box of food.

"I can only tell you how it was when we left it," Clara said stoically.

"What's happened?" Jill asked.

Clara took the phone from her ear. "The vampires, the dead ones in the sewer: his men didn't find any bodies."

A deep confusion settled on Jill's mind, and she stared at Clara blankly until something Johnny Bathory had said the night before rose to the surface.

The reason your world doesn't know about us is not because no one's ever thought to study us . . . but because no one's lived long enough to tell their tale.

"Oh," she said heavily, and touched Clara's sleeve. "Tell him . . . tell him there was one more vampire. He was the one who killed them. He cleaned up after we'd gone. I think he doesn't want people to know; he's protecting himself. And Officer Dunes."

Clara frowned, but repeated the words into the phone.

More indistinct, fuzzy voice. It sounded angry.

"You can tell him we are confident there will be no more vampire murders," Jill offered. Her voice must have come through loud enough for Dunes to hear, for the chattering stopped.

"I am sorry," said Clara into the phone. "That is all I can tell you."

She hung up.

"I think it's time we left," she said, slipping her phone into her pocket.

Jill, her mouth full of breakfast, silently agreed.

They decided to go north, on the grounds that Selene was driving, and Selene had driven through Arizona enough times already, and the only other two directions were southwest toward Los Angeles or northwest, back the way they had come. Jill didn't much care at this point. She had never been to Utah or Arizona before, so it was all new to her. It was just a relief to be *moving on.* She was so tired from the restless night before that as soon as they were clear of Las Vegas, tearing north along Interstate 15, she leaned back and let her eyes drift shut.

At last, she thought. *I can sleep.*

And then she did. Deeply and soundly.

And then . . .

Then she *dreamed.*

It was one of those horribly realistic dreams. At first she thought she was back in the hotel, that it was still night and they had yet to leave the city. She could see the silhouette of Selene in the window against the curtains, and by that filtered light she could make out the mountainous hump that was Clara clumped on the other bed. But there was a thick, white fog drifting through the room that she did not remember, and she opened her mouth to ask Selene about it; Selene would know what to do.

She couldn't speak.

And, now that she tried, she couldn't move either. She was stuck, lying on her back, as the mist swirled up and around her, engulfing her.

It was cold. *Cold like six feet underground on a snowy night* she knew, and didn't know how.

She could not shut her eyes. Then again, in the convenient way of dreams, she didn't need to blink either.

The fog was thickening before her, twining together into a shape roughly man-sized.

It was terrifying to watch, and yet Jill felt no surprise when the form of Johnny Bathory solidified out of the mist.

He looked a little different in her dream; his hair was down, hanging loosely around his shoulders, and he wore a simple black cloak which faded into the mist.

Jill tried to sit up (she couldn't); she tried to call for help (no sound came out). She wasn't sure if she was even breathing anymore, but in the dream she didn't need to.

She could hold her breath forever, lie silent in the ground, safe under the snow.

"You'll have to forgive me," the vampire said, coming forward to stand at her bedside. "It's been a while since I had such a frank conversation with anyone. It was more unsettling than I expected."

Jill didn't answer. She couldn't.

Johnny Bathory seemed to withdraw into his cape. He hovered at the edge of Jill's bed and looked down at her thoughtfully. Slowly, a smile crept up and out of his mouth, leaving his face like some distorted mask.

"You asked for the wrong thing," the vampire said. "Considering your age, it was an understandable oversight." A hand emerged from his cape, ivory white and thin. Jill felt something she thought were bones close around her wrist, and realized it was his other hand.

Gently he lifted her arm, turned her hand palm up, and pressed something hard and cold into it with his other hand, curling her fingers to close around it.

"You should not fear the dark, Jill Hamilton," he said. "But you should show it some respect."

He lowered her hand back onto the bed and took a step back.

Then he dissolved, melting back into the cold, white mist, like a tumble of water in slow motion.

At last, Jill screamed.

The world suddenly got a lot brighter. It was also a good deal warmer; sweltering, in fact, and Jill felt sticky with sweat.

There was a sickening swerve as Selene jumped in the driver's seat.

"*Jesus* woman are you okay?"

Jill's eyes came all the way open as she realized she was not in bed, but in Arcana. That it was *daytime,* and they were traveling almost seventy miles per hour.

Jill gasped, breathing in large, life-affirming gulps. "Just . . . a dream. Bad one. It's nothing."

"Didn't *sound* like nothing," Selene said, signaling to exit the highway. Clara, riding ahead on her motorcycle, noticed and began drifting to the right.

They pulled off onto a lonely desert road, raising a cloud of dust as Arcana rolled over to the shoulder and jerked to a halt. Clara kicked the stand down on her bike and walked over.

"Jill had a bad dream," Selene said, by way of explanation, as she came around the front and pulled the passenger door open.

"Can you remember it?" Clara asked practically as Jill climbed out.

Jill was feeling rather silly by this time. She'd just had a nightmare. Not surprising, all things considered. And here were Clara and Selene, acting as if she'd been assaulted or something.

She shook her head and managed a weak laugh. "Not really," she said. "It was just a stupid dream."

Selene patted her gently on the shoulder. "Sometimes stupid dreams *ain't* 'just' stupid dreams, hon."

Jill frowned at her, feeling suddenly cold in the bright desert sun.

"Jill," said Clara, looking seriously at Jill's right hand, which was curled into a tight fist, "What have you got in your *hand*?"

It took a surprising amount of effort for Jill uncurl her fingers. They felt so cold and stiff, she had to use her other hand to force them open in the end. There in her palm was a small bottle, full to the brim with a thick, dark liquid.

Jill wanted to scream and hurl it into the desert.

She didn't. Instead she handed it to Selene, who inspected it closely, then abruptly cupped her hands around it.

"This is *vampire blood*," she practically yelped. "Jill, where did you *get* this?"

"Bathory . . . gave it to me," Jill said, pressing herself back against Arcana's side.

"Bathory?" Selene looked around sharply. "*When*?"

"Just now," Jill said quietly. "In my dream. He was here. There. He came in mist. He . . . he put that in my hand."

Selene stared at her, eyes bulging.

"He is a dream-walker," Clara said.

"Is that a bad thing?" Jill asked.

"It's a ghost skill," Clara said. "Not many vampires can do it, let alone to the extent that they can transfer physical objects from one realm to the other."

"Forget vampires," said Selene. "Not even many *ghosts* can do that." She shook herself. "Wait, you said he *gave* this to you?" She indicated the bottle still cupped in her hands.

Jill nodded, suppressing a shudder.

"He gave you his blood," Clara said, her voice a dull monotone. Then she gave a low whistle.

"I don't understand," Jill said. "What does that mean?"

Selene shook her head, carefully wrapping the bottle in her bandana and passing it back to Jill. "I've got no idea," she said. "This one's all you, girlfriend: you always did want *samples*."

Jill, still feeling cold and shaken, looked out at the bleached desert surrounding them, and found she couldn't argue.

"A lot of people say you're only in it for the money and the sex," the interviewer said. "What do you say to those who insist you're just a shallow rock 'n' roll star?"

The man in makeup and yellow contacts shrugged. "Well I think that's an over simplification," he said mildly. "I mean, I'm also in it for the *blood*."

"Is there a message you'd like to send to your fans?"

Johnny Bathory laughed, and for a moment his hoarse, weak voice dropped and filled. It was a rich, dark laugh, with an undertone like a growl.

"Well, my fans . . . you know my whole work is my message. If I could say something in particular, I suppose I'd say *thanks*. You know I get to do what I love because of you, so I love you guys, I really do. You people make me feel alive."

"Any parting words for your critics?"

"Not really," Johnny Bathory said with a wide grin. "I don't pay them much attention. It's all for my fans, you see. I'd do anything for those guys. Seriously, anytime someone mistreats a JB fan I'm like . . . I kinda want to hunt them down and eat them."

"You look after your own, eh?"

"I try, Jenny. I do try."

"Well, that's all the time we have. Once again, *thank you* Johnny Bathory for coming on the show. That's *Johnny Bathory*, ladies and gentlemen. You can buy his music from retailers worldwide and on the internet, and he's playing live at the Castle, Las Vegas, for the next week. It's a mind-blowing show, and you should *definitely* go check it out."

Well I'm a jack ripper
And I'm a greedy god
I'm an idol for the opiate masses
Maybe I'm not your savior
But I'll still have your
Love and lust and guts and blood.

Sex, blood
Rock and roll
Sex, blood
Rock and roll

You wanna give me life
Well I will give you death
I will give you all the things that you want to fear
In return I ask for your worshipful heart
And the hearts of the gods you created!

You say you'll give me devotion
You want a Christ for your night
But all you get is revulsion, sin
And you'll go down without a fight.

Wait 'til you see my teeth
Wait 'til you see my teeth
Wait 'til you see my TEETH
Wait 'til you see me.

You say you'll give me devotion
Let it go without a fight.
But all you get is revulsion, sin
You're gonna give me your life's light.

Sex, blood
Rock and roll
Sex, blood
Rock and roll

Sex, Blood and Rock 'n' Roll

The more that you fear me
the stronger I grow
The more that you love me
the stronger I grow
Well I am no Christ, oh, I am no Christ
I'm no Christ but which Christ do you know?

Sex, blood
Rock and roll
Sex, blood
Rock and roll

You say you'll give me devotion
A way to get through the night.
But all you get is revulsion, sin
And you'll go down without a fight.

Sex, blood
Rock and roll

Wait 'til you see my teeth
Wait 'til you see my teeth
Wait 'til you see my TEETH
Wait 'til you see my TEETH
Wait 'til you see me.

—See My Teeth/*Johnny Bathory*

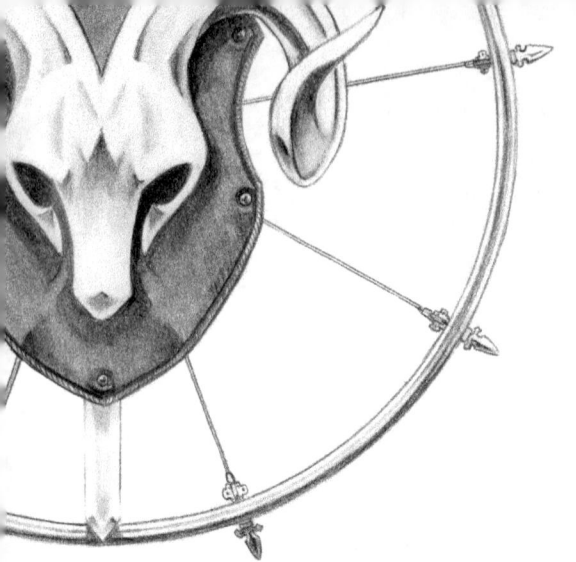

GOD, 5.
or
ALIENS

Green River Campground, outside Roosevelt, Utah

THE BASIN ELEMENTARY SECOND GRADE NATURE CAMP TRIP WAS, in Amar Dresner's opinion, a big letdown. He had been camping before and enjoyed it thoroughly, but that had been with his family, in the summer. It had been rather full of bugs and dirt, but his dad had taken him on wonderful, ranging hikes and let him light the campfire.

Now it was March. It was cold. They would not let him go for hikes off the well-beaten trails, and Miss Matthews would not let him anywhere near the campfire. Once it was alight she had the class gather round and gave them metal skewers with which to roast marshmallows. In the ordinary way Amar liked a roast marshmallow as much as the next seven-year-old, but found that when he went to roast one himself it came out burned and blackened and tasting mostly of charcoal. His classmates laughed at him when they saw his sorry, black lump of a marshmallow. Amar thought this was singularly unfair of them, since theirs were not much better.

He raised his hand and asked to use the bathroom.

"Of course Amar," said Miss Matthews. "Sarah, would you take him?"

Sarah was an imposing seventh grader who gave the impression of having been roped into assisting Miss Matthew's class as a form of punishment. She was able to roast marshmallows perfectly, and looked across at Amar over the beautiful gold-and-brown melting lump on the end of her skewer with a sour expression.

"Yes, Miss Matthews," she said, in a voice which tiptoed up to the line of goody-two-shoes, but didn't quite step over it.

Amar got up, dusting off his jeans and carrying his skewer with him; he did not put it past his classmates to hide it while he was gone.

The bathroom was an outhouse a little way outside and uphill from the campground. Its door was covered in rude graffiti, and it smelled horrible. Amar had put off using it for as long as he could, hoping he would get a chance to sneak off into the shrubby woods, but Miss Matthews and Sarah had so far prevented him.

Now he walked up to the door, and stopped.

"Well, *go on*," said Sarah, eating her marshmallow with delicate care and extreme relish. How Amar envied her that marshmallow.

"It smells bad," Amar said, hoping he could appeal to Sarah's sense of reason.

"*Yeah*," said Sarah, swallowing the last of the marshmallow. "And the longer you take, the longer *I* have to stand here and smell it. *Go on.*"

Amar went . . . but not into the stinking hut. Instead he darted around the side, slipping between the bushes, and pelted off among the trees. Heedless of Sarah's shouts, he skipped over half-seen rocks and stumbled over others. He was terrified, and exhilarated. He hit upon one of the well-beaten trails, followed it for a few feet, and then spying a deer track leading off to one side, he took that.

There was a great pounding all around him: his feet, his heart, and the more distant pounding of Sarah's feet. Finding a small clearing he put his back to a tree and was just about to fulfill his original purpose when an enraged arm snaked around and grabbed him by the shoulder.

"Come *here* you!" Sarah snapped, dragging him out of his hiding place and back toward the campground. "What *are* you, a little savage?"

Amar kicked and screamed. Sarah called him a rude name and twisted his arm. That made Amar cry.

"Shut *up*," she hissed in his ear. "You want to get me in *trouble?*" She pulled him roughly out of the bushes, and Amar found they were back at the outhouse. He must have run in a circle. Sarah pulled open the door and pushed him inside. Then she shut it and leaned her back against the scummy surface, panting. She fixed her hair, then she adjusted her top and jeans. In his flailing, the boy had grabbed the silver cross she wore around her neck and the chain it hung on had bit into her flesh. She adjusted it gingerly, cursing inwardly.

"Everything all right, Sarah?" Miss Matthew's voice called.

"We're fine, Miss Matthews," Sarah replied, dropping an extra dose of sweetness into her words. The little turd would probably go crying to teacher as soon as he got out, and she'd have to be on best behavior to win a word-off with him. Amar Dresner might be the only kid in Basin Elementary's second grade who wasn't peach and creamy white, but his mother was known to be a terror. She'd raised a huge stink when it came out that each student had been given a complimentary Book of Mormon upon enrolling in Basin Elementary, and made them change it.

"Muslim oppression!" Sarah's mother had cried.

Ayana Dresner was not, in point of fact, Muslim, but Sarah's mother thought everyone who was darker than a vanilla smoothie and didn't have a Biblical name was a Muslim, and the unfortunate tendency had perco-lated down a generation.

It had made a rather ugly impression on Sarah, who now felt a twisted sense of satisfaction in being able to strike back, as it were, through Ayana's son.

Who was, it must be said, not making a sound within the stinking building. Sarah gave him a good minute before she banged on the door.

"You finished in there?" she asked, keeping her voice down so she could use a tone that threatened trouble if this was not actually the case.

Silence.

"Amar?" she called, louder this time.

Still nothing.

"Amar, this is *not* funny," said Sarah, leaning on the door. "Finish your business and come *out.*"

All she got was the scubby door's graffitied face gazing mutely back at her. Someone had scribbled an obscenity over a smiley face right in the middle. It made Sarah feel like the door was mocking her.

"*Amar,*" she said, "I am going to count to *five,* and if you're not out here I am going to Miss Matthews. One."

Not a sound.

"Two. Three. Four . . . "

Sarah trailed off. She did not actually want to fetch Miss Matthews, for the topic of why Amar was hiding in the outhouse might come up, and the kid could make difficulties. On a whim Sarah tried the handle and found to her delight that it was unlocked.

"*Five!*" she cried with vicious triumph, and flung the door open.

For one horrible moment there was a blast of bright, multi-colored light, and a snap of something that was both white-hot and deeply cold at the same time. It seared Sarah's skin and she fell back, throwing up her arms to guard her face. She hit hard on the dirt and yelped, then screamed in earnest as the pain from her hands reached her brain.

Abruptly the light shut off and there was darkness again; the air was the right temperature, and Miss Matthews was at her side.

"What is it Sarah? What happened? Oh my *god!*" There was a frantic beeping, and then the teacher's voice, shrill from fright and shock, said: "Yes, my name is Laurel Matthews, I'm at the Green River Preserve campground off 88. I'm with a student who has been badly burned. No, I *don't* know how, she wasn't anywhere near a fire—but it looks *really bad.* Yes, thank you . . . "

The words washed over and around Sarah, but none of them penetrated her mind, which was quickly becoming consumed by the blinding pain radiating up from her hands and arms.

It wasn't until later—*much later*, after the ambulance had arrived, and she'd been taken to the hospital—that she was made to understand that the reason the outhouse had been so quiet was that Amar Dresner had not been in it: he had disappeared without a trace.

Interstate Highway 15
Cedar City, Utah

STANDING IN HER JEANS AND BRA in front of the motel mirror, Selene Shields inspected the damage with the detached objectiveness of one assessing the usability of a piece of equipment.

The cracked rib she had acquired escaping from Death Valley had finally finished healing during the month they'd spent in Cedar City. Now the only signs of that struggle were the three thin, shiny black lines that began just below her neck and stretched down, across her back and over her shoulder in a wide arch, and the small pebbly scars on her left forearm. Experimentally she clenched and flexed the muscle there, taking deep satisfaction in the complete lack of pain. Really, the bruising had been almost as bad as the puncture wounds. Now, however, the skin was new and fresh, and Selene rolled her shoulders, delighting in the feel of intact skin stretching effortlessly over her bones.

She had to hand it to Clara; the woman knew how to suture a wound. In time, she fancied, these scars might fade away entirely. Quite unlike the sloppy job she'd done on her own leg five years ago—that one was still rough, and the skin pinched in around it—or the scuffed elbows and knees she had acquired from those funny shallow scrapes that never bled, but left the nastiest-looking scars behind. Selene examined one of her elbows now, idly running a finger over the darkened and mottled patch of skin. What had that been from? The strange night in Death Valley? Or more recently, in the drains of Las Vegas? Or was it from sometime much earlier? Selene couldn't remember. She had layered the scars on her elbows, one on top of the other, over the years.

It was all so much superficial damage in the end, she thought as she pulled her shirt on. Banged up elbows might look gnarly, but they didn't stop you doing your job. And if you weren't being paid for how you looked, why worry about the marks at all? Selene had long since given up caring about the aesthetics of her physical appearance beyond keeping it clean and in clothes that were not too dirty or worn out. With this in mind she bundled her hair back into a lumpy braid and tied off the end with a piece of leather shoestring, pulled on her work shirt, and strode out into the main area of their room.

To her surprise, she found Jill awake and seated at the little desk with her laptop open, a plate containing the best food the motel's complimentary breakfast could provide pushed over to the side. She was sipping an orange juice and had the little frown between her eyebrows of someone whose computer was not magically giving them exactly what they wanted.

"You're awake," Selene said.

Jill looked up, and her face broke into a triumphant grin. "Slept through the *whole* night," she said. "Woke up around one AM to use the bathroom but went right back to sleep again. *No dreams,*" she added. "I'm catching up on email and then Clara says she might have found us something."

"Glad to hear you've managed to return to the ranks of the pleasantly diurnal," Selene said dryly, coming over and taking a piece of thin brown toast off Jill's plate and smearing it liberally with all the little jam samplers. "What sayeth the emails?"

"Spam and junk, mostly," Jill said. "Lots of requests for interviews from sketchy magazines—some vampire website wants me to write them a blog. I *told* Okedo not to give out this email, but I suppose they got it from the college or something."

"Any news from the good professor?" Selene asked, her mouth full of toast.

"Not as such," Jill said, snatching the other piece before Selene could grab it. "They've been trying to figure out how the chimera mother worked—remember when you killed her, all the others keeled over? And none of them tried to regenerate? Why did that gland cease to work?—but so far nothing conclusive. It's hard, as the subjects are all dead and staying that way."

"Tough life," Selene said.

Jill adjusted her glasses and looked Selene over critically. "Not as tough as yours," she said. "How's the rib?"

"I can't even tell which one was broke," Selene said proudly, thumping her side for emphasis. "So, what has Clara got?"

"Nothing online, as far as I can tell," Jill said. "She's been over in the lot all morning, running some sort of scanning algorithm."

"Running a what now?" Selene asked. Jill had a way of applying inscrutable sciencey-sounding names to perfectly ordinary spells that made them unrecognizable to Selene's ears.

Jill screwed up her face in distaste. "She called it the Savannah Circle or something like that. I made her explain. Essentially it's a scanning algorithm, using sticks and stones balanced on top of each other to sense disturbances in the fabric of our world ... " she trailed off as Selene waved a hand.

"Yeah, yeah," she said. "I know what a Savannah Circle is. What did she find?"

"She wouldn't say," Jill said without rancor. "Apparently, the first result wasn't definitive enough. She's running a refined search now. You want to finish that?" she asked, seeing how Selene was eyeing the plate of food. "Then we could go meet her. She's set up in that empty lot just around the corner."

Under a pale blue sky streaked with thin, high clouds, the mountains rising blue and white beyond the low houses and trees of the city, Clara Nordstern leaned against her motorbike and pulled the collar of her leather jacket tighter around her neck against the wind.

Anyone passing on the road might have seen her: a tall, leather-clad figure in black with a black motorcycle parked in the middle of an empty lot covered in scratchy dead grass. They probably would not have seen the careful series of stone cairns with sticks balanced at their tops that were arrayed in a circle around her. The stones had been hard to come by; she'd been obliged to use bricks, pieces of cinder blocks, and chunks of old concrete in places. It was close enough. The irregularities in her ingredients did not explain the extraordinary reading she'd got. It had been so extraordinary that she hadn't been able to tell Jill. Not right away. Not until she'd confirmed it.

Now, as the little pendulum she'd hung from a branch propped in a hollow at her feet—out of the wind—swung gently to a stop, she looked up to find Jill and Selene both approaching down the edge of the road.

Clara shook her head violently, and Selene put a hand on Jill's arm to stop her. Clara liked that about Selene; she could understand her in a way few people did. And she was good at explaining things to Jill, which Clara *hated* with a passion. She felt as though the woman was judging her, but Selene always made things sound simple and obvious and got Jill to leave her alone. Like now.

Clara watched the little pendulum swing to a halt, its smooth motion going slower and fainter with each successive pass. And then . . .

It did it again. A sharp jerk to the northeast, stretching so that the string it hung on was parallel to the ground. Then it was back to its almost still, minute motion.

It was against all the proper laws of physics and the theories of gravity and momentum, and Clara knew seeing it would have sent Jill into fits. She being unable to accept the easy answer: magic.

Low grade, rudimentary, simple magic, but magic nonetheless. Clara liked this sort of magic; it was practical and it worked, and it didn't cause any lasting harm to the order of the world.

Reaching down she stilled the pendulum and began walking in the direction it had pointed. Like this she came eventually to the small cairn of stones set in the northeast extremity of the circle.

It was no longer a cairn. The stones had tumbled outward as if blown by a small explosion, and the stick had been shredded. Clara frowned and rubbed her chin. When at last she'd made a decision she looked up and beckoned to Jill and Selene, who still waited patiently by the side of the road. As they made their way over, Clara bent and picked up one of the scattered stones. She couldn't feel anything through the thick glove she wore, but bringing it close to her face, she sensed warmth and a faint smell of something. Maybe ozone.

"Whaddaya got?" Selene asked cheerfully.

Clara looked up, her eyes wide and clear and icy blue. Her angular face opened in honest bewilderment.

"I don't know," she said.

*   *   *

The fresh paper of the map crackled as Clara spread it out over the hotel bed. Using pillows and one of Selene's boots, she carefully weighed down the corners so it was pulled flat.

"You know, we do *have* Google maps," Jill pointed out.

"Your screen isn't big enough," Clara said. She had produced a pen and was making little notations on the paper, beginning with their current location (Cedar City) and working her way up and to the right. "The field stood for the state of Utah. The affected cairn represented the Uintah Basin. I need to see the towns and how they relate to the whole. *These . . .* " She drew a broad circle in the upper right-hand corner of the map. "One of them is the town affected."

"Duchesne . . . Myton . . . Roosevelt . . . Vernal . . . " Selene read out. Jill promptly looked them up on her laptop. "But what is *going on* there?"

Clara pulled up a chair and sat in it, leaning back to survey the map.

"A bent stick means a malicious nature spirit. A broken stick means demonic activity. A blooming stick means increased magical activity."

"And *your* stick?"

"Stripped of bark, shredded, the cairn stones scattered."

Selene's eyebrows wagged and she let out a low whistle.

"It suggests something unusual, something drastic. Something big."

"No kidding."

Jill made a little sound like "*Oh!*" and looked up. "Something big, like, 'boy disappears from class camping trip in bizarre freak accident, one injured'? *That* kind of big?"

The two hunters turned to stare at her. "I expected something a little more . . . drastic," Clara said.

"No, no, wait until you hear the rest," Jill said, raising a hand for silence. "'Amar Dresner, 7, of Basin Elementary, has been missing for two days since he disappeared from his second grade camping trip. Sarah Wightman, 13, is still in the hospital from burns sustained in a freak accident. According to eyewitness reports, Ms. Wightman had been supervising Dresner in using the campground restroom, when her teacher, Laurel Matthews (38, of Roosevelt) heard screaming. Upon reaching the scene she found Wightman with severe burns on her arms and hands. Wightman was hospitalized at the Unitah Basin Medical Center, and a search of the surrounding park was unable to locate Dresner. No signs of foul play have been found, but local authorities are treating it as a possible kidnapping. Any persons with information pertaining to the case are encouraged to contact the Duchesne County Sheriff's department at . . . ' number number, number number . . . " Jill trailed off. "And if that's not enough, there's an interview with this Sarah Wightman girl. *She* says she opened the door of the outhouse to check on the kid and saw a bright, blinding light right before she was burned. There are a bunch of posts on alien conspiracy blogs saying this is a case of alien abduction." She looked up expectantly to find Selene rolling her eyes.

"Alien abductions are *never* worth the trouble," she groaned. "It's *always* only so many pranksters or government airplanes or flat-out delusions."

"Yet, there is my stick," Clara said. "You say this occurred near Roosevelt?"

"Green River Nature Preserve," Jill said. "Just off Highway 40."

Clara nodded. "I'll go check us out," she said.

Sarah Wightman lay in a haze of pain and confusion. Her burns were slow to heal, and they were puzzling to the doctors. She had not been allowed to see her hands, but from the deep aching pain she felt under the bandages, she knew they must be very bad. Her arms hurt too—everywhere she had been burned hurt—but not in the same way. It was almost a relief when, on the third morning after the incident, she woke up and couldn't feel her hands at all. But when she told the nurse, the man blanched and fairly ran out of the room. Doctors came pouring in. They gave her more painkillers and then took off her bandages. Sarah got one glimpse of her right hand—it looked like a mummy's hand, gray and mangled, with chunks missing from the fingers—and screamed. They gave her sedatives then, and after that she didn't remember much. Eventually her mother came in, crying, and hugged her and stroked her hair. In her still groggy state the words bubbled up in Sarah's mind and out her mouth before she realized she was speaking aloud.

"It's my own fault," she said, muffled against her mother's bosom.

"Sorry sugar?" her mother said.

"My fault," Sarah repeated. "'M being punished. I did a bad thing, so I'm being punished."

"You did nothing wrong, sugar," her mother said. "This is all a horrible accident."

"No, I did," said Sarah, stronger now. It seemed important that she get it out. "I was being mean. So I'm being punished."

"Jesus loves you, sweetheart," her mother said. "He'd *never* punish you like this."

"You love me," Sarah pointed out. "You still hit me with a ruler that time I broke granny's vase."

She felt her mother still. In the stillness and the silence things became perfectly clear in Sarah's mind. She pulled back and looked her mother in the face. "This time, He's going to take my hands. You watch and see."

EXTRAORDINARY BURNS GOD'S PUNISHMENT TO TEEN FOR BULLYING (*Tearful Mother Claims*) read the front-page headline of the garishly colored newspaper insert. Jill lifted it by the corner from where it lay in the center of the breakfast table as if it were a rotten animal carcass.

"What," she said, wrinkling her nose, "is *this?*"

"Propaganda rag," Selene said cheerfully, sliding her plate piled high with eggs and bacon onto the table. "They can be useful if you read between the lines."

"Or misleading," Clara said. She had Jill's laptop open, her own breakfast of oatmeal and fruit remaining untouched.

They would have been standouts in the comfortable, western-style diner, except that word of the unusual incident had apparently drawn a crowd of disaster tourists and UFO hunters that made Jill, Clara and Selene look comparatively normal. At the next table over sat a fat white man and his equally large, white wife, both of whom wore denim jackets with little green alien appliqués on the back. A trio of young hispanic men who would have ordinarily been written off as farm workers stood out with their crisp clothes. They also had the better part of a telescope laid out on their table. A pair of weatherbeaten older men who would have been white had they not been so thoroughly tanned hunkered in a corner. They wore evidently hand-decorated t-shirts so well worn there were holes around the collars. The shirts had slogans printed on them in fading dye: one said "Ask Me About Aliens" while the other read "I Had a Wife but Her Planet Needed Her More."

Jill had been able to spot the locals easily enough by the dirty looks they were shooting at all the obvious intruders. By comparison, the trio of women at the table by the window—even if one of them was exceptionally tall and dressed in black biking leathers and one was *actually* black—were refreshingly mundane. Selene had also made a point of tipping the cashier when she'd paid for the breakfast buffet, and that was enough to secure the congeniality of the entire staff.

"Coffee?" asked a perky freckled waitress with blond pigtails. Her name tag said Fay, and she looked like an out-of-place elf. "Oh, here, let me take that—someone must have left it," and she reached out and plucked the offending paper out of Jill's unresisting hand.

"We were actually kind of curious," Jill admitted, indicating the headline. She waved her hand at the proffered coffeepot, but Selene held out her cup gratefully.

"What? Rebecca Wightman's tearful interview?" Fay said, filling Selene's mug with practiced ease. She made a face. "Tasteless, I call it. With her daughter still in the hospital and everything. And the poor Dresners—that's the parents of the kid who's gone missing—have to sit back and read stuff like that when they've actually *lost* a kid. I ask you, who's really being punished? So are you ladies on a road trip then? Plan on staying here long? Roosevelt's not usually so full of . . . um . . . well, so upset. You know." She rolled her eyes at the diner.

"I can imagine," Jill said tactfully. "We might stick around a while."

That brought a smile to Fay's open face. She happily stood and chatted at them about this new park that just got renovated and that band that was playing at a local bar the coming weekend. She seemed singularly unwilling to leave their table, and when Jill cast around and saw some of the looks the other patrons were giving her she found she hadn't the heart to make the poor woman leave.

The upshot was they left breakfast with little knowledge of the contents of the rag, but a lot of minute details about the daily goings-on in Roosevelt.

"Where to now?" Selene asked, pulling open the driver's door of Arcana. The big Ram truck completely filled the parking space outside the diner, but the locals seemed to give it an honorary resident card based on the fact that it could obviously haul a fully loaded four-horse trailer without breaking a sweat. They got friendly waves from passing traffic just by standing next to it.

"I want to see the campsite where the incident happened," Jill said, climbing in. "I doubt it's been thoroughly examined. Do you think we'll have any trouble getting at it?"

"If we do," Selene said with a shrug, "I can probably handle it. You coming, Clara?"

Clara had wheeled her motorcycle around and now stood astride it, looking up something on a pad of paper.

"If my presence is not required," she said diffidently, "I would like to speak to the missing boy's parents."

"That sounds like a good idea," Jill agreed. "We'll meet back here for lunch then and compare notes."

Clara nodded, putting the pad away and pulling on her helmet. Her motorcycle, with its spike of black anodized aluminum mounted above the headlamp, barked roughly as she accelerated onto the road.

The Green River campground was crowded with tents and RVs, and here they found the bulk of the pilgrims. These had erected a clear zone around one of the outhouses—a big, blockish wooden structure with graffiti on the door and a pervasive stench—more secure than any police line. It had a constant sort of honor guard comprised of picture- and note-taking enthusiasts, who were quick to pull anyone back who was getting too near. A bemused sheriff's deputy sat in his truck nearby, reading a paperback and occasionally checking texts on his phone. Jill pulled Arcana up behind him and got out.

"What do you think you're doing?" Selene asked, catching her elbow.

"I'm going to ask permission," Jill said, all open innocence. "What? It's worth a try!" she said in response to Selene's look of doubt.

"For you, maybe," she grumbled, and remained steadfastly in the truck while Jill climbed down and went around to the deputy's door.

"Hi," said Jill cheerfully to the man in the truck. He looked young for a deputy, comfortably large and brown-haired, and he was reading a Stephen King paperback. Jill thought he looked more bored than anything else.

"Hello," he said, blinking at her rather. "You need help?"

"I'm Jill Hamilton of UCSC," Jill said briskly, handing him a small white card. It was one of a batch of several dozen she had ordered during their downtime in Cedar City. It had her name on it and two numbers: her cell phone, and Professor Okedo's office phone. Since Jill had been able to ship him some small but incredible samples, her old professor had become increasingly willing to swing whatever weight he could muster in her favor.

The deputy inspected the card dubiously.

"I'm a field researcher," Jill breezed on. "I'd like to document the site of the disappearance you had here a few days ago, and my assistant and I would also like to take some samples."

The deputy blinked at her. "You mean the outhouse?" he said.

Jill nodded.

"You do know we don't think the boy *actually* disappeared from there," he said, gently, as though breaking an unpleasant truth to a child. "We did have that thing taken apart and put back together again: the kid's never been in there. His babysitter probably told a lie to cover up her mistake— or she's too out of it on pain meds to remember. She got burned pretty bad. I'm just here to make sure no one does anything stupid."

"Yes, so I heard," Jill said briskly. "Well, if you have no objection, I'd like to take some measurements, photographs, and minor samples."

"Wait what," the deputy put down his paperback at last and gave her a good look. "What *samples?*"

"Wood scrapings," Jill said. "Swabs. That sort of thing. Nothing that would damage the integrity of the structure."

Back in Arcana, Selene had her face pressed against the steering wheel in embarrassment. In the deputy's truck, the man gave Jill an incredulous look.

"Do you want a sample of waste to go with that?" he said. "You know, in case someone's taken a magical dump or something?"

"I don't think that will be necessary," Jill said, perfectly serious.

The deputy gave her a long, hard look, as if weighing the chances of her being crazy with the chances of her being a *harmless* crazy. He must have settled on the latter, for in the end he shrugged and said: "Well I don't see why not. At least you're more polite than half the other loonies here." He slid down out of his seat, throwing his book onto the passenger side and offering Jill her card back.

"Keep it," said Jill. "You might need it later."

With a shrug the deputy slipped the card into his pocket. "Deputy Rich Gordon," he said, extending his free hand. "Just don't be offended if I don't call."

"Wouldn't dream of it," said Jill, taking the hand. "C'mon Selene, bring my case, would you?" she called back to the truck.

Selene, who was watching the scene unfold with annoyed admiration, shook her head as she grabbed up Jill's briefcase and hopped down out of Arcana.

The crowd of pilgrims did not welcome the presence of Deputy Rich Gordon in their midst, and turned downright resentful when he lifted the yellow tape and ushered Jill and Selene under it.

"Why do *they* get a closer look and *we* don't?" someone young and male called out.

"Field researchers for UCSC," Deputy Gordon called back, grinning a little. "And they asked nicely."

"*See?*" whispered Jill.

"Yeah, yeah," said Selene, pushing the briefcase into her arms. "Only because you got a softie this time."

Jill ignored her. She set the briefcase down on the steps of the outhouse and began taking pictures.

The outhouse was the solid wooden type with a deep cesspit below. It sat on a concrete base and had a heavy shingle roof with a skylight and a ventilation shaft. It also smelled so bad Jill had to consciously breathe through her mouth in order not to get sick to her stomach. From the reports she had read, the missing boy had been reluctant to use the bathroom, and now she understood why.

With a gulp she opened the door and had Selene come and hold it that way. Inside was a single pit toilet, a urinal, and a small sink with a cistern of water above, a little bottle half full of liquid pink soap clamped to one side. There was a roll of paper towels, a trash bin, and strips of wet toilet paper on the floor. It smelled, if possible, even worse.

It was also obviously, painfully, *normal.* Just to be certain, however, Jill went to the toilet and lifted the lid. Taking a small flashlight from her pocket she cast its beam down into the depths. It illuminated a shiny pile of brown muck with bits of white paper and a couple of cigarette ends. She let the lid fall closed with relief and went to leave.

She stopped in the doorway, resting her hand on the frame, only to freeze when she felt something *give.* Turning abruptly she saw that the wood beneath her hand, which she thought had been painted gray, was actually disintegrating, like ash disturbed after a fire. She took her hand away, and little flecks of door frame floated free with it.

"What in the world . . . " she murmured, and turned to have a closer look. Now she saw that the line of gray began abruptly midway through the door frame—at about the place the closed door would have rested, Jill thought—and ran all the way around, up and down both sides and across the top and bottom—except the concrete there, which had been scorched black. Jill ran her finger across it, and though it was firmer than the wood, it too gave way with a little scraping.

"Deputy Gordon," Jill called, and the man—who was chit-chatting with one of the sightseers—looked over and waved. "The girl who was burned," Jill went on. "It happened *here*, didn't it?"

"Around here, yeah," said Deputy Gordon agreeably.

"No, I mean, *right here,*" Jill said, gesturing to the door frame.

Deputy Gordon frowned at that and walked over. "What did you say?" he said, quietly now.

"This wood," Jill said, pointing at the line of gray, "and this concrete," she tapped her foot, "all show signs of having been exposed to extreme heat. Of being *burned.*" She looked intently at the deputy.

Deputy Gordon cleared his throat awkwardly and glanced around. "I didn't want to say so here," he said, leaning in, "because we've got enough UFO-seekers already. But, we're not exactly sure *how* Sarah Wightman was burned. *She* says she went to open the door to check on the Dresner boy, and then she was burned. But her teacher didn't *see* any fire."

"But the girl *was* burned?" Jill asked.

Deputy Gordon gave a little shudder. "Oh yes," he said. "Yes, she was. Is. It's very bad, actually."

Jill looked around at the little line of scorching, and frowned. *"Huh,"* she said.

Selene obligingly leaned forward and inspected the line of black, scorched wood. It ran all the way around the interior of the door frame, just where the door itself would rest when closed. On the side of the hinges it had scorched neatly between the door and the frame, leaving a mirror of blackened wood on the edge of the door itself. Selene nodded patiently as Jill showed her how the scorching started cleanly on the inside but then flared outward, leaving flame-like streaks.

"And all this means . . . what?" she asked eventually.

"*I* don't know," said Jill excitedly, taking a panorama of the door frame with her phone. "This is the part where you lend your expert opinion."

Selene looked critically at the door and shook her head. "Sorry," she said. "I got nothing."

"Really?" said Jill, lowering her phone. *"Really* nothing?"

"Really nothing," Selene repeated, rolling her eyes emphatically in the direction of Deputy Gordon.

Jill, bless her, had learned enough to take the hint, and finished up taking samples and documenting the area without insisting on an explanation there and then. When she was done she thanked Deputy Gordon politely, nodded to the bitter-looking pilgrims, and led the way back to Arcana.

"So, what *do* you think happened?" she asked, once the doors were safely closed.

"Honestly, I don't know," Selene said, putting the truck in reverse and backing carefully out of the campground. "Looks to me like someone opened some kind of portal there. Big one too, considering the burn. If there *was* fire then I suppose it could have been a demon. They go in for that type of thing. Don't think it was, though; demons leave behind a rather noticeable smell, and this place, well . . . "

"It smelled *horrible*," Jill pointed out.

"Yes," allowed Selene. "Horrible and *normal*. Demons, they leave behind this residue which . . . well, it don't smell like no outhouse. Just as well, really. Demons are slippery bastards and a royal pain in the butt."

"Perhaps Clara will have some ideas," Jill mused.

"One can always hope," Selene said, checking both ways before turning onto the highway.

While Jill and Selene had been investigating the door of the outhouse, Clara's bike came to a purring halt outside a generous two-story house with oak trees, now covered in tiny green buds, lining the street beside it. Its windows were shuttered, but a bright blue SUV sat in the driveway, which Clara had to edge past in order to reach the front door.

After ringing the bell she waited upward of a full minute before there were footfalls from inside and the door cracked open. The face on the other side was as dark as Selene's, though at a slightly higher elevation. Clara took a step back, holding her helmet modestly at her side.

"Mrs. Dresner?" she asked, bowing her head slightly.

The face on the other side of the door frowned. "Who sent you?" it asked. There was a gruffness to the woman's voice and a puffiness around her eyes that told Clara she would have to tread very, very carefully.

"My name is Clara Nordstern," she began, and considered the words she would use next. "I am here to find your son," she said at last.

Mrs. Dresner glared at her through the cracked door, her brows creasing an impressive ridge between her eyes.

"You with the police?" she asked.

Clara shook her head. "No," she said simply. "I'm a . . . an independent investigator."

"Uh-huh," said Mrs. Dresner. "And how much do you charge?"

Clara shrugged. "You? Nothing."

She waited. Mrs. Dresner was a fine looking woman, and gave her a cold, imperious stare. Clara bore it patiently.

The door creaked as it was pulled open the rest of the way.

"Wipe your boots before you come inside," she said by way of invitation.

The house looked to have been a neat and tidy place that had recently suffered some catastrophe. Books and articles of clothing and shoes were scattered everywhere, and a child's playset was spread across the living room. Understandable, Clara thought, as she carefully stepped over a pair of pink sneakers and toward the kitchen, where Mrs. Dresner was running water.

"Tea? Coffee?" she asked as Clara entered. "I only have instant."

"Just water," Clara said. "I do not wish to put you to any unnecessary trouble."

"*Huh*," said Mrs. Dresner, pouring Clara a glass and putting the kettle on to boil anyway. She took down a mug and a packet of instant coffee, which she shook viciously before pouring the contents into the cup. "So, how are you going to find my son?"

"I am not sure, yet," Clara said truthfully. "First I must find out where he has gone. This has turned out to be a difficult task. I was hoping you might help me determine whether any similar incidents have occurred in the past."

"*Similar incidents?*" Mrs. Dresner asked, pouring the hot water. "Well, *no,* Amar's *not* gone mysteriously missing ever before."

"Granted," Clara said with a nod. "But has he ever . . . well, has he mentioned anything to you? Bizarre stories, tales of improbable adventures? Does he have any imaginary friends?"

Mrs. Dresner gave Clara a cold look. "*No,*" she said decisively. "And no imaginary friends either, except the ones he *knows* are imaginary. We try not to go in for that sort of thing. No offense," she added.

Clara, who knew just how dangerous imaginary friends could become if allowed to run rampant, shrugged. "None taken. Does he have any friends with whom he plays complicated games of make-believe?"

Mrs. Dresner turned right around and frowned at Clara.

"What does this have to do with finding out what's happened to him?" she asked, a slight trill to her voice suggesting a steel trap, ready to spring.

"It could have quite a lot to do," Clara said plainly. "Or, nothing. I am merely collecting information, at the moment."

Mrs. Dresner narrowed her eyes and wrinkled her nose. Then she cast her eyes down and sighed heavily.

"The truth is," she said, going to lean on the counter. "Truth is Amar doesn't *have* many friends. Not any that he plays with outside of school. The closest you could say would be his sister, and they do get up to flights of fancy now and then. They built a fort out in the living room last week and insisted it was a castle." She stopped and swallowed hard.

"I see," said Clara, glancing in the direction of the living room. "And . . . where is his sister now? May I speak with her?"

"Desta?" said Mrs. Dresner. "She's up in her room. But I've been trying to keep her calm about all this. I don't want you upsetting her."

"I will do my utmost," Clara said. "Do you wish me to fabricate soothing lies or simply conceal the truth?"

Mrs. Dresner gave her a sharp look. "Just don't tell her her brother's *missing,*" she said. "Josh and I have made sure she thinks her brother's still on his camping trip. She's only *five,*" she added, seeing the look of shock on Clara's face.

Clara's phone rang. Clara excused herself, while Mrs. Dresner called upstairs: "Desta? Desta darling, there's someone here who wants to talk to you!"

"What did you find?" Clara asked. She listened intently to Jill's answer, covering one ear against Mrs. Dresner's repeated calls.

"Say that again?" Clara asked, watching keenly as Mrs. Dresner went upstairs. She followed at a safe distance.

The calls were becoming annoyed now. Doors opened and shut upstairs.

"Desta? *Desta* come out! Desta, you stop hiding this minute! Desta? *Desta where are you?*"

Clara reached the landing and saw Mrs. Dresner, eyes bulging in alarm, come out of the master bedroom.

"I can't find *Desta*," she gasped, more shocked that anything. "I left her in her room, but she's not there ... she's not *anywhere* ... " The woman ran down the stairs, still calling for her daughter.

"What's happened?" Jill's voice asked.

Clara stood in the doorway to the girl's room. It was decorated with blue cloud wallpaper and there was a model castle on the bedside table. The window was shut, fastened on the inside, and it was entirely deserted.

"Explain what you found," Clara said grimly. "Very, *very* thoroughly."

"It's what I *haven't* found that bothers me most," Jill said, scratching her head.

They had regrouped back at their motel, as Mrs. Dresner had been less than enthusiastic about suddenly entertaining more guests. They had left her standing in the drive talking animatedly on the phone with her husband, and gone back to their base for Jill to run tests on the samples she had collected. These had turned out to be singularly disappointing.

"As far as I can tell," Jill said, pushing dishes of wood scrapings and ashes about. "These are all perfectly normal. They show regular molecular structure—as far as I can tell with my field microscope—apart from damage sustained by the burn. But the *pattern* is all *wrong*. You don't get sheets of fire appearing and disappearing at the drop of a hat—or the opening of a door!"

"No signs of sulfur?" Selene asked.

"None!" cried Jill. "Wait, why sulfur?"

"The fact that there is none rules out the possibility of this being a demonic abduction," Clara explained. She dipped one shoulder suggestively. "Unless, of course, it's a very special demon."

"So essentially it's inconclusive," Jill said, leaning back in her chair. "What I wouldn't give for a high-purity, germanium-crystal detector."

"A *what*, now?" said Selene.

"To check it for radioactivity," Jill said. "There could be something going on here that I simply don't have the equipment to test for."

"There is *obviously* something going on here that you don't have the equipment to test for," Selene drawled.

"I don't see you offering any options," Jill snapped.

"Honestly, I'm as stumped as you are, sister," Selene said with a shrug. "Doesn't feel like a demon. Or a fairy. *Or* a mundane kidnapping."

"I want to see the girl who was burned," Jill said, frowning. "There may be evidence in her injuries that the doctors have missed."

"And how are you gonna do *that?*" Selene said, trying—and failing—to mask a sneer. "Just walk in the front door and *ask?*"

Jill looked up and adjusted her glasses. She raised her eyebrows in an expression of perfect innocence.

To Selene's astonishment and Clara's bewildered amusement, this was exactly what Jill did. And it *worked.* The doctor in charge of Sarah Wightman—an overweight, pink-faced man with neat gray hair named Carlston—spent almost half an hour on the phone with Professor Okedo back in California before he would let Jill into his office, and even then he insisted they all sign confidentiality agreements before ushering them into chairs, but then he laid a folder down in front of Jill with a *smack* and said:

"*There.* You take a look at that and see if it makes sense to *you.*"

With an air of a child opening a Christmas present, Jill flipped open the file and began going over the reports, photos, and x-rays within.

It was not a sight for the faint of heart. Jill had to clench her teeth and force herself to think as analytically as possible when she found the pictures that had been taken upon Sarah Wightman's admittance. The burns *were* horrible, the skin blistered and hanging off the muscle and bone beneath, vividly red and white except where it had been singed purple.

"It was a close thing she didn't lose both hands," Dr. Carlston said, leaning forward. "But we were able to successfully debride the wound and excise the dead tissue. We transplanted skin from her thighs to serve as a graft, and *that* appeared to be working well, but ... "

"But what *then?*" Jill said, flipping through the pages.

"Her arms rejected the grafts. The flesh had necropsied to a greater extent than we thought—well, that's how it first appeared."

"I'm sorry?" Jill said.

The doctor sighed and flipped through to a couple of horrific photos. They each showed a hand, practically skinless save for a few patches of pale white flesh that hung limply off them. The muscle and tendon visible beneath were all a dead, gray color.

"That was *healthy* flesh when we first treated the burns," he said, slapping the paper. "It was healthy, with *no sign* of burn or necropsy."

"A slow burn?" suggested Jill.

"She's not a *tree,*" said Dr. Carlston. "And that's not *burn* damage either. I took a biopsy and ran it through every test we have. The cells *are dying,* but not from burns."

Jill held up a glossy printout. The hand there looked almost like a piece of preserved cadaver—not like a living thing at all.

"Spontaneous cell death?" Jill asked.

"Not *exactly* spontaneous," said Dr. Carlston. "The effect is definitely localized to the area of the most severe burns. But it *is* spreading."

"Are the hands still attached?"

"For now," said the doctor unhappily. "But a double amputation looks likely at this point. We can't have it spread to other parts of her body, and we're risking a systemic infection as it is. I've explained all this to her mother but . . . " He made a frustrated sound in his throat.

"Understandable," said Jill, setting the picture down. "And . . . I'm not sure an amputation would stop it at this point."

Dr. Carlston began gathering up stray sheets, a look of horror growing on his face. "Why is that?" he asked.

"I believe Sarah Wightman was exposed to something—I don't know what yet—which severely injured her. It may have caused other damage—somewhat like radiation poisoning—that was not immediately apparent. I would encourage you to find out *why* these cells are dying, and try to find a way to stop it, because if my hypothesis is correct, you will begin to see spontaneous necropsy all over her body."

Dr. Carlston leaned back in his chair with a sigh. "And what makes you think that?" he asked.

"Habit," said Jill. "I have a habit of imagining the worst possible outcome. Now, may I speak to Miss Wightman herself?"

This turned out to be more difficult. They had to acquire her mother's permission to do so, and at the description of the woman Selene promptly excused herself ("I'll hurt your cause more than help it, I *promise* . . . "), and Clara decided she wished to have another look at Desta Dresner's room.

So it was that Jill was alone when Rebecca Wightman bustled into the waiting room. She was a large sort of woman: her midsection bulged out over the line of her tightly belted jeans, and her western-style suede vest had silver studs on it. Her hair was improbably yellow and buttery, and she wore a lot of very colorful makeup. So even though she was actually rather short, she gave the impression of being much taller. Jill didn't know whether to be impressed or disconcerted.

"Mrs. Wightman," Jill began, but didn't get any farther.

"You're the doctor from California," Rebecca Wightman announced, only the subtle upturn at the end of her sentence suggested that maybe, possibly, what she had just said might have been a question.

Jill opened her mouth to correct the woman, but found she had wandered into deep water with this one, and the current was strong.

"It's about time they gave me someone new: that man Carlston is a *butcher*. Did they tell you he wanted to cut my Sarah's arms off?"

"So I heard," Jill said. "Mrs. Wightman, I wanted to speak with your—"

"I'm sure *you'll* be able to sort this out," Rebecca Wightman said, now clasping Jill by the hand. Hers sported long red nails, Jill noticed, and a silver bracelet with a large silver cross hung from one wrist.

She extracted her hands as quickly as politeness allowed and then clasped them protectively behind her back.

"Mrs. *Wightman*," Jill said sternly. "What I really need is to speak with your daughter. *Would* you allow that?"

Rebecca Wightman blinked eyes with mascara so heavy it had clumped together on the individual lashes, and pulled away from Jill.

"Yes, yes of course," the woman said. "I'll just tell her you're on your way, and you can go get *changed.*" She made a disparaging gesture at Jill's tidy, plain street clothes, and bustled off.

Jill rolled her eyes at the receptionist, who had witnessed the entire interaction. The woman gave her a shrug and a nod, as if to say: *yes, that is what I have had to put up with for the last week. Just roll with it.*

Sarah Wightman lay propped up on pillows in a monstrous hospital bed, hooked up to an IV and a heart monitor. She was staring vacantly off into space when Jill entered, following Dr. Carlston into the little room. Rebecca Wightman, who had been sitting fretfully at her daughter's side, jumped up at the sight of them. If she noticed that Jill had done nothing to alter her appearance she didn't say, but said instead:

"There's no need for *him* to be present," jerking her head toward Dr. Carlston.

Dr. Carlston sighed and went over to check the clipboard hanging from the foot of the girl's bed.

"Hello Sarah," he said, quite gently and kindly. "How are you doing?"

"Mrs. Wightman," said Jill, very seriously. "You need to know that I am *not* a doctor. I am a scientist. I wish to understand what is happening to your daughter, and hopefully from that understanding I will be able to develop a successful treatment plan. But I *need* Dr. Carlston in order to conduct my research."

Whatever Rebecca Wightman was going to say in response was cut off by a little sound from the bed: Sarah had spoken. That is, she'd tried to speak, and coughed instead.

"I'm sorry, I didn't catch that, sugar," her mother said, shoving past Dr. Carlston as she rushed to her daughter's side.

Sarah Wightman, however, was not looking at her. She was staring over the blankets at Jill, her eyes very wide and unfocused.

"You said you were a scientist?" she asked in a small, dry voice.

"That's right," said Jill, smiling encouragingly. "I research extraordinary phenomena . . . like this." She gestured awkwardly at the two bundles of white wrapping that were all she could see of Sarah Wightman's hands.

"Oh," said the girl, sinking back into her pillows. "Then you won't find anything here."

"We'll see about that," Jill said, unable to help the grim edge that crept into her voice.

"No," said Sarah Wightman, listlessly shaking her head. "No, you won't find anything. It's my punishment from God, you see. God is beyond science."

Jill frowned.

"Now Sarah, you know you've done nothing wrong," said Dr. Carlston as Jill circled around the bed to stand beside the girl's head.

"Why?" she asked, and when Sarah Wightman rolled her head to look at her she continued: "*Why* is your god punishing you?"

To her surprise Sarah Wightman pursed her lips and began to cry. Immediately her mother and Dr. Carlston began shushing her, but Jill just listened. Through the sobs, the girl was speaking again.

"B-because I p-put him in the bath-r-room," she choked. "I p-pushed him in when he-e didn't w-want to g-go. And when—when I tried to check on him it *burned* me."

"The door to the outhouse *burned* you?" Jill said, attempting to puzzle out the discombobulated admission.

"I took him to the bathroom," Sarah Wightman whispered. "He ran off into the woods. I chased him. I was angry. I grabbed him. I think I *hurt* him. I put him in the bathroom. He didn't want to go. I pushed him in there anyway. He was quiet. He was *too* quiet. He took too long. So I tried the door to see if I could check on him. And it burned me."

"The door did?" Jill asked.

"The *light*," hissed Sarah Wightman. "The light *inside* the bathroom!"

"There was light inside the bathroom?"

Sarah Wightman nodded.

"What did you see?"

"Just the *light*," said the girl. "Just the *light*. I thought it would burn my eyes out, so I . . . "

"So you threw up your hands," Jill finished, letting her gaze travel down the limp arms once more. "Thank you, Sarah. You've been very helpful. A word, doctor," she said, beckoning to Dr. Carlston.

Once out in the hall and a safe distance away from Rebecca Wightman's withering glare, the older man turned to her and said:

"Now, Miss Hamilton, I'm as good a Christian as anyone in this town, but there's some things you just can't go believing at the drop of a hat. The girl is traumatized; *clearly* she is fabricating a story. There's no *knowing* what went on that night."

"Actually, the evidence supports her statement," Jill said simply. At the doctor's incredulous look she explained: "I found traces of fire—*very hot* fire—around the door of the outhouse in question. *Something* burned there, from the inside flaring outward. What she says about the door—or the *doorway*—burning her, looks to be true. Now, I've taken some samples of the burns at that site. I'd like to compare them to a sample from *her* damaged tissue. And I'd like to use the strongest microscope you have. Also, I need to check for any radioactivity. And . . . I'd like to have a sample from an *undamaged* part of her body, for control. I don't know yet what I'm looking for."

Dr. Carlston frowned and leaned toward her. "That would be . . . extremely irregular," he said.

"This *entire incident* is irregular," Jill agreed fervently. "Now, will you call a nurse to take the samples or shall I?"

Selene lay in the back seat of Arcana, her duffle bag full of weapons lodged behind her head and one arm thrown over her face. She was drifting on a pleasant cloud of sleep, secure in the knowledge that it was broad daylight, and that she was in the middle of a concrete parking lot with many cars to provide cover, and a fully functioning hospital nearby, no less. Then her phone rang.

It was a new phone, purchased for her by Jill on the grounds that her old one was cracked and unreliable and probably water damaged. In reality Selene thought it was because this new phone had a camera and the ability to send pictures over the cellular network, and Jill just wanted another person who could document supernatural events. She'd tried to buy Clara one, but Clara—who did not like having a cell phone in the first place—refused on the grounds that her phone was still new and undamaged, thank you very much. Selene thought, if given the chance, this phone might have changed Clara's attitude. It was slim and black and had a shiny, vibrant display whose keyboard changed from numbers to letters depending on what you wanted. It also had a wide variety of ringtones, some of which were so musical and soothing that they did not immediately sound like ringtones.

One of these was playing now, and Selene listened to it for several moments before she realized it was her phone. Slipping a hand into her pocket she pulled it out, and had a moment of discombobulation when she automatically tried to flip it open and discovered she couldn't. Then she blinked at it, and remembered she had to slide her finger across the bottom half instead.

"Yellow?" she said, pressing the phone to her cheek and rolling onto her back.

"Any word from Jill?" Clara's voice said on the other end.

"Nah, not yet," said Selene. "Though she's been in there long enough, I think she probably managed to see the girl. Where you at?"

"Desta Dresner's room," came the answer.

"Oh. Find any scorch marks?"

"No," said Clara. She sounded a little irritated. "There is nothing. Only . . ."

"Only what?"

"Her boots are missing."

"Her boots."

"She had pink rubber boots," Clara explained. "She always kept them by her bed. It was this . . . thing she liked to do. They're gone."

"So wherever she is, she's got protective footwear," Selene said, suppressing a yawn.

"Whatever came and took her, gave her time to put on her boots," Clara said.

Selene's phone made an impatient *beep, beeeeeep* noise, and she took it away from her head to see a flashing display that said "Boss Jill Calling . . ."

"Hold on a sec, Clara," she said, and with a little smugness she put the other woman on hold, and then pressed the little "merge" button that had appeared on the screen.

"Say hello to the boss, Clara," she said, putting the phone back to her ear.

"Selene?" said Jill. "Selene, I need you to . . . *what* Clara?"

"Yes, I'm here," said Clara, sounding a little confused.

In the truck, Selene grinned, then felt bad, and covered her mouth with her fist.

"Jill, Clara was just telling me that wherever Desta Dresner went, she's got her favorite pair of pink rubber boots," Selene said. "Clara, anything else you want to tell the boss while I have her on the line?"

Silence—from both ends—and then Clara said: "No," and hung up.

Boop, boop, boooop, said the phone.

"Selene, Selene are you there?" Jill asked, sounding urgent.

"Yeah, yeah," said Selene, smiling a little guiltily. "What's up?"

"I need you to bring me the samples I took from the outhouse this morning. They're in my case marked *evidence,* and you'll see them labeled with today's date."

Selene pulled herself up using the back seat as a handhold. "On my way, sister," she said, then paused. "Wait, just where are you?"

It turned out Jill was in the hospital's pathology department, and it took Selene almost half an hour to navigate her way past what felt like dozens of unfriendly receptionists and through as many doors with "private, no entry" signs on them. It was exhilarating, in a way.

She found Jill seated behind an elaborate machine made of tubes and pipes with little knobs. To Selene it looked like some sort of bizarre robot, but Jill was manipulating it with as much calm detachment as if it were a coffeemaker.

"What you got?" she asked, setting the tray of little bottles on the counter beside Jill.

"A few skin cells from behind Sarah Wightman's right ear," Jill said, not looking up from the eyepiece.

"Oh, that's exciting," said Selene, pulling up a stool and sitting on it.

"It *is,*" agreed Jill with total seriousness, "when you compare it to the cells from the palm of her right hand. Are those the samples from the outhouse? Give them here . . ."

She took a bottle labeled "door frame" and popped it open, taking a new dish from a stack to one side and, with a pair of tweezers, transferred a single splinter from one to the other.

"So . . . you *found* something?" Selene asked, scooting closer.

"Maybe . . . possibly," said Jill, sliding the new dish under the microscope. She peered in, adjusted the focus on the machine, slid the dish around, and then peered some more. Then her whole body went stiff and she made a little sound of indrawn air and the word "*Yes . . .* " slipped out.

Pushing back from the microscope she spun to face Selene, the pupils of her eyes blown wide behind her glasses. "I *thought* so, but this proves it—well, pretty much."

Selene frowned and wagged her head. "Proves *what?*" she asked.

"These . . . muscular tissue cells," Jill pointed at a slide with a few flecks of gray between two pieces of glass. "The ones from Sarah Wightman's hand. They are exhibiting a strange form of cell death. I can't see any sort of damage—not from a virus or infection or *even fire.* They're just . . . dead. Not just dead, but disintegrating too. These skin cells . . . " she placed her hand next to another slide, "from behind her ear, are perfectly normal and healthy—as far as I can tell. But *these . . .* " She slid forward to the dish that held the blackened door frame splinters. "They *do* show damage from extreme heat, and of course any cells within the wood had died a long time ago. But they *also* show the *exact same* disintegration process."

Selene blinked at her. "And . . . this tells us . . . what?"

"Well, that Sarah Wightman is telling the truth when she says she was burned by the open door," Jill said. "Her testimony is supported by actual physical evidence."

"Okay," said Selene, hooking her feet behind the legs of the stool and resting her elbows on the counter. "Does this tell you *what it was* that burned her?"

"Nnoo . . . " said Jill, stringing the word out uncertainly. "Only that it was something very *hot* and with some highly unusual properties. But I have some ideas about that, too."

"Oh," said Selene, straightening up. "Let's hear 'em."

Jill swiveled around on her stool and clasped her hands between her knees. She pursed her lips and looked very hard at Selene. "I was thinking. About what you and Clara said about demons. You don't think this is a demonic abduction—but I'm thinking it's safe to say that whatever burned Sarah Wightman also took Amar and Desta Dresner."

Selene nodded her head. "Demons are tricky though," she said. "I mean, it *could* be . . . but it would be the *weirdest* demon I've ever seen. It doesn't feel like any demonic possessions or abductions I've witnessed. Put it that way."

"Fair enough," said Jill, and took a deep breath. "Well, if it's not a demon . . . what about an *angel?*"

Selene leaned back on her stool and let out a long breath.

"There *are* angels, aren't there?" Jill pressed. "It follows, if there are demons."

"*Yeee*aahh . . . " said Selene, letting the word out in heavy sigh. "Angels . . . that's a really . . . *distorted* area. Depends on what *kind* we're talking about. There are tons, you know. The Abrahamic angels are what most people think of when they *say* 'angel,' but those usually turn out to be fravashi or Amesha Spentas. Devas and garuda have also been mistaken for angels. And then *within* the Abrahamic angels you get this really complicated hierarchy that's always given *me* a headache. You could ask Clara to explain—she probably knows more than me."

"But ... could it be possible that an angel abducted Amar Dresner and burned Sarah Wightman?" Jill pressed. "I remember something about angels burning people."

"Those are eyes you're thinking of," Selene said. "Abrahamic angels are known to burn out the eyes of anyone who looks at them directly." She shrugged. "It's worth considering. Though I should warn you; angels are harder to deal with than demons. There's not much you can do but put your head down and wait for them to finish their business and move on."

"But there would be a way to test for angelic activity?" Jill asked. "Or ... I don't know ... some residue we could sweep for?"

Selene made a noncommittal shrugging motion. "We could run a Celestial Gunn Sweep—that should tell us if an angel manifested in this plane within the last week or so."

Jill nodded. She had been nervously fidgeting with the dish of splinters, and now she took a new one and filled it with splinters from a different bottle and placed that under the microscope. "None of this tells us what we can do for Sarah Wightman ... what the *hell?!*" She shot to her feet so fast she sent the stool skidding backward. Selene caught it before it could tip over into a glass-fronted cabinet full of bottles and syringes.

Jerking the dish out from under the microscope she slid the old one in, checked it, then checked it against one of the slides. Then she picked up the new dish of splinters again and thrust it under Selene's nose.

"The bottle this came from? *Where was it?*"

"Er," said Selene, going a bit cross-eyed. "Right next to all the others. Why?"

"*This,*" said Jill, wagging the dish, "doesn't *match!* There's no sign of the cellular disintegration!"

"Er ... good?" said Selene.

"No, no, *bad,*" said Jill. "These splinters were *also* taken from the outhouse door frame. They *should* show the same type of damage as the others. But they *don't.* Unless they've been tampered with somehow. But the only difference I can think of is *where* they were placed within my case. So ... *what was next to them?*"

Someone else might not have been able to say at once, but Selene had solved enough problems by noticing little things that did not fit to make her memory unusually strong. She also had good reason to remember what had been next to the little bottles of door samples.

"Er ..." she said, unsure how Jill would react. "It was the ... um ... the bottle Johnny Bathory gave you. Y'know, the one with his ... um ... blood?"

Jill's eyes widened and her brows dropped, and Selene could almost see the gears turning in her mind. She was half expecting the woman's next words by the time they were spoken.

"I need it," Jill said. *"Now."*

"Gimme me a minute." Selene raised her hands defensively as she backed off her stool. "I can't *teleport*, you know."

Selene's phone rang as she was hiking across the parking lot.

"Yellow," she called into her phone.

"I'm back at the hotel," Clara's voice said. "Where are you?"

"Running errands for our very own mad scientist, of course," Selene said, unlocking the truck and climbing into the back. This time she grabbed Jill's entire briefcase, mentally scolding herself for not having done so in the first place.

"Now...ungh...now she thinks it could be *angels*," Selene said, tucking her phone against her shoulder. It was too thin and slippery, however, and nearly fell out immediately.

"Angels," repeated Clara's voice.

"Yeah ... so ... think you could round up the ingredients for a Celestial Gunn Sweep? I mean, *I* don't think it's angels but at this point who knows. Oh, and be ready to explain to her the difference between angels and fravashi and stuff."

"There is no difference," Clara said promptly. "They are all the same thing called by different names."

"Really?" said Selene, sliding back out of the truck, briefcase in one hand, phone in the other. "That makes things *much* simpler. I'll tell her. Thanks."

"Selene?" Clara said, and this time there was a note of concern in her voice. It made Selene pause before shutting Arcana's door with her foot.

"Yeah?"

"I fear wherever Amar and Desta Dresner are, they are beyond our reach."

"Never say never, sister," Selene said, briefly setting the case down so she could thumb the lock button on the remote key. "Don't forget the ingredients for the Gunn Sweep, and remember: you can always hope for a miracle."

Clara made a derisive snorting sound and hung up. Selene shook her head as she slipped the phone into her pocket and began the long hike back to the pathology lab.

The frustrating thing about dealing with supernatural specimens, Jill thought as she compared once again the two splinter samples, was that there was clearly *something* going on—she just didn't have the instruments to measure it. As it was she was reduced to a sort of trial and error that was not only inefficient and time consuming, but also held enormous room for error. Yet when Selene arrived—carrying her entire briefcase this time, bless the woman—she noted with satisfaction that the sample of vampire blood was indeed right next to the slots where the bottles of door-frame samples had lain.

Carefully moving the disintegrating samples to the end of the counter, she pulled out the little bottle and set it on a dish of its own. Then she took a single splinter of affected wood and the slide of damaged tissue and set them on the dish beside the bottle, before putting the entire arrangement away on a shelf.

"It would be best if I knew how to isolate its effects," she grumbled. "But as I have no idea how this stuff interacts with physical barriers, I don't know what to use."

"Iron's usually a pretty good magical insulator," Selene offered.

"Iron?" said Jill, retrieving yet another dish. "Not lead?"

Selene shook her head vehemently. "Lead's actually a bit of a magical conductor."

"Huh," said Jill, taking an eyedropper and drawing out a tiny sample of blood, which she squirted onto the center of a new dish. Taking another splinter and a fresh sample of tissue she laid these directly in the blood, before immediately slipping it under the microscope. Pressing her eyes to the viewfinder, she carefully refocused the machine.

"Oh my god," she whispered.

"What's up?" she heard Selene say, and felt the warmth of the other woman leaning over her shoulder. It was only with distant attention, however, because of what was going on before her eyes.

The samples of wood and tissue, which she had ascertained *were* damaged before coming into contact with the blood, were rebuilding themselves as she watched.

Jerking her head back she removed the dish and went and got down the slate with the bottle on it. Removing the bottle she slid the slate, with the splinter and tissue samples, under the microscope. Here the change was not nearly so pronounced, but already she could tell some of the damage had been reversed. She looked over at Selene, her mouth slightly agape.

"The vampire blood," she whispered, "is acting as a regenerative agent. It's counteracting whatever is causing the disintegration."

Selene raised her eyebrows.

"Tell me *that* is a good thing," she said.

"It's *astonishing!*" cried Jill. "And yes, it is also a *very* good thing— certainly for Sarah Wightman. Here, could you bring me some of those sterile pads? Ask a nurse—*any* nurse. I want to test this on her *actual* hands."

Sarah Wightman was dozing, but in that shallow, unsettled way that was not true sleep. Her hands no longer hurt—she couldn't feel them at all— but now there was a slow ache spreading up her arms. It made her feel extremely tired. So tired she couldn't even be bothered to rouse herself when a crowd of people bustled into her room. Her mother was there, her mother would see what they wanted.

She watched in detachment as Dr. Carlston gently put her mother aside, and a nurse came forward and began changing the dressing on her hands. She noticed the woman with glasses from earlier, and a black woman with messy hair who she'd never seen before. She watched them fuzzily as the nurses gently re-wrapped her hands and arms, and her eyes lingered on the doorway after they had left.

"I would give it overnight at least," Jill told Dr. Carlston once they were in the hall. "Remember: you're not looking for *dead* tissue, but that particular disintegration pattern I showed you."

Dr. Carlston nodded, but he was frowning. "I don't understand," he said. "What exactly is in those bandages?"

"I can't say for certain," Jill said primly, and behind her Selene let out a silent breath. She would not have put it past Jill to say, with perfect innocent honesty: *"It's two-month old vampire blood diluted in saline solution brushed onto sterile pads,"* and expect the doctor to just *accept* it the way she did.

"You're getting better at this," she told Jill as they made their way out of the hospital for good.

"It was the *truth*," Jill insisted. "I don't know if it's actually the blood that's doing it, or something *about* the blood that is reacting with whatever is in the damaged samples. It's too early to tell."

"Whatever you say, boss," Selene said agreeably.

"That's just the thing. I *can't.*" Jill sighed. "Where are we with Amar and Desta Dresner?"

"Still where we were," Selene told her, holding a swinging door open. "Clara found absolutely zilch—no burns, no nothing. So I had her pick up the ingredients for the sweep. We can start that as soon as it gets dark."

"Why—" Jill began, but this time Selene anticipated the question.

"Elementary magic, girlfriend," she said, "tends to work better in the dark. And don't ask me to explain it—that's just the way things *are.*"

Jill pursed her lips, clearly biting down on a swell of skeptical remarks, but managed to contain them.

"Good," she said at length. "Then we'll have time to eat beforehand."

They ended up back at the same diner they had patronized for breakfast, this time sitting clustered around a little table in the back as Clara laid out the plan for the night. Fay was nowhere to be seen now, and the staff shot them a number of dirty looks as Clara shoved plates of food down to the end of the table to make room for her chart.

"The Celestial Gunn Sweep is a modified version of a seventeenth century divining spell first developed by Romani wizards," Clara explained as she laid out a burnished brass bowl filled with little glass bottles. "Originally it was used to detect the presence of a wide range of supernatural entities, but the Gunn brothers refined it in the 1970's to specifically target angels. They had many opportunities to perfect it, and it is still the best method to tell whether an angel has been or will be present at a given place for a short duration of time."

"Hold on a second," Jill said, chewing her overcooked steak and peering into the bowl. One of the bottles definitely contained lavender, and another rosemary. There was also a small tub of oil. "You said has *or* will? What does that mean?"

Clara looked pleadingly at Selene, who hastily swallowed her bite of cheeseburger and wiped her mouth on her sleeve.

"Angels don't exist in linear time, like we do," she explained. "They can drop in and out of our world as they please. They can *literally* be in two places at once—at least, that's what people who study the Brothers Gunn say. Truth to tell, there have been few confirmed reports of angelic activity since the attempted apocalypse of 1970—"

"There was an *apocalypse* in 1970?" Jill exclaimed.

"It was averted," Clara said.

"*Anyway,*" continued Selene. "The thing about the Gunn Sweep is it scans for angels in the near vicinity—in the past, present *and* future. So you can use it to check and see if an angel is going to make an appearance, as well as seeing if one has been around lately."

"Or if one is standing right behind you," Clara added.

"Can they sneak up on you like that?" Jill asked.

Selene and Clara looked at her and nodded in unison.

"Behind you, beside you, in front of you, *in you*," Selene said. "Angels can pretty much go wherever they want."

Jill pursed her lips and nodded. "Okay," she said, poking at the copper bowl. "How does this work?"

The night was dark and the sky scattered with stars by the time they set up at an empty campsite not far from the outhouse in question. It would have been best, Clara had remarked bitterly, if they could have run the sweep at ground zero, as it were, but Jill had felt this would be trying the patience of the volunteer officer who was currently keeping watch on the crowd of pilgrims—who were for the most part clustered around a bonfire and chatting happily—and so they set up at a prudent distance. They were still close enough, Selene assured her, to get an accurate reading.

"The sweep is actually pretty wide, space-wise," she explained as they laid out the bowl, and Clara began mixing ingredients. "It's just more specific the closer you are to the exact location."

"And how long is this going to take?" Jill asked.

Clara paused in the middle of sprinkling crushed rosemary into the bowl. "About four hours," she said after some thought.

"Four *hours?*" Jill exclaimed. She checked her watch. It was a quarter past nine.

"This is magic, hon," said Selene wearily. "Not . . . um . . . *magic.* I mean, it's not called a *sweep* for nothing. Think of how long it takes you to find a missing sock or bra in your bedroom, when your bedroom is a mess and that sock or bra may or *may not* be there, oh, and you also have to check the hours, days, and even *weeks* before and *after* that moment to see if it appeared in those times as well."

"Oh," said Jill, leaning back against Arcana's door. "That makes sense, then."

Clara dipped her fingers into the tub of oil and smeared a wide streak around the rim of the bowl. She wiped her hand on a black handkerchief and sat back on her heels.

"Would you like to perform the incantation?" she asked Selene deferentially.

"Why not all of us?" asked Selene. "It'll be more powerful that way. Do you have the English version?"

Clara nodded. She had produced a battered little book and was leafing through its pages.

"Here," she said, opening it and placing her finger in the middle of the spread. "You may read from it. I memorized it when I was eight."

"Handy, that," Selene said, taking the little book.

Switching on her flashlight Jill came over to stand at Selene's elbow and peered over.

The book appeared to be a handwritten journal. The lettering was neat and precise, and in a foreign language she did not recognize. One page, however, was covered in tidy red letters that spelled out recognizable English words. She read it through, mouthing the words under her breath.

"Don't," said Selene, giving her a gentle nudge with her elbow. "Wait until Clara gives the word."

"I was only practicing," Jill objected.

"Yeah, well, the great mystical ether don't know that," Selene said with a wry grin.

"Are you ready?" Clara asked. She was kneeling above the bowl, a match in one hand, box in the other.

"When you are, sister," Selene said.

Clara nodded, and struck the match. It flared to life, briefly illuminating her bony face—in the stark light her eyes appeared unusually dark: black pools save where the fire was reflected as a tiny golden spark. She began to speak, and only a little off cue, Selene and Jill fell in behind her.

"*Find,*" they spoke in more or less unison. "*Messenger without message. Out of maker, out of order. Find the doors, find the footsteps. Find the flame behind the light. This is what we charge:* melohinon elozere."

Jill tripped a bit over the last two words, and feared what came out of her mouth was closer to "melanin-hello-there," but she was drowned out by Clara and Selene's more assured pronunciation. To her surprise the sound of their voices intensified and took on a strange echoing quality—as if there had been nine of them speaking instead of three. Clara dropped the match into the bowl, where it went out with an anti-climactic *puff.*

"That's it?" Jill asked, moderately disappointed.

"It has begun," said Clara. "Now we wait."

Selene brought out her duffle bag and used it as a cushion while Clara stood over the bronze bowl. Jill went and sat in Arcana's back seat, typing up a report of what they had just done. She was particularly intrigued by those last, alien words—which apparently had no English equivalent.

"How did you spell those last words?" she asked, her fingers hovering over the keyboard. "Mellow-high—"

"*Shush!*" Selene and Clara hissed in unison, and Jill bit off the end of the word.

"What?"

"That's a . . . how do you say?" Selene said, waving a hand as if trying to catch the right phrase out of thin air.

"A Word of Power," Clara intoned, so clear and defined that Jill could almost hear the capital letters.

"Which is . . . what?" Jill probed.

"The closest thing you get to *abra cadabra,*" Selene said. "They're um . . . well we actually don't know exactly where they came from."

"They are all that remains of the Language of Making," Clara said.

Jill wrinkled her nose. "Wait . . . isn't that something from a book?"

"It has been alluded to in many books," Clara said. "It is one of the Universal Truths that permeate the human subconscious and often manifest in the stories you think of as . . . well, as fairy tales and fantasies. There was a Language of Making, but it was lost a long time ago. I do not think it was originally *words* as you or I understand them. It was something else. What we used was only a fragment of it, but like a drop of dye cast into clear water it will have a profound effect."

"Basically those aren't words you want to risk saying lightly," Selene said. "I mean, they *might* do nothing . . . or they might do *anything.* Without the proper context to guide their actions—the bowl, the lavender, the oil, the chant—it's almost completely random whether it has any effect or not."

"Like getting radium from thorium decay," Jill said, nodding sagely. "I see."

"Getting what from *what now?*" Selene said.

"Radium," said Jill. "Specifically, one of its more unstable isotopes. You can get radium when thorium decays, but it doesn't *stay* radium for very long before *it* decays into something else. So you can have a lump of, say, uraninite, which *may* or *may not* have any radium in it, all depending on what is happening at a nuclear level."

Selene put her head on one side, digesting this. "Yeah," she said with a sort of half shrug. "I guess you could put it that way. Just imagine if you could also, I dunno, find a way to make *sure* there would be radium in that lump of ura-whatever at a given time. And if that radium could then make *really weird* things happen."

Jill opened her mouth to begin expounding upon all the weirdness radium was capable of, but thought better of it. She returned to her computer, and Selene and Clara returned to their silent vigil.

The night slowly crept by: one by one the dark figures in the neighboring site left their bonfire, and the conflagration itself burned down into a pile of dimly glowing embers. Jill finished entering her report and went to sit on the cold ground next to Selene. Clara shifted occasionally from foot to foot, but never actually sat. Jill's knees grew stiff from sitting in a folded position, so she uncrossed them and sat with her legs stretched out until her rear began to ache. Then she went and lay down across Arcana's back seat.

She had thought herself too wound up to sleep, and she doubted she ever properly drifted off, but she was in a slight doze when she was roused by a word from Clara.

"M-wha?" she mumbled, pulling herself upright and lowering her feet to the ground.

"I said: it begins." Clara's voice came drifting through the darkness.

Jill checked her phone: it was fifteen minutes after midnight. Slipping it back into her pocket she made her way over to where Selene had gotten to her feet and was standing opposite Clara across the bowl.

The bowl, which now contained a faint purplish glow. It lit the faces of the two women from beneath, casting vague shadows up around their eyes. For a moment Jill felt a wave of disorientation as she saw different features highlighted in what she had come to think of as familiar faces: the tense lines around Selene's mouth and brow, the sharp planes of Clara's cheekbones and the flare of her nostrils. They stared intensely down at the bowl and made no move to acknowledge her as she came to stand between them.

The glow turned out to be coming from a single ball of light that was slowly growing as little drops of light condensed on the rim of the bowl and slid down to pool in the bottom. As they watched, it grew in intensity until it was so bright Jill had to avert her gaze.

She was aware of it still; in her peripheral vision she saw it begin to rise up out of the bowl, and there was a subtle pulsation in its radiance that suggested rotation. Up, up it went, until it hung at about head height. Then it went out abruptly.

Jill blinked, trying to rid her mind of the afterimage left by the light. Instead of fading, however, the negative image only intensified, and to her amazement began to move again—as if whatever was creating the light was *still there*. It rose high above their heads, and Jill had to crane her neck back so she could track its motion.

When it reached a height of about fifty feet it halted—and then began to grow, throwing out arms that twisted as it slowly spun, forming a shape that put Jill in mind of a spiral galaxy. As the arms of the negative light passed over them, Jill thought she felt a chill settle on her skin.

The strange form hovered above them, rotating majestically against the starry sky, and after a while she began to see faint traces of lights at the tips of the arms, like dimly flashing stars. Once, one flashed brightly, far out at the very tip of the longest arm, and then the whole thing slowly faded from view. The chill left Jill's skin, and the gentle murmuring of the wind picked up in her ears, sighing across the campground.

"What . . ." she began. "What was that?"

"That was the Celestial Gunn Sweep," said Clara. "It read nothing in the vicinity either in the near past or future."

"But . . . but there was a flash," Jill protested. "I *saw* it, out on the end of the arm."

"That was somewhere far away from here," Selene said gently. "And at least two weeks in the future, I'd say."

"Colorado, at the closest," Clara added. "Maybe Kansas."

"So . . . no angels have been around here?" Jill asked, stamping down on her disappointment.

"Not in the last year," said Selene. "Or the next."

Jill sighed and helped Clara pack up the bowl and the remains of the ingredients. They put them in Arcana, and Jill drove them back to the motel. They fell into bed—even Clara—tired and deflated.

They were woken in the early morning by the trill of both Jill and Clara's phones ringing at the same time.

"Arrrgggh!" cried Selene, fumbling in Jill's coat, even as Clara rolled out of bed and flipped open her phone.

"Nordstern," Jill heard her say, and then her face went perfectly blank.

"Yellow," said Selene, putting Jill's phone to her ear. "Yeah," she said. "Yeah, she's right here. Phone call for you, boss," she said, passing the phone to Jill, who took it and peered at the name on the display before bringing it to her ear.

"This is Jill Hamilton," she said. "How can I help you, Dr. Carlston?"

"You can tell me what you were doing in Sarah Wightman's room last night," came the clipped voice of the doctor, in a mix of anger and hysteria.

"I . . . *what*?" said Jill. "I was never *in* Sarah Wightman's room last night."

Behind her, Clara was speaking into her own phone:

"I assure you I have no knowledge of—they said *what*?"

Jill put a finger in her other ear and turned up the volume on her phone.

"I was at Green River campground until past midnight—ask the volunteer patrol," she said. "What's *happened*?"

"What do *they* say happened?" Clara asked.

"What's *happened*?" repeated Dr. Carlston over the phone, the anger subsiding and the hysteria growing to fill in the gaps. "Sarah Wightman has *completely* recovered, *that's* what's happened!"

"Really?" said Jill, blinking in disbelief. This was a far more dramatic result than she had dared hoped for. "Then my treatment worked?"

"That's just the *thing,* Hamilton," Dr. Carlston said. "When the nurse came in this morning the bandages were all stripped off. She found them in a pile next to Wightman's monitor with a *note* on top. I thought *you'd* left it."

"What—a *note?*" said Jill. "No, no I never . . . wait, what does it *say?* And what does *Wightman* say happened?"

"Girl was under the influence of painkillers and sedatives," snapped Dr. Carlston. "She's saying an *angel* came and healed her. Needless to say, her *mother* is having a field day."

"I can imagine," said Jill, dropping the phone to her shoulder. "*Selene,*" she hissed. "The reading from last night . . . are you *sure* it was from out of state?"

Selene nodded. "Nowhere closer than a hundred miles. And not due for another two weeks."

"So no chance it could have indicated activity, say, at the hospital *last night?*"

"What?" said Selene, sounding almost offended. "Naw, no way. What's happened?"

"I don't know," said Jill. "Doctor, I need to see Sarah Wightman. No, no, I *assure* you I had *nothing* to do with this."

She hung up.

"I need to get to the hospital," she explained. "Something happened in the night and Sarah Wightman's been healed." She stopped. Clara had also gotten off the phone and was looking like she'd been hit by a truck and hadn't quite accepted it yet.

"What's wrong?" Jill asked.

"Amar and Desta Dresner," Clara whispered. "They're back."

Jill nearly dropped her phone in shock.

"*What?*" she cried.

Amar and Desta Dresner turned out to be amber-skinned children with vigorously curly black hair and large, almond-shaped eyes with dark lashes. They were the most enchanting children Jill had ever met, and they were entirely unharmed. Indeed, they were in high spirits, running wild over the large house, when they arrived.

Clara, who'd gone ahead, ushered them downstairs while their mother hovered protectively above them.

Martin Dresner, even taller and somewhat bulky, rambled around the kitchen making coffee while Jill tried to interview the children. They regarded her with serious dark eyes, and did not seem inclined to answer her questions.

Where had they been?

"Exploring," Amar said firmly.

"Castles," said Desta. "Big castles, small castles, cloud castles, star castles ... "

"Desta has been in a castle phase for the last three months," Martin explained self-consciously.

"Yes," said Jill. "But *where?*"

Amar shrugged. "Around," he said.

"We saw a ... we saw a *giraffe-bird*," said Desta, raising her hands to illustrate. "It cackled and carried me on ... carried me on its *shoulders.*"

"Was it the giraffe-bird that took you?" Jill asked.

"No, *silly*," said Desta, grinning. "*Amar* came and got me."

"Amar, you came back *home*?" his mother asked.

"I didn't want Desta to be left out," he said. "So after waffles I brought her along. We didn't fight or make any messes," he assured his parents.

"How did you get out of the outhouse?" Jill asked.

Amar shrugged and looked up at her with the perfect innocence only a seven-year-old could manage. "I went somewhere else," he said, and that was all she could get out of him.

"They seem *perfectly* fine," Ayana told them as they left. She sounded like she was still trying to convince herself of this fact.

"And they just appeared in their beds this morning?" Jill asked.

The woman nodded. "They must have sneaked in through the back door. They were horribly dirty—but fine. They must have been off playing make-believe for the past few days. I can't imagine how they weren't seen ... but here they are."

"Do you have any intention of making a statement to the police?" Clara asked.

Ayana Dresner looked ready to throw them bodily out of the house, but her husband stepped in and said, with a good approximation of a soothing voice:

"Only to tell them to call off the dogs, as it were. I mean, we have them back, and that's the important thing."

"Let's hope Sarah Wightman is a bit more forthcoming," Jill grumbled as they pulled into the hospital parking lot.

"Don't count on it," Selene said, putting the truck in neutral and setting the parking brake. "This is looking more and more like a GOA to me."

Jill, distracted with her briefcase, didn't question this. She hopped out and fairly pelted up the steps to the main lobby and into the restricted-access corridors before anyone could stop her.

Dr. Carlston was hardly surprised to see her when she burst into his office.

"If you're hoping for a clear explanation," he said heavily, "this is the *wrong* place."

"Sarah Wightman doesn't remember what happened?" Jill all but wailed.

"Oh, she *does*, that's the problem," Dr. Carlston said bitterly and spun his open laptop around so Jill could see the web page displayed there.

"'Roosevelt teen cured by miraculous angelic visitation . . . '" Jill read in the blog's headline. "But that's *wrong!* We *checked!* There were no angels around here!"

"You checked," said Dr. Carlston blankly. "For *angels?*"

"I need to see her. Can she receive visitors?"

Sarah Wightman was sitting up in bed eating yogurt from a plastic cup when Jill was shown in. Her mother fairly bounced to her feet and shook Jill's hand in both of hers.

"It's a miracle!" she cried, her eyes shining. "Thank *God!*"

Even to Jill's skeptical mind it looked pretty miraculous. Sarah Wightman's hands, uncovered and clearly useable, were the healthy brownish pink of healing skin, and apart from a few minor discolorations there was no sign of the burns or the horrible necropsied tissue. The girl herself was vibrantly pink and smiling blissfully.

"Sarah," said Jill seriously, sliding a chair up next to the bed, "Sarah . . . what happened?"

Sarah Wightman sighed rapturously. "I was *visited*," she said. "By an *angel*."

"Can you *describe* this angel?" Jill asked. "What did it *do?*"

Sarah Wightman swallowed a spoonful of yogurt and stared airily over Jill's head.

"I was lying in bed, praying for forgiveness," she said conscientiously. "When suddenly there was this blinding light and an angel stepped out of it. I could tell he was an angel because he had this glowing halo around his head. Anyway, he came and undid the bandages on my hands, and he told me everything would be all right, and I *knew* it would be, so I went to sleep—and when I woke up I was healed!" She set down her yogurt and waved her hands.

"Has Amar been returned yet?" she asked, suddenly concerned. "I need to apologize to him."

"Amar Dresner is fine," Jill said. "As is his sister. They reappeared at approximately the same time you had your . . . visitation."

"That's *good*," said Sarah, leaning back in her pillows.

"Is that true?" Dr. Carlston asked as Jill made to leave.

"Yes," she replied. "Their parents believe they were off playing somewhere."

Dr. Carlston shook his head. "Oh," he said, picking up a small box from a trolley in the hall. "Here are the wrappings we found on her table this morning. They appear to be the dressing you applied yesterday."

Frowning, Jill opened the box, and there sure enough were the stained pads and medical tape. There was also a scrap of paper, clearly torn from a corner of Sarah Wightman's treatment record. Taking it out and holding it up Jill peered at it.

"And there is the note . . . " Dr. Carlston said unhappily.

In sloppy, blunt pencil was scrawled a single line:

Good try, but look harder.

"I was hoping you could tell me what that meant," the doctor said.

Jill, who'd stopped in her tracks to read the note, practically shuddered with frustration. "Apparently," she said, stuffing the note back into the box, "*apparently* I need to *look* harder."

Selene and Clara were waiting in the parking lot, standing between Arcana and the motorcycle, Unicorn, when Jill stormed out the doors and down the steps.

"I take it Wightman was not a perfect witness . . ." Selene hazarded.

Jill practically growled as she stuffed the box into the back seat and then thrust the scrap of paper at Selene.

"*Someone* was there," she said. "They healed Sarah Wightman, took off her bandages, and left *that*. I think they left it for *me*."

Squinting rather, Selene read the note. Then she let out a low whistle and passed it to Clara, who read it in turn and responded with one of her inverted shrugs.

"Well?" said Jill. "What do *you* make of it?"

Clara looked up at her, then over at Selene, and said in tones of mild wonderment: "It's a GOA."

Selene put her head on one side and nodded. "Yep," she said. "I'm calling GOA."

"*What*," said Jill, "is a 'gee oh ay?'"

Clara dipped and raised her shoulders again. "An initialism," she said. "It stands for God Or Aliens."

"Basically," said Selene as Jill groaned and rolled her eyes. "It's something we don't know what it was and there's no way of finding out. Might as well be God . . . or aliens. *We don't know.*"

"*Ugh*," said Jill, snatching the piece of paper out of Clara's gloved hand. "That is *not* an acceptable answer."

"It isn't an answer," said Selene. "It's just a way of admitting that *we don't have an answer for this.*"

"It happens sometimes," Clara said gently. Then she said, in a rhythmic way as if quoting someone: "Does the trapped spider understand the human intervention that frees it? We, as humans, must accept that there are beings in this universe that are so far beyond our understanding that their actions are as incomprehensible to us as ours are to the spider."

Jill glowered at them and climbed into Arcana.

"Hey," said Selene, putting her head in after her and grinning. "It could have been a lot worse. At least nobody *died* this time!"

Jill sighed, and though she was still stewing in her own impotent frustration, she found she had to admit that Selene was right.

Still, she couldn't help muttering under her breath: "But I *will* figure this out one day . . . "

"Whatever lets you sleep at night," Selene said amiably, climbing in beside her. "Now, if you'll give this a break, maybe we could get something to eat? I'm *starving*."

Jill felt her stomach grumble, and decided this was something she agreed with whole-heartedly.

Did you see that?

My child, this might be a disaster
Young lovers, watch out for the blaster
See that flash from the sky, it's
God or aliens!

That's right, you choose one or the other
Tonight, do your best to discover
What's that sound that you hear? It's
God or aliens!

If you pick one you can bet some people will get quite upset,
But you've nothing to fear.
Look up into that blue sky, say you've got big fish to fry
Your intention is clear.

All ways, they lead you in a circle
What now? You act like it's a surprise.
Don't you see it's got to be
God or aliens!

If allowed to have your say, we could be stuck here all day.
It's getting harder to hear.
All the crazy in this verse, still your courage won't disperse.
Immolation is free—so is this:

God or aliens!

A ship no ship a door no door oh how
Can you figure out this big mess now?
Things you can't explain, might as well be
God or aliens!

God, or Aliens

You've got no lines of inquiry just magic and some wizardry.
Cooperation is key.
I don't know why you reject all the things that I expect
But now all we have is
God or aliens!

God or aliens!

—God or Aliens/*The Laughing Hands*

MISSIONARY ^{6.}MAN

Pearson, Kansas

ANDREW BELL WAS SMALL FOR HIS AGE and he knew it. He felt even smaller than usual seated at his mother's enormous kitchen table. The vast expanse of hard-scrubbed wood stretched out in front of him, striped with afternoon sunlight from the kitchen window. He was grateful for it, however, because it kept the man on the other side a safe distance away.

This man was only the latest in a string of well-brushed men in neat dark suits who had been through his mother's kitchen ever since the *incident,* and in Andrew's experience, they were mostly well-intentioned people who were unable to listen to the words Andrew said.

It didn't stop them asking questions, though.

"Who was the first person you saw about your condition, Mr. Bell?" the latest man asked.

This man was different, Andrew had to admit. He was white, for starters, and while the others had all called him Andrew, or even *Andy,* this man spoke to him as though he were an adult. It was all "May I speak with you, *Mr. Bell,*" "How are you doing today, *Mr. Bell?*" It was enough to convince Andrew to come down to the kitchen when his mother called, instead of leading them on a mad chase all over the house and into the backyard like he had done with the others.

"I already told you that," Andrew's mother said. "We went and saw Dr. Chaser over in Wichita—"

"Thank you, Mrs. Bell," said the man. "I appreciate your information, but I would like to hear what young Mr. Bell has to say."

And Momma, by some miracle, fell silent. Andrew was shocked. Nothing and no one had been able to get Momma to be quiet ever since the incident if she didn't want to. It gave him the tiniest spark of hope that things would be different this time, and that gave him the courage to speak.

"Yes, Mr. Bell?" said the man. He had muddy blond hair neatly trimmed, and a sprinkling of stubble across his strong, squarish chin. He looked, Andrew thought, rather like Captain America, if Captain America forgot to shave for a couple days and traded in the red, white and blue spandex for a priest's black coat and collar, and the star spangled shield for a white cowboy hat. This, which was now hanging neatly beside the front door, had positively shone in the sun as the man had crunched up their driveway in his leather cowboy boots.

"I wen' an' saw Dr. Chaser, yeah," said Andrew, then kicked himself for not finishing his words. That made him more nervous, which made him begin to stammer. "H-he s . . . said ah . . . ah . . . said ah ah ah I am fine. Buh . . . buh buh but Momma say no so she brung in Mr. Palm."

"Mr. . . . . Jeremiah Palm," the man said, producing a small book and making a notation. "The local priest? What did he do?"

"H-he he he say I un g-got got demons inside me—"

"Demon, darling," said his mother. "Just one."

"Could be more than one," the man disagreed cheerfully. "Dual possessions are rare, but they do happen. What sort of demons did he say you had?"

"A bad kind. Devil spawn an' darkness," said Andrew. "He ah . . . had me eat salt an' it brought my dinner back up. I kept blowing an' blowing, so I thought all the demons got blown outta me, but he say they still inside so he put me in a bath an' wrapped my head in towels."

Andrew shivered. The water had been cold and the towels had gotten soaked. He could hear Mr. Palm's chanting and feel his mother's hands holding him still, so he couldn't reach up and yank the towels off. He'd begun to choke, struggling to breathe. He'd thought, certainly *this* would get the demons out of him, but when the towels were finally removed Mr. Palm had declared the demon only weakened, and told his mother he'd have to come back next week.

"I see . . ." said the man, making a little mark in his book. "And . . . how many times did this happen?"

"I forgotten," said Andrew. "Once a week since Chrissmas? I dunno how many weeks that is, but is a lot, innit?"

The man nodded gravely. "And you still have demons in you?" he asked.

"Don' I must?" asked Andrew. "Momma says I scream at night an' paint my walls in blood. Ya *seen* it, I know. I don' remember doing any of it, but is *there* every morning an' it *scares* me."

"Yes," said the man, "they're meant to." He gave Andrew such a sympathetic look that suddenly he knew—he *knew*—that this man not only believed him, but understood how he felt. "Well," he went on. "I think you've been through enough. Lets get those demons out of you right away, what do you say?"

"Will it need wet towels?" Andrew asked.

"None at all," said the man, smiling broadly. He had perfect white teeth, just like Captain America should, Andrew thought. "You don't even have to move. Sit tight, this will only take a minute."

Getting up, the man came around the table and gently pushed it away from Andrew, so his chair now stood alone in the middle of the kitchen floor.

"Comfortable?" he asked. "Need to use the bathroom?"

When Andrew nodded, and then shook his head, the man smiled reassuringly and opened his briefcase. Inside Andrew glimpsed a lot of little bottles on silver chains, a couple knives, leather pouches, and several flasks of dark liquid. Removing one of these and a large brush, the man unscrewed the lid and began painting a circle around Andrew's chair.

"Wha's that for?" Andrew asked.

"Well," said the man. "I'm going to draw the demons out of you, carefully, so you don't get hurt. Once they're free, however, I need to make sure they can't just run off and jump inside someone *else*."

"So the circle is to protect *us*?" asked Andrew's mother.

The man, bent over the floor and concentrated on his work, didn't answer at once. He finished the circle by painting a smaller circle that joined the two ends, inside of which he painted a little sigil, like an *S* with an extra squiggle and some dots. Then he opened a pouch and sprinkled some powder around the legs of Andrew's chair.

"Right," he said, replacing the bottle, brush and bag and getting to his feet. "Whatever happens, don't leave the circle. Got that?"

Andrew nodded.

"The circle is for protection," the man said, turning to Andrew's mother. "But it's to protect *him*, not us."

Momma stared at the man. Andrew tried to understand. He knew something had changed about his mother since the incident, but it had never been so obvious as it was now. Her face was still Momma's face, but it was the wrong expression. Her eyes were too wide, too bloodshot, and her breathing was too fast. Her teeth bared in a humorless grin; she began to laugh.

"You-huhuhu have the *wrong* idea, Mr. Freeman," she said.

"No," said the man with a sigh. "Stop messing around, Lashka, and come out."

"You-huhu *summon* me?" said Andrew's mother. Or, rather, the thing *inside* Andrew's mother. Andrew found he had to admit, it hadn't really been his mother since the incident.

The man held out his hand, as if offering it for the taking. "I do, Lashka, I summon you."

And then . . . then Andrew's mother began to laugh in earnest. Her mouth opened wide—wider than it should have. Her skin turned blue, and some *thing* crawled up her throat and out her mouth. It crouched on her tongue a moment and then leapt at the man.

Almost too fast to see, the man snapped his hand back and thrust the other out. He held something in it that glinted like crystal, and the thing dissolved into a thick, blue-black smoke in midair. This billowed out, cloaking first the man, then Andrew's mother, before rushing to fill the room.

All except a narrow pillar of air around Andrew's chair, which remained clear as day.

Peering into the smoke, Andrew heard a grunt of pain, a hastily bitten-off swearword, and finally a triumphant *"Gotcha!"* Then there was some confused thumping, the sound of someone running into the table, and then a grinding as the window over the sink was pushed open. Almost at once the smoke began to clear, and a moment later the shape of the man was visible, bent over Andrew's mother and gently fanning her face.

"Doing okay, Mr. Bell?" he asked, his voice a little hoarse.

"Is Momma okay?" Andrew asked.

"Yeah—she should be," said the man. "Could use a drink of water though, I think. Would you mind? I don't know where you keep the cups. Oh, you can get off your chair now. Demon's gone."

"They said the demons was in *me* though," said Andrew, cautiously climbing down off his chair.

"Nope," said the man. "Only one demon, and that was in your mother. All you've got inside you is a whole bunch of bad memories. Which, I can assure you, no matter what you may hear people say, aren't nearly as bad as a *real* demon. Easy there, Mrs. Bell. Looks like there was a bit of an accident, but no harm done. Can you manage to sit up? Your son is bringing you some water."

Somewhere on the outskirts of Denver, Colorado

CLAYMORE DREAMED. This was unusual: she had gotten rather good at *not dreaming* and usually shut dreams down before they got too strong, if she couldn't avoid them entirely. This one, however, was persistent. It had dogged her sleeping mind for the past two weeks, and it was becoming difficult to get any rest with all the waking up she had been doing to escape it. So, finally, worn out from a day of riding and an evening listening to Jill and Selene bicker, Claymore allowed herself to sleep. And to dream.

In her dream she was walking through a thick dark wood. Unless she was floating. She had become her name: her legs had fused into a long, gray blade; her arms were quillons and her hands were quatrefoils.

She was lost. This she knew. More than that, she had lost everything else. She was alone. Even Bellatrix and Unicorn were gone. Though, if she had become a sword, perhaps Bellatrix was now a woman and Unicorn was a unicorn. She could see them clearly in her dream, though she knew they were not there. Bellatrix made a tall, narrow, sharp-looking woman, and she wore a gray dress that glinted like metal. Unicorn was a huge, dark shadow behind her. Big as a Shire, graceful as an Arabian, she held her neck in a proud arch. Her horn was made of anodized aluminum and glimmered faintly in the reflected light from Bellatrix's dress.

Claymore could see them, knew the feel of them, but could not find them in her dream. The wood closed in thickly about her, and she did not know where to go.

A light bloomed behind her, and Claymore turned her stiff neck to find a deer standing over her. No, not a deer . . . a *stag.* He was white as fresh snow, and the two magnificent antlers resting on his head had a translucency like ice. Colors shot through them, brilliant like a rainbow.

He stood over her for a moment, and then with a leap took off through the wood.

Claymore followed as best she could. The stag knew the wood. He knew the way out of it. And he would lead her, if she could but follow.

She shot through the wood after him, keeping the pale leaping body always in her sight. She was gaining on him, she was closing on him. She could not stop.

I am a sword, and he is a soft, beautiful, innocent animal, she realized with a sense of horror. Then, grappling frantically for control of the dream, she remembered something else: *I am going at him hilt first. I will not hurt him.*

They cleared the wood just as Claymore reached the white stag, and for a moment the two were suspended in air over a dark city while the wood crowded away behind them.

Then the white stag gave another bound—across thin air this time— and shot away into the sky. Claymore watched him leaping among the stars, toward the face of the moon, even as she fell.

"I think it's a demon," the moon said.

"No it's not," said Claymore.

"What do you mean it's not?" asked Jill.

She opened her eyes, and like the lights going on at the end of a play the dream vanished. Bellatrix was at her back, and Unicorn she knew was parked just outside their motel room door. Claymore was gone, replaced with Clara, and the stag remained only as a memory of snow-white fur and a brilliance shot with a rainbow of colors. Selene was staring at her from across the other bed, Jill's computer balanced on one leg, with an amused expression on her face.

"Didja just fall asleep on us?" she asked.

Clara rubbed her face, assuring herself that she did have *hands.* She was also pleased to find that her legs had gone back to normal.

"Sort of," she said. "There was a dream that wouldn't leave me alone."

Selene raised an eyebrow, and Jill, who was sorting through newspapers at the little desk, shot her a curious look.

"So you mean in your *dream* it wasn't a demon?" she asked.

Clara nodded. "It was a white stag," she said.

Selene chuckled. "Well, it *sounded* like you'd been listening, which if you had, you'd admit this is pretty quintessential demonic activity. Listen here . . . " she straightened the laptop and began to read. "'A boy in Pearson, Kansas, was reportedly found asleep in a pool of blood late last year. Afterward he began exhibiting signs of extreme stress, disorientation and schizophrenia. Doctors have been unable to determine the cause of his illness, and his mother hired a priest to perform an exorcism.' Now, compare that to *this* report, also from Pearson, of an outbreak of graffiti defacing local storefronts. They've also had an increase in cases of rabid dogs and other animals."

"Graffiti doesn't mean—" Jill began.

"*Look* at the graffiti and tell her," Selene insisted, shoving the laptop at Clara.

Taking the computer, Clara scrolled through the collection of pictures and felt an uncomfortable prickling in her gut. They were all of comfortable, modest buildings, some with wide windows, others with inviting expanses of brick wall. All of them had been decorated with copious amounts of red and black paint which, to an untrained observer, might have been a disordered jumble of lines, circles and dots, but to Clara they spoke volumes.

"This is a master *unbinding*," she whispered, tracing a finger over the first one. "This is the sigil of Lashka the Tormentor. And *this* . . . is that a partial *odegra*?" She raised her face to Selene. "How is this town not *crawling* with demons?"

"For all I know, it *is*," Selene said grimly, taking the computer back.

"Okay, okay," said Jill, waving a hand. "Someone explain to me how demons work, and how they're different from gods and angels and stuff."

Clara and Selene exchanged a look. The look said, "Oh, won't *you* please take this one?" at which Selene groaned and rolled her eyes.

"So, near as I can tell," she began, "demons are non-corporeal entities that can manifest within a person's mind. That's what we call a *possession*. They can also manifest in—that is, *possess*—an inanimate object. They are generally pretty nasty, and the best thing to do is stay as far away from them as possible."

"Unless you are an exorcist," Clara added.

"Or us," said Selene, with a dark grin. "They can't be killed—not in this dimension, anyway—and they have all sorts of powers over their environment that makes fighting them a royal pain in the butt."

"They exist in a strict hierarchy," Clara took over. "The exact structure is unknown, but it is generally accepted that there are an infinite number of lesser demons, somewhere on the order of thousands of greater demons, and several hundred legendary demons. Also, theoretically, there are maybe a handful of elder demons, but these have never been directly observed. The greatest power you can hold over a demon is to know its true name, but this in itself is risky, since their name is intrinsically linked with the demon. To know its name is to invite the demon into your mind. You have to be strong enough to keep control of the demon at all times, otherwise it will consume you."

"Interesting," said Jill. In place of her computer she had pulled over the motel notepad and was scribbling on it.

"As for how they relate to gods," Clara sighed. "It's complicated."

"That never stopped me before," Jill pointed out.

"It's sort of like this," Selene said. "*Gods* feed off human belief. No belief, no god. The entity *behind* the god can still exist, however. These are the entities that make up the class of beings *we* refer to as angels, demons . . . and gods."

Jill nodded. "So basically, what makes it a demon or an angel or a god . . . all depends on how we perceive it?"

"Pretty much," said Selene. "And by their behaviors. There are certain things a demon will do that an angel won't. But yeah, it basically comes down to: are they nice to us or not? And whether or not they have a cult following."

"It would be useful," Jill sighed, "if there was a clear way to organize these different entities."

"There a number of ways of categorizing demons," Clara remarked. "But most of them have to do with their culture of origin. It's not the best, however, since demons aren't cultural—it's just that different cultures have seen them differently and so perceive them to be different."

"So what you're saying is . . . "

"Take a demon like . . . oh . . . *Lilith*," said Selene. "Everybody likes Lilith. She's primarily a Judeo-Christian demon, but the actual *spirit* behind her *isn't*. It's more likely that she's similar to Echidna—in fact they may be the same person."

"Hold on, hold on," said Jill. "Lilith, Echidna . . . those are both *mythological characters*."

"Yep," said Selene. "And, like a lot of them, they existed—just not in the way the stories make it out. Most gods and stuff, when you start to dig a bit, turn out to be real things that humans have plastered all these names and legends on."

"So . . . what about other monsters? Gorgons and trolls and ogres and things like that? Are they demons too?"

Selene wagged her head from side to side. "It's hard to tell, actually. Since, the way we use the term, a *demon* is just a malevolent spirit that can't manifest corporeally. *If* they could, they might turn out to be a gorgon or something like that. But they can't, so we don't really know."

"Demons are wide and varied," said Clara. "It is likely that the things we call demons contain multitudes of different entities."

"But mostly, when a hunter says '*demon*' they mean a nasty piece of work that possesses people and causes all kinds of trouble." Selene explained. "It's like . . . fish. Fish all live in water and stuff, but there's *tons* of different *kinds* of fish, and some are so different that you'd never guess they were both fish. *And . . . *" she continued, warming to her metaphor. "There's even things that *look* like demons, but aren't. Same ways not everything you find in the sea *is* a fish."

She sat back, smiling proudly, while Jill continued to scribble notes.

"This is hardly conclusive," she said with a frown. "But it's a place to start. Very well. What do you propose we do about the demon in . . . " she leaned over to check the computer screen, " . . . Pearson? Would it be possible to study it up close?"

Selene laughed nervously. "Sure . . . I mean, same ways you study a *tornado* up close. Wait until it goes away and then examine the wreckage. Or, in this case, wait until we *make* it go away."

Jill's mouth twisted in disappointment. "So . . . there would be no way to . . . well . . . *catch* it for study?"

"It's possible," Clara said, while Selene's jaw dropped. "But unwise. Many have sought to harness demons, to use their power for their own ends. It . . . never ends well."

"I don't *want* to use its power!" Jill exclaimed. "I just want to understand how it *works*."

Selene and Clara looked at one another despairingly.

"Look," said Selene. "We'll go sort out Pearson, and you can take whatever you can from *watching us work*, and collect whatever evidence is left over. If, after that, you still want to have a pet demon . . . well, we'll see."

Jill pursed her lips, but didn't press the issue.

They stayed only one night at the hotel outside Denver, and left early the next morning.

After spending the last several months in mountains of varying dryness, the great open *flatness* of Kansas took a little getting used to. Jill, who had never considered herself a mountain person, still found herself surprised by the sheer amount of sky that stretched over them as they chugged along Interstate 70. It was enough to wonder, if she didn't keep a firm hand on the wheel would Arcana float off into that great blue ocean? She couldn't help smiling inwardly at the flight of fancy, and shook her head. Jill was fond of reason and logic, but that didn't mean she couldn't indulge her imagination now and then.

Arcana, big and red and loud, ate up the miles as they traveled east, following in the wake of the sleek black form that was Clara riding Unicorn. They traveled across a sun-bleached asphalt road that cut a straight line between the flat green plain and the blue arc of the heavens.

Stopping for fuel on the outskirts of Pearson, Selene left Jill in charge of cleaning the windows while she headed into the foodmart. She returned a few minutes later, a frown on her face and a folded newspaper in her hands.

"Something wrong?" Jill asked, shaking the excess fluid off the window scraper.

"Take a look," said Selene, passing Jill the paper in exchange for the squeegee. She got up onto Arcana's front bumper to reach the middle of the windshield. "That article lists no less than *four* probable cases of demonic possession. Oh, yeah, they're *calling* it the flu, but look at the symptoms!"

"'Archie Davis, 27, claims to have hallucinated walking on his ceiling and biting the ears off the neighbor's dog . . .'" Jill read. "'Said neighbor, Julie Christopherson, denies having seen the man on her property, but reports her dog did get in a fight that left it with a mangled ear.'"

She looked up at Selene incredulously.

"Keep going," said Selene.

"'Two minors have been admitted to Pearson Memorial Hospital with extreme cases . . .' what are *extreme cases?*"

"Probably vomiting pea soup and spinning heads," Selene remarked casually. "Or something along those lines. Keep going, though, it gets better."

"'Laurel Fletcher, 32, was diagnosed after *painting her children black and locking them in the attic?*'"

"All fun and games now, but just wait until they start eviscerating each other," Selene said grimly.

Clara, who as always finished refueling first, had wandered over and now stood reading the paper over Jill's shoulder.

"We should begin with the woman Fletcher," she said. "She appears to be the prime host."

"Can't argue with that," said Selene. "You thinking straight up exorcism or should we try to catch it?"

"I don't have any lamps with me," Clara said. "We can salt the earth to prevent a repeat possession."

"One problem," Jill pointed out. "How do we *find* her?"

Selene laughed at that, and even Clara managed a sort of smile.

"If she's got a demon in her, hon, she'll be *easy* to find," Selene said. "Now let's find us a room so I can set up my gear."

The room was provided by the Happy Pear Inn, and Selene's gear turned out to be a greasy, wax-stained cloth and a bunch of candles. Clara hunted down a paper map of the town and spread it out on the bed, then sat down at the little table where she opened one of her panniers and unpacked a bottle of dark liquid, a roll of brushes, and several pieces of cloth—they looked to be torn squares of old jeans.

"More magic?" Jill asked, a little tiredly.

"If it helps, you can think of it like a test," Selene said, spreading the cloth on the floor and sticking the candles to it. "These are moth-wax candles; they don't burn with physical fire. They will, however, react to demonic activity. Do we have any oil? I need it to prime the map."

Wordlessly, Clara produced a small tube and handed it to Selene.

"Thanks." Selene took the tube and squeezed a generous dollop onto her hands, which she began to rub into the paper. "The oil makes the candles read the map as if it were the place it represents," Selene explained as she worked. "Don't ask me *why*."

"I see," said Jill. "Then what is Clara doing?"

Clara had laid out her little squares of cloth and was now painting things on them. They were unrecognizable to Jill, save in the most abstract sense. One of them looked a little like an A.

"This is not magic," said Clara. "It is *protection*."

"Since demons aren't physical, they can pass through walls and armor and things," Selene explained. "So to protect yourself from them, you need to make ... erm ... non-physical walls."

"Place this under your clothing," Clara said, handing one of the squares of cloth to Jill. "Make sure it lies flat."

This was easier said than done. Jill retreated into the bathroom to solve the problem, and by the time she returned Selene had lit the candles and was holding the oil-soaked paper map over them.

Jill made an involuntary move to look for a fire extinguisher, but Clara held up a hand to stop her.

"It's moth wax," she said, as if this explained everything.

"I don't understand," Jill said, creeping cautiously forward.

"We're not sure we do either," said Selene, but absently, as she was concentrating on moving the map over the flames in a systematic pattern.

Sure enough, the paper wasn't burning, though Jill could see the light from the candles shining through it. Then, sparks. A glow of orange and yellow.

"Got one!" Selene cried, as a small portion of the map caught fire. Before Jill could become alarmed, however, the fire died out, leaving a dark, burnt circle behind.

Only for another fire to start up at a different place on the map.

"Two ... " said Selene.

And another. And another. And another. This last was the biggest of them all, and left a hole in the map the size of a quarter.

"Damn," said Clara.

"What does that mean?" asked Jill.

Selene lifted the map away and blew out the candles. Laying the paper back down over the bed she took out a small flashlight and began examining the surface of the map.

"Put simply, sister, it means we're gonna have our hands full."

"We'll take the one on Pleasant Drive first," Selene explained as they packed. "That'll likely be the lead demon. Get rid of that, and the smaller ones will probably hightail it out of here."

Jill followed mutely in the woman's wake. The manner of her two employees had changed so dramatically that, for once, she'd managed to rein in her curiosity and desire for knowledge and simply let them work. Almost as if in gratitude, neither of them had suggested she stay behind. So she drove while Selene dug through her duffle bag pulling out strange little artifacts and tying them to her wrists and ankles. They weren't crosses or other religious paraphernalia, as far as Jill could see. They looked more like twisted little bones.

The house on Pleasant Drive—as indicated by the huge scorch mark on the map—looked ordinary enough in real life. A comfortable house with a wide lawn, it was missing only the white picket fence to be something out of a suburban fairytale.

"Stay in the truck," Selene said, opening the door as soon as Arcana stopped.

"But—" Jill began.

"*Trust* me on this one," Selene said, sliding her legs out. "If we find anything you can safely study, we'll bring it back to you."

And Jill was forced to accept that. Leaning on the steering wheel she watched as the two women—looking almost like a humorous double act, Clara was so much bigger than Selene—walked up the path and boldly rang the doorbell.

After a moment the door cracked open and a conversation, inaudible to Jill, took place. Then the two women were permitted inside, and the door shut behind them.

In the truck, Jill prepared for an interminable wait and so was surprised when the door opened less than ten minutes later and Selene and Clara re-emerged, looking puzzled.

"That was fast," Jill remarked as Selene opened the door and climbed in, pulling out the map and spreading it open on the dashboard.

"It's clean," she said with a frown.

"What?"

"I mean, there's no demon in there anymore. Sure, there *was* or this wouldn't have pinged," she tapped the scorchmark. "But *apparently* it left on its own."

Jill frowned. "I take it that doesn't happen very often?"

"Often?" said Selene. "Try *never*. There's something fishy going on here."

"I recommend we check the other houses," said Clara. "It could have moved on."

"Hells yeah," said Selene. "Let's try the one over on McCormack Street next."

McCormack Street held a modest block of apartments. Jill parked across the street and watched Selene and Clara approach Number 12A like a pair of lions stalking prey. After a considerably longer conversation (during which the occupant refused to take the chain off the door), they returned with nothing but puzzled expressions, and in Selene's case, mounting frustration.

"It's like the thing keeps jumping hosts right before we get there," she said. "No doubt that guy *had* been possessed—he had the look. But I didn't pick up *any* signs of possession, did you?"

This to Clara, who shook her head gravely.

"Well, let's try Fifth and Cottonwood," Selene sighed.

Fifth and Cottonwood found Jill waiting in the truck for almost an hour, but as it turned out, this was only because the little old lady who lived there felt compelled to invite Selene and Clara in for coffee and cake and proceeded to tell them all about the nice young man who cured her migraine that morning.

"I think I have heard my fill of handsome young men with miracle cures in neat, black suitcases," Selene said, rolling her eyes. "What's next?"

Next turned out to be a small cottage on the back lot of a larger house on the outskirts of town, where a prickly young couple informed Selene and Clara that the gas leak in their home had been fixed two days ago, thank you very much, and the pair came away with nothing.

After that it was a trailer. Clara went to talk to the inhabitant on her own, while Selene crept around the back.

"I found his stash," she confessed as she climbed back into the truck. "But no demon."

At last they found themselves in front of a small bungalow on a dingy street. The yard was mostly dirt and littered with children's toys, and there was a battered Honda sedan in the drive.

"What are we at now?" Selene asked tiredly as they trudged up to the house.

"This is our sixth," Clara replied, indomitably.

"Right," said Selene. "Let's get this over with."

She knocked on the peeling front door, and from within came the sound of small feet pattering on tile. A moment later the door opened, and the two women found themselves staring down at a small boy of maybe ten or eleven. He had very large black eyes set in a dusky, umber face, which was in turn surrounded by a halo of frizzy black hair.

"Can I help you?" he asked in a small voice with a hint of a stammer.

"Yes," said Selene. "Can we talk to your parents?"

"Or," said Clara, leaning her head down over Selene's shoulder. "Can you tell us if you've seen any demons around lately?"

"*Clara,*" Selene hissed, elbowing the larger woman in the ribs.

Unfazed, Clara peered down expectantly at the little boy, who was staring back up in shock.

"What we mean is . . . " Selene began, but then the boy began to speak.

"Momma had a demon in her," the boy said, quickly and quietly. "Demon did bad things. But the man came and got it outta her. He like you . . . " he pointed at Clara, then leaned conspiratorially toward Selene. "*White* man," he explained. "But wears black all over. An' a white hat."

"Did this man have a *name?*" Selene asked shrewdly.

The boy shook his head. "He ah . . . like a missionary. Missionary man."

"Like a priest?" Clara asked.

"He no priest," the boy said, drawing back inside. "No priest helped Momma."

"And the demon is totally gone now?" Selene asked.

The boy nodded.

"Well, that's good," Selene said. "Glad to hear it. Thanks, uh . . . kid. Yeah. You don't have to tell your parents we were here."

The boy nodded gravely and withdrew into the house, and Selene and Clara walked back down the drive in thoughtful silence.

"Let me guess," said Jill as Selene climbed back inside. "No demon?"

"Nah, there really *was* a demon in that house," said Selene. "It's not there anymore."

"What happened to it?"

"I think it got exorcised . . . or . . . " Selene frowned and gave a small shudder. "It jumped hosts."

"How do you mean?"

"Sometimes a demon gets bored of one person, and hops onto a new host. Sometimes it kills its old host, sometimes it just leaves them alone to live with the trauma."

"So you think the reason we haven't been able to find any *actual* possessed people . . . is because the demon's *moved on*?" Jill pressed.

"That's *one* possibility," Selene said, spreading the map out and tapping a spot near the center of town. "This is our last hit," she said to Clara, who had come to stand outside the window, helmet on but with her visor raised. "If it's not there . . . "

Clara nodded. "I'll lead you in," she said, flipping down the visor and striding off to her bike.

Downtown Pearson was in a sleepy, mid-afternoon lull when Arcana pulled up across from a dusty shop with TATTOO above it in red-and-purple letters. The door stood open like the black mouth of a cave, but nothing moved inside.

Clara was already there. Having parked Unicorn around the corner she was now approaching the little parlor slowly, with one hand outstretched as if she expected to run into an invisible barrier. Inside Arcana, Selene checked her gun—"Special cartridges for the special occasion"—and the talismans hanging from her wrists before jumping down into the street.

"You think this is the one?" Jill asked, coming around the side of Arcana to peer skeptically at the shop.

"It's the last place on the map," Selene said, a little shortly. There was a smell just on the edge of her senses, like something foul and wrong, that she had begun to associate with demons. In the other places it had seemed old and stale, but here it was definitely fresh.

Whatever it was, smell or no, Clara could sense it too. She had one hand up behind her shoulder, resting on the hilt of her sword. Selene bit back on the urge to remind her not to harm the human host; Clara was a warrior, a hunter like herself; she didn't need Selene telling her how to do her job.

The silence of the afternoon was broken by the purr of an engine as a white sedan turned onto the street and rolled to a gentle halt directly in front of the tattoo parlor. There was the muffled sound of music, which shut off a moment after the purr of the engine ceased, and a creak as the driver's door opened and a long leg, encased in a black trouser with a black cowboy boot on the end of it, reached out to rest on the asphalt of the road. A hand on the window frame followed, and a trim, square-shouldered masculine body stood up, adjusting the pair of aviator sunglasses perched on his face as he ducked out of the car. He reached back in a moment later and re-emerged carrying a white cowboy hat, which he placed jauntily over the crop of short, golden-brown hair that decorated his head.

He wore a black suit and a priest's collar, the little snip of white at his throat being the only bright thing about his clothing, apart from the hat. Even under all this, Selene thought, he looked like the kind of generically handsome model one found in clothing magazines or on television shows. His jaw was too perfect—strong and angular without being overly square and blockish—and when he smiled at them in passing he flashed dimples and perfectly straight, white teeth. He walked with an easy, rolling step that showed off his long, well-formed legs and kept his back straight and his shoulders broad and confident.

He was altogether unreal, a perfect specimen of the sort of beauty not usually found outside of a cinema, and this unrealness fixed Selene and Clara to the spot as they watched him stroll up onto the sidewalk, swinging his black briefcase, and disappear inside the tattoo parlor. There was a tinkle of a bell, and the sound of low male voices.

That sound brought Selene to her senses. Either that man was the exorcist—in which case he'd just walked into a demon's lair without a spotter—or he was some poor missionary about to get his ridiculously well-formed butt handed to him. She started across the street, called to Clara—who seemed to be distracted by the man's car of all things—jerking her into action.

They made it to the door of the shop this time, at the same time there was a deep and bone-shaking *thud* from within, and *something* whipped past them, ricocheted off Arcana's side, and billowed up into the sky like oily smoke before shooting off across the town.

Hardly had this happened when there was the crash of a door from within, and the man came pelting out again. He had a greasy smudge across one chiseled cheek, and his glasses had been knocked off, but he fairly leapt into his car, tossing the briefcase into the back seat, and peeled off into the street with a screech of tires.

All this happened so fast that Clara and Selene were still more or less where they had been when they'd felt the *thud,* though Jill had wandered halfway across the street in her confusion.

"*Stay* where you *are*!" Selene shouted at her, and rounded on Clara.

"It was an Impala . . ." the woman whispered. She still didn't move.

"A *what*?" Selene said.

"That car, *his* car," said Clara.

Selene, who had only registered the car as *generic, white, sedan* glared at her in consternation.

"Chevrolet Impala, named after the antelope," Clara continued, raising her face to stare at Selene, her crystalline eyes wide and bright. "*He's* the white stag . . ." she whispered, and took off down the street in the direction of Unicorn.

Seconds later, with a deafening engine roar, she came skidding around the corner and shot off down the street with a scream of rubber on pavement.

"What on earth . . . " Jill murmured, coming to stand next to Selene, "was *that*?"

Others had sensed the disturbance as well, and now a few cautiously curious heads were poking out of doors and windows.

"Honestly, I have no idea," Selene said under her breath. She shrugged expansively when one of the heads turned to stare questioningly at her, smiled and waved. "She said something about that dude being a white deer and then just took off. No idea what she was thinking. I mean, *you* know Clara."

"No, no," said Jill, waving her hand. "I mean the thing that came out of the shop."

Selene lowered her hand, and the plasticky smile faded from her face. "That was a shadow," she said. "It's what we can sometimes see when a demon leaves its physical host."

"So the demon's not *in there,* anymore?" Jill asked, indicating the tattoo parlor.

"We'll see," said Selene. She glanced around the street, frowned, and turned back to Jill. "Spot me, will ya?"

"How do I do that?" Jill asked, but gamely.

"Just . . . keep an eye out. You see anything fishy, give me a holler."

So Jill waited, fidgeting, by the door while Selene crept inside. The lights had been blown out, so she walked, crablike, with her flashlight trained along Elvis's barrel.

The shop was long and narrow and deserted except for the form of a man on his back on the floor. He was pasty white and bald, wearing a denim shirt, jeans, and the kind of pretentious leather vest with artistically frayed edges. Switching the flashlight to her mouth, and keeping her eyes moving around the room the whole time, Selene checked his pulse. It was steady, and the man was visibly breathing. Taking his right arm she pulled at it gently until it was raised above his head, then she grabbed a fistful of leather vest and dragged until she'd rolled him onto his side, his head resting on his raised arm. She hooked a foot behind his left knee and pulled it forward until it met the floor, preventing him from rolling onto his face. She then checked the back area, the office, and the tiny bathroom. Then she ducked back into the office and used the landline to call an ambulance. Then she left.

"Nothing here," she said to Jill, who was waiting anxiously outside.

"No what?" came the predictable reply.

"Get that map out again," Selene said, pocketing her flashlight and holstering Elvis. "And my candles. We gotta find out where that demon went."

"What about Clara?"

"I would bet good money she's already there," Selene said with a wry grin.

Clara leaned as far as she dared into the turn, and *there* was the flash of white. They were headed for the highway, which meant she could catch them. She leaned forward into the wind as Unicorn picked up speed, banked for another turn (behind her someone honked) and found the white Impala in her sights once again. Whether its driver knew he was being followed was uncertain: he made no attempt to lose her but pulled onto the highway and headed out of town.

Wind whipped up along the road. It buffeted the car, but Clara sliced clean through it. A partially disassembled cardboard box was sent cartwheeling across the road only to be crushed beneath the car's tires, then thrown up into the air once again. Leaning serenely to the side, Clara dodged it by inches and closed on the car. Looking past it, now she could see the billowing black cloud that ripped through the air in front of them, so faint it could be mistaken for a shimmer on the air. With her experienced eyes she could clearly see the miasma that trailed behind the disembodied demon like thick exhaust.

They cleared the town, and the demon jerked suddenly sideways—as if it were a puppet pulled by a string. Almost as abruptly the white sedan turned down a road, hardly more than a dirt track, kicking up a huge cloud of dust, its rear wheels skidding along the turn. Thrown wide, Clara cut a sharp track through the sparse grass growing on the shoulder and tailed the car all the way down the road, where it ended in an empty lot behind a dilapidated warehouse.

The man was out of his car before it completely stopped, sprinting across the dirt toward the small cairn of stones he'd constructed earlier. Now they were belching a stream of truly angry-looking smoke: flames licked like orange tongues in its depths, and it took only a very little stretch of the imagination to see a face glowering out from the dark cloud. This dwindled to a narrow funnel above the cairn, one that was narrowing further by the second.

Shaking in his hurry the man threw out an arm, a single flash of white cuff visible beneath the black sleeve, and something else swung forward: the smooth round bodies of rosary beads, suspended in the air before the outstretched hand.

The beads touched the edge of the cloud, and he felt it connect even before there was a shriek like ripping stone and it condensed inward, pouring itself into a shape somewhere between a man and a spider. Legs flicked out, clawed at the man's face, but he jumped backward just in time.

Words drifted forth from the shape, clawed their way into his mind, biting, ripping. Mentally he brought up his guard to resist them, and then—

Then they were drowned out by other words. Ancient words. Foreign and yet familiar, they rang clear in his ears from the throat of a living being, and against every instinct he turned his head from the demon to look toward their source.

He saw an impossibly tall woman appear out of the swirl of dust, standing astride a muscular, black motorcycle. A long leg kicked over the back of the bike, and she approached, one hand held awkwardly behind her shoulder. The reason for this pose became apparent when she brought it around and in a flash of cold steel plunged the broadsword into the shadow.

For a moment the shadow swallowed the sword. Then there was a crack like a thunderclap, and bolts of lightning shot through the haze, jumped about within it, and eventually found their way to earth. They took the last of the smoke with them, leaving the man staring down the length of the woman's sword, which glinted brightly in the sun.

She put him in mind of a modern black knight, right down to her tinted visor, though clad in leather instead of steel. Slowly she lowered her sword, and from behind the helmet a voice emerged—the same voice that had spoken before. This time it spoke words he understood, though once again their meaning escaped him.

She said: "I come hilt first. I will not harm you."

And sure enough, she had turned the sword around in her hand so the blade pointed behind her, and all he saw was the smooth round end of its pommel.

For his part the man pushed the rosary back up under his sleeve, and then extended his free hand.

"That's good, I think," he said. "Ariel Freeman. Thanks for the assist."

This gesture seemed to perplex the woman, who stared down at his hand awkwardly. Eventually she reached forward with her free hand and took his in a light, careful grip.

"Claymore Nordstern," said the black knight.

They stood there for a moment, connected by their hands, until the tentative silence was ruptured by the growl of a truck's engines, and the huge red pickup lurched into view at the head of a billow of dust. A dark-skinned woman with an impressive mane of black hair stuck her entire upper half out the passenger window, and shouted over the sound of the engine:

"Okay, I've had about enough of this god-forsaken snipe hunt. You stay right there, mister, and tell me who the hell you are!"

The man was surprised, but not offended. He tipped his white cowboy hat respectfully, and laughed at the expression on the new arrival's face.

"So you're, like, a demon *specialist*?" Jill asked, much later. After an awkward round of introductions. After Selene had carefully inspected the contents of Freeman's briefcase, the trunk of his car, the little cairn of stones, and finally proclaimed him to be "legit."

The sun had set on them, and a bright spring night rolled over the sky. Freeman had set up a small bonfire and produced a six-pack of warm beer and a foil-covered tray.

"The lady I saw this morning insisted on giving me a casserole," he explained sheepishly. "There's no way I can eat it before it goes bad."

So they had eaten cold casserole around the bonfire and drunk warm beer. That was, Selene and the man drank the beer. Jill sipped reluctantly at hers, and Clara just sat on the opposite side of the fire and glowered at them through it.

Selene had begun to grill the man—Freeman—on his activities. He answered readily enough, with the good humor that was apparently his natural state, and they discovered they had been only a little behind him in their circuit of the town.

"Seems like you were practically stalking me," he said, with a sly grin. Selene punched him lightly on the shoulder. The man swayed with the blow and didn't take offense. Indeed, he practically radiated amiability.

At last Jill posed her question.

Ariel Freeman tilted his hat so he could scratch his scalp under it, letting a few locks of golden-brown hair escape, glinting in the firelight.

"Exorcist is the more generally accepted term," he allowed, but nodded. "Same thing, though. I always liked 'infernal plumber' but people tend to take that the wrong way."

"And what sort of priest are you?" Jill asked, gesturing at his clerical collar.

Freeman paused with the bottle halfway to his lips, then gave a sort of shrug and took a swig from it before answering.

"Not a priest," he said. "A minister. Was, anyway. Baptist."

"Was?" asked Jill.

Freeman shrugged and grinned sheepishly. "There was a time in my life, earlier, when I was confused about a lot of things. I believed in a perfect and just universe created by God, and I saw it as my duty to protect that." He shrugged again. "Like you do."

"Yeah-huh," said Selene knowingly. "And now what? You just keep the collar for the casseroles?"

Freeman cocked his head at her, but he was grinning. "Not so much for the casseroles. But it does help you get in the front door. Also . . . well, people just don't ask so many questions of priests. I think mostly they're afraid I'll try to convert them. And I'm not a complete fraud," he added. "I still *believe*."

"Yeah . . . but in *what?*" Selene asked.

For the first time the man frowned. He looked at Selene shrewdly, before pushing his gaze on to the other two women.

"Have any of you actually *read* the bible?" he asked.

Jill was obliged to shake her head, and Selene rolled her eyes, but Clara nodded gravely.

"Okay." Freeman drained his beer and set the bottle aside. "It's like this. You read the bible—and I mean *really* read it—and you have to come to one of three conclusions." He held up the same number of fingers to illustrate. "Proposition: our world was created by a benevolent, omnipotent god. But if you read the bible several things become clear: firstly, *bad things* happen. Our world isn't perfect."

"You don't need the *bible* to tell you that," Selene pointed out dryly.

Freeman shook his fingers at her. "Yeah," he said. "True enough. But here's something you only learn from the bible: God is an insecure bastard. He changes His mind. Makes mistakes. He lets some really messed-up stuff happen."

"People say that is because the Nameless God has a great plan that encompasses everything and is beyond the scope of our experiences," Clara intoned from beyond the fire.

"Yes, that's *one* of the three conclusions," Freeman said, with a nod of his head.

"Another option is that there is no god," Jill pointed out practically. "That the bible is a work of fiction created thousands of years ago and mutilated by centuries of translations, rewriting, and political bias, and frequently used as an excuse for people to do what they wanted to do in the first place."

Freeman nodded. "That's two," he said. "And the third . . . is that everything in the bible is true . . . except for the bit about god being omnipotent."

"I'm sorry," said Selene. "*What?*"

"If you look at the events of the bible," the man said, "you could see how they could all come to pass . . . *especially* if God wasn't all-powerful. Maybe He's just a bigger, more powerful version of an ordinary guy. One who's trying his best but makes mistakes, has attacks of insecurity, and loses his temper sometimes. Someone who made something amazing, and then let it get away from Him. His creation got too big for Him to handle, and now He's just clinging to its coattails, trying to keep up."

"There is one more option," Selene said, a dark grin spreading across her face. "Maybe your god's a malicious little bastard. Maybe all the suffering and bad things in the world *are* for a reason: he thinks it's *funny*."

Freeman pulled another beer from the box and expertly twisted the cap off. "And you know," he said, bringing it to his mouth. "I just can't decide which of those last two I believe in. It's one or the other. Point is I believe in *something*. I don't know what that makes me, but I'm not what you'd call an atheist."

"Atheists can believe in things," Clara said softly.

"Nuh-huh," said Selene. "That's the whole *point* of being an atheist. It's that you *don't* believe."

"I think," Jill cut in with finality, "that it's less important what you *call* yourself and more important what you *do*."

"I'll drink to that," Freeman said, raising his beer. When he had finished he wiped his mouth on the back of his hand and stared into the fire for some time. In the quiet left by the lull of their voices the only sound was the crackle and pop of the flames.

"So about you," he said, sloshing the remainder of his drink around the bottom of his bottle. "You're on a bit of a quest then?" He nodded at Jill. "Like a modern-day Brothers Gunn."

Selene snorted, and Clara frowned.

"It's not like that," the large woman said, but Jill cut her off.

"I've heard of them before," she said. "But I've never gotten a clear explanation. Who *were* the Brothers Gunn?"

Ariel Freeman shot an incredulous glance toward Selene. "You haven't told her?"

"Oi," said Selene. "Most of what we know about them is legend. What do you want me to do? Sing her their song? Buy her those stupid novelizations that came out in the eighties?"

Freeman's face twisted in disgust. "Okay," he said. "The novels *were* awful. But the song is good. Matches up with all the historical facts we could dig up. The Brothers *Gunn*," he continued, turning to Jill, "were a pair of hunters. David and Adam. Very interesting pair. Got up to no end of hijinks and died *several* times. Helped stop an apocalypse . . . once. Nearly brought one on once or twice. Adam was an antichrist, you see."

"Hold on," said Jill. "*An* antichrist?"

Freeman nodded. "There's one for every generation. They don't usually amount to much, otherwise . . . *poof* . . . old John's prophecy would've come true a dozen times over by now."

"You mean Armageddon?" Jill said.

"I do mean the great *reboot*," Freeman said, nodding.

"So what happened to them?"

Freeman smiled. He was rather ridiculously good-looking, Jill noted with detached interest. Like a benevolent, golden angel. He rolled his head back to look at the stars, the fire highlighting the sharp curve of his jaw and the faint dusting of stubble there. After a quiet moment, he began to hum. It was a rudimentary melody, but it made both Selene and Clara sit up a little straighter. Then to Jill's surprise, Selene joined in, this time fitting words to the tune.

"*Somewhere out there the wayward sons, Jimmy's amber-eyed boys, are blown by a Kansas tornado—they landed who knows where . . .*"

The song had the simple rhythm and cadence of a folk song, and Selene—though she had a pleasant, throaty voice—was a somewhat hesitant singer. Then Freeman picked up the words and Jill realized she was listening to an immensely talented musician—albeit one rather out of practice.

"*David was born in forty-nine and Jimmy was his dad. He hollered high, he rolled strong. He drove his mother mad,*" he sang in a reassuring baritone. "*Adam was born in fifty-three and Jimmy was his dad. Though he was quiet, before one year, his mother she was dead.*"

Then Selene joined in and they both sang together . . .

"*Somewhere out there, the wayward sons, Jimmy's amber-eyed boys, are blown by a Kansas tornado, they landed who knows where . . .*"

Selene dropped off, but Freeman continued.

"*Adam ran off to college, but that there didn't last. David came a-knockin' on his door, and they blew town but fast. They say David loved no woman, but he took them all to bed. Adam loved but one (it's true) but in a year she was dead.*"

"I don't like what happens to women in this song," Jill remarked dryly.

"Oh, it gets worse," Selene assured her as Freeman launched into another verse of *Somewhere out there the wayward sons . . .* "Proper old-boys club, they were. And white as lilies. No offense," she added, with a nod to Clara, who shrugged.

"*Adam had been dead two days before David sold his soul,*" Freeman sang on.

"*Life don't come cheap,*" Selene chimed in.

"*A year he had skirting the Pit before he took the plunge . . .*"

"*Hell's river runs deep.*"

"*Oh, Adam went near crazy, he took a demon's hand. As he danced to the devil's tune he sang 'they don't understand.' Somewhere out there, the wayward sons . . .*"

"Can you possibly skip the refrain?" Jill cut in. "What happened next?"

"Oh?" said Freeman. "It's kinda important to the ending, and leaving it out makes me lose my place."

"Next is the bit about the angels," Selene prompted.

"Oh, right," the man cleared his throat. "*It took seven angels to raise David from the Pit. One broke his back, one broke his bonds, and one, he broke his heart.*"

Now Selene joined in, and gustily. "*Oh, those seven angels, where have they gone? One died in thunder, one died in ice, and one, he broke his heart. When those seven angels raised David from the ground, one was lost, one was found, and one, he broke his heart.*"

"That's nine angels," Jill pointed out.

"The one who broke his heart is mentioned three times for some reason," Selene said. "He became kind of important later on, you see. Anyway, after that there's another bout of the refrain, and then . . . "

Freeman took over.

"They said Adam raised the Devil, they say David closed the gate. They say the angel with the broken heart was bent on tempting fate. They say Adam beat the Devil, they say David went to ground, and the angel with the broken heart was lost and never found."

"And another refrain," Selene cut in. "And then there's rather a lot of cryptic verses about boxes and the various crimes the brothers got up to and from the sound of it our poor angel had a bitch of a time."

"He did," Freeman added.

"Anyway," Selene continued, "after the bits about the blood of hell and earth and how the boys lost their angel and how the angel found his heart too late and one last bit with the Devil, it ends with . . . *They drove their bird into a storm, they stopped the world turning. They were strong and silent, and they vanished in the storm.*"

"That's not how it ends," Freeman protested.

"Oh right," said Selene, mock-slapping herself on the forehead. "We get one more reiteration of that lovely refrain and then . . . "

"Then there's the ending, but I can't start up on it now, I have to sing the whole thing," Freeman admitted.

There was an awkward silence, and then from the other side of the fire came a soft and haunting voice, and it took Jill a moment to realize it was Clara singing.

"So if you pass a weeping angel, best stop and pay your leave, for he's waiting on his amber-eyed boys—Jimmy's wayward sons—but they are blown by a Kansas tornado . . . "

Then Selene chipped in, singing louder and faster, and Freeman joined her, clapping his hands along with the beat.

"They are blown by a Kansas tornado—"

"They are blown by a Kansas tornado!"

"They are blown by a Kansas tor-NAY-dooooo . . . "

The other voices faded out, and left Clara's alone to finish, softly, delicately . . .

" . . . and they landed, who knows where."

"Am I to take it they went to Oz?" Jill asked, once it was clear the singing was good and done with.

"One would like to think that," Freeman said, finishing his beer. "Truth is, last anyone saw of the Brothers Gunn, they were driving their car—a black Ford Falcon, hence the lyric about their bird—along a road in Kansas when a tornado whipped up and ran right into their path. The car was found—upside-down in a tree two miles away—but the boys never were. So . . . they landed *who knows* where."

"And the angel?" Jill asked.

Selene shook her head, but Freeman spoke up.

"Oh, he's still around. In a graveyard not far from here, actually. But you wouldn't know it to look at him."

"How do *you* know so much about the Brothers Gunn?" Selene asked.

The man shrugged innocently. "I made it a special study. Mostly to figure out what *not* to do . . . " he added with a grin.

"Now, that I *will* drink to," Selene said, raising her own beer and clinking it with his.

Clara, Jill noticed, was silent even for her usual stoic self, and remained so as the fire was put out and the other three bedded down for the night.

Jill spread herself out in Arcana's bed, staring up at the stars and wondering about demons—Freeman had promised to lend her some of his "souvenirs"—with the melody of the song still stuck in her head. In the end the words *they are blown by a Kansas tornado* morphed smoothly into dreams, and she slept.

It was Clara's voice that woke them, when the dawn was still dim and gray. Her words were indistinct, but spoken so sharply that they roused Jill from her fragile slumber. Feeling gingerly over the side of the truck, she found the surface moist with dew and withdrew her hand at once to wipe it on her sleeping bag before carefully propping herself up.

"Say what, Clara?" she asked blearily.

Clara didn't answer her right away. Jill heard her talking, but it seemed she was speaking to someone else. The words, " . . . and you're *sure* that's the shape the blood made?" drifted over and Jill rubbed her eyes, coming more awake by the second.

Clara was kneeling in front of a small black boy, who had just straightened up from drawing something in the dirt. An old bicycle, two sizes too big, lay on the ground behind him.

Beside the remains of the campfire Selene and Freeman were coming to life, shaking themselves out of their cocoons of blankets. Selene staggered over, but Freeman lounged with the ease of a cat, smoothing his tawny hair before jamming the white cowboy hat down over it. He stretched, and fairly strolled over to where Selene and Clara stood by the boy, staring down at the ground in consternation.

"Mr. Bell," he said, tipping his hat to the boy. "How can I help you?"

The boy stammered something, but Selene picked up her head and rounded on Freeman.

"You *missed* one," she said, and jabbed her finger at the dirt.

By this time Jill had pulled her shoes on and was staggering toward the little group, her sleeping bag wrapped around her shoulders like an oversized feather boa.

"Hold up, hold up," she said. "What's happened? How did you know to find us here?" she asked the little boy.

"Went looking for you," said the boy, not meeting her eyes.

"I told him to find me here if there were any problems," Freeman sighed, and pointed at the ground. "By the look of *that*, our work here isn't done yet."

On the dirt was scratched a symbol, unfamiliar to Jill, like a circle with a sort of twisted tree in the center. Unless it was a giant eye.

"*Our* work?" Selene protested.

"Of course I will assist you," Clara announced.

"Great," said Freeman, flashing her a dazzling smile. "Demon first, then a shower and breakfast, maybe? I still owe you for yesterday."

"Like hell you're going in there without a spotter," Selene said. "Jill will want to come anyway. Here, kiddo, we'll put your bike in the back and give you a ride home. Don't suppose your ma is around this time?"

But the boy—whom Jill realized must be Andrew Bell—nodded. "She stuck," he said quietly.

"Well then," said Freeman brightly over Selene's curses. "No time to waste."

Jill helped Selene hoist the bicycle into Arcana's bed, made sure Andrew Bell was safely buckled in the back, and then climbed in only to find Selene already in the driver's seat.

"What's happened?" she asked as the other woman started the engine and began turning the huge truck around.

"Missed one, didn't we?" Selene said shortly. "Our boy back here"—she jerked a thumb at Andrew Bell—"his ma was one of the folks that preacher man exorcised. Only the demon's not *gone*. Or there was more than one. Anyway, he found that sigil in blood on his ceiling this morning and high-tailed it out here as fast as he could."

"So, now what?" Jill prompted.

"Now we follow our leading lady and gentleman," Selene said, gesturing as first Clara on her bike and then Freeman in his car, peeled out of the dirt lot. Arcana followed at a more sedate pace, maneuvering cautiously through the thick dust the other vehicles had left in their wake.

The sun was just peeking over the horizon when they arrived at Andrew Bell's house, which looked much the same as it had the day before. Except . . . not. As Clara rolled Unicorn to a stop a safe distance away she became aware of a faint miasma that hung over the building, fuzzing its edges and making her nose itch.

Ariel Freeman—she kept thinking of him by both names for some reason—had parked around the corner and now came strolling toward her at his strange, rolling gait that was deceptively fast. He had his hat tipped at a jaunty angle and his black briefcase swinging, but he paused when he came in sight of the house, and sniffed the air experimentally.

"You smell that?" he asked, coming even with Clara.

"No," said Clara. "But I can see it."

Ariel Freeman shot her a penetrating look from under the brim of his hat, his light green eyes focused briefly on hers, then turned back to the house.

"What do you think?" he asked.

"I think one of the demons you exorcised yesterday might have left a door open behind it," Clara remarked.

"That's what I was afraid off," Ariel Freeman said. Kneeling on the pavement he set down the briefcase and opened it. Clara couldn't help staring a little as she found herself looking at a perfect anti-demon kit.

There was silver, and blood-ink, a battered copy of the Red Book of Sigils, and a jar full of small, twisted bits of iron that looked like they had been melted at some point. A similar—if fainter—miasma hung about that jar, save that where the one cloaking the house was oppressive and dark, this one was light and golden.

"Something wrong?" Ariel Freeman asked her.

Clara blinked, breaking her line of sight to the artifact.

"Sorry?"

The man grinned nervously. "You look like I've done something to royally piss you off. Everything okay?"

Clara stared down at the man, then realized that could be construed as glaring, and shook her head.

"It's just"—she pointed at the jar of twisted metal—"is that holy shrapnel?"

"You have a good eye," Ariel Freeman said, picking up the jar and rattling its contents. "Picked these up myself after an angel sighting in Arizona five years ago. They're too potent to wear full time, so I just keep them for emergencies."

Clara nodded. She didn't ask if this was an emergency—that was something only Ariel Freeman could decide.

Their stilted conversation was given a merciful death by the sound of Arcana rolling up to the house. Selene got out almost as soon as the vehicle had stopped and marched over to them.

"Right, so what's the plan?" she asked.

"Well, I go in," Ariel Freeman began.

"*We* go in," Clara told Selene. "Can you hold a perimeter?"

"I can shoot whatever comes out of the house," Selene said dryly.

"Do you have bullets that work on demons?" Ariel Freeman asked. Not accusingly, just with natural concern.

Selene laughed. "I got something that'll *make* them work," she said with a sly grin.

The exorcist inclined his head respectfully. "Great, perfect." He reached into his briefcase, took out a small string of beads like greenish pearls, and wrapped it around his hand. Closing the case he gestured with his beaded hand and made a slight bow to Clara. "After you," he said.

Clara did glare at him then, having heard enough mocking *ladies first* jokes in her life. Ariel Freeman saw the look, and gave her a short, small smile—somehow worse than his huge blinding one, because this was personal; it was just for her, and it said, *I realize how that must have sounded and I'm sorry; please don't hit me.*

"Your eyes are probably better than mine," he explained.

"If you say so," Clara said.

She advanced on the house as if it were a wild animal. Drawing her sword as she reached the edge of the lawn she saw Jill and the boy Andrew staring out Arcana's windows.

"You should be further away," she told them.

"I told them that," Selene called, climbing up to sit in Arcana's bed. She had her shotgun out and was tying a soaking-wet rag around the barrel. A heady, golden miasma hung thick about it, and with a jolt Clara realized the cloth must have been soaked in holy oil. Where Selene had managed to get it Clara would have loved to know, but the curling, twisting presence in the house was only growing stronger.

Still, she insisted on waiting until both Jill and Andrew had withdrawn to the far side of Arcana, then with a nod to Ariel Freeman she pushed the door open.

Or tried to. It was locked. Selene could probably pick it, but she didn't want to take her off guard duty. Clara tested the deadbolt, got a feel for the wood under her hand, and then concentrated very carefully on her left arm—the one that held the door handle. Then she opened the door.

Splinters went flying as the bolt ripped through the soft wood and one of the hinges gave out. Clara carefully set the door to the side and stepped into the small living room.

The miasma was thick in here, and now she could smell it as well. The ceiling was dark with a thick, reddish ooze that dripped in puddles on the carpet, and from these puddles rose the heavy scent of burned Dacron and brimstone.

Ariel Freeman stepped forward into the room and made a wide sweeping gesture with his beaded hand. Then he repeated the motion, slower this time, but keeping his hand low to the ground.

"She's in the basement," he said. Then gave a wry smile. "As usual."

Clara appreciated the joke but didn't laugh. She was all too aware of the oppressive presence of the demon, stronger than any she had faced alone before.

Well, she wasn't exactly alone now, but she had yet to construct a firm grasp of Ariel Freeman's abilities. She only hoped he'd had the sense to be warded against non-consensual possession. She didn't ask, either, because considering his profession he probably would have found the question insulting. So she only nodded and began searching for the stairs.

They found them without much trouble, and she was pleased to see Ariel Freeman lay down a holy shard at the top of the stairs. It was wrapped in a silk handkerchief to prevent anyone touching it directly, but Clara could still see the glow of its power through the thin cloth.

Taking a small flashlight from a pocket of his coat he led the way down the stairs until they ended in the concrete floor of the basement. Clara heard him locate the light switch, and then the click as he flipped it, but the darkness remained.

"Hello there," he said pleasantly, and turned up the power on his flashlight, aiming it at the ceiling so its beam was reflected back down, filling the whole room with a soft, diffuse light.

The demon was there, twined around the form of a woman standing very still in the center of the floor.

Her eyes were directed at the ground, and they were blank and unseeing. Her body had a contorted, scrunched-in look, as though the bones and muscles were trying to force themselves into a form that the human body simply couldn't take.

"Mrs. Bell?" Ariel Freeman asked, experimentally.

The woman's head twitched, but her eyes didn't move, and her expression didn't change. Clara felt a sinking feeling in her chest: the demon was so closely wrapped around the woman that she wouldn't be able touch it without harming the human host.

Ariel Freeman, however, seemed perfectly confident.

"Right Mrs. Bell, you just stand there. No need to . . . move. Just relax, and this will be over very, very soon . . . "

As he spoke, Clara noticed the man was carefully running the pale beads through his fingers, stroking them gently with his thumb.

The demon turned to watch him. Clara could see its eyes, like two points of darkness that made her own ache, tracking Ariel Freeman as the man began to circle slowly around the woman.

"Claymore?"

The sound of her true name sent a thrill of nerves through Clara's body, before she realized it was Ariel who spoke, and she forced herself to calm down. She had given him that name, it was only to be expected that he would use it.

"Here," she said, trying to keep the hoarseness out of her voice.

"If you want to light up that sword of yours, now would be a good time."

"I can't use it without harming the woman," Clara told him tightly.

"That won't be a problem in a moment," came the reply.

Clara chanced a glance at the man, and saw him looking back at her, steady and confident. Half his mouth tipped up in a grin, showing a flash of perfect white teeth in the dim light. "Trust me," he said.

Clara inclined her head, eyes narrowing, and carefully drew her sword. She didn't want to risk alarming the demon, so she laid her free hand along the blade and traced the words onto the cool metal. When she felt the hum of power in response she gave Ariel Freeman a short nod, then lowered the blade to a less threatening position.

"Little girl . . . " came a voice that hissed and breathed like the gasping of a dying animal. Clara felt the demon's eyes; its gaze burned on her skin, then faded as it turned its attention to Ariel Freeman. "Little boy . . . you are very . . . confident . . . for so delicate a . . . creature."

"Oh, I'm sure I'll grow on you," Ariel Freeman replied with easy self-assurance. "We'll have a *lot* of time to get to know each other, once I've got you safe in a lockbox, that is. So why don't you let Mrs. Bell go, and we can talk about what it is you think you're doing here."

The demon laughed, sending waves of nausea through Clara's body. She stomped down on the feeling, consciously loosening the muscles in her shoulders and widening her stance.

Ariel Freeman seemed unaffected. He raised his beaded hand, beckoning, and smiled at the demon—or rather, at the human woman the demon had possessed. Clara wasn't sure if she could see the demon itself.

"I won't ask again," he said, closing his eyes briefly. When he opened them his face had gone cold and hard as a piece of marble. A tendon in his jaw tensed, and he grimaced briefly. Then he shouted, the words racketing out of him and shooting around the room like an angry animal.

"*Ashkazural*, I hold your name and I summon you!"

The demon screamed—a physical shockwave that shot through the room, through the walls, through Clara and Ariel, and sent a shower of dust and plaster and other, less pleasant debris, down from the ceiling. It leapt from the woman, toward Ariel, bounced off him and streamed for the door—where Clara intercepted it with a decisive slash of her sword.

She felt the energy sing along the blade, rush through her arms and rattle around in her chest, before it dissipated into the air, leaving a strangely clean, bleached smell and a faint ringing in her ears.

Ariel had dropped the flashlight in the blast, having been knocked down by his impact with the demon, but was now getting stiffly to his feet.

"Mrs. Bell?" he asked, sounding as though he'd just inhaled a lungful of smoke.

"Son of *God* . . ." came a bleary, drunken voice. "What are you doing in my *basement?*"

Ariel Freeman just laughed, warm and rich, and a little bit wheezy.

Clara sheathed her sword with an inward sigh of relief, and went to help Mrs. Bell to her feet. The woman was shaken but seemed uninjured. It was difficult to tell in the uncertain flashlight, so Clara gently wrapped an arm around the woman and began leading her tenderly up the stairs.

It was slow going, the woman still being wobbly on her feet, and with every step Clara noticed how the stairs creaked, how there seemed to be more cracks in the wall, and how—did the ceiling always sag like that?

They reached the threshold, and Clara turned to find Freeman still at the bottom, curiously looking around the room.

In that instant Clara felt a strange wave of energy flow through her. It felt bad, like a deep ache in her bones, and she heard an ominous crack.

"Freeman! *Move!*" she shouted.

Ariel Freeman looked up at her, puzzled. At the sight of her expression, however, he began to climb the stairs. Slowly, though. Too slowly.

A step gave way and things jerked back into motion.

There was no time to think, so Clara didn't. She gave Mrs. Bell a shove, didn't bother to watch the woman land, and fairly dove back down the stairs.

She reached the man just as the ceiling came down around them.

Outside, Jill tapped a finger against Arcana's side. She'd heard muffled shouting, felt a tremor like a small earthquake, and seen Selene tense, alert. But nothing happened. Nothing came out of the house. Eventually she grew bored and climbed up into the bed alongside Selene and the boy Andrew.

"Can I ask a question?" she asked.

Selene jumped, but nodded after a moment.

"Why the rag?" She waved at the piece of dripping cloth tied around the barrel of her shotgun.

Selene glanced at back at her, and without taking her eyes off the house she explained: "It's holy oil. Hard to come by, but effective. Not holy water, which only works against some types of demons. What it does is give the slugs that pass through the barrel a charge of power, which lets them damage noncorporeal monsters. Like demons."

"Fascinating," said Jill. "Why is it so hard to come by? I should think any church..."

She was cut off by movement at the front door, and a bedraggled woman staggered out. She clutched the door frame for support, her chest heaving, then took another step—but without the support of the house she staggered and fell.

"Momma!" cried the boy, and tried to climb down out of the truck. Selene caught him by the arm, shook her head, and pushed him back.

"If it's really your momma," she said, "I'll bring her back." She swung her legs over the side and slid to the ground, landing lightly on the asphalt. She approached the fallen woman with her gun down, but still ready.

Jill saw her kneel, check the woman's pulse, turn her face skyward, look at her eyes, and finally press two fingers briefly to her forehead. Then she seemed to relax and took the woman gently under the shoulders and supported her down the rest of the drive.

She sat her on the curb but kept looking back over her shoulder at the house, which remained silent.

"Watch her," she said to Jill. "I don't know what's happened in there, but I don't think it's over yet."

Jill nodded, all too aware that there was no sign of Clara or Freeman. She hopped down, using the running board as a foothold, and went to support the woman's shoulders while Selene turned back to cover the house.

* * *

It was dark and hot, and what air they had was filled with plaster and brick dust. But after the shock of the collapse had passed, Ariel realized that he had not been crushed to a bloody pulp, and in fact all his limbs were perfectly intact.

"Are you injured?" came Claymore's voice, strained, and very near his right ear.

Ariel tried to raise his head and felt his hat catch on something. He realized he was crouched in a very small space with nowhere to go, and thanked his lucky stars he wasn't claustrophobic.

"Not that I can tell," he gasped, choking on dust. "You?"

No answer. There was a creaking sound and the squeak of leather as the woman moved above him. He was aware of a pressure that had been on his back shifting, and realized it was one of her arms. She must literally be spread over him like an umbrella.

"What happened?" he tried.

"I do not believe the demon was vanquished," came the reply, now slightly muffled, as if Claymore was looking somewhere else.

"Oh," said Ariel, his heart sinking. "It trapped us."

"It tried to kill you," said the woman. "Now please be quiet. I have to concentrate."

There was a sound from inside the house like rocks tearing apart. Jill, Selene and Andrew all jumped, and Andrew's mother even turned her head, dazed though she was, toward the front door. A billow of whitish smoke came rolling out, but Selene relaxed as soon as she caught a whiff of it: it was ordinary plaster and dust, not brimstone.

Two figures materialized out of the smoke, solidifying into Clara and Freeman as they staggered out. Their dark clothes were covered in white and red dust, and there were splinters stuck in the shoulder pads of Clara's jacket. Freeman was holding his hat, disappointedly trying to bend it back into shape, but he gave up and squashed it back on his head when he saw them.

"What the hell *happened?*" Selene asked, lowering her gun.

"Demon was uncooperative," Clara replied, wiping debris off her shoulders and shrugging.

"Is it gone now?" Andrew Bell asked with wide eyes.

Ariel Freeman opened his mouth. Jill thought he was going to say something reassuring, like *yes*, but instead all that came out was a puff of black smoke.

The man frowned, coughed, and then doubled over, choking.

Jill froze, uncertain what to do, but Clara reached over and pressed a steadying hand against his shoulder, before giving him a firm whack across the back with her other.

Something came loose in Ariel Freeman's throat, welled in his mouth, and then fell to the pavement with a *splat*, where it began to steam faintly.

"What is—" Jill began, but Selene had already jumped down, ripped the rag off the barrel of her gun and spread it over the puddle of black liquid, as though she were mopping up spilled milk.

"Don't *tell* me you got your ass *possessed*," she snarled, glaring up at the man.

Ariel Freeman looked back, his eyes unfocused. There was a drop of the same black liquid rolling down his chin as he shook his head.

"C-car . . ." he whispered, and then swallowed, painfully.

Clara looked up, spotted the white sedan, and then scooped the man up, bridal style, and carried him across the street.

"Is mister going to be all right?" Andrew Bell asked, clearly torn, but he did not let go of his mother's hand.

Selene didn't answer. She'd grabbed her duffle bag and vaulted out of Arcana's bed to follow Clara. Jill, reaching in back for her sample kit, paused.

"I don't know," she said, frankly. "But we'll do our best to take care of him."

"Take him to hospital!" the boy called after her as she made her way across the street.

Clara had set Ariel Freeman down in the shadow of his car, leaned him carefully against the rear wheel, and after fishing in his pocket she found his keys and opened the car's trunk.

"Where is your asphodel?" she asked, fingers reaching unerringly for the handle to lift out the false bottom, revealing a small space crammed with bottles, books, and an assortment of bladed weapons.

There was an impatient tap on her leg, and she looked down to see that, through all this, Ariel Freeman hadn't let go of his briefcase.

Leaving the trunk Clara opened the case and immediately saw the little bottle of grayish-yellow powder in the middle of the top rack. She pulled it out and popped the top off, looked around for a cloth or rag, and found Ariel calmly holding out a small white handkerchief.

His eyes were focused now and seemed steady, but Clara noticed how he was keeping his jaw clenched shut and how there was black liquid oozing out of his right nostril. His breathing was rapid and whistled through his nose in an alarming way.

Clara poured a generous amount of asphodel into the cloth, folded the ends over to make a neat little package, and even remembered to re-cork the bottle before she presented the bundle to Ariel.

The man opened his mouth—and a torrent of thicker black liquid poured out. Clara pulled his shoulders forward so most of it went onto the pavement, but a significant amount had already run down the side of his face, soaking into the fabric of his collar and staining the little white snip an ugly brownish-purple.

"Breathe," Clara said quietly.

This got her a few gasping breaths. A shaky laugh. Ariel reached for the packet of herbs, but his hand was trembling so badly Clara was forced to steady it with her own as he placed the folded cloth in his mouth and bit down with relief.

Clara took one of her own rags and gently wiped the side of the man's face, where the liquid had already begun to congeal and harden. She folded it over so a relatively clean side was presented, and held it up to Ariel's nose.

"Blow," she told him.

Ariel snorted out through his nose obediently, and a distressingly long string of black, tarry goo came away with the cloth.

"What's happened? Is he *possessed?*" Jill asked, her head appearing from over the side of the trunk.

"Nah, sister," said Selene, even as Ariel shook his head vehemently. "I thought so at first, but this looks like he's been *hooked.*"

"Hooked?"

"It happens sometimes when a demon tries to possess someone, but can't—for whatever reason. If that someone, say, knows the demon's true name." She looked at Ariel, hard, before continuing. "Well, the name *is* the demon, and the demon *is* the name. That's why knowing a demon's true name is so powerful. But if the demon is strong enough, they can turn the tables on you."

"They can manifest inside your head," Clara said.

Ariel ripped the little packet out of his mouth, spat—spittle and black goo—and shook his head.

"I spoke its name," he said, his voice thick and hoarse.

"I did not keep it," Clara assured him, and he gave a sigh of relief.

A sigh that turned into a violent coughing fit. Clara didn't ask this time before sticking the packet of herbs back in his mouth.

"What's *that* for?" Jill asked.

"Asphodel," Clara said, shortly.

"Helps alleviate the ... er ... symptoms," Selene said.

"We need to get him to a sanctuary," Clara said.

Jill opened her mouth, saw the looks on Clara and Selene's faces, and decided not to ask what a sanctuary was.

"The nearest sanctuary is in New Mexico," Selene said. "We'll never make it in time."

Ariel Freeman shook his head violently and removed the packet. Of course all that came out of his mouth was another torrent of black slime. Now Jill noticed its smell—sharp like iodine but with an undercurrent of rotten plants.

"Not ... not ... " His words were drowned.

Clara, her brow bunched and her cold blue eyes glaring, moved a hand behind the man's neck and traced a pattern there, as though she were trying to soothe him.

And amazingly, it appeared to work. Ariel Freeman let out a short gasp and shuddered. He raised his head and looked wonderingly at Clara.

"Thank you," he said, smiling weakly.

"I did not know if it would work on a human," Clara replied.

Ariel shrugged and turned back to Selene.

"If you can get me to the Angel's Graveyard, I think I can take it from there."

"The *Angel's* Graveyard?" Selene repeated. "But no one knows where that is!"

"I do," Ariel said. "I found it. It's not far. Load me up in the back, I'll give you directions."

"I'll stay with you," Clara declared. "I will return for Unicorn later."

"Fine, *fine*," said Selene, waving her hands. "Jill, you better follow in Arcana. We might need the arsenal."

Jill, who had been pondering whether she wanted to take a sample of the black goo, looked up alertly.

"Where are we going?" she asked.

"The Angel's Graveyard," Clara said.

"You *remember* the song, right?" said Selene. "The one with the broken heart. Supposedly, he's *still here*, in a way."

Clara installed herself in the back seat of Ariel's car, laying her sword down on the floor, and pulled the man in beside her. As Selene started the engine she cast a look back at Unicorn, sitting resolutely at the edge of the street, and her mouth hardened. Then her line of sight was cut off by Arcana pulling in behind them, and then the view was fading. She caught a glimpse of the woman, Bell, her arms around her son, as they watched them leave in bewilderment.

Perhaps it was best for them. They would be confused, and haunted for some time, but whatever was left of the demons that had plagued them was now confined within the man next to her on the back seat. The best thing they could do was get him away from them.

"Talk to me, missionary man," Selene said, weaving slightly on the road as she shoved the seat forward and adjusted the mirrors. Clara braced one leg against the back of the passenger seat in order to hold Ariel steady. The man groaned, his eyes fluttering closed, and a thin trail of black ooze ran down from his nose.

"Get on the highway," he said, wheezing a little. "Head south. It's in Dodge City. Suburbs."

"Got anything more specific?" Selene asked. She *didn't* say "In case you can't talk by the time we get there," and Clara appreciated it.

"It's called Mercy's End Cemetery." He had to pause and cough. Clara braced his shoulders between her knees and started making a fresh packet of asphodel. "End of Mercy Street. Can't miss it."

"You got that, Jill?" Selene asked, driving one-handed as she held her cell phone up to her face.

"Copy," came the answer, a little fuzzily. "That's about … two and a half hours away."

"Well, no time to lose," Selene said, and hit the gas.

They made the highway in no time, speeding southeast once they cleared the last of the lights, and Clara was just daring to hope, daring to imagine something other than an ugly death for the man in her lap, when they passed the "Now Leaving Pearson, come again!" sign, and the car's engine abruptly stuttered, stalled, then died and refused to start.

"What the ever-loving—" Selene let out a string of curses as she tried to restart the machine.

Ariel's eyes opened, very wide and bright in the dimness of the car. Clara noticed the green of them was shot through with bolts of amber. They were also red around the edges, and the tears that sprang from them were ugly, dark and brown. Raising a shaking hand he took the packet from his mouth and whispered, "It's gaining on me."

"*Pus buckets!*" Selene shouted, guiding the car to the side of the road as they coasted to a halt.

Arcana rolled past a moment later, its right turn signal blinking, and stopped with a crunch a few feet ahead.

"What's happened?" Jill demanded, climbing down.

Selene, who had popped the hood and gotten out, shook her head.

"Demon's messing with the car. Doesn't want us to leave."

"But we need to get him to this sanctuary, right?" Jill said, frowning.

"That *was* the idea," Selene said. "But if this demon's strong enough to meddle with machines without being fully manifested we are in *big* trouble."

"We can't just ... er ... load up in Arcana?" Jill asked.

"Probably wouldn't get far ... " Selene admitted.

"But worth a try?"

Selene glanced back into the white car. Clara met her gaze, and then took matters into her own hands as she grabbed her sword, pushed open the door and began dragging Ariel out.

"Open up the back," she said as she strode past, Ariel draped limply in her arms. "Get his briefcase. Don't forget to lock his car."

"Clara, the demon will just shut down Arcana—"

"It's worth a try," Clara said through clenched teeth.

Selene didn't argue. She went back, pulled Ariel's briefcase out of the back seat, closed and locked all the doors, and then jogged forward and hopped in next to Jill.

"All right," she said. "Let's try this."

Arcana coughed ominously when Jill went to start him up, and in the back Ariel rolled his eyes heavenward. Clara took his meaning, and figuring it couldn't hurt, whispered a short prayer.

With a heavy growl the diesel engine came to life, and the truck shuddered as Jill pulled gently onto the road.

"Now's not the time to drive like a granny," Selene said. "That man needs a sanctuary *ASAP.*"

"This is no time to get pulled over, either," Jill replied primly, and insisted on driving exactly the speed limit.

But she drove. She drove, and Arcana *did not stop.* Out of Pearson, mile upon mile, the black tread of the highway falling away behind them as they crawled under a blue sky that became increasingly overcast as they drove into the rising sun.

In the back, Clara went through Ariel's supply of asphodel and dug into Selene's, keeping the packet fresh. She refreshed the words on his back once, but dared not do it again when she felt how hot his skin had become. The black goo flowed freely from his nose and eyes, puddling on the floor when Clara failed to wipe it away in time.

In the front, Jill had Selene put the address for the cemetery into her phone's map app, and kept eyeing the directions as they told her they were two and a half hours away . . . two hours away . . . one and a half hours away . . . It was a lucky thing they'd filled the tank so recently; Jill suspected they could not afford to stop.

Arcana himself appeared to be running smoothly, yet the way in which Clara and Selene had been acting made her more sensitive to the truck's performance. Perhaps because of this she noticed at once when the engine began to rev faster every time she put her foot on the gas.

Had Arcana always handled that way? Was this just her nerves? Even if it was new, it certainly wasn't *slowing them down.* Jill had, true to her meticulous nature, been maintaining the vehicle faithfully and saw no reason to suspect a mundane mechanical malfunction, yet she made a mental note to have it checked out the next time she brought the truck in for service.

The sky was an ominous swirl of black and gray by the time they entered the outskirts of Dodge City. Jill had the headlights on as she slowed and got off the highway, squinting at the directions on her phone's screen. In the back, Ariel moaned as they swung right abruptly.

Coming to a stop at an intersection Jill flicked a finger over the map, trying to get an idea of where they were going. The light changed, and Jill eased Arcana forward while still squinting at her phone.

The truck had barely rolled two feet before it took off like a rocket. The engine blared. Jill found herself thrown back against the seat and Selene swore. Ariel let out a pained moan and Clara grunted.

"Now is *not* the time to start a drag race!" Selene shouted.

"That wasn't *me!*" Jill screamed back. She had taken her foot off the gas at the first wild leap and slammed her other down on the clutch, but even though they were slowing down the engine revved faster and faster.

"It's the demon," announced Clara.

"*Runaway,* more like," hissed Selene.

Jill had already put the truck into sixth gear, but she kept her foot on the clutch until they had pulled off the road and come to a complete stop, engine practically *screaming* by this time, like an animal in pain.

"Don't forget the parking brake," Selene said, and Jill remembered to set it before she slammed her foot down on the brake pedal, took a breath, and then let out the clutch all at once.

The huge truck shuddered, jerked, and the engine died with an ugly gurgle. In the silence there was the faint hiss of steam, but everything else was still and calm. Almost apologetically, Jill put the machine back into neutral and patted the dashboard.

"Sorry, big boy," she whispered.

"Are we there yet?" came a wavering voice from the rear of the cab.

"Almost," replied Selene, hopping out and pulling the back door open. "We're gonna have to hoof it from here. Can you walk? No, stupid question," she admonished herself when she laid eyes on the man. Ariel's mouth was stained black, and there were tears like dirty water running from his eyes. "Clara, can you carry him? That's probably *also* a stupid question . . . "

Clara merely rolled her eyes as she gently lifted Ariel out of the back seat, being careful to keep his head elevated.

"Can you get my sword?" she asked, and obligingly half knelt so that Selene could slide the blade into the sheath she wore strapped to her back. Then she looked around. "Which way from here?"

"Keep heading north another quarter mile," Jill said, coming around the truck's nose, her phone in one hand and her sample kit slung over her shoulder.

Selene, who had climbed up into the bed and was hastily packing one of her small duffle bags, looked up at the sky worriedly. "And then?"

"Then it's not far at all. Less than a mile."

"Well thank the stars for small favors," Selene said, sliding down. She had Freddie slung casually under one arm, a fresh rag tied around the long barrel, and at her back bounced the sawn-off shotgun, Elvis, similarly treated.

It felt somehow wrong—like an admission of defeat—to leave Arcana there, by the side of the road. Jill shut off the emergency lights and locked all the doors before she left, and kept sending worried looks back toward the truck as they made their way down the street.

Which was largely empty—probably thanks to the evil-looking sky—which was just as well. They made a truly bizarre spectacle: Clara in her black biking leathers carrying what was clearly an injured man in her arms as if he were a child, and Selene with her guns. Jill in her jeans and backpack was probably the only one who could have passed for normal.

Even walking they almost missed Mercy Street—something had come through and ripped the sign down, and it was only because Jill could track their location on the map with her phone that they knew to turn right when they did.

Here they quickly passed into a residential district, the street lined with conservative homes huddling behind scrappy lawns with pickup trucks in their driveways. They passed only one other person—a dog-walker who crossed the street well before their paths met and studiously avoided looking at them.

The wind, which had been gusting fitfully since they'd left Arcana, strengthened, growing to buffet their faces, as if pushing them away.

"Let me guess, demon again?" Jill gasped as her hair lashed her face.

"No . . . " whispered Ariel, his voice barely audible. But his eyes were bright and alert, and they focused intensely on Jill as he answered. "This is from the angel. It means he doesn't want to be disturbed."

"Too bad for him," said Selene, and quickened her pace.

The sky was downright inky, and the clouds crouched low above them by the time they reached the end of the street. Here they had to slip between two houses and through a rusty gate before they at last emerged into a rundown cemetery. A sign above the main gate—which was fused open by all the tangled weeds growing around it—declared that this was Mercy's End Cemetery, and a white piece of cardboard had been tacked under it, on which had been written: "Closed Permanently: Do Not Enter"

"Some sanctuary," murmured Jill.

The place did appear more depressing than comforting; many of the gravestones were chipped, crooked or knocked over. What flags or fake flowers remained were bleached from the sun, and only added to the pervasive atmosphere of abandonment.

Ariel, however, perked up the moment Clara carried him under the sign. He writhed in her arms until she grudgingly let him down, but allowed himself to be supported as he staggered off between the headstones.

The cemetery was filled with trees: scraggly oaks whose boughs drooped and whose leaves from the previous fall still lay upon the ground in thick mats. The hanging branches, the new spring buds still small upon them, clattered in the wind like bones rattling.

"So, you said the Weeping Angel is *here*?" Selene asked the man, who had come to a stop in a wide path between the headstones.

Ariel Freeman didn't answer. He swung his head about, as if scenting the air, then turned and staggered off down the avenue, Clara at his side.

There were a number of statues in the cemetery, Jill noticed. Most of them were high up on pedestals, smaller than life-size. Some appeared to be ordinary humans, but a few had half-unfolded bird wings.

Through a gap between the trees Jill thought she saw someone standing over one of the graves, and gave an inarticulate shout. The sound alerted Selene and Clara, who turned to look, and Ariel let out a feeble laugh.

Jill looked again, and found it was not a person, but another statue. Trudging through the leaves, she saw it was set on a low pedestal, made of a dark brownish stone that was strangely free of lichen or moss. The figure was that of a man in an old-fashioned coat with a long scarf draped over his shoulders. He had a sloppy mop of short hair, and stood with his eyes downcast, staring at his empty hands which were held palms out, hanging limply in front of him.

Staggering out of Clara's grasp, Ariel collapsed at the foot of the statue, resting his back against the pedestal and closing his eyes in relief.

"Do you require any other assistance?" Clara asked.

Without opening his eyes, Ariel shook his head. "Just time," he said.

Feeling worried and helpless, Jill took a turn around the statue, and frowned when she saw its back: sprouting from the man's shoulder blades were the stumps of what must have once been wings, but the material had been ripped, twisted, as though the appendages had been torn off. Coming around to his front again, Jill finally took a good look at his face, and was surprised to see a discoloration of the stone beneath his eyes: greenish, freckled with white. It lay in two streaks from each eye down across the cheeks, in the exact path that tears would follow.

"*If you pass a weeping angel, best stop and pay your leave,*" Selene whispered at her side.

"From the song?" Jill asked.

Selene shrugged. "You'd be surprised how much of the old songs and legends turn out to have a grain of truth to them. Though, to be honest, I never believed the bit about the angel until now."

"Is he . . . uh . . . a real angel?" Jill asked. "Looks just like a weird statue to me."

Selene tilted her head to one side. "That's hard to say," she admitted. "It's pretty clear the Brothers Gunn *did* have interactions with angels. It's not too much to believe that *this* is one of those angels, but . . . well. Things happened toward the end. Weird things. Ultimately, I'm not sure if their angel was *still* an angel by the time they disappeared."

"Is that why he's a statue now?"

There was a raspy cough from by their feet, and the two glanced down to find Ariel Freeman looking back at them.

"If he wasn't an angel," the man said, hoarsely, "then how'd he turn himself into a statue?" He managed a weak smile, one that vanished a moment later when he started coughing.

"Selene," Clara said, her voice harsh.

Selene came around, and saw immediately what had warranted the change in Clara's tone.

Black liquid was pouring out of Ariel's mouth, streaming from his eyes, and where it pooled on the ground it steamed, smoke that rose white before going black as the sky above them.

Ariel gulped, trying to stop the flow, but Clara put a hand on his back, forcing him to keep his head bowed.

"Let it out," she said gently. "Let us worry about it."

"You don't—understand . . . " for the first time, his voice sounded not only hoarse and weak, but actually frightened. "This—demon—shouldn't be this strong. Think—there's—more . . . "

A vicious wind whipped through the cemetery. It lifted the damp, half-rotted leaves and flung them into the air. The trees creaked, and above them in the burgeoning clouds a fork of lightning flashed. The smoke hung in a thick haze all around them, and within it Jill thought she could glimpse a solid shape growing.

"Selene . . . " she began, reaching to tug at the woman's sleeve.

Selene, however, had already seen the shape, brought her gun to bear, and fired.

There was a horrible, soundless scream. It sang in Jill's bones and made her ears and eyes hurt. Unthinking, she clapped her hands over her ears and shut her eyes.

Clara, who had been kneeling beside Ariel, was on her feet in an instant, sword in hand, and she shouted the words aloud into the smoke.

Below her, Ariel retched, shuddered, and lay still. The pool of black liquid had almost entirely evaporated, but now the smoke was twining around them with almost solid tendrils. The wind howled, and somewhere a branch cracked threateningly.

"What are they trying to do, create a Hell Gate?" Selene swore, firing off another shot into the smoke. The bullet left a streak of clear air behind it, through which could be seen the barren trees and banked leaves, but the vision was quickly swallowed as more smoke poured in.

All of a sudden the shapes in the smoke became a great deal more solid. They moved like tigers, or maybe like sharks, and slipped past Clara's blade, aiming for the man on the ground. In response the large woman threw herself bodily in the way, and there was an electric crackle in the air as the demon connected. She dropped to one knee, apparently winded, and buried a hand in the thick bed of leaves. Above her, Selene was firing shot after shot into the smoke.

Then there was a *bang* of an entirely different variety, and with a crash one of the oaks let fall a huge branch, which landed barely a yard from where their group was huddled.

Jill opened her eyes to find herself staring into Ariel's face. The man's eyes were closed now, his skin dangerously pale and his lips stained black. His tears had dried in a dirty streak down his face, and with a jolt she realized he wasn't breathing.

She looked up and around instinctively for help, and found her gaze landing on the statue of the angel.

The angel, whose face was now turned up and away from them, looking out upon the scene surrounding it. Surely it hadn't been like that before? Surely, it had been looking *down* . . .

But even as she watched, Jill saw the angel move. The stone shifted, shimmered behind the haze, and slowly the face turned down upon them again. Its eyes were open now, and Jill swallowed when she saw they were dark, empty hollows.

Something she had read once about angels—you weren't supposed to look at them. But it was too late for that now, and Jill continued to stare, transfixed.

The angel frowned, and turned his hand over, palm down.

It was a little motion, but done with such finality that Jill felt a shiver run through her body.

The next instant the winds ceased. The shapes in the smoke disappeared, and the smoke itself lifted abruptly. Above them the clouds hurtled up and away, lightening from black to gray, from gray to gray-blue, until a beam of strong midday sun broke through and lit the entire cemetery in hues of gold and green.

The angel shut his eyes.

For Ariel, the haze of fog and pain and the screaming in his head faded slowly. Like recovering from a bad fever, he felt weak and cold and incredibly gross. His mouth tasted awful and his face felt crusty. He did not quite trust his mind not to seize and clench every time he tried to think, and he kept expecting the demon's name to muscle itself to the front of his mind and sit there, grinning at him. It took a moment of careful prodding before he was satisfied this was not the case, and after another moment he was surprised to realize he no longer remembered the demon's name at all. There was no blank space, no scar where it had been. It had been lifted out of his mind, cleanly and carefully, like a splinter being removed from a wound.

He inhaled. That cleared the fog further. Above him someone said, "Never mind, I think he's okay," and Ariel cracked an eye open to find three concerned faces peering down at him.

"Oh, yeah," he said, and was surprised at how easy it was to speak. His throat hardly felt sore at all. "I am *fantastic.*"

"You're unbelievable, is what you are," Selene said. "And you look *awful.*"

"We all gotta have grungy days," he replied. "Though I gotta say, demon slime makes for terrible eyeliner. Zero of ten, would *not* recommend."

"Are you always like this after near-death experiences?" Jill asked.

Ariel sat up gingerly, expecting a rush of dizziness. Instead, he only felt his head clear further. He was feeling stronger by the minute. Cautiously he put a hand to his face and began picking dried slime off his cheek. It caught on his stubble, and he winced. "Nah, sometimes I can actually *be clever.* Are you ladies all right?"

To his dismay he saw Jill's face harden. He looked around, feeling a tightening of fear in his chest, but the woman appeared perfectly fine, as did Selene. For a moment he panicked, but then his eyes landed on Claymore, who was stomping through the leaves a little way off, clearly hunting for any residual demonic presences.

"Then what—?" he began, but the small woman cut him off.

"*Arcana*," she said with a heavy sigh. "My truck. I've probably blown his clutch even if that demon of yours didn't destroy the engine. I hope you have friends in Dodge, because we're gonna be here a while."

It was a beautiful spring afternoon, and in the abandoned cemetery two figures in black sat on a mossy stone bench. They would have been sharing a beer, but Claymore refused every time Ariel offered.

"You should be drinking water," she only said.

"I'll get to that," he said, taking another sip from the bottle. "For now, I need the alcohol. Helps put some distance between . . . things." He grinned at Claymore, who only looked back, blankly. Ariel shook his head and sighed.

"I'm sorry," he said.

Claymore's left brow twitched. "For what?" she asked, sounding genuinely confused.

"For whatever it is that's making you look like you just ate a lemon," he said. "I can't think of anything I've done, but if I have, I'm sorry about it."

Claymore turned to look at him. Her eyes were cold and blue and glittered in the sunlight. She frowned, the motion crowding her forehead with wrinkles. Then, like clouds passing, her expression cleared and she turned away, sighing faintly.

"You have done nothing," she said in that abrupt way of hers. "This is just . . . the manner of my face."

"Oh? So my presence is not like sandpaper on an open wound to you?"

Claymore actually smiled at that. Not a big one, and it was gone almost as soon as it appeared, but it was there nonetheless. She shook her head.

Ariel sipped his beer and the two sat in companionable silence for a time.

"That's good," he said eventually. "Thanks."

Claymore's shoulders dipped and rose, and she tipped her head to one side. "I did what was required," she said. "Thank *him*." She gestured toward the statue.

Ariel looked over at the stone angel. According to Claymore, Jill had seen it move. Ariel couldn't be sure if it was in the same pose as before— hadn't the hands been different? He couldn't remember. Admittedly, he hadn't been in a position to get a good look at it before. Now he could clearly see the streaks of discoloration on the angel's cheeks, and the mangled stump of his right wing was just visible over one sagging shoulder.

"Do you ever wonder what happened? You know, what broke his heart?" he asked after a while.

Claymore did her little inverted shrug again. "Lots of things, I expect," she said.

Ariel laughed. "That's what everyone says. 'What broke his heart?' 'Oh, *things*, you know . . . ' But, like, what exactly? Was it that Adam turned out to be an Antichrist? Was it his rebellion against Heaven? Saying someone has a broken heart implies an unhappy romantic relationship, but if you look at actual records there's no sign of anything like that."

Claymore frowned. "Didn't he have a wife, once?"

Ariel nodded. "Twice, actually. Once from before he was woken, and once when he turned human and lost his memories."

"That happened more than once," Claymore pointed out. "Which time?"

"Uh, the second, I think. But in both cases it wasn't really *him*. Not all of him, anyway. That was the man, Calvin McGovern, not the *angel* inside him. Nah, I think it must have been something else."

There was a crunching sound behind them, and the two turned to find Selene wading through the leaves and fallen branches. She had a crooked grin on her face, as though she had been eavesdropping and wasn't sorry about it.

"Innit obvious?" she said, coming up next to them and putting her hands in the pockets of her jeans. "The angel was in love with *David*. Right from the start."

"David Gunn?" Ariel echoed, arching an eyebrow at her.

Selene cocked her head at the despondent statue. "It's all there if you care to *look*. Not even forty years of straight whitewashing could hide it completely. *Besides*, that there," she jerked a thumb at the dejected angel, " . . . is *definitely* the look of someone who tried to date someone in the closet."

Ariel finished his beer and grinned blindingly up at Selene.

"Glad to hear it," he said. "I was beginning to think I was the only one who thought so."

It was Selene's turn to stare blankly down at Ariel. Claymore interrupted the awkward pause by asking: "What is the damage to Arcana?"

Selene gave herself a little shake. "What? Oh, would you believe it? *Nothing.* Needed some more oil, but that was all. No damage to the clutch *or* the engine. It's giving Jill fits, but I told her, I said: 'Jill, you just saw a statue come to life and banish a demon—now you have problems with your precious truck being miraculously unharmed?' And do you know what she said to me? She said: 'Yes, Selene, because *this* doesn't make *sense.*'" Selene rolled her eyes. "She's got him down by the gate now, on the phone with that professor of hers."

Claymore, however, was frowning thoughtfully. "I will go take a look," she said, and stood up.

"Have fun with that," Selene called to her retreating back. Turning to Ariel she went on. "Anyway, we can take you back to your car any time. Unless you want to grab something to eat. Me and Jill already did."

Ariel lifted a hand to stem the flow of words. "Just a sec," he said, getting slowly to his feet. He went over to the statue of the angel and, after looking into its face for a moment, gently laid one of his hands over the angel's stone fingers. He closed his eyes briefly, and murmured something almost inaudible. Selene thought it was Latin.

"If you pass a weeping angel," he said by way of explanation as he came away, "best stop and pay your leave."

"Aye," Selene said. She threw a ragged salute toward the statue. "Better luck next time, ya poor bastard."

They walked slowly back together through the leaves and tombstones. Ariel, though he claimed to be fine, still looked greenish and wobbly.

Then Arcana came into view, parked on the far side of the gate. Its hood was up and Clara was leaning over the engine, inspecting something in its depths. Jill was next to her, waving her arms and exclaiming over something.

"Can I ask you a kind of personal question?" Ariel said while they were still out of earshot.

"Sure," said Selene. "Mind, I might not answer."

"Of course," said Ariel with a laugh. Then his face sobered. "What is she?"

Selene sighed. "She's this crazy chick we picked up in Santa Cruz. She's *obsessed* with finding the *reason* and *science* behind what we do. What we fight. Me and Clara, we just work for her. It's aggravating, sometimes, but we—"

"Not Jill," Ariel said. "Claymore."

"*Clara*?" Selene returned. Her eyes narrowed. "What *about* her?"

Ariel stopped, forcing Selene to pause and turn back.

"A *house* fell on us," he said quietly. "Or a lot of its floor. I was under her. I couldn't see, could barely move. But she just sort of . . . *burrowed* us out of there. Like a mole. Only I looked back when we got out and there were two-by-fours that had been snapped like twigs, shattered pieces of concrete and bent rebar. It looked like a *bulldozer* had been through."

Selene raised a heavy eyebrow.

"Clara's . . . very strong," she allowed.

Ariel smiled and shook his head. He started off toward the truck. "I'm just saying. If you're ever in a tight spot and all hell breaks loose? I'd stick to her like glue."

"Son," Selene said, turning to follow him. "You don't have to tell me that."

The late afternoon sun lit the white sedan by the side of the road like a beacon, flashing so bright it was impossible to miss. Arcana lumbered past, executed a hasty three-point turn before trundling back along the shoulder. The truck stopped. Jill, Selene and Ariel got out and made their way over to the car. While Jill wiped down the back seat, Ariel checked the car's fluid levels, before climbing in and starting the engine.

"All good?" Selene asked.

"As ever," Ariel replied. "Thank you," he said to Jill, who'd extracted his white hat from the back seat.

"You're not going to explain what just happened?" she asked.

"You mean about the angel?" Ariel asked, slipping on a pair of aviator-style sunglasses.

"No, I mean about the demon," Jill said. "How did it hook you? Why was it so strong?"

Ariel's lips pursed and he swallowed. "To tell the truth, I don't know why. It *shouldn't* have been that strong. Then again, maybe I slipped up. I'm only human, after all." He smiled, dazzlingly.

Jill was unmoved. "Very well then," she said, and produced a card from her wallet. "If you ever find yourself in a similar . . . *situation.* Or if you discover anything particularly *out of the ordinary.* . . . Give me a call."

Ariel took the little white card, studied it, then smiled and stuck it in his hatband.

"You know, usually I'm the one handing these out at the end of the day."

"Well, the world is full of surprises," Jill said dryly. But she got out her phone. "Do you want to give me a number, anyway?"

Ariel did.

"Now, if you'll excuse me," he said, almost apologetically. "I'm going to find myself a nice, cheap hotel room with a hard bed and a hot shower. I recommend you do the same." He pulled his shades down far enough to wink at Jill, gave one last flash of his remarkably straight, white teeth, and pulled his car onto the road, and away.

Clara was dozing in the back seat when Jill and Selene returned.

"I gotta say I agree with him," Selene admitted. "I'm all greasy, and I shudder to think what Clara's got on her."

"First stop, Unicorn," Jill reminded her.

From the back came a mumbled agreement.

"Surprised you didn't come out to say good-bye to him," Selene chided. "I think he *liked* you." She leaned around to find Clara's eyes had cracked open.

"No need," she said. "We will see him again."

She shut her eyes and turned toward the window as Arcana shuddered to life. In her mind she felt a dream, but it was receding, like the sound of light hoofbeats fading away into the distance. Somewhere out there the white stag was running. Clara let it go.

Well he's a man with a missionary collar
He's a man with a missionary's pride
But if you ask for absolution baby can't you see
He's no gentle preacher he'll take you for a ride

Whether he's been lost, whether he's been found,
Believe what you want to once he's in the ground
Doesn't matter if he loses or wins
'Cause he's got it coming
'Cause he danced with a visionary sin

He danced with a visionary sin

A visionary sinner, he comes in like the tide
A man on a mission, he's got nothing to hide
A rod and a spoiled god
He's a man with a vision
of the world on fire.

There was a man with a vision and an angel lost at sea,
His visionary sin it was going to be
The best and the worst and the
only true reality
Oh listen to the roar as the tide recedes
recedes
recedes
recedes
recedes . . .

Well he's a man with a missionary collar
He's a man with a missionary's pride
(Missionary's pride)
But if you ask for absolution baby can't you see
He's no gentle preacher
preacher
preacher
preacher
preacher . . .

It don't matter, lose or win
Oh honey (He danced with a visionary sin)
See what you done (Visionary sinner)
Take a step back from that door (Visionary sinner)
(Visionary sinner) He danced with a visionary sin
(He's got it coming to him now)
Visionary sin

—Visionary Sinner/*Technorhyme*

7. SONS of FIRE

The suburbs of Kansas City

THE MOTEL ROOM was quiet and dark, despite the lateness of the morning. The thick curtains which had been drawn against the harsh streetlight now served to keep out the piercing sun. While the temperature steadily climbed in the asphalt parking lot outside, inside the little room all was dim shadow and vague, lumpy shapes. The only light came from Jill Hamilton's computer screen, which she hunched over guiltily, trying to block as much of its glow as possible.

Though most of the time her bodyguards took it in turns to keep watch through the night, with the rising of the sun Selene had declared herself done, and fell into the bed not occupied by Clara. Now their sleeping forms were but a rumpled twist of blankets in the shadows, and Jill—who was the only one who had slept through the whole night—after breakfasting in the motel's cafeteria, had muted her computer and silenced her phone and now sat, trying to type as quietly as possible, while she listened to the two women peacefully breathing.

There was an ear-splitting, tooth-grinding chime, followed by an insipid melody rendered with all the musical acumen of a nineteen-eighties arcade game. It blared out of nowhere, filling the room, and beneath it was a soft, and accordingly aggravating, buzzing noise.

It was unmistakably the ring of a cell phone, but not any that Jill knew. With some of the money brought in by the sale of her childhood home she'd bought both her employees smartphones which, in addition to allowing her better access to them when they were out and about, had a far more pleasing selection of ringtones. This was not any of them.

"Y'all realize this means *bloodshed*," Selene gasped, rising out of her cocoon of blankets like a monster from Greek mythology. With her thick, tightly curling hair half-pulled from its ponytail and pushed out in all directions she did look a little Medusan, and though she had not yet managed to open her eyes, her teeth were bared in an awful grimace. She flailed, shedding blankets, and began feeling around the bedside table for the source of the noise.

Jill shut her laptop at once and began homing in on it. Being more awake than Selene, she soon figured out it was coming from the dark pile of leather panniers that Clara had left in a corner by the door.

That gave her pause. Clara fiercely valued—and guarded—her privacy. Also, having seen some of the things to have come out of those panniers (magic rings, armor, special knives) Jill was reluctant to begin pawing through them—even to silence such an awful noise.

As it happened, however, she didn't have to. Clara turned over and, without ever actually sitting up, crawled over the end of her bed, and then over a good three feet of floor, until she could reach the topmost pannier and flip it open. She was so tall her hips and legs still rested on the bed, while her torso stretched out over the floor as she began rifling through the contents of the satchel.

"Clara, you make that noise stop—or I *will* kill something!" Selene cried, crumpling back into her bed and mashing the pillows into her face, from which further threatening murmurs continued to emanate.

Clara said nothing, but single-mindedly dug through her pannier until her hand came out holding a small, battered, and very much outdated cell phone. It was the simplest, cheapest kind of phone—just a keypad and a small digital display—and it looked like it had been sat on at one point.

Clara, her face illuminated by the glowing screen, blinked at it, read the number displayed, and then she answered.

"What is it?" she asked, sounding both irritated and strangely fragile. As Jill watched, however, her face darkened, and something like fear flashed in her cold blue eyes—though this was quickly pushed down and hidden.

"*Who* is this?" she asked, her tone suddenly changing. Now she sounded angry. "How did you get this number? How did you get his *phone?* . . . You are *what?* Oh. *Oh.* Why are you calling me?"

A silence stretched on after this last question, and Jill saw Clara's eyes widen briefly, her nostrils flare, and her already thin mouth tighten.

"When did you last see him?" she asked. Now she sounded tense, and a little shocked.

"Oh. I see. Yes, that's to be expected. Look, have you tried . . . *oh.* Oh. No, I understand. Listen, you *stay where you are.* Where are you?"

Silently, Jill passed Clara a pad of the motel's complimentary notepaper and a ballpoint pen. Clara, collapsing to sit on the floor, took them both with her free hand and began to jot down an address.

"Okay, I have it. Thank you. I can be there in . . . " Clara's eyes went to the ceiling; she frowned, and then looked back down at the paper, " . . . seven hours. I will call his phone if there are any delays. If you notice anything . . . suspicious . . . call me at . . . " she fumbled in her pocket for her other phone. Jill took pity on her and looked up the number on her own phone before holding it out for Clara to read. " ... 7803, area code 831," Clara finished. "Do you have that? No, area code eight three *one*, like a one dollar bill. Yes. What?"

Clara paused and looked past Jill. Selene, who had gradually re-emerged from her fortress of blankets and pillows as she listened to the phone call, blinked at them owlishly. Clara looked past her as well; to Jill it almost seemed like she was looking out of the motel room entirely, to a very different place.

"I'm his sister," Clara said at last. "I'll see you soon." She ended the call and lowered the hand holding the phone. Finding both Jill and Selene staring at her with the obvious question printed bold across both their faces, she merely shrugged.

"I have to go to Chicago," she said simply.

"You have a *brother?*" Selene said incredulously. Jill could almost see what she was thinking, too: what someone with Clara's genetics, but with a Y chromosome, would have to look like. He was probably a bonafide titan. Then her analytical brain caught up with her imagination, and she came down off her cloud with a thump.

"What's happened?" she asked. "Is he all right?"

"I don't know," Clara said. She was repacking the pannier, glancing at the clock by the bed. "He's missing. Has been for three days. His ... his *girlfriend* just called me. Using *his* phone—apparently he had my private number listed as 'Emergency.'"

"How come we don't got your private number?" Selene asked, brazenly.

"Because I have not given it to you," Clara replied, without rancor. She moved over to the bed and reached down, drawing out her heavy, leather biking boots.

"Three days is more than long enough to file a missing person report," Jill pointed out. "Shouldn't she call the police?"

Clara paused with one boot on, the other held poised over her foot. Her face worked into a grimace and then out again. "She did. They aren't ... Flammard's not ... " she sighed, finished putting on her boot, and shrugged into her leather jacket. "The kind of person he is ... any trouble he can't get himself out of, the police wouldn't be able to help—even if they wanted to." She reached for the leather harness that held her namesake—a two-handed claymore broadsword—and buckled it on. She turned to Jill.

"I apologize," she said. "But I must request some ... time off. I will meet you in five days, wherever you wish."

Jill blinked dumbly at her, but fortunately Selene spoke for both of them.

"Hell with that, we're coming with you!" she said, bouncing out of bed and fumbling around for her own boots.

Jill looked around at the disaster area that was their motel room. She frowned.

"There's no way we can be in Chicago in seven hours. It's more like eight, and that's if we leave *right now*. Which we can't," she pointed out.

Clara nodded. "Precisely," she said, slinging her panniers over one giant shoulder and making for the door.

"So give us the address, at least!" Jill shouted, starting after her. "We'll meet you there!"

Clara stopped, ponderous, turned around, and glared at them. "This is personal," she said, quiet and deadly.

"It's common *sense*," said Selene. "Look, girlfriend, I get it. He's family. And family is complicated—good *lord* I know that—but if he's anything like you, and *he's* in *trouble,* then, I'm just saying you might want yourself some backup is all."

Clara's nostrils flared, but she did not open her mouth and spit fire at them—which Jill had thought looked ready to happen a moment ago.

"Fine," she said, digging in her pocket and pulling out the notepad on which she'd scribbled the address, and flung it at Jill. "I will see you there," she said, and pulled open the door.

"Don't you need a copy?" Jill called after her.

"I've memorized it already," Clara replied, not even bothering to turn her head. The door slammed behind her, and a minute later they heard the muffled roar of her motorbike, Unicorn, coming to life and tearing out of the parking lot.

There was one stunned moment of silence in the room after her departure, and then Selene whipped into action, pulling back the curtains and turning on all the lights so she could see to pack. Jill carefully entered the address—a residential on the north side of Chicago—into her phone, and went to help Selene.

They found Clara's toothbrush and sharpening kit in the bathroom, as well as a pair of her socks hung over the towel rack to dry.

"See, *see?*" Selene said, waving a brown hand at the articles. "She hasn't even barely *started* yet, and she needs our help!" She carefully packed the toothbrush in a clean plastic bag, and put it and the rest of Clara's possessions in a corner of her backpack. "*See you there,* my fine ass. Jill, you let me drive. We'll make it in *six!*"

The stone was cold and a little damp under his cheek, though that might have been condensation from his body heat. Somewhere in the distance was the sound of a generator; it was dull enough that he guessed it was in a different room. There was light, that much he could tell even through closed eyelids, and he kept them closed as he listened with all his might for any clue as to where he was.

Waking up from a drugged sleep was not the most pleasant experience at the best of times. Waking up from a drugged sleep in an unknown location without the use of one's hands—his were bound tightly behind his back—was even more disconcerting. To Flammard Nordstern it brought back a flood of memories, most of which were associated with extremely unpleasant events in his life, but with the memories came old habits, reawakened with the rising tide of adrenaline in his system.

He reached out with his senses—the regular kind like hearing and smell and touch, but also that particular *sense* that belonged to him alone. It was the sense that could tell him, for example, if that soft *patting* sound was a flap of cloth in a breeze, or the footsteps of his captor.

It turned out to be the latter. Flammard held himself dead still, relaxed and hardly breathing, until the owner of the footsteps retreated out of earshot.

Only then did he dare crack open an eye and look around.

He was wedged into a tiny cell; four feet long and high, and barely wide enough for him to turn around in. There was a bucket in one corner and a drain in the floor; the grate was digging painfully into his thigh. The only light shone in weak beams through the bars at the front, where there was a door of the sort found on animal cages, secured with a heavy chain. Beyond the bars he could glimpse another wall of similar cages; some dark and still, others with their doors hanging open. In the one directly across from him were visible a pair of feet in worn sneakers, which twitched periodically.

The first thing Flammard did was free his hands. This was easy enough, though he had to cheat a bit. He felt a pang of regret at having to do so—he'd sworn off cheating in *that* way when he'd moved in with Lalai—but he figured the situation warranted it.

With his hands he gave himself a thorough check; discovered bruises on his neck and shoulders consistent with being carried, but none in the more vulnerable areas of his body. He also found a circular band-aid at the base of his neck—impossible to reach with bound hands—and he ripped it off at once. There was a little patch of gel underneath, and this he carefully wiped away with the hem of his shirt—and then wiped the excess on the bars with a shudder.

The bare necessities done, he retreated to the farthest corner of his cell, curled his knees into his chest, and assessed the situation.

The lock on the chain would give him no problem, if cheating was back on the table. Where he went from there, however, was less certain. Judging by the temperature (dangerously cold if Flammard had been an ordinary person) and the sound of the generator, he guessed he was somewhere underground. That could be problematic, especially if there were guards. Which there most likely were. People who knew how to incapacitate someone like Flammard and take him somewhere he couldn't easily locate probably knew better than to leave him unattended. It was surprising, though, that they hadn't thought to lock him up properly. It made him suspicious.

No, things did not look good.

And that was *before* the screaming started.

Chicago, Illinois

MALALAI AHMADZAI HEARD THE ROAR of a motorcycle distantly from where she sat at the kitchen table. She'd been sitting there ever since Satsuki had dropped her off after grocery shopping—all but the milk and eggs still sitting out on the counter. Lalai hadn't had the energy to put them away.

The roar of the engine intensified, but instead of retreating down the street it came to a stop. There were footsteps on the walk, and from the window Lalai looked down to the front door and saw it open for a tall—was that a woman? It was hard to tell. She was tall for a woman, if she was one, her head a bright, bald orb perched atop black, leather-clad shoulders. It bent, and Lalai caught a snatch of conversation. Gem had intercepted the visitor. That was a relief.

Then there was a step on the stair that started Stirling barking in the apartment below, and then a knock on her own door that sent butterflies up to Lalai's throat and down her arms. It had been over seven hours since that strange phone call in the morning, and she'd all but written off the harsh voice of Leonard's sister—if it was his sister at all.

Another knock. Not exactly impatient, but sharper this time. It spurred Lalai to action, and she dragged herself from the little kitchen to the door and cracked it open—leaving the chain in place.

She was met by the sight of a snugly zipped leather jacket and a gloved hand raised to perform a third knock. Readjusting her gaze to point upwards, Lalai at last found the face attached to this impressive body. It was a plain, roundish face, with ice-cold blue eyes and a thin, unfriendly mouth, but there was an angular jut about the cheekbones and a concerned wrinkle between the fine, platinum eyebrows that was achingly familiar. Lalai felt her mouth fall open slightly.

"My god," she whispered. "He *does* have a sister."

The concerned face frowned. "He has two, actually," the woman said. "I am the only one . . . available. I am Clara Nordstern. May I come in?"

Lalai took a deep breath and undid the chain. Clara didn't move, however, until she'd opened the door the whole way, stepped back, and ushered her in.

It was almost like watching a robot, or a particularly well-disguised alien, walk into the room. Clara was so tall her head nearly brushed against the slanting ceiling (one of the charms of living in an attic apartment, but as neither Lalai nor Leonard were above five and a half feet it had never bothered them), and her wide shoulders were made even wider by the hilt of the sword she wore strapped to her back, which jutted out to the right of her neck. She was dressed from head to toe in black motorcycle leathers, with matching black gloves. The only thing not black was the harness that held her sword, which consisted of crisscrossing brown leather straps that buckled around her waist.

For someone so big she moved softly and with an assurance that radiated stability. If someone tried to punch her, Lalai thought, they would probably bounce off.

Icy blue eyes found her, harsh as a searchlight. Not at all like Leonard's gentle hazel ones, but the expression behind them was like enough for Lalai to see the resemblance. Perhaps not a full sister, though. A half-sister, maybe?

"And you are?" Clara asked. Her voice was light, but clipped.

"Malalai Ahmadzai," she said, feeling the butterflies rise in her arms again. "Lalai for short. I, uh . . . I appreciate you coming so . . . fast."

Clara shrugged. She had a funny sort of shrug: first lowering her shoulders and then raising them again. She moved further into the little apartment, taking in the carefully stacked bookcases, picture-lined walls, and the old *rubab* hung in a place of honor between the two wide windows.

"Flam—er, *Leonard,* lives here?" she asked. There was a curious fragility in her voice, and Lalai noticed the flub over his name. She didn't remark on it, however.

"Yes," she said simply.

"How long?"

Lalai found she had to think about that a moment. "Three years?" she said. Had it only been that long? That wasn't long enough. The butterflies were lumping in her throat now, and she had to fight to keep them down. "We moved in—together—when he got his job with the fire department."

"The *fire department?*" Clara said sharply, sounding a little alarmed.

"He's an EMT," Lalai reassured her. "Just made paramedic."

"Oh," said Clara, and a small, bitter smile flitted across her face. "Good for him." She unclipped her sword from the harness and leaned it carefully next to their oldest, most battered armchair. It had a very long hilt with downward-sloping—what were they called? Quillions?—with four little rings arranged like the leaves of a four-leafed clover at the ends. It was an impressive, businesslike sword.

"May I?" Clara asked, indicating the chair.

"Yes, oh yes, of course," Lalai said, realizing what a poor host she was being. "Can I get you anything? Coffee? Lemonade?"

"No, thank you," Clara said. "Please, just sit down, and tell me what happened."

Lalai took a deep breath, and went and got a chair from the kitchen. The only other seat in the little living room was the loveseat under the window, and sitting in *it* only made Lalai miss Leonard even more. It was sitting in that seat, one rainy afternoon in April three years ago, that they had curled around each other and Lalai had realized that *yes,* this—the house, her career, his job, *their relationship*—was going to work.

Now she pushed the chair between her legs and sat, leaning her chest against the backrest. "Where do you want me to start?" she asked.

* * *

Clara had been interested to find the musical, intelligent voice belonged to a diminutive brown woman with smokey black hair and dark, red-rimmed eyes. Dressed in a flowing silk shirt and a neat black-and-red floral print skirt with stockinged legs in sensible flat sandals, she looked like a well formed, stylish person gone a little off the rails. Which was understandable. What had surprised Clara was moving into the space of their little attic apartment. To her it felt cramped, but she was sure this was due entirely to her size. It was clearly a comfortable, well loved and well lived-in place. The walls were covered with bright, colorful watercolors depicting flowing, flowery animals. There was half a week's worth of mail and two grocery bags on the kitchen table, and the sink was filled with dirty dishes, but these seemed to be symptoms of the calamity that had just occurred, not indicative of the regular state of affairs.

It was with a small pang—both of loneliness and jealousy—that Clara realized the reason she hadn't heard from Flammard in four years was because he'd been busy building himself a life. A happy one with the name Leonard and a brilliant woman named Lalai.

Clara ground her teeth and resolved to do her best not to ruin it.

"When was the last time you saw him?" she asked.

"Tuesday," Lalai replied, as if she'd answered this question before. "He had—was supposed to have—night shift at the station, so we got dinner together. He went to work, I went to bed . . . I heard him come in around seven in the morning—at least, I thought it was him. I didn't actually *see* anyone. But it must have been him, because when I got up, his phone and keys were on the table. But he wasn't." Lalai swallowed visibly. "He wasn't *anywhere.*"

"Did you hear anything?" Clara asked, patiently.

"Outside? No . . . well, I mean, nothing unusual. I heard Stirling bark— that's the dog on the second floor—but it was her friendly, hello bark. That's why I thought it was Leonard."

Clara frowned, rubbing her chin with one hand.

"How had he been acting . . . lately?" she asked. "Anything . . . seem to be bothering him?"

Lalai shook her head, tears welling up under her big dark eyes. She was the opposite of Flammard in so many ways, and yet Clara could imagine how they complemented each other.

"No . . . everything was . . . everything was *fine.* More than fine, *good.* He was . . . we were . . . he got a double break this weekend, and we were going to go downtown and do the museum walk—can you believe we've lived in Chicago three years and never been to Millennium Park? He was *happy.*"

To Clara, Flammard being openly happy usually meant he was up to something—and it wouldn't always be pleasant. On the other hand, that was ten years ago. Now things might be different, as they obviously were in so many other respects.

"What have you done, in the meantime? You mentioned you already tried the police."

"Yeah," said Lalai, with a roll of her eyes. "The minute forty-eight hours were up. They weren't . . . well, he's *your* brother. You know."

"I know," Clara said. And she did know. More than Lalai did, if she thought Flammard had been abducted by ordinary humans.

"It's *ridiculous*," Lalai hissed, clearly trying not to scream. "He's an *EMT*. He works with the fire department! You'd think a whole crew wanting to know what's become of their paramedic would, maybe, you know, *motivate* them? But *nooo* . . . as soon as they found out about, well, *that*, it was suddenly . . . 'we see this a lot, Miss Ah-mad-zai. That kind go missing all the time, Miss Ah-mad-zai.' *That kind.*" She wrinkled her nose in disgust. "That's what they called him. Sorry." Lalai reached up to wipe her streaming eyes with the sleeve of her shirt, but paused before moving on to her nose. "Excuse me," she choked, and moved into the kitchen, from which she emerged a moment later, blowing her nose on a hand towel.

"Anyway, that's where I've been the past three days. Just this morning I woke up around two, and after trying for hours I couldn't sleep, so I just started going through all of Leonard's contacts, calling them and asking if they'd seen him. Then I got to an entry labeled 'Emergency' and that was *your* number."

Clara nodded. "That is probably because I told him to call it if there was one. May I see it? His phone, I mean."

"Oh yes, yes, of course."

Lalai produced a sleek black smartphone in a rubbery case with little birds on it. Clara took it, but didn't wake it up. She held it in her hand, trying to get a sense of Flammard from it. But either it was a new phone, or he hadn't cared for it very much. Even after she took her glove off she felt nothing but cold, hard glass and metal.

In the distance, from the street below, came a rumble of an engine. Not the soft purr of the small city cars that coasted down the quiet, residential street, but a big, gutsy growl.

Arcana crept down Dayton Street like a self-conscious bull in a china shop. He stopped in front of a tall house made of cheerful red bricks while Jill squinted at the address.

"This is it," she told Selene after a moment.

"Nice digs," Selene murmured appreciatively.

And they were. The house was large, the type that had an extra floor in place of a basement, with a scooped out yard in front, out of which peeked the crowns of little trees. Stairs led up to the recessed front door, which stood beside two narrow, arched windows. Above that was a second floor, and above that a terrace and what looked like an attic floor—the kind where the shakes of the roof bent over and came down in a wall around bright windows reflecting sky.

Most of the house was in shade from the vigorous trees that lined the street, and there was a black metal fence surrounding the front yard, with a simple latch gate leading to the front path. There was a well-chewed dog toy lying in the middle of it.

They had to go on past the house a little ways before Selene found a place where she could squeeze Arcana. On their way they passed Unicorn, which had been defiantly walked up onto the curb and parked next to a tree.

Jill had to get out and spot her as she parked, the street was so tightly packed with small cars, and it was a wonder they found a parking space at all. Even hugging the curb, Arcana's rear wheels bulged out into the street, and his red coat stood out against the pervasive grays, blacks, silvers and blues of the other vehicles.

As they approached the house its front door opened, and Clara walked out, followed by a small, middle-eastern looking woman in a loud print skirt, stockings, and a loose shirt. She looked like she had been crying, but Clara was as blank and composed as ever.

"Selene," she said, by way of greeting. "I need your ring."

"I'm sorry?"

"The one I gave you," Clara said, and gave Selene a meaningful look.

"*Oh,*" said Selene. "*That* ring. Righto, you got it." She turned on her heel and headed back to Arcana, returning a moment later with a small cloth bundle. She shot Jill a look as she passed her a second time. *See? Hopeless*, the look seemed to say. Jill rolled her eyes.

Selene dropped the bundle into Clara's waiting, ungloved hand, and stepped back.The other woman's long fingers closed around it, and she shut her eyes, concentrating.

"Are you . . . friends of Clara?" the little woman asked timidly.

Jill and Selene exchanged looks.

"You could say that," Selene began cautiously.

"They work for me," Jill said frankly. "Jill Hamilton," she said, extending a hand. "This here is Selene. Um . . . Clara left us in a bit of a rush this morning. You are . . . ?"

"Lalai," said the woman. "I'm her brother's girlfriend. But you, er . . . probably knew that."

"Honestly," said Selene, watching as Clara began turning in a slow circle, the hand that held the little cloth-wrapped ring stretched out in front of her like the needle of a compass. "We didn't even know she *had* a brother, before this morning."

Clara's eyes flew open and her nostrils flared. She said nothing, but began to walk . . . off the path that led from the sidewalk to the front door, past the sunken yard, and around the side of the house.

The other three women followed in a confused line, with Jill bringing up the rear. They found Clara in the tiny backyard, staring down at a patch of curly grass as though she could bore through the earth with her eyes and see what was beneath.

"Clara, what—" Jill began.

"Shovel," said Clara, not looking up. "I need a shovel."

Selene turned to Lalai, who pointed mutely at a tiny shed wedged into a corner of the yard. Stepping over a pot of tulips Selene opened the door and found a mildewy shovel tucked between a rake and a moldy tarp. She returned, bearing the desired implement, and presented it to Clara.

Clara looked up, surprised, and took the shovel gently.

"Thank you," she said quietly.

"Clara, what on earth is going on?" Selene asked.

Clara dug the shovel into the dirt and began prying away the grass. "My brother, Flam—*Leonard*—is missing. I believe he has been abducted. I am looking to see if that is indeed the case."

"By digging up Lalai's yard?" Jill asked, shooting her an apologetic look.

Clara turned over a mat of grass and, laying aside the shovel, began scooping the soft, brown earth away with her gloved hand.

"There are some things we Nordsterns always take with us, wherever we go," Clara said by way of explanation. She glanced over at Lalai, her eyes narrowing. "They are not our wallets and cell phones," she said. Then her expression changed as her hand caught on something that was not earth or rock. She began pulling at the soil, excavating a long, narrow strip that revealed what looked like a cloth-wrapped bundle.

"What *do* you take, then?" Jill asked.

For answer, Clara gripped one end of the bundle and pulled, dislodging more dirt, and raised up on end a long, stick-like package. Having pocketed the ring, she used her free hand to brush away the last few clinging clods of dirt, and began teasing at one end, where there was a free strip of cloth.

The cloth, half rotted already, came off in pieces, revealing what was to Jill and Selene an already familiar object.

Lalai let out a gasp of consternation.

"What," she said, "is a *sword* doing buried in our backyard?"

Clara turned to her, holding what was indeed a sheathed sword. It had an intricately carved pommel with red leather around the long grip, loops of metal sprouting around the guard, and a further stretch of leather-wrapped metal that ended in a downward-facing crescent—after which the blade disappeared into the sheath, which was wide and heavy and wrapped in a complicated pattern of straps and buckles that, Jill guessed, would translate into something like the harness Clara wore if they were untangled. It was considerably shorter than her own massive claymore, despite the impressive hilt—though Jill imagined it would still be too big and heavy for herself.

"He chose to leave his old life behind four years ago," Clara explained, grimly. "But he would never, *ever* leave his sword."

Flammard was beginning to wish he'd kept his sword strapped to his back, the way Claymore did. But they probably wouldn't let him drive the ambulance if he did that—let alone treat patients. And his captors would have taken it away first chance they got. No, Flammard thought as he watched a pair of men—their heads hidden by black hoods—drag a third man be-tween them back to a cell and throw him inside, what he really wanted was to have Feuermann in his hand *right now*. With Feuermann, he could slip out of his cell and calmly walk out of whatever torture chamber he was trapped in. Feuermann had that effect on people.

But he was alone, and empty-handed. Oh well. Time to use what he did have. This consisted of the jeans and shirt he was wearing (they'd taken away his shoes) and—this was the important part—his *wits*.

The men in black hoods had been in and out many times over the last few hours. Each time they were either dragging someone out of their cell, or dragging someone back into one. In between there was screaming—awful screaming—and a particularly horrible smell that anyone else might have been hard pressed to identify, but Flammard knew to be that of burn-ing human flesh. It was difficult to see the state of the people when the men dragged them back in, but they were silent. That didn't bode well.

Now the men were coming back, and one of them was knocking a stick against the fronts of the cells as he went.

"Check number five," his partner said, and the two forms paused in front of Flammard's door.

Flammard squished himself as far back into the darkest corner as he could, and cheated as hard as he could.

The door opened.

The hooded head which gazed in had a perplexed air about it. A thick arm reached up and shined a flashlight into the little area. Flammard shut his eyes as the beam passed over his face, and held his breath.

"What the ever-lovin' Christ," said a voice from under the hood. "There's no one in here!"

"What the hell?"

"The door was locked—bolted. But there's no one in here. *Someone's* been having a laugh." Their tone suggested they knew exactly who this *someone* was, and that *someone* was going to get some rather unpleasant payback.

"Give it a rest, Charlie," said their partner. "We'll take the one in six. I think he's good to go."

The hooded head disappeared, letting the door swing closed. It hit the wall of the cell and bounced, twice, before coming to a rest about an inch from the doorframe. They hadn't even bothered to latch it.

In the shadows at the back of the cell, Flammard dared to breathe.

His breath caught almost at once as he heard the man in the cell next to his—unlucky cell six—begin to shout and cry as he was dragged out.

"No, man—*no!* Don't take me—I got—I got—*no!*"

"Listen, bucko," one of the men in hoods growled. "You know how it goes. You come quiet, or Charlie here takes his stick and *makes* you quiet."

A strangled gulping sound. Another clang of a cell door. Whimpering, and the whisper of cloth on stone as the unfortunate man was dragged away.

Flammard waited. He waited until the noises had faded away entirely, and then—ever so slowly—he crawled forward and gently pushed his cell door open, and slipped out.

Immediately the room around him erupted into surprised shouts.

"What are *you* doing?"

"How did you get out?"

"Hey, kid! Hey *kid!* Let me out!"

"Yeah, man, let us out!"

"You can't leave us here!"

"*Please* be *quiet!*" Flammard hissed. "They'll *hear* you!"

This got exactly one cell to quiet down. The rest were too agitated, and the cacophony of voices continued to rise.

"They'll *kill* us!"

"I don't want to die here!"

They had a point. Flammard sighed, and went over to the one cell that had fallen silent. The man on the other side of the bars stared back at him, tight-lipped, but said nothing.

"Hi," whispered Flammard. "I'm . . . call me Leonard."

"Hey, Leonard," the man replied softly. "I'm Marcus. Listen—could you? I mean, *can* you?"

"Yeah," said Flammard. It was more cheating that he strictly wanted, but at this rate, if he was using his powers, he might as well make them *really* useful. "Just stay quiet."

Marcus nodded, and Flammard turned his attention to the lock. This was the good kind, and would have been almost impossible to pick from the inside. From the outside, however, Flammard was able to get it at the angle he needed, and a moment later he was helping Marcus out of the tiny cell.

Marcus turned out to be a large black man with an improbable halo of carroty curls framing his face. He stood up—and up and up and *up*—*almost as tall as Claymore,* Flammard thought—and the noise in the room redoubled.

It must have been partly from seeing another of their number released, but also, Flammard realized, behind the shouting in the room, the screaming had started up again. He felt his heart twinge at the thought of the man who had gone in his place, but at the same time he knew this would give them that much more cover.

"I'm only letting you out if you can *be quiet!*" Flammard shouted.

A few more cells grudgingly fell silent, but a couple shrill voices continued to cry out.

"All y'all shut *up!*" Marcus bellowed. He had a good, deep bellow, and the noise of it knocked the room into a brief quiet.

"I'll let you out, but only if you can *keep* quiet," Flammard explained quickly. "If you can't, then we'll *all* get it."

Silence. Flammard took that as a go-ahead, and got to work on the other locks.

All in all, he found nine more occupied cells. Seven of which divulged similarly agitated young men. And two of which . . .

Flammard braced himself in the doorway so that the growing crowd couldn't see inside. He'd felt obligated to check on the men who had been brought back, but after the second one he decided to spare himself the pain.

It only made him more determined to upset what was happening to the man who had recently occupied cell six.

Closing the door to the ninth cell—shutting out the sight but not the smell of burnt flesh—he turned to survey the crowd that had grown in the center of the room.

They were of every size and shape, from small and lithe, like Flammard, to huge and hulking, like Marcus. The only thing they had in common was that they were all male, and their hair was all some shade of red. He was not the only one to notice.

"Dude, what *is* this?" one of them asked. "Some sicko with a League of Red-Headed Men fixation?"

Flammard said nothing. He'd noticed something else they all had in common, but it was so subtle, and so weak in some cases, that he was fairly certain only he was aware of it.

Every single one of them had a faint, flame-like aura—when Flammard forced his eyes to look for it. None of them were as strong as his own—which he was aware of as a sort of orange glow on the edge of his vision—though Marcus's was fairly distinct. In fact, apart from Flammard, Marcus was probably the only one who might have picked up on it.

"We need to get out of here," he began.

"Ya *think* so, Sherlock?" said the man who had spoken before. Marcus hushed him.

"Mostly, *you* need to get out of here," Flammard went on, turning to Marcus. "I think I might know what they have in store for us, and after me, you're the one most at risk. Think you can lead them out?"

Marcus stared at Flammard. "I got no idea what you're talkin' about, man," he said. "But yeah, I'm ready to blow this joint. Which way is out, though?"

"You'll have to figure that out for yourself, I'm afraid," Flammard said. "But I think anywhere that goes *up* would be a good idea."

"Where are *you* going?" someone asked as Flammard fought his way through the press of bodies toward the door.

Flammard paused, and in the ensuing quiet they all heard, faint but distinct, a strangled, anguished sob.

"I'm gonna go find out what *that* is," he said.

"Dude, you *crazy?*"

"Old habit," Flammard snapped. "Marcus, get them going!" And he ran. Before his courage ran out. Before he lost the tenuous conviction singing in his veins. He ran. Behind him he heard the commotion as the crowd erupted in argument, with Marcus booming over them all. But Flammard ran, down unfamiliar corridors, bare feet stinging on the cold stone, and he did not look back.

Lalai frowned at Clara. "Is there something about Leonard you're not telling me?" she asked, a little accusingly.

"Many things," Clara said, dusting off the scabbard. "Now is not the time, however. When I return . . . with him. Then you may . . . talk. Or not. I know there are things that he would rather remain buried, like his sword. Now I must go . . ."

"Oh whoa, whoa there," Selene said, stepping into Clara's path as she tried to stride away. "Keep in mind some of us aren't exactly up to speed yet. Which we *want* to be," she added, earnestly, to Lalai, "We're here to help."

"I believe you," the woman replied, smiling shakily. "I . . . um . . . appreciate it."

Clara seemed torn. She groaned softly and looked up at the sky for a few moments. "I need to find an open area. No houses."

"Oz Park is just a few blocks from here," Lalai offered. "I can show you . . ."

"No," Clara cut her off, then continued, more gently. "No, thank you. Directions. We'll walk. I'll explain on the way," she added to Selene.

Lalai looked disappointed, but she gave the directions to Jill, who pulled up a map on her phone and led the way.

They left the red brick house with Lalai standing in the walkway, hugging herself miserably. Jill felt a stab of sympathy for the woman, and wished there was some reassurance she could offer—but she knew from agonizing experience that maybe the only thing they brought back to her would be a terrible sort of closure.

"All right," Selene said, punching Clara lightly on the arm. "What's the scoop? I take it you're convinced your bro didn't just take off for Belize or something . . . so what happened?"

Clara sighed and recounted what Lalai had already told her. When she had finished, Selene frowned and scratched under her ponytail.

"So . . ." said Jill, also frowning. "Did I miss something? Why aren't the police involved? Did Lalai even *call* them?"

"She did," Clara replied bluntly. "They wouldn't help."

"Wouldn't . . . or *couldn't?*" Selene pried.

"Most likely, they looked at the type of man my brother is, and decided he wasn't worth their time. It's happened before." There was a note of bitterness in Clara's voice, and under that, a softly boiling rage.

Selene wrinkled her nose and frowned. "That doesn't follow. What's he like, this brother of yours? To borrow a phrase from his girl: *is there something about Leonard you're not telling us?*"

"Many things," Clara replied. Selene groaned.

"Some of them may prove relevant," Clara admitted. "Some not. I will inform you of the relevant information as soon as it becomes so. For now, understand that, for many years, my brother was—like me, and our sister—a warrior. A hunter of monsters. A guard against the ancient night. He . . . has skills. No ordinary person would be a threat to him. Whoever took him must have extraordinary powers. This will be a dangerous situation, and I do not wish to put you in unnecessary peril."

"Sister, you know we deal with *tons* of peril every time she gets some harebrained idea," Selene pointed out.

"It's for *science*," Jill protested. "Oh, we go right here."

Turning right necessitated crossing the street, which they did in a line. Jill wondered what the car that stopped at the intersection thought of them. Clara especially, in her biking leathers and carrying two swords.

"You *know* what I mean," Selene said as they crossed. "Point is, it'd be crappy of us to bow out of a little extra peril when your very own *brother* is in the stink."

Clara smiled, briefly, harshly, like she didn't quite believe it. "That's very . . ." she began, then stopped. "Thank you," she finished, quietly.

They walked in silence for a while, passing more brick-and-plaster houses, speckled with shade from the leafy trees lining the streets and lit in golden, sideways light from the setting sun. Up ahead a break in the buildings, with the crowns of larger trees encroaching on the skyline, heralded their approach to the park.

"His name is Flammard, not Leonard," Clara said eventually. "That will be important for you to know, if you are to help me find him. Flammard. Leonard is just what he calls himself . . . back there."

"Sort of the way your name's Claymore, but everyone calls you Clara?" Selene asked.

"Sort of," Clara allowed, and said no more.

The road they were on bent to the right, and from there a pedestrian path led off between a baseball diamond on the left and a wide, grass-covered swell on the right. Chattering from the diamond announced the presence of a woman's softball team getting in some evening practice, and Clara made instead for the swell, which was perfectly deserted.

"So . . . what are we doing, exactly?" Jill asked as Clara paced around, testing the ground with her foot.

"Locating Flammard," Clara replied shortly. She had found a place that was relatively flat, and holding the exhumed sword out in front of her, she gently drew the blade from its scabbard. It was silvery and clean, with an extraordinary wavy pattern down the length, which made the edges ripple. Jill had seen a sword like that, once, in an animated film. It had been the villain's sword. But this sword, while sinister, also had an elegance about it that was enchanting. With its long hilt, looped cross guard, crescent prongs, and wavy blade, it almost looked more like a decorative ornament than a weapon.

Clara twirled it expertly in her hand, causing the evening sunlight to dance along the blade. Because of the ripples, it almost looked like the thing caught fire for a moment.

"Uh . . . Clara? You're not gonna go all Inigo Montoya on us, are you?" Selene asked.

Clara shot the other woman a confused look, then she turned the sword down, plunging it abruptly into the earth, where it sunk in by almost a foot.

"What *are* you doing?" Jill asked.

"*Shh,*" said Clara. She had sunk to her knee, one hand on the hilt of the sword and the other resting on her bent leg, her head bowed. She stayed that way, perfectly still, for almost a minute. In that time Jill looked questioningly at Selene, who shrugged expressively. They waited.

After a while Clara began to speak, but in a whisper, as if to herself.

"We are our swords, and our swords are us. Find yourself, *foyaman.* Find yourself."

To Jill and Selene it appeared nothing happened, but to Clara it felt as though the sword turned under her hand. Its blade warmed, causing the damp roots of the grass surrounding it to hiss as the water turned to steam, and a bright, hot speck appeared in her mind.

It was such a relief that she nearly let go of the sword, which would have been disastrous. Clenching her hand around the rapidly warming hilt, she focused on that speck until she could sense its location in relationship to her own.

Flammard was still in this world. He was still alive, and all things considered, he was not so very far away.

Clara looked up. To her companions her eyes appeared a little glassy and far off, but she sounded perfectly normal when she said:

"I know where he is . . . I can't tell you where, but I *know.*"

She stood up, drawing the blade out of the earth as she went. Jill took a step back when she saw its tip, which was glowing orange-hot.

"Clara . . . " she said, uncertainly.

Clara felt the hot speck in her mind fade to a warm glow as the sword left the earth, and she shut her eyes to hold it there.

"I cannot let go of the sword, otherwise I'll lose him," she said, hoping for once Jill would take her words literally.

Selene understood, at least.

"Let's take Arcana then, all three of us. I'll drive. Here, I'll carry that scabbard—you probably shouldn't sheathe it anyway, even once its cooled."

Clara nodded, and together the three of them climbed down off the swell and began retracing their steps.

One of the women on the diamond saw them go out of the corner of her eye, and was so distracted by the sight of Clara and the wavy, red-hot sword, that she nearly got brained by an incoming ball. It bounced and rolled off into some bushes, and by the time it had been recovered the three women were gone, and none of her friends believed her when she told them about it.

At first it was easy. All Flammard had to do was follow the screams. These eventually died down to a low moaning, and when that stopped altogether he had to pause and consider his position.

He was definitely underground. The air was cold, and the passages were all carved out of stone with sections of concrete to shore them up. Furthermore, he could feel the weight of all that earth pressing down around him, closing in tightly, holding him in thick, gnarled hands as strong as time and darkness.

He was cheating again, quite by accident this time, which was unsettling. He checked himself over to make sure he wasn't actually *glowing*— he wasn't—and leaned against the wall to catch his breath.

What bothered him most about his predicament was that he had no idea how he had been taken. He remembered coming home from his shift, leaving his things on the kitchen table, and noticing that the recycling needed to be taken out. He'd pulled the box out from its niche by the refrigerator, walked it down the stairs, out the front door, and around to the side where the wheelie-bins were kept. He remembered lifting the heavy, plastic lid . . .

And there it cut out. Sight, smell, touch, and memory. Only the sound of a word remained, faint and unrecognizable. And the voice . . .

Thinking of voices made him perk his ears up, which was how he caught the sound of actual voices speaking in the immediate present. He couldn't tell if any of them were the voice from his memory, but he edged his way softly down the corridor so he could hear them better.

There were three voices: two deep and rough, one high and sharp. Probably female. That one was easier to understand, and so for a while it was liking listening to one side of a three-way telephone conversation.

"That one was even more pathetic than the last. Are you even *checking* their auras before you take them?"

A rumbly, indignant answer.

"Yes, yes, he was a Son of Fire, but so are *you*, remember? Do *you* want to have a go at it?"

Indistinct speaking. The female voice laughed, humorlessly.

More rumbling. A question, this time.

"No, gut him and throw him back in with the others. I need a rest. We'll try again in an hour or so."

Flammard inched closer, exerting a tremendous effort not to be heard. Now he could understand one of the gruff voices when it said, "Yes, Mistress," and the shuffle of feet that followed.

Flammard just had time to press himself back against the wall of the passage as torchlight flared around the corner, and the two hooded men came through it, dragging a limp object behind them. Flammard caught a glimpse of an arm, a naked torso with blood on it, and in one unfortunate flare from the torch, a ruined face.

He'd seen worse. Once. When the fire crew had rescued a woman from a burning car. The burns had been all over her face and neck and chest, and he'd had to cheat to keep her alive on the way to the hospital.

Flammard wasn't sure if it made it better or worse that he couldn't do anything for the man. The turmoil of emotions in his chest made him shudder, and he hung in the corridor for a long moment after the sound of footsteps and dead weight being dragged over stone had faded into the distance. Then he jerked into action.

How long until they noticed the empty chamber? Well, that depended on how long it took them to "gut" someone. He could try to double back—meet up with Marcus and make a break for the surface—but something about what was going on rubbed him the wrong way. It was wrong beyond just the empirical wrongness of killing someone—it was *wrong* in that something was trying to happen that *should not* happen. And that passing reference to the Sons of Fire . . . that couldn't possibly mean what Flammard thought it meant . . . except it probably *did,* considering the way all those men had auras and red hair. In which case, Flammard had to stop them.

He rounded a corner and was nearly blinded by the blaze of light pouring out from the room beyond. Light and *heat,* he realized as he crept forward, for the illumination came from a solid wall of fire that took up one side of the room.

Concentrating *very hard* on not being seen, Flammard entered the room and looked around.

It was a long, rectangular chamber—the wall of fire taking up the far, narrower side, opposite from the door Flammard had entered by—with a rough sort of da s halfway down that had a high-backed chair on it. The walls were lined with coarse hangings with rudimentary figures woven into them. Flammard caught an odd tingle from these, as though they did not wholly belong to this world.

The long sides of the room were also lined with narrow tables, on top of which were an assortment of clay pots, bleached bones, and some nasty looking knives. Flammard gave them a wide berth as he crept toward the wall of fire.

As he moved forward around the da s and throne, a crude altar hove into view in front of the fire. It consisted of a lumpy, cold, gray stone twice the size of his kitchen table, with iron rings hung from posts driven into either side. Charred remains of something limp and reddish hung from those rings, and the whole thing gave out a feeling of terrible menace.

This stone did not do bad things to you, Flammard realized, but bad things happened on it. It breathed off coolness, even in the face of the fire, whose angry orange light did not touch it. If the hangings were not entirely part of this world, then the stone was completely alien.

Flammard came right up to it, reached out a hand to touch it experimentally, and then recognized what the charred remains hanging from iron rings actually were.

He'd seen intestines, once, outside the victim of a particularly brutal car crash. The sight had stayed with him longer than he'd liked, and now the memory rose up again, matching perfectly the ten or so inches of reddish-black wrinkly tubing tied off neatly to the iron ring.

Flammard took his hand away.

"I thought you'd be an interesting one," said a voice from behind him.

At the sound, Flammard felt all the hairs on his body stand on end, and his heart speed up. But he forced himself to turn, slowly, and face the high-backed chair—which he now could see was occupied.

There was a woman sitting in it. She was wearing a long, belted tunic made of black velvet, with supple leggings and knee-high boots with lots of buckles. Her legs were crossed, one foot kicking idly, and she had her hands knitted together over her chest, her elbows on the armrests of the chair. Her bright red nails gleamed in the firelight. She had dark red hair and dark brown eyes and very pale skin. Her lips had been painted red to match her nails, and they stood out vividly against the white oval of her face.

What struck Flammard the most, however, was her aura: it was a bright, angry flame that surrounded her whole body, with tongues of fire licking upwards, spitting and arcing. Like the corona of the sun. Her aura was hardly bigger than Marcus's, really, but it was so fierce and violent Flammard rather thought she was holding it back.

"I know you're there," the woman said, her mouth twitching in the suggestion of a smile. "You're good, though. I still can't see you—not really. But a bit rusty, maybe? I'm surprised you didn't notice me. Do come forward, so I can see you properly."

She uncrossed her legs in a whisper of cloth, resting her boots—which had impressive, four-inch heels—on the stone slab in front of her. She smiled briefly, her yellow teeth like a flicker of flame in her red mouth.

Flammard's heart was hammering in his chest. Beyond his recognition of her superficial appearance as a conventionally attractive woman, he was also feeling a subconscious longing plucking at the core of his being. A sinuous, insidious desire to take, to conquer, to devour.

It was such a foreign feeling to him that he recognized it at once as a cheat of the very worst sort. He blinked and shook his head.

"Stop that," he said, giving the intruding sensation a metaphorical kick in the muzzle.

The woman actually jerked back physically in her seat, a look of surprise crossing her face.

"Don't you like that?" she asked, sounding genuinely confused.

"No," Flammard ground out. "I really don't. I also don't like what you're doing here. You need to stop."

"Are you a submissive, then?" the woman asked, and a whole different set of feelings assaulted Flammard's mind. A desire to serve, to get down on his knees and crawl up the steps of the daïs. To lay himself out at her feet, open, exposed . . .

"I said *stop* that," he ground out through gritted teeth.

"Let me *see* you then," said the woman, with an annoyed flick of a finger. "I'm even more curious now; you're not like any man I've met before. There's something . . . *different* . . . about you."

Oh gods, she could tell, Flammard thought frantically. Mostly, people who said they could sense male and female energy were full of baloney—energies were so much more diverse and complex than just male and female, saying so only proved one's ignorance—but if she could sense him to that extent through his strongest invisibility cheat, who knew what else she could see?

Unless she was picking up on the *other* thing that set him apart from most men. He almost hoped it was that. That, he knew he could deal with.

His fear only made him shrink further away, backing around the horrible stone altar and its grisly decorations, until he could feel the warmth of the fire against his back. It felt . . . oddly comforting. Unlike the fire of this world, which was angry and wild, this fire recognized him. It knew him. Knew him and welcomed him. That alone was unsettling, but Flammard tried to draw strength from it. He wasn't sure why he was so *frightened* of this woman finding out about his heritage—she clearly suspected it already, that was why he'd been grabbed—except that from what he'd seen it could only make his situation worse.

She had gotten to her feet and stepped down off the altar to follow him, her hands resting on her hips and her head cocked to one side. Her dark eyes sparkled in the firelight as a slow smile curved up one side of her face.

"Interesting," she said, and began slinking toward him around the stone.

Flammard was backed so close to the fire now he could smell his clothes beginning to burn, but the flames were licking comfortingly at his neck, and he didn't pull away.

Heedless of the fire, the woman walked right up to him—in her heels she was a good two inches taller than he, and when she thrust an arm into the flames to block his escape, the fire surged forward and welcomed her as well.

Smiling widely, the woman raised her other hand to cup his face, and while one part of Flammard screamed in protest and began putting up mental barricades, another, treacherous part of him sang for joy at contact with a kindred spirit.

For they were kindred. As close, in fact, as he was to Clara and Schiavona.

"Oh my dear boy," whispered the woman, her eyes blazing in the light of the fire. They were both well into it by now, and Flammard could feel a hard stone wall at his back, from which the flames sprung. "You're no ordinary Son of Fire," she went on, stroking his cheek with a finger. "You are like *me*." She smiled hugely, and reminded Flammard of nothing so much as a dragon. "You're a *first generation* Child of Fire. A child of Loki himself!"

So she could tell, Flammard thought despairingly, wishing he could disappear into the flames.

They made good time once they got onto 41. They were apparently counter-commute, if the solid wall of headlights in the northbound lanes was any indication, and they headed along the lakefront at a good clip, until—as they were nearing Millennium Park—Clara shouted from the back seat, "Take the next right!"

The next right took them away from the lake and toward the city, passing brightly lit skyscrapers on one side and a large, green park on the other. There was something like an amphitheater set up in the middle of this, and the road was choked with cars. Arcana slowed to a crawl, and in the back seat Clara growled impatiently.

"Easy there, sister," said Selene, who was driving. "We are, quite literally, *not* in Kansas anymore. I can't go any faster on account of the car in front of me. Now, it's one of those dinky convertibles, but if I were to run her over—like I'm sure Arcana *could*—the maggie up ahead *might* take exception, and that's a barrel full of monkeys we do not want to play with tonight."

"Maggie?" Jill whispered from the passenger seat.

Selene flicked her hand over the steering wheel to the police cruiser two cars ahead.

"I don't suppose . . . " Jill began hopefully.

"*No,*" both other women said at the same time.

Somewhere a light changed. The traffic crept forward. On their left, the park opened up and Jill glimpsed, through some trees, a flash of something huge that reflected the lights of the city and the lights of the park around it. Like a giant mirror. Ahead of them, above the traffic, a train hurtled between the buildings—some fifteen feet off the ground—its wheels flashing on the elevated rails, whining as it slowed to a stop.

They crossed an intersection, passed under the tracks, and Clara shouted "Stop! Here!"

Of course, Selene couldn't stop there, but she turned down the next alley and squeezed Arcana between a couple of dumpsters.

"Close enough?" she asked, twisting around in the driver's seat.

Clara was already kicking the back door open and sliding out of the truck, the sword held out in front of her as though it were a glowing brand. Jill and Selene were a little slower to follow—the latter retrieving her trench gun, Freddie, from under driver's seat before going after the other two.

Clara was pacing up and down the alley, the wavy sword held aloft, and sweeping the air in front of her like it was a torch and she needed to illuminate their surroundings.

Evening had crept over the city, and it was darker in the alley with the high buildings looming overhead and cutting out all but a thin strip of quickly fading blue. At the same time lights were coming on in the upper windows, and from a sunken door the steady thrum of a bass could be felt, reverberating up through the brick and concrete.

Clara led them past this door, to another whose window was shuttered and dark. Drawing aside the screen Clara tried the handle. It was locked.

"I got my picks," Selene began, but the next moment Clara had pushed the door open, the frame shattering as the deadbolt tore through the wood.

"Oookay," said Selene, glancing around nervously.

"What is this building?" Jill asked, automatically reaching for her phone.

"The building doesn't matter," Clara said. "He is not here, but this is the way to him." She disappeared through the door, and Jill didn't wait for Selene's impatient nod to follow her in.

The door led them to what appeared to be the back room of a bakery. Jill caught sight of shadowy rolling shelves stocked with bread and pastry boxes. There was a smell of flour and sugar, and a single light flickered in an adjacent room.

The place was deserted.

"Down," said Clara, and Jill instinctively ducked. But it was a description, not a warning, as she looked and saw Clara pointing to a set of stairs leading to the basement.

"Charming," said Selene, and reached into her pocket for the flashlight that clipped to Freddie's barrel.

Clara led them down, and in the dark Jill could pick out the wave-bladed sword, as it still glowed faintly. Behind her there was a quiet *snap* and then harsh light flooded them, throwing out long, dark shadows as Selene turned the flashlight on.

The stairs were concrete, chipped and cold, wet in places, and led down to a dusty cellar. Clara moved through the maze of exposed pipes and cardboard boxes, still with the sword held out in front of her, until they ran up against the back wall. Here she paused, and then began moving along it until they came to a large, metal cabinet. It had rusty corners, and one door was dented so the two didn't meet in the center, leaving an odd, grinning crack.

"Something tells me that ain't the way to Narnia," Selene said dryly.

Clara just grunted and, putting her shoulder to the cabinet, shoved it firmly out of the way. There was a horrendous scraping, and a sudden draft of cold, damp air blew out at them.

Moving the cabinet had revealed a dark, ragged opening in the concrete wall, like something had taken a bite out of the structure. Dark, wet wooden stairs were just visible down at least thirty feet when Selene cast her beam into the passage.

"I'll take point here, if it's all the same to you," she said. "Stay close behind me, Jill. This place has bad news written all over it."

It did not get bad right away. The woman had given him new clothes, as his own had been irreparably burned when he'd backed into the flaming wall. He'd had to hold them onto himself while the woman procured a pair of coarse, black cotton trousers and a sort of robe-like top with a hood—similar to the outfit her assistants wore—and offered them to him.

Flammard took the folded cloth, and as the woman made no move to give him any semblance of privacy he turned his own back and changed as quickly as possible. He pulled the robe on and tied it with the attached sash, being careful to cross it securely over his chest, and only then turned to face her.

"You *are* interesting," said the woman, her dark eyes glittering. "What is your name?"

"Flammard," said Flammard, resignedly. "Yours?" he asked.

A flicker of a smile. "You may call me Mistress," she said coyly. "Tell me, Flammard, surely you have figured out by now what is going on?"

"I have some ideas," Flammard allowed, narrowing his own eyes. He did not like the way Mistress was looking at him, like he was a dish of cooked veal and she was longing to eat him up. "You want . . . descendants of Loki. Specifically men."

"Sons of Fire," said Mistress, with a regal nod. "Like you."

Flammard sniffed. "And you want them for . . . sacrifices? You've got a piece of the eternal flame there. It could stand as a proxy for Loki. I can't imagine what you hope to achieve, though."

Mistress gave a crackling laugh. "It's true some of the sons have died. They were weak. But they allow me to capture more powerful specimens. I'm not *sacrificing* anyone, per se. I can't help it if they're not strong enough, or that the fire won't accept them. All I want is what, I think, all any child wants. I wish to meet my father."

The words rang in Flammard's ears like a gunshot, and he took a step back. "You want *what?*" he gasped.

"I wish to meet my father—your father," Mistress said, as if this should be the most obvious and reasonable thing in the world. "All my life I've had powers and abilities that set me apart from my fellow humans. It took me a long time to realize that it was because I was *not* fully human. You and I . . . we are also part . . . something else. Something ancient and powerful. So I gathered to myself other like-minded individuals, and we set about devising a way to meet the person responsible for our gifts."

Suddenly everything clicked into place, and Flammard felt his stomach drop.

"You're using the door in the fire," he whispered. Behind him, the burning wall flared as if in response. "The door in the eternal flame, the one that can open anywhere . . . "

"*Almost* anywhere," Mistress corrected him. "I can open it—that part was easy—but I cannot open it into Loki's prison. *That*," she said bitterly, "I eventually learned, can only be done by a *son* of fire. A *male* descendant of Loki." She sniffed disdainfully. "Patriarchal scumbags. But, that's where *you* come in," and she smiled, ever so sweetly. "The others didn't understand, but I think you do. You'll help me, won't you? You'll open the door?"

"*No*," said Flammard before he could stop himself. It was a stupid thing to say, but he was horrified at the thought of opening up a door to *that* realm, the realm of gods and spirits and giant snakes that wrapped themselves around the world; the realm where a man's heart could be weighed against a feather—literally—and where, he knew, all the things that made him just a little more than other people came from. All the things he'd tried so hard to suppress.

"I mean, look," he said, backpedaling a little. "Have you thought about what it is you're doing? Never mind, of course you have. I mean, have you thought about *who it is* you're wanting to meet? This is *Loki* we're talking about. The god of mischief and fire. The one who killed Balder—for *fun!* He's not exactly the nicest guy, if you read the stories, and there's probably *lots* more we don't know about him. He could be a *lot* more trouble than you seem to think he'll be worth." *And,* he thought internally, *Mother never wanted me to meet him. That says more than anything.* "Besides," he said. "How do you even know he'll still be in prison? If he's managed to get out and seed all these descendants—not to mention you and me—chances are he won't be *there* anymore."

Mistress was watching him, her expression of scorn slowly fading into one of disappointment. Idly she went over to one of the tables and began pulling on a pair of elbow-length, black gloves.

"The exact circumstances of my conception are rather blurry," she said. "I don't imagine your mother ever described how *you* were conceived? No? I thought not. Loki is the cleverest of all the gods, don't you forget that. And his prison is the last solid recorded location I have for him. It is, at worst, a start; but I also believe it is my best chance. Now, I'll ask nicely one more time, since we are half-siblings: won't you *please* open the fire door to Loki's prison? Think of my request with a cherry on top, if it helps."

Flammard eyed the woman, who was now resting one hand casually on the lid of a clay jar. He gauged the distance between them, and the distance to the door, and made his choice.

He leapt, vaulting over the high-backed chair, and sprinted for the door. He heard Mistress shout something behind him, and suddenly his way was blocked by a large man in a dark, hooded cape. Flammard ducked the first reaching arm, imagined himself like a slippery fish or snake, and dove for the gap between the man and the wall.

He would have made it, too, had not something cold and clammy closed around his ankle, and he felt himself jerked roughly into his proper size and weight. He tripped, fell hard on the stone floor, and the pain of the impact was more immediate and intense than anything he'd ever experienced. It rendered him immobile as large hands closed around his shoulders and pulled him back into the room, and even after the searing pain had subsided and he'd caught his breath, he found to his astonishment and horror that he could *no longer cheat.*

"According to some texts," came Mistress's voice, sounding triumphant and a little smug. "Loki was restrained, in his prison, beneath the earth, by the guts of his son. Well, one of his sons. Now, you might say this could be a result of a mistranslation somewhere along the centuries. It turns out, however, that it is quite likely *true.* Because, and this is a fact that took me *ages* to find out, the lineage of Loki is adversely affected by the blood of its kin—and *especially* by their sinews and intestines. Put Loki in regular chains, he'd break them in an instant. Tie him up in the entrails of his child, and poof! Welcome to your eternity of snake venom!"

Flammard tried to curse, but it came out as a groan. He felt like he'd chipped a tooth, and there was blood in his mouth from where he'd bitten his cheek in the fall.

"Don't worry," Mistress said as he was carried bodily over to the stone. The stone that did not *belong* here. The stone from the spirit world. "I'll loosen them up enough so you can open the door, just as soon as we have you properly bound."

No, no, no, no, *no,* Flammard thought, and the thought trailed into verbal speech as he was laid across it, and another cold length of slimy organ used to secure each wrist to one of the iron rings on either side. He tried to thrash, to kick, and found his feet caught and a frightening twinge in his elbow.

"You can't force me," he remarked, leaning his head back against the cool stone and staring up at the ceiling.

"True," said Mistress's voice from somewhere around his chest. He felt her shadow move coolly across him, and realized she must be standing between him and the fire.

He considered craning his head down to look at her but instead kept staring up at the ceiling and tested his restraints. They held with surprising strength.

He was spread out across the stone and elevated so that he had to stand on tiptoe if his feet were to support any of his weight. His jaw ached. It was remarkably uncomfortable.

There was a tickle at his collarbone as someone fiddled with his robes, and that caused his head to snap up. Mistress had a paintbrush in one hand and was carefully parting his robes with her other, nails dragging lightly over his skin.

"Now, now, don't look so worried," she began, seeing the look of horror on his face. "*This* part won't hurt at all . . . unless you're ticklish. In which case you'll just have to lie back and think of . . . oh . . . "

Mistress had succeeded in pulling open the folds of Flammard's robe so that his entire upper torso was exposed, and she was staring at it with such a look of surprised confusion that it would have been quite funny, except that Flammard knew *this* was where things got *really* bad.

The stairs ended in a dirt-covered stone floor, and Selene stopped at the bottom of them, shutting off her light. Jill flattened herself to one wall, fearful of Clara and the unsheathed sword she carried. It was then she noticed that things were not as dark as they should have been: a faint, warm glow was coming from the rippling sword. Not enough to light their way, but enough to illuminate its bearer, whose face was pinched in concentration.

"Heard something," Selene whispered after a moment. "Think we better go silent for now . . . if we can't go completely dark," she added, with a sour look at the glowing sword.

"We're getting close," Clara said defensively.

"Yeah," said Selene. "I figured."

They felt their way forward from there on out, and as the tunnel widened Clara moved to walk at Jill's side, holding the sword pointed downward so as not to accidentally stab Selene in the back.

Several paces on, Jill heard what must have originally alerted Selene: a snatch of conversation, distant and broken, and now a low sound of someone moaning.

Beside her, Jill felt Clara stiffen, then relax.

"Not him," she whispered.

The passage branched before them, and after a moment where Clara swung the sword like a pendulum between the two, she indicated the right-hand passage. They took it, and after that the sounds grew faint again.

"Jill," Selene said out of the dark in front of them. "Just so's you know, this is probably gonna get ugly. When it does, I want you to drop and run."

"What if I can do something to help?" Jill asked.

"Only do that if it's safe," Selene warned. "Maybe think of helping *your-self* first, okay?"

Jill knew better than to argue.

"Okay," she said.

Mistress was laughing. Which was, on the whole, not the worst reaction Flammard had ever experienced. There was a manic edge to it, however, that made his hackles prickle and his heart pound. Someone who laughed like that was definitely capable of making things *very* unpleasant for him.

"I should have known," Mistress let out in a long wail. "I should have *knooooown*. . . . Why, it's obvious to look at you, once you actually *look*." She prodded him with one nailed finger, just above the faded brown scar on his left side, and he flinched. "We're *even more alike* than I first thought," she said, grinning widely. Bringing her painted lips up to his ear, she hissed with bitter triumph: "*Sister.*"

Flammard weighed the benefit of explaining what being transgender *actually was* against his continued chances of survival, and settled on rolling his head to one side so he could glare at the woman, and say, "*Not* your sister," through gritted teeth.

"Puh," said Mistress, and flicked his cheek. It stung, but not as much as her next words. "You can call yourself whatever you like, I don't care. It doesn't change *what you are* at the most fundamental level. On the level that counts for *this*." She gestured at the burning wall.

And . . . yes, there was the rage, Flammard noted with detached interest. There was the indignation, the fury, and behind it all, a little bit of despair. And now . . .

. . . now Mistress was unhooking his arms from the iron rings, pulling him off the stone, binding his hands behind him, and giving him a shove toward the corner.

Flammard, dizzy and a little bit nauseous, took two steps and felt his legs give out from under him.

Time to take new stock, he thought dully. *Good bit: not on the stone any more. Bad bits: entrails seem to be sapping physical strength as well as magic strength. Emotions not as strong as they should be.* Unless that was a result of the stress. It was a phenomenon Flammard had noticed before, and even actively practiced in order to remain calm with difficult patients. Now, however, he had a feeling that only a sweeping, consuming emotion like hate or rage could cause him to draw up the energy he needed to break free, and while he understood he had a perfectly good reason to get angry, he simply couldn't muster up the energy. Which he needed to do, and soon.

The realization was enough to panic him, except he seemed unable to do even that. Fear and pain dulled as he pushed himself up and rolled over so he could look up at Mistress, who was standing by the stone looking stormy and disappointed.

Then, to Flammard's amazement, she gave a little sigh and her anger seemed to dissipate. "Well, of all the setbacks I've experienced this is the most . . . *twenty-first century*," she remarked with dry resignation. "Your organs might still be useful—worth a try considering you're still a *child* of Loki. But there's no hurry. I had one other I meant to try tonight . . . "

She was interrupted by the sudden appearance of two disheveled men in dark robes. They had someone held limply between them, and they were panting.

"Forgive the delay, Mistress," one of them gasped. By his voice, Flammard recognized him as one of the men who'd managed the room full of prisoners. There were more than two, total, he now realized, taking in the additional robed figures who had caught him earlier, now standing to either side of the door.

"What?" snapped Mistress.

"I don't know how they did it, but they were out of their cages. Took us a while to get them all rounded up again."

"They got *out?*" Mistress said, and she turned on Flammard, one eyebrow arched accusingly.

Flammard decided he didn't have the energy to answer that question, so he just shrugged carelessly.

"Did any get away?" Mistress asked.

"No, Mistress," came the dutiful reply. "We got them all. Though this one gave us the most trouble." So speaking the pair moved further into the room, and dropped the body they had been carrying on the floor.

It was Marcus, and he groaned softly as he curled onto his side. One wide eye darted around the room, lingered apprehensively on Mistress, then settled on Flammard.

"Hey, Leonard," he croaked.

"Hey," said Flammard.

"Sorry," the man mumbled. "Tried my best."

"Wish I'd done the same," Flammard said, feeling the bitterness like a vague cloud around his throat. If he'd led the men out when he had the chance . . . but even the regret was muted now.

Flammard was beginning to feel lightheaded as Mistress marched over and inspected Marcus critically.

"Yes, I suppose you'll do," she said briskly. "I have the patience for one more attempt tonight. And if this doesn't work I'm taking out my disappointment on *her.*" She flicked a glance at Flammard, and then moved over to the table with the clay jars. Clay jars full of entrails.

"Marcus," Flammard said, forcing himself to focus. "Can you run?"

"Nggh," said Marcus. "Knee's all jacked. Can't even walk."

"Okay . . . " Flammard groped, mentally, for the desperation he needed in order to keep talking. "Look, whatever she asks you to do . . . just do it, okay? If you can, you probably won't even die."

Marcus rolled an eye at Flammard. "And if I don't? Or can't?"

Flammard thought of the screams, and felt disgust roiling in his stomach—but it was far, far below him, like a storm in a valley and he was stranded on an exposed mountaintop. "Definitely you die. And badly. Just . . . "

Mistress was coming back, swinging a length of wet intestine between her gloved hands. Briskly she cast a loop around Marcus's neck, and the poor man cried out.

Flammard watched in muted horror as Marcus was hoisted to his feet and marched—and he nearly had to hop to keep the weight off his right leg—over to the stone. His hands and arms were secured in the same manner Flammard's had been, though he was tall enough that he could rest his weight fully on his one good leg.

The men in robes retreated to the sides of the room, well away from the fire, and Flammard wondered randomly if they were even aware of their actions. Mistress had said they were also Sons of Fire, but perhaps they were ordinary men she had enchanted—just as she had attempted to enchant him.

Mistress returned, a small knife in one hand, and briskly cut Marcus out of his t-shirt.

"What the *hell*—?" Marcus began, then yelped as the woman took a brush, dripping in bright red paint, and started applying it to his naked chest.

"No unpleasant surprises *this* time," she said, glancing scathingly at Flammard.

Flammard frowned, seeing the figure she was painting take shape.

"But that's a *binding* rune," he said, dumbly.

"Of *course* it is," Mistress said. "I can't keep them wrapped up in entrails while they try to open the fire gate, can I? It stops *all* their powers, you know."

"I'm getting that," Flammard said.

"Right, now then, what's your name, son?" Mistress asked, giving Marcus a sharp pat on the cheek.

Marcus blinked down at her. "M-Marcus," he gasped. "Lady, I don't know what'chu think you're doing, but—"

"Hush," said Mistress, putting a finger to her lips. She stretched the end of the word out so it became a long, soft, "Shhhhhh . . . " She tapped Marcus lightly on the nose. "Marcus, I'm going to take these nasty things off you, so you'll be in full possession of your powers, and you're going to open a door in that wall over there. The one that's on fire. Can you do that for me?"

Marcus gaped at her. Then his gaze flicked to Flammard, and understanding dawned in his eyes.

"Lady, I don't know how the hell I'm gonna do that," he said. "But you believe me, I'll *try*."

Mistress smiled briefly at him. "*Good* boy," she said. "Now, concentrate on the *door*. It's already there, you see. All you have to do is *open* it."

Mistress yanked sharply on the length of intestine that secured Marcus's left hand, pulling it away, and Flammard saw his eyes widen in horror as he realized his arm was still stuck there.

Mistress only smiled, and removed the entails from his right hand, and the ones still draped around his neck. She coiled them in her hands, like someone winding a length of rope, and stepped back. Then, with a grand flourish, she tossed them into the fire.

As soon as the guts hit the wall of flames it exploded outward, the flames reaching into the room, washing over Flammard and obscuring his view. He caught a glimpse of Marcus's horrified face, mouth open, and a moment later heard the scream.

Then the fire banked, receded, and Flammard blinked down at himself to find his clothes steaming faintly, but unburnt. The guts securing his wrist smelled singed, but they still held when he tested them. The effort nearly made him throw up.

Then he raised his head and saw that a part of the fire had not receded. It was reaching for Marcus, gladly, and Marcus was doing his best to flatten himself against the rock.

The fire did not recognize him, Flammard realized dully. He had more power than any of the others, save himself and Mistress, but he was at least three generations removed from anything non-human. He might be able to open the gate, but he could not survive the fire.

"Marcus!" Flammard shouted. "Marcus, you have to open the gate!"

"What *gate?*" Marcus shrieked.

"The one in the fire. You can't *see* it. You'll *feel* it." He swallowed, gathering strength, before going on. "Marcus," Flammard said, desperately. "Marcus, have you ever had any time in your life where something *crazy* and *inexplicable* happened to you? Some *wild* coincidence that was too good to be true, but *was?* If you have, go back to that time. Go back, remember whatever *wild, mad energy* possessed you, and use it to *open that gate!*"

Marcus stopped screaming abruptly. His eyes were so wide the whites were showing all the way around his dark irises, and his eyebrows were encroaching on his ginger hairline. He blinked once, twice, and then shouted something.

It was not a scream. It was a wholly different sound. It was direct. It had *purpose.* It was like no word or words that Flammard had ever heard before, but it resonated in his body and he felt an answering hum from within him, somewhere around his ribcage. Somewhere deep inside him, he knew those words, and from the triumphant expression on Mistress's face, she knew them too.

The fire was blown back suddenly, letting out a soft *whoomphing* noise, and retreated to burn in a narrow line around the edges of the wall.

In its wake it left, not bare stone, but a dark, empty void that breathed out a foul smell like wet, decaying plant matter, and a cold draft that made Flammard shiver.

With a faint cry Marcus collapsed to the ground, his head flopping limply onto his arms, and lay still.

There was an astonished murmur from the hooded men, and they shuffled hopefully forward.

"No!" shouted Mistress, stepping up over Marcus's limp form. "You shall not enter his prison. I alone will journey there, and I will bring our father back to us."

Boots clicking on the stone, she stepped forward through the door that had opened in the fire, gathering a piece of flame into one hand and raising it high above her head.

With all the attention focused on her, Flammard managed to scoot himself backward so his arms were planted firmly in the little strip of flame in the corner, and there he waited while he felt the entrails that bound him blacken, smoke, and finally give out entirely.

When Mistress had disappeared into the darkness he struggled to his feet, casting the horrible things away, and into the full swell of all his powers—and emotions. Behind him, he felt the fire flare up in sympathy.

His first thought was to close the gate—Mistress and Loki, if he was indeed still in prison, certainly deserved each other—but then he caught sight of Marcus, and all his training took over.

Unthinkingly, he moved for the fallen man.

That jerked the hooded men out of their daze, and as one they came for him.

There was a strangled cry from the back of the room—one of both surprise and pain—and a black-robed body went hurtling through the air, smacked up against the rock, and fell to the ground.

Flammard raised his eyes, and thought for a moment he was dreaming.

Claymore was standing in the doorway, and in her hand was not Bellatrix, but Feuermann, and she held him blade down, his blade glowing white-hot.

The men were rallying, recognizing the new threat. Claymore swung her arm meaningfully.

"Flammard!" she shouted, and at her voice Flammard realized this was, in fact, no dream. He felt a mad grin spreading across his face.

"To you!" Claymore shouted, and flung the sword, hilt first, across the room.

It was a long way to throw a sword, but Claymore had always been freakishly strong—even for their extraordinary family—and the sword arced true, diving gracefully toward Flammard like an eagle returning to its handler.

Midway its blade burst into flame, causing the robed men to duck and roll, as it fell like a comet toward him.

Flammard hardly had to reach; just raised his right hand, palm open, and felt it meet the smooth hilt of Feuermann. With the contact the last of the nausea and light-headedness left him. He felt whole and grounded, yet weightless at the same time. He was the fire in the sword and the wall, and the material world was a thin film that he could push around with the merest nudge of his mind.

He breathed out, long and slow, and the fire kissed his breath and danced around his face.

* * *

322

The long, rectangular room was bright and hot and alive with moving bodies. Jill hung back in the doorway and let Clara and Selene dive into the fray. She heard Clara shout something and toss the sword—which caught fire in midair—to a small, red-haired man who was crouched by the gaping black opening ringed in fire. He caught it, amazingly, and stood up. He was thin in a spare, sinewy sort of way, dressed in a dark robe that had been pushed off his shoulders and hung around his waist. He had two old, curving scars, one under each lean pectoral muscle, and his pale skin was thickly freckled.

Standing up with the sword, he seemed somehow to enlarge—though he remained the same size—his presence filled that end of the room, and the hooded men who had been approaching him turned instead to Clara.

Clara, who had drawn her own sword and was swinging at them lustily. Jill caught a glimpse of her face and was surprised to see, instead of her usual stoic blankness, an expression alight with excitement and anger. Fury, almost. She lashed out at the men, and each one she struck fell and did not rise again. Selene snuck out in her wake, pulling back the hoods of the fallen men, revealing a mottled group of unconscious humans.

"Clara," she said sharply. "Clara, hold up a second!"

But Clara did not hear. She'd caught the last man by the collar of his cloak and held him, her sword raised. It gleamed in the light of the fire, but there was something dark and red dripping down its length.

"Claymore, hold! They are human!" the red-headed man with the flaming sword—Flammard, Jill guessed—shouted.

He had a surprisingly high voice for a man, very much like Clara's, but it rang out through the chamber and reverberated in Jill's ears.

Clara paused. The man under her hand struggled uselessly against her iron grip.

"Are you sure?" she asked.

"More human than me," Flammard said gently. "Thank you, Clara, you've done enough."

Almost regretfully, Clara lowered her arm, forcing the hooded man to his knees. Using the hilt of her sword she knocked back his hood, revealing a white, terrified face with a bloody nose.

"Are you going to give me trouble?" she asked him.

The man shook his head.

"Here, Clara, I'll take him," Selene said. She'd holstered her gun and deftly took the fabric of the man's robe and twisted it behind him so his hands were pinned together. She gave Flammard an odd look, and then turned away quickly. Too quickly. Jill wondered if she was missing something.

"Claymore, help me with him," Flammard was saying. He'd put his sword—no longer flaming—aside, and was kneeling on the ground.

Daring to creep into the room, Jill saw he was referring to another man, a large one with African-American features and improbably red hair. He'd been stripped to his waist, rather like Flammard, and was lying in a heap on the far side of a strange, grayish stone.

"We need to get him away from the stone," Flammard was saying as Jill approached. "Be careful of his right knee—I think it's sprained."

"What happened?" Jill asked as Clara, after sheathing her sword, took the man gently under the armpits and dragged him slowly around the stone, away from the gaping black hole.

Flammard looked up at her, and Jill found herself staring into vibrant hazel eyes that seemed to catch the light of the fire—even though he faced away from the fire that burned along the wall. There was something about his chin and the expression on his face that reminded her of Clara, but other than that they looked nothing alike.

"They made him open the gate," he said, as if this would explain everything. "He's probably been burned, too. Lay him down here, Claymore—mind his head!"

For Clara had nearly dropped the man in her hurry to get up and look around.

"Is that *the* gate?" she asked.

"*Yes*," said Flammard. "The woman responsible for this mess just crossed over. We'll worry about her in a minute—I have to get him stabilized."

Clara gave a frustrated grunt and turned to Selene, who was keeping herself busy checking on the robed men and not looking at Flammard. What *was* going on there?

"Selene, it's not over yet!" Clara shouted, drawing her sword and striding toward the dark hole—which, now Jill thought about it, hurt a little to look at and breathed out damp, fetid air.

Jill saw Selene turn to follow Clara, and was about to trail after them both, when she was distracted by the clatter as Flammard tossed his sword away and cursed softly.

Looking down, she saw he was removing his hand from the unconscious man's face, while the other gripped frantically at his upper arm.

"No pulse?" Jill asked, remembering her first-aid training.

"Or breath," Flammard said and began arranging the man so he was lying flat on his back.

Jill, who knew what came next, abandoned any thought of following Clara and Selene, and knelt down next to Flammard.

"I know CPR," she offered.

"Hopefully we won't need that," Flammard said, gently straightening the man's head, pushing the man's chin down to open his mouth, and then placing one hand on either side of his lower jaw and pulling forward to open the airway.

And then he paused. He got a strange, inward sort of look, and then he leaned in, placing one hand gently on the man's chest, took a short breath, then sealed his lips around the open, slack mouth, and breathed out.

Jill saw the chest rise, faintly, and then Flammard was sitting up. He exhaled, inhaled, and then went back down.

Another breath, and a longer one this time. Jill could see the muscles on Flammard's back—also freckled—straining under the skin.

There was an odd kind of spark in the air when Flammard sat up this time. The fire on the wall flared, and Jill felt a heat begin to rise from the man on the ground.

"Marcus," Flammard said, quietly and intently. Then, a little louder, "*Marcus.*"

The man on the ground drew in a weak breath, hoarse and wheezing, then blinked his eyes. These were dark brown, but for a moment they too held the same kind of fire as Flammard's. Then the light faded, and it was a perfectly ordinary—if somewhat distressed—face that was gazing up at Flammard and Jill.

"What . . . " he began, and coughed.

"Hello, Marcus," Flammard said. "Try to relax. I'm here to take care of you. You might be feeling some acute nausea, so I'm going to roll you onto your side, okay? Tell me if this hurts your knee—or anything else. Help me lift his shoulder please, ma'am."

Working together they got Marcus, who was almost as big as Clara, over on his side, with his good leg bent to provide a brace so he wouldn't roll all the way onto his face.

"You don't seem badly burned," Flammard was saying. "So I'm going to cover you with my robe. You'll be going into shock soon, if you're not already. Just stay awake, and stay with me, okay?"

"Whah the *hell* happened, L'nard?" Marcus mumbled.

"You did great, Marcus," Flammard said, and he really seemed to mean it. "You opened the gate. Everything's going to be fine now, just try to relax."

"*What gate?*" Jill hissed.

Flammard barely glanced at her, and he smiled sadly.

"Go ask Claymore," he said. "Oh, and don't touch that stone, if you can help it."

Jill rose and wandered off through the bodies, some of which were beginning to shiver and moan. Per Flammard's instructions she gave the strange, gray rock a wide berth, and came around to the other side to find Clara and Selene standing at the lip of the hole, both with their weapons out, and Selene casting her flashlight into the dark beyond.

"*What*," demanded Jill, "is going on here?"

Clara didn't move, but Selene spared her a short grin.

"You'll like this one, boss. It's a transdimensional gate. A big one, too. According to Clara, it leads somewhere *you* might have heard of."

Jill frowned into the dark. Selene's flashlight barely illuminated the first ten feet, and all she could see was a field of wet, lumpy rocks—similar to the one in the room behind her—with green slime clinging to the cracks between them. It was cold, and smelled of decaying water plants.

"According to Norse mythology," Selene said, "Loki, the god of fire and mischief, killed Balder, who was the favorite son of Odin and the god of purity and light and all that whaffery. Anyway, this pissed Odin off, so he had Loki chained to a rock in a cavern under the earth, with a serpent to drip venom on him, for the rest of time. Or until Ragnarök."

"I know what happened to Loki," Jill sighed. "Didn't he also have his wife there to catch the snake's venom?"

Selene nodded. "That's not so important now. The important thing is, somehow, someone's managed to open a transdimensional gate to *that* place. Loki's prison. *There.*" She jerked her head at the hole.

"Wait," said Jill. "So . . . *Loki's* in there?"

"Not necessarily," said Clara. "There are . . . conflicting records as to what happened next."

"Stories, you mean," Jill said. "There are *lots* of stories about Loki."

"Those too," said Clara. "They can influence people like him."

"*Someone's* in there," Selene said, cutting off Jill's next question.

Sure enough, there was a sound from beyond the gate. A faint voice, and fainter than that, a slick, sliding sound. Like scales over wet rocks.

"Oh no . . ." said Selene, and then there was a high, anguished scream.

Fire flared briefly in the dark, and by its light they saw the silhouette of something huge and snake-like. It was writhing down from the ceiling of the place, where scaly coils gleamed in the light of the fire. A shadow of a woman stood up from the rocky floor, one arm thrust out as if to ward the serpent off. It was undeterred. The long neck lunged, a huge mouth opened, and the scream cut off in a startled gasp.

There was a rumbling from within the cave.

"Get behind me!" Selene shouted, grabbing Clara's elbow and pulling ineffectually. "Jill, *get out of here!*"

All of a sudden a face appeared, lit faintly from all sides by the fire that ringed the portal. It was a wide, flat face, with a blunt, scaled snout and two weeping, yellow eyes. Venom sacks bulged menacingly at the back of its head, and it was currently in the middle of swallowing someone. Jill caught a glimpse of a flailing arm and a tangle of dark red hair, before Selene knocked her away.

"*BEHIND ME, CLARA!*" she roared, and fired at the giant snake.

She hit it squarely in its right eye. Jill saw the spurt of vibrant, red blood, and the snake withdrew, hissing.

Not before Clara, stepping boldly over the fire, reached up and grabbed the dangling arm.

The snake recoiled. Clara skidded a few feet, then caught a foothold and stood fast. Between the two of them, the body emerged from the snake's mouth and flopped to the ground. Clara grabbed it roughly by the shoulders and began dragging it—*her*, it was a woman—over the threshold and into the room, while Selene covered her with more shots from her gun.

No sooner had Clara set her burden down then the snake struck again. This time its head shot past Selene and into the room, trailing a length of thick neck covered in glistening yellow-brown scales. Its open mouth struck upon the gray stone, caught it, and crushed it.

For a moment the head retreated back into the cave, spitting chunks of rock, and then it returned.

This time, however, Selene and Clara were ready for it.

Selene shot it again, in the same place as before. And again. And again.

At the same time, Clara swung up and lodged her sword in its throat.

The snake hissed and flailed; its right eye was a pulpy red mess, and Clara's sword, when it was yanked from its neck, left a deep wound that began to bleed profusely.

The snake flailed, hitting against the edges of the portal and once nearly smashing into Jill. But it was a retreating flail, and soon the snake was once more a vague shape in the darkness behind the flames, and then it was only an anguished hissing in the shadows, and then it was nothing at all.

In the wreckage of the room, Selene and Clara stood, the former calmly reloading her gun, the latter breathing heavily. Between them on the floor the crumpled, wet remains of what had been a glamorous woman in a black dress and boots lay in a bleeding heap.

"Flammard!" Clara called, sounding a little winded. "We need you!"

Flammard looked up from where he was crouched protectively over Marcus. "I can't leave him!" he shouted back.

Clara shot him a distressed look. "We need to close the gate, Flammard. The serpent nearly got *out*. You know I'm useless at these things—*please.*"

Flammard looked torn. His searching eyes landed on Jill, and he gazed at her imploringly.

Taking pity on him, Jill picked her way through the debris and fallen bodies—she tried not to think too hard about whether they were corpses or not—and resumed her position at Marcus's side.

"I'll watch him," she said. "You go do . . . go close the gate."

Flammard picked up his sword and used it as a cane to push himself to his feet. Visibly shaking, he staggered over to Clara and Selene.

There was a dull moaning sound, and the crumpled heap on the floor shivered. Jill had to suppress a swell of bile in her throat as she realized the woman must still be alive.

"*You . . . cannot close the gate. It is opened, and must remain, so that our father may come into this world.*"

"Wasn't he there, tied to the stone?" Flammard asked, a note of sarcasm in his voice Jill did not wholly understand.

"*No . . .*" admitted the woman on the floor. "*He has gone . . .*"

"I thought he might have," said Flammard. "Then I don't think he'll mind me sealing off his prison once and for all."

This was greeted with a broken-sounding laugh that was part gurgle.

"*You cannot close the gate. Just as I could not open it.*" Now there was a note of bitter triumph in the wrecked voice. "*Only a male descendant of Loki may open or close that gate. And you are no man!*"

Flammard stilled and Selene looked aside awkwardly, but Clara bristled in rage.

"He is my *brother*," she hissed, going down on one knee so she could hold the edge of her sword to what had been the woman's throat. "You will show him the respect he deserves."

"*What's this . . . another sister? No . . . no you are not a Child of Fire. You are . . . something else. A half-sister, then. What will you do, knight errant? You cannot kill me, for I am already dead; the serpent saw to that.*"

"Then why are you still here?" Flammard asked. He sounded more annoyed than anything.

"*Our bodies die . . . our spirits go on.*"

"Yes, so I've heard," said Flammard tiredly. "So *go on* somewhere else."

"*Or you will do what? You don't have the strength to banish me, and your half-sister has not the skill to—*"

"I can do *this!*" Clara shouted, throwing aside her sword. She grasped the body firmly with both hands and lifted it clean off the floor. Raising it above her head she rocked back on one foot, and then hurled it over the threshold and into the darkness. There was a wet, messy-sounding *thud* and then silence. Jill found she had to look away.

"That was unnecessary," Flammard said mildly.

"I didn't like her," Clara responded.

"Neither did I," Selene agreed. "She the one running this mess?"

"She was," Flammard said.

Selene sniffed. When Jill looked up, she found Selene was staring intently at the flames. She seemed to have a hard time looking at Flammard. "Hate to say it," she said after a while. "But she did sort of have a point. These gender-specific things are stupid as hell, but they're sort of anal about their requirements and . . . well . . . you're not exactly a . . . a . . . "

She trailed off. Clara had gone bristly again.

" . . . you might not be man enough for *it*," Selene finished cautiously. "Just . . . you know, *in this case*. Is all I'm sayin'."

Jill blinked. Her brain was processing many things at once, and only now were certain facts gelling into a firmer understanding.

Looking at Flammard, at the smooth shape of his lean body, at his graceful profile and small, nimble hands—not to mention the old scars on his chest—suddenly the reason for Lalai's trouble with the police and the feeling that she was hiding something, and Selene's odd behavior, became immediately clear.

And then the words of the dead woman came back to her and swept that realization aside.

"Wait, wait, *wait*," said Jill, breaking the tense moment. "*You're* a descendant of *Loki?*"

Flammard half turned to glance at her, and in the mixed light of the fire his face took on a strange quality: both ageless and genderless, it was both male and female, young and old. But mostly, it looked tired.

"You could say that," he said. "I'm his son."

Jill felt her brows knotting as she stared at the three of them.

"Oh, you people!" she cried. "You guys *have* read those stories about Loki, right? I mean, if *anyone* is *not* going to have *any problems* with having a transgender child it's going to be *Loki!* So go—go *on!* I can stand not taking samples this time since that snake looks even worse than a vampire. Go *on!*" She flapped her hand at Flammard.

Flammard didn't move at once. He was looking at Jill with a sort of wonder. Then he shook himself and turned back to Clara and Selene.

"Give me space—a lot of space," he said. "I don't want anyone else getting hurt."

Silently, Selene fell back to Jill and Marcus, while Clara, after Flammard jerked his head at her, retreated a few steps, retrieving her own sword and holding it, point down, in front of her.

Flammard shrugged and turned back to the gaping hole. With an effort he raised his own sword. He seemed suddenly very small, and very delicate, and very, very tired.

The man named Flammard Nordstern faced the open gate and raised his sword. Feuermann rested in his hand like a warm assurance, and at this point that was all that he had going for him. Days of drugged sleep and the aftershocks of the magical binding and the stress in general had sapped him of all but his most dire supply of emergency energy.

And yet he needed to do this. For Claymore—because she was right and only he could—but also for Lalai, and the life he had built for himself. The life *he* wanted. And, also, a not insignificant part of him wanted to prove Mistress wrong.

Flammard was a little surprised at how certain he was that Mistress *was* wrong—Claymore's partner had made a good point, even if it had hurt. Yet he knew, deep in the core of his bones, that this was not only his power, but his right.

Taking a deep breath he opened all the little gates within himself, all the gates he so carefully kept closed most of the time. It was slow going, as some of them seemed to have fused shut, and by the time he had finished he was shaking. Not from fatigue, not anymore, but from the effort needed to hold all that energy in.

The fire felt it too, and rose up to greet him, as it had Marcus. But unlike Marcus, it found Flammard a friend, and he let out a sigh of relief as he felt the warm flames embrace him.

He reached out—Feuermann's blade began to glow—and drew in the edges of the door, and began to drag them shut.

It was hard going. The door did not want to be closed. It had been closed for a long time and now it was finally open it wanted to stay that way. More so, it wanted to rip wide, tear a channel between the worlds. Flammard shuddered at the thought of what might flow through that channel, and pulled harder.

Both of his hands were on Feuermann's hilt now, and he noticed only vaguely when his hair caught fire. Not ignited by the flames caressing him, but of its own accord.

We are our swords, he thought to himself with an inner shrug. And his sword was Feuermann, the fireman.

Slowly, slowly, the door shut. Flammard held it there, feeling the seams knit together, sealing it thoroughly, until not even he could tell where the handle of the door was. Then he took a step back, and surveyed the wall—which was complete once more, covered in flames as before.

It would not do to leave it like this, he realized. So, almost regretfully, he coaxed the eternal flame out of the wall and onto his sword, and then, weeping for the waste, he pushed the fire down, pulled it in, and extinguished its physical presence.

As the fire died, the strength in his arms abruptly gave out, and he heard a *clang* as Feuermann's blade hit the floor, cold as stone now. His hair went out, and darkness surged in around them—the only light coming from an electric flashlight someone had thoughtfully turned on and pointed at the ceiling.

A dull chill spread up his body, and utterly spent, Flammard felt himself collapsing forward, powerless to stop his own fall.

Only he never met the hard floor. Instead he was caught by strong, steady hands, warm under their soft, leather gloves. They lowered him gently, lifted Feuermann from his own lax hands, and Flammard felt himself pressed into a huge, welcoming body. Welcoming, even though it had odd poky bits. Claymore still wore the armor he'd made her. That made him smile.

The presence of the body retreated briefly, and then he felt the weight of a jacket being wrapped around his naked shoulders. It soothed the aching chill, and Flammard breathed in the familiar smell of clean leather and sweat that permeated everything Claymore owned.

He leaned his head forward and found her chest. Turning his face sideways he rested it there and took a deep breath.

"Claymore?" he mumbled.

"I'm here," came the immediate reply.

"'M tired, Claymore," he said. "Take me home."

Strong arms passed around him and held him. He closed his eyes.

Clara insisted on carrying Flammard back up to the surface, which left Jill and Selene to handle Marcus. He was marginally more alert now, but that didn't make things any easier.

"We can't just . . . leave," he groaned, when Jill explained to him what was happening. "There're *others*. They got put back in the cells. We can't . . . "

"We'll come back for them," Selene assured him. She had been search-ing the robes of an unconscious man, and stood up holding a folded piece of paper. Shining her light on it, she gave a little cry of satisfaction.

"Clara, hold up. I found us a faster way out."

It was a map, Jill realized. It was not such a surprise, now she thought about it. Just because you worked in an underground labyrinth didn't mean you could automatically find your way around.

"I can walk," Marcus said when they tried to get him up. "Y'ladies shouldn't haf'ta carry me."

"Don't give me any of that, son," Selene told him sharply, and had Jill get on his uninjured side. Selene took the other, and hoisted one arm over her shoulders, while Jill did the same. Like that they were able to walk him out of the room, while Selene held her flashlight between her teeth to light the way.

They went first, since Selene had the map, and Clara followed, carrying Flammard bridal style. The way they took this time was indeed shorter but involved a lot more stairs. That slowed them down, and every time they stopped to rest, Jill worried that more hooded, angry men would appear out of the darkness and attack them.

Nothing came of that, however, and the corridors and stairways were silent.

"Who built this place?" Jill asked, once.

"Probably lots of people, over the years," Selene huffed next to her. No one had the breath for anything more, after that.

The stairs ended abruptly in a flat, stone ceiling.

"Oh, no," Jill said, imagining them having to retrace their footsteps, and Marcus moaned.

"Let me," said Clara, laying Flammard carefully on the steps and squeezing past them. She felt all around the seam of the stone panel, trac-ing the lines with her fingers, and then abruptly slammed her fists into it. Once, twice, three times. A little shower of mortar fell from the ceiling, but the stone didn't move.

Undeterred, Clara spread both her hands flat across the stone, planted her feet firmly, and *pushed*.

The slab of rock came free, and Clara slid it aside, letting in a confusion of yellow light and the sound of people talking.

At first Jill thought they were speaking gibberish, until she realized she was listening to overlapping conversations in several different lan-guages.

"Here," Clara said, offering her arm to Selene.

Selene came and gave Clara her knee, equestrian style, and Clara boosted her up through the hole. Then she did the same to Jill, who found herself thrust into a loud, glittering world—made even more confusing by the myriad reflections whirling around her.

She was sitting on dry pavement, and Selene was standing over her. Over them arched a swooping, curving ceiling made of mirrors, and around them was a confused gaggle of tourists in bright clothing. The mirrors came down to the ground on either side, but in front of her Jill could look out, and there she could see the familiar Chicago skyline, and the orange-gray night sky above it. The air was cool and fresh, and smelled faintly of wet grass.

Ignoring the crowd gathering around them, they both reached in and helped drag first Marcus, and then Flammard up out of the hole. At last, Clara hoisted herself out and crouched, glaring around at their audience as she carefully slid the lid back over the hole. Not entirely, so you could still see where it was, but enough so that someone couldn't accidentally fall in.

"Are you all right?" a concerned voice asked in earnest, if heavily accented English.

Jill looked from Clara to Selene, to the two prostrate men.

"Now?" she asked Selene. "*Now* can we call 911?"

They did, and Jill waited with Marcus on some nearby benches while Selene went to get Arcana. From there she could see the confusing mirrors were actually a gigantic, bean-shaped sculpture, and she realized they had come up in the middle of Millennium Park.

Clara, waiting a few yards away, still with Flammard in her arms, beckoned to her the minute she saw the ambulance arrive.

"We can't stay for this," she said gently. "They will take care of Marcus. He will tell them about the others. We must leave now."

Jill swallowed a lungful of protests and went back to where Marcus was huddled under the black robe.

"Listen," she said to him, fishing in her pocket. "I've got to go, but if you ever feel like talking about what happened, give me a call," she pressed her card firmly into his hand and gave him a pat on the shoulder. "I'm sorry about this. Good luck."

She left him there, but lingered on the edge of the plaza until she saw the EMTs find him. She saw Marcus trying to brush them off and pointing at the mirror bean, where the dark hole was just visible.

Satisfied that things were going in the right direction, Jill trotted off down a flight of stone stairs, to the red hulk of Arcana waiting by the curb—Selene, Clara and Flammard already inside.

Lalai was sitting at her tiny kitchen table, pondering the bottle of rum left over from making eggnog the previous New Year's Eve, and wondering whether now was a good time to try getting drunk, when she heard the sound of a huge truck turn onto the street, coming to a halt right in front of the house.

Hardly daring to hope, yet feeling a flutter in her chest, she went to the window and pulled aside the curtains ... and there was the giant, dual-rear-wheeled red monster that the three odd women had driven off in earlier that afternoon. Its rear door opened, and Clara got out, followed by ...

Lalai was out the door and pounding down the stairs the next second.

"Darling, what's wrong?" Gem asked, putting his head into the hall as she passed.

Lalai didn't answer. She was wrenching the deadbolt off the front door and flinging it open, hurtling down the path.

Leonard looked somehow smaller than before, but maybe that was because he was almost swallowed by the huge leather jacket zipped up under his chin. He was leaning heavily on Clara's arm, but looked up when he heard the door open. He had a graze on one cheek and he looked dead tired, but he was alive. He was alive and looking at her.

"Oh, my—*Leonard!*" Lalai screamed, and ran forward and grabbed him. She kissed him, trying to be careful of his scraped cheek but probably failing, because suddenly she was shaking and sobbing and clutching his head and *he* was shaking too, his arms settling weakly around her waist, and together they sank to the ground in the middle of the path, holding onto each other and gasping for air.

Only after Lalai had caught her breath did she think to ask any questions.

"Where *was* he?" she asked, sparing a glance up at Clara, who was towering above them with an unreadable expression on her face. "And ... what *happened?*"

Something flickered across that blank visage, and Clara sighed.

"He was kidnapped by some *very* unpleasant, and rather crazy, people," Jill said, appearing from around the nose of the truck. "I got some fluids into him on the drive back, but he probably needs more. And food. He wouldn't let us take him to the emergency room."

"Yes, he's like that," Lalai said with a sigh, and pulled herself together. "Come on, Len, let's get you into bed. You can tell me all about it in the morning."

She caught a look, then, that bounced around the three women, too fast for her to make out what it was.

"What?" she asked.

"Yeah," said the dark one—Selene. "About that ... "

It was on the news the next morning. A cult of religious extremists living in the sewers underneath Chicago had been exposed when one of their captives had miraculously escaped and been found, dazed and confused, on a bench in Millennium Park. Investigation of the network of tunnels had uncovered a chamber of injured men—some in quite bad shape and one who was still in a coma—as well as a horrific prison in which were held six more men who had previously been reported missing, and some truly disturbing remains.

"The victims look to have been burned alive and then gutted," the reporter announced with a blink of her perfectly made-up eyes. "Who was behind this operation, and how Marcus Bowerman escaped, is still unknown—though many of the suspects recovered have now been linked to an obscure group called the Sons of Fire, which until now was thought to be a harmless role-playing club based online. Quite an unsettling occurrence, and right under our noses here in the heart of downtown Chicago. More from this story as news becomes available, I'm Amanda Casey."

Lalai looked up from Jill's laptop, on which the reel had been playing, and stared at them.

"You," she said quietly. "You're how Marcus Bowerman escaped."

"I wanted to stay and talk to the police," Jill said primly. "There was more going on that . . . " she stopped. Leonard, from his nest of pillows and blankets on the couch, had gone white under his freckles, and Clara had stiffened ominously. Meanwhile, Selene took the more direct approach and mimed zipping her lips.

"What?" said Lalai. "What *happened?*"

Leonard looked miserable. "Lal," he said brokenly. "There's some things about me I haven't told you . . . "

"Flammard, don't . . . " Clara began, and stopped.

"Len," said Lalai, more gently. "You know I love you more than anything, and I've been worried sick about you this last week, but you can understand why I'm *curious*, right? Whatever it is, I promise won't be angry." She paused, and turned to Clara. "Why'd you call him *Flammard?*"

"Because that is his name," Clara replied blankly. "His true name."

"It's embarrassing," Leonard said, drawing a hand over his eyes. "It's a type of sword. *Flammenschwert*, they're properly called. Means 'flame-bladed.' *That* kind of sword . . . " he gestured to the sword with the wavy blade that was lying across their coffee table. He gazed apologetically at Lalai, and she could see he was nerving himself up to tell her something. It reminded her of the moment when he'd come out to her as trans—except then she'd already suspected as much. Now she not only had no idea what was coming, but it seemed to be weighing on him even more.

"The truth is . . . Lal . . . I'm . . . "

"*Hold on a second,*" Jill interrupted, taking her laptop back. "Stop right there, please. Sorry Flammard—or Leonard, if that's what you prefer—I'm sorry but you *can't* go about explaining it like *that*. She'll think you're crazy."

"No, I won't," protested Lalai.

"You *will*, but you shouldn't, because he's not. So let me explain things the way I *wish* it had been explained to me."

"Explain *what?*" Lalai wailed.

Jill patted the back of her hand comfortingly. "Do you mind coming out to my truck?" she asked. "I've got some things to show you."

* * *

Lalai and Jill were out by Arcana for almost an hour. Clara could see them, heads bent over Jill's sample case, when she went to the window.

"What's she got in her truck?" Flammard asked from the sofa.

"Bits and pieces," Clara said. "Ashes from a summoning, notes on a dead unicorn, some demonic ectoplasm."

"Don't forget the vampire blood," Selene added. Selene, Clara noticed, was still acting a bit weird; she kept glancing all around the room without ever really looking at Flammard.

"Yes," she said. "And vampire blood."

"What on earth does she want with all that?" Flammard wondered.

"She's studying them. It. She's trying to make sense of the supernatural," Clara told him.

"And you're helping her?" Flammard asked.

"We . . . uh . . . work for her," Selene offered, staring out the window.

"Huh," said Flammard. Then he shot a twinkling grin at Clara, almost back to his old self. "I like her," he said, and leaned back on his pillows. "I think I'd also like to lie down again. Help me get into bed?"

Clara helped Flammard sit up. He and Lalai didn't have a bedroom, per se, but a loft over Lalai's workroom that housed a double bed and a long, low dresser. Clara boosted Flammard up the ladder, and stood on it while he got himself tucked in.

"Claymore," he said, once he was settled. "Loki wasn't in his prison. That's why the snake attacked Mistress."

Clara's face clouded over. "Then what the Book of Hecate said was true . . ."

"Not necessarily," sighed Flammard. "But I think it's worth noting for other reasons as well."

"Such as?"

"Well, consider that the freeing of Loki is supposed to precipitate the coming of Ragnarök."

Clara frowned, and nodded. "I will keep that in mind," she said. "Do you need anything? Or shall I go?"

"I think I need sleep," Flammard said. "Thank you."

Clara began to descend the ladder, when he spoke again, making her stop.

"I'm glad you came," he said quietly, and when Clara poked her head over the railing again he was smiling at her. "I'm sorry I . . . sorry I disappeared on you."

"You had things to do," Clara said, and glancing around the little apartment, she added, "It looks like you did them well."

"I still miss them," Flammard whispered. The fire in his eyes was banked, and they were drifting shut. "And you. You haven't heard anything . . . ?"

Clara shook her head.

"I also worry about you. Don't laugh."

"I'm not laughing."

The greenish eyes opened again, focusing briefly on her. "There's this saying," he said. "The fire department uses it in their training, to remind us that we have a duty to keep *ourselves* alive before anyone else. They call it *courage to be safe*. Clara . . . I won't ask you to stay safe, but have the courage, okay?"

"I'll try," Clara said. "You too."

"Thanks," said Flammard with a wry grin, closing his eyes at last. "I'll try."

Lalai was quiet and thoughtful when Jill led her back into the house. She went into the little kitchen and made herself a cup of tea. As she filled the kettle, she glanced questioningly at Jill and Selene. The former shook her head, but Selene said: "I could really appreciate a beer right about now—if you don't need me to drive tonight," she added.

"I think we have some left over from Gem's birthday party," Lalai said, going to the refrigerator and poking around in its doors. "And unless you guys have somewhere you need to be, you're welcome to stay as long as you want. That sofa folds out, and we have an extra futon around here somewhere . . . "

Selene raised her eyebrows and looked at Jill. "What did you *tell* her? She's taking this better than you did!"

Jill shrugged. "Just the truth: that we don't really *know* what's going on, only that strange things *are* happening and we need to find out more about them. I told her I'd take a sample of Fla—Leonard's DNA and see what I could find out from that."

Selene took the beer Lalai offered her, but didn't open it. She rubbed the back of her neck thoughtfully. "I dunno, boss," she said. "Demi-gods are tricky things. A lot of them don't look extraordinary unless they want to—or have to. It's a way of . . . like that protective coloration some animals have."

"Camouflage?" Jill suggested.

"Yeah," said Selene. "Just like that."

"How convenient," Lalai said dryly, pouring her tea. She turned around and leaned back against the counter, gazing past Jill and Selene to the door of the back room. "So if Leonard's the son of Loki," she said, thoughtfully. "What does that make you?"

Turning to look, Jill found that Clara had appeared in the doorway, ducking her bare head to pass into the living room.

She stopped at Lalai's question and got an inward, considering expression. Jill was suddenly very conscious of how little she really knew about Clara's family, and how many questions she'd carefully left unasked, for fear of offending the woman.

Clara didn't seem offended now, however, just uncomfortable . . . and perhaps a little sad.

"We share a mother," she said after a pause in which one could hear a pin drop. "All three of us do. But we have three different fathers. Schiavona and Flammard . . . well, you know about Flammard now. Schiavona made me promise not to tell, but she is also what you would call a demi-god. And I . . . " she gave one of her inverted shrugs. "We do not know."

"Surely your mother knew who your father was," Lalai said.

Clara's mouth twisted unhappily, and she went and sat down on the little sofa. Her knees came up almost into her chest, but even trying to make herself small she seemed to loom in that little room like a giant.

"I think mother knew, but she never said," Clara sighed at last. "I always got the feeling though, that I wasn't . . . well, I wasn't an *accident,* but I wasn't exactly part of the plan, either. I don't know. Flammard and Schiavona both had—both *have* fairly potent powers, whereas I . . . " she shrugged. "I'm just *me.* I don't know. I am the daughter of Dana Nordstern, and that's always been enough."

She looked miserable though, and Lalai looked as if she had more questions. Frantically Jill cast about for a means to change the topic, but since many of the questions she imagined Lalai was going to ask were ones *she* wanted answers to as well, this was proving difficult.

Selene came to her rescue, in a way, when she rolled her head to look at Clara and said, in her driest, long-suffering voice: "Jill wants to take samples from your brother."

"Only with his consent!" Jill added hastily, throwing her hands up in defense of the glacial glare being leveled at her. "And then only some hair, at *most.* Fingernail clippings would do, if that's easier. *Maybe* some saliva."

"He's *sleeping,*" Clara said, stonily.

"Then we'll wait," Jill said. "Lalai has invited us to stay. I can write up my report for Okedo, and, uh . . . can I buy you dinner?" she asked their host.

Lalai chuckled. "We usually cook our own food," she said. "But you can wash the dishes."

This was, more or less, how they passed the afternoon. Jill found herself chained to the sink, while Clara intercepted the string of visitors that began starting around noon. Most of these were Flammard's co-workers from his shift at the fire station and took some convincing to go away again. Eventually Flammard woke up and stumbled out into the living room, still wrapped in his blanket. Clara set him up on a throne of pillows there, where he received the remaining guests, while she towered over him like his personal bodyguard. The little apartment became quite crowded, and Selene disappeared sometime in the middle of it all, though that hardly made a difference in the crowd.

Lalai finally emerged from the kitchen and ordered everyone out so Leonard could get some rest. No, they weren't filing charges and he'd be back to work in two weeks. Out.

"*Now* we can eat," she said, closing the door behind the broad back of a firefighter. "Can someone tell Selene we're having dinner now?"

Since Jill was still elbow deep in dirty dishes (some of which she was washing for the second time that day), Clara was the one who got sent out. She went, looking like she was carrying a raincloud around her shoulders.

Clara found Selene sitting in the back of Arcana, sipping at a now-warm beer. Clara told her dinner was ready, and the woman nodded.

"Aye," she said. "You go on and eat. I'll be in inna bit."

Clara hesitated on the sidewalk, then she hoisted herself up next to Selene and dropped a small, cloth-wrapped object into her hand. Selene's eyebrows went up as her fingers closed around it and she realized what it was.

"You're giving me his ring back?" she said, uncertainly.

"He gave it to me," Clara explained, a little tightly. "When he . . . left. I gave it to you. I needed it to find his sword, which I needed in order to find him. I am returning it now."

"I just thought . . . after what I said . . . you might not want me to have it," Selene admitted, staring down between her knees.

Clara did one of her inverted shrugs. "I thought about it. Then I talked to Flammard. He's not angry. I thought if anyone has a right to be angry it's him, so I am trying not to be angry."

"Sorry anyway," said Selene.

Clara nodded, but didn't leave.

Selene took a deep pull from the bottle, then said: "It's just . . . there's this obvious, insensitive question I wanna ask, and if you keep sittin' there I'm gonna ask it."

Clara's face shuttered, but she didn't move. When it became clear she really wasn't going anywhere, Selene took a deep breath and began to speak.

"What was it like for you, growing up with that? I mean, how did you handle it when this person you *thought* was a woman, female, thing—everything that implied and all—was actually a . . . a man?"

To her relief Clara's expression cleared immediately. She almost smiled.

"Flammard came out to our mother when he was seven—a full year before I was even born. I never knew him as anything *other* than my big brother. It was the same for Schiavona—she was four at the time—but really, I don't think she noticed any changes except Flammard wanted to be called her *brother* now, and she was suppose to use 'he, his, and him' when referring to him. She got used to it. I didn't even have to. He was just *normal* to me, even after I found out most men *aren't* like him. He just . . . is." She rubbed her chin thoughtfully. "I don't forget that he's transgender, I just forget it sometimes makes otherwise good people act weird. I *don't* forget it makes him more vulnerable. He's my brother. My *only* brother.

He's the only family I have left in this world, and I would lay down my life for him."

They sat together in silence, both looking straight ahead, for a moment.

"What did your mother think, when her seven-year-old daughter told her she was actually her son?" Selene asked.

Clara smiled wanly.

"She never talked about it. But Flammard told me she just shrugged and said: 'You come by it honestly, at least. Goodness knows, if the gods can get their genders wrong and have to swap them about then what's to be expected from poor, fallible humans?' And that was that."

Selene nodded thoughtfully.

"You know, Clara, I'd lay down my life to have a family like yours."

Clara sighed, settling down next to Selene to watch the sun set through the trees.

"I don't have a family anymore. Schiavona and mother are gone. It's just me and Flammard now, and . . . well. He doesn't want to be a part of my life anymore."

"Have . . . had . . . whatever," said Selene. "Most of my family's still in *this* world, but they won't have anything to do with me—or I them, honestly. Do you know what *my* mother said when *I* came out to her? She told me I was sick and that I was gonna go to hell. Where I would burn. She went into a *lot* of detail."

"I am sorry," Clara said, and Selene could tell she meant it, in her stiff way.

"Thanks," she said. "Sorry if I was weird."

"Good people sometimes are."

"I got history, is the thing."

"I understand."

"You want to hear about it?"

"Only if you want to talk about it."

Selene drew in a deep breath, then let it out again in a long sigh.

"You know," she said, finishing her beer. "I think I've had about enough of history. Yours, Flammard's, and mine. I say, let's think about tomorrow. I mean, we're *in* Chicago! Is there anything you'd like to see?"

Clara still looked a little fragile, but she was also smiling.

"You know, honestly, I hadn't thought."

"Well get *thinking*, sister—oh crap. Is that, like, a bad word to use around you? You know it's just a word to *me* but . . . uh . . . "

Clara shook her head, smiling a little sadly.

"I don't mind. I find it endearing, actually."

"*Endearing?* Wow, you sure have melted. But that's good, right?" Selene chanced a nervous grin at her companion, who responded with one of her signature shrugs and a nod of her head.

"Yeah," said Selene. "I'ma call that good. Good? Good. Let's go eat."

They climbed down off the truck, and together, they went inside.

I'm gonna carry the light
I won't let go of my right
I'm a son of the flames
You don't need my name tonight

I'm gonna carry the fire
Gonna make love to your ire
Drown your rage in my bright conflagration
I'm a fireman

I'm gonna carry the fire
I'm gonna carry the light
I'm gonna marry your ire

I'm gonna carry the fight
I cannot be chained anymore
I'm gonna carry the light
Like nothing that you have seen before

C-c-c-carry
C-c-c-carry
C-c-c-carry
the fight

I'm gonna ignite my sound
Dig up my sword from the ground
Hold it right to the sky
Scream to heaven that I
am a fireman

Well I've got nothing to prove
But I can take it from you
That you want to see my fire
So I'll raise my sword higher
I'm a fusion

And I will carry the light
I'm gonna carry the fire

I'm gonna carry the fight
I cannot be chained anymore
I'm gonna carry the light
Like you can't find the strength to ignore

C-c-c-carry
C-c-c-carry
C-c-c-carry
the fight

Sons of Fire

Love is too cruel
To take me from you
The serpent is not the source of my pain and fuel
Spark in the night, turn to the sky
Stuck in the earth I am a slave to my birthright
So get to the ground when I spread my wings wide
I can't tame my flame with my doors all unlocked
I cannot hide

Now watch me rise
Ignite me and I will rise

And I will carry the fight
I will send up the smoke and the fumes
I'm gonna carry this fight
I'm a fire, I was made to consume

C-c-c-carry
C-c-c-carry
C-c-c-carry
the fight

I'm gonna carry
Carry
I'm gonna carry
Carry
C'mon, c'mon
The light, the fire, the fight
The fight!

—Carry the Fight/*Princess Die*

DYING
TO
LIVE

8.

River View, MO
Population: 983

MOTHER JUNE ALWAYS TOLD CYNTHIA not to go home through the wood. The wood was a bad place, with bad trees. Take the river path, Mother June had said. Take it in daylight, walk past the tall white houses where the rich, white men lived, but don't look at them. Keep your eyes down, walk (don't run), and you'll come home safely. Cynthia followed these instructions with a religiosity that only a nine-year-old could manage. Every afternoon, once school let out, she would walk the two miles from the bus stop on the edge of River View, down the river path, past the tall white houses, through the center of the little town—using back alleys and side streets—and eventually come to Mother June's back door, which she unlocked using the key she kept on a string around her neck.

One day, in the beginning of summer, there were three tall, white men standing beside the river path outside the three tall, white houses. Cynthia tried not to stare, but she might have, a little. That was probably why one of them spoke to her.

"Hello, miss," he said. His face was round and his cheeks very pink, and he had a thick head of greasy gray hair.

Cynthia's first instinct was to run, but Mother June had always told her that if a white man saw you running, he'd think you'd stolen something, and run after you. So Cynthia made herself stop and say, "Hello sir," as politely as she could.

"You walk past here a lot, do you?" asked another man. He was thin and black-haired, and wore a crisp, pressed shirt with long sleeves, despite the heat.

"I take the river path," Cynthia explained earnestly. "Because the wood is bad."

All the men nodded understandingly. Then the third one, who had not yet spoken, said: "That's a good girl. You keep on taking the river path. We keep it safe, see?"

He was older than the other two, with a bushy white beard. He had short, white hair, neatly trimmed, and he was wearing a comfortable cotton shirt over lightweight trousers and sandals. Yet he seemed somehow better dressed than even the black-haired man.

He reached into his pocket and produced a tiny object wrapped in crinkling plastic.

"Here you are, miss," he said, offering it to her. "You just keep on taking the river path."

The second thing Mother June most often told Cynthia was not to take candy from strangers, but in this case Cynthia thought she would be in more trouble for not taking it.

"Thank you," she said meekly, slipping the hard candy into her pocket. Then she turned and walked stiffly away. She didn't look back, but she could feel the gazes of the three men on her as she went.

The next day was Friday, the last day of school, but even so Mother June could not get off work early to pick her up at the bus stop. So Cynthia began her long walk home, consoling herself with the thought that this would be the last time she'd have to make the walk for the rest of the summer.

At the place where the trail split—one path forging straight through the wood, the other turning to wind along the river—Cynthia hesitated. She had not liked the men. She would almost have preferred the wood—even though it was awfully dark and humid. But Mother June had told her never to go through the wood. And besides, Cynthia had heard stories: people died in the wood. One every year. Always a tourist, or someone from out of town, but still. The wood made you crazy, people said.

With a sigh, Cynthia turned to walk down the river path one last time. She might have been better off going through the wood. She *might* have.

Bloomington, IL
Early September

Selene Shields sat in the dark of the motel room they'd rented outside the city, the only light coming from the screen of Jill's laptop, which was currently open and resting on a pile of pillows in front of her.

It was her watch, but since the possible poltergeist activity they'd driven down to investigate had turned out to be a dud, she was more relaxed now than she would have been normally. It was hard, staying awake when everyone else was asleep, but the bright light from the computer monitor was helping.

Idly, she scrolled through her usual favorite websites. She'd become accustomed to regular internet access during the months spent working for Jill Hamilton, and was now beginning to take advantage of it. She'd joined several (under aliases, of course) and discovered to her joy that they were far better sources for leads than any of the papers or official news reports.

Then she came across a post that made her stomach drop, and all her joy evaporated like steam off a hot iron pan.

When Jill woke that morning, it was to find Selene still hunched over her laptop, her nose wrinkled in a snarl.

"Pack up, sister," she said. "We gotta get to Missouri."

Jill rolled her head over, glancing at the mountainous lump that was all they could see of Clara, then back to Selene. She pushed some stray hairs out of her face and blinked sleepily.

"What's in Missouri?" she asked, her words a little fuzzy.

For answer, Selene turned the computer around and set it on Jill's lap.

Rapidly coming awake, Jill fumbled on the nightstand for her glasses and pushed them onto her face. Squinting a little, she frowned at the screen.

"A Tumblr post?" she asked, skeptically.

"Just *read* it," Selene said, her mouth tight.

"'Justice for Cynthia Jefferson,'" Jill recited, reading from the graphic displayed on her screen. Under the headline was a picture of a young girl with strong African-American features, her frizzy hair up in two pigtails, secured with the kind of bands that had little balls on the ends. Pink ones. She was wearing a denim jumper, and she was smiling widely.

"'Cynthia Jefferson, 9, of River View, Missouri, disappeared on the evening of June sixteenth. She was last seen leaving the Hawk Point bus stop. Her grandmother, June Freeman, reported her missing to the county sheriff, but no action was taken. One week later ...' *oh damn,* 'One week later her body was recovered from the Cuivre River. She had been brutally murdered. The police are doing nothing. This is an outrage. Please reblog, and sign the petition at ...' oh, there's the link. 'We must let the Lincoln County law enforcement know that we demand justice for Cynthia Jefferson ...' Gosh, that's horrible," Jill said, looking up at Selene. "Do you want me to sign the petition?"

Selene snorted and rolled her eyes. "If ya want. It doesn't matter. Naw, I need you to drive me to River View ASAP."

"But ..." said Jill, slowly closing her laptop. "This isn't really ... I mean, it's awful. *Really* awful. But what are *we* gonna do about it? This doesn't look like anything supernatural. There's no reason for us to get involved."

Selene looked at her, a small, humorless, triumphant smile crawling across her face. "That's where you're wrong," she said. Taking the computer, she switched tabs. "I did some more digging," she explained. "Turns out, little Cynthia ain't the first girl to go missing in River View—though she's the first one to turn up so promptly. Look, here's Sabrina Mulaski, 24, disappeared in 1998. And Nadine Horner, 21, in 2001. Lucy Odayama, 23, in

2005 . . . and more. They *all* disappeared around River View, at about this time of year, too. *And* . . . they were all last seen heading into Live Wood."

"What's that got to do with anything?" Jill asked, bewildered.

"Look at the road," Selene said, switching again, this time to a map of rural Missouri. "Here's Hawk Point, here's the Cuivre River—River View's that little bunch of houses on the other side. Here's the bus stop Cynthia Jefferson was last seen at. Now look at her route home. There's a path that leads *directly through* Live Wood."

Jill blinked, then her eyes widened. "So . . . there's something in the wood?"

"There's *always* something in the woods," Selene said. "This time, though, there's something *bad.* It's been taking girls, almost yearly, for a *long* time. Now, I'm not saying it couldn't be one of those gas-mask wearing, prostitute-murdering scumbags, but it *might not be.* And *if* it is," she added, raising her hands defensively. "I promise I won't go all Batman on you. We can turn over whatever evidence we find to the stuffed shirts of Lincoln County and go on our merry way. But it's worth a *look* . . . "

"All right, *all right,*" Jill said, waving her own hands. "Okay, fine. You go . . . pack, or something. I need a shower, and breakfast, and then we can hit the road. Assuming Clara's okay with that . . . "

Clara, however, didn't question Selene's assertion that there was something fishy going on. She looked at the blog post, she looked at Selene's list of names, and nodded stoically.

"Could be a kobold," was all she said. "Or a river spirit."

"Or a crazy guy with an axe," Jill couldn't help adding, at which both the women glared at her.

Midmorning found them motoring southwest on Highway 55, the summer sun high in the sky, and the fields of wheat turning golden under its gaze. Clara rode in front, the black shape of Unicorn like a shadow on the bleached asphalt of the road. Her voice, a little jumbled from the sound of wind and engines, spoke into the relative quiet of Arcana's cab, thanks to the bluetooth headset Jill had installed in Clara's helmet.

"Tell me more about River View," she said.

"Tiny little nothing. Hardly a town," Selene said from where she lounged in the passenger seat. She'd forgone Jill's laptop in favor of her own smart phone, and was busy doing research even as Arcana bumped over the highway. "Kids gotta bus all the way to Troy for school. Nearest grocery outlet is Hawk Point. It's basically just a little cluster of houses, some shops, and a church. Dunno why it hasn't turned ghost, honestly. Which in itself is suspicious."

"Why is that?" Jill asked.

Selene stretched, one leg reaching up until her toes nearly touched the ceiling of the truck's cab. "Little towns like this," she said. "Ones that shouldn't, by rights, still exist. Sometimes they're just *lucky.* Sometimes they got . . . let's say they got a little supernatural *assistance.* Guardian spirits, that sort of thing."

"That's . . . nice," Jill said, sounding a little surprised. She liked to think that the supernatural, for all it seemed to cause a lot of problems, might also exist in a more symbiotic relationship with humans.

"*Yeah*," said Selene, reluctantly. "Thing is, most of these spirits? They have a price. The kind of price people get tired of paying, eventually. Or worse, they *don't*. Remember that corn god up in—what was it? Nebraska?"

"*Yes*," came Clara's immediate response.

"Nasty stuff. Took kids. *Little* kids. Liked babies the most. That was bad. You know what the worst part was?"

"I'm not sure I want to," Jill said with a shudder.

"The worst part," Selene went on anyway, "was that the people did *nothing*. Just kept on letting the god take their kids. They *knew* something was going on, but they didn't want to look too closely, because they were so comfortable and happy. 'Cept the people who lost kids, o'course. Took *both* the Eisenfausts to clear it up."

"No," Clara corrected. "Just Faraday."

"Wasn't it both?" Selene asked, conversationally. "I heard it were *two* of us, so I assumed . . . "

"The other one was *me*," Clara said.

"Oh . . . " said Selene, her eyes widening. "But that was *years* ago."

"Yes," said Clara, blankly. "Yes it was."

There was silence in the truck, while from the speakers the ambient sounds of Unicorn's engine got progressively louder and louder.

"Please say something," Clara said eventually. "Or I'll hang up."

"Some places could use guardian spirits," Selene said, obviously casting about at random. "Like Detroit? Whooo . . . yeah, *Detroit* could use a whole *army* of kobolds. Lemme tell ya, the *last* time I was in Detroit . . . damn washing machines on fire in the street. It's getting ugly up there."

"Explain to me about guardian spirits," Jill said, trying to drag the conversation back on topic. "How do they work?"

The following explanation, teased out of Clara once Selene dropped off to sleep, lasted all the way to the Missouri state line.

According to Clara, a *guardian spirit* was a designation along the same lines as *soldier* or *doctor*. There were a variety of creatures that could act as guardian spirits, each in their own different way, but that didn't mean all creatures like them would be guardian spirits. It was a job description more than anything else.

"So any creature with supernatural abilities could act as a guardian spirit?" Jill asked.

It could, Clara allowed. Though there were some who seemed predisposed to the role.

"Like what?"

"Kobolds, hobgoblins, old gods, demi-gods. They all have their price, though."

Jill waited, but when no answer was forthcoming she said: "Can you give me some examples?"

There was ambient motorcycle noise from the speaker for almost a minute, before Clara replied.

"Most of them aren't . . . pleasant."

"You *do* remember how I got involved in all this?" Jill asked, dryly. She was referring to the fact that she'd met Clara and Selene, almost a year ago now, when her boyfriend had been brutally killed by a chimera.

"Yes," said Clara, heavily. "I do."

"So tell me. It can't be worse than that."

Engine noise. Jill began to grow uncomfortable.

"Most of the time, they require some sort of sacrifice," Clara said at last. "For lesser spirits, hobgoblins and demi-gods, it's something like a pitcher of milk or some other kind of food."

"Makes sense," Jill said. "Like cultivating a garden to attract bees."

"Yes. Perhaps. But the bigger the field of protection, the bigger the sacrifice. If you find a spirit that's guarding an entire *town*, then its probably taking *human* sacrifices."

"And that's what you think we've got here?" Jill said, her stomach giving a cold twist.

"That is what we will find out."

The June sun beat down on them. In the cool, air-conditioned cab of Arcana, Jill wondered how Clara could stand to be out biking in all that black leather. But Clara seemed perfectly happy to ride though the hottest part of the day, with only one short short stop in Troy to refuel and relieve. Selene woke up while Jill was paying for gas, and after raiding their supply of granola bars and fruit leather (Jill insisted on stocking snacks that at least pretended to be healthy, if Selene was going to eat in her truck) offered to drive the rest of the way.

They made Hawk Point by the early afternoon, and then proceeded to get fantastically lost. The map app on Jill's phone didn't think it was possible to drive to River View, and eventually they had to stop and ask for directions.

"I'd ask at the post office," Selene said. "They usually know at the post office."

"I don't know if this town *has* a post office," Jill said.

Hawk Point *did* have a post office, and they *did* know. The rotund woman with vigorously permed hair behind the counter gave Selene detailed instructions, and a suspicious side-eye, all the while calling her "my girl," in that specially proprietary way that made Selene want to hit things, but in the end she returned with a piece of paper bearing a crudely drawn map, and a humorless smile.

"I'd forgotten that Missouri's really part of the *South*," she said, climbing into the driver's seat. "A'right, there's our map, you can read me the road signs if you want, but I think I got it."

The way to River View lay north from Hawk Point, across fields and past shambling houses that thinned the further they got from the little town. The horizon was an even line of green, broken only by the odd power pole or spreading oak. The double roar of Arcana and Unicorn's engines sent flocks of blackbirds up from the fields to crowd on the lines overhead, where they watched the passage of the vehicles judgmentally.

Then the road curved, and to their right was a thick swath of woodland—dark and brown with a green crown, the trees packed in tightly together so that it was impossible to see more than a few feet. Now and then they would pass little roads that disappeared into the wood, but each time the way was blocked by a rusty metal gate half grown over with blackberry vines.

The road curved again, and they passed a beautifully painted sign that said "Welcome to River View," with a picture of an oak-lined river winding away under the letters. Then they drove right past the little road leading off to the right marked "River View Drive" and over a bridge, and Selene cursed as she executed a hasty three point turn and drove back across the bridge.

Clara, who'd been following them on her bike, stopped and waited at the turn, until she saw the red bulk of Arcana appear on the bridge. Then she turned her bike down the narrow road, and led the way into town.

It was hardly a town, though. It reminded Jill of those little English villages she'd read about: basically a street with houses on either side and a church at one end. River View was pretty much like that, only there were a couple other streets, and the houses were all on one side because of the lazy, green river that slunk by on the other. There was a church, however: a white, clapboard building with a simple but well-tended spire and a modest cemetery beside. Selene parked Arcana in front of it, for lack of a better place, and got out her phone.

"Right, so first thing I want to do is check in with June Freeman— that's the girl's grandmother," she said when Clara presented herself by Arcana's side.

Clara, still wearing her helmet, nodded. "I will meet you there," she said.

"Um . . . yeah. About that . . . " Selene wiggled her shoulders awkwardly. "I'd *kinda* like to talk to her myself. Just me, I mean. No offense," she added, glancing over at Jill. "It's just, with the three of us . . . gets a little intimidating, yanno? Also, place like this," Selene glanced around, as if expecting something ugly to come crawling out from behind the church. "Might be better if it were just me."

Jill blinked at her. Then her expression cleared. "Oh . . . this is because you're both *black*, isn't it?"

Selene winced. "I wasn't gonna put it quite so *bluntly*, but yeah. Don't say anything," she said, turning on Clara, who'd taken off her helmet and looked ready to speak. "I put up with you going all mother hen over your brother, you gotta let me do this."

Clara only nodded, however, and thrust the helmet at Selene.

"If you know how to ride," she said, in response to Selene's questioning stare. "I will take Jill in Arcana, and we will go investigate the wood."

Selene stared at her. "I...oh...*damn* Clara," she said, taking the helmet reverently. "I mean...I was planing on *walking* but...um. You sure? 'Cause I thought that bike was like one o' them temperamental horses. Only one rider."

"Unicorn is a motorcycle," Clara said, blandly. "She will carry whoever knows how to operate her."

"Yeah, but *still*," said Selene, climbing down out of the truck, holding the helmet as though it were a sacred relic. "She seems . . . special."

"She is," Clara said, dipping and raising her shoulders.

Selene's eyes grew wide as she realized how serious the other woman was. "Wow," she said, turning the helmet around so she could put it on. "Well...I mean...*thanks*. I'll, uh...bring her back with a full tank."

"I do not believe there are any gas stations in this town," Clara remarked, looking at the sky.

"You *know* what I mean," Selene said, giving her a light punch in the arm. "But seriously, *thanks*," she said, as her face disappeared into the helmet.

"We will rejoin here at sunset," Clara announced, unstrapping her sword so that she could climb into Arcana.

"Aye, sister," Selene called, before striding away to mount the huge, black bike. She did so gingerly, and Jill noticed that Clara didn't budge until she'd watched Selene start the bike, wheel it around, and ride off at a sedate pace. Jill wasn't much of a judge, not being a motorcyclist herself, but she thought Selene had the look of a skilled rider somewhat out of practice. She was a lot smaller on the bike than Clara, almost childlike in comparison, and her bushy mane of hair streamed out behind her from under the helmet as she went.

"So . . . about the wood?" Jill said.

Clara shivered a little, and tore her eyes away from the place where Selene had disappeared.

"Yes," she said. "The wood." She turned to Arcana, and hesitated. Jill realized that in all the months they'd spent traveling together, Clara had barely set foot in the truck, much less driven the thing.

"I'll drive," Jill said, unbuckling herself and making to scramble over the center divider.

"No," said Clara, stepping up into the truck. She was so tall, Jill noticed, that she didn't have to use the running board, and her head fitted neatly into the recessed portion of the ceiling directly over the seat. Arcana had been made with people her size in mind.

"Do you even have a *license*?" Jill asked.

Clara did one of her inverted shrugs. "I think so, but it doesn't matter. I know how to drive."

And she did, even though she killed the engine twice before they could get going. On her third attempt, Clara leaned over the wheel, pressed one hand briefly against the dash, and then pressed forward, easing the clutch out and gently revving the engine.

Arcana rolled forward over the uneven asphalt, as smoothly as any automatic. Jill clapped.

Clara gave her an indignant glare. "I told you I could drive," she said.

June Freeman lived at the end of a street that ran perpendicular to River View Drive. It was called Wood Lane, and when Selene got to the end of it she saw why.

The wood they had passed through on their way came right up against the back of the house, save for a tiny strip of yellowing grass bounded by a low wooden fence. The house itself was white clapboard, like the church, only the paint was old and chipped with a lot of brown showing through. Its ancient shake roof had a sunken, broken-backed look, and there were copious spiderwebs under the eaves. There was a battered Honda station wagon sitting in the drive, blue with pockmarks in the enamel, the back stuffed with boxes and barrels and what looked like a mop. Long ago someone had painted "Mother June's Cleaning" along the side, but this was as faded and scratched as the rest of the car.

All in all the place looked like whoever lived there was either too busy to worry about appearances, or didn't care, or both. It was not unlike the kind of places Selene had lived in as a child, and for that reason she felt both strangely at home, and a little trepidatious about what she might find inside.

She parked Unicorn at the edge of the front lawn, which was mostly weeds with one scraggily rose growing in a corner, and patted its fuel tank lightly as she hung the helmet off the handlebars. She crunched up the gravel path, past the old Honda, and up onto the creaking wooden porch. This had once had a nice screen all around it, but long ago the thing had turned brown and brittle and now hung in tatters. There was a rocking chair with a mildewed pillow on it, and the far end was filled with more boxes. A little porcelain pig with blue flowers painted on it stared up at her with blank eyes as she knocked gently on the door.

"Hello?" she called, when there was no immediate sign of life. "Mrs. Freeman?" She knocked again.

This time there was a clatter from inside, and a deeply southern voice swore colorfully. In spite of the gravity of her errand, Selene had to bite her lip to keep from grinning.

More clattering; heavy, uncertain footsteps, and some angry muttering. Then the door was jerked open, and Selene found herself face to face with a short, round, woman. Her dark face was heavily lined and there was a shock of gray in her wild, flyaway hair, but Selene thought she didn't look much older than fifty. Awfully young to be the grandmother of a nine-year-old. Then again, Selene's own mother had been nineteen when she was born. If both generations got started early enough, she figured, it could happen. It did.

"Mrs. Freeman?" she asked, and sniffed a little at the smell of alcohol that poured out around the woman. "I'm Selene Shields. I'm not ... well I'm no one official. But I'm here about what happened to your granddaughter. I'm here to ..." she trailed off, grappling for the right words, and eventually settled on the most honest ones she could find. "I'm here to help," she finished, a little lamely.

June Freeman stared at her, her wide eyes bloodshot and her nose running a little. She was wearing a plain, black dress, but even so Selene thought it looked dirty and disheveled.

Then the woman burst into hacking, dry sobs, and crumpled forward. Selene thought she would fall flat on her face, and rushed forward to catch the woman under the arms. Something hard clunked against her thigh, and she looked down to find the source of the fumes: a mostly empty bottle of George Dickel #12.

"All right, all right," she said soothingly, trying to maneuver the woman back into the house. It was difficult. She had collapsed with the weight of all her sorrow and despair as well as her natural, not insignificant body-weight, and Selene staggered a little as she half-carried the older woman inside.

The interior of the house smelled even more strongly of liquor, and after depositing the still-sobbing Mrs. Freeman in the nearest chair the first thing Selene did was to go around and open as many windows as she could find. In the process she disturbed a black cat who had been sleeping on the sill of one, and after initially objecting to Selene's presence, it began meowing pitifully and twining around her legs.

Selene put her hands on her hips and regarded the mess: the house was small and had the look of an ordinarily neat place recently gone to seed. There were dirty clothes on the floor, shoes everywhere, and empty booze bottles decorating nearly every flat surface, except where they'd been knocked on the floor when the cat had taken issue with them. Three weeks worth of mail was piled on the little coffee table, surrounded by more bottles, and there was an intermittent smell of cat pee. Glancing into the kitchen, Selene saw the sink was overflowing with dirty dishes, and there were pots on the stove that had something fuzzy and green growing in them. She sighed. Clearly, help of the more prosaic nature was needed, before they could get on to the business of avenging Cynthia Jefferson.

Going back to Mrs. Freeman, Selene found the woman had sobbed herself to sleep. Taking the bottle from the dry, limp fingers, she rinsed it out at the sink and refilled it with water, before jamming on a stray cap and setting it on the floor next to the unconscious woman. Then she went and found a plastic bag and a shovel, and hunted down the cat's litter box. It turned out to be tucked in beside the tiny stall shower in the bathroom, and was just as much of a disaster as the cat's actions had indicated it was.

The cat became very interested whenever Selene went into the filthy little kitchen, and she took the hint and discovered a barrel of dry cat food in the corner. She made a little pile of it on the cleanest bit of floor she could find, and while the cat ate (with happy purring and gobbling sounds) went and refilled the water dish that rested under the window.

She took down the sunflower-printed apron hanging on the wall, put it on, and pulled on the pair of rubber gloves hanging above the sink. Digging out a new sponge and a fresh bottle of detergent from the cupboard, she set to work washing dishes with a sigh.

The lumbering grumble of Arcana's engine sent the birds feasting in the blackberry bushes growing along the road up in a storm of flapping wings and small, dark bodies. Clara stopped the truck just outside an over-grown gate, chained shut, and hesitated for a moment, until Jill pointed out where the parking brake was.

"Thanks," Clara mumbled, giving Jill a grudging smile. Jill patted her arm reassuringly.

"Let's go for a walk in the woods," she said.

Clara stepped down from Arcana into soft, springy green grass, then reached back inside and retrieved her harness, sword and sheath and all. While she fastened the buckles, Jill crawled into the back and began pack-ing up what she called her "kit." This was a backpack that contained a set of small, glass bottles with metal caps, a case of eyedroppers, plastic sy-ringes, and a bag of livestock-grade hypodermic needles, each in its own sterile plastic sheath. There was also a packet of clean, lint-free cloths, a magnifying glass, a spiral-bound notebook with a pen tucked in the spine, a swiss army knife, a bottle of rubbing alcohol, and an old makeup case that had had the cosmetics scraped out and the little dishes filled with vari-ous kinds of powdered metal and minerals—which Jill had put together after a lengthy discussion with Selene. There was iron and salt, gold, sil-ver and copper leaf, as well as aluminum, titanium, and carbon—because Jill was curious how different elements would react to the various phe-nomena they encountered. There were a pair of cotton gloves, a brush, and a little palette. There was also a box of vinyl rubber gloves and some disposable face masks.

Jill refilled her water bottle from the cooler in the bed of the truck and slipped it into the side pouch of the pack, shrugged the whole thing onto her shoulders, and slapped a baseball cap on her head.

"Right," she said, coming around to join Clara, who was waiting pa-tiently by the gate. "Let's go!"

They climbed over the gate, one after the other, and forged off down the grassy track—which must have once been a road, but was so overgrown—trees encroaching from either side and a few saplings sprouting from the center—that it would have been impossible to get any vehicle that wasn't a bulldozer down it. Sunlight lay in warm patches, illuminating the road, but doing hardly anything to the forest on either side. The trees were closely packed, old oaks and walnuts mostly, with here and there the pale, peeling bark of a river birch showing through the mottled browns and greens.

It was a warm afternoon, the hum of insects filling the thick air of the road, while above them the branches rustled in a light breeze. The smell of earth and grass rose up out of the road and engulfed them, and despite the heat, Jill felt inexplicably complacent and comfortable. The only thing that kept her from forgetting their mission was the way Clara seemed even more on edge than usual. Though she had her sword sheathed, she nevertheless gave the impression of being armed. She was clearly on guard as she stalked down the disused road, peering suspiciously into the shadows, and occasionally reaching down to inspect the lower-hanging tree branches.

"See anything . . . odd?" Jill asked.

"Not yet," Clara admitted, but reservedly, as if she was expecting something odd to happen any minute.

But they walked for almost an hour and saw nothing more alarming than a small, dusky deer, which stared at them out of wide, white-ringed eyes, before bounding off into the forest. Eventually Jill grew tired, and when they came to a wide part of the road where a large maple grew close to the edge of the forest, spreading its leaves like a gentle curtain, Jill announced she needed a break. She let her pack slide off her back, and sat with relief, leaning against the maple's trunk, while she sipped water.

"We should not linger," Clara said, hovering nervously.

"Just give me a minute," Jill said, and offered Clara the water bottle. "It's important we don't get ourselves into trouble, trying to figure out what the trouble *is*."

Clara took the bottle and sipped from it, then handed it back. "That's exactly what I wish to avoid," she said, but she let Jill be.

Jill rested her head on the trunk of the maple and shut her eyes. She was feeling suddenly exhausted, the way you do when you sit down after a long walk in warm weather. She felt herself slowly sinking into slumber. In some part of her mind, she knew she had to get up and keep hiking. Whatever had got Cynthia Jefferson was still out there, probably in this very wood. But Clara was nearby, with her sword, and Jill was so, so sleepy . . .

Something rough and cool curled around her wrist, and Jill woke with a start. She tried to scream, but her breath was stopped as something equally cool and rough—and frighteningly strong—closed around her neck. She thrashed, panicking, and then Clara was there. Her sword flashed in the sunlight, and Jill had to squeeze her eyes shut.

Then there was a hard hand on her shoulder, fisted in her clothes, dragging her forward. There was still something wrapped tightly around her neck, and when Jill opened her eyes it was to see Clara pull a knife out of her boot, and come at her with it. She shut her eyes again and tried to hold still.

Something smooth and cold slid against her skin and she gasped, then heaved in relief as she realized she *could* gasp. Whatever had been around her neck was ripped away, and Jill fell to her knees, coughing, as she felt something warm and wet begin trickling down her chest. She hoped it wasn't her blood.

"Away from the trees!" Clara hissed in her ear, grabbing the front of Jill's shirt and dragging the smaller woman up and forward, squashing her against Clara's chest, while the other arm rose to brace Jill's shoulder, holding the sword up defensively.

Jill clung to Clara's wall-like body, shuddering, gasping, and coughing. It took a minute or so, but when no further attacks came, she pushed herself feebly away and felt gingerly at her neck.

The skin was sore and slightly abraded, but she felt no wound. Looking down, she saw her front had a long stripe of bright red blood, and at her feet was the source: a thick, gnarly, twisted tendril of tree root, slashed off at one end, and stabbed multiple times. For each break in the tough, brown bark, there was a swell of lurid red.

"What—" Jill gasped hoarsely. "What—"

"Stay," said Clara, gently lowering Jill to the ground and creeping over to the edge of the trees. Jill saw her backpack, still resting by the trunk of the maple, and made to reach for it.

"*I'll* get it," Clara snapped, and stretched out a hand for the pack, as though she expected the tree to bite her.

Suddenly it appeared the pack came to life, writhing, and then Jill saw this was because more tendrils of root had emerged from the forest, curling around the straps of the pack, dragging it off into the undergrowth just as Clara lunged for it.

"*Damn* it," Jill cursed, reaching up to straighten her glasses, and found there was another piece of root still clamped around her left wrist. It too had been neatly severed after only a couple circuits of her limb, and the point of amputation was an ugly red mess.

As the oxygen levels in her blood returned to normal, Jill's vision cleared, and with the diamond-hard focus of adrenaline she reached down and pried the root—it really *was* a tree root—off her wrist. She held it up and examined it carefully.

It *looked* like an ordinary tree root, except the wood inside was unusually soft and pliant—and still oozing blood.

"Clara," Jill said. "What is this?"

Clara was standing as close to the edge of the wood as she dared, peering into the dark. The roots had disappeared, taking the backpack with them, and now everything was still.

"*Clara*," Jill said, louder this time. "Talk to me."

"I don't know," Clara snapped, not turning around. "Possibly a dryad. Maybe even a green man. We should leave this place. We are not properly prepared."

"But it took my pack," Jill said, limply.

"We will replace your pack," Clara said, turning around at last and coming toward her. She'd managed to recover the water bottle, at least, and now this hung from one hand, while in her other she still held her sword. "Can you walk?" she asked.

"I think so," said Jill. She was beginning to feel dizzy, but she also knew that she couldn't stay here. The feeling of quiet complacency was gone, and suddenly the dark wood looked unfriendly and the sun was too hot. The insects buzzed around her, and she swatted at them uselessly.

Clara must have noticed the signs, for she handed Jill the bottle and then offered the woman her arm. Jill clung to it gratefully as they made their way back the way they had come.

Mother June's consciousness drifted to the surface of her hazy, alcohol-soaked mind. Her head ached and her mouth tasted of fermented leather, but there was an amazing smell drifting in from the kitchen.

For a moment this confused her, since Cynthia's culinary skills only went as far as scrambled eggs and toast. Then she remembered that Cynthia was dead and buried up on the old hill, and that by rights *no one* should be in her kitchen making *any* kind of smell.

She shot to her feet, grabbing for a bottle from her coffee table, only to find the thing swept clean—even the old beer stains had been wiped away.

"Rise and shine, grandma," said a lilting southern voice, like honey mixed with dark chocolate. The accent made her think of Arkansas—or maybe Georgia. It was hard to place.

Mother June whirled around, and beheld a complete stranger standing in her kitchen, wearing her apron, and flipping pancakes on the stove. There was a pile of fried bacon laid out on the plate nearby, and the kitchen seemed to have been attacked by an army of cleaning gnomes while she was out.

Mother June was beginning to feel the creeping presence of sobriety intruding on her hazy state, and she groped instinctively again for a bottle. Finding one on the floor she raised it to her lips and took a deep swig, swallowing half of it before she realized it was water.

The resulting spray reached all the way into the kitchen and hissed on the stove.

"Don't do that, grandma," said the woman in the kitchen. "It's good for you. Don't make me come over there and crack a raw egg into your mouth."

Letting the bottle drop to the floor in defeat, Mother June stared at the woman all over again.

She was a young woman. But then again everyone under forty looked young to Mother June, and this woman struck her as barely a woman at all, though realistically she was probably somewhere between twenty-five and thirty. She had long, fiercely curly black hair, tied back into a simple ponytail at the base of her neck. It flared out like an angry, frizzy bush over her shoulders. She was rather darker than Cynthia had been, and her eyes, though very black, were ever so slightly slanted. She had a graceful, round face, marred only by the dusting of acne scars over her forehead—but her whole presence was so composed and self assured that even these flaws looked more like intentional decorations. She was a little taller than most women Mother June had met, and though her body was lithe and athletic-looking, she wasn't exactly thin either. There was a substantialness about her legs and shoulders and around her midsection that hinted at powerful muscles lying low under a comfortable layer of padding. She was wearing a pair of ragged blue jeans and an olive tank top, and around her right wrist there was a strap of leather tied with a piece of string.

As Mother June watched, she took a spatula and expertly tossed a couple of golden-brown pancakes onto the plate next to the pile of bacon. She set this aside and ladled more batter into the pans, before grabbing a fork and knife from the drying rack and, setting the utensils one on either side of the pancakes and bacon, laid the whole arrangement in front of Mother June.

"Your milk was bad," she said apologetically. "And if you got any syrup I couldn't find it. But I fried them in the bacon grease, so they should be good. You go feed yourself, grandma. It's literally the least you can do for me."

Now her accent sounded more Louisianan, with maybe a hint of Texas. It rambled all over the South, and Mother June gave up trying to place her. She stared at the pancakes critically, as if she expected them to turn to ash any minute. It was what food had been doing to her lately, hence all the whiskey.

"What'd you do with my drink, girl?" she asked.

"Bottles rinsed and bagged," the intruder replied cheerfully. "If you got one o' them recycling centers nearby you might get fifty bucks for 'em. Always nice to turn trash into change, I say."

Mother June took a tentative bite of the nearest pancake. The woman might not have found her precious bottle of real maple syrup, but it still tasted too sweet. Too strong. She took a strip of bacon up between her fingers and ate it, letting the fried meat crunch satisfactorily between her teeth.

She *was* hungry, in a distant, shaky way, and when her stomach accepted the bacon without complaint she wrapped the next piece in the top pancake and took a small bite. All the while she kept glancing at the woman in her kitchen, who, after watching her eat for a moment, turned back to the stove and flipped the next batch of pancakes.

"You an angel?" she asked, doubtfully.

The woman laughed. She had a rich, deep laugh, like a guffaw, but there was a bitter undertone to it.

"Naw, grandma. No angel. Just me."

"You got a name?"

The woman raised an eyebrow at her. "I told you. It's Selene Shields." She forked a pancake off the stove, waved it through the air a couple times, and took a bite. "I'm here because of . . . well, like I said before, which you clearly don't remember, I'm here 'cause of your granddaughter. I'm here to help, I mean, in any way I can."

Mother June looked at her critically, but kept eating the pancakes. They were making her thirsty, and the only thing to drink was water. She took a grudging sip.

"You a friend of Shona's or what?" she asked.

Selene Shields blinked.

"Sorry," she said. "Who?"

"My girl, Shona," said Mother June. "One what dumped Cynthia on my doorstep when she were hardly outta diapers, and she takes off saying she's gonna get *cleaned up.* Only she never did. She probably out behind a Seven-Eleven somewhere, more messed up th'n me. But if you don't know then why you care?"

Selene Shields finished the pancake in one swallow and shrugged, licking her fingers. "It's just what I do, grandma," she said. "You want my help or what?"

"Depends," said Mother June, shrewdly. She chewed. "You gonna hunt down the swine-asses that killed my bae?"

Selene Shields nodded.

"You gon' make them pay?"

"As much as I can," the woman said, grimly. Mother June was struck by the fact that, although her skin was a pleasant, rich brown, her face looked thunderously black, like storm clouds. And for a moment, Mother June thought, maybe she'd heard wrong. Maybe this woman *was* an angel and she actually *could* avenge poor Cynthia. But the reality of the situation hung heavy on her shoulders, and she turned away.

"Ya can't help," she said, defeatedly. "I *know* what got my Cynthia, and it ain't nothing anyone short of an angel could touch."

There was a *click* and a *scrape* as Selene Shields turned off the burners on the stove and flipped the last pancakes onto another plate. "Maybe not," she said, casually. "But I won't know unless I try. Tell me what happened." She came around into Mother June's vision, pulling up a footstool so she could crouch, the plate of hot pancakes on her knees, across the table from her.

"You wouldn't b'lieve me," Mother June warned. "You'll think I'm a bat-nuts old lady. You kids, what grew up with the *inter-webs* and vid'yo games, you lost touch with what's *really* out there, and it ain't the stuff you see on the teevee, hon. It's worse than that."

When she looked up, Selene Shields was smiling at her, sadly. And though her face was young, her eyes looked so, so old and tired, it was like Mother June was looking into a mirror.

"I *know*, grandma," she said, softly, her hands gripping the edge of the plate. "I know."

And the thing was, she *did* know, Mother June realized, staring across at the woman with the face like storm clouds. Something stirred in her chest. Not hope—she was beyond the reach of any hope—but the despair hardened into something stronger, something hotter; a weaponized kind of sorrow with sharp edges, ready to spring out.

"If you're not an angel," Mother June said, "d'you b'lieve in them?"

Selene Shields grinned at her. "Don't have to, grandma," she said. "In my 'sperience, they're out there whether you believe in them or not. So go on, tell me what'cha got."

And, after a brief moment's thought, and somewhat to her own surprise, Mother June did.

Selene sat and listened to the old woman—who in all fairness actually *did* remind her of her own grandmother, what she could remember of that woman, anyway—as she began, haltingly at first and then gaining confidence when Selene nodded and listened patiently, to explain.

"First thing you gotta know," she said, picking up the whiskey bottle, then remembering it was water, and putting it down again. "First thing you gotta know: this town ain't s'posed to even *be* here. We got no reason t'be. Can't fish the river, can't log the wood, only one gas station and no dentists. Just a doctor and him on vacation more often than no. Everybody who could find work elsewhere did and left. Years ago. Some folks, they come here to die—that is, for their *retirement*. They think it's *pretty*." She laughed dryly. "But they's not rich themselves. So where's the money come from, then, that keeps the streets paved and the lights coming on and the water flowing? Who pays the drudges like me to keep this place lookin' so good? I tell you where," she said, before Selene could open her mouth. "It comes from the white boys' row. That's the one street what lies along the river. Three big white houses, all in a row, with three big white men a-living in them. Always been that way, s'long as I can remember. They pays for the roads, for the doctor and the baker. They hire me to come in and clean for them, since their wives either left or dead, and no kids to take care of 'em.

"They pay me, they pay the entire town. But no'n pays *them*. They just always gots the money. No'n knows where it comes from. No'n asks. No'n dumb enough *to* ask, because we all know where it really comes from."

She trailed off. Selene just raised her eyebrows. There was a soft, rumbling sound from around her feet, and she found the cat had come to twine around her ankles, looking intently at her plate. She put it down on the floor without a second thought.

"It comes ... from the *wood*," June Freeman said, raising a knobby finger significantly. "The *wood* keeps the town alive. That's why it's called *Live Wood*. Long time ago, some'n planted a tree—special kind of tree, from a special kind of seed—and they fed it on blood and bones, and the tree grew up big and strong, and it brought the wood with it. Now that tree's still a-livin' in the Live Wood, and it remembers the town, and it knows the people whose blood it sucked up all those years ago, and it looks after them. Thing is, this tree ain't like no other tree. This tree gets hungry, and no sunlight, no rain, no good, honest earth can feed it. So abouts every year, it takes a human, crunches them up under its roots, and eats them."

Selene felt her eyes widen. She'd heard of carnivorous trees before, of cursed trees, or even trees that weren't really trees, but enchanted people, but nothing quite like this before.

Still, that explained those recurring disappearances. She made a face.

"And that's what . . . ?" she began, not wanting to finish the question.

June Freeman raised her leathery hands and covered her face with them, her shoulders beginning to shake.

"I *tol'* her not to go through the wood," she said, her voice quavering. "I *tol'* her to take the river path. It's longer, sure, and it goes right behind white boys' row, but *anything's* better 'n the wood. Only the Jack O'Green can live in the wood . . . anyone else goes in . . . "

She crumpled backward into her chair, and Selene hesitated only slightly before reaching across and patting the woman's nearest arm. Then what the woman said caught up with her.

"Wait," she said. "You've got a *greenman* living here?"

"Not a greenman," June Freeman said, startled out of her grief. "Just old Jack O'Green. He lived in the wood, looks after the tree. Sees it fed. *He's* the one who took my Cynthia. But he stays in the wood, and I can't go in there. And them fancy detectives from St Louis don't believe me, don't even believe Jack O'Green exists. Say I'm imagining ghosts."

Selene froze. "You say there're cops here?" she asked, trying to keep the edge out of her voice.

"For a little while," June Freeman allowed. "They come around asking questions, all good and proper. But they know nothing. Ain't got no power. No knowledge. They'll be gone soon. Nothing they can do."

Well, *that* was a relief. Selene hated having to dance around cops when she was investigating a case. They nearly always suspected *she* was the problem, they got in the way—sometimes got themselves killed, too—and were never, ever any help.

"Right," she said, putting her hands on her knees. "You got any books on this town that might mention this tree? Anything more I could learn?"

"You could try the old library," June Freeman allowed. "Most of what I know is what my mama tol' *me*, years ago. But I heard they was pretty open about the tree in the beginning. You might find something."

"And what else did your mama tell you?" Selene asked, sweetly.

"Stay outta the wood," June Freeman repeated. "Tree is bad, *bad* news. Evil. Not meant to be fed blood. It got turned bad long ago and never got better. It hungry, always hungry. And it *everywhere* in the wood. Runs through the whole thing, like poison. Have to salt my fence line every year or it creeps in."

"Salt works on it?" Selene said, her head perking up. "That's good to know, *thanks.*" She got up, taking the empty plates with her, and rinsed them briskly in the sink. She left them to dry and put away the cooled pans, filled the bowl she'd used to mix the batter with water, then scrubbed it out. When she'd finished she took off the apron and pulled on her work shirt again.

"I'll go check the library," she said. "I think I passed it on the way here. I'll call, if I need your help again."

Then she was going out the door. A clatter from behind her announced June Freeman's pursuit, but she was almost to Unicorn before the woman poked her head out the front door.

"Hold up there, girl!" she shouted after Selene. "What'chu do with my *drink*?"

Selene glanced back, and grinned at her as she picked up the helmet. "You'll see me again!" she called, and pushed it onto her head.

June Freeman shouted something after her, but it was drowned out as Selene revved Unicorn's engine, and rolled away down the drive.

Maybe it was the adrenaline, or the shock, but it seemed to Jill that it was taking them longer to get out of the wood than it had to get in. The heaviness had left her senses, leaving them so sharp that she jumped at the smallest sound. She was painfully aware of the all the little rustlings in the undergrowth, and every slither of leaves jostled in the wind made her think of creeping tendrils, reaching out for her.

It was only natural that it would *feel* longer, now they knew what danger lurked here. Jill had had the fortitude to grip one of the severed pieces of prehensile root in her hand, but she was satisfied to stave off investigating it until they were (literally) out of the woods.

They walked, and walked, and Jill was beginning to feel a dull brick of dread settle in her gut when Clara tensed and looked around. It wasn't just *seeming* to take longer. It really *was* taking longer.

Clara stopped and took out her phone. She checked the time against the position of the sun, and frowned in a way Jill did not like at all.

"Don't tell me we're *lost*," she said, her voice still rather hoarse. "We *can't* have gotten lost. There were no turns!"

"This wood is stronger than I estimated," Clara said, grimly slipping her phone back into her pocket. "It has cut off my reception, and it is twisting space."

"Twisting . . . space?" Jill echoed weakly. Her mind immediately went to wormholes and science fiction spaceships that could travel outside of three-dimensional space.

"It is shifting the road," Clara said. "No matter where we go, we can only go where it wants us to."

"So . . ." Jill said, taking another sip of water. "How do we get out?"

Clara lowered and raised her shoulders. She seemed more resigned than alarmed. "We go where it wants us to, and do what needs to be done."

Jill groaned, but she followed Clara when the bigger woman resumed walking.

Now she thought about it, the track was definitely unfamiliar, and not just because the angle of the light had changed. They passed distinctly twisted trees she had no memory of, and the road seemed to be sloping gently down, with the branches growing higher and thicker above them. She stayed practically at Clara's elbow, glancing into the dark undergrowth suspiciously, but nothing tried to molest them.

They passed deeper and deeper into the wood, and the branches closed together above their heads, shutting out the sunlight. At first the cool shade was soothing, but soon a deep chill settled into Jill's bones, and she shivered.

"We are close now," Clara said. She had her sword out and ready, the other hand poised to either grab Jill or her knife, depending. The trees were thick and brown and hung with wreathes of lichen and moss, and there were crackings and cooings in the undergrowth that suggested the presence of birds.

Then the road turned a sharp corner and ended in a small clearing. A well-defined path led off from the far end, toward where they could just glimpse, through the shadowy trees, a truly enormous trunk of a dark, reddish color.

Crouched next to the path was a small cottage, half overgrown with grass and bushes, its thatched roof sprouting and the ridgeline bowed like the back of an old horse. Its mean little windows were boarded up, but the door was cracked ajar. Despite its dilapidation there were signs that someone lived there: a tin can with a lid over it that looked like it was used regularly sat next to the porch, and a long, polished walking cane rested against the wall. And beside the door, crumpled but still intact, was Jill's backpack.

Jill exclaimed, and Clara made to cautiously advance, but as they approached, the door was pulled open, and something very much like a man walked out.

That was to say, he *was* a man, but as overgrown and dilapidated as his house. His brown leather coat was worn and cracked, his hair was greasy and matted, and his skin was brown with dirt. His clothes appeared to once have been green, but years of wear with no washing had rendered them as brown as the trees around him. He sniffed, his wiry gray beard twitching, and then reached out and grabbed the nearby staff.

"'Bout time you showed up," he said, walking toward them purposefully. "Don't know what McCleaver's thinking, putting this off so long. But now you're here, just stand still, this won't hurt a—"

He stopped talking, for he'd nearly run right into the point of Clara's sword, which she'd raised the moment he began advancing.

"I am Clara Nordstern," Clara said calmly. "This is Jill Hamilton. We mean you no harm, and if you show us the way out we will leave peacefully."

The man seemed perplexed by this, and tried sidling around the tip of Clara's sword. It followed him, of course, and made a little jab when he tried to duck around it.

361

"That's not how this is s'posed to work," he said. He had an accent a little like Selene's Jill thought, only more gravelly and unkempt, like he didn't talk to people much.

"If you do not let us go," Clara said, her voice as cold and sharp as her sword. "I will have to cut you down."

The man laughed at that, coughing and spitting. It was an unsettling sight.

"Go'n and cut me down," he howled. "Tree raises me back up again, like she always do. I look after her, she looks after me. It's the deal, okay? The *old deal.*"

"Then I will cut down your tree," Clara said, blandly.

That made the man stop laughing all at once, which was almost as bad. He stared at them out of red-rimmed, furious eyes, and clasped both hands around his staff. It was a big staff, thick and heavy, but Jill still didn't like his chances against Clara and her sword. And since he was obviously human, this worried her.

"Clara, don't hurt—" she began, but the man had already raised his staff to attack them. In response Clara shifted her stance a little.

Violence, however, was averted by the sound of a car engine and the squeak of suspension as it bounced ponderously through the wood. It caused Clara and the man to stop what they were doing and look around for the source of the noise. That was when Jill noticed that there was *another* road leading to the cottage. This one was better cleared and had brown ruts where the tires of vehicles had once driven. As she watched, one of these vehicles—a shiny, red SUV—came bouncing along, branches brushing off its windshield and whipping along its sides.

It came to a stop at the edge of the clearing and, with a faint creak, the driver's door opened and a thick, pink, hairy leg stretched out. It was followed by a large, older man with well-groomed white hair, wearing a comfortable linen t-shirt and a pair of canvas shorts. He reached back into the truck and took a straw sunhat from the dash, which he put on before ambling toward them.

"See here, Jack, what's this all about?" he said, his voice rich and pleasant.

The wild man looked at him, wide-eyed, and then slowly lowered his staff. Clara shifted her stance again, but didn't move her sword. She was glaring at this new arrival, and it made Jill look at him twice. But there seemed nothing sinister about him; indeed, Jill felt a wave of relief at his arrival.

The man Jack mumbled something, and the new man shook his head.

"Don't be so impatient, Jack. Everything'll be just fine, now don't you worry. And stop scaring these nice ... uh ... *ladies.* I'm sure they're just lost, don't mean you no harm ... " he said this, even as he glanced questioningly at Clara's sword.

Clara didn't move; she seemed frozen, but Jill had the presence of mind to tuck the hand holding the severed piece of root behind her back as she stepped forward and said:

"You're right, sir, we *are* lost. I was looking for my backpack, when we must have gotten turned around. But it looks like *he* found it," she said, pointing with her free hand. "I'd just like it back, and then we'll leave."

"This true, Jack?" the new man asked.

Jack muttered something about "the wood brung it to me . . ." and the white-haired man laughed.

"You mean you did find it, good for you," said the man. "Well, why don't you give it back to the nice lady, and I'll take them off your hands."

Jack stared at the man with something like betrayal in his eyes. Then he threw down his staff and marched over to the cottage, where he grabbed the pack and slung it toward Jill. She dove for it, and while the men were occupied arguing with each other ("I can't keep her happy for much longer, she needs—" "I *know* what she needs, Jack, and I'm working on it. You just keep calm now, ya hear?") she hid behind Clara's legs and tucked the severed root into the largest pouch. By the time she got it stowed and the pack hung off her shoulders again, the white-haired man had walked Jack to the door of the cottage and was speaking to him in a low, soothing voice.

"Go ahead and make yourselves comfortable in my ride, ladies," he said, glancing over his shoulder at them. "I'll be along in a quick minute."

Jill looked at Clara, who gave one of her inverted shrugs. Jill decided she'd take her chances in the car, and walked over. The doors were unlocked, and she climbed gratefully into the back.

Clara, after sheathing her sword, stood outside, keeping an eye on the two men. She stayed that way until the white-haired man returned, and motioned her inside.

"After you," Clara said, blankly.

The man seemed a little surprised, but didn't take offense. He came around and climbed into the driver's seat, at which point Clara finally squeezed in beside Jill.

"Sorry about ol' Jack O'Green," the man said. "He's sort of a community project. Do the best we can for him, but some things . . . eh . . ." he shrugged expressively. "I'm Rafe McCleaver, by the way. Sorry I didn't introduce myself earlier, but . . . *well*. Where are you ladies coming from, if you don't mind my asking?"

"California," Jill replied, before Clara could stop her.

"Oh, road trip then?"

"Yes," said Jill, with perfect honesty.

"Bit dangerous for a couple of ladies, isn't it?" Rafe McCleaver said. "I mean, I see you take precautions," he added. His head twitched to glance at Clara in the rearview mirror.

"Haven't had any problems yet," Jill said, with slightly less honesty. "Except for that . . . uh . . . Jack O'Green. But it's no problem, really. Thanks for the ride."

"Just doing what I can," Rafe McCleaver said, jovially. "How long are you in River View for? You got a place to stay?"

Jill did not like the way he kept asking questions, though she supposed it was only to be expected. Judging from Clara's face, however, she guessed the less she told this man the better.

"Not sure," she said. "We're sort of playing it by ear." She smiled, trying to keep the nerves from showing.

"You take a tumble out there, missy?" he asked, with a little more interest than Jill thought was strictly necessary. She felt her skin prickle.

"Tripped on a root," she admitted. "It was embarrassing."

"I see," said the man, and Jill worried for a moment that he *did* see—see that she had red welts coming up around her neck in addition to the bruises and scrapes—but after that he changed the subject and began telling them about all the things they should see in River View, as if it were his own personal backyard, and he was showing it off. There were a surprising number of things, for a town so small.

Clara kept looking nervously out the window, but before Jill could start getting concerned they came out of the wood and met a wide, paved road. Checking her phone, Jill saw she had reception again, and that they were were only a little ways from where they'd parked Arcana.

"Our truck is out the road to the left, about half a mile," she said, and then held her breath to see which way Rafe McCleaver turned.

He turned left, and Jill let out a silent sigh of relief. Clara was just being paranoid.

When they reached the turnout where they'd left Arcana, however, Jill discovered their adventure was not over yet. In addition to the big, red truck, there was also a sleek, black sedan with a row of blue lights on top. Two men were standing outside it, facing each other across the roof, and broke off what seemed to be a heated debate when Rafe McCleaver pulled up.

For a moment, Jill thought she saw a crack in the man's jovial demeanor. He looked furious, frustrated, and a little disgusted. But it was only for an instant, and then he was saying, "Sorry about this, ladies, looks like some of our local problems are trying to disrupt your vacation." He put on the parking brake and hopped out, greeting the two men as cheerfully as he had Jack O'Green.

Jill slipped out immediately, followed by Clara, and together they went around to Arcana so Jill could stash the pack in the back seat. While they walked she couldn't help overhearing the conversation taking place among the three men, and what she heard made her hackles rise.

"Gentlemen, you're still here," Rafe McCleaver had said, the congeniality in his voice audibly strained. "I hope there haven't been any problems?"

"No problem," said one of the men. He looked young; tall, with luscious brown hair and neatly pressed pants, his cotton button-down was dark with sweat under the light blazer he wore, and Jill glimpsed a flash of silver at his belt before her view was cut off by the bulk of Arcana.

A detective, then? Had that internet petition worked, after all?

"We've just been . . . *discussing* . . . some of the particulars," said his partner. This one was significantly older; his hair was as white as Rafe McCleaver's, and he had a rather impressive mustache; it drooped down on either side of his clean-shaven chin, neatly trimmed and bushy on top. The man's skin was reddish from too much sun, and he had bright, crinkling blue eyes. He was leaning on the car, and as Jill came around from stowing her pack, she saw he was distinctly bowlegged.

"Nothing to concern you, sir," said the younger detective, mildly, shooting the older one a warning glance. "We should be out of your hair by tomorrow. Ladies," he said, touching his brow with a nod.

"Some outta-towners," Rafe McCleaver explained. "They got a bit turned around in our little wood, so I gave 'em a lift back."

"Yes," said Jill, rather too eagerly. "Thanks, by the way."

She found herself on the receiving end of two very different gazes. The one from the younger, brown-haired man was tired and bored. The one from his older partner, however, was sharp and keen and put her on edge. His face looked like it belonged to someone who'd seen some messed up stuff, and could smell wrongness like so much cow dung. The wrinkle in his nose suggested he smelled some now.

Jill had to fight against all her instincts in order *not* to give him her card. Partly because she didn't want Rafe McCleaver to realize she'd seen anything suspicious, and partly because she knew Selene would hit the roof if she found out Jill had talked to the cops.

But still, a girl was dead, and the last time someone had died, it had been the police who brought the case to *them*. It only seemed right.

Rafe McCleaver didn't seem willing to leave them alone with the detectives, however.

"I hope you won't disrupt their day any further," he said, looking earnestly at the younger detective.

The brown-haired man shrugged and rolled his eyes, then waved dismissively at Jill, but the older one must have seen something in her expression, because he ambled over, smiling slightly. He had, Jill thought, a nice smile, in a comfortable, worn-out sort of way.

"Jus' one second," he said, with such a heavy, relaxed Texas accent that Jill thought he could have walked right out of a movie. She glanced down compulsively and—yes—he was wearing cowboy boots.

"I'm sure you ladies have heard about the difficulty that happened here a while back," he said casually, thrusting his thumbs into his pockets. "Me and Detective Karl here, we been looking into it."

"*Have been* looking into it," Detective Karl said, tiredly.

"And I'd just like to take your contact information," the older man went on smoothly. "In case something turns up and I'd like to get your input."

"Oh, yes—of course," Jill said, trying to hide her relief. "I have a card, will that be okay? We haven't *seen* anything, of course," she added, for Rafe McCleaver's benefit. "We only just got into town today." She said this as she opened Arcana's driver's door, and leaned across to pull one of her contact cards out of the center cup-holder.

"Don't see why not," said the older detective with a shrug.

Jill passed him her card. She saw his eyebrows go up when he read her job description, and when he glanced at her she pursed her lips and rolled her eyes significantly in the direction of Rafe McCleaver. To her relief, the man smiled understandingly, and reached into his own pocket.

"Thank you, Miss Hamilton," he said. "And if you think of anything you'd want me to know, you just give me a call."

Jill found a sharp square of paper pressed into her hand, and she looked down to find the words "Detective Ronald J. Wilco, SLMPD" stamped under a fancy seal, with two phone numbers below that. She felt her own eyebrows rise, but decided to return Detective Wilco the favor he had paid her, and said nothing.

"Thanks," she said. "Yes, I will. I mean, if I think of anything. Which I probably won't." She laughed nervously, and felt for the doorframe of Arcana. Rafe McCleaver was giving her a considering look, and she wanted to leave before he decided on what he was going to say.

"Well, I think we're done here," said Detective Wilco, ambling back to his car. "Unless you want keep expounding upon my failings as a detective now you got a proper audience, Karl, I say we go find ourselves some dinner."

Detective Karl went a little red in the face, but nodded shortly and got into the car. Jill fairly scrambled into the driver's seat of Arcana, only to discover she had to adjust practically everything, since Clara had configured things such that she could barely reach the pedals. Clara watched her sympathetically from the passenger seat while she did so, then looked up sharply.

Rafe McCleaver had come to stand just outside her window, and was waving at them cheerfully. Jill started the ignition and rolled the window down, in lieu of opening her door.

"Yes?" she said, trying to smile as innocently as she could.

"Don't let them fancy city detectives scare ya," he said, his own smile looking rather forced. "River View is a safe place; we look after our folk."

"That's—that's nice," said Jill, her voice bright and fragile. "I mean, I can tell. *Thanks* for the ride, and all." She waved, rolled her window up, and started Arcana with a roar, backing out onto the road without bothering to adjust her mirrors.

"*Whew*," she said, once they were safely headed back to town. "*That* was creepy."

"It was interesting," remarked Clara. "It was a pity you gave him your card."

"No, no, *not* a pity," said Jill, trying to adjust her rearview mirror as she drove. "I'd *like* him to call. I think we might need some help on this one."

"You will only endanger—" Clara began sternly.

"A girl is *dead*," Jill said. "There will *be* law enforcement involved. Or there *should* be. And if what they discover is that she was killed by some weird, prehensile tree-monster, then . . . then . . . "

"Then what?" Clara asked, her voice unusually small and quiet.

"Then *good*," said Jill, surprising herself with her own vehemence. "People should *know* about these things. They should *know* that they are happening."

"Most people are not ready to know," Clara remarked.

"I don't give a *damn* if they're ready," Jill said, thumping the steering wheel in frustration. "*I* sure as hell wasn't ready. Ready or *not*, people should know. They should know so that they can understand and they can *do things* to prevent stuff like this."

Clara was silent. Jill simmered. After a while, the larger woman shifted in her seat.

"Selene called while we were in the wood," she said. "She left a message saying to meet her at the library. I think she may have found something."

"Great," said Jill. "Where's the library? We can *both* show and tell what we've found!"

The library turned out to be on a low hill overlooking the town surrounded by spreading oaks. Jill shivered at the sight, but was comforted when she saw Selene sitting on the steps outside, doing something on her phone. A moment later she spotted Unicorn, parked in the shade by the side of the building.

"They closed early today," she said by way of explanation as Jill and Clara approached. Then she saw Jill's neck, and her eyes widened. "What the hell happened to *you*?"

For answer, Jill reached into her pack and pulled out the piece of severed root. She tossed it to Selene, who caught it reflexively, then recoiled.

"Oooookay," she said. "I was gonna say, I think I know what's been killing folks all these years, but it looks like you've already been introduced."

"I think it is a corrupted wealth tree," Clara said.

"You're not far wrong," said Selene, peering closely at the root. "*Yyeep*, that's blood. Okay, so, why don't we take this somewhere private, and y'all can fill me in."

Since River View lacked a suitably anonymous motel they ended up settling for the cab of Arcana, parked in the shade outside the library. Clara and Jill related their adventure from the afternoon, and Selene filled them in on her visit to June Freeman.

"Suddenly I don't mind washing all those dishes," she said with a dry smile. "But I did manage to dig up some stuff at the library, and it makes even more sense considering what you found. They wouldn't let me take anything out, but I took lots of pictures." She brought out her phone and started thumbing through them. "Right, so the first disappearance I could find was in the year the town was founded, 1836. Says here it was a native girl—well, young woman—who'd married one of the white founders. They don't *call* her Native American, you understand, but I can tell that's what she was. Anyway, she goes missing, and then suddenly the town's fortunes pick up. There's gaps in some of the records, but someone disappears every summer—and I bet the years that don't have a record you could find one, if you looked for a missing person report from farther away. That's how I found the one for last year," she added, darkly. "Jordan Ames, who was on a road trip by herself. Took a wrong turn coming out of Hawk Point and was never seen again."

Jill thought of what Rafe McCleaver had said to her and Clara, and suppressed a shiver.

"All this," Selene went on, "is from the official records. As for what's been squatting in that wood, well, I had to range a bit farther afield. Here, this is from *Local Myths of the Cuiver River,* which is about the most disgusting, whitewashed collection of tales I've ever seen, but it's got one about Live Wood that was *very* interesting. Dunno if you can read it."

Jill took Selene's phone and squinted at the screen. By enlarging the picture she was able to make out the words, but they were blurry, and it was hard to keep track as she scrolled through the picture.

"Don't worry, I remember most of it," Selene said. "Basically, it was just what June Freeman told me. Supposedly the family that founded River View brought with them this special tree from the *old country*—wherever that was. Sounds like they carted a sapling over with them and planted it in what was then an open field. Now, this is where it gets *weird*. According to the story, they mulched it with blood. From their livestock, *supposedly*, and according to the myth the tree repaid them with wealth, and the town sprang up around their homestead. There's no date on this story, but I bet this coincided with the disappearance of that native girl."

Jill frowned, and Clara sucked in a breath.

"It's a *blutra*," she whispered.

"A what?" said Jill.

"She means a *blood tree*," said Selene, tiredly. "It's sort of a loose definition, but basically it works like this: there are trees, magic ones, which can provide an area with protection, good fortune, that sort of thing. Any story you've heard about a magic forest with a special tree in the middle, that's one of those trees. They crop up in mythologies from all over the world. Here's the thing: sometimes, what people did, was to feed them blood. They'd sacrifice animals—sometimes humans—at the base of the tree, and leave the body to decompose at its roots. Sometimes they'd even *bury* the body there. The tree absorbs the blood, and gets special powers. It protects the people who feed it in ways trees—even *magic* ones—don't normally do. Thing is, trees like this, they get hungry. They keep needing more blood, or... well, or bad things happen. Like grabbing random people who get too close."

"But that wood," Jill said, trying to wrap her mind around the events of the afternoon. "It . . . *moved* around. We couldn't get out. And those roots, they must have stretched at least a *mile* from where we met Jack O'Green."

Selene nodded. "That's what I mean; *special powers.* I think this one's also driving the economy of River View, such as it is."

"So what you're saying is, people here have been sacrificing *humans* to this magic tree for over *a hundred years*, and in return it's been keeping the town alive?" Jill asked incredulously.

"That's about the size of it," Selene said.

Jill frowned. "Do you have, like, a *list* of the known victims?" she asked.

Selene smiled. "I thought you'd might want that," she said, and pulled up a note on her phone, handing it to Jill.

Taking the little device, Jill frowned at the list of names, then handed it to Clara.

"Notice something odd?" she asked.

Clara, peering at the list, wrinkled her forehead. "They are all women," she stated, blankly.

"*Yes*," said Jill. "But more than that: notice how they're mostly listed as *missing*?"

"Yeah, but it's pretty obvious they're dead," Selene said.

"I know, that's not the point," said Jill, snatching the phone back. "What's odd is that Cynthia Jefferson's *not* missing. Her body was found in the *river*."

Silence fell in the truck's cab. It was a big cab, but with Clara looming in the back seat, it suddenly felt stifling. Then Selene shrugged.

"Tree couldda rejected her," she said. "It happens. Which would explain why it went after you—it still needs a body for this year."

"And why Jack O'Green was trying to capture us," said Clara disdainfully. "He is clearly the tree's keeper."

"I wonder how old he really is," Selene mused. "From the way June Freeman talked, he's been there all her life, and she ain't no spring chick."

"So . . . what do we do?" Jill asked. She was feeling a little queasy. While the physiology behind a tree that drank blood and grew prehensile roots and could manipulate space-time was a fascinating prospect, she found she had no desire to go back into the wood, and would have been satisfied to let Clara and Selene deal with it, and then pick through whatever was left.

"I believe Rafe McCleaver is involved as well," Clara said. "He sounds like one of the men June Freeman told you about."

"Yeah, what live in the houses built over where the first homestead was," said Selene. "We'll have to go carefully here. Spend the night making a game plan, and move in sharp tomorrow morning. If that tree is still waiting on its body for this year, we don't got a lot of time."

They spent the night camped out beside the river in an abandoned field which Clara announced was perfect for a circle of protection. While she set it up, Selene sat in the back of Arcana, rolling some very interesting slugs. She also brought out a pair of hatchets from her weapons case, and sharpened them dutifully. Torn between which one to watch, Jill set herself up in the back of Arcana, opposite Selene, alternately glancing between the two women. As such, it was she who first noticed the white-haired figure ambling toward them from the direction of the town.

For a horrible moment she thought it was Rafe McCleaver, until she recognized the bowlegged gait, and let out a sigh of relief. Then realized Selene was still holding one of her axes.

"You might want to put that away," Jill suggested. "Casually. Like it's no big deal."

Selene looked up, and her eyes widened as she took Jill's meaning. She calmly tossed the hatchet back into her trunk, stretched extravagantly, and then kicked the lid closed and turned around. She turned back immediately and swore under her breath.

"Don't tell me—" she began.

"Hello, Detective," Jill called, hopping down from Arcana to go intercept the man, and hopefully give Selene enough time to hide the rest of her arsenal. "How can I help you?"

Detective Wilco was wearing tinted, aviator-style glasses, but he took these off and nodded to Jill as he drew closer.

"You don't care for the two-bit B and B over on Main, then?" he asked casually, glancing at Arcana. "Can't say I blame ya," he added. "The department sent me and the boy wonder there as a matter o' course, but I'd just as soon camp out in the back seat of the cruiser than spend another night there, to be honest. The beds are so soft they feel like they're tryin' to eat'cha, and the food is too good."

"Oh," said Jill in a small voice. "*Too* good?"

"Feels like they're fattening you up for something. Or maybe they're slipping poison in it." The old man gave her a grin, but with a sideways, clever slant that made it seem like he was evaluating her based on her reaction.

Jill thought carefully, and then said: "I don't quite feel safe here; I'm not sure who I can trust."

Detective Wilco nodded understandingly. "I can agree with you there. Knew there was something fishy goin' on, but my boy Karl, he's a very by-the-book sort of fellow. Fresh out of school. He's convinced some drifter killed that girl, based on some psych analysis he read last month, but in thirty years a man learns to trust his nose, if you know what I mean, and my nose tells me there's something rotten here."

Jill swallowed around the lump of nerves in her throat. She was acutely aware of Clara, who'd finished her protection circle, glaring at her from the far side of Unicorn. She was also certain that Selene would be livid if she brought this man into their confidence.

And perhaps that was the wrong thing to do, but Jill was finding the more she listened to him talk the more she *liked* Detective Wilco. He reminded her of a wrinkly old dog, stubborn but good-hearted. Most of all he seemed a man not easily deterred, and his instincts *were* on the right track, after all. She took a deep breath.

"What Rafe McCleaver told you earlier, it's not strictly the truth," she said.

"Oh, isn't it now?" said Detective Wilco, smiling in a way that showed he was not surprised at all. "And something tells me he didn't know it wasn't strictly the truth."

Jill shrugged. "I think ... that is, *we* think he was involved in the murder of Cynthia Jefferson."

The detective put his head on one side and regarded Jill thoughtfully. "If ya don't mind my asking," he said. "Just who are you, who is thinking such things?"

Jill looked at him blankly. "You've seen my card," she said.

"Yee-ah," came the reply. "And I talked to your Professor Okedo. Nice man, very patient. Still don't explain why you're running your own personal Sherlock Homes investigation here."

"I suppose, technically, we're *not* investigating a murder," she allowed. "Just the cause of it."

Detective Wilco raised both his bushy white eyebrows. "That's a mighty fine distinction," he said.

"Yes, well ... " Jill looked around. Selene was shaking her head, but Clara only rolled her eyes. She decided to take a chance. "Detective Wilco, there's something I need to show you. And I feel I should tell you what really happened in the wood today."

Selene and Clara sat side by side on the locker behind Arcana's cab, staring down to the tailgate where Jill was calmly laying out the twisted root she'd brought back from the wood, and telling the grizzled detective all about their day.

"He has seen nothing," Clara said softly. "He won't believe her."

"He's a menace, he is," said Selene. "His sort always are."

"He's a detective, not a cop," Clara pointed out.

"Same thing, really. Full of themselves men who wanted to grow up to be bullies," Selene said bitterly. "You watch. He's gonna get the wrong end of the stick and think *we're* the ones to blame. That's how it goes, every damn time."

Clara thought about it.

"Not every time," she allowed.

"Yeah, but *enough* of the time," Selene muttered darkly.

Clara's face crumpled a little.

"Yes," she sighed, leaning back against Arcana's rear window. "It happens enough."

Jill, meanwhile, was warming to her subject, beginning to gesticulate excitedly, when Detective Wilco raised his own hands to stop her.

"Thank you, Miss Hamilton, I think I've heard enough," he said.

"Don't feel like you need to *believe* what I'm saying," Jill said, immediately. "Just . . . *look* at the facts. Look at the *evidence*."

"Honestly, all I see here is a funny-lookin' root with some brown goop in it. Could be anything's blood."

"It's got *veins—*" Jill protested, but Detective Wilco spread a palm in her face to keep her quiet.

"Point is, this don't help me," he said. "Now, you bring me some solid evidence implicating Rafe McCleaver, and that I can do something with."

Jill looked beseechingly at Selene.

"Can you tell him what June Freeman told you? You know, about the economy of River View and all?"

Selene pursed her lips.

"Hold on," said the detective, really looking at her for the first time. "You got something out of that Freeman . . . woman?" he finished, almost defiantly.

"Yeah," said Selene, jutting her chin out. "What's it to you?"

"Lady, I spent the better part of my first day here tryin' to get some sense outta that woman, but all I got was a bunch of sobbing and second-hand alcohol fumes. How'd you get one coherent sentence?"

Selene scratched behind her ear, sucked a wad of snot up her nose, coughed it back up, and then spat it over the side of Arcana. "Maybe I asked nicely," was all she said.

"Selene . . ." Jill said, torn between a plea and a threat.

"Look—how am I s'posed to know he's actually gonna help us?" Selene asked, gesturing at Detective Wilco. "Last time I checked, the law enforcement was more interesting in confiscating your beloved samples than actually solving a crime!"

Detective Wilco coughed.

"Now see here," he began, then caught the look Selene shot at him. He paused, visibly re-calculated what words he should use, and then started over. "If you'll just let me have a moment," he said. "I am not interested in whatever hokey-dangle you ladies are into. I knew some Neo-Pagans back in Austin who, maybe they got a little doo-lally come midsummer, they had their heads on straighter than most of my Sunday neighbors. We all got a little bit o' crazy in us, and s'long as we keep that line between what is and what's not drawn clear in the sand, I don't see why we can't get along. I don't know what your past experience is," he nodded at Selene. "But I can promise you my number one concern is finding out who killed Cynthia Jefferson, and bringing him to justice."

Selene stared at him, disbelieving. In the ensuing silence, Jill murmured: "*Could* be a woman . . . "

Detective Wilco turned to her, putting a hand on his belt. "You know," he said conversationally. "In all the years I've been catching killers, not one of them were female? You can rake me over the coals if I'm wrong, but I like my odds on this one."

Selene chewed her lower lip.

"According to June Freeman, and as far as we can tell from independent research," Clara said, speaking slowly and cautiously, "River View subsists on the money of three individuals: Lyle Richmond, William Ashcroft, and Rafe McCleaver. These men have no known profession or independent means of income. We believe they derive their wealth from a god-tree that they have been feeding human sacrifices to for the last century or more. That is why they killed Cynthia Jefferson."

Selene put her face in her hands.

Detective Wilco, after gazing wide-eyed at Clara for a moment, put his head on one side and stretched his mouth down at the corners.

"Well," he said, a little at a loss. "Well that is . . . it *sounds* like complete hokum. A *god-tree*, you say? Like one o' them ladies what wears willow bark and dances around?"

"Those are dryads," Clara informed him, stoically. "And they do not *wear* bark. It is their skin."

"Right, right," said the detective, raising his hands defensively.

"This is something different," Jill said, and held up the piece of root significantly.

Detective Wilco gave her a tired look. He seemed ready to slouch off in a huff, and Selene held her breath in anticipation. Then Jill ruined it.

"Look, even if you don't accept that there's a magic tree in the middle of Live Wood making all this happen, you must have noticed all the other people who've gone missing throughout this town's history. *Even if* you take out the supernatural element, it's not hard to imagine a group of heavily delusional people who've been systematically killing folks every year. You're not just dealing with one madman or even a serial killer—this is *traditionalized* homicide."

Detective Wilco gazed at Jill thoughtfully for a moment. Then he shrugged to himself.

"And you think these three—Rafe McCleaver and his boys—are at the heart of it?"

"It seems highly likely," Jill said.

Detective Wilco nodded. "And he caught you poking around in his wood."

"Yes, but I didn't tell him anything," Jill said.

"Right," said the detective. He raised his head and sniffed the air—moist and cool, now that the sun had gone down. The mosquitoes were rising, and in the distance was a clamor of birds settling down for the evening. "You know," he said. "I think I will camp out in my car tonight. Right here, if you don't mind. Which I hope you don't. It'd be for your own protection."

Clara pursed her lips, and Selene rolled her eyes. Jill just smiled tightly and said, "Whatever makes you feel comfortable, detective."

True to his word, Detective Wilco fetched his car, driving it cautiously over the spongy ground, to park it a tactful ten or so feet away from Arcana. Clara had to go back and fix the part of the circle he'd run over, but she seemed satisfied when she returned.

"I will take first watch," she announced, and Selene agreed gratefully. She unrolled her pad in the bed of Arcana and pulled over her duffle bag for a pillow, while Jill curled up across the back seat of Arcana's cab. It was not her favorite bed, but she didn't envy Clara and Selene out at the mercy of the insects. She was enchanted, however, to see the fireflies winking in and out of sight, their glowing yellow bodies dancing in the gathering dark, and she spent a long time gazing at them through Arcana's windows. Everything seemed so beautiful and peaceful, and such a long way from her scare in the wood. With Selene and Clara near to hand, not to mention the detective, Jill felt confident that nothing bad would happen that night.

In a very limited, technical sense, Jill was absolutely right. Something bad *did* happen, but not to them. It was a close thing, though.

Around two in the morning, when Selene and Clara were changing shifts, something stirred in the grass beyond the protection circle. It could have been the wind, except there was none. It could have been a wild animal, too, but it sounded too big. Stare as she might, Clara could glimpse nothing.

When Selene woke up she heard it too, and got out her flashlight. Its beam illuminated the stalks of still grass, and beyond them the indistinct shapes of trees.

Then the noise came again, but all the light caught was a patch of grass where the seed-heads were bobbing gently.

"Something is out there," Clara said.

It was at this point that the shining beam roused Detective Wilco, who was understandably grumpy, but at the same time seemed to take it as his gentlemanly duty to investigate.

"Everything's fine," said Selene, switching off her flashlight. "Prob'ly nothing. Imma stay up a bit anyhow. No big."

Detective Wilco collapsed back into his car gratefully, and Selene took over the watch. Lying in the bed of the truck, however, Clara still caught the sound of whispers in the grass—whispers that seemed to be moving in a counter-clockwise circle around them. And there was a smell, faint but distinct, of old dirt and must and something sour. It was the smell of death, Clara realized.

She didn't get much sleep that night, drifting off only when a gray glow began to spread from the eastern horizon.

She woke again, after what must have been at least an hour, to the sound of Detective Wilco's voice, talking on the phone and sounding progressively more frustrated.

" . . . and pick up yer god-damned *phone* you green-horned son of a b—" the last words were bitten off when the speaker looked up and perceived both Selene and Clara's bleary faces peering at him from the back of Arcana.

"My rookie of a partner isn't answering his phone," the detective explained apologetically. "Which ain't normal fer him—unless he's givin' me the cold shoulder 'cause I took off with our ride. You ladies sleep well?"

Clara's attention had already moved on, and she was scanning the field around them. It appeared undisturbed, but she longed to go and hunt for tracks. Under cover of needing to relieve herself she went and checked the boundary line, and noted with grim satisfaction that it was scorched black—burned into the soft earth—with a line of yellow grass on either side.

Something *had* been out there last night. It had been strong enough to test her circle, but not strong enough to pierce it. That, or it had decided it was simply not worth the effort. She'd have to double ring them tonight, and maybe even salt the earth as well, to be safe.

In the distance behind her, the detective's phone rang. His amiable, cracked voice answered, and then abruptly changed tone. The change made Clara turn her attention away from her spent circle and back to the man by the sedan.

"Ol' right Mrs. Hanson, you just take a deep breath and explain things nice and slow," he was saying, but his voice was pinched and worried, not soothing. Clara edged closer, angling so she could see his face.

"You said what? How? *When?* Don't *move*, Mrs. Hanson. Don't move, and don't you dare call anybody else, I'm on my way."

"Something wrong?" Jill asked, poking her head out of Arcana's back passenger seat.

Detective Wilco looked up from his phone, and Clara saw his face was white, his pupils dilated, and his breathing had gone ragged. He looked to the sky, then back down to Jill, then back up at the sky again.

"I gotta run, ladies. Take care of yourselves. Don't get into trouble."

He was climbing into his car as he spoke, but Clara could see how his hand was shaking as he pulled the door shut. She exchanged a look with Selene, and the two women nodded at one another.

"I'll tail him," Clara said, as the sedan made deep brown tracks leaving the field.

She left Selene to explain the situation to Jill, and shoved on her helmet, not bothering with the snap as she threw a leg over Unicorn's back and followed in the wake of the detective's car.

This was easy enough, even after she hit the paved road. Such was the nature of the landscape that Clara could glimpse the car as it turned down a distant road, and she made an educated guess as to its destination. Sure enough, when she reached the tall, green house with "Hanson's B&B" on an artistic sign at the head of the drive, there was the dark sedan, parked sideways across it.

Coming to a stop beside the sign, Clara fished out her phone and called Selene.

"Y'ello, sister," came the immediate reply.

"It's the B and B," Clara told her. "Something's happened. Not sure what yet. I'm going in."

"We'll be there in five," said Selene. "Jill says to take pictures."

Clara grunted and cut the call. If the *something* that had happened was at all related to the *something* they'd heard last night, she seriously doubted anyone would want to look at pictures of it.

The moments after a catastrophe was discovered were usually the best ones in which to get a look at it. While people were still shocked and panicked, and before the first responders and law enforcement arrived. Though, Clara supposed, law enforcement was already *here* in the form of Detective Wilco, but judging by his reaction in the field, she guessed he wouldn't be the best representation of overbearing rationality.

The door opened under her gloved hand, and she entered a bright, clean hall crowded with wooden cabinets displaying china dolls. An ornate guestbook lay open on one, surrounded by an apple-cheeked milkmaid and a little herd of black-and-white cows. To one side was a dining room, the table laid for breakfast, and to the other a parlor with a glass-top coffee table and several overstuffed chairs. Straight ahead were a flight of stairs, and Clara made for them with a purpose. Arriving at the first landing she heard voices from up ahead, and saw the first clue to the nature of the disaster:

A bullet had come clean through the plaster wall and burrowed down the polished wooden banister, coming to a halt just as it exited. It gleamed in the morning sun streaming in through the open door, and Clara noted its presence before she went to the doorway and peered inside.

Detective Wilco was there, leaning shakily against the wall, while across from him, a round, gray-haired woman sat huddled in a wicker chair, shaking and sobbing.

In between them, lying flat out on the floor, his lifeless eyes gazing up at the ceiling, was the body of the younger detective they had met the day before. Clara recognized his shiny brown hair and square face, but not the expression on it: that of fear, horror, and utter shock.

He was dressed in a sleeveless cotton shirt and a pair of comfortable-looking sweatpants, his bare feet protruding from the ends. His hands were thrown up, the gun that had no doubt fired the bullet Clara had passed in the hall still held between the stiff fingers of his right hand.

He'd been killed by a single blow to his chest: a deep gash that had cleaved right through his sternum and into his heart. His entire midsection was a mess of brown and red, and the glimmering blood lay in a pool around him. Clara could see the horrified face of Detective Wilco reflected in it.

Whether the detective saw her, or merely sensed her presence out of the corner of his eye, he suddenly looked up and glared at her.

"I'm sorry miss . . . sorry. You can't be here," he said.

Clara ignored him. She crossed the pool of blood and body in one stride, and came to stand beside the bed. This had clearly been slept in, and it looked as though Detective Karl had gotten violently out of it, throwing the blankets aside. Turning to the window Clara found, to her satisfaction, a pair of gashes on the sill, and the glass of the lower pane shattered. There were no signs of blood, and a quick inspection turned up no shreds of cloth or other evidence. There was a smell, however, lingering on the edge of perception: something like old dirt and musty caverns, with a sour undertone. Clara felt her nostrils flare at the scent, and she bent to look closer.

Something pale gold glimmered in the sun, and Clara pulled off a glove with her teeth before teasing it out between her finger and thumb.

It was a hair, crinkly and curled, that shimmered gold and silver in the light. Running it between her fingers, Clara felt it fizz gently against her skin. Anyone else might have put it down to static electricity, but in Clara it sparked a sympathetic response, making her own skin feel alight with power, her tattoos standing out like cold spots against the warm glow.

Suddenly she understood Jill's insistence on bringing sample containers everywhere. She turned around, and found Detective Wilco gazing at her across the grisly remains of his partner.

Clara, for all she felt a strange disassociation from the mundane world, could sympathize with what he was going through. It didn't mean she had the faintest idea of what to say.

"This was not meant to happen," she tried.

"Oh, you *think* so?" the man said.

By the wall, the woman who Clara surmised was Mrs. Hanson whimpered.

"I believe it was you who were meant to be killed," Clara said.

Detective Wilco just stared at her, speechless. She took the opportunity to cross the room and took out her phone.

"You would be wise to leave River View," she said, though she knew the advice was likely falling on deaf ears. "Leave this to us. But if you require assistance laying your partner to rest . . . " she paused, and realized she had no idea how to figure out what her number was. She had Jill and Selene's saved under their respective names, Flammard and Lalai's landline, and the last known contact number for the Isenfausts, but not *her own.* She'd never needed it before.

"Jill Hamilton has my number," she finished. She raised her phone and snapped a picture of the scene, then put it away and walked out into the hall.

She made it halfway down the stairs before the detective called her back. She paused, looking up at him.

"You can't leave," he said, sounding like he was reading from an internal script. "You've disturbed a crime scene. You have to . . . " he trailed off, the script clearly evaporating.

Clara felt for him.

"Leave River View, detective," she said, trying to sound kind. "What is here is beyond you. Let us handle it." She turned and finished descending the stairs, leaving Detective Wilco at the top of them.

Coming out into the sun, she went around the house until she could look up at Detective Karl's window. It was easily thirty feet up, and there were no additional signs of someone having climbed the side of the building.

Except . . . except there *was* a sign on the soft green lawn some ten feet away. Two deep impressions, as if from a pair of feet, and then a few shallower ones, which faded into nothing in the direction of a line of trees that marked the border of the property. Clara didn't bother following them; she knew they would disappear into nothing but the smell of death.

She went and stood over the two deepest impressions, which still held the rough shape of feet. Placing one of her own alongside, she was interested to note that they were almost as big as hers. Turning to gaze back up at the window, she calculated their owner must have taken the shortest route possible down.

Someone tall, but relatively light, then. Someone who was strong enough to drive an axe through a grown man's sternum in one strike, and land a jump from thirty feet.

Anyone else might have assumed this person to be male, in addition to whatever supernatural abilities they possessed, but Clara knew of three people who could perform such feats, and they were all female, and so she found herself thinking of this person as female by association.

But of those women, one of them was herself, and the other two were her closest female relations. So there was now a fourth in the world. And, Clara realized with a shiver, she would probably have to fight her.

The rumble of Arcana's engine raised her from contemplation of impending battle, and she left the prints to meet Jill and Selene down by the gate.

In brief words, she explained what had happened.

"Holy crap," said Jill in a small voice, as Selene let out a low whistle.

"I took a picture," Clara offered, but Jill raised a hand.

"Actually, that's okay," she said. "Just tell me how did he—I mean, is this related to the blood tree and all?"

"Probably," said Clara. "Though I doubt it was the tree itself. More likely it was an agent of some sort."

"Like the Jack O'Green you met yesterday?" Selene suggested, to which Clara gave one of her inverted shrugs.

"I don't suppose you found any evidence?" Jill asked.

For the first time that day, Clara felt a spark of pride flare in her chest, and she held up the bare hand in which she still grasped the curling golden hair.

Jill blinked at it, adjusted her glasses, and blinked again.

"It was in the window, which was broken," Clara offered.

"Nice catch," Selene said.

Jill, who'd taken the hair between two hands, now spared one to reach into her pocket for a vial. Winding the hair tightly around her pinky, she nudged it carefully into the little container.

"Looks pretty normal to me," she said. "You sure we shouldn't leave this one to the police? I mean, Wilco's already here."

"If I were him," Selene mused, "I wouldn't *want* to handle this one. But I s'pose he'll call in reinforcements now."

"If he is wise," Clara said, "he will leave."

"Yeah but that's no guarantee he *will*," Selene pointed out.

As if on cue, Detective Wilco came out the front door and ordered them off the property.

"If it weren't for the fact that I *know* where you three were last night," he said, his face flushed and red, "I'd arrest the lot of you. Out, out, *out*. And you, give me what you took from the window up there." This last was directed at Clara, who spread her hands innocently.

"Just a cobweb," she said.

Detective Wilco let out a low growl, then shouted: *"Out!"*

They left. Clara called as soon as they were moving, and told them about the prints she had found.

"So . . . what's our next move?" Jill asked.

Silence from both ends of the phone. Then beside her, Selene said: "No sense waiting for more dead bodies to show up. If it were up to me, I'd go in and torch that tree. Now."

"Agreed," said Clara.

"And if Rafe McCleaver shows up?" Jill asked, nervously.

"I'll handle him," came Clara's voice, cold and emotionless.

Jill was not comforted.

But Rafe McCleaver was not in the wood. He was in his house—his basement, to be precise—and the pair of women he'd escorted out of the wood the day before were the last things on his mind.

"What part of my order did I not make perfectly clear?" he asked, trying to keep a hold on his temper. "I needed those detectives gone *yesterday*. They're interfering with your mission—*my* mission—and I need them gone. *Especially* the older one—Wilco."

"Your orders were transparent," came the reply from a shadowy corner, where a human-like shape sat cross-legged on an overturned wooden crate. "I was simply unable to carry them out in their entirety."

"What . . ." said Rafe McCleaver, and stopped to rub his temples. When he was calmer, he tried again: "What stopped you? You didn't have any problems killing that greenhorn Karl . . . "

"Detective Wilco was not in the specified location," came the ice-cold reply.

"So you wrote him off because he wasn't where I *expected* him to be?" Rafe McCleaver growled.

"No, I surmised you would wish me to hunt him down. I did so. Detective Wilco passed the night in a field by the river, inside a circle of protection that I did not have the power to break."

"A circle of . . . *what* now?" Rafe McCleaver said, trying to keep the squawk out of his voice.

"Protection. Old magic. Powerful magic. It was well-laid and would have required considerable energy on my part in order to break it."

"But you *could* break it?"

The shadow was silent. "If you wished it so," it said after a time.

"Then get back out there tonight, and finish the job *properly*," said Rafe McCleaver.

"That is what you wish?"

"It is!" Rafe McCleaver resisted the urge to stomp his foot like an angry child.

There was a shiver in the dark, like a shadow nodding its head.

"Understood," it said in a stony voice.

It was nearing midday by the time they reentered the wood, using the same road Rafe McCleaver had when he'd picked up Jill and Clara. The latter rode in front now, like a vanguard, into the green shadows of the wood. Jill drove Arcana, while beside her Selene rode with the window down, her shotgun Freddie resting in her lap. She'd spent the remainder of the morning rolling very specific slugs for him, and Clara had woven them strange little totems out of grass. One hung from Arcana's rearview mirror, while the other was fastened to Unicorn's saddlebags.

"They're like portable protection circles," Clara had explained. "Not as powerful, but they will help us reach the tree."

They must have been powerful enough, for it wasn't long before they came to the end of the road and the clearing where Jack O'Green's cottage sat. There was no sign of the other road, the road that Jill and Clara had taken the day before, but the ground in front of the cottage was well worn with tire tracks.

There was also a mound of fresh earth near the edge of the clearing, which Jill was sure had not been there last time, and she felt her stomach tighten as she saw the door to the cottage was cracked open. It looked like it had been torn off its hinges and then propped back up against the frame.

Clara noticed as well. She parked and dismounted from her bike in one smooth motion, drawing her sword and walking the perimeter of the clearing, covered by Selene from the open window of Arcana, before she allowed them to get out.

Selene and Clara then went over to the cottage, and Clara lifted the door aside while Selene waited, and then whipped herself in, her shotgun at the ready.

It was dark in the cottage and smelled of mold and decaying plants. Dirt was caked on the floor, and only the boards on the windows had prevented the forest from taking root inside as well as out. Selene tore them down as she moved through the little structure—the rotting wood coming away easily in her hands—letting in the filtered sunlight from outside.

Despite the general mess, signs of a struggle were obvious: a moth-eaten sofa had been overturned and there was a broken bottle with strong-smelling alcohol puddling around it. It looked like it had been thrown at the wall.

Checking the tiny kitchen, the closet-like bathroom, and the main living area (where the broken bottle was), Selene then moved cautiously toward the back, where a curtained doorway led into what she assumed was the bedroom.

She was right; there was a bed and a bookcase and not much else. Everything was covered with a thin layer of dirt, and there was moss growing on the corner of the bookcase that caught some sun from a gap in the curtains.

The bed itself was cleaved nearly in two by a long gash running down its center. Lying on either side were the pieces of a staff. It had been a heavy, well-worn staff, and was the only thing in the room not covered in dirt.

There was a backdoor here, hanging unlatched. Selene nudged it the rest of the way open with the nose of her gun, and stepping out into a little yard, she found the place where the kill had happened.

Blood, brown and old and black where it had soaked into the dirt, covered half the yard and had splashed up against the side of the house. There was an impression in the ground, like that of a body being dragged away, and then some hastily kicked up leaves, to hide the trail. Selene thought she had a good idea of where they would find it, though.

Following the path that led from the yard around the side of the house, she found herself back in the clearing, with Clara and Jill looking curiously at her.

"I don't think we need to worry about that Jack O'Green fellow anymore," Selene said dryly. "Something came through and butchered someone in the backyard. Looks like the body was dragged over that way." She nodded significantly at the pile of fresh dirt. "Do we got a shovel?"

They did not ("I'll put it on the list of equipment we need," Jill said), but Clara found one propped against the wall at the end of the porch. It looked to have been recently used.

"This is so strange," said Jill, as Clara set about digging into the pile of fresh dirt.

"What, the shovel?" Selene asked.

"Yeah," said Jill. "I mean, why be so obvious? Like, they took the time to bury the body, but they didn't put it anywhere inconspicuous, or even bother to take it away with them. *That's* strange."

Selene rubbed her chin thoughtfully. "They might not have thought anyone would be back here for a long time," she suggested.

"I have something," Clara said, making both the other women jerk to attention. She had stopped digging, and was using the shovel to scrape away layers of dirt. She had hardly made an impression in the soft earth—whatever was buried was only under a minimal layer of dirt. Jill got out her phone automatically, and then felt her hand drop to her side as a flick of the shovel's blade revealed a swatch of familiar brown jacket, and a few wiry white hairs.

Clara laid the implement aside and finished excavating the body with her hands, brushing the dirt away. Slowly a form was revealed, and Jill forced herself to watch, even though she found the sight revolting.

Jack O'Green had been killed by a single strike to his chest, ripping clean through his clothes and crushing his ribs. The dirt was a bloody mud down there, but it seemed most of his blood had seeped away beneath him. His upturned face was covered in dirt, the eyes obscured by the thick paste of soil and twigs that had formed over them. His mouth had been forced open, and this was stuffed—deliberately, it looked like—with green leaves.

When the entire body had been uncovered, Clara took it by the shoulders and made to lift it out from the shallow grave it had been put in.

It wouldn't budge.

Clara frowned and tried again. This time there was an angry snapping, and a cracking like some creature howling in agony. The earth around Clara's feet roiled, and Jill scrambled back as she saw tentacle-like roots bursting through the surface, some of their ends shiny red with blood already.

But they did not attack: instead they retreated, writhing away into the undergrowth, and when Clara at last dragged the body free she turned it over, and Jill saw where all the blood had gone.

Jack O'Green's back had been perforated by the roots; it was a mess of torn clothes and holes, with bits of root still protruding from them. It reminded Jill of the stage in the decomposition of a corpse when the birds and other scavenging animals have had at it, tearing it open and pulling out the innards. Only this had all been done by a plant.

As fascinated as she was by the sight, Jill found herself growing dizzy. So, trying not to look directly at the grisly spectacle, she took some pictures which she hoped to study later. She also took pictures of the shallow grave from which the body had come, and the disturbed earth where the roots had beaten their retreat.

"I think it's time we followed those to their source," Selene said, grimly. "I'll get the gasoline . . ."

"Wait," said Clara. She had put Jack O'Green's body aside, and had gone back to the grave. Taking up the shovel again, she resumed digging.

"What are you doing?" Selene asked, pausing halfway to the truck.

"He was buried here for a reason," was all Clara would say, and a moment later her shovel hit something. She gave a darkly satisfied grunt, and proceeded with more caution. A few minutes later she had uncovered a piece of what looked like denim. A dirty plastic rhinestone glittered on it.

"*That's* not from Jack O'Green," Jill exclaimed, feeling horror and excitement race each other to the top of her throat.

"Do you have the list of the missing women?" Clara asked, businesslike, as she worked to uncover more. The cloth was half decayed and collapsed under pressure, but eventually Clara's work revealed a bony hip, and above that, a torso clothed in the remains of a white cotton shirt.

"Aw *damn*," said Selene, when she saw it.

This body was almost unrecognizable—the face had been obliterated by a year in the ground, though a matted tangle of yellow hair remained. What was left of the rest had been shredded—just as Jack O'Green's body had been—and aside from the skin and bones there was little left inside it.

Jill made a quick search on her phone, and discovered the list she had compiled of the previous victims.

"If I had to guess," she said, uncertainly, "that's probably Eileen Gillespie. She's the most recent name on the list—disappeared two years ago."

"Did she have blond hair?" Selene asked.

"I don't remember," Jill admitted. "I only have their names here. I'd look her up, but the reception's gone out again."

Selene just grunted. Clara, having excavated most of the new body, continued digging, this time just above its shoulder. Almost immediately she uncovered a mummified foot in the disintegrating remains of a sneaker.

"Aw *jeez*," said Selene.

Clara was unable to complete her exhumation of that body, however, because the vegetation began halfway up its midsection, and she set her shovel aside with a grim expression.

"In time these should all be removed and re-buried—properly," she said. "Their presence here only feeds the corruption of the wood."

"Yeah," said Selene. "In the meantime, why don't we do something about the wood itself?"

Clara nodded, shortly, and the two women were moving toward Arcana—where the bag containing their tree-burning supplies waited—when there was a rumble in the distance of a car approaching.

Immediately they redirected themselves to stand on either side of Jill, with Selene facing the road and Clara the forest. Jill felt her heart leap into her throat, and then felt it retreat again as Detective Wilco's black sedan rolled into view.

Selene cursed under her breath, but Jill brushed her aside and went forward to meet the man as he threw a leg out the car's door and pulled himself up to stand behind it.

"Detective, I'm glad you're here," she began. "There's something you should see—"

"Damn right there's something I should see," the older man cut her off. "The part where you ladies get off your all-fire rush to put your noses where they don't belong and get out of town—"

"I'm sorry, we can't, there's—"

"I don't care if you've found Amelia Earhart," Detective Wilco said. "What I see is—"

"*Three dead bodies!*" Jill shouted, practically in his face, and pointed. Reluctantly, Selene and Clara drew apart, allowing the man to look past them, to where the lumpish forms of Jack O'Green and the unidentified woman lay, and the mummified foot was just visible, poking out of the earth.

Detective Wilco's jaw actually dropped, creating a dark circle under his drooping white mustache.

"Don't tell me that's who I think it is . . . " he groaned.

"One of them is Jack O'Green," Jill said, businesslike. "The other two haven't been identified, but at least one is a woman. Detective, I think we know where the bodies of the people who've disappeared here over the last century have ended up. If we could get a professional team in here I'm sure we could find—"

Detective Wilco raised a hand to stop her, and Jill wisely shut her mouth while the man stalked around to get a better look at their excavation. He pulled a thin, blue rubber glove from out of his pocket and put it on, carefully using that hand only to touch the bodies. When he stood up, his face was even whiter than before, and his mouth was a thin, grim line.

"It is the same attacker who killed your partner that also killed Jack O'Green," Clara told him, blankly.

"Oh, you know that for certain, do you?" said Detective Wilco sarcastically. "Did you *see* them?"

"No," said Clara mildly. "But I can smell them."

Detective Wilco stared at her, then he shook himself and pulled out his phone. "This is well and truly beyond me," he muttered. Then he cursed, shook his phone, and cursed again.

"We don't have signal, either," Jill told him. "Your radio might work, but then—"

"Either way you're not staying here," Detective Wilco said, stripping off his glove. "Now, one of you can drive the truck, but the other two are getting a ride in the justice wagon over there."

Jill shot a look at Clara and Selene, who were both looking quietly furious. She saw Clara's hands twitch, and for one awful second she thought the woman would try to strike Detective Wilco.

It didn't matter what she intended, however, for the next second there was a rustling in the undergrowth, and roots erupted from everywhere around them.

Without thinking, Jill ducked and threw herself toward Arcana. Selene spun around, whipped out Freddie, and shot the two nearest, their ends exploding in reddish goo, then retreating with a hissing noise. She reloaded immediately, but the tendrils seemed to lose some of their tenacity as they entered the clearing, drooping and writhing along the ground like snakes.

There was a sharp *Bang! Bang! Bang!* as Detective Wilco got out his own pistol and shot at them as well. The metal bullets did little to deter them, however—whatever Selene had put in her slugs was clearly paying off—and they found themselves needing to retreat anyway.

"Protection's gone out," Selene said through her teeth. "We got maybe a minute—time to leave."

"Like *hell*—" the detective said, and then a huge root exploded from behind them, wrapping itself around the sedan, partially crushing it, and then dragging it off into the undergrowth.

"You'd better ride with us," Jill said, grabbing him by the sleeve of his gun hand and pulling him toward Arcana.

Clara had already mounted her bike.

"I will clear you a path!" she shouted as she rode past.

"Great!" Selene called after her. "Jill, you better drive. I'll ride in the back and cover you. *Move!*"

Jill didn't need to be told twice. Already the bodies they had uncovered were being reclaimed by the twisting roots, and the circle of space wherein they lost their vigor was rapidly shrinking. She bundled Detective Wilco into the back seat, then climbed in and started the engine. Selene vaulted into the bed and pounded on the roof.

"*Drive!*" she shouted, and Jill did. Clara had cut a path through the encroaching brush, but it was still a tight squeeze for Arcana, and Jill cringed in sympathy as she heard branches and leaves scrape along his sides. She didn't envy Selene, being out in the thick of it, but by the sound of her gun firing she knew the woman was still with them.

On the dash, the carefully woven wreath had gone brown and was smoking faintly. Her inclinations toward tidiness told her to get rid of it, but another instinct told her *no, that was their only chance of escape.* She just hoped the road would still take them out.

It did, but it was a long time coming, and Jill's knuckles were white on the steering wheel by the time she saw the yellow glow with patches of blue that heralded the end of the wood. The dark form of Clara, standing astride her motorcycle, was silhouetted to one side, and as they passed, Jill saw she had her sword raised, pointing back the way they had come.

Jill turned onto the paved road and gunned the engine, driving blindly away from the wood, Selene clinging to the back of the cab and Clara hot on their tail.

Mother June woke to the sound of a diesel engine grumbling down her drive, and the bark of a familiar motorcycle. For one confused second her mind went back in time and she wondered if it was Selene Shields coming to talk to her. But Selene Shields had been and gone, and though Mother June had made some new dirty dishes in the intervening time, the kitchen was still immaculate compared to what it had been.

No, Selene Shields had gone, but now she was back—and by the sound of it, she had brought friends. Mother June staggered to the door and pried it open, peering out into her front yard. Then she opened it all the way and stared.

The sound of the diesel came from a huge red truck—the kind with two rear wheels stacked next to each other, on either side. Its body was sleek and curving, and it would have been a beautiful vehicle except it was covered with broken branches and bits of tree. Leaves were plastered to the windshield and the grill, and there was a streak of dirt—almost like claw marks—along one side.

The burly black motorcycle, carrying the remains of a ward crown, crunched to a halt at the foot of her porch. Even before its rider took off their helmet, Mother June could tell it was not Selene Shields. This new person was taller, broader across the shoulders, and—when the helmet did come off—turned out to be as white as a newborn lamb.

Mother June blinked at the sight of a fine-boned, feminine face with near-invisible eyebrows atop six-foot-high shoulders.

Then Selene Shields kicked open the back door of the truck and hopped out. There were twigs in her hair and a graze on her cheek, and she looked a little out of breath. She was grinning apologetically.

"Sorry to bring the whole crew down on you," she said, ambling over to the porch. "I couldn't think where else to go."

Mother June looked at her, then at the truck, and then at the foliage decorating both vehicles and Selene Shields herself. She sniffed, caught the tang of wood magic, and scowled.

"Ya damned fools," she muttered, but she stepped aside so they could come in—four of them, it turned out. Besides Selene and the giant on the motorbike, there was another, smaller woman with glasses and long hair tied up in a ponytail, and a white man with whiter hair who looked like he'd seen a ghost.

Mother June stopped him in the doorway.

"I know your face," she said, almost accusingly. "You've come poking around here before."

"Detective Wilco," said the man, his voice a little shaky. "Yes I have, ma'am. We weren't able to talk before . . . I think, if we had, things might have gone a bit differently."

Mother June squinted at him. "Maybe," she said. "Come inside and get comfy. I've made coffee."

Coffee was the last thing Jill wanted after their scare in the wood, and besides, it was a hot afternoon. But she took a cup to be polite, and pretended to sip it while Selene filled June Freeman in—and by extension Detective Wilco—on what had happened.

"It's a blood tree, all right," she said, throwing herself down on the dingy sofa as if she was in her own living room. "Big one, too, judging by the size of its roots. We got three bodies without hardly trying, and I bet there's more."

"Hold up," said Detective Wilco. "What exactly *is* this blood tree you're talkin' about?"

June Freeman, Selene and Clara all spoke over each other answering his question, and in the end it was Jill who edited together their answers into something comprehensible. When she had, the detective leaned back in his chair and covered his eyes.

He sat like that for so long, Selene must have decided he was no longer interested in their conversation, and turned back to June Freeman.

"What are your protections like around this house?" she asked, all business. "You've got to have them, being this close to the wood. And I'll need to juice them up a bit, seeing as how the tree's got itself a mobile agent or avatar or something."

June Freeman frowned at this. "I got the strongest wards the goddess ever sent," she allowed. "But I ain't never heard of the tree leaving the forest—in any kind of form. You sure it's from the wood?"

"What else could it be?" Selene asked.

June Freeman didn't have an answer to that, but Jill made a mental note: Selene was uncertain, and Clara did not offer up any concrete evidence either way.

From the armchair, Detective Wilco shuddered to life again with a moan. "Damn me to hell—sorry, ladies—but this is like that Bellefontaine mess all over again."

"Sorry?" said Jill. "*You* have experience with prehensile, flesh-eating trees?"

"Not flesh-eating," Selene corrected her. "Blood-drinking. Like a vampire." She mimed drinking from a glass.

"*No,*" said the detective, answering Jill's question. "What I *do* have is an embarrassment of a case from ... gosh, from twenty years back. It's the reason I'm gonna retire as a *junior* detective, while boys like Karl will"—he choked off for a moment. "*Would,*" he corrected himself. "Would have positively *floated* up the ranks."

Jill, Clara, Selene and June Freeman all gave this revelation a respectful silence, but when Detective Wilco declined to elaborate, Selene returned to the older woman and the matter at hand.

"We're gonna try to burn it out," she said. "Might not be enough, if the tree's as strong as I suspect, but it'll give us time to think of a more permanent solution—or it might weaken it enough that we can chop it down and pull it out by the roots. There's got to be a backhoe somewhere in this town we could borrow."

"Father Brown had a backhoe," June Freeman allowed. "Oh, but he died last year. Son came and took it away. Doesn't matter—*them* boys from the white houses won't let you anywhere near the tree."

"I think," said Jill, "that by tomorrow those *boys* will be in no position to get in our way." She said this while looking pointedly at Detective Wilco.

"I think we agree now, that tree is a menace and needs to be taken out for the good of everyone involved?"

Detective Wilco, though he still looked like the shadow of the man they had met yesterday, nodded his head. "I've called in for backup," he said. "Should be here by this evening, and by tomorrow morning we'll have county fire as well—we can blow up that whole wood if you like."

"Great," said Jill. "Just let me take at least *some* of the ashes."

Clara sighed, and Selene rolled her eyes.

They spent the rest of the afternoon collecting items for the following day. Selene and June Freeman sequestered themselves in her kitchen, mixing up a batch of what Selene called "fire juice."

"It's the stuff we use for Gunn Classics these days," she explained. "Salt, with a combustion agent to speed up the burn."

"Don't know why it's still called after those lily white bastards," June Freeman muttered, dumping an entire carton of salt into a huge stainless-steel mixing bowl. "When my mother, and her mother, and her mother, and all the way back to our first mother, knew that the thing to discourage a spirit was to cover its avatar in salt and burn it. Recipe older than the hills 'round these parts . . . " her grumble trailed off as she stirred the salt in with the rubbing alcohol.

Clara, meanwhile, walked the border of June Freeman's backyard, where it butted up against the wood. She had intended to strengthen the wards there, but she was impressed to find they were already quite strong and well maintained. You did not live right next to the wood of a blood tree for so long, it seemed, without good protection.

It had not been enough to protect Cynthia Jefferson, a small voice in the back of her head reminded her, and Clara found herself shivering, even in the late afternoon sun.

Still, she could say only good things about June Freeman's wards, at which Selene just nodded, a little proudly.

They had an improvised dinner made of canned soup from June Freeman's cupboard and the stock of dried fruit and meat that Jill kept in Arcana. It was an odd combination, but everyone was pleasantly full afterwards.

While Jill and the detective bedded down in the living room, Clara and Selene sat out on the front porch, watching the fireflies, to share the first watch. However, what with the stress from the previous day and night, and the knowledge that they were as well protected here as anywhere, neither of them tried very hard to stay awake, and soon Selene was fast asleep.

She woke suddenly to a smell like old coffins and sour milk. It wafted down from the wood behind the house, and brought with it an uncomfortable sense like pins digging into the back of her neck. Years of experience triggered a surge in adrenaline and she unconsciously reached for Freddie—which she'd stashed under her chair.

Clara was a black mountain beside her, head stooped in slumber, and all was silent and dark inside.

Nevertheless, Selene got up and went over to the screen door, which she pulled open just enough so she could stick her arm inside and flick on the porch light. It fizzed and tinked in protest, but came on eventually. By its light Selene could see the cluttered porch and a few feet of gravel and scraggily lawn, and nothing much else. The moon was cut off behind a thick layer of clouds, and the air was heavy and humid.

Still, behind the smell of wet, decaying grass and the green scent of the wood and river, there was that peculiar odor Selene had come to associate with vampires and ghouls and other physical manifestations of dead things. Dead and dry, like a dust-filled cavern, and behind that, something sour.

"Hey, eh, wake up there sister," she said, nudging Clara's knee with her own. "Whatever paid us a visit last night, I think it's back."

Clara woke up so smoothly Selene wondered if she'd even been asleep. Her newly opened eyes were very bright and blue and stared piercingly out into the dark.

She rose from her chair, her leather clothes creaking faintly, and went to stand at the top of the porch steps.

"Death," she said quietly.

"Sorry?" said Selene.

"Death is what you sense. That smell. It is death."

"You mean like the big D, Death?" Selene asked. "Grim Reaper, skeleton in a cowl with a scythe, all that jazz?"

"I don't think so," Clara said. "But someone touched by it." She paused a while, leaning forward into the air. "I believe the boundary is holding them," she said. "I think . . . I think I would like to see who it is." She glanced back at Selene, her face open and vulnerable, as if on the cusp of a question she didn't want to ask.

"Go on then," Selene said, waving a hand. "I'll watch your six."

Clara nodded. She shrugged her shoulders, feeling the weight of the sword on her back, and stepped off the porch and into the night. Selene grabbed up the flashlight she kept handy, and followed.

At first everything seemed perfectly normal, aside from the smell. The night was quiet, save for the distant croaking of frogs, and dark from the lack of moon; the fireflies had long since gone dormant for the night.

Clara followed the well-trodden path that ran along June Freeman's boundary, occasionally stopping to peer out into the night. Once or twice she poked an experimental finger over the border, but nothing happened.

Then, just as they were approaching the house again (from the opposite direction this time), Clara stopped so suddenly that Selene, who was dutifully facing the other direction, trod on her heel.

"Sorry, *sorry*," she hissed, but Clara hardly reacted.

"Turn off your light," she said, her voice quiet and chill.

Selene knew better than to argue with that tone. She flicked her flashlight off, and stood there in the dark while her eyes adjusted.

"It's here," Clara breathed, and Selene felt the pins travel down her spine, out her arms, and gather in her hands.

"Can you see it?" she whispered back.

"Barely," admitted Clara. "I think . . . I think there is only one. Come and see."

Slowly, Selene turned around.

Clara was facing the boundary of June Freeman's property, where the fence line ran between her backyard and an open field. This was just visible as a dark gray patch in the otherwise black night, which was the only reason Selene could distinguish the darker shadow that was currently standing in it.

They—it was impossible to determine any kind of gender—were easily as tall as Clara, though perhaps a bit narrower, with long, sinewy arms hanging loosely by their sides. Angular shapes around their waist suggested weapons, and their shoulders were wide and pointed.

"Heya," Selene called to them, seeing no point in a silent standoff. "Are we gonna have a problem with you?"

Movement in the shadow: a twitch like the tip of a curious head.

Then it was gone—blurred into the rest of the night, leaving only a puff of air smelling of dust.

Clara whirled around, one hand on the hilt of her sword.

"Did you see where it went?" she asked.

"Sure," said Selene, sarcastically. "I have *perfect* night vision, that's why I always carry a flashlight—of *course* I didn't see where it went."

Clara cursed and began jogging off along the fence. "Check in with Jill," she called back over her shoulder. "I don't think it's the tree after all."

"You don't think—" Selene began, and then put together what Clara had just said.

Protection rings could be fiddly, specific things. The one Clara had used last night had been a sort of all-purpose spell, good against a variety of supernatural beings. But June Freeman, living so close to the wood, had developed a *specialized* sort of ring, one that was incredibly effective at blocking intrusions from the blood tree, but wouldn't do a thing against, say, a ghoul or a vampire.

Selene didn't bother to stop and wonder *why* something unrelated to the tree would be coming after them—such questions were only a distraction and could get people killed—she just ran back to the house, pulling open the front door and fumbling for the lights.

"Up and at 'em, folks!" she shouted, making Jill jump awake and Detective Wilco groan and curse. "We got a live one, and we might have to go mobile any minute!"

"I thought you and Clara took care of the *protections*," Jill moaned, groping for her glasses.

"I thought we did too," said Selene. She found the switch for the living-room lamp, but the moment before she flipped it, chanced to glance out of the window above the couch where Jill was sleeping.

There was a darker spot in the night outside. A tall, slender, dark spot, and a smell like musty rooms and sour milk rose in her nostrils.

"Jill—get—*Jill!*" Selene lost the capacity for coherent speech, and dove forward and grabbed Jill, pulling her off the couch, just as the window above her shattered, and the shadow came crashing into the room.

"Behind me, *behind me!*" Selene heard herself shouting, her instincts running on ahead of her words, causing her to raise her gun and fire twice into the shadow before Jill could even get to her feet.

The flash gave her a brief glimpse of black armor that shimmered gold around the edges; wicked, curving forms and a visored helm that stared back at her blankly. Selene sent a third shot directly into it, and she heard a *thud* as the figure was thrown back into the sofa.

"Lights please, someone!" Selene ordered, and the next moment the living-room lamp—which had been knocked on its side in the confusion—fizzed to life.

It showed Selene in more detail that which she had only glimpsed before: six feet of armored body, covered head to toe in intricately interlinked plate armor, its head covered by a ridged helmet with a grill in front of the mouth and a series of slits for eye holes. Half of it was dusty black, and there was a noticeable dent in the forehead from Selene's shot.

"Aw *hell*," Selene said, as the figure shuddered and rolled to its knees. It had a pair of battle-axes, which it still clutched—one in each hand—and these caught the light as the figure used them as braces to push itself to its feet.

"Everybody *out!*" Selene shouted, so loud and fierce she felt her voice break. It got Jill and Wilco moving, however, and she caught a glimpse of June Freeman, in her nightgown, fleeing back into her bedroom.

The strange warrior didn't seem interested in the old woman but launched itself at Selene, who caught one axe under the blade with Freddie's barrel, kicked the hand with the other, and then *twisted* herself so she could get a shot right off into the warrior's neck.

The figure jerked violently and went down on one knee, and Selene took the opportunity to follow Jill and Wilco out the door, slamming it shut behind her.

"What *is* that?!" Jill gasped. She and Wilco were crouched on the porch steps, and the detective had his piece out, trained on the door.

"Don't know, don't want to stay to find out," Selene said, her voice hoarse from shouting. "Into Arcana, both of you. I don't think it's interested in June Freeman."

As if to prove her point, the black-armored person chose that moment to come hurtling through the house's front window, rolling nimbly to its feet amid a shower of glass shards. Selene, though she'd put her arm up to shield her face, felt one bite into her thigh through her jeans. She ignored it and reached into her back pocket for the spare rounds she kept just for moments like this.

She didn't rightly have the time to reload. The armored figure paused once it had rolled upright, rising slowly to its feet, one axe held loosely in each hand.

Behind her, she heard Detective Wilco swear.

Still the figure waited. Waited until Selene had finished reloading, waited while she snapped Freddie back together, and still . . . waited. Selene realized she had not yet raised her gun, and for a mad second she thought *it's waiting for me to be ready; whatever it is, it's being sporting.*

Then something whizzed out of the air, clipped the figure's metal shoulder, and buried itself in the soft wood of the porch.

Another dark figure, just as tall and even broader, advanced out of the night. Clara had put on her own helmet, and now the two faceless fighters stared at one another: one tall and shiny, with curling prongs on its metallic armor, the other in flat, unadorned leather. To Selene they seemed of a kind, both set slightly apart from the world that she and Detective Wilco stood in. They drew about them a dim electric feeling like a distant storm.

There was a *shing* as Clara drew her sword, resting the blade on her free hand to level the point at the warrior on the porch, who at the same time turned to face her, twirling the axes and shaking the last of the broken glass out of the notches in its armor.

Then they were upon each other. Impossible to follow in the dark, Selene heard the clash of their weapons, the dull *thunking* of blunt blows, and then there was a grunt, and a black body came sailing through the air, twisting, landing with a tumble on the porch.

It was Clara, sword still in hand, and she rose to her knees before Selene could help her.

"Get them out, Selene," she said, her voice sounding strained. "June Freeman is already away."

"Define 'out,' sister," Selene replied.

"Out of River View," Clara snapped. "I'll give you as much time as I can."

"Clara, what—" Jill began, but Clara was already off, leaping off the porch and coming at the armored warrior, her sword a pale flash in the night.

"C'mon guys, this isn't a cage fight," Selene said, herding them down the steps. "I think it's after *you*, boss," she added when Jill hesitated, "let us do our jobs, for *once*."

That got Jill moving. Together they sprinted for Arcana, Jill sliding into the driver's seat while Wilco scrambled in back. Selene vaulted into the bed, grabbed the duffle with her arsenal in it, and then, as Jill backed around, getting ready to tear out of the driveway, she jumped back out.

"*Go!*" she screamed at Jill when the latter rolled down her window in confusion. "We'll catch you up!" She kicked Arcana's bumper for emphasis.

Jill shot her an unreadable look, but she accelerated down the drive so fast she nearly buried Selene in the dust.

Selene was already moving, running to where Clara had left her bike and—*yes*—the keys were in the ignition. Standing astride Unicorn, Selene opened her bag and made for the gun tucked in a special pocket in the lining. Checking the barrel she found it only had two shots—which, when you were only planning on using one, was more than enough. She dropped the duffle on the ground, slung Freddie onto her back, and started the bike one handed.

Unicorn fairly roared to life, and in the beam of her headlight Selene could see Clara and the mystery warrior going at each other still. Their fighting had devolved into a brawl, with as much kicking and punching as clashes of weapons. Clara was making the warrior work for it, that was certain, but not without cost. She was visibly favoring her left side, and even as Selene watched, the warrior came at her, lightning fast, and the next moment Clara was on the ground, while above her the warrior raised an axe. Selene, for all her conditioning, found herself frozen.

The axe descended, and Clara dropped her sword, raised her hands, and *caught* it, clawed her way up it to grasp the warrior's arm, and held it there while she bent her body in half and delivered kick after kick to the warrior's midsection.

When at last her opponent struggled free, it was only to stagger away and hunch, doubled over, as Clara rolled to her feet—picking up her sword as she did so.

Selene jerked into action, barreling down toward the pair of them. She tried to shout, but her voice came out in a choked croak.

But Clara recognized the sound of Unicorn's engine and took one step to the side, giving Selene a clear shot at the warrior.

Selene took it, and under cover of the resulting explosion, slid to a halt in front of Clara.

"Sorry I didn't ask," she gasped.

"Apology accepted," said Clara, weakly, as she climbed on behind Selene. An arm like a steel band clamped around her waist, and with one last glance at the clearing smoke—lit yellow from the porch light—she saw the quivering form of the warrior, slowly struggling to its feet.

Selene didn't wait to see more. She spurred Unicorn down the drive, feeling the damp night air pummel her face and whip in her hair. She was aware of Clara, big and warm and breathing heavily, pressed up against her back, and something hot and wet dribbling down her shoulder.

"They get you?" Selene asked against the roar of the wind.

"Ride on," was all Clara said, but it sounded like she spoke through gritted teeth.

Selene rode. She rode south, out of River View, and did not stop riding until she cleared the wood, and the fields on either side turned to pasture. Around that time she felt Clara's grip begin to loosen, and she pulled Unicorn gently off the road and stopped on a wide piece of shoulder. Clara began to topple almost immediately, nearly taking Selene and the bike with her.

"Easy, *easy*," Selene gasped, holding tight to Clara's arm so she could set the kickstand and then, slowly, lower the larger woman to the ground. There was a dull *thunk* as Clara let go of her sword.

"Where'd they get you?" Selene asked, slithering off the bike. She still had Freddie strapped to her back, and by extension the flashlight that went with him. She snapped it off and turned it on, holding it in her mouth so she could work on unbuckling Clara's helmet. Her hands were batted away immediately, however, and Clara did it herself.

The face this action revealed was whiter than Selene had ever seen it. There were greenish tinges around her eyes, and her cheeks were startlingly red.

"It's not bad," she said shakily.

It was hard to see in the uncertain light, but Clara's whole right side looked wet and shiny. It was impossible to tell where most of it was coming from, though.

Selene plucked the flashlight from her mouth. "Like hell it's not," she said. "Let me see it. Looks like you're leaking pretty bad."

Clara froze, her face twisted in panic.

Selene wanted to slap her.

"I ain't gonna *stare* or do anything awkward, sister," she said, trying to keep the anger and the hurt out of her voice. She swallowed it down, and went on, more gently. "Let me help you."

"Just don't," Clara said abruptly, when Selene moved to unzip her leather jacket. "Whatever you see," she went on, her voice gone soft and a little blurry. "Don't ask questions," she finished. Then she reached up and unzipped her jacket herself, unbuckled the leather armor she wore under it, and allowed Selene to take them off her. The tight-fitting, stretchy turtleneck beneath everything gave them the most difficulty, since Clara wouldn't allow Selene to cut her out of it. Eventually, however, by pulling it off her left side and then carefully—*oh so carefully*—lifting it away from her right shoulder and stripping it off her right arm, she managed to remove it.

If it had been modesty that made Clara hesitate, she needn't have worried. Selene had seen enough shirtless women in her life that the novelty had worn off, and she was nothing if not practical. Though she could see why Clara assumed she would have questions—she did—but in all honesty she was more concerned with the wound in the woman's shoulder, which was still bleeding profusely. It probably looked deeper than it was, however, since Clara had been able to move that arm and still had full control of her right hand.

"Oh my," said Selene. "That's gorgeous, that is."

"I've had worse," Clara said stoically. Her voice was a little shaky, and she looked ready to tip over. She remained conscious, however, long enough to direct Selene to the first-aid kit in Unicorn's saddlebags, and even held the flashlight with her left hand while Selene rinsed the wound and applied disinfectant. She didn't even twitch when Selene started stitching it shut. She put a sterile pad over the site, and wrapped it tightly with the bright purple, slightly tacky tape Clara kept in rolls at the bottom of the kit.

"Vet wrap never goes out of style," she assured Clara as she draped the woman's jacket over her broad shoulders and helped her lean back against a nearby fence post.

"Ha ha," said Clara, weakly, and shut her eyes at last.

Selene then gave the rest of her a cursory once-over, and after she discovered no further injuries in need of immediate attention, packed up the kit, putting it carefully back in Unicorn's pannier. She checked that Freddie was as fully loaded as he could be, and then at last she got out her phone and called Jill.

When Clara woke she was surprisingly warm and comfortable. Then she tried to move and all the checks her body had written the night before got cashed in at once. She opened her mouth and a sound came out, something between a groan and a whine.

Immediately her view of the bright, blue morning world was eclipsed by the concerned face of Selene Shields, her frizzy hair escaping from its ponytail like a dark corona.

"Hey sis," she said. "Glad you could join us. Had me a little worried, there."

Clara blinked, and gingerly rolled her head to one side. She saw gray plastic molding, and the corner of their aluminum equipment locker. She was in the bed of Arcana, propped up on lumpy pillows, the rest of her body buried under Selene's sleeping bag—which had been unzipped so it could serve as a blanket. Judging by the chafing around her legs, she was still in her pants, and her leather jacket was zipped up to the neck under her chin.

"How long?" she asked, her voice coming out weak and disoriented. She coughed.

"Only about seven hours," Selene answered. "But you were *out* out. Didn't wake up even with the three of us hoisting you up here. How you feeling?"

"Oh," said Clara. That was sobering. But she was feeling progressively better the more she came awake. The sleep had done its job. "I am hungry," she said.

"That's good," said Selene, cracking a smile. "Let me just check the stitches and then we'll load you up with ham and eggs."

"No," said Clara, tensing. Then, at the expression on Selene's face, she found herself explaining: "Last night I trusted you. Trust me, now. I will ask for help if I need help."

Selene heaved a big sigh. "*Ooo*kay, if you say so."

"Thanks," Clara said, to make up for it. "For last night. And for not asking."

"No problem." Selene shrugged. "Lots of folks got tattoos they regret getting. I mean, I could show you . . . wait, no, I won't." She peered down at Clara, who, despite putting on her blankest expression, felt like the other woman was reading her soul.

"But I take it, those weren't *your* idea?" Selene said softly.

Clara swallowed.

"I've had them my whole life," she admitted. "I don't know where they came from, or what they mean. I asked Mother, over and over, but she only smiled and told me not to worry. '*I'll explain when you're older,*' she said."

"Did she ever?" Selene asked.

"She left before I got old enough."

"*Ah-oh,*" said Selene, and twisted her mouth. She glanced over, out of the truck, and then looked back at Clara. "You want breakfast in bed, or will you be joining us?"

"Us?" Clara said, dully.

"Turns out our Detective Wilco can grill a mean sausage. Also, June Freeman's here; we've been talking about what happened . . . last night."

Clara nodded infinitesimally—it was as much as she could manage. "Where is *here*?" she asked.

"Here" turned out to be the selfsame turnout where Selene had pulled over the night before. Arcana had been parked as far off the road as they could manage, while June Freeman's dinged-up station wagon acted as a sort of buffer between it and the road. Unicorn had been crammed up against the fence to make room for the little fire pit, over which Detective Wilco had rigged a makeshift grill to cook their breakfast, using supplies provided by June Freeman—who had taken Jill into Hawk Point for groceries.

It was a better breakfast than Jill had had in days, she thought ruefully. If her stomach hadn't been so tied up with nerves over Clara, she might have enjoyed it. Detective Wilco had been staunchly calm all night, as though he'd pushed all the feelings of shock and horror and guilt down into the back of his mind while he dealt with the crisis at hand. Jill could sympathize, but she was also grateful for it. The sight of Clara, limp and unconscious and so white she looked almost green, had affected her more than she realized. She'd tried to get Selene to take her to a hospital, but Selene had just looked at her stonily and shook her head. She tried distracting herself by talking to June Freeman, since the events of last night had made her reconsider their hypothesis about the blood tree, the forest, and why Cynthia Jefferson had been killed.

"That warrior last night," June Freeman said with a shake of her head. "They no from the wood. They no part of the tree. They different."

"They didn't *look* tree-ish to me," Jill agreed. "But how are you so certain?"

"My wards," the woman replied. "They good. They old. They *strong*. They don't let nothing bad from the wood get near my house. But that warrior, they come busting in like wards don't mean a thing. They not from the wood."

Jill nodded, thoughtfully. "But I think it's likely they're the same person who killed Detective Karl and Jack O'Green. I saw their axes; they nearly did the same to Selene and Clara last night." *Only Selene seemed to think they were coming after me,* she thought to herself, with a shiver. Then another thought occurred to her. "What if *they* were the one who killed your granddaughter?"

June Freeman pursed her lips and looked down at the ground.

"Sorry," Jill said, automatically. She could imagine, probably more accurately than any of them there, the vortex of grief that was whirling inside the older woman. But when she was upset she always buried herself in the technical, in the cold, emotionless world of hard facts. And she was, she realized, very upset right now. She turned to Detective Wilco, who was studiously frying another panful of eggs, like it was the only thing keeping him sane.

"Cynthia Jefferson," she said. "Were her fatal wounds caused by an axe?"

Detective Wilco shut his eyes, his face contorted at the unpleasant memory.

"Now you have to understand," he said after a moment. "They'd already buried her by the time we were assigned the case. I only got the coroner's report which was ... well, he was a god-damn amateur, pardon me, ma'am," he added, nodding at June Freeman. The old woman gave him a strange look, as though she was not used to being addressed this way. "Fact was," the detective continued, adjusting his seat. "She'd been ... well ... her throat was slit," he said, jerkily. June Freeman shut her eyes. "Now, *could* be done by an axe, but probably not."

"And not at all what we've seen from the previous victims," Jill finished, nodding. She bit her lip in concentration as she felt the fragmented puzzle pieces in her mind beginning to snap into place, creating a bigger, more disturbing picture. "And ... the sacrifices ... Cynthia wasn't like those either. Her body was found in the river, right? *Not* under the tree. Selene thought she'd been rejected, which makes sense, if she went through the forest and Jack O'Green caught her ... "

"I *told* her not to go that way," June Freeman moaned.

Jill looked at her, and another piece slotted into place.

"Mrs. Freeman," she said, as gently as she could. "Your granddaughter, was she a pretty trustworthy kid? She'd follow instructions, I mean, if she knew they were important?"

"Of course," said June Freeman, as if it were an insult to imply otherwise. "Cynthia was a good kid. She know when her Mother June mean business. I trusted her with the house when I was out working late. She *good.*"

"And you told her never to go through the wood?" Jill pressed on.

"Every mornin'!" June Freeman exclaimed. "That's what I been *saying*—"

"Right, *right*," said Jill, having to shut her eyes so she could better see the picture unfolding in her mind. "So what I'm saying is . . . suppose she actually did what you *told* her. Suppose she *didn't* go through the wood? Suppose she took the . . . the . . . whatever other path it was you always had her take."

"The river path," June Freeman said with a sad nod. "It longer. Goes behind the white boy houses. But it safer."

"What if it wasn't?" Jill said in a small, hard voice. "That last time, what if the river path *wasn't* safe? Because . . . because there are *other things* killing people. Besides the tree. Besides even that axe-murderer. There's at least *one other thing*. And *that's* what killed Cynthia."

She looked up to find June Freeman and Detective Wilco both staring at her.

"Rafe McCleaver," said Jill, with the same small, hard assurance. "He's involved. Him and his friends. I bet *they're* the ones that killed Cynthia."

"Yeah, but if not for the tree, then *why?*" asked Detective Wilco.

Jill leaned forward and gripped her head between her hands. She almost had it. She *almost* had it. Rafe McCleaver and the other two, they were the ones who benefited directly from the tree. But they were somehow linked to Cynthia Jefferson's death, and that death, Jill was certain, was somehow linked to the axe-murderer, and it all was related to the blood tree. There was one last piece that needed to be fitted into place, and Jill hoped that if she just kept still it would present itself to her.

There was a moan and a *thump* and Selene said, "Take it *easy* sister," and Jill looked up to find Clara walking wincingly toward them, leaning rather on Selene.

And like that the fractured picture was gone, replaced by a huge torrent of relief.

"*Clara,*" Jill said, standing up so quickly she went dizzy for a moment.

Clara just nodded stoically, and allowed Selene to help her sit down.

"Are you . . . um . . . all right?" Jill asked.

"I am *hungry,*" said Clara, looking meaningfully at the grill.

"Don't have to ask twice," said Detective Wilco, and dumped the contents of the pan onto a paper plate, forked some sausages over it, and handed the whole thing to Clara, who balanced it on her knee and ate it left-handed.

"We've been talking," Jill explained. "About what happened last night. The warrior who attacked us, I don't think they're related to the tree. *From* the tree, I mean. I think all of this is *related*, somehow."

"She," Clara said, swallowing a mouthful of eggs. "The warrior last night, was a woman."

"Thought so," said Selene. "She fought like one."

"She fought like some kind of *demon*," Jill pointed out.

"Exactly," said Selene, giving her a significant look.

"How could you tell?" Jill asked, genuinely curious.

"Because I recognized her," Clara said shortly. "At least, I think I did. I've never actually met one of her kind before, but Mother told me about them. And you're right, she is not a part of the tree. The opposite, in fact. I think . . ." Clara broke off to chew thoughtfully for a few moments. "I think she's here to fight it."

"Fight . . . the tree?" Selene said, surprised.

"Fight on behalf of one who is opposed to it," Clara amended.

"Then why kill my partner?" Detective Wilco said, bitterly. "Why come after Miss Hamilton?"

"Because we were getting in the way," Jill said, realization dawning. "First you and Detective Karl—though I think *you* were the real target. Because you wanted to keep investigating. And me . . . because I . . . well . . ." She shrugged.

"Because we were investigating the death of Cynthia Jefferson," Detective Wilco said, and like that the final piece snapped into place. Jill's fingers *itched* with excitement, and she felt butterflies rise in her stomach.

"Rafe McCleaver," she said. "It *all* comes back to Rafe McCleaver. I don't know why, but *he's* the one behind Cynthia's death. *He's* the one's pulling our axe murderer's strings. For some reason . . . somehow . . . We need to investigate *him.*"

Detective Wilco sighed. "I can put in a request for a warrant," he said. "Though I can't promise anything."

"No, *no,*" said Jill. "We need to do this *today.* Today, or we get the hell out of here. Because that *thing* will be back tonight, and I don't think we can fight it—her, I mean."

Detective Wilco stared at her.

"Do you mean to ask me to *unlawfully* enter a civilian's house and detain him while you conduct an illegal search?"

"It's that," Jill said, nodding, "or more people will die. Possibly us included."

"This is Bellefontaine all over again," Wilco said, rubbing his eyes with a gnarled hand.

"Maybe," said Jill. "But I thought you were gonna retire soon, anyway?"

Detective Wilco gave her a crooked smile. He shook his snowy head and shrugged. "Heck," he said. "At least we'll have backup this time."

"Don't count on that," Selene warned. "Things getting stirred up like this, I doubt the tree'll be letting anyone else close to River View."

"Now, see here," said Wilco. "Do you really think it can stop a whole unit of Missouri law enforcement?"

Selene shrugged. "When was the last time you actually *heard* from your dispatcher?"

Detective Wilco's face went perfectly blank. He pulled out his phone, tapped it, wiggled it, and then cursed.

"I couldda sworn I had service here—"

"I did, last night," Selene said. She turned to Jill. "It knows we're here. It knows, and it's scared. You sure you want to do this?"

Jill thought of Cynthia Jefferson. She thought of the bodies under the tree—they never did manage to positively identify the ones besides Jack O'Green. She thought of June Freeman. Then she looked across at Clara.

Clara appeared almost her normal self now. Aside from the huge gash in her jacket shoulder and the stiff way she held her right arm, she appeared to be fine. She caught Jill's gaze and returned it steadily.

"No, I don't want to do this," Jill said, a little snappishly. "But I'm gonna. If . . . if you'll help me," she added, suddenly uncertain.

Selene laughed and came around to clap her on the back, and Clara smiled, small and brief.

"Now you're talking like a hunter," Selene said, grinning.

"Y'all *crazy*," said June Freeman, flatly. "What'chu think you are? Big damn heroes or something?"

Selene gave her an arch look. "You prefer if we weren't, Grandma?"

"H-yell no," said June Freeman. "Jus' you take care of this lot. I ain't burying them." She dusted off her hands. "I'll lead you in, though. Tree gets fidgety like this, times are you need someone like me to make the roads behave."

"Someone like you . . . like what?" Jill asked, her eyes narrowing. "Are you a . . . a magician?"

"Lordy *no*," said June Freeman with a hoarse laugh. "Magician? I? That's for white men too proud to call 'emselves witches. Me? I'm just someone who *knows* stuff." She gave them a cheeky grin and tapped the side of her nose.

Rafe McCleaver sat on his front porch, wearing Bermuda shorts, a cotton, button-down shirt, and a straw sunhat, sipping a tall glass of iced lemonade. He was projecting an air of studied relaxation and innocence, and hardly glanced at the two men who came to stand down by his garden gate. He was forced to look, however, when one of them coughed pointedly.

"We need to talk, Rafe," said Lyle Richmond (tall, dark-haired, wearing a starched white shirt and patent leather shoes).

"About our joint benefactor," added Billy Ashcroft (short, red-faced, hair perpetually greasy).

Rafe McCleaver found himself hating his neighbors then, in the light, casual way born of over familiarity. Suddenly it struck him what boring, small-minded, sheep-like men they really were. Billy Ashcroft wheezed, and Lyle Richmond seemed to think of himself as a tall, dark, mysterious character, but came off as pretentious. It had been *his* idea to get rid of that damned tree. *He* was the one who hunted up that stupid book that had showed them how to do it. And when push came to shove—or rather, when knife met flesh—it was Rafe McCleaver who'd had the courage to go through with it. Sure, they'd mocked him, had told him it was useless; that he was making a fool of himself.

But who was coming 'round for help now? Rafe McCleaver thought, as he lazily got to his feet and ambled down the path toward the gate, still sipping his lemonade.

"What's got you boys in such a tizzy?" he asked, between pulls from his drink.

"I'd rather not say, *out here*," Lyle Richmond said, rolling his eyes toward the houses further down the street.

It was ridiculous, Rafe McCleaver thought; between the three of them, they *owned* River View. By rights they should be able to talk about whatever they liked, wherever they liked.

"Come inside then," he said, with a sigh.

Both men swayed on their feet—as though they were prepared to obey Rafe McCleaver purely out of habit. But they didn't budge, which made Rafe McCleaver frown.

"Truth is, Rafe," sniffed Billy Ashcroft, "we'd just as soon talk about this in Lyle's backyard, if it's all the same to you. Wouldn't want our benefactor to overhear and get the wrong impression."

Rafe McCleaver sighed and tossed the remainder of his lemonade into the bushes. Lyle Richmond had one of those stupid Chinese Rock Gardens in his backyard—or something; Rafe McCleaver just saw something, called it *oriental* and didn't think on it any more. But it was behind tall, thick hedges and about as private as you could get.

"Lead on, gentlemen," Rafe McCleaver said.

"It's not that we don't *appreciate* its contributions to our cause," said Billy Ashcroft, once they were seated on the uncomfortable wooden benches amidst the neatly raked sand and random rocks. The bushes rustled in a light breeze, and somewhere down the road a truck went by. But the noise was distant, and Rafe McCleaver was more interested in gauging his co-conspirator's moods.

He'd left the warrior to rest in the basement; it seemed to like it there. He'd been shocked that it hadn't managed to kill the woman Hamilton outright, but judging from the destruction he'd seen when he went to check on June Freemen, he didn't think he'd be seeing any of them again any time soon.

Still, it had given him a thrill, having someone he could order about that way. It felt *right*. Right for *him* in a way that being the defacto head of some nowhere town had never been. Richmond and Ashcroft—they'd gone soft. They didn't want to deal with feeding the tree anymore. He could agree with that—mostly because he wanted to leave River View. So he'd cooked up a way out for all of them. Only *now* . . . now maybe Rafe McCleaver didn't care so much what the tree did or didn't do to the inhabitants of River View. He had a seven-foot-tall warrior who could cut down men like a chain saw cut saplings. He could *go* places with this.

If he could just get away with it.

The two main reasons he couldn't were currently huddled on the bench opposite him, looking mulish.

"I just don't think we have our priorities synchronized," Lyle Richmond said. "Jack O'Green had to go, that much was clear. But now you have our warrior running off after *cops* and *tourists* and . . . I'm sorry, Rafe, wasn't this just the sort of thing we were trying to *stop?*"

Rafe McCleaver leaned back on the uncomfortable bench, folding his hands casually behind his head. He did this so Richmond and Ashcroft couldn't see that he'd teased the talisman out from its leather pouch and was now fingering it purposefully.

It came down to two options, it really did. Rafe McCleaver could explain, could soothe, could *reassure* these men . . . just as he had been doing with curious reporters and confused law enforcement for *years.* Or, he could simply make them go away.

Rafe McCleaver did not think of himself as a violent or bloodthirsty man. He considered killing to be abhorrent; terrible. He supported the death penalty, but only for murderers. But he was also so very, very tired of *explaining.*

"My friends," he said, tugging hard on the talisman. "It's really quite *simple . . .* "

Selene parked Arcana at the head of the street marked River Path Rd, and squinted down past the line of trees to where the peaked roofs of three tall, white houses were just visible. She climbed out and made a sweep around Arcana, then beckoned to Jill and Clara, who got out, followed by Detective Wilco. They walked the remaining distance to the houses, and paused.

Detective Wilco took the lead then, striding boldly up to the nearest and largest and reaching for the bell.

"Ah—*no*," said Selene, catching his hand before it could touch the little button. "Honestly, I'd rather see what we can see *before* he finds out we're here."

"That's not the way we do things," the detective replied.

"Yeah, I know," said Selene. "But these guys have been getting away with murder for over a century, thanks to people like you doing things *your* way. Now give a sister some space, man, and, if you must look, promise to forget you ever saw me do this."

So saying Selene dropped to one knee, producing her lock-picks and beginning work on the door.

Detective Wilco sighed and tried the handle.

The front door swung open.

"I ain't seen nothing," he said as he stepped inside.

Jill stayed back, beside Clara. Not because Clara was moving slowly, but because Jill had heard all about the big woman's injury, and knew it would be better if *she* moved slowly. So while the detective and Selene stepped inside and cleared the front rooms, she and Clara lingered in the doorway.

Clara, leaning gingerly into the house, sniffed experimentally. Following her lead, Jill inhaled as well, and nearly sneezed. There was a strong smell of bleach and rug cleaner, and it made her nostrils tingle.

"Get anything?" she asked Clara.

"She's here," came the firm reply.

"You can smell her?" Jill asked.

"No, but I smell the mask. Blood was spilled here. This was where they summoned her."

"You keep talking like you know who this warrior is," Jill said as they advanced slowly into the house. It was tall and airy and full of light, with tasteful rugs and drapes and displays of delicate china plates. There was a pitcher of lemonade on a table by the door, the ice cubes still floating in it.

"I am not yet certain," Clara admitted. "But if I am right . . . it would explain many things. Come, it's this way."

Confidently, as if following a trail only she could see, Clara led Jill down the hall and into a comfortable kitchen. She opened a door off to the side, revealing a set of stairs leading down into the basement.

"Basements," said Jill. "Why is it *always* basements?"

"Now you're *really* sounding like one of us," Selene said, coming up behind her. "You let me take point here, yeah? Wilco, watch our backs. Clara, watch his."

Jill followed Selene down the worn steps, following the beam of her flashlight. It turned out not to be necessary, however, as the first light switch she tried caused a wide array of recessed lights to go on, bathing the basement in perfect, white-balanced light.

Which in turn revealed a curious and unsettling sight.

Boxes and crates had been shoved aside and stacked upon one another, leaving the middle of the concrete floor open. In this space someone had arranged a circle made of dried, broken twigs, at four points of which were little piles of black ash. In the center was a large stone, wrapped in chains with metal cuffs on the ends. There were still splatters of blood on the stone and chain, and one part of the circle of twigs had been obliterated, as if there had been a disturbance—or a struggle. Around the circle were painted angular, Nordic-looking runes, and on the bare wall that faced them, there was a blast mark of black soot, as if something had exploded on it.

"What in the name of God . . ." murmured Detective Wilco, coming to stand next to them.

"Yeah," said Selene. "But which one?"

"Vjor," came Clara's voice, quiet but clear.

"Sorry, *who*?" asked Jill, tearing her eyes away from that awful stone.

"V-yor," said Clara again, carefully. "That is the name of the god you want. A goddess, actually, and an old one."

"Define *old*," Selene said, poking at a twig with her toe. "This looks kinda like a summoning array . . ."

"It is, after a fashion," Clara said. She sounded numb. Jill went over and grabbed the nearest available crate, and hauled it over for her to sit on. It spoke to the severity of her injury that Clara sank down on it gratefully.

"And she is very, very old. Before Ares-Tyr-Mars there was Sekhmet and Kali, but before them all there was Vjor. She might not be the first god of war, but she is the earliest one whose name is still spoken. For you speak a form of it every time you mention the thing that she was a sovereign of."

"Wait . . . " said Jill. "*War*? Vjor is a god of war? Er, a war goddess?"

"God of war, mother of battle, she bleeds fury and revels in destruction," Clara said.

"Never heard of her," Selene said.

"Most people haven't," Clara said mildly. "But mother was insistent we learn about the gods that came before the patriarchal revolution; before even the advent of the Triple Goddess, and Vjor was a major part of that."

"So this," Jill said, waving her hand at the circle of twigs and the bloody stone. "This is part of a spell to summon *Vjor*?"

"Not . . . exactly," said Clara. "I do not think—with no worshippers living, Vjor can no longer manifest in this world. But . . . well, the principle thing about Vjor was that she kept a standing army of elite warriors. Warrior *women*. And, if you were willing to make the necessary sacrifice, you could summon one of these warriors—they were called *Vjorkrige*, and were the forerunners of the Valkyries—to serve you. It is called the Rite of Varriger, and that . . . " Clara nodded at the circle. "That is its sigil."

"And the necessary sacrifice?" Jill asked, feeling a little sick to her stomach.

"The life of a girl," Clara said, her voice hollow and cold. "An innocent life, in exchange for the life of a Vjorkrige."

Jill shut her eyes.

"Cynthia Jefferson," she whispered. "Wasn't killed by the wood at all."

"But this makes no sense," said Detective Wilco, albeit a little shakily. "Why summon one of these *v-yor-kree-gays* in the first place?"

"What if you got tired of feeding your blood tree?" Selene suggested, darkly. "Ya can't just dump those things like a crazy girlfriend, yanno? You need to take them *out*. But that ain't easy. You'd need someone with a lot of power."

"And these *v-yor-kree-gays*? They're that strong?" the detective asked.

"Vjorkrige," Clara corrected. "Refers to both the singular and the plural. And yes, they are. You saw one in action, last night."

"So . . . Rafe McCleaver summons a Vjorkrige," Jill said, beginning to pace around the circle, taking pictures. "He has her kill Jack O'Green, 'cause he's this tree's keeper or something. Has her try to kill the two detectives who're investigating their sacrificial victim, has her try to kill *us*, who're just investigating, period . . . just how much control does he have?"

"I am not sure," Clara said, sounding disappointed in herself. "The Rite of Varriger has not been performed, to my knowledge, in at least a thousand years. Presumably the old cult of Vjor had ways of determining the amount of control they would have, and possibly the rank of Vjorkrige they would get, sort of like a contract. But it's a summoning, so at the very least they need to have a specific task for the Vjorkrige to perform, which, once done, the summoner's control would be greatly diminished."

"Well, *thank* you for that," drawled a smooth, satisfied voice from the head of the stairs. "I'll definitely keep that in mind when I summon the next one."

Selene snapped to attention, training her gun on the chest of Rafe Mc-Cleaver, who was standing in the doorway to the kitchen, looking a little red under his snowy hair. He chuckled when he saw Selene, and touched his brow to Jill.

"Nice job, ladies. You're a persistent bunch, I'll give you that. But, as you can see . . . " he laughed, spreading his hands. Jill did not like the sound of that laugh. It sounded like the laugh of someone who had taken a step off the proverbial cliff of sanity and was free falling toward madness. "You are entirely too late, and I might add, *terminally* unprepared."

There was a soft sigh as Clara got to her feet.

"Rafe McCleaver," she said. "How did you find out about the Rite of Varriger?"

"Same place as my ancestors found out about that bloody tree," he replied, easily enough. "A book you won't find in any library. It's right there, as a matter of fact. Practically *under your feet*. I'd invite you to peruse it, but I am entirely done with you occupying the same realm as me. Good-bye, ladies, Detective . . . " his eyes passed disdainfully over Selene. "Give my regards to Cynthia Jefferson, when you see her. Tell her, *her sacrifice is appreciated*."

"You *asshole!*" Selene roared, and shot him.

Rafe McCleaver disappeared in a burst of black smoke. He was replaced by a tall, armored figure, who stood hunched in the doorway. It was recognizably female, now that it could seen in a proper light. The Vjorkrige had beautifully crafted armor, metal overlaying leather, with golden details etched in its surface. Gracefully arching pauldrons topped sleeves with plates like snake scales, and her chest plate was a convex wedge, like the prow of a ship. She carried a longsword strapped to her back, much like Clara, but both her hands were currently occupied holding twin battle-axes—short shafts of wood tipped with a dual blade and spike. The business ends of these were dripping blood onto the steps under her booted feet.

There was a *clap* of a door closing, and the sound of retreating footsteps.

"*McCleaver!*" Detective Wilco shouted, but there was no answer.

"Everyone," said Clara softly. "Get behind me."

"Like hell," said Selene, coming to stand, elbow to elbow, with the taller woman. "We do this together, sister."

Clara gave her a look then. It was unreadable to Jill, but it made Selene break into a smile.

There was a *click* as the Vjorkrige took a step down the stairs.

Clara, wincing, drew her sword.

"*Wait!*" Jill practically screamed.

"Not now, Jill," Selene said tiredly.

"Not *you*," Jill snapped. "*Her*, the Vjorkrige—you *can* understand us, yes?"

The Vjorkrige paused. She wore a visored helmet that gave her a face reminiscent of a horse's skull, which sloped back to a sharp ridge that ran down the back of her head and joined a similar ridge on her back plate.

Taking a deep breath, Jill stepped between her two guardians, and addressed the warrior directly.

"Clara tells me, when your kind is summoned, you've got to have a *reason* to come. Is that right?"

Slowly, the helmeted face nodded. Encouraged, Jill went on.

"Can you tell us why *you* were summoned?"

A pause. Then, with a rasp like rusty gears, a voice spoke from within the helmet.

"I am here . . . to subdue the *blutra* of Live Wood. And . . . to protect Rafe McCleaver."

"But you're *mostly* here for the tree, right?" Jill pressed on.

Another pause. Then a nod.

"So . . . killing us must come under *protecting Rafe McCleaver*, right?"

A nod.

Jill exhaled.

"Well, I'd just like to point out, we're *not* threatening Rafe McCleaver. Not anymore. He's *perfectly* safe. So really, you don't have any reason to kill us. In fact, you've got a *big* reason *not* to."

The Vjorkrige inclined her head at this, as though she wasn't convinced, but she was listening.

"Thing is, we're not too keen on this *blutra* either," Jill went on. "In fact, we'd love to help you, er . . . *subdue* it. And . . . once that's done, you're released from your contract, right? You won't have to do anything Rafe McCleaver says . . . and, I think that's what you want. Because . . . I don't think you *like* killing on his orders. That's not what you're here for . . . yes?"

The Vjorkrige stood frozen. The only movement was the blood that slowly dripped from the blades of her axes.

Behind Jill, Selene and Clara looked at each other, shocked.

"Yes . . ." said the Vjorkrige, slowly. She nodded. "Yes," she said again, firmer this time. She hooked the ends of her axes into hidden loops on her belt, then reached up with gauntleted hands, and after some fiddling, removed her helmet.

Jill wasn't sure what she expected to see underneath—a skull, perhaps?—but whatever it was, it was not a face as black as Selene's, with high, proud cheekbones and full, red lips, eyes like orbs of obsidian, and improbably light, creamy, tightly curling hair.

The Vjorkrige had the face of a woman in her mid-twenties, one that was handsome rather than beautiful, with an expression like a stone cliff. Her eyes, narrowing, passed over them, and then she nodded once more. Her lips parted and she said, "Yes."

"Great," said Jill, grinning in relief. "Then let's get to it, shall we? My truck's at the end of the street." She started toward the stairs, and there was one tense moment when the Vjorkrige just watched her with those impassive black eyes. Then she took a step backward and to the side, and allowed Jill to pass. Then, to Selene and Clara's utter astonishment, she turned her back on them and followed Jill out of the house.

"Aw man," moaned Detective Wilco. "Bellefontaine's got *nothing* on this."

Before they left the basement, Selene and Clara made a quick search of the floor and turned up an ancient book in a new binding, which had been laid in a place of honor beside the circle. A red ribbon marked a spot near the back. Selene whistled when she saw it, and Clara tucked it inside her jacket.

"There will be a reckoning," Clara said.

"No kidding," said Selene.

Jill drove and Detective Wilco rode shotgun, while Selene and Clara sat on either side of the Vjorkrige in the back seat. Selene felt like her heart was going to pound clean out of her chest, but the Vjorkrige seemed entirely uninterested in harming either of them. She spoke only once on their way to the wood, when she turned to Clara and said:

"I am glad we were unable to finish our fight. Two daughters of Vjor should not destroy one another."

"Vjor is not my mother," Clara replied, coldly.

"Nor is she mine, in actuality," the Vjorkrige allowed. "But in spirit."

Clara smiled, small and bright and brittle, at that, and inclined her head. "It was an honor, though," she said.

"Likewise," said the Vjorkrige.

The tension in the cab seemed to ease after that, and they passed the remainder of the drive in steady, if not exactly peaceful, silence.

Jill pulled off the road and parked at the entrance to the wood. The gate there had been completely overgrown, and the road itself was covered in twining vines.

"We walk from here," announced the Vjorkrige. Jill couldn't help but notice how her speech patterns were somewhat similar to Clara's. She wondered if it was a Nordic thing . . . or something else.

"I'll get my machete," said Selene, sliding out.

"That will be unnecessary," said the Vjorkrige.

"Bring it anyway," said Clara, to which Selene nodded.

Jill got out and went to join Detective Wilco, who was standing beside the gate, peering inside curiously.

"That's somethin' you don't see everyday," he remarked, dryly.

"Stand aside, please," said the Vjorkrige, causing them to jump. For someone in full armor, she could be silent as a cat.

Jill and Wilco sidled aside, and then stepped further back when the warrior drew her sword. This was a long sword—though not quite as long as Clara's claymore—with a shorter hilt and a crescent moon decorating the pommel. Its blade was black, like her armor, and soaked up the sunlight like a piece of black velvet.

Raising this shaft of night, the Vjorkrige swung it in a wide arch, rolling her shoulder, as she came to stand directly before the gate. Holding her hand up and behind her head, she leveled the blade at the road—as though she would do battle with the forest itself. Which was, Jill realized, not entirely wrong.

The warrior paused, then turned to look at them.

"Give her more room," said Clara, and beckoned to where she and Selene stood, well away and nearly in the road.

"What's she doing?" Jill asked as they hurried over.

"Clearing us a path," said Clara. She was holding the Vjorkrige's helmet in both hands, as though it were a priceless artifact.

"Ah," said Jill. "That's nice of her."

"It's what she's here to do," Selene drawled. "Nothing *nice* about it."

Wilco looked like he was about to comment, but then the Vjorkrige began to move.

It reminded Jill a little of the time she'd come upon a group of elderly Chinese ladies doing Tai Chi in a grassy park. Even though they were of all shapes and sizes, they moved with a uniform assurance, going smoothly from form to form like a slow dance.

That was what the Vjorkrige did, only she did it with a sword, and much, *much* faster. Rocking backwards and forwards on her feet, she brought her sword around in a smooth arc, as though she were winding a huge gear. Over and over again she repeated the flowing poses, and a wind rose around them, temporarily lifting the heavy, wet heat. It chattered in the leaves of the wood, and ripped up the grass around the Vjorkrige's feet. This rose in a flurry around her, and Jill was astonished to see the blades of grass forming a stream that flowed around the warrior, tracing a pattern in the wake of her sword.

Watching, Jill felt something tighten in her stomach, a winding tension like watching a huge boulder being lifted high into the air by a thin chain.

Then, when the wind was practically a gale around her, the Vjorkrige abruptly changed her dance, tightening her movements, and then all at once she thrust *out,* toward the wood, shooting it down the blade of her sword and through the gate.

It was like watching an invisible rocket tear through the trees. The gate gave way with a *clang,* followed by the crashing and cracking as the tree limbs and vines were ripped apart, shattering and flying up into the air. Jill could hear them long after the road in front of them was cleared: a rolling thunder of tearing wood that faded slowly into the distance.

The wind vanished, letting the grass fall to the ground around the Vjorkrige, who crouched in her final pose, her sword still held in front of her, and her feet planted in a wide stance, one in front of the other, pointing into the wood.

Slowly she stood up, the plates of her armor settling like bird feathers, and she shook her shoulders, as if to loosen them. In a graceful motion she sheathed her sword and turned back to look at them, gathering her feet beneath her.

"The way is clear," she announced. She paced over, and Clara wordlessly held out the helmet. The Vjorkrige slipped it on, fastening the latch under her chin. "You may follow if you wish," she said, then turned on her heel and marched through the shattered gate and down the road.

After a stunned moment, they all hurried after her.

The trail of destruction left by the Vjorkrige's attack ended abruptly at the cottage—though it had cleared the area around it. A crumpled metal husk was all that remained of Wilco's car, and the bodies they had unearthed had been partly reclaimed by the roots of the tree.

This tree—the *blood tree,* Jill realized—was now visible through the ravaged undergrowth. It was impossible to miss, really: by far the largest tree in the wood, thick and bloated with a vivid, reddish-brown bark. Like the color of a Giant Sequoia, Jill thought, only instead of being soft and pulpy, this bark was smooth and hard, like a manzanita—but all twisted and bubbly, as though it had melted and re-hardened. Reddish sap dripped from the crevices where boughs branched off from the main, squat trunk, and these rose like a thorny crown above them, their dark shapes making a latticework against the pale sky. The tree had no leaves, and malevolence breathed off it along with a stench of putrefaction.

At their approach the twigs rattled, sounding like bones, and Jill saw one of the great branches move closer, in a position to swipe them off the ground.

The Vjorkrige didn't give it the chance. She leapt across the twining roots, nimbly dodging the branch that came crashing down, and buried her sword almost to the hilt in the tree's bloated trunk. Raising her free hand she made a complicated motion and pressed it against the bark, next to her sword.

For a moment a pattern glowed against the trunk, around her palm, picked out in red light. Then it faded, and with a shudder the tree went still.

"Nice," said Selene, appreciatively. "Shall I get the torches?"

"This will not be resolved by fire," said the Vjorkrige, stepping down from the tree—but leaving her sword.

"Oh?" said Selene, genuinely curious.

"I knew trees like this," said the Vjorkrige, her harsh voice taking on an odd, soft quality. "They are not inherently evil, but exist at the mercy of their keepers. They should not be destroyed for the fault of those who have failed them."

"So . . . what'chu gonna do?" asked Selene, folding her arms.

"I will do what any gardener would," replied the Vjorkrige, taking up one of her axes. "I will prune away the bad growth, take away its poison, and hope . . . " she raised the axe, and buried it into a nearby root. "I will hope the *heart* is still pure."

They watched in amazement as the warrior began to hack away at the tree, systematically pulling off the roots that lay near the surface, and then diving into the trunk itself. The tree shuddered a little when she did this, and Jill couldn't help wincing. The Vjorkrige was merciless as she stripped off the outer layer of bark, carving footholds in the wood so she could climb up and chop off the fat, leafless branches.

Selene and Clara helped awkwardly, dragging away the trimmings and piling them in a heap by the cottage. Jill and Wilco, after watching dumbly for a few minutes, went around to where the bodies were still partially exposed, and began extracting them. Jill found the shovel they had used before, half buried, and set to work excavating.

The work went a lot faster than it should have, since, as the Vjorkrige cut further and further away at the bad growth, the roots writhed and snapped, bringing more bodies up to the surface. Like a sick animal being made to throw up, Jill thought. She worked with Wilco, pulling skeletons and other remains out of the mess, and laying them out in the road. They kept coming, boiling up to the surface as the dying roots rejected them. There were dozens and dozens of them.

Over a hundred, Jill realized, numbly. *One a year for over a century.*

"You better get on the horn to your HQ," she told Wilco. "Get a forensics team out here and start *identifying* these folks."

Wilco nodded, mutely. He was sweating and red in the face, but worked with energetic determination.

Like this they missed most of what the Vjorkrige did, only dimly aware of the growing light as more branches came away, letting the sun shine in on the destruction below.

Then, all at once, the Vjorkrige was *there,* standing over them. She'd taken her helmet off and was holding it in the crook of her arm, her sword back in its sheath, and her axes hanging from her waist. She was looking at them thoughtfully.

"It is done," she said.

Jill looked over at the tree, and saw that it was.

It was hardly a tree anymore: there was a stump, with a single piece of bark rising up on one side, to which was attached a thin layer of pulpy, white wood. The rest of the tree had been cleared away, and Clara and Selene were just stacking the last of the chopped wood.

"You'll want to bring a chipper in here," Selene said. "If you won't burn them, they should at least be mulched."

"So the tree . . . won't kill people anymore?" Jill asked.

"The tree never killed anyone," said the Vjorkrige. "It ate what it was fed."

"But, I mean," said Jill. "It's safe now?"

"Safe?" said the Vjorkrige, looking confused.

"It will not harm anyone," Clara said.

The Vjorkrige nodded. "Yes," she said. "My task is complete. It is over."

"Does this mean you're not beholden to Rafe McCleaver anymore?" Jill asked.

The Vjorkrige thought this over, and then nodded decisively.

Jill smiled triumphantly. "Then this isn't over," she said. "This has only just *begun.*"

Jill was right, of course, Selene thought bitterly. Because with Jill, you couldn't just melt off into the background once the job was done. No, you had to *stick around* and make sure the state troopers (called in by their newly restored cell phones) found the site, set to work properly exhuming the bodies, talk to the chief forensic investigator, and insist on accompanying Detective Wilco to arrest the three men.

That was where they ran into problems. Rafe McCleaver had vanished, taking all signs of the Rite of Varriger with him, and the other two . . . well, Selene wasn't entirely surprised when they found the bodies. It explained why McCleaver and the Vjorkrige were away when they entered the house.

Selene heard most of this through Clara, who came and found her in the little cemetery on the hill overlooking the river. Selene was sitting, hunched over, gazing at the wire-and-metal tag that labeled the area of dirt in front of her as the final resting place of Cynthia Jefferson.

Selene swallowed what felt like bile. *Of course* Rafe McCleaver got away. Save the town, lose the battle, she thought bitterly. They'd defeated the original evil at the cost of letting a greater wrong go unpunished. It didn't help that people like Rafe McCleaver had been getting away with doing what he'd done to people like Cynthia Jefferson for longer than River View had been a town.

"They *picked* her," Selene said, not certain Clara was listening. "Little black girl in a town like this—*who'd care?* I bet they thought. Hardly a sacrifice—to them. Probably thought no one would even *notice.*"

"But we did," Clara said, quietly.

"Not that it *matters*," Selene snarled. "The bastard will get away, you mark my words. It'll all evaporate, without the evidence. Even if they did catch him...what could they prove? It wasn't actually *him* that killed those other men—and in the end that's all that matters as far as law enforcement is concerned."

She sniffed. There was a smell drifting up from the river, like old, dusty coffins and sour fruit.

Getting to her feet and turning around, Selene saw the Vjorkrige walking up the hill toward them. She had her helmet off, tucked under one arm, and there was a heavy traveling cloak thrown over one shoulder. She must have been baking under it and all her armor, but Selene figured she was probably like Clara in terms of heat resistance. Or, more likely, Clara was a bit like the Vjorkrige.

She looked dark, even in the afternoon sun, as though the light didn't fully touch her. And, Selene noticed with a start, cool air wafted off her when she moved.

Maybe not baking after all, she thought.

"You taking off, then?" was what she said aloud.

The Vjorkrige nodded. "My work here is done," she said. "I came to pay my respects."

Selene wondered if she was referring to them, or to the occupant of the grave at her feet. Then a thought occurred to her.

"I don't suppose," she said, "if *you* leave, we get Cynthia back?"

The Vjorkrige shook her head solemnly. "It does not work that way."

"No," said Selene, turning away. "It never does."

"We require a life," the Vjorkrige went on, earnest if a little awkward. "To walk in your world, it is necessary, as we no longer have lives of our own. A life must be given, so that we, in turn, may live."

"And what about *her* life?" Selene said, whirling round. "You've used— what?—a couple *weeks* of it? She was only *nine*—she should have had *decades* more!"

The Vjorkrige looked down at her feet—in armored boots, of course. She seemed, Selene realized, almost *sad.* If someone with such a stony face could be thought to show emotions at all—really she was *worse* than Clara.

"What is given to Vjor cannot be taken back," the Vjorkrige said eventually. "But it is not an end. Not at all. Already her soul will have been welcomed into Vjorhallen, and she will, in time, become a great warrior. As I did. Given enough time, she may even walk this world again, as I have done."

The Vjorkrige looked up, and her eyes were indeed very black, but alone among all her features, they caught the light of the late sun, flashing briefly with a distant fire.

Selene felt her mouth drop.

"That is where the Vjorkrige come from," Clara said, quietly, as if only just now realizing. "That is why Vjor requires a young girl . . . " she trailed off.

"To take the place of the Vjorkrige she will send," said the Vjorkrige with an approving nod.

"But you're going back now," Selene said, wanting to be *sure* she understood.

"Yes," came the simple reply. "In this way every Varriger strengthens Vjor's army—though we have not had a new recruit in many centuries."

"But . . . " Selene pressed on. "You don't *have* to leave now? Like you said, you've got Cynthia's life, which should be lots of time."

The Vjorkrige shrugged—in a manner similar to Clara; down and then up.

"The time is superfluous; I do not see any reason to stay."

There was a growl of an engine down by the road, and the three women turned to see Arcana pulling up beside Unicorn. Jill hopped out and came around the nose, walking purposefully up the hill toward them.

Selene felt her heart begin to hammer in her chest, torn between her desire to put the whole mess behind her—and the great, black, angry need for justice.

"Listen," she said, quickly and quietly to the Vjorkrige. "If you want to leave, fine. But you'd better do it *now*."

The Vjorkrige only looked at her, confused. Selene held her breath.

"Oh good, you're still here," said Jill, slipping around Clara and addressing the stoic warrior.

"Don't say I didn't warn you," Selene muttered, though she didn't think anyone heard. Jill was talking again:

"I was worried you'd gone poof, like all my other candidates. But you're here, so that's good. I need to ask: how long can you stay? In this world, I mean? Have you got a timer or anything like that?"

The Vjorkrige blinked at her. "My time in this world is limited," she said. "Like anyone's. I do not know how much I have, exactly. But I do not foresee leaving save by my own volition any time soon."

"Great," said Jill. "I was hoping you'd say that. See, it turns out we really need your help."

"I am not obligated to give you any," the Vjorkrige remarked.

"Yeah, I know," said Jill, with a sideways sort of grin. "But I'm hoping you'll want to, anyway. Here's the deal: that asshole who summoned you? He's skipped town. Clean got away and I do mean *clean*. Like, *leave no trace* clean. Now, all the big guns have been called in since he—well, *you*—killed those other guys, but Wilco's not too hopeful about finding him. And even if they *do,* there's the problem of . . . well the fact is . . . they really don't have any evidence except what we saw in that cellar. Once. Which isn't there anymore. Oh, and some really bad phone photos. Point is, the way Wilco is talking, even if they caught the guy, they probably couldn't make anything *stick.*"

"Probably because they ain't *trying*," Selene said, turning away in disgust.

"Yeah, well," said Jill, squaring her shoulders and putting her hands on her hips. "*I'm* trying. I'm asking *you*," she pointed a finger at the Vjorkrige, who frowned. "If I'm not mistaken, *you* could probably find Rafe McCleaver with your eyes shut. And you could testify as to *exactly* who killed Cynthia Jefferson, and how. *You're* the best piece of evidence we have."

The Vjorkrige went very still, like a cat that has spotted a mouse. "You wish me to help you," she said slowly, "to help you bring this man . . . to justice?"

"Yeah," said Jill, but there was something shifty in her voice. Something just a little bit off. It made Selene turn around again.

"You are giving me a reason to stay," said the Vjorkrige. It wasn't a question.

"Only if you want to," Jill said. "But . . . well, I'd really appreciate it. Wilco would too, and Selene"—she looked up at the woman in question, an apology lurking behind her eyes. "I know this was what you were really after."

The Vjorkrige looked from Jill to Selene, and then—almost beseechingly—to Clara, who shrugged.

"You will have to guide me," she said, a little stiffly. "I am not as familiar with your laws as I am with your warfare."

Jill drew in a deep breath, and smiled expansively. "No *problem*," she said, grinning ear to ear. "I'm sure Wilco can get you protective custody or something—though you won't really need it. Do you eat? The fire department brought pizza."

"Pizza," repeated the Vjorkrige, perplexed.

"It must be seen to be believed," Jill assured her. "Come on, I'll introduce you to the wonders of pepperoni."

They turned to go, but Selene reached out and caught hold of Jill's sleeve before she could follow the Vjorkrige down to Arcana.

"You do realize," she hissed. "You put her on the stand—no one'll believe a thing she says."

Jill blinked up at her, innocently. "Why not? After she proves to them she really is an undead warrior summoned by ancient magic, I think most people are bound to believe her."

Selene gaped at her.

"Sister," she said, a little nervously. "The way her kind prove themselves . . . I'm just gonna say . . . it won't be like *anything* folks have seen before."

Jill returned her gaze, her own steadfast and assured and not a little triumphant.

"I know," she said. "That's another reason this *needs* to happen."

And she turned, sliding out of Selene's grasp, and followed the Vjorkrige down to Arcana, where she showed the warrior how to open his doors.

"Do you think she'll do it?" Clara asked, coming to stand behind Selene.

"Our boss?" Selene asked. "Or the Vjorkrige?"

"Both," said Clara.

"Hell if I know," said Selene. "I *do* know it's gonna be messy."

"They have to find McCleaver first," Clara remarked.

"With *her* helping them?" Selene snorted, jerking a thumb at the Vjorkrige. "That won't be hard."

Out of the corner of her eye, she saw Clara nod.

"That book we grabbed outta his basement," Selene said, quieter now. "You get a chance to look at it?"

Another nod.

"It what we thought it was?"

"Yes."

Selene whistled. "Do we show it to Jill?"

Clara sighed, then winced as the motion dragged on her shoulder. "Eventually," she said, after a pause. "When she's ready."

"Sister, that girl was *born* ready."

That got a small smile. "When *we* are ready, then."

"Amen to that," said Selene. "C'mon. Let's make sure she doesn't get herself killed."

And together, they left the little hill and walked down through the graves toward the road.

Hear my heart; it beats
I have starved for ten thousand years
Blood dried in my veins.
But now I wake.

See me rise from ash
Out of smoke and out of mind
You can't say my name
'Cause you know it's wrong
But remember that I am
just dying to live!

Hear the beast at night
She's on a prowl—a rampage
Can you see her teeth?
You can run and you can hide
You've been so wrong.

Still convinced you're right
You're like a plague on my house
Won't you look at me?
Or are you afraid of what you'll see?

You've been so wrong
And I have grown strong
I'm raging in the night
I'm dying to live!
Rage in the night
I die to live!

Hear those cries so true
They're just the sound
Of our tortured minds
You can't ignore us now.
Go run and hide you can't escape

Hear my heart; it beats!
I have starved for ten thousand years
But now I'm awake
I'm hungry and angry—I'm rising

And you were wrong
While we have grown strong!

We're raging in the night
We're dying to live!
Rage in the night
We'll die to live!

Raging in the night
(You've been so wrong)
Rage in the night
(You've been so wrong)
Rage in the night
While
we
grew
strong!

—Rage in the Night/*Deanne Stiletto*

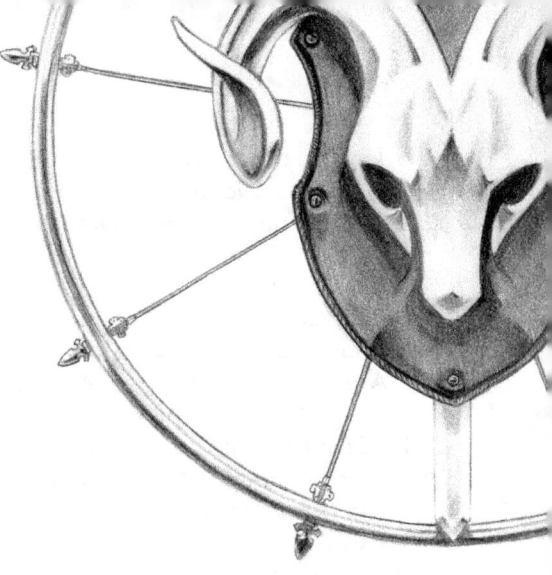

9. BY MOON *and* STAR

St Louis, Missouri
September

Dᴇᴛᴇᴄᴛɪᴠᴇ Rᴏɴᴀʟᴅ J. Wɪʟᴄᴏ sᴀᴛ ᴅᴏᴡɴ opposite the imposing figure in the small, windowless room, and not for the first time wished he were elsewhere. Or at least that that damned Hamilton woman was here—she had promised to come, but five minutes before the interview was due to start he'd received a text that said *moving house. sosorry. tell the V i said hi.*—so here he was, alone save for the court recorder, and whatever it was that was sitting on the other side of the table.

Six and a half feet tall even without her boots and helmet, the Vjorkrige (which was apparently pronounced "v-yor-kree-gay") had a face like carved obsidian and an expression to match. She had taken off most of her armor, revealing a thick wool garment of deep crimson that put him in mind of an oriental robe, only this one had what looked like Nordic runes embroidered along the collar. Her hands—which were as black as her face, except the palms, which were an unsettling gray—rested on the desk in front of her in a studiously relaxed position. Even though she'd been waiting for almost ten minutes, she showed no sign of impatience—not a twitch of an eyebrow or a tap of a finger. He had to watch her keenly for almost half a minute to discern whether or not she was even *breathing.*

She was. Just barely. Wilco tried to take some comfort in this and failed.

But it had been thanks to her eerily precise directions that they'd been able to find their suspect before he even made it out of the state, and it was thanks to her willingness to testify that they had a workable case against him at all. So he swallowed down his nerves and cleared his throat.

"Sorry for the wait," he began, adjusting himself in his chair. Then, at a look from the recorder, he added: "Let the record show that this interview, between Detective Ronald Wilco and the...er...Miss...er...Ms....the

Vjorkrige, is taking place at the St Louis City Municipal Court, beginning at . . . " he checked his watch. It was a quarter past two in the afternoon. He gave the time and date, and then cleared his throat. "Miss . . . er . . . look, not to be overly blunt about it, but what do you prefer to be called?"

The black face, with its bright black eyes, blinked at him.

"I do not understand the question," the Vjorkrige said, her voice calm and smooth and cold as a slab of rock.

"Are you a Miss Vjorkrige or a Ms. Vjorkrige, have you got any other names . . . ?" Detective Wilco trailed off. The Vjorkrige's attention had drifted from him and now seemed to be floating somewhere over his head, beyond the confines of the little room.

"I had a name, once," she said, and her voice was incrementally lighter— almost wistful. "But it died long ago. Now I am just Vjorkrige." Her attention shifted, refocusing on him, and Detective Wilco felt something cold run up his back.

"Vjorkrige, then," he said, filling in the form in front of him. "Do you know why you are here?"

"I do," said the Vjorkrige, emphasizing the first word in a way which suggested she doubted anyone else did.

"Could you please state that reason, for the record?" Detective Wilco asked.

The Vjorkrige considered for a moment, as if she were entertaining the possibility of not answering. Then she said:

"I am here to bear witness to the death of Cynthia Jefferson, so that the lies perpetrated by Rafe McCleaver may not be sunk into oblivion. I am here to speak truth, where no other can. I am here to serve my own will. I am here to live."

Detective Wilco mentally chewed on this statement before going on.

"So you agree that you are here of your own free will, and that what you are about to say is the truth, given freely and without duress?"

The Vjorkrige thought about this. At his elbow, the court recorder was beginning to fidget.

"Yes," said the Vjorkrige eventually, almost as though she were surprised at her own answer.

"Good," said Detective Wilco, ticking a box. "Now, please give your name, for the record—or, whatever it is you are legally recognized by," he added, seeing the Vjorkrige's mouth open in protest.

"I am Vjorkrige," she said, settling back into her chair.

"Is that your first name or your last name?" Detective Wilco asked.

"It is not my first," said the Vjorkrige. "It would be presumptuous to assume it will be my last. For now it is merely sufficient."

"What does that mean?" asked Detective Wilco.

"It is what I am."

He sighed. This was the part he had been dreading.

"And what . . . for the record . . . exactly is that?"

No response. Then the Vjorkrige said, in tones somewhat more halting—as though she was having to sort the words out carefully beforehand:

"I am a Warrior of Vjor, one of the legion of dead who serve the Grand God of War. I exist here by the life of Cynthia Jefferson, who was sacrificed per the Rite of Varriger, and whose soul was traded for mine so that I might fulfill the needs of an earthly commander."

The court recorder was giving Detective Wilco curious looks, and no wonder.

"In plain speak, then," he said, rubbing his eyes. "You're a resurrected ghost-warrior summoned by Rafe McCleaver when he murdered Cynthia Jefferson?"

A slow nod. "That statement is factually correct."

"I almost hate to ask this, but do you have any way of verifying your identity? It's a pretty serious business, trying someone for murder—and you're the key witness. Can't say the defense will be much impressed if I put you on the stand and you just *say* you're a resurrected ghost-warrior . . ."

It was a problem he'd been wrestling with ever since Jill Hamilton had talked him into this mad scheme.

But the Vjorkrige was nodding, a small, satisfied smile creeping over her face.

"Your people lack the perceptiveness to see me for what I am," she said. "Gillian Hamilton has explained I will need to offer you some form of proof. I have thought long on this, and arrangements have been made which should satisfy even the most near-sighted of your kin."

The cold was back, creeping up Detective Wilco's spine and lodging between his shoulder blades.

"What do you mean, 'arrangements'?" he asked.

"At present I can offer you nothing but what I am," said the Vjorkrige, lifting her hands from the table and spreading her arms. "You say this is not enough, so I have requested the aid of one whose word should satisfy all as to the validity of my existence."

Detective Wilco found himself glancing nervously around the little room.

"I don't suppose . . . they're here now?" he asked.

"Not yet," said the Vjorkrige, lowering her arms. She leaned forward over the desk and repeated, with deep sincerity. "*Arrangements* have been *made.*"

Roads are treacherous things. A bad road might have obvious problems, like washouts and broken pavement. Good roads have other problems: they give drivers a false sense of security, such as the erroneous impression that they can drive as fast as they like and still be perfectly safe. Because when you are comfortably ensconced in a large metal object with soft seats that responds instantly to your commands, it is easy to forget that roads are not their own sovereign states. They exist in a world much older and wilder, which can—and frequently does—forget that things like roads and cars are there.

Tragically, most of the time this results in roadkill. Never mind that the raccoons and bunnies and deer were there first. When pitted against a fast-moving piece of metal the result is almost always a fatality on the part of the non-human participant.

Except when it's not.

Such as when the red BMW, speeding out of St Louis one late summer night, its driver operating under the dangerous assumption that the wide, empty road before them would *remain* wide and empty as they pushed seventy mph along a fifty mph section.

Suddenly a dark lump appeared on the horizon of their headlamps. Too late they braked; too late they tried to swerve. There was a sick, thumping *crunch,* and then the road was smooth again. The driver winced—partly out of sympathy to whatever had just been run over, but mostly at the possible damage that had been done to their car.

Though perhaps it would not have made a difference if they had felt particularly bad about it. To the lump in the road—whose nap had been so rudely interrupted—the emotional state of the driver was of less importance than the fact that they been run over in the first place.

The lump shivered to life, scales gleaming in the distant light of the waxing moon, and opened a wide, red mouth in a wail of anguish that sounded more angry than pained.

Snug in their speeding metal shell, the driver remained blissfully unaware until there was another thump, and then a horrible screech of tearing metal, then a scream of skidding rubber, and then the car was flipped off the road as neatly as an expert chef flips a pancake.

It might have been of some comfort to the doomed driver to know that, as far as the lump in the road was concerned, it did not bear them any personal grudge. Its issue was with the heavy thing that had run it over. Then again, as it took out its issues by pummeling said thing into something resembling a crooked pretzel and leaving the crushed remains smoking in a ditch, the driver was in no condition to think anything by the end of it.

Roads were treacherous things. Clara knew this. In some ways, she often thought, there was nothing more dangerous than innocent-looking roads. They could be hiding potholes, traps, or might not lead where you wanted. Sometimes they led exactly where you *didn't* want.

And sometimes you met things on them that it was better you had not.

Which was what had obviously happened to the smart red car folded into thirds and lying, tires up, in a ditch.

"Lucky how you can find these things before the police," Jill said, an edge of dark humor in her voice. She was beginning to get used to the sight of broken bodies and dead people, and that in itself was unsettling. But she kept right on taking pictures, careful not to disturb the cold, crumpled car or the cold, crushed human inside.

"It wasn't luck," said Clara, flatly. "I was on patrol."

Selene looked around from her post up by the road (where she had been directing traffic around Arcana—strangely, though passersby were more than happy to slow down and stare, none so far had insisted on *stopping,* which was actually a small mercy).

"You were *looking* for something like this?" Selene asked, raising an eyebrow.

Clara did one of her inverted shrugs: shoulders slumped, then rose again. She could not precisely explain the itching feeling which had nagged her mind all night until she'd gotten up with the crack of dawn, got on her motorcycle, and gone for a ride. The itching got less the further she got from the city, until suddenly it got a lot worse, and then she'd seen the wreck.

The itch was gone now, replaced by a general feeling of growing unrest, like whatever this was was part of something much bigger. In the avalanche of a catastrophe, this was the first pebble that clattered down and struck someone on the forehead.

But she knew she couldn't explain it like that, especially not to Jill. So she shrugged.

"Could it be unicorns again?" Jill asked, putting away her camera at last and starting to take notes.

"Nah-ah," said Selene, coming down from the road to stand alongside the car. She pointed at a concave piece of its door. "See them?"

Jill scuttled around in the thick, damp grass and came to stand beside her. In the way of someone taking pictures, she had not gotten a good look at the thing she'd been taking the pictures *of.*

"Not hoofmarks," she said, with enough certainty for it not to be a question.

"Teeth marks," said Selene, running two dark fingers several inches in the air above said marks. Then she switched hands and did the same to some other deep gashes. "*Claw* marks."

"So not unicorns . . . "

"It could be a werewolf," Clara mused.

"You ever met a werewolf who could do *this*?" Selene asked, kicking at a shredded tire.

Clara did one of her inverted shrugs, and didn't answer.

"Oh, hi," said Jill, and Clara and Selene instinctively stepped away from the wreck and looked around for whoever Jill was talking to. But Jill was pointing at the grass on the other side of the ditch, where an embankment of soft earth ran up to join a sparse wood. The embankment had been torn by the footprints of something very big and heavy with rather long claws. A depression in the earth between the tracks suggested that the creature had a heavy, dragging tail.

"Looks like it was the size of an alligator," Jill said, pulling out her camera again.

The itch was back in Clara's mind, sharper now—almost painful. It surprised her into speaking.

"It's a worm," she said.

"Say what?" said Jill. "What kind of worm's got *legs*?"

"A kind of dragon," said Clara, distracted by the itch in her mind. Was it close by? Or was it angry? Her hand twitched instinctively for the sword on her back.

"Naw," said Selene, shaking her head. "Not here . . . not *here*."

"Dragon . . ." repeated Jill, blankly.

"Small, flightless, but strong. Very strong," said Clara, cautiously climbing up the embankment and peering into the trees.

"No *way* could a dragon turn up here," Selene was saying. "Not even a worm. Too many humans. It's even harder for them than *unicorns* to manifest in this world. Clara?"

Clara had reached the top of the embankment, and stood there, balancing, as she stared into the light forest.

At least, it *should* have been a light forest. She should by rights have been able to see through it to the outskirts of St Louis and even a couple high-rise buildings.

Instead, the space beneath the branches was dark, and in the humid air the shadows seemed to crawl. There was a thickness in the atmosphere, and a smell like burned rubber and rotting plants.

Clara had carefully removed all the hair from her head, but even so she felt her scalp prickle, and unthinkingly she drew her sword.

"Clara?" someone asked.

It was Selene, who had in response slid her sawn-off shotgun out of its holster.

"It's in there," said Clara, nodding toward the wood, and set off with long strides through the undergrowth.

A dragon—a proper, high dragon—would have been too much for her. They were worse than gods, in their way. But even a worm was bad enough. Like the worst sort of invasive species: drop them into the comparatively soft, warm, defenseless human world, and they would soon devastate the native population of . . . well, of everything.

The itch had hardened now, focused into a single, sharp spike in Clara's mind. But she could think around it, at least—use it like a very specialized form of hearing—as she crept carefully through the wood.

For a large person, Clara could be surprisingly silent if she wished. So when she heard a sharp *crack* of a twig underfoot she knew it wasn't her.

She spun, swift and silent, and found Selene standing in the gap between two trees, looking both annoyed and concerned. She had her gun out, pointed conscientiously at the ground, with her index finger resting against the outside of the trigger guard.

"*Stop*," Clara commanded, in a voice that was more air than sound.

Selene froze.

It was *here.* So very close. Clara scanned the undergrowth of dead grass and drifts of leaves, while all around the thick air pressed in. The spike in her mind that was the dragon's presence practically burned.

Then the dragon blinked.

It was all the movement Clara needed.

In an instant she had stabbed her sword into the suspiciously large pile of leaves, but an instant before *that* the leaves erupted, and something like an alligator, only darker and spikier and with horns and claws like minia-ture scythes, sprang from under her sword and made for Selene.

Selene took one step back—to steady herself—and then calmly put two rounds into the creature's face.

The worm paused, momentarily stunned, and Selene began to reload.

Clara took advantage of the distraction to mount the worm from the rear and ram her sword into its neck—through the gap in the scales that was just big enough for a sword to fit sideways. She pushed until she felt the tip meet the spine, and then she *really* pushed.

The worm shuddered violently, and Clara *yanked* sideways.

There was a satisfyingly horrible *snap* and the creature went still.

The hot spike of awareness slowly faded from Clara's mind, and she blinked up to find Selene looking down at her with guarded respect.

Then there was a crashing from the embankment as Jill arrived, snap-ping branches and spitting leaves.

"Oh *no,*" she said, upon seeing Clara and the worm's corpse. "Don't tell me you *killed* it!"

In a hotel room it would have been out of the question. Luckily (or *un*luckily, if you asked Selene) they had acquired a more permanent base while they waited for Rafe McCleaver's trial. Well, his *arraignment,* tech-nically, since that would be the first time the supernatural, undead war-rior known as the Vjorkrige, who was the only surviving witness, would be asked to testify. Jill had originally found them an apartment in Midtown, but after one look around the neighborhood Selene declared it unusable, and insisted they move south of Interstate 44, to where she had (by means of a few favors and some heavy glaring) secured access to an abandoned schoolhouse.

This was a long, rectangular building of red brick with a small living area attached to the back, and while it had no air conditioning, bad heat, and questionable electricity, it did have the advantage of a very large room with lots of big windows up by the ceiling, which Jill lost no time in con-verting into a lab—with the help of a lot of fans and a rented chest freezer.

It was also surrounded by a heavy chain-link fence decorated with barbed wire, which served to limit the reactions of their neighbors to curi-ous glances from the church across the street on the first Sunday. Selene was grateful. She'd been out walking every day the first week, and while she felt safer here than anywhere else in Missouri, she still preferred the locals to keep to themselves. Besides, she was uncertain how they might react to Clara.

"It's not that you're white," she'd told Clara. "It's that you're six-foot-four-blue-eyed-and-shaved-head-*white.* You look like a neo-Nazi waiting for his first ink."

Clara had considered this.

"But I am a woman," she'd said.

"Sister," Selene sighed, patting her on the arm. "That ain't exactly obvious to some folks."

Now, however, in the relative safety of the warm, drafty schoolroom, Selene allowed herself to relax with a cool beer while Clara helped Jill maneuver the stiff, plastic-wrapped package that was the worm out of the freezer and onto the makeshift exam table (three school desks put together with a plywood board over the top), and begin to unwrap it.

"He'll need to thaw first," Clara pointed out.

"So we'll wait, what? Five minutes?" Jill said, wiping her brow with a cotton bandana and then tying it around her head.

Selene regarded the corpse on the table while they waited. It was not a big worm, all things considered; could be and probably had been mistaken for a large alligator. But the horny ridges rising from its spine spoke otherwise, and its protruding lower jaw had a spiny beard that sprouted at the chin and ran up each side before terminating in long spikes on either cheek. The eyes had clouded over now, but they had—Selene remembered vividly—been a piercing shade of gold streaked with orange, and the strange, star-shaped pupils were still clearly visible.

Its body was long and its legs were short, but it retained an elegance similar to that of a snake. Its scales gleamed, even in frozen death, and where its blood had poured out from the fatal wound it was not black, but bright like molten gold.

"He should'na been there," Selene sighed.

"What, in the road?" asked Jill.

"In this *world*," said Selene. "You can listen to me an' Clara wax all poetical about worms and dragons and such, but it's all so much . . . what'd you call it? Book-learnin'? We don't *know* anything: the last person who saw a live dragon probably died over five hundred years ago. You don't *see* them here anymore 'cept in TV shows and movies."

Jill sniffed. "Why'd you have to kill it, then?" she asked.

"Because it was going to kill us," Clara answered. She gazed down at the corpse, and frowned. "I suggest we find another method of containment," she said, and pointed to where a faint steam was rising from the plastic-covered table. It smelled of burning rubber.

"Is that—holy cow is that its *blood?*" Jill said, half horrified, half excited. "I think we've got some aluminum foil—will one of you take a sample?"

"With *what?*" Selene asked, downing the last of her beer.

"Try glass!" Jill shouted, heading for the kitchen.

Clara looked from the corpse, to Selene, and then down at her beer bottle.

"Aw, heck," said Selene, offering it to her. "I'm done with it."

Getting the blood into the bottle was a tricky business, since Clara didn't want to get the blood on any of her leathers—let alone her skin—and Selene wasn't going near the stuff. She'd never encountered a real dragon before—even a worm—but she'd heard stories.

When you worked daily with the stuff of legends, myths, and nightmares, you learned to *trust* the stories.

"Careful there," she was saying as Clara held the bottle under the table to catch the drops of golden blood. The lip was already splashed, but so far the glass was resisting better than the plastic had.

There was the sound of an engine outside, a creak of a car door, a slam, and a knock. Distantly they heard Jill getting the door, and Selene felt herself biting back the impulsive order of "No, don't answer it!"

Jill, who read as "Not Black" to anyone with a working pair of eyes, was still safer dealing with the locals here than Selene would have been just a few miles south. Besides, the voices coming from the kitchen didn't sound angry. One of them did sound upset, though, and it wasn't Jill.

It was a man's voice, pitched higher than normal and speaking fast. A few moments later the owner followed Jill back into the main hall, carrying an extra roll of aluminum foil in his hands and a bewildered expression on his face.

He was, as far as Selene was any judge, a good-looking young man with a narrow face supported by a precisely trimmed goatee and severely short hair. He was wearing the uniform blues and official cap of an SLMPD officer, which put him a little below the dead worm on the table, in Selene's opinion.

" . . . and you're saying the painting came to life?" Jill said, continuing a conversation that had begun in the other room.

"Not the whole thing," said the police officer, a little defensively. "Just the woman. She's gone missing now, and she took the knife with her."

"I see," said Jill, and Selene could almost believe she did.

"Hey now, what now?" she asked.

Clara stood up, gingerly holding the bottle, and paused at the sight of the newcomer, her free hand reflexively twitching as if to cover the dead worm, then realizing it was too late, she moved around in front of it and glared at the officer.

"Guys, this is Officer . . . Wheeler?" Jill asked. The policeman nodded.

"Officer Wheeler," she went on. "He's got something sort of up our alley, I think. Officer, this is Clara Nordstern and Selene Shields, my . . . colleagues. Have you got my blood there?" she asked, marching over to Clara and taking the bottle out of her limp fingers. She sniffed it.

"Did you even wash this *out* before?" she gasped in horror. "It had *beer* in it."

"You said something about a painting of a woman coming to life?" Clara said over Jill's head, leveling her cold, blue gaze on the unfortunate officer.

Officer Wheeler straightened up, puffing his chest out in a way that put Selene in mind of a pompous frog.

"Tell them what you told me," Jill said, wandering off to the side of the room where she kept her field kit. She set the beer bottle down and then came back, unrolling the aluminum foil as she did.

"Lift the head up, will you Clara?" she asked.

Clara obliged, and whatever Officer Wheeler was going to say came out as a long wheeze when he finally noticed what was on the table.

"What the *hell*?" he exclaimed, one hand going for the piece on his belt. Jill didn't even turn a hair.

"You said Detective Wilco sent you to us," she said dryly. "*This* is why. Don't worry, it's perfectly dead. Now tell them what you told me—only slower, with more details."

Officer Wheeler was so distracted, however, that his story came out in bits and pieces. But eventually there were enough of them that Selene was able to construct the following picture:

Officer Wheeler had responded to a domestic disturbance call put in by one of the neighbors of a man named Richard Stein. The neighbor had been frightened, and stammered something along the lines of Mr. Stein not being right in the head ever since his wife had died.

If he didn't have a wife, Officer Wheeler had thought, then who was he having his domestic disturbance with? The neighbor couldn't say.

So Officer Wheeler and his partner (who he referred to as Peaches) went around and, finding the house dark and quiet, made every attempt to contact Mr. Stein before making entry through the back door—which was unlocked.

They found the house in disarray; furniture overturned and bookshelves knocked aside, papers scattered over the floor, all the mirrors broken and every picture in the house pulled down from the walls and smashed. No sign of Mr. Stein, though his car was in the garage, and they found his wallet on the floor by the overturned bed.

Then Peaches had discovered the painting, which was remarkable purely on the basis that it was the only thing in the house that remained intact, hanging in a place of honor over where the dining room table had been.

It had been a portrait painted of Mr. and Mrs. Stein around the time of their marriage, but someone had been through and defaced the thing, slicing the canvas across Mr. Stein's throat and giving Mrs. Stein horrible black holes for eyes and a mad, toothy grin. There was also a kitchen knife embedded in the floor in front of the portrait. Officer Wheeler had barely entered the room, when the image of the woman in the painting came to life, surged out of the canvas, grabbed the knife, and took off through the ruined house and out the back door.

Officer Wheeler got rather hung up at this point and, after listening to him say, "And then she—I mean the painting—she—the painting—thought I'd piss myself—she—the painting—" for almost a minute Selene gave a great sigh and cut him off.

"She came out of the painting, didn't she?"

Officer Wheeler nodded.

"She take the knife?"

Another nod.

"Gods *damn* it," said Selene, casually.

"You know what this is?" Jill asked sharply.

Selene shrugged.

"Sounds like a pretty standard haunting, though you gotta wonder what went on between those two before she died, for her to leave a ghost behind that was strong enough to manifest corporeally—even with the help of an image."

"Haunting . . ." echoed the policeman, weakly.

"What did you *think* we'd say?" Selene asked. "'No problem, officer, it's a perfectly normal occurrence, here's some scopolamine, take the rest of the day off'?"

"Have you found his body yet?" Clara asked, quietly.

"His body?" said Officer Wheeler, blinking at her. "Whose body?"

"The body of Richard Stein," said Clara.

"You think he's dead?"

"All signs point to a revenge haunting," said Clara. "Normally, such things never amount to more than a run of bad luck. However, when there is enough free-floating spiritual power, it can allow some ghosts to manifest corporally and take more . . . material actions."

"You're saying Richard Stein was killed by the ghost of his dead wife?" Officer Wheeler looked ready to bolt, or arrest the lot of them. Selene began sidling around behind Clara.

"It's happened before," Clara said, lowering and raising her huge, leather-covered shoulders.

"Fairly often, actually," added Selene.

"So what do we do about it?" Jill asked, rewrapping the worm corpse, which was beginning to smell faintly of burned pepper.

"We-ell," said Selene, drawing out the single vowel for all it was worth. "Time was you could do the old Gunn Classic—that's, er, find the bones of whatever it is that's causing the haunting, pour salt over 'em, and some gasoline, and set the lot on fire—but so many people did that, nowadays most ghosts are resistant. So we do it the hard way."

Jill passed a hand over her face. "Do I even want to know?"

"You'll see," said Selene, with a humorless grin. She peered around Clara's elbow at Officer Wheeler. "So you wanna take us 'round to Mr. Stein's house, or you gonna field this one on your own?"

* * *

Detective Wilco stood outside the door to Rafe McCleaver's cell, idly wishing he could choke people just by staring at them, like in those *Star Wars* movies. If ghosts and monsters and undead warriors could be real, why couldn't he have some special powers? But no matter how hard he concentrated, Rafe McCleaver kept right on breathing as easy as ever.

"I ain't gonna confess, if that's what you're waiting for," the man said, leaning smugly back against the wall of his cell and crossing his legs. "Got nothing to confess to, and you got no one to say otherwise."

"Don't I?" asked Wilco, absently. He was imagining all the wonderful colors McCleaver's face might turn if deprived of oxygen for long enough.

"Some wacko who thinks she's an undead warrior?" said Rafe McCleaver with a snort of laughter. "What's she got? Some driver's license from the Queen of the Underworld? No judge in their right mind is gonna believe a word she says—and her *word*, Detective, is all you have."

All I have to get you on first degree murder, thought Detective Wilco. *There's still Hamilton, Shields and Nordstern—not to mention myself— who could bring charges of assault and kidnapping.* But he had a point. The murder charge was what had allowed Wilco to bring McCleaver to St Louis. It was what was keeping him locked up, at present, and if the judge didn't take the case up after the arraignment . . .

Suddenly Wilco was faced, in his mind, by the memory of the Vjorkrige, and her silent, still strength, as she had said *"Arrangements have been made . . ."*

It gave him shivers. He just wished he could share that feeling with Rafe McCleaver.

Richard Stein's house was a cheerful blue two-story with a wide, welcoming front porch, in a neighborhood of St Louis very different from the one where Jill and her crew had been staying. All the houses on the street were large and prosperous looking, with painstakingly watered lawns decorated with roses and hydrangeas.

From the outside the Stein residence maintained a respectable fa ade, save the single broken window which had been covered with a black trash bag. From the inside it was, as Officer Wheeler had described, a complete mess.

"Was this a ghost or a tornado?" Jill asked, picking her way over a chair whose legs had been snapped off to stand in the blown-out doorway to the living room.

"Sometimes it's one and the same," Selene admitted. She had made straight for the problematic painting, and was now looking up at it with a frown creasing her brow.

"You do this a lot, do you?" Officer Wheeler asked, smiling nervously.

Selene gave him a blank look and the policeman quailed, then turned back to the wall.

The portrait must have been a nice one, and expensive to commission. It posed the couple like a pair of Regency lovers, clasping hands as they stood on a bridge covered in flowers with a bucolic pasture in the background.

Which made the defacement all the more unsettling. The canvas under the husband's throat cut, and his face splashed with black paint so it was completely hidden, and the woman . . .

. . . where the woman should have been there was only blank canvas, with a faint discoloration where the paint ended, that suggested burning.

"You find any other reports of . . . domestic disturbance?" Selene asked after a few moments.

"Well," said Wheeler. "The lady's been *dead* for over five years . . . "

"I meant *before* that," said Selene.

Officer Wheeler pulled a face and rubbed the nape of his neck. "Hadn't actually got around to checking that yet . . . hey, Peaches!"

Peaches—whose name tag said he should rightly be called Officer Max Pudonovski—had turned out to be a large slavic man with short dark hair and eyes like sapphires set in caverns under a foreboding brow. He was almost as tall as Clara, and the two had had a brief staring contest before Jill tactfully suggested Clara check the basement.

Now he put his head around the corner and glared at them. Wheeler ignored the expression of his partner and went on.

"You ever run that search on Stein? See if there was any previous reports?"

"No," said Peaches.

"No, you didn't run the search, or no, there were no previous reports?" Jill asked, brazenly.

Peaches hesitated. He seemed troubled by Jill—whether by her tenacity, her fierce concentration, or his inability to intimidate her—and took this question a little more seriously.

"Ran a pass," he said. "Nothing pinged."

"Which doesn't mean there wasn't *something*," Selene sighed.

"I don't get that," said Wheeler. "Like, you got someone hurting you, you pick up the phone and call for help. That's what we're *here* for."

This got him humorless stares from both women. Jill weighed the benefits of giving him a 101 on spousal abuse statistics against the cost of the time that might take, paused when she realized she was considering explaining *spousal abuse* to a *police officer*, and felt a wall of red anger rise up in front of her eyes.

"Right," said Selene, with the sound of someone swallowing a particularly bitter pill. "We'll need this painting taken down. *Gently*, mind you. It's our best bet at catching her ghost."

"So . . . it's really a ghost?" said Peaches, his tone an odd mix of derisive scorn and cautious hope.

"Ghost, spirit, really angry lifelike afterimage," said Selene. "Something like that. They're all basically the same thing. What we gotta do now is find out where she's gone, get her back in the painting, seal it and . . . well, ordinarily you gotta destroy these things, but seeing as it's probably too late for Mr. Stein, she should be harmless once she's back in the painting."

"I don't suppose . . ." Jill began.

"No, you can't keep it," Selene sighed. "That'd be asking for trouble. Naw, we'd best bury it. With her actual body, too. That should keep her spirit well enough chained that it won't get out and cause problems. O'course, doing that's gonna require some prep work. We'll need a summoning array, for starters, some sulfur, and salt. Lots of salt."

There was a muffled crash from the direction of the basement stairs, and a scream that made Jill's ears ring and her teeth hurt.

"She's coming at you!" Clara shouted through the wail, and Selene leapt into action.

"You boys didn't see this," she said, swinging her sawn-off shotgun, Elvis, out from under her jacket. In an instant she'd cracked the barrel open, pulled out four slugs from her pocket, loaded two of them and stuck the remaining pair between her teeth.

"Eff'ry buddy *drrn!*" she shouted, as well as she could through her mouth full of bullet.

Something had exploded from the floor and was hanging over the trashed dining room table like a thick, buzzing cloud of flies. Blood dripped from it onto the floor, and its whirling interior seemed to be made of strips of dried paint, flicking in and out of the dark shadow.

From her vantage point on the floor, a piece of broken chair digging painfully into her side, Jill saw the buzzing, roiling, dripping cloud advance on them.

Bang, said Selene's gun.

The cloud rocked sideways, pieces of it scattering and dissolving into the air.

Bang, went the gun a second time, and the cloud shrieked in pain. It had dissipated so far now that Jill could see Clara, looming like a vengeful, leather-clad whale, her sword unsheathed and gleaming in the smoky light.

"The *painting*, Selene!" she shouted, and brought her sword around in a careful arc—narrowly missing the kitchen cupboard and a piece of table. It caused the tip of her sword to circle what remained of the buzzing cloud, leaving a faint, sparkling trail in the air behind it.

The cloud screamed again, but Selene had already leapt back, holstering her weapon, and was dragging the painting down.

"Outta the way, *outta the way*," she said, shoving her way past the officers.

The cloud must have seen her coming. It shot out a tendril, and Jill saw the knife only at the last second.

Selene jumped, the painting held in front of her like a shield, bringing it down on the cloud even as the knife shot forward.

It sliced clean through the canvas, coming out by Selene's ear, and whizzed through the air to hit the ceiling fan and drop—luckily handle first—in between the police officers.

The painting hit the floor with a loud *whap* and Selene landed on top of it with a pained *oof*, as Clara hurried forward and, once Selene had crawled off it, stabbed it through with her sword.

There was a muffled moan, and a thick cloud of black smoke belched from under the painting, hanging heavy along the floor, before slowly fading. It left behind a smell of rotting fruit, undercut with a sharp tang of salt water.

Clara prodded the picture frame with her finger. It didn't move.

"Well done," she said, the respect audible in her voice.

"Thanks," said Selene, a little hoarsely. Gingerly she leaned back on her heels and, spitting out the slugs that had still been in her mouth, wiped them on the sleeve of her jacket and popped them back into her pocket.

"'Kay boys, coast is clear. Though, ah, I'm thinking maybe we wanna burn this after all?"

Clara did one of her inverted shrugs. "She has no reason to act again: Richard Stein is already dead."

"Then go stick it in her grave, you should be okay," said Selene. She turned to the two officers, who were only just now daring to get up. "You boys got that? Good. Right. Here, Jill, I think there's some splinters of the frame you can take for samples. Did anyone get the knife? Yeah, you'll want to bury that, too."

Selene pulled Arcana into the little drive of their makeshift base and sat slumped at the wheel while Jill went around and closed the cyclone-fence gate behind Clara. When she got out of the truck it was to find Jill walking back up the drive accompanied by a small girl with huge, bushy pigtails, leading a bicycle that might have once been pink, but was now so covered with scratches, dents, and stickers, that only bits and pieces of the original color peeked through. She looked up at Selene with large, frightened brown eyes, and she clutched the handlebars of her bicycle like it was the only thing keeping her upright.

"Hey," said Jill. "This is . . . uh . . . *Kida*, I think. Kida, right?" she asked, bending her head a little.

In reply, the girl shivered so hard it was difficult to tell whether she had nodded or not.

Jill sighed. "Anyway, I think it's you she wants. Kida, this is Selene."

Selene looked down at a face which, given enough years and close encounters with monsters, might have looked very much like her own, and found herself met and held by those eyes.

Maybe the close encounters had already started.

"What's up?" she asked, digging her hands into her pockets. "Did Shawneel send you here? S'okay if she did. Won't get her in trouble."

But the girl—Kida—was already shaking her head.

"Shawneel says I stay away," she said, her voice faint and fluttery, like a dried up autumn leaf. "But Jolly, he tells me Imma gone crazy if I just sits all day waitin' on it to get gone. So I say, who'm I gonna ask when Mama don't believe me? And Jolly, *he* say you was the one helpin' Shawneel when her man went pop-eyes and I could tell you 'bout it because you already gone crazy."

The words came out in a rush, and the little girl's shoulders slumped after she had finished, as though they had been building up inside her for some time.

Selene thoughtfully rubbed the bruise on her side that she had acquired in the scuffle with the ghost, while she watched Jill slowly register what had just been said.

"We're not crazy," she said. "And neither are you. Why don't you come inside and tell us—or Selene—what's happened."

Kida looked ready to bolt at this suggestion, until Selene took over.

"Jill, I need you to run to the grocery store," she said.

"You what?" said Jill.

"We need lemonade," said Selene, and turned to the child. "You come put your bike on the porch, hon, and I'll have Clara get some ice tea going. You look like you could use an ice tea. And then, when you cooled down a bit, you tell me what it is got you so scared."

So saying she led the girl up to the house end of the hall, stuck the bike securely in a corner of the porch, and opened the door to the kitchen. She looked around. Jill was still standing beside Arcana, looking bemused.

"Well get goin', girl," Selene said, flapping a hand in her direction. "I told you we need *lemonade*."

In the kitchen Clara and Kida moved around each other like two cats who weren't certain if they were going to be friends or foes yet. But everyone was hot and sticky, and the iced tea served to soothe the tension somewhat. Kida wouldn't speak, however, until she had drunk down a tall glass of milk as well. Then it all came pouring out.

There was a monster under her bed. A *real* monster. It had got her mother's pet dog, which everyone thought had run off, but Kida had heard the bones crunching at night, and she smelled it slowly rotting. That morning she'd woken to find her room a complete mess, and laced through the clutter something that looked like a rope, but wasn't. It was black and a little gooey, and smelled of dead dog.

"So I go out my window," she explained, wiping a stray drop of milk off her cheek. "Hang on by my fingertips and drop. Jolly sees me and comes into the garden asking what happen. So I tells him, and he tells me I go to you, only I have to go in for breakfast and then Mama makes me go to school—but I ride as hard as I can soon as it's over and I sees you pullin' in. So I ask the lady at the gate can I be talkin' to the sister in the truck and that's how I found you."

432

She played with her empty glass for a while, turning it around in little circles where water, having condensed on its side, had trickled down and formed a wet patch on the tabletop.

Outside there was the rumble of Arcana, the clatter of the gate, and a further crunch and grind as the truck was parked, and then Jill was walking in the door carrying a jug of lemonade in one hand and a can of concentrate in the other. "I didn't know which one you wanted," she said, by way of explanation, setting both goods down in front of Selene.

For answer Selene took the jug and, after offering it to Kida, who shook her head, opened the top and drank straight from the bottle.

"Kida has a bogart under her bed," Clara told Jill, matter-of-factly.

"Swell," said Jill. "What do we do with bogarts?"

"We drink our lemonade," said Selene, taking another sip. "And then we go kill 'em."

Kida's house was only a couple blocks from their own base, so they walked—Selene with her duffle bag stuffed full of weapons and equipment slung over her back, and Clara with her sword swinging with the roll of her shoulders as she strode along. Kida walked practically in Selene's shadow, one hand on her bike and one hand in Selene's, while Jill brought up the rear.

It was a hot, humid, muggy afternoon, and soon Jill was sweating. The houses were dark and still, and the only other people they saw were a pair of boys sitting in the back of a pickup truck. They wore oversized t-shirts with the arms cut off and the kind of baseball cap that only works when worn backwards (which they were) and sneakers with the laces untied. One of them had a basketball balanced on his knee with the help of his hand, but it nearly slipped from his grasp when he saw the four of them round the corner and go marching past.

Kida led them to a small house with peeling red paint and a composite roof much the worse for wear. The drive was empty, but a patch of gravel black with oil indicated where the family car usually sat. They waited on the sunny porch while Kida unlocked the front door and then followed her inside, through a living room cluttered with game controllers, CD cases, and little plastic action figures, and along a hallway with a dusty carpet. The girl finally stopped outside a plain white door with "Kida's Room" written awkwardly on it in purple crayon.

"It here," Kida said, and pointed.

She needn't have bothered. There was a thick, black fog seeping out from under the door, sending tendrils like searching roots twining into the hall.

Selene bent forward, sniffed, and then set down her duffle bag and began pawing through its contents.

"Rosemary," she said, pulling out a bundle of herbs wrapped in string. She handed it to Clara. "Rue," she went on, handing over another sprig. "Aaand . . . I'm thinking we want iron *and* silver, yeah?"

"It would be best," said Clara, her hands full of herb.

Selene cursed under her breath, but a moment later she straightened up, holding a bar of black metal and a thin, tarnished chain—which she began to wrap around the bar.

"Some lead would be nice, too," she sighed.

"What for?" Jill asked.

"Bogarts are mostly magic, ain't they?" said Selene. "Iron and silver both good against them, but so's lead. Don't know what our fella here is gonna dislike more, so it's good to cover all the bases. 'Kay," she said, handing the chain-wrapped bar to Clara. "Tie on the herbs, will ya? I got some iron shot in here I need to load up. Ah, y'all might want to stand behind me for this one." She pulled her trench gun, Freddie, from the bag as she said this, and as one they crowded to the far side of the hall—if only to keep from being whacked by the butt of the long rifle as Selene swung it around to point at the door.

When the shotgun was fully loaded, and Selene was standing with the butt resting firmly against her collarbone, Clara edged around, hefting the strange bundle of rosemary, rue, iron and silver, as she took hold of the handle.

"Mark?" she asked.

"Three and go," replied Selene.

"One, two, three . . . *go*—" said Clara, and at the "go" shoved open the door and tossed the bar of iron with silver and herbs into the room.

Black smoke billowed out into the hall. Jill heard the bundle land with a muffled *clunk,* and then a horrible retching noise filled the air.

It made her stomach curl and she backed further down the hall, only to bump into Kida, who'd had the same idea.

Through the smoke she saw Clara dive behind Selene, and the dark woman leveled her gun at the door and fired.

The *bang* temporarily canceled out the retching sound, and before it could come back Selene fired again. She took a step forward and was lost into the smoke, but another *bang* proved she hadn't moved far.

Something screamed. It lifted the hair on Jill's arms and made her ears hurt. She clapped her hands over them, but the noise seemed to have burrowed into her brain and clung there, like the ringing that sometimes came on out of nowhere—only ten times worse. Kida was on her knees, fingers dug into her ears, but still peering fearfully into the smoke.

Jill looked up in time to see Clara's bulk disappear into the room, and then Selene shouted, "I *got* it Clara! Get the *window!*"

There was a panicked scrabbling sound, more choked screams—Clara grunted, Selene cursed—and then there was a scrape and a *thwump* and the screaming (which had never really stopped) suddenly got a lot fainter.

The smoke still hung heavy in the hall, but the next moment Selene and Clara came stumbling out of it. Clara had her sword sheathed and Selene was pointing her gun at the floor, but they rushed past Jill and Kida as though the fight wasn't over.

Jill hesitated, wondering whether to follow, but Kida had no such doubts. She was on the hunters' trail in an instant, following them out of the house and around to the backyard, where *something* was burning and shriveling in the sun.

"Oh ... *yuck*," said the girl, and Jill agreed.

The bogart looked like an odd cross between a wolf and a giant spider. There was a mouth that took up most of its midsection, and the possibility of a second head sprouting from its neck, but what made Jill's stomach turn was that the whole thing appeared to be melting. Teeth—yellow and blackened in places—slid in the ooze as the jaw dissolved, and the spidery legs dried and shriveled like stalks of grass in a wildfire.

Jill only took a moment to stare in horror, then she was fumbling out her phone and in lieu of taking pictures, went straight to video.

It was just as well she did: the monster continued to disintegrate, and within another minute there was nothing but a black patch of stinking goo, one remaining tooth floating in the middle of it.

"Is that—" Jill began, but then something rose up out of the goo.

It was hard to describe what, and it happened too fast for Jill to even raise her phone.

Even if she had, she thought later, it probably wouldn't have captured anything. Whatever *it* was felt more like something happening inside her own eye, rather than in the real world. It looked like a spot of flickering light that hovered above the puddle of goo, a strange discoloration on the surface of reality.

Jill became aware of a low hum inside her ears. The hum slowly grew along with the discoloration, and as it grew it formed into words.

You ... will ... pay
When ... the gate ... opens
You ... will ... pay ...

"What gate?" Clara asked at once, unfazed by the strange form of communication.

But the scintillation in the air only faded, taking the hum with it, and then there really was nothing but a puddle of goo. Selene pulled a scrap of cloth out of her bag and dropped it over the tooth, reaching gingerly over the puddle and lifting it out.

"Here," she said. "These are actually useful, so I want it back when you've done collecting samples off it. But we're gonna hafta bury the rest of this. You got any shovels around here, Kida?"

Kida found them shovels, and then watched thoughtfully as they dug a pit next to the puddle of goo, and then a trench between the two so the goo drained away, leaving a black patch like an oil slick, which Clara covered with leftover dirt after they'd filled in the hole.

"You won't wanna disturb that for about a year," Selene told the girl. "And you probably won't see anything growing in it for a while after that. But you're generally in good shape. Bogart's got no power once you seen 'em."

Kida nodded gravely.

"If you have any other problems, you can call us," Jill said, offering her a card.

Kida just stared back. Eventually Selene took the card and gave it to the girl, who pressed it close to her chest as she went back inside.

They were just walking down the path to the street when a battered station wagon turned into the drive, and Selene hurried them around the corner before Kida's mother could get out and ask awkward questions.

It was early evening by the time they got back to base, and Jill found she was rapidly falling asleep even as she tried to log their results for the day. Clara and Selene seemed equally exhausted, and after their weapons had been cleaned and put away they had a brief round of coin flipping to determine first watch (Selene won), Clara wearily stationed herself by the door leading from the house to the hall, and Selene collapsed onto the sofa.

Jill fell asleep at her computer, woke when Selene and Clara changed shifts, and hauled herself to the bathroom to brush her teeth and go properly to bed. She was just on the edge of sleep for the second time when the bogart's parting words came back to her with unnerving clarity.

When the gate opens . . .

And Clara had asked *"What gate?"*

Jill fell asleep to those words chasing themselves around inside her head.

At six-thirty in the morning Jill's phone beeped, then vibrated so hard it made a *brzzzznt* noise against the hardwood table where she'd set it to charge the night before. It was the buzz that woke Jill more than the beep, since it reminded her of unpleasant things with teeth that waited in dark places.

Mumbling curses, Jill groped for the phone before it could make another sound.

Brrzzzn—"H-hello?" Jill said, trying to make her voice sound more awake then she was.

"G'mornin', it's Wilco," said a gruff voice on the other end. "Sorry about the early call. Did Officer Wheeler ever find you?"

"Wheeler . . . " said Jill, her brain slowly coming online. She found her recollection of the policeman had been heavily washed out by the encounter with the bogart, and she had to think for a little longer yet before the memories swam to the surface. "Oh, yes. He found us all right. We got him and Peaches sorted out—should be no more trouble for them."

"I'm glad to hear that," said Wilco. "Because I got five more cases in Downtown alone this morning, and I'm a donkey if I know what to do with them."

Jill, coming rapidly awake now, sat up in bed.

"What?" she said. "*Five*?"

"*Five* new cases overnight?" Selene said disbelievingly, when Jill came out in her pajamas to break the news.

Sitting at the kitchen table with a bowl of sliced apple and almonds in front of her, Clara frowned.

"That is extremely irregular," she said.

"Ya *think*?" said Selene.

"Whatever the reason," said Jill, trying to steer them back to what she felt was the important point, "there was a vampire reportedly sucking blood out of tipsy club-goers, an attack by what sounds like a giant ape-man, something that is probably a demonic possession, a fire-breathing snake in a toilet, and a house that has gone sentient and won't let anyone out—all reported last night."

Her phone rang. She took a look at the caller ID, and her shoulders sagged.

"This is Hamilton," she said. She rolled her eyes upward as a male voice yammered in her ear.

"I understand," she said after a minute. "Me and the crew were gonna stop in at the central station this morning anyway. Just keep her there for now, I'll see you soon. Yeah, yeah, you're welcome. Bye."

She hung up and slipped the phone back into her pocket.

"That was Officer Wheeler," she explained. "He says now there's a mad old woman claiming to be a witch camped out in front of their station and she won't budge."

Selene blinked. "What's her name?"

Jill shrugged. "He didn't say. Just that she'd set herself up outside their doors and was handing out good-luck charms to anyone who came too close. And apparently she's got a pet raven. What?"

Both Selene and Clara had looked up sharply at mention of the bird. They exchanged glances. Selene's eyebrows worked expressively, but Clara just did one of her inverted shrugs.

"Oh come *on*," said Selene. "How many witches do you know of in this country ballsy enough to say so and then be *obvious* about it. And the *raven*."

"Lots of witches have familiars," Clara pointed out. "It might not be her."

"Be *who*?" Jill demanded.

They looked at her like they had forgotten she was there.

"Only one way to find out," Selene said, grabbing up Arcana's keys from the counter. "Sorry, Jill, looks like dissecting the dragon's gonna hafta wait another day."

437

* * *

The St Louis Metropolitan Police Department turned out to be a humorless, square building built of tannish stone with a lot of rectangular windows and large, heavy sliding glass doors set some feet into its side. Creeping down Olive Street, Selene nearly plowed into the car ahead of them when she saw the figure sitting on the front steps.

"Holy mackerel, tuna and flipping halibut," she said, slamming on the brakes. "That's *gotta* be her!"

"Gotta be *who*—Selene you can't park *here*!" Jill exclaimed, but Selene had already pulled Arcana up behind the line of cars filling the designated parking spaces in front of the station. He was still half blocking the eastbound traffic, but Selene didn't seem to care. She put on the parking brake and vaulted out of the truck, dodged round the front and then slipped between the properly parked cars up to the heavy doors of the police station. Jill saw the figure sitting on the steps there for only a moment, before she got out of Arcana herself and made to chase after Selene—with a vague notion of getting the keys back so she could park Arcana properly—and then she actually saw who it was that sat on the steps in the shade of the building.

She was, as Officer Wheeler had described, an older woman whose age, though safely over fifty, was otherwise hard to guess. She had a brown, weathered face with bright, shining blue eyes, and her hair was dark gray with streaks of white in it. She had an odd discoloration about her skin, like someone had splashed white paint over her left cheek and neck a long time ago, and there was a piercing in her right nostril.

She was wearing an outfit which Jill could only describe as Steampunk, but with less pretentiousness and more utility. Her white cotton shirt was wrinkled and stained around the sleeves, and the leather vest that went over it was shiny from wear and cracked in a few places. She had half a dozen belts tied around her body in various arrangements (two over each shoulder, so they crossed over her midsection, one high around her waist, one a little below it, and two more hung slantwise off her hips, making another cross. The sagging ends of these were secured to her legs by leather thongs that tied onto metal buckles stitched into her trousers). There were no sign of decorative gears, although slung from one of her hip-belts was a disc with jagged outer edges, like a bicycle chainring, but this looked like more of a weapon than a piece of jewelry. All the belts had little pouches in or tied onto them, and there were more bulging pockets in her trousers—the hems of which had been tucked neatly into a pair of tan, calfskin boots with buttons up the outsides and one-inch heels. Their toes were covered in metal, Jill noticed.

The woman also wore a pair of goggles, with thick, greenish lenses and more lenses held by articulated arms, and a small LED flashlight strapped to one side. Currently the contraption was pushed up onto her brow to hold her fluffy gray-and-white hair out of her eyes, and beyond it was perched, shaggy and disapproving, a very black, very large raven.

"Can I interest you in a lucky charm?" asked this peculiar character, rattling a small jar she held in one hand. It contained a lot of small, hard round things which Jill thought might be buttons. "Wards off demons, spirits, ghosts. Good against vampires and lots else besides. Can't be too careful, can we?"

"No," said Selene, stepping up onto the sidewalk. "I don't think we can. Especially these days, for some reason."

The woman squinted up at Selene, who put her hands in her pockets and coughed. She looked *nervous*, Jill realized, and looked again at the old woman.

"I don't think the normal ones will do much for the likes of you," she said, pulling the jar back and fumbling in one of her belt pouches. "But I might have something—ah, *yes*—you'll want this," and the woman lifted a small, circular amulet with a pin on the back, and dropped it into Selene's waiting hands.

"Selene Shields," said the old woman, causing Selene to jump. "It is good to meet you at last."

"Excuse me," said Jill, coming up to the steps and folding her arms across her chest. "You know each other?"

She was met for a moment by the woman's bright blue eyes, and felt something like an electric shock run down her spine. It made her shiver.

"And the fool," she said, grinning. She had remarkably straight teeth, though they were stained yellow. "You could have been a lot worse."

"*Excuse* me?" said Jill, but then the woman was pushing past her and striding down the sidewalk, the raven on her head flapping to keep its balance.

For a moment Jill worried the woman was leaving them, but then she saw that Clara had found a space for Unicorn and was coming up the sidewalk. A flash of recognition crossed her face, and then settled into a smile that, while still a little cold and distant, was the warmest expression Jill had ever seen on her.

"Claymore, what have you done with yourself?" cried the old woman, throwing her arms out and embracing Clara around her midsection.

This caused Clara's face to work in unexpected ways, and Jill couldn't help glancing down.

"Faraday," she heard Clara say, sounding a little odd.

"Faraday?" Jill asked, sidling up to Selene.

Selene looked up from examining the amulet that the old woman had given her. She stared at Jill for a moment before answering.

"That's Faraday Isenfaust," she said, nodding toward the woman as though she could scarcely believe it herself. "The Witch of Monongahela."

When she turned back to find Jill still looking at her questioningly, she gave her shoulders a little shake.

"Sorry. Keep forgetting you're not actually one of us. The Isenfausts are sort of legendary. Among hunters, I mean. Like, everyone learns about the Brothers Gunn, but any hunter worth their blood will tell you, it was the *Isenfausts* who kept the world together. They were the ones who picked up the pieces after the brothers . . . um . . . left. There's Tesla, the older one: blacksmith by trade. They say she can make a knife that kills demons on contact. Faraday's her younger sister."

"And she's a witch," Jill said blankly.

Selene swallowed. "Strongest one in North America, they say."

Jill frowned. "Why'd she call me a fool?"

"She didn't call you a fool, she called you *the* fool," said Selene, her eyes drawing wide. "Oh gods, she knows what's going on."

"I hope so," said Jill, marching over to where the witch and Clara were still in conversation.

"How is Bellatrix?" she heard the old woman asking. "Not that I can do anything if she's gone out of true, but Tez would be disappointed if I don't tell her."

"She is well," Clara replied tightly, looking over the woman's shoulder at Jill.

Following her gaze the woman pivoted around and looked quizzically at her.

"I haven't got anything for you," she said, bluntly. "Other than these two, you're on your own. Things are precarious enough without you muddling around in them."

"Sorry?" said Jill, momentarily off-put.

"You mean all the new cases?" Selene asked.

The woman—Faraday Isenfaust—sniffed. "I mean the displaced magic. It's bleeding through this whole city. Gonna be like Detroit all over again if we don't do something."

"What happened in—" Jill began, but she was cut off by Officer Wheeler coming out of the police station and catching sight of them.

"Oh good you're *here*," he said, and then stopped, seeing Faraday. "Oh," he said, his face falling. "*You're* still here."

"I told you, son," Faraday began, raising a hand, but Clara covered it with one of her own and stepped forward.

"Officer Wheeler," she said. "Allow me to introduce another of our . . . colleagues. This is Faraday Isenfaust."

"She said she was a *witch*," Officer Wheeler said, narrowing his eyes.

"That is because she is," said Clara, blandly.

Wheeler opened his mouth and took in a breath, then thought better of whatever he was going to say, and deflated a little. He turned to Jill.

"We got two more calls while you were on your way over," he said. "Not my cases, but they sound like more of your type."

"Then let's take this inside," said Jill, who was beginning to sweat standing out on the broiling sidewalk. "Including you," she said, jabbing a finger at Faraday.

Selene and Clara both flinched, as though they expected a spontaneous explosion, but Faraday just looked at Jill (along her finger and up her arm before settling on her face), and smiled very slightly.

"Why?" she asked, her crackly old voice honey-sweet.

"Because you probably have the most extensive knowledge about supernatural phenomena, and if we're having an unexplained local spike in them you're our best chance at understanding it." She started toward the big, double doors.

Wheeler coughed, and nodded his head at Arcana. "I assume *that's* not gonna stay there?"

Selene swore, but went over and got back into the truck as the rest of them—even Faraday—filed inside.

It didn't seem like a busy morning at the station, but as soon as Officer Wheeler led them through the door with a large "Authorized Personnel Only" sign on it Jill found they had entered a cramped world filled with desks overflowing with paperwork and harried-looking people sitting behind said desks or hurrying this way and that, talking on headsets.

Some of the commotion halted when Faraday entered the room, mostly because she still had the raven perched on her head, but Jill thought some of the stares were also directed at Clara, who loomed taller than Faraday and her bird combined, and took up even more space thanks to the hilt of her sword jutting out over one shoulder.

Then a familiar figure detached itself from the crowd and came strolling over.

"Hello, ladies," said Detective Wilco, snowy-haired and bow-legged, a little red in the face but otherwise unchanged from the last time Jill had seen him. "You here to lend a hand? Because God knows we could use one. Or three."

"We have also been busy," said Jill, and briskly gave him a rundown of their encounter with the bogart.

"Speaking of which," she said, swinging around to face Faraday, who had begun sticking little silver coins under all the monitors she could reach. The woman guiltily retracted her hand and straightened up when addressed. "Right before it . . . evaporated . . . the bogart said something that I didn't understand."

Faraday snorted, a little derisively. "Not a surprise," she muttered.

"Fara," said Clara admonishingly, before Jill had a chance to be offended.

"He said something about a gate opening," Jill forged on. "And some unimaginative threats. But I couldn't think what he meant by a *gate*."

"It's *obvious*, isn't it?" said Faraday, her bright blue eyes widening. "All of this? Isn't it obvious?" She looked around the busy station, at the officers and clerks in varied states of distress, at Jill and Clara and Wheeler, and finally at Wilco.

"Not to us," Jill said, dryly. She folded her arms. "Please explain," she said, just as Selene slipped in through the door behind them.

Faraday Isenfaust looked around, nodded in recognition at Selene, and then went over to perch on a corner of a relatively clear desk. She pulled up one booted foot and rested it on the nearest chair.

"Okeydokey folkeys," said the old woman, reaching up a veiny hand to take the raven off her head. It went with a disgruntled squawk, but rested on her arm while she stroked it. "Here's the deal. You are experiencing something of a transdimensional dust up. Something big is coming through from another world. Big enough that it can't just pop through one of those little rabbit holes, like a unicorn or a demon. It's gotta open a big old door—that's what Jill's bogart was on about. Now, something that big, just moving pushes of wave of magic in front of it, and there's lots of stuff that's happy to ride that wave. Bogarts and beasties, mostly, but even your local supernatural flora and fauna are going to feel this rising tide. They're gonna get more excited, more active. That's what we have going on right now. Not a lot of new blood coming in, but everything that's *already here* is gonna be more excited. And that's just the beginning.

"This big thing, now, how's it gonna get here? Like I said, it's got to open a *gate*. Well, when that gate opens, lots of other stuff is gonna come through with it. So you're looking at a flood of new supernatural entities along with the local lads, all amped up on extra juice. In short, ladies and gentlemen, you've got a tornado full of hurt on its way to this city, and no which way I can see of diffusing it or shunting it off somewhere else. S'why I'm here, though I'd much prefer to be in Vermont with my feet up and a bottle of bourbon, I can tell you."

The office, which had slowly quieted down as the witch spoke, rolled back into gear as soon as she finished. Questions were shouted at and about Faraday, and a tall man with a long, lined face began forging purposefully toward them through the sea of desks.

"Do you know *what* is coming?" Clara asked, bending low to speak into the witch's ear.

"If I knew that I wouldn't be dispensing general protective charms, now would I?" Faraday snapped, and then the tall man arrived.

He was wearing a pair of navy slacks and a crisp cotton shirt with a rather impressive badge on his belt. By this and the way that Wilco and Wheeler deferentially made room for him, Jill guessed he must be someone important. He loomed over Faraday in a way that was probably meant to be intimidating, but it didn't work. The witch looked up at him, making a bother of craning her neck around and then shading her eyes, like she was looking into the sky on a bright day.

"You got questions, boss man?" she asked, shooting him a creaky smile.

"Who the hell are you and what the hell are you doin' in my station?" the man asked, the lines of his face folding themselves into unfriendly shapes.

Wilco cleared his throat.

"Not now, Ronnie," said the tall man, holding up a hand to silence him without looking. "You've dragged enough crazy in here over the years, but this is the last straw. Madam, I have to ask that you take your . . . *animal* . . . and leave these premises immediate—"

His last word was cut off by a crash from outside, and then something hit the door leading to the public area of the station, causing it to rattle. There were muffled shouts from outside and then a horrible scream.

"What the f—" the tall man began, turning to make for the door.

Clara's arm came up like a solid, black tree branch, catching him in the chest and shoving him backward. She took two strides forward, so that she was closest to the door, and unsheathed her sword in a careful arc, so as not to catch it on anything.

"Selene, do you have weapons?" she asked, not turning her head.

"Left 'em in Arcana," Selene said, bitterly. "Thought takin' Elvis into a *police station* would be pushing it."

"Someone get my friend a shotgun," Clara ordered, and with such authority that Jill saw a clerk make an involuntary motion as if to obey.

"Lady, put that sword away," shouted the tall man, beginning to look truly angry.

"You'll want one of these," Faraday said at Jill's elbow, pressing a small coin into her hand. It was cool and silvery, and felt a little odd for having a hole in the middle of it.

"Lucky charm?" Jill asked.

"Only the best," said Faraday. She wandered off through the crowd, and Jill didn't see what she did after that, except that the blinds on the windows began opening, letting in strong shafts of hot sunlight.

Outside in the public area there was silence now, and then a creak as the door handle turned.

"Everyone *behind me!*" Clara shouted, leveling her sword as the door burst open and someone dressed all in black shot through.

They looked a bit like a cartoon ninja, Jill thought in bemusement. Black pants, long-sleeved shirt, boots, gloves, and a head scarf that covered their hair, ears and neck. Their face was further hidden behind a sophisticated mask: it had a grill in front of the eyes and a ventilator at the mouth. The figure had a long knife in one hand and a small revolver in the other.

Which was promptly knocked away by Clara, who then took a direct hit from their knife.

They moved *fast.* Too fast for Jill to follow.

"Oh *boy*, it's a vampire!" Selene shouted the next instant. She had found a gun—a pistol—from somewhere, but she wasn't firing. She wasn't even aiming at the struggling pair. Instead she was edging around to cover the door, and a sharp *bang! bang!* sent a second black-clad figure that had followed the first skittering away instead of diving in to help their companion.

Who, it must be said, after the first lucky strike had not be nearly so fortunate. Despite being at a disadvantage with her long weapon in such cramped quarters, Clara had managed to get a hold of them by their neck and was now beating their mask in with the hilt of her sword.

Eventually it cracked, and Clara got her gloved fingers under the chin of it and pulled.

The mask flew off, revealing a greenish-white face with blood-red eyes and flaring nostrils. Clara turned, dragging the figure with her, and started for the nearest splash of direct sunlight.

The vampire started screaming, and the next instant their companion was back—only to be blown off their feet when Selene unloaded four shots directly into their head, causing their own mask to shatter. It flew off in pieces, along with a lot of gooey, black blood.

People were shouting—Clara was trying to drag her vampire closer to the sunlight—the tall policeman had drawn his own weapon, as had several of the other officers, but they weren't pointing them at the vampire—either vampire—they were training them on Selene . . .

"Oh for the love of Christ," said Selene, ejecting the pistol's clip and then putting her hands in the air.

"Put those *down*," Jill snapped at the nearest officer—who turned out to be the tall man.

"Lady I don't know who the hell you are, but—"

"Will you *look* at what is going on?!" Jill practically screamed in his ear. She grabbed hold of his upper arm, digging in her fingers for all she was worth, and dragged him around so he could see Clara shove the head of the struggling vampire into the square of sunlight.

Smoke started pouring out from around the scarf, and with it a horrible, tortured howling. It made Jill's insides curl, and she at least had known what was coming. Several of the officers—the tall man included—started looking a little green.

"That'll do, Claymore," said Faraday Isenfaust, working her way through the crowd.

Wordlessly, Clara pulled the vampire out of the sunlight, shoved him—Jill was pretty sure it was a him—to the ground, and looked around for something to secure his hands.

"Here," said Wilco, offering his pair of handcuffs.

Clara took them with a nod of thanks and briskly clapped them onto the vampire, who was still moaning faintly.

"What the hell," said the tall man, who had seemed to have forgotten Jill, who was still gripping his arm.

"Vampires, told ya," said Selene, who still had her hands up—even though most of the guns in the room were pointing at the floor now. "Don't think y'all'll be happy with the front desk, but someone should check it. I know I got the other guy but sadly it takes more than a headshot to kill a vampire."

"Vampires . . . " repeated the tall man.

"Yes, sir," said Jill, pulling on his arm again. "Officer . . . er . . ." she squinted down at his badge. "Captain *Miller*. Those were vampires. And the haunting Wheeler found yesterday, that was real too. And there's gonna be more."

The tall man—Captain Miller—was peering down at her out of his lined face and blinking rapidly.

"I know it's a lot to take in," Jill said. "But you better do it fast, because the sooner you do the sooner we can figure out what's going on and get to fixing it."

"I *told* you what's going on," Faraday said. She had opened one of the windows and was putting her raven out through it as she spoke. Once the bird had flapped away she turned back to the baffled crowd.

"Something powerful is coming, and it's pushing a wave in front of it as big as anything I've seen." She put her hands on her hips and glared at them. "And here you nearly lose your marbles over a couple of desperate vampires. Oy, you," she said, kicking the one that Clara had captured.

"It's like that rising tide lifts all boats sort of thing," Jill explained, mostly for Captain Miller's benefit. "Only here the tide is . . . um . . . ambient thaumaturgic energy, and the boats are all the supernatural stuff that usually creeps around in the dark corners where we don't notice it."

"Lady," said Captain Miller. "That is the craziest bullcrap I've heard all week."

"Won't be by the end of the day," muttered Selene.

"What's gotten into you?" asked Faraday, and everyone looked around, confused, until they realized she was talking to the vampire on the ground.

The vampire moaned, and raised his head—it looked blotchy and brown from where Jill stood, but his eyes were still very bright and red.

"Like you said, grandma," he rasped. "Somethin' big is coming. Thought we'd . . . you know . . . get a head start."

"I *know*," said Faraday darkly. "Do *you* know what's coming?"

The vampire cracked a grin. "How's that saying go? It's something old, something strong, something dead, something wrong."

"That's not how it goes," Jill said, flatly.

"It's how *our* saying goes," snapped the vampire, rolling his eyes at her. "And you can stop trying to talk sense into these cretins. They're all gonna be so many walking hamburgers when the gate opens. You think we're bad? Just wait till you meet what's coming through from the other side. You lot—" he spat the words as if they tasted bad. "You won't know what hit you. *Literally.*"

"Maybe not," said Jill, coolly. There was an odd sort of excitement growing in her belly, like panic tempered with experience and steel. She was beyond frightened—she was terrified—and she was elated, eager, and determined. "But we'll find out."

The vampire twisted around so he could look up at Clara.

"Who the heck is that psycho?" he asked.

"She is my boss," said Clara, stonily, and pushed his head back into the floor.

"Uh . . . guys?" said Selene, who was leaning back to peer through the open door. "Guys? About that other vampire? Yeah, might wanna follow through on that before he comes around. I can see 'im from here, and he be twitchin'."

"Wheeler, take Selene and go get him," Wilco said, ignoring Captain Miller's half-hearted protest. Then he turned to Jill.

"Do you mean to tell me that all *this*," he waved a hand at the disarrayed office. "All the weird cases. It's all because of *something big* that'll be coming from . . . where exactly?"

Jill took a big breath and prepared herself to explain the vague picture she'd got from Selene and Clara talking about the Spirit World and how it wrapped around their world, but Faraday spoke over her.

"From the other side of shadows, my friend," she said. "From where dreams are made manifest; where hopes go to die. Did you ever wonder what happens to gods when no one believes in them anymore? They do not vanish—no, they cannot merely *vanish*. They hang on at the edges of the world, beyond the reach of mortal minds, and there they fester. Now something is stirring, spreading, tearing up roots from that raggedy edge, and it is coming *here*."

Wilco swallowed, and then he nodded with surprising acceptance.

"I thought it might be something like that," he said. "See, I think I know who's calling it."

"Oh for the love of Jesus, Ronnie," said Captain Miller. "Not your mystery witness *again*."

"Yes, my *mystery witness*," said Detective Wilco, as Selene and Wheeler reentered the room, dragging something behind them. Wheeler looked terrified; Selene looked grim.

"You mean the Vjorkrige?" said Jill, and she felt more than saw Faraday's eyes snap to her.

"Yes the—" Wilco began, but Faraday cut him off.

"What did you say?" she said, her voice like a hot knife through butter, so sharp it hurt.

"There's a Vjorkrige," Jill said. "She's a . . . a servant? Warrior? Special envoy from this old war god—"

"I *know* what a Vjorkrige is," hissed Faraday. "And you say there is one— *here*?"

"Well, not *here* precisely," said Wilco uncomfortably. "Thing is, she comes and goes. Sometimes she's at the safe house, and sometimes not. We can't keep track of her, but she always turns up when we need her."

"And what," said Faraday, her voice like needles. "Do you need her *for*?"

"I asked her to testify," said Wilco, raising his chin defiantly. "Against Rafe McCleaver."

"He's the one who killed the girl they sacrificed to summon her," Jill put in. "And a lot of other people besides. But the Vjorkrige was the only reliable witness we had, so—"

"Only her reliability depends on people believing she is who she says she is," said Wilco. "And when I explained this to her she just . . . well she didn't actually smile. But she looked really smug and said that 'matters had been arranged.'"

"Matters had been . . . " Faraday repeated, and trailed off. Then her eyes screwed up, her cheeks pulled back, her yellow teeth parted, and she began to bellow with laughter. She laughed and laughed, cackling louder and louder, and then abruptly stopped. She coughed a little, bringing one hand up to cover her mouth. "You are all in deep, deep trouble. Walking hamburgers my magically gifted ass, you are *spiders in a bathtub.*"

"Faraday?" asked Clara tightly.

"Oh, not you, honey," said Faraday quickly. "I'll see you right through this, and your friend Selene. But the rest of you—*ha!*" She threw back her head and choked out a couple laughs, then sobered up again. "You are going to die, because you have been idiots. Idiot move one," she held up a finger to indicate. "You asked an extremely potent, undead, magical entity to take part in your mundane, flawed, tiresome justice system. Two: you expect her to play by *your* rules. Which she very well might. But in doing so, she is going to break some even bigger ones. Because you want your idiot *sources* and your *validation,* well, she'll think, if they don't believe me when I say I'm me, who would they believe?" She gazed at them, her eyes very wide and her face open.

"Oh, holy heck," said Selene, quietly, in the background. "She's calling in the big guns, isn't she? The real deal."

"From the raggedy edge," murmured Clara.

"*Who?*" Jill practically screeched, and found herself caught once more by Faraday's needlepoint gaze.

"She's calling Vjor, my pretty fool," said the witch. "Her master: conflict incarnate, She Whose Name is Hell on Earth; the Grand God of War. *Vjor.*"

Jill found her throat had gone dry, but she managed to swallow anyway.

"Ah," she said eventually. "That's what counts as something big, does it?" She turned to Wilco. "How long until she has to testify?"

"McCleaver's arraignment is tomorrow," Wilco offered. "But we'll need her for the trial after that, if it takes."

"Well," said Jill, stomping down the excited panic in her gut. "Make sure you get a good record of what happens there, because I don't think anyone wants *this* to happen *again.*"

Wilco nodded, subdued.

"Yeah, um . . . about *this,*" Selene said. "Why don't we all agree to do exactly what the witch tells us, point guns at the monsters—not me—and maybe we can survive the next twenty-four hours? If you ask me, it's worth a try."

* * *

Jill had never been so busy and so far out of her depth at the same time; not even her freshman year of college had been so overwhelming. The thing was, even after they'd talked Captain Miller around, even after they'd teamed up with the other precincts—who admittedly needed little convincing—and even after they had successfully contained the vampires (iron spikes through the heart; locked in coffins; stuck in a holding cell), it was *her* people kept coming to for advice.

"Animal control says they just picked up a dog the size of a buffalo," said one of the dispatchers, tugging on Jill's sleeve.

"Alive?" Jill asked.

"Sedated," said the woman.

"Tell them to bring it in, I'll take a look."

Others adapted frighteningly fast.

"I have another haunting in Princeton Heights," someone said. "Large, blue, threw a table out a window."

Jill knew this one. She'd heard Selene giving advice to another officer being dispatched to something similar.

"Give the response salt-filled slugs," Jill began, then she had an idea. "Or, better yet, have you got any pure sodium?"

The dispatcher blinked at her. "I'll ask the lab," she said.

The calls kept coming in. When Jill had no idea what to tell them—like the time someone reported a ten-foot-tall humanoid made of flames walking down Arsenal Street—she would send them over to Faraday, who had put a chair on top of a desk and sat herself down on it so she could survey the growing chaos. She was working a rope between her fingers, tying it into complicated knots, while her raven flapped in and out through the open window.

"If Tez can't put down her hammer for *one minute* to deal with a near-apocalypse level breach, see if there is *anyone* else we can get," she was saying.

The raven squawked.

"*Gods* no, not him. Have you found Girion? Well, look again!"

The raven flew off, scattering some nearby papers.

"What?" said Faraday, when asked about the flame-person. "Well don't send the fire brigade, they'd just make it mad. Sounds like an ifrit, or an especially powerful salamander. Probably hungry. Give it a pile of kindling and it'll be busy for a few hours. With any luck it'll burn itself out."

Jill felt torn. On the one hand she wanted to be *out there*, actually *seeing* everything that was happening. On the other hand, so many things were being reported now, she worried that if she left the station she would miss something.

Then word came that they'd brought the giant dog in, and who was taking charge of it?

Jill put up her hand, and found herself briskly shunted down some back stairs and along a concrete corridor to an underground parking bay where a dirty van was in the process of unloading something the size of a cow.

Only it was not a cow. It had paws and a fluffy tail and erect, triangular ears and a muzzle with gray whiskers. Its mouth lolled open, but it was breathing steadily.

"I've been in this town thirty-eight years," said the grizzled officer who'd driven the van. "Ain't seen nothing like this."

"Was anyone hurt?" Jill asked.

"Derkensen's had to go to the emergency room for stitches and shots," said the driver with a shrug. "We got lucky. Thing seemed more confused more than anything."

Jill bent over the creature as far as she could. It was maybe a little more muscular around the shoulders than an ordinary dog, and there was a thin, golden chain around its neck, stretched tight to the point of snapping. There was a tiny locket in the shape of a heart dangling at eye-level. Jill poked it with a finger, and the animal shuddered.

The officer who had led Jill down pulled out his weapon, but she raised a hand to stop him.

"Something's not right," she whispered.

"That's the understatement of the year," scoffed the driver.

On a hunch, Jill took the little coin that Faraday had given her and touched it gently to the dog's wide forehead.

The whole animal shivered, sighed, and then began to deflate like a punctured balloon. The men made startled noises, and no wonder. As the creature shrank it changed shape, losing its hair, legs growing longer even as the body contorted and the tail disappeared entirely, until it was a human woman who lay on the makeshift gurney, stark naked save for the gold necklace, and breaking out in goose bumps. She was middle-aged, white, with freckles across her face and shoulders and rusty brown hair.

"Get me a blanket," Jill ordered. "And get word to Faraday: what do you do with werewolves?"

It turned out, if the werewolf was asleep and not hurting anyone, Faraday couldn't be bothered.

"Give her a hot drink, I think," was all she said. "Oh, and keep her away from the vampires."

Jill did more than that. She sat with the woman in one of the more private cells until the tranquilizer wore off and she blinked awake.

"Hi," said Jill, calmly, as she saw the woman's eyes focus, and then jerk all the way open. "I've never met a werewolf before, but if I were you, I'd probably want to know that, one, I didn't kill anyone, two, I'm not technically under arrest, three, there are some clothes over on that table—I'll turn around if you want to get dressed—and four, it's not just me, er, you. Everything's going crazy today."

"Who..." said the woman, slowly. She had a rough, hoarse voice. "Who the hell are you?"

"I'm Jill Hamilton," said Jill, reaching over and pouring the woman a glass of water. "And, if you don't mind, I'd like to ask you some questions."

The day crept by without Selene really noticing, in the way that hideously busy days do. It felt like a million years. It felt like the blink of an eye. The police changed shifts, but she and Clara and Faraday remained. Jill was around somewhere, too, but in all the chaos Selene had lost track of her.

And then... then it was night, and Selene and Clara were sitting behind the front desk of the station doing weapon prep. Selene had decided it was worth getting out her own guns, since, while she'd gotten inexplicit permission to carry firearms, no one wanted to be responsible for actually giving her any.

"You ever worked with law enforcement before?" she asked Clara, who was methodically sharpening all her knives. She had a surprising number, for all she usually made do with her sword alone.

"Mother had a friend, once," she said. "A US Marshal. He helped us... sometimes."

"Yeah," said Selene. "Me neither."

At some point Wilco turned up with Chinese takeout, and dumped the boxes on the desk in front of them.

"Some of us aren't going home tonight," he said by way of explanation.

Clara nodded in recognition, and Selene swallowed her pride so far as to say "Thanks," before she dug into the chow mein. "It's gonna be a long one."

And yet, as if the universe just wanted to prove her wrong, for a while nothing happened. They finished eating, and Selene finished prepping her guns. She had just taken out the little amulet that Faraday had given her—it was a slightly convex silver disk with the face of the moon beaten into it, artfully stained so that only a crescent was brightly shining. It had a needle and latch on the back so it could be pinned onto things. After some consideration, Selene pinned it to the inside of her work shirt—when Jill reappeared.

She looked rumpled and tired, but unhurt, and her eyes focused at sight of the takeout containers.

"Are you gonna finish this?" she asked, finding the leftover rice, and wouldn't say anything else until after she'd cleaned out all the containers.

"So, what happened with the dog?" Selene asked, once she had finished.

"Not a dog," Jill said, shaking her head. "A werewolf. Woman. Name's Janine. Nice lady—confused, but nice. She let me take samples."

"Such a saint," Selene drawled. "What did you do with her?"

"She's downstairs," said Jill. "Seemed to think it was safer for herself. I guess... well, she says normally she can control the change, right? Easier to be a wolf when the moon's in its second or third quarter, but she can always control it. This afternoon though—bam, out of nowhere, it was suddenly wolf! And she doesn't remember much of what happened afterwards."

"The rising tide," said Clara. "For those of us not adapted to it, an increase of magic can be problematic."

"Anyway, it's something to keep in mind," said Jill, poking around in the plastic bags for any missed food. "Not everything we run into—or that runs into us—is actually malevolent. You'll tell your people, right?" she said, turning to Wilco.

The older man sighed, nodded, and pushed himself out of his chair. "I'll tell Captain Miller," he said. "But don't expect he'll listen."

More time passed.

Selene and Clara took turns napping at the desk, while Jill bedded down in a corner. Around two in the morning one of the night shift officers brought them coffee.

"What time is McCleaver's arraignment?" Selene asked as she sipped her drink.

"Eight AM," Jill replied, not opening her eyes.

"Six more hours," Clara remarked, casting her eyes up at the clock above the door.

"A lot can happen in six hours," Selene said.

They almost made it through the night. In retrospect, Selene supposed, it had been too much to hope for. Still, when the phones started ringing at four in the morning she was a little disappointed to find out they were *not* mundane reports of robberies or accidents.

The door to the back room flew open and Faraday strode out.

"Up and at 'em, Claymore," she barked, causing the raven on her shoulder to cackle in response.

Clara stood up immediately, flipping open the divider to join Faraday in her march toward the front door. Jill automatically moved to follow, but found herself halted by a brown, veiny hand held up in front of her chest.

"Not you," said the witch, sternly. "And not you, either," she said, looking over Jill's shoulder to where Selene had also stood up. "You need to stay and watch over your fool. Look, she's already lost the protection I gave her."

"I gave it to Janine—the werewolf," Jill said, feeling her nerves begin to prickle. "It helped her keep calm."

"You gave it to the werewolf, of course you did. Fool," said Faraday, and rolled her eyes.

"Stop calling me that," Jill said, her voice gone tight and quiet.

"Why not? It's what you are," said Faraday, blandly. Then she turned and pointed, first at Clara, then at Selene. "Star-sword," she said. "Moon-shield." She swung back to Jill and jabbed a finger at her. "Fool." She shrugged. "Don't be angry with me, it's not *my* prophecy."

Jill's mounting fury went out like a candle in an open widow. The prophecy—she'd almost forgotten about the prophecy. But it was the prophecy that had gotten her going in the first place—that and mad, blinding grief coupled with steely curiosity—and the prophecy had been divided into three verses, one each for Clara, Selene and herself. And while Clara and Selene both had names that seemed to fit with what the prophecy called them, Jill had never thought *she'd* been called anything... until now.

For the fool that takes a rod to wield...

She was the fool. The fool with the rod. What else had it said? She could only remember the next part... *before the shadows that surround them yield*... but she had it written down somewhere.

While she was busy thinking this, Faraday had gone over and tugged on Clara's sleeve, leading her out the door. It shut behind them with a click.

"Well..." said Selene, drawing out the word for all it was worth. "That's a load of bullcrap if I ever saw one." She began picking up her weapons and methodically strapping them to her person. Lastly she took up her trench gun and slung it over her shoulder. "C'mon, boss. I'll drive."

They almost made it to the front door when the office door opened and one of the night shift stuck his head out.

"Just thought you should know," he said. "There's something—we think it's a protest—coming toward us up Tucker Boulevard. They're not... well ... that is... they're not all *human*..."

"Yeah," said Selene. "And what're you gon' do about it?"

The officer swallowed. "SWAT teams are already gearing up," he admitted.

"Right," said Selene. "Tell them not to wait for us." She grabbed Jill by the arm and hurried her out the door.

They did not have to go far: South Tucker Boulevard was just around the corner from where Arcana was parked, and they only had to cross under the freeway before they hit the roadblock that was still hastily being erected. Beyond it, however, Jill could see that all four lanes were filled with pedestrians, walking shoulder to shoulder, and advancing slowly toward them.

They parked Arcana a safe distance from the squad cars, and jumping the barricade they slipped through the lines of policemen—who by this point all knew Jill and Selene on sight and let them through without comment.

They were halted, however, by a line of SWAT officers with riot shields and full-face helmets. Captain Miller was standing just behind them, shouting into a megaphone. For a moment Jill assumed he was talking to the crowd on the road in front of them, and then she began to pick out his actual words.

"Lady," he was saying, his voice blaring harshly through the speaker. "I'm only gonna warn you this once: you need to get the hell outta there, or I won't be responsible for what happens to you."

Leaning over the shoulder of the nearest SWAT officer, Jill found she could see the tall, dark figure of Clara, harshly illuminated by the searchlights. At her side, Faraday appeared almost child-sized, but stood with the same, determined erectness.

The witch tugged on Clara's sleeve, and the tall woman bent her head to listen. After a moment she nodded, and then turned and marched back toward the line of officers.

"Thank you—" Captain Miller began, and then Clara reached over and snatched the megaphone out of his hands.

"I need this," she said, by way of explanation. "Keep your soldiers back."

"What the hell are you—" the captain stuttered, but Clara had already turned around and was marching back to rejoin Faraday.

"Can you see what's going on?" Jill asked Selene, only to find the woman had gone. Looking around, she saw a figure jump the railing on the edge of the road, and begin handing herself along it, past the line of SWAT officers. A moment later the figure—who was indeed Selene—jumped back onto the road and trotted over to join Clara and Faraday.

Jill gave out a frustrated sigh, and followed in her tracks.

It was more difficult than Selene had made it look to crawl along outside the railing, for the road was elevated here, soaring over a dirt parking lot with railway tracks crisscrossing below. The railing was made of white-painted metal, with bars perfect for handholds, but the concrete ledge was barely more than three inches, and Jill became very aware of the whistle of the wind around her as she inched her way past the human blockade.

I would never have done this a year ago, she thought in a daze, as she scrambled back to safety.

Behind her, someone shouted, but she was already staggering over to the other three women, who had turned to face the crowd in the road.

This, now Jill had a clear view, was the most unusual collection of people she'd ever seen.

Only a few of them appeared human, for a start, even though most of them were human shaped. Mostly.

In the first line alone Jill saw people the color of dead fish, people with blank, black eyes, and one person who seemed to be covered in fur. Another was covered in scales. Another didn't seem to have skin at all . . . Jill found her gaze moving on rather swiftly from its oozing mass, and found her eyes drifting up and over their heads, to where something loomed, just beyond the reach of the searchlight.

This thing, whatever it was, was tall and spindly and made mostly of legs with large, bulbous knobs on them. One of its appendages reached forward into the light as Jill looked, and she saw with a start that the bulbous thing was a face, but with the features all twisted and jumbled about.

"What is *that?*" Jill couldn't help asking.

Faraday shot her a resigned glance, then answered with a shrug. "Slender Walker. Usually prays on children. Very solitary. *Usually.*"

"What are they doing?" Jill asked. For the crowd, which had shuffled just into range of the police lights, seemed unwilling to come any closer.

They just stood there, filling the road for as far as Jill could peer into the dark, and there was a faint noise of humming conversation.

"That's what we're tryin' to figure out," Selene said.

Clara cleared her throat and brought the megaphone to her mouth.

"Citizens of St Louis Below," she said, her magnified voice covering the empty space with ease. "I am Claymore, daughter of Nordstern. I stand with the Witch of Monongahela and Selene Shields, and we charge you to state your purpose."

She lowered the megaphone.

The humming conversation intensified, then sagged, and there was confusion on the front line as the various beings turned to one another. There seemed to be some argument over who should speak for them. At last a small figure, hunched under a huge, tattered sack, crawled forward between the legs of the Slender Walker, and stumbled out into the light.

Then it raised a head—and kept on raising it as its neck extended like the body of a snake. It blinked huge, inky eyes, and Jill realized with a start that it had three of them in a line across its forehead.

A dark line appeared underneath the eyes, which widened, growing red and turning into a mouth. The creature let out a long, low cough, and then spoke in a wet voice that snapped the ends off its words as though they had been bitten.

"We are not St Louis Below," it said. "We are below and above and beside you. We are here to ask for one thing."

"Ask it," Clara said.

The humming of hundreds of voices rose behind the three-eyed creature as it cried out: "*Block the gate!* You must not let it open—it will be a holocaust for us all!"

"And if we do not?" Clara asked.

There was a growling from the Slender Walker. It was a horrible, low sound that crawled up Jill's spine and dug claws into her heart.

Someone deep in the crowd howled, and then as one they all surged forward.

This caused shouting from behind them, and Jill looked around just in time to see steaming canisters go sailing through the air over their heads. They landed in the crowd of monsters, exploding dully, and in seconds the whole road was covered in thick, white, acrid smoke.

"*Will* you stop interfering?!" Faraday screamed, rounding on the line of police and SWAT officers. She raised her arms, and Jill felt something tug on her, like an invisible rope.

Then the witch brought her arms down in a powerful, sweeping motion, and the tear gas cleared away as though blown by an unseen wind.

It left the road deserted and empty, not a single creature remaining. The only sign of their presence was a small dark patch where the thing with no skin had stood, and a flutter of something that might have been a scrap of cloth. A tear gas can, now spent, rocked slowly to a halt.

"I don't understand," Jill said into the silence that ensued. "What just happened?"

Clara strode forward into the space recently vacated by the crowd of monsters. She drew her sword and swung it around, testingly, but met no resistance. Walking back to them she sheathed her blade with a shrug.

"Okay," said Selene. "Okay. *Okay.* Now I'm getting nervous."

Monday morning came, bright and quickly warming the sidewalk outside the police station. Clara and Selene sat on the steps outside, drinking tea and coffee respectively. Selene was in the process of devouring an egg sandwich, while Clara picked at an energy bar.

Things had been impossibly *normal* since the crowd of monsters' sudden disappearance. Faraday had spent the remainder of the night tramping through downtown St Louis, only to return at dawn, her face twisted with displeasure.

"Everyone's lying low," she'd said. "I don't like it." Then she had gone inside, gotten the biggest map of the city they had, spread it out in the middle of the floor, and begun running spells on it to see where the promised "gate" would open. Jill had been fascinated by this, and was currently inside as well, leaning over the witch's shoulder and trying to make sense of what she was doing.

Outside, Clara checked her watch. It was a quarter to eight.

"The hearing's starting soon," she said.

"Yeah," said Selene. "Where is that happening, anyway?"

"At the courthouse, I assume," said Clara.

Selene licked the last bits of egg off her fingers and waved a hand. "Yeah, *which* one? There's like . . . dozens."

Clara rolled down the wrapper on what was left of her energy bar, pulling a trademark shrug. "Shall we go inside and ask?" she suggested.

"Sure," said Selene. "Maybe they'll let us watch!"

As a matter of fact, they did let them. Word had gotten out, and someone had set up a television in the back room that was playing a feed from the courthouse. It showed a large room with wood paneling and uncomfortable-looking pews at the back. People were still filing in and taking their seats, but Selene spotted Rafe McCleaver immediately. He was sitting back in the defendant's chair next to a smooth-headed attorney in a navy suit, and looked condescendingly amused about the whole thing. She saw Detective Wilco too, standing with a small, rabbity woman who, Selene assumed, represented the prosecution. All in all, it looked very much like the courtrooms she had seen on television, except things went slower and faster in different places, and the procedure was more difficult to follow.

"Where's the Vjorkrige?" Jill asked, coming to stand beside Selene's elbow.

Behind them, Captain Miller coughed. He was a white and shaken version of the man they had met the previous day, and seemed thoroughly humbled by the night's events, but he still glared at them a little as he explained: "Witnesses don't usually have to testify at evidentiary hearings. Wilco got a statement from her, which the prosecution gives to the judge. Who then decides whether the case goes to trial, and if it does, whether it should be tried by *this* court."

"Would it?" Jill asked, curious.

The police captain shrugged.

"This fellow, McCleaver? Were any of his victims from outside Missouri?"

"Most of the bodies we found under the tree were," Jill said.

"Then it might need to go to federal. It's already been bumped over to St Louis since the county court couldn't handle it."

Selene rolled her eyes. This was why she liked taking care of things on site, without involving the authorities; someone like Rafe McCleaver could spin in the criminal justice system for *years*, and at the end of it might not even get that harsh a sentence.

Except . . . except in this case they had the Vjorkrige, and though Selene had been skeptical of Jill's plan at first, now she had to admit she was almost looking forward to seeing the United States justice system try to meander around something like *that*.

On the screen the judge was reading something. It was full of legalese and terminology that made Selene's head hurt to think about.

The defense got up and said a few words. Then the prosecution said something. Finally the judge made a waving motion, and the rabbity woman approached the stand and handed over a thick manilla folder. The judge flipped it open, took one look at the first page, and frowned.

"The witness has no last name," she said.

The rabbity woman looked at Wilco expectantly, and the old detective cleared his throat.

"No, your honor," he said.

"She has no date of birth, either," remarked the judge. "And her occupation is . . . *undead warrior?*"

In the room, Selene noticed Jill was smiling, an odd light dancing about her eyes. When she saw Selene looking, she grinned even wider.

"Here it comes," she said.

"Detective Wilco," said the judge. "It's hard enough when a witness has no identification, but I don't think it's possible to believe this one is what she says she is. It goes against the laws of *nature*, Detective Wilco."

In the room, Jill let out an impatient breath. "Come on," she whispered. "*Ask.*"

"I understand your reservations, your honor," said the detective, gamely. "I shared them with the witness, and she has agreed to appear in the court today to . . . er . . . validate herself."

"She can prove she is an undead warrior?" the judge said skeptically.

"She *said*," Wilco began, and paused. He looked around, and shrugged. "Just ask her yourself," he finished, raising his hand and beckoning to someone off-camera.

There was no sound that announced the Vjorkrige's arrival, only the sudden commotion in the audience as they all turned to look toward the camera. Rafe McCleaver turned too, and Selene saw the smug look on his face flee in terror at what he saw.

Advancing into view, walking up the aisle between the pews and onto the floor, was the Vjorkrige. She had come in full battle armor, her axes clanking at her hips, her feet clacking on the hardwood floor. The one concession she had made was the removal of her helmet, which she carried in the crook of her arm.

She walked, like a spiky, black crustacean, into frame and past the defendant and prosecution desks, until she stood below the judge's stand and looked up at the woman in the robe.

"You wished to see me?" she asked.

The judge stared down at her, wide-eyed but incredulous.

"You are Ms. Vjorkrige?" the woman asked.

"I am the Vjorkrige," the Vjorkrige corrected her. "I am a Soldier of Vjor, one of the undead legion. I have no faith and no master in this world; I serve only my will and my will is true. Is this not enough for you?"

"That's an impressive way of saying you're not lying," admitted the judge. "But no, I'm sorry, it is *not* enough."

The Vjorkrige nodded. "Then I shall waste no more of your time. I will not stoop to performing cheap tricks in order to convince you. If you have issue with what I claim, you can take it up with a higher authority."

"And what higher authority would this be?" asked the judge.

Jill let out a satisfied sigh. "And there . . . " she said.

"The highest that there is," said the Vjorkrige. She stretched out an arm and made a sweeping gesture, turning so that she faced the camera—and the door behind it. She shouted something. Words in a language guttural and harsh, but among them Selene distinctly heard the name Vjor repeated several times.

Outside the screen, outside the building, Selene felt something like a small earthquake. There was a distant *boom*, and then a rushing, whining scream.

Behind them, the door to the front desk slammed open, revealing Faraday, her raven perched once more on her head. Her eyes were flashing and her cheeks were flushed.

"That's torn it," she shouted. "Dam broke and the cows are coming home to roost!"

"You mean the gate has opened," said Clara. It was not a question. "Where?"

Faraday rolled her eyes at them. "*Don't* tell my sister I didn't predict this—I'd never hear the end of it—*where do you think?*"

Clara blinked at her. Selene felt like there was something big and obvious she was probably missing.

"It's so *obvious*. I mean, if you're an ancient god and someone calls you to this city, where do you think *you'd* open the gate? Remember, this is *St Louis!*"

Of all of them, it was Jill who said it first.

"The gate!" she shouted. "*The* gate—the Gateway Arch!" She whirled on Captain Miller. "Where is *that*?" she demanded, pointing at the screen which still showed the interior of the courtroom. "Which courthouse are they in?"

The captain hesitated. "They're at the Circuit Court, why?"

"*Where is that?*" Jill demanded.

"Just down the road, corner of Tucker and Market," said the confused policeman.

"Right," said Jill, almost snarling. "Clara, Selene, you're with me! We gotta move—oh, and captain?" she rushed on, not giving the man time to answer. "Better close down Market Street. No traffic, no pedestrians. In fact, if you could evacuate everywhere between that courthouse and the Gateway Arch, that'd probably be best!"

Then she was running out the door. Selene didn't have to think twice before following close on her heel.

Market Street was three blocks south from the police station, but Jill knew it before she even saw the sign. There it was at the intersection of Tucker Boulevard and Market Street—a tall, square building topped with a pyramid-shaped roof. To the right it was a straight shot down the street, past the dome of the Old Courthouse, to where the Gateway Arch, slender and graceful, cut an arc out of the city's skyline.

She'd seen the arch before, many times, in person as they drove around the city, and also from numerous postcards and movies. Erected to celebrate the European expansion into western America, her fact-hoarding mind supplied, helpfully.

Now it was celebrating something very different, she thought, as she watched the smoke rise from the earth around it. The arch itself was still clearly visible, but the interior of it was glowing an angry red, which brightened to a golden shine, like something hot was burning through, as she watched. In the distance there was the wail of sirens, cut with alarming cracks and bangs.

Market Street was full of people when Jill, Clara and Selene arrived, and there were cars pulled haphazardly over to the curb, their drivers standing halfway out of their vehicles, looking back toward the arch. The reason for this, Jill soon saw, was a huge crack that had appeared in the asphalt down the center of the street. It ran in a jagged line from the direction of the arch, past them, and on down the street to their left, where Jill could glimpse the impressive faade of the courthouse.

A shadow fell across them, muting the warm rays of the morning sun, and Jill looked up to see pillows of inky, black clouds, rolling in out of nowhere.

Literally, nowhere. They formed out of thin air, curling and frothing, and streamed toward the arch in waves. She could see them boiling, throwing off flecks of cloud, and in their depths, when they opened, she glimpsed flashes of lightning. The following thunder almost drowned out the sirens, and it went on and on, growing louder as the clouds grew.

"Good gods," murmured Clara, audible only because of her proximity to Jill.

"Sorry," said Selene, dry as a desert. "Don't think this is a good one." She swung her gun around so it rested across her back, and then began trotting down the street toward the arch.

"Hey y'all!" Jill heard her shout. "Get *out! Out* of the street! Get *away!* Everyone, *run!*"

No one was listening. Because almost at that moment there was an almighty *crack,* like the sharpest clap of thunder Jill had ever heard, and the air inside the arch caught fire.

At least, that's what it looked like to Jill. There was certainly a flash, like an impossibly bright light, and an explosion of smoke that billowed out on the far side of the arch, rising up like a wall of ash before drifting forward, meeting the dark clouds, and cutting off the last of the clear morning sky.

In the strange, unnatural twilight that followed, the arch itself began to shine, and then a shadow appeared, slipping through the light and advancing toward them, stepping carefully over the buildings but clearly making for Market Street.

Jill saw the tops of trees, just peeking above the roofs of Downtown, suddenly bend and whip about, and that was all the warning they got before a wall of oven-hot air hit them.

Selene must have seen it coming, because she dove into the lee of a parked car, while Jill, taken by surprise, staggered back into Clara.

Firm hands came up, gripping her arms, and Jill felt herself moved with equal firmness so that Clara stood between her and the hot wind. It still whistled and buffeted around her, but now she could blink her eyes open (she spit out some hair too) and look around.

The light from the arch had vanished, replaced by a blank darkness that was, somehow, even worse. It hurt to look at in the same way it hurt to look at the sun, only instead of blinding brightness there was blinding blackness, and that incongruity just made Jill's head hurt even more.

"You'd best return to the station," Clara said, twisting her neck around so Jill had a hope of hearing her.

But Jill just gripped the leather harness that Clara wore to carry her sheathed sword and shook her head. Despite all the chaos her brain had continued working, and just then it had seen fit to drop the remaining words from her verse of the prophecy into her head.

Follow the path by moon and star . . . Ride a red ram with a sword and shield.

"Staying with you!" Jill managed in a coughing yell. "Gotta see. Gotta *understand.*"

Clara said nothing, just shrugged, a dip and rise of her broad shoulders, and then she began forging through the wind toward Selene.

One good thing had come from this, Jill thought: all the pedestrians had fled the street, and those with cars had locked themselves inside. It left them with a clear path toward the arch, where the shadow had solidified into a recognizably human-shaped being, though it was so tall its head and shoulders were lost in the rolling black clouds.

"Stay behind me!" Clara called to Selene, who nodded and made a running dive through the whipping wind to latch on next to Jill.

Like that they crept down the street—first on the sidewalk, and then, when this was blocked by a Suburban that had run off course and crashed into a power pole, in the center of the road itself, next to the ugly crack.

Behind them, Jill heard more sirens, and chancing a glance back she saw a number of police vans and one armored car pull onto Market Street. One stopped and let out a short, squat figure in a leather vest, and then Jill had to duck when Faraday's raven came screaming in out of the sky and cut in behind Clara, flapping wildly until it reached its mistress.

Clara kept on marching, however, and Jill didn't see what the witch did after that. Selene was beside her, shouting at anyone they saw to get away, even going so far as to brandish one of her smaller guns when they didn't listen.

They'd barely made it past the park beyond the courthouse when the hot wind disappeared all at once. It was replaced by a dead stillness and a deep cold that came rushing in, soothing at first, and then alarming as Jill saw her breath rise before her eyes and felt the chill settle on her skin.

Now, however, she could step out from behind Clara and look up, and up, and *up,* at the shadow that was marching down the street.

It was less of a shadow now; in the dim light it was clearly a solid person covered in thick, pock-marked armor. This armor was not black, as Jill had first assumed, but a very dark red that was hard to look at in the same way as the darkness inside the arch.

The giant vision had also shrunk, ever so slightly, so now she could see a tiny head, encased in a spiked helm, set between two impressive pauldrons.

The ground trembled, and Jill realized with a jolt that the giant was no vision: it was a real, physical thing, and its footsteps were sending shockwaves over the asphalt. There were explosions of dust with every step, and now it was drawing closer, Jill could see a crowd of people walking in its shadow.

No, not walking, she realized. *Marching.* They marched in the shadow of the giant, perfectly in step, though the sound of them was all but drowned out by the booming of the giant's footfalls.

They were soldiers, Jill saw, as they drew still closer. Soldiers in the same style of dress and armor as the Vjorkrige, and some of them carried banners of flapping cloth, others torches. The tiny lights flickered in the shadow of the giant, who had shrunk still further, and was now only the height of the tallest buildings. The clouds and smoke trailed after them, lying low over the city like a streaming cape.

A hand like a metal claw closed on Jill's arm, and the next moment she found herself being dragged out of the street and down a side alley by Clara, where Selene was already waiting. Jill had been so awestruck she had lost track of them, and now looked around guiltily.

"Sorry," she gasped, shivering. "What do we do now?"

Selene stared at her.

"Search me, boss," she said. "This is a first for all of us, I think."

"We must wait," Clara declared. "One does not come between a god and their business."

"That . . ." Jill choked. "That *thing* . . . that's—?" she couldn't finish.

"Yeah," said Selene. "That's Vjor."

"One of her avatars, at least," Clara amended. "Faraday was right, as usual." She didn't seem happy about it.

"The p-problem," Jill stammered, and found she was shaking from cold and nerves. "Th-the problem is wh-what comes through the g-gate *after* her, r-right? Can we c-close it?"

Selene pursed her lips. "Wouldn't try it. Gotta leave Vjor somewhere to *go* when she's finished."

"We might contain the influx," Clara said, peering out at the street. "At the very least, we should try to save as many civilians as we can."

"S-sounds like a p-plan," Jill chattered.

"Can't move until *she* goes past, though," Selene pointed out, nodding toward Market Street.

Forcing her head up, Jill looked just in time to see a foot the size of a small car come down in the middle of the road, cracking the asphalt and sending up a small explosion of debris. It was smaller, however, than the previous ones, and the ground hardly shook at all.

There was a clatter of gunfire from the direction of the police vehicles. Then a panicked silence, and then a *boom* and a whistle, followed by another *boom*.

"*That* was a tank shell!" Selene cried. "What are they still doing with a *tank*?"

"Faraday has the authorities under control," Clara remarked, as the foot rose off the pavement and disappeared, only to be followed moments later by the spiky army marching behind it.

"And we take the rest," said Selene, tightening her grip on her gun. She was shivering too, Jill noticed, though Clara remained unaffected. Perks of wearing all that leather, she thought. "Just as soon as they clear us," Selene said.

It took several minutes for the army of the war god to march past. By the time the last of them passed by the alley where Jill, Clara and Selene were crouched, Jill's fingers and toes were hurting from the cold and her limbs had gone stiff. Clara had to help her to her feet, and then she was limping after the two warriors as they trotted back to Market Street.

Jill looked back and saw that Vjor had shrunk again, and was now only as tall as a double-decker bus, though her cape was still made of black clouds and smoke and stretched away forever into the sky. It looked like she had nearly reached the courthouse.

Then Jill turned away from the god and followed Selene and Clara toward the arch—which was still glowing with the painful blackness—and the devastation that had been left in the war god's wake.

I'm probably missing something important, Jill thought, as she climbed up a pile of asphalt. There was a car on its back at the bottom, bent and dented as though the army had marched right over it. Selene had broken one of its windows and was leaning down to speak to the person trapped inside.

This was also important, Jill realized, and made her frozen limbs work faster as she stumbled down the far side to see what she could do to help.

What was happening at the courthouse *was* important, of course. And so it shall be told.

It had taken most of Faraday's energy and all of her patience to push back the police cars—and their tank—to give the approaching god a clear path. She did this, not for fear they would prevent the god from reaching her destination, but for fear of what would happen to whatever got in her way.

The god walked down the street, and if she saw the huddle of small, crunchy bundles of flesh packed along the sidewalk and in the alleys, she didn't find them worth her interest. She was drawing herself in as she walked, Faraday saw, the giant vision shrinking, but at the same time growing more intense, until she appeared to be a figure only a little taller than Claymore—but with so much energy packed into one place that it distorted the air around her. She left ripples in the fabric of the world when she moved, and an afterimage, a faint glow, lingered where she had been. Her footsteps burned the pavement, searing red-hot impressions that immediately began to smoke. This smoke twirled upward to join the smoke of her mantle, which billowed from her shoulders to feed into the heavy clouds that had cast the city into twilight.

Faraday stood at the head of the SWAT team, feeling them slowly come under the influence of the god's magic, and a small portion of her relaxed.

No one moved. Everyone was frozen in place. They couldn't have fired their weapons even if they'd been ordered to.

Vjor might be the Grand God of War, but she didn't incite bloodshed and bravery, like Sekhmet, nor did she inspire strategic thinking, like

Athena. She was all the faces of war, bound up and packed into one space, and just seeing them together was enough to freeze you in your tracks.

Or make you sick, Faraday amended, hearing someone behind her begin to retch.

The god climbed the steps to the courthouse, leaving smoking footprints in her wake, the building buckling and bending as if in an attempt to get away from her.

She came to the door, pulled herself in just a little more so she could fit comfortably under the lintel, and stepped inside. After that, Faraday's view was blocked by line upon line of Vjorkrige who marched up and arranged themselves upon the steps, facing out toward the street. They stood at ease, shields by their sides and spears held in the crooks of their arms, and yet appeared more threatening than the cops with rocket launchers in riot gear, who were cowering behind Faraday now, as the waves of intense, otherwordly power breathed off the assembled Vjorkrige.

Even Faraday felt a little nauseated, and she did not envy the people in the courtroom. No, she did not envy them at all.

From Detective Wilco's point of view, what happened was this:

A little while after they felt the first tremor there were some distant booms, and then the light from the windows was abruptly blacked out. While everyone was getting up and murmuring and the judge was demanding silence and order there was an awful *cracking* noise and he was nearly knocked off his feet as the floor shook under him.

It was shaking because a crack had appeared, beginning under the Vjorkrige's feet and running jaggedly between the benches and out the door.

Everyone who had been standing suddenly sat down, and the judge was thrown back in her seat. Then, before anyone had a chance to get up again, a heavy, hot wind whistled up from the crack, filling the room and lifting papers off the desks.

Then, just as the temperature was becoming unbearable, it suddenly turned icy cold. The wind ceased. Detective Wilco felt his joints begin to ache, and he saw the windows fog over almost immediately.

Because of that, no one saw anything of what was happening outside until the doors to the courtroom flew open and *something* walked in.

Detective Wilco assumed they were a person, but he had to assume so because they were too painful to look at. They wore a spiky helmet and red armor; that was as much as he could see before he had to cast his eyes aside.

The image of the figure lingered in his vision, however, as if it had been burned there. And, as he stared determinedly at the floor, he saw this image—a glowing red silhouette—begin to move. He saw legs step, saw the billowing cape that streamed from the person's shoulders. He saw it extend a hand, and realized it must have reached the Vjorkrige. He could just see her, out of the corner of his eye, and she was kneeling before the figure.

Detective Wilco found he was sweating, despite the cold, and that he seemed to be crying. His heart was pounding, his blood was probably more adrenaline than anything else, and he felt like he might throw up. If he didn't die first.

Then a voice spoke. At the time he thought it was spoken softly into a silent room, but later he realized this would have been impossible. The thing behind the red shadow had brought a screaming, roaring sound with it, and the voice had been in the screams and the roars as well. It had been everywhere, even inside his own head.

It asked,

WHO DOUBTS THE WORD OF MY WARRIOR?

And to his horror, Detective Wilco found he could not speak. And he *needed* to speak. Because he realized *this* was the Vjorkrige's proof, and if they didn't make it clear it was accepted it would *stay* and if it stayed, Wilco was certain, people really would die.

It was the judge who answered. Perhaps because the red shadow let her.

"N-no one *doubts*," she stammered. "We simply require ... *authentication*."

IS HER WORD NOT ENOUGH?

It should have been, Wilco realized, coldly.

The judge seemed to have realized the same thing. Looking up (it didn't matter where he looked, the red shadow was always *there*), he saw her mouth was open in a silent scream of horror, and she was weeping too. Not tears, though. Too dark. Too red.

He had to get the red shadow to leave. He just hoped he knew how.

Summoning up all the strength he had, Wilco ground out: "No, but *your* word *is*."

If he had thought the red shadow was bad before, it had nothing on the feeling of the thing behind it actually *looking* at him. Wilco felt something wet running down his face and *hoped* they were tears.

THEN YOU SHALL HAVE IT.

Something hot was pressed into Wilco's hand. He curled his fingers around it and tried not to scream. He probably whimpered anyway, but what with the constant roaring, he didn't think anyone heard.

Things went distant for Detective Wilco at that point. He was aware of the red shadow turning to speak to the Vjorkrige again. It was asking if she was ready to come home.

The Vjorkrige shifted awkwardly on her feet.

"If I am allowed," she said, "I feel that my work is unfinished here."

The red shadow said she was allowed. And then—mercy of mercies—it turned and walked out of the courtroom.

Only to stop at the defendant's desk. Rafe McCleaver fell off his chair in his attempt to get away from it, but the red shadow did not pursue him. Instead it said, a little blandly,

THE VARRIGER WORKS BOTH WAYS. HE WHO DEMANDS SERVICE WILL IN TURN SERVE.

And *then* it was going. Walking out through the ruined doors, taking the smoke and the roars and the screams with it.

In the relative calm that lingered in its wake, Detective Wilco staggered over to the judge's podium. Climbing up on the witness box, he grabbed the file containing the Vjorkrige's testimony in his free hand, and pressed the red shadow's word onto the front page. It transferred to the paper in the form of a burning red mark that Wilco knew better than to look at. Instead he raised his face defiantly to the judge and said:

"There is your authentication, your honor."

His voice was weak and hoarse, but the courtroom was so quiet that everyone heard him loud and clear.

Step. Step. Step.

The Grand God of War walked out of the house of justice, collected Her retinue of warriors, and began retracing Her steps back to the gate from which She had come.

Step. Step. Step.

See the smoke rise. See the figure grow tall as the clouds that still covered the sky. See Her mantle of streaming ash, see Her footprints like pools of fire, feel the rumble of Her tread.

Step. Step. Step.

See the Vjorkrige, striding over the ground, following closely in the deep shadow of Vjor as they march in Her wake. They go, heedless of the chaos and destruction that surround them—it always surrounded them—but heedless also of the half-invisible beings that were still creeping out through the gate.

Some of these were timid, curious, and skittered off into the shadows of the new world. Others were sly and malicious, and took root in the sewers and the attics and the backs of people's minds, where they would not be found until it was too late to send them back. Others still were brash and bold, and ran joyously into the city, uprooting trees and turning over cars.

Many of these were unpleasantly surprised to find that the new world they had discovered was not as defenseless as it had first appeared.

The beast was ten feet tall and only moderately stunned when Selene shot it in the face. It was boar-like in appearance, with two huge, curving horns. And it could spit fireballs.

"He has no armor on his belly!" Clara shouted, diving over a slab of ripped concrete to land next to Selene.

Selene reloaded first one gun and then the other. Ten shots, between the two of them. And then there was her knife.

"But can you get close enough?" Selene asked.

Clara looked at her. Looked down at her guns. Then back up. Their eyes—one pair ice blue, the other inky brown—met for only a moment, but a moment was all they needed.

"I trust you," was all Clara said, before she vaulted the slab of concrete and began pelting over the ruined street toward the—Selene was just going to call it as she saw it—boar-shaped fire monster.

She took a deep breath, then held it as she broke cover and aimed—over Clara's head—at the monster.

Bang! between the eyes.

It staggered. Snorted.

Bang! closer to the nose this time. It bellowed into the ground, sending out a stream of fire.

Clara was almost under its feet now, and Selene saw a flash as she drew her sword.

Bang! and that one went into an eye.

The beast threw its head sideways and began spewing fire wildly. It had to open its jaws to do so, and Selene promptly put another slug in the roof of its mouth.

Clara had disappeared now, but then the beast *really* howled, and she reappeared, dodging out from between its legs.

It didn't die at once. It toppled first, thrashed, but the black blood coursing into the street took its strange life with it, and within a minute it was still. Smoke rose from the blood, its mouth, and its ruined eye.

The air smelled hot and burnt and a little metallic when Selene at last inhaled properly.

"Atta girl," she said. She wasn't sure if she meant herself or Clara.

"Thanks," said Jill, at her elbow. Selene blinked down at the woman, whose face was streaked with soot and whose knees were sporting bloody grazes. "I got the woman from the Suburban to the hospital. Now what?"

As if on cue, the ground shook. Selene looked up. Half lost in the smoke she saw a shadow that hurt her eyes and left a red afterimage even when she glanced away.

It was directly above them.

Step. Step.

The Grand God of War paused. The next step, when it came, was especially loud, as though it had been rather longer than the others.

On the ground, Selene, Jill and Clara watched numbly as the giant foot that had landed just beyond the slain monster lifted, leaving behind a bright ring of fire, before disappearing into the fog. Then they were surrounded by the dark, cold shapes of the host of Vjorkrige as they marched through, somehow managing to find their way neatly around Selene and Jill and Clara—*and* the giant monster's carcass—without breaking formation.

In the distance the Gateway Arch was beginning to glow again. Tendrils of invisible light licked out, spreading like a blooming flower, at the approach of the God.

She bent Her head just slightly, so the horns of Her helm did not catch on the flimsy arch, and then she was beyond the gate, drawing the smoke of her mantle after her.

The Legion of Vjor marched in her wake, and it was as though they carried the shadow with them.

For a moment, through the arch, there could be seen a gray and desolate land, with mountains in the far distance, crowned with spiky black trees. Things soared in the ebony sky that might have been birds, and might have been something else. They were only visible for a moment; then the God walked into Her domain, and shut the gate behind Her.

The shaky camera footage showed mostly smoke, but in it there was a shape, roughly human, and so tall its head was lost in the clouds. A cut, and then the screen showed a foot shaped crater, still aglow like a burning ember.

"Experts disagree as to the cause of the devastation in downtown St Louis," the news anchor said in clipped tones. "While there has been no official statement, theories from terrorist attack to a natural gas explosion have been put forward as a way of explaining the sudden environmental chaos that has engulfed the city's center. Eyewitness reports, however, tell an even more frightening story."

The video cut to a young black man wearing a backwards baseball cap and a stained white t-shirt. His skin was shiny with sweat, and he was shaking.

"It was the craziest, man. Just the craziest. Like a spider the size of a house, ma"—*bleep*—"came walkin' in like anything, all stompin' and snarlin' . . ."

Then there was an older, white woman, her hair blown about her head and a soot stain across her cheek. "It came through the *arch*, I *saw* it. First everything was normal, and then the arch caught *fire* and there was smoke and dust *everywhere* but I *saw* it. Whatever it was, it was *huge* and it wasn't an alien or a robot—I am *not* crazy—and where it walked there were these explosions, like little volcanic eruptions . . ."

"While the strange catastrophe has only affected a small portion of downtown St Louis," the news anchor's voice cut in, smoothly, "the tremors were felt as far away as Kansas City and Indianapolis. Local law enforcement have evacuated Downtown and Downtown West, Midtown, and parts of Grand Center, and banned anyone from entering the affected zones until a threat analysis has been completed."

The footage came back to the recording studio at this point, and the news anchor, who looked visibly shaken herself, went on: "In the wake of what has been dubbed the Gateway Incident, reports of animal attacks and other unexplained phenomena have become increasingly common in St Louis County, including one of a man whose teenage son supposedly came back from the dead. What is certain, however, is that there will be no easy answers for what happened earlier today."

The video ended. Mutely, Clara clicked over to the next tab. It was an interview with Captain Miller of the SLMPD.

"Listen," he said, glaring at the reporter off screen. "What we are dealing with here is beyond anything we've ever seen before. This isn't a smart bomb, it's not a drone strike, it's not even a nuclear meltdown. What we have is . . . it's something that's beyond our capabilities to understand, and anyone pretending to have some quick and easy answers is a lying monkey. I've got men and women who've stared down robbers, murderers, angry mobs—a lot of them are lying in the fetal position right now, crying. There's nothing I know that can explain what happened, except to say that it was the strangest"—*bleep*—"I've ever seen."

This time, when Clara reached to switch tabs, Selene raised a hand and laid it gently on her arm.

"I think . . . I think I've seen enough for now," she said, weakly.

Clara nodded and instead shut the laptop. She leaned back against the couch next to Selene, and folded her hands neatly in her lap.

"Damn," said Selene, after a while. "This is really happening, isn't it?"

"Yes," said Clara.

"Damn," said Selene.

Clara nodded.

In the other room they heard Jill's phone go off. It was her generic ringtone, and neither of the hunters moved a muscle. After a moment they heard Jill pick it up, and then her indistinct voice. They caught "Oh," and "Ah, I see," and "Okay, thanks for telling me. I'll keep in touch. Yes, yes and you too."

Footsteps. The creak of the door opening. Jill's freshly scrubbed face poked into the room.

"That was Detective Wilco," she said, her voice strangely small and quiet.

"Oh yeah?" said Selene.

"He just called to say that . . . well. Rafe McCleaver was charged with first degree murder, and . . . and he took a plea bargain."

Selene raised an eyebrow.

"Oh, and what's that mean?"

Jill made a face. "Basically? I think they skip the trial and go straight to sentencing? Something. Anyway, it seems the Vjorkrige was *very* convincing."

Selene perked up a little at that. "So . . . he's goin' to jail?"

"At *least*," said Jill.

Selene twisted her mouth, considering. "A'ight," she said. "Guess it was worth it, then."

Jill came all the way into the room, pushing her laptop gently aside and sitting down on the coffee table to face the other two women. She seemed tense—but not frightened. Excited, that was it. She was turning her phone over and over in her hands, and tapping one foot on the ground.

"What?" asked Selene.

Jill looked up, her eyes big and bright.

"I've been thinking," she said. "About what we're gonna do next."

"Oh?"

"What with . . . what happened yesterday. The Gateway Incident. Lots of people have questions. Questions not even I have the answers for. And here's the thing, they keep coming to *me*. Asking *me*. Like I'm supposed to have the answers."

"Now you know how *we* feel," Selene said with a dry laugh.

Jill blinked, as if this remark had derailed her train of thought. She shook her head.

"Point is," she went on. "People are so desperate for answers . . . I think. I think I can actually make this *work*."

"This?" said Selene.

Jill spared a hand from her phone to wave it between the three of them. "This, *us*. What we've been doing for almost a year now. Enough people saw enough yesterday that they're asking the same questions I did. And they want answers just as much. Thing is, now they're willing to *pay* me to do just what I *have* been doing—only *better*."

Selene raised her head to stare at Jill.

"And this means . . . what to us?" she asked.

Jill looked at her like she was the mad one. "I'm thinking of investing in a mobile lab. Like a modified camper—I mean, Arcana's got the muscle for it. Oh, and you get a raise, of course. I mean, if you're still willing to work for me."

Selene rolled her head over to glance at Clara, who did an inverted shrug.

"Aw hell," she said, grinning despite herself. "Sure thing, boss. 'Sides, yanno you wouldn't last five minutes without us."

"I know," said Jill, dead serious. She looked over at Clara. "And you?"

Clara was frowning, but not like she was annoyed or angry. She worried her lower lip for a few moments, before looking up at Jill.

"Was this your intent?" she asked, very even and sincere.

Jill's eyebrows went up. "Intent, what?" she asked.

"This . . . outpouring of the supernatural. Something so big and obvious no one could ignore it."

Selene's head snapped around so fast she felt her neck twinge.

"*What?*" she spat.

Jill had gone very still, but then she sighed.

"It wasn't . . . " she began, then stopped. "I didn't have anywhere near like such a clear idea in my head," she admitted. "And I'm sorry for the people who got hurt. I didn't *want* anyone to get hurt. But . . . it happened, okay? It happened and . . . and I'm *not* sorry it did."

She lifted her chin and gazed at them, challengingly.

Selene didn't know what to say, but apparently Clara did.

"I think the oracle was wrong," she said. "You are no fool."

Jill actually laughed at that, her eyes crinkling. She seemed a little embarrassed, but honestly amused. It was the first time, Selene realized, that she had ever seen the woman with a genuine smile. It made her seem infinitely soft and vulnerable and endearing all at once.

"No," said Jill, her smile fading—but slowly. "I'm the fool all right. But I think I'm foolish in all the right ways." She sat up, straightening her glasses. "So, what do you say?"

Clara stretched, her leather garments creaking with the motion. She rolled her shoulders, flexing muscles that Selene knew had to be horribly bruised. Her icy blue eyes fixed on Jill, and she said: "When do we start?"

Ow!
Ow!
O-ow!
Ow-oh-ow!

Ow,
ow-oh-ow
Ow,
ow-oh-oh
ow!

We were facing down a red nightmare
Racing toward a dark horizon made of fear
We just wanted the word to be heard
Our choice, a butterfly.
Streets shaking, throwing up their guts
Quaking with each step from a god of war
We were soldiers, but we could not see
Though the black, smoke-filled sky.

We were fools, not tools
Just looking for a way out
We found the ground
We were children in the dark.

Coda I

St Louis, Missouri

CAPTAIN MILLER AND DETECTIVE WILCO looked everywhere for the so-called witch, but all they found was a ragged woman with especially long canines who introduced herself as Janine.

"I hear you've been getting some funny calls," she said, a little cagily.

"Funny isn't the word I'd use," Captain Miller said, stiffly.

Janine nodded, as if conceding the point. "I guess . . . I was wondering if you could use some help. From someone who . . . uh . . . has got a good nose for these things?"

Captain Miller looked at her critically, a vague memory trickling up through the haze of the last forty-eight hours. A werewolf in the basement. He shook himself, and turned to Wilco.

"She's all your's Ronnie," he said, and stomped off to find the damn witch. She had to be around here somewhere. No one could just *disappear* like that . . .

Behind him, Detective Wilco and Janine regarded each other. Eventually the older man coughed.

"So, um," he began. "What do you know about *ghouls?*"

Far from laughing at him, the woman just grinned. Her teeth were very long and sharp indeed.

We woke up to a morning where the world had been changed
The tides had turned, the players rearranged.
Everything that we had lost cannot now be regained
The thunder fades and now begins the rain.

Coda II

River View, Missouri

MOTHER JUNE SAT IN HER BATTERED HOUSE and stroked her cat. Some days were bad. Some were—not good—but less bad. Some days had a bit of both. Yesterday she'd received a call from the DA in St Louis that, while providing her with a feeling of grim satisfaction, hadn't really made her day any better.

This day had started off badly, but now it was stretching into the late hours of the afternoon, and with the creeping evening shadow—coming earlier and earlier as the autumnal equinox approached—and the breaths of cool air it brought, Mother June felt a stirring in her that called on her to *do* something. Cook, maybe. Or clean.

There was a knock on the door.

She hadn't heard a car in the drive or the step of feet. It sounded as though whoever it was had magically appeared on her front porch.

Gently tipping Marlowe off her lap, she got creakily to her feet and stumbled over to the door. She opened it a crack, saw what was on the other side, and slammed it shut again.

She stood there, listening to the blood pounding in her ears, until she realized two things. One, that the thing on the other side of the door hadn't torn it down and stormed inside. Two, that it had *knocked.* You didn't knock on doors you could tear down unless you were trying to be nice.

Mother June opened the door again.

The Vjorkrige stood on her porch, her hands in the pockets of a large, tan overcoat. It was clearly too big for her, but a bulkiness around the shoulders suggested she had her armor on under it. Her helmet was gone, however, and Mother June peered up into an inky-black face with bright, glittering eyes the color of the night sky. Framed with platinum curls, she realized with a jolt what a shockingly young face it was. Smooth and curving, with big, soft lips and a nose that, had it not been so high up off the ground and attached to an otherwise terrifying body, could have been called *cute.*

"What do *you* want?" Mother June asked, her voice rough from disuse.

The Vjorkrige seemed surprised she should ask. She blinked her dark eyes and drew back a little from the door.

"Life," she said, uncertainly. "I have not had . . . much practice at it. I apologize. It is . . . more complicated than I remember. Things, once begun, must be finished. But it takes time, and I must do something in between."

Mother June sighed and leaned against the doorframe. "I suppose it's no good holding any hard feelings against *you,*" she said. "You didn't *ask* to be put here."

The Vjorkrige looked away. "Even so," she said quietly. "I am living a borrowed life. I feel it behooves me to live it in such a way that would make its rightful owner . . . " her mouth worked soundlessly as she searched for the correct word.

"Happy," she finished, at last.

Mother June stared at her incredulously.

This seemed to make the Vjorkrige even more uncomfortable. She shifted restlessly from foot to foot, and would not meet Mother June's gaze. This caused her to look past the porch, over the neighboring field, to where the tops of the trees were just visible, gold and red in preparation for winter.

"Many things grow in the shade," she said, thoughtfully. "It would be . . . good . . . if someone were here to look after them."

Mother June blinked. In her grief she had completely forgotten about the stripped god tree which still lived—if only just—in the heart of the forest. They had cut out all the bad growth, but that didn't guarantee it would grow back *good.*

She found herself looking at the Vjorkrige more closely now. Under the overcoat, and the dark robe, and the leather straps and bits of armor still visible, she could see a faint movement of breath. The Vjorkrige still smelled of grave dirt, but only faintly; now it was overlaid by the scent of clean leather and a faint whiff of—was that strawberry shampoo?

It was Marlowe who decided things. The cat twined out between Mother June's legs and through the door, and after sniffing the Vjorkrige uncertainly, he began purring and rubbing up against her armored shins.

Mother June felt something tight uncoil in her chest.

"A'aight," she said. "Come in, why don't you. But no weapons in my house; the axes stay *out*."

The Vjorkrige nodded contritely, reaching inside her coat to remove her battle-axes, which she leaned carefully against the wall of the house, below the taped up window.

"And you can help put this place back together," Mother June said, beginning to find her stride.

"I will do all I can," said the Vjorkrige.

"And I'm gonna need a name for you," said Mother June. "You want to make a go of living, can't just call yourself *Vjorkrige*. That's like calling me *old woman*. Not gon' work."

The Vjorkrige nodded, thoughtfully. "There have been precedents," she said. "Living Vjorkrige are allowed to take on the name of the life they were given."

"I *ain't* calling you Cynthia," said Mother June, her voice turning harsh and scratchy.

The Vjorkrige looked lost at this. She seemed so woeful Mother June took pity on her.

Really, just a big child herself, she thought.

"You can be Shona," she said. "How you like that?"

The Vjorkrige picked up her head. "Shona?" she said, her voice small and hopeful. She shut her eyes, seeming to concentrate. "Shona was . . . the name you gave your daughter?"

Mother June pursed her lips, but the Vjorkrige nodded.

"Shona," she said, more firmly this time. "I believe it will serve. Yes, I can be Shona."

That evening found Mother June rocking gently on her front porch, as a tall, thin figure cut wood and nailed the railing back on. They took a break for dinner, and then returned to work.

The night fell, but the darkness didn't bother them.

It didn't bother them at all.

> *Ow,*
> *ow-oh-ow*
> *Ow,*
> *ow-oh-oh*
> *ow!*

> *We saw wonder in a world filled with love and hate*
> *We were blinded by the dark beyond the gate*
> *Reason said we should have made a break*
> *and fled*
> *but we stood still.*

We were fools, not tools
Just looking for a way out.
We found the ground
We were children in the dark.

We woke up in the nighttime, heard a voice out of the world
screaming smoke and ashes rising, curled.
All the things we thought were true were crushed beneath her feet
The light has gone, the nightmare is complete.

The nightmare, the nightmare
The nightmare,
is complete.

Ow,
ow-oh-ow
Ow,
ow-oh-oh
ow!

We woke up to a morning where the world had been changed
The tides had turned, the players rearranged.
Everything we thought was true has gone up in the flames
The thunder fades and now begins the rain.

Ow,
ow-oh-ow
And now begins the rain!

Ow,
ow-oh-oh
ow!
And now begins the rain!

—Children in the Dark/*We3*

ALTHOUGH THE FOLLOWING STORY *does not contain any of the principal characters from* Driving Arcana, *it takes place within the same universe, at about the time that Jill is discovering that chimeras exist. It was originally published in* The Urban Green Man anthology, *EDGE Science Fiction and Fantasy 2013, and bears on the* Wheel 2 *story, "The Earth It Weeps."*

ABANDON ALL ____

Evening in the city. The cooling air is filled with the sound of traffic: the roar of cars; the grumble and screech of trucks. A train barrels through, adding to the din. The sky is half pale blue gray, half black clouds hanging ominously in the south. A soft wind ruffles the topmost leaves of a majestic oak tree, but there is no sound; the quiet rustling of the leaves is eaten up by the pervasive rumbling, honks and occasional squeaks of rush hour.

The sound washed over and around Marvin like a blanket. He had been born in the city, raised in the city, and to him the sound of car engines was as natural and reassuring as birdsong—when he noticed it at all. At the moment, he had other things to think about.

It was getting dark. That meant that the lights had come on along the pedestrian path that ran beside the canal, casting little circles of orange light that marched away into the distance. Marvin wished they hadn't: he liked dark places. In dark places he could hide. In dark places he was safe. He didn't understand why people were afraid of the dark. A place was a place whether it was light or dark, except that if it was dark and Marvin was in it, then people didn't see him and left him alone.

Marvin liked being alone. There was no one to hurt you if you were alone. His mother didn't like it. She said he had borderline social dysfunction disorder, or something like that, and encouraged him to make friends.

Marvin didn't like friends. His friends at school called him Starvin' Marvin, because he ate so much. The fact that he was also quite fat was hilarious to them, and they spent most of their time around him talking about how funny this was. Sometimes they pushed or poked him, just to make him squeal, and that was even funnier. They called him stupid and retarded, and talked about him like he wasn't there.

At that moment, Marvin was trying to avoid some of these friends. He had decided to take the detour home to avoid them, but was now realizing the error in his plan: the detour meant taking the pedestrian path over the freeway and along the canal and then through the abandoned cemetery. It was deserted at this time, which meant Marvin was alone. His friends were more likely to play with him if they found him alone.

Marvin hated playing with his friends. It was never any fun. One time they'd lifted him over the fence along the canal and he'd spent all afternoon trying to get out. His sneakers had been ruined, and he'd smelled of algae and bird poop when he got home. His mother hadn't been happy about that, though when he told her he'd been playing with his friends she cheered up. She always cheered up when he told her he had been playing with his friends, which was the only reason he kept doing it.

This evening, however, Marvin was tired and didn't want to play. So he walked quickly along the path, darting from shadow to shadow. He veered off across the cemetery, and here thankfully there were no lights.

There were also three teenagers lounging on broken headstones, drinking from bottles in paper bags. Marvin stopped dead in his tracks. These were some of his least favorite friends; they were the ones who had dumped him in the canal. Marvin thought about turning around and going home another way, but they had already seen him.

"Heeeey, look 'ere guys, it's Starvin' Marvin," said the tallest of the teenagers, a lanky boy with black hair and a thin beard.

"Hey Marvin, wanna drink?" said the shortest of the teenagers, a skinny boy with a buzz cut and a large zit on his nose.

"No, no thanks," said Marvin politely. He had tried one of their drinks before, and it had reminded him of the way his vomit had tasted when he'd had the flu last winter.

"Whatsa matter Marvin, you *scared* of a little beer?" said the middle teenager, a girl with her hair in pigtails and a book bag over her shoulder. She was the worst, because everybody liked her—including the teachers—and were forever telling Marvin she was a good influence on him and he should spend more time with her. This was because they never saw what she was like when she was alone with Marvin: she would stab him with her pencil and snap at him.

"Nah, nah," said the tallest teenager. "He's not *scared,* he's *hopeless.* That right, Marvin? You're *hopeless!*"

Marvin didn't think he was hopeless. He hoped, for example, that they would all step in dog doo on their way home. But he didn't say so.

The short boy chuckled. "Yeah, hopeless I'll say. Hey, hey Marvin—you know where you belong? In with *them.*" He pointed at one of the largest graves. Instead of a headstone it had a small house with a battered wooden door and words carved in blocks over the lintel. At one time ivy had grown over the front, and when it had been ripped away by some long-ago gardener, one of the blocks had been pulled free as well. Where once there had been a complete couplet, there now only read:

Abandon All ----
Ye Who Enter Here.

"That's s'posed to say '*Abandon all hope, ye who enter here,*'" the short boy chuckled. "That's from litra-cher, that is. Dante. Classic, man. Invented Italian. It means *welcome to hell.*"

Marvin peered at the little building. "I don't think so," he said carefully. "Hell is a big place. That is too small."

"What do *you* know about it, huh, *re-tard*," said the girl. She pronounced the word 'retard' like it was two words: re tard.

"Hey, hey," said the tall boy. "Maybe Marvin should go in and see for himself, yeah? He'll learn a thing or two about *hell* in there!"

The other two thought this was a great idea, and before he could protest Marvin found himself stripped of his backpack and marched up to the door, which the short boy kicked open. They pushed him inside and hauled the door shut behind him, and when he turned around to try to open it again, he found it immovable. They probably had all their backs pressed up against it. In fact he could hear their muffled giggles close by on the other side.

Marvin turned around and sat down with his back to the door. He was getting hungry and wanted to go home, but though he explained this in a loud voice so his friends could hear, they only laughed harder. This made Marvin frustrated and a little angry.

But he was not afraid.

He sat in the dark, waiting for his eyes to adjust. At first he had thought the place was pitch black, but now he realized there must be a skylight up in the arched ceiling, for the longer he waited the more gray shapes swam into view.

He was in a little stone room with a large stone slab in the middle, on the far side of which was a dark doorway. Marvin considered it for some time, before deciding to make his way around the stone slab to peer cautiously through the door. Perhaps there was another way out?

He stepped through, into a pile of dead leaves, which gave way under his feet. He staggered, then tumbled down a steeply sloping passage, the leaves rustling and whispering all around him. He landed in another pile of leaves at the bottom and clawed his way to the surface, spitting twigs and bits of leaf out of his mouth.

He blinked. It was light down here. A dim, pale light, ghostly and white—not at all like the orange streetlights. Marvin was reminded of the time when he was ten and his mother had taken him to visit his grandparents in the country. He had gone outside one night to find the world bathed in pale white light, and the moon full and round and blindingly bright above him. This then . . . this was *moonlight*. Wonderingly, Marvin looked up.

High stone walls stretched up all around him, but there was no ceiling, and beyond that was an impossibly black night sky, pricked by impossibly bright stars. Sure enough, there was the moon, milky white with a faint aura around her. It was wrong, how bright the moon was, and Marvin got the uncomfortable feeling that if he were to climb the stone walls he would find himself in a completely different place than the abandoned cemetery.

Drifts of leaves, muted brown in the moonlight, half filled the room. It was absolutely silent, as if the whole world was holding its breath. And at the far end, resting on the leaves as though on a bed, was a human skeleton.

Marvin frowned. It was hard to tell in the moonlight, but he thought it was the wrong color: too dark, and some of the bones looked wobbly and wrong. Curious, he waded through the leaves toward it for a closer look.

It was a tall skeleton—much taller than he was—and the reason it looked so dark was because it was not made of bone, but of perfectly carved wood. Marvin could see the grains of it, like in his mother's best chairs, making patterns in the ribs and the skull.

There was something in the skull's mouth that glinted in the moonlight. Marvin reached forward with his hand . . .

No sooner had his fingers brushed the skeleton's wooden teeth than the whole thing shuddered and twitched. Marvin was so surprised that he fell backwards and could only stare in astonishment at what happened next.

A little green sprout, color vivid even in the moonlight, pushed its way out of the skull's mouth and twined around the side of its head, sprouting more leaves as it went. Another sprout appeared, twining up the other side. Their leaves grew shiny and wide, then opened revealing pale buds. These quivered a moment, then unfurled gracefully into white, star-shaped flowers.

At the same time more leaves were curling out from its eye sockets, pushing together in the center of its forehead. A sharp shoot sprang up between them, arching back from the brow like a crest.

Even as all this happened, the rest of its body was undergoing a similar transformation: leaves crowded out from its shoulders, covering its ribs and pelvis. Vines ran down its arms, joining the wooden bones together, and little green buds bloomed on its fingertips.

Then the skeleton—which was not really a skeleton anymore but a body made of leaves and vines and blossoms—sat up with a jerk (more leaves burst out across its shoulders), writhed to its feet (a curtain of leaves like ivy tumbled down its legs like the folds of a robe), arched its back, rolled its shoulders, and finally looked down at Marvin. Its eyes were two dark pools between the leaves of its forehead and its cheeks, with little points of light in them like distant stars. Its chin was bare and its mouth slightly open because of the shoots of leaves that poured out on either side.

Marvin was not sure what to do. Nothing he had ever read had told him what to do about wooden skeletons that sprouted leaves and came to life. So he did what he usually did when he met a new person: he stared, trying to figure out if they were threatening or not.

"Hello," said the leafy thing. Marvin didn't see its mouth move, and its voice had a swishy, rustling quality that made him think it was the *leaves* doing the talking, not the head.

Marvin decided the leafy thing was *not* threatening. It was too polite.

"Hello," he replied solemnly. "I'm Marvin."

"Hello Marvin," said the leafy thing with equal gravity. "Why are you here?"

Marvin sighed. He didn't like being asked questions. Answering them usually got him into trouble. But the leafy thing did not strike him as the same sort of person as his teachers or his friends. He felt like he could talk to it without worrying what it thought.

"My friends wanted to play, so they locked me in the hell house in the old cemetery," he said. A thought occurred to him. "Is this hell?"

The leafy thing rustled, but no words came out. Marvin thought it was laughing. Eventually it said: "No. I cannot be in Hell, and Hell cannot be with me. We are . . . incompatible." It pushed its finger buds together to demonstrate. The leaves of its face drooped then, as if it was sad. "You keep strange friends," it said. "When last I walked, friends took up arms against one's enemy, defended one's honor, brought one solace and comfort in times of trouble. They did not lock one in houses of the damned." The leaves of its forehead bunched together, crowding over its brow in a frown. "Do your friends do any of those other things?" it asked.

Marvin thought about it, and had to admit that they did not.

"Then," said the leafy thing, it's face firming up as it came to a decision. "They are not your friends."

The statement hit Marvin like a blow. *They were not his friends.* That made so much more *sense.* He felt a brief pang of sadness at the thought that this meant he didn't have any friends, but mostly he was so relieved not to have to call those horrible bullies—which was, he realized now, what they were—his friends, that he laughed out loud.

This puzzled the leafy thing, but it leaned back against the wall, folding its hands under the wide leaves hanging down from its chest, and waited patiently for Marvin to finish.

"I understand that now," Marvin said. "They only *said* they were friends, but they were not."

"They lied," said the leafy thing. Marvin found he liked how it stated things so neatly and clearly. It made it easy to talk to.

"I like you," he told the leafy thing. "What's your name?"

The leaves along the thing's shoulders rose and fell, like a sort of shrug. "I have been called by many names," it said. "I'm not sure which one you would know me by."

"Well," said Marvin, who had given a lot of thought to what he would have called himself if given the chance. "What do *you* like to be called?"

The thing ruffled its leaves, and its eyes glowed brighter.

"Green," it said decidedly. "I am . . . Green."

"Are you a boy or a girl?" asked Marvin.

"I am neither," said Green. "But you may refer to me as whichever you wish."

Marvin shook his head. "I won't call you either, then, if you're not. It's only fair."

Green was pleased at this. Marvin found, now he was growing used to the face, that he could read its expressions better than normal human faces: something about the way its leaves perked or sagged confused him less than the way cheeks and eyebrows would bunch and squish.

"I think," said Green, "that we should go talk to your other friends."

"They're not my friends anymore," Marvin said, and felt warm and good just saying that. "They never were. I was confused."

"Still," said Green, offering Marvin one twiggy hand. "I believe we should explain how matters stand, don't you?"

Three teenagers sat in a cemetery drinking beer from bottles in paper bags. One of them, the tall one, said:

"He's been awfully quiet in there, think we should let him out?"

"He's jug . . . he's jug . . . " the shortest (and the drunkest) boy replied. "He's juz tryin' to scare uz. Yanno . . . make uz tink he'z inter . . . in trouble."

"He's prolly just waitin' for us to let him out. Thinks it's all a big game . . . re-tard." The middle one—the girl—giggled. So did the short one. The tallest—who was also the most sober—laughed nervously and glanced at the little crypt . . .

. . . and turned pale and let out a ragged gasping sound.

In the middle of the old wooden door had erupted a profusion of bright green leaves, and in the center of the leaves, stained a sickly green, was Marvin's pudgy face.

"Hello . . . children," said Marvin's face. But it was not Marvin's voice: it was too knowing, too old, too *wise*. It was the voice of something ancient beyond reckoning that knew each one of them personally. *Intimately.* It knew all their darkest little secrets, and it was not pleased.

The other two found themselves sobering up fast. All three of them stared at the green face in the door, speechless. The shortest one made a retching sound.

"I know what you've been doing," continued Marvin's face in the old, knowing voice. "I know what you've been dreaming. I know what you've been *fearing*." The old voice trailed off into laughter like wind in trees. When it spoke again it was definitely all Marvin now, and the face scrunched up in anger.

"You're *not* my friends anymore," he said. "You never *were!* And if you don't stop bothering me . . . I'll *get* you!"

As he spoke the last words the leaves writhed around his face, and it lunged forward out of the door, supported by tendrils of strong, black vines.

There was a crash and a tinkle as the tallest boy hurled one of the bottles against a tombstone, turned tail and fled. The other two followed suit, stumbling, blind with panic, until they found each other and hobbled off together at a stilted run.

Marvin stepped out of the door and craned his neck to watch them go. Behind him the vines and leaves retreated, weaving back together, and Green emerged, its disgorging mouth stretched into an unmistakable grin.

"That was good," Marvin said, when the sounds of the teenagers had dwindled to nothing.

Green didn't answer. When Marvin turned to look he found it staring back up at the lintel above the door, at the inscription missing a word.

"I see the problem," Green said, and bent over, sending shoots and tendrils out along the ground, searching. Eventually it found what it was looking for and stood up, a block of stone held in one hand. Carefully it reached up and fitted the block into the space of the missing word and stepped back.

"Oh," said Marvin, after reading what the inscription now said. "That's much better."

"I think so too," said Green.

Marvin was very late getting home. His mother was upset at first—she had been worried—but when she saw him all rosy cheeked and brimming with happiness she relented, and gave him a slice of pie with his dinner.

"I made a new friend tonight," Marvin said through his pie. "We played in that old cemetery."

"That's wonderful," said his mother. "Maybe tomorrow you can bring him around for dinner, I would love to meet him."

Marvin nodded vigorously, his mouth full of pie. It occurred to him, distantly, that there might be some complications involved with bringing Green home for dinner—he wasn't sure Green even ate human food— but that was a problem for another day. For now, he had a friend—a real, proper friend—and pie. He was happy. His mother was happy. Things would be all right.

In the cemetery, standing so still that any passerby would have mistaken it for a shrub, Green stood and listened to the sound of the traffic roaring in the distance. This world was drastically changed from the one it had known, but all the old principles were still in place. There was material to work with, and all things considered, Green was happy too.

Above and behind it, over the lintel of the door to the crypt, the repaired sign now read:

Abandon All Fear
Ye Who Enter Here.

The black clouds parted, and the moon shone down on the little cemetery. It was unusually bright that night.

THE SAGA CONTINUES ...

Jill, Selene and Clara will return in

PAVING
THE ROAD
TO HELL

The Earth It Weeps · Out of Space · Half Lives
Critical Magic · On the Surface Die · Free Man Running
Follow the Dark · Paving the Road to Hell · Escape Plan

ABOUT THE AUTHOR

Goldeen Ogawa is an author and illustrator of science fiction and fantasy whose works include the *Professor Odd* novellas, *The Adventures of Bouragner Felpz*, and the webcomic *Year of the God-Fox*.

She has been telling stories since before she could read or write and has been drawing pictures the whole time. Her chief inspirations are the natural world, science of all kinds, and frustration with the inherent unfairness of the world in general. She lives in Bend, Oregon, where she rides her bicycle year round.

Her official website is **goldeenogawa.com.**

TEXT AND DESIGN

The body of this book was typeset using LaTeX in Skema Pro Livro.

Cover art and book design by the author.